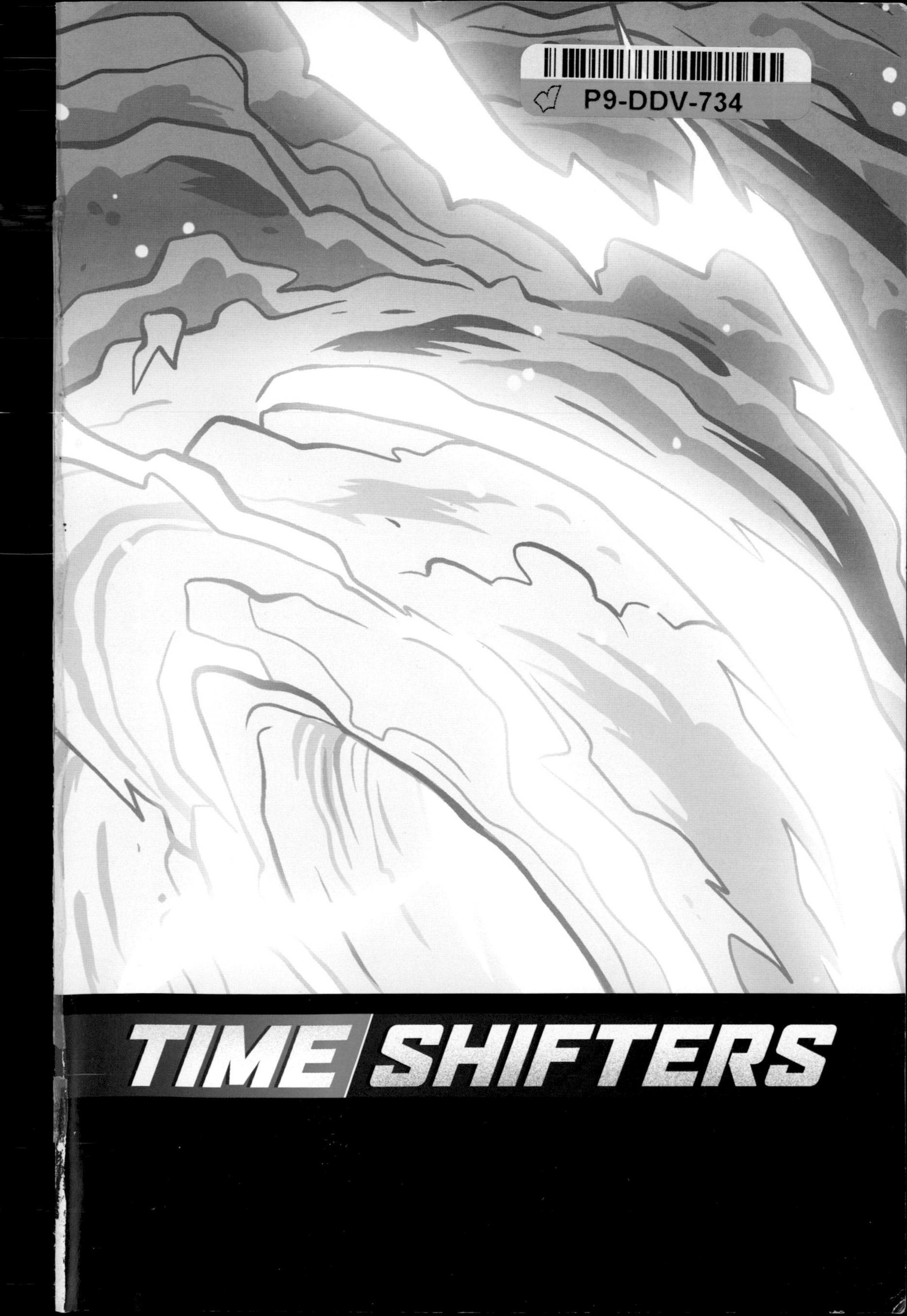

TIME SHIFTERS

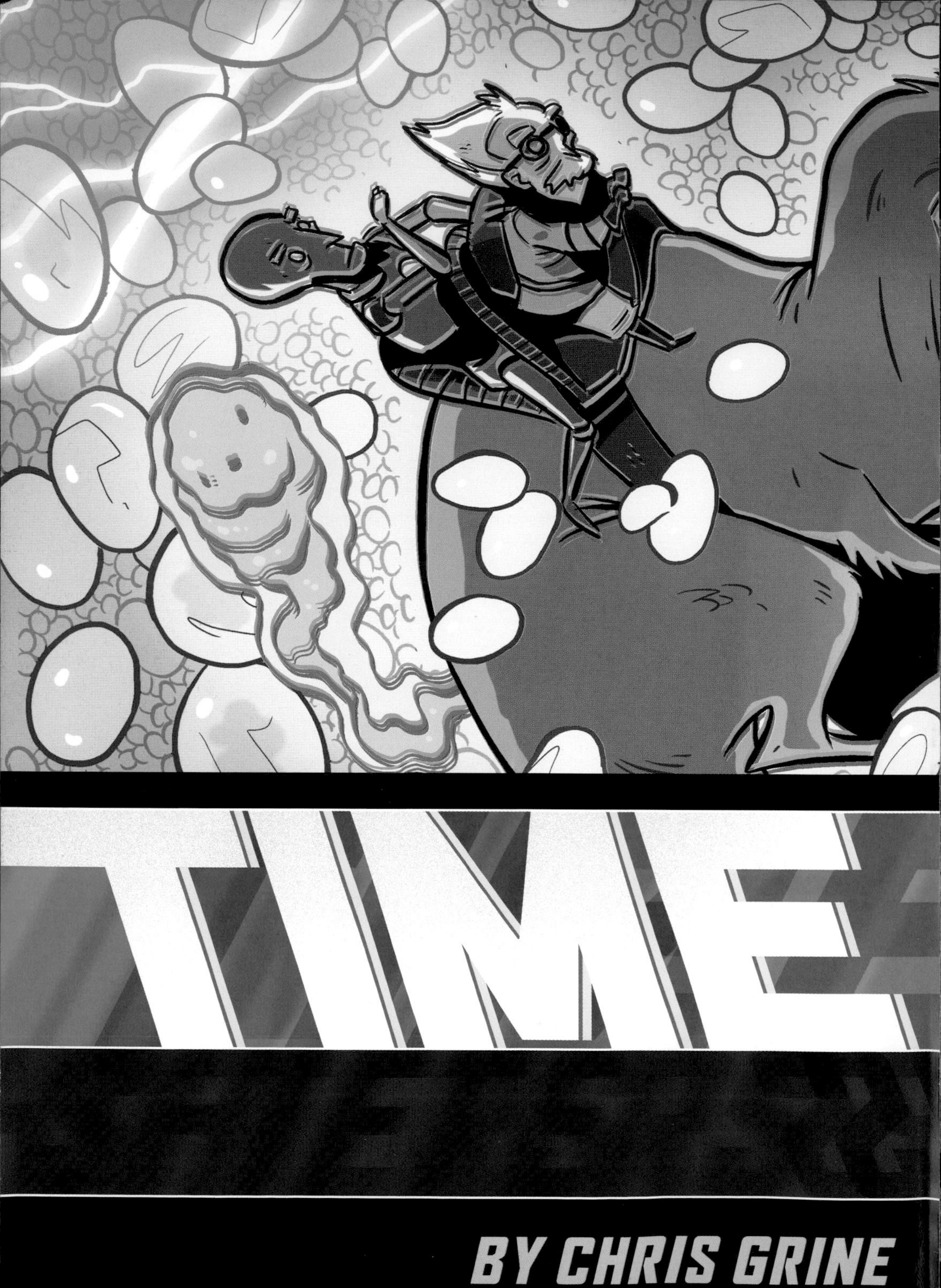

TIME

BY CHRIS GRINE

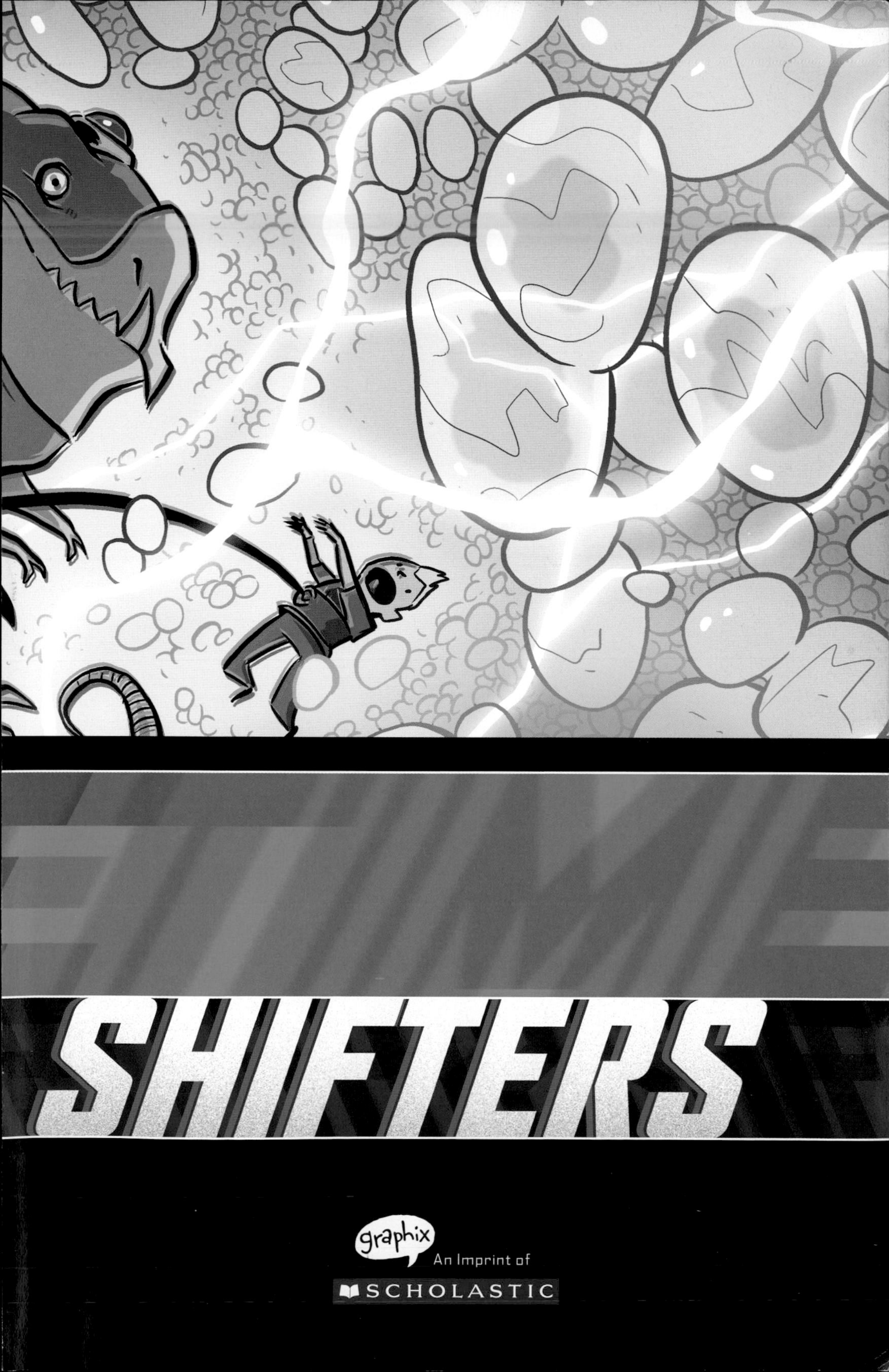

SHIFTERS

graphix
An Imprint of
SCHOLASTIC

For my dad, whom I miss every day.

Library of Congress Control Number: 2016951424

ISBN 978-0-545-92659-1 (hardcover)
ISBN 978-0-545-92657-7 (paperback)

10 9 8 7 6 5 4 3 2 1   17 18 19 20 21

Printed in China   38
First edition, June 2017
Edited by Adam Rau
Book design by Phil Falco
Creative Director: David Saylor

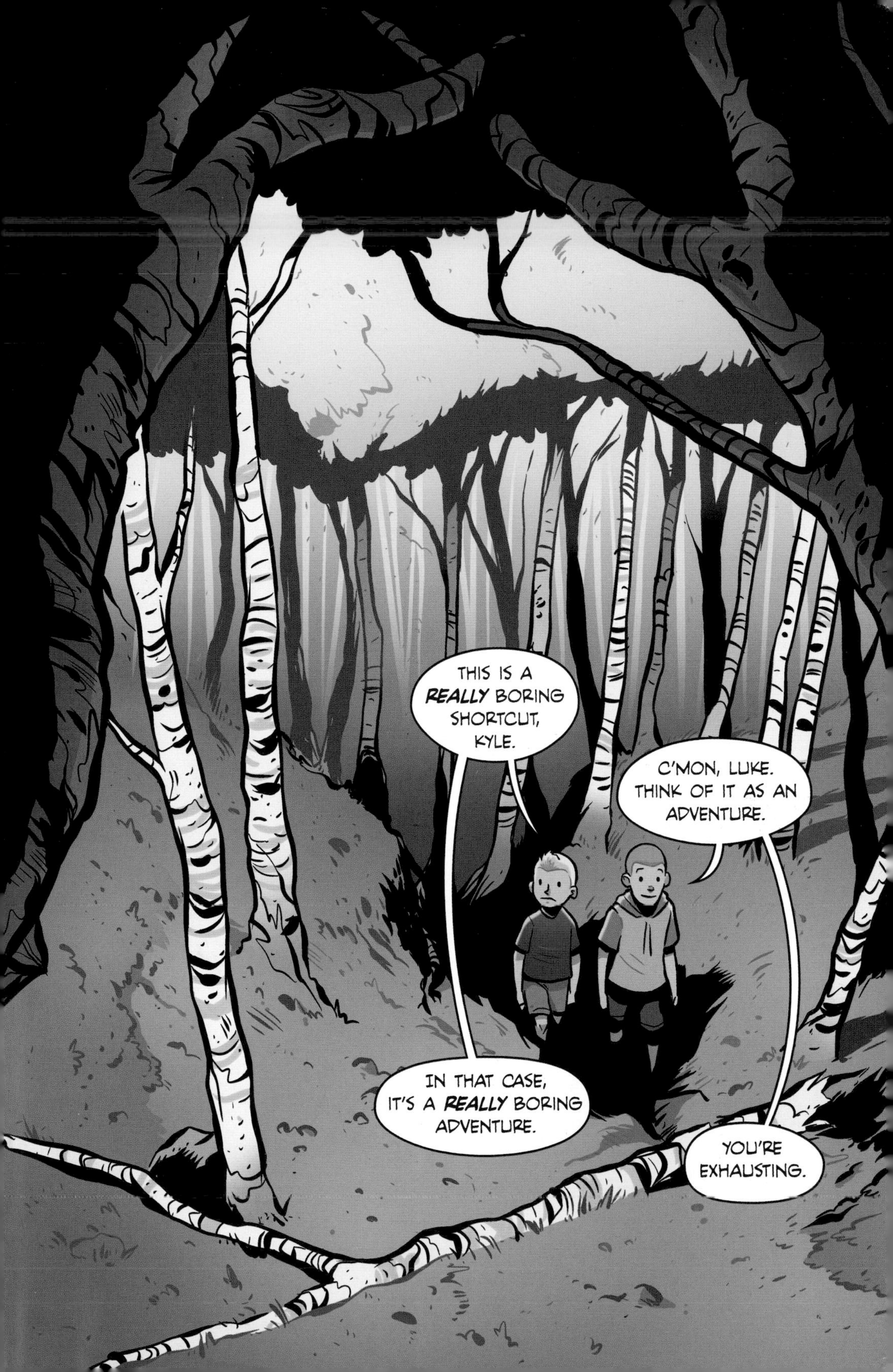
THIS IS A *REALLY* BORING SHORTCUT, KYLE.
C'MON, LUKE. THINK OF IT AS AN ADVENTURE.
IN THAT CASE, IT'S A *REALLY* BORING ADVENTURE.
YOU'RE EXHAUSTING.

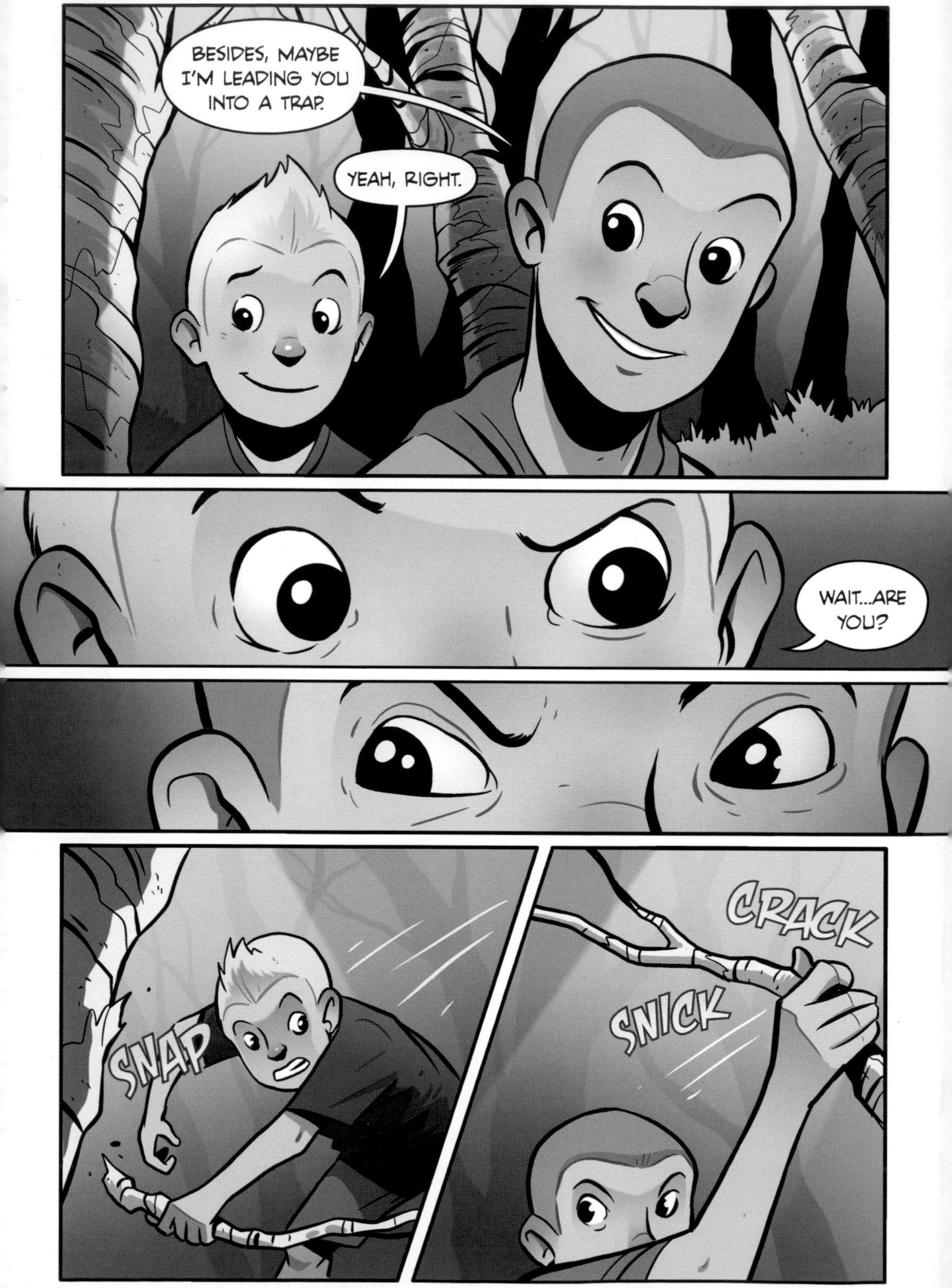
BESIDES, MAYBE I'M LEADING YOU INTO A TRAP.
YEAH, RIGHT.
WAIT...ARE YOU?
SNAP
CRACK
SNICK

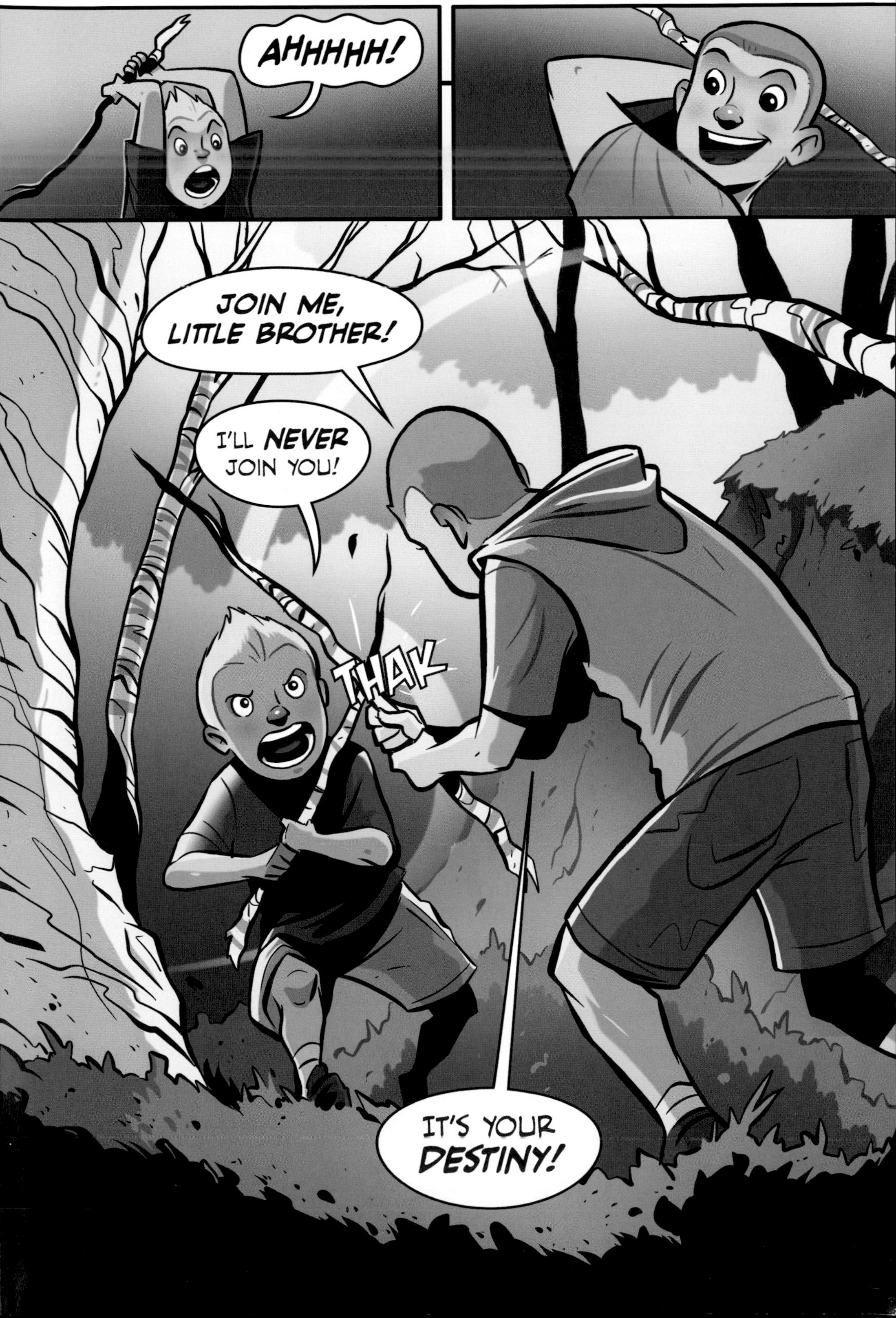
AHHHHH!
JOIN ME, LITTLE BROTHER!
I'LL NEVER JOIN YOU!
THAK
IT'S YOUR DESTINY!

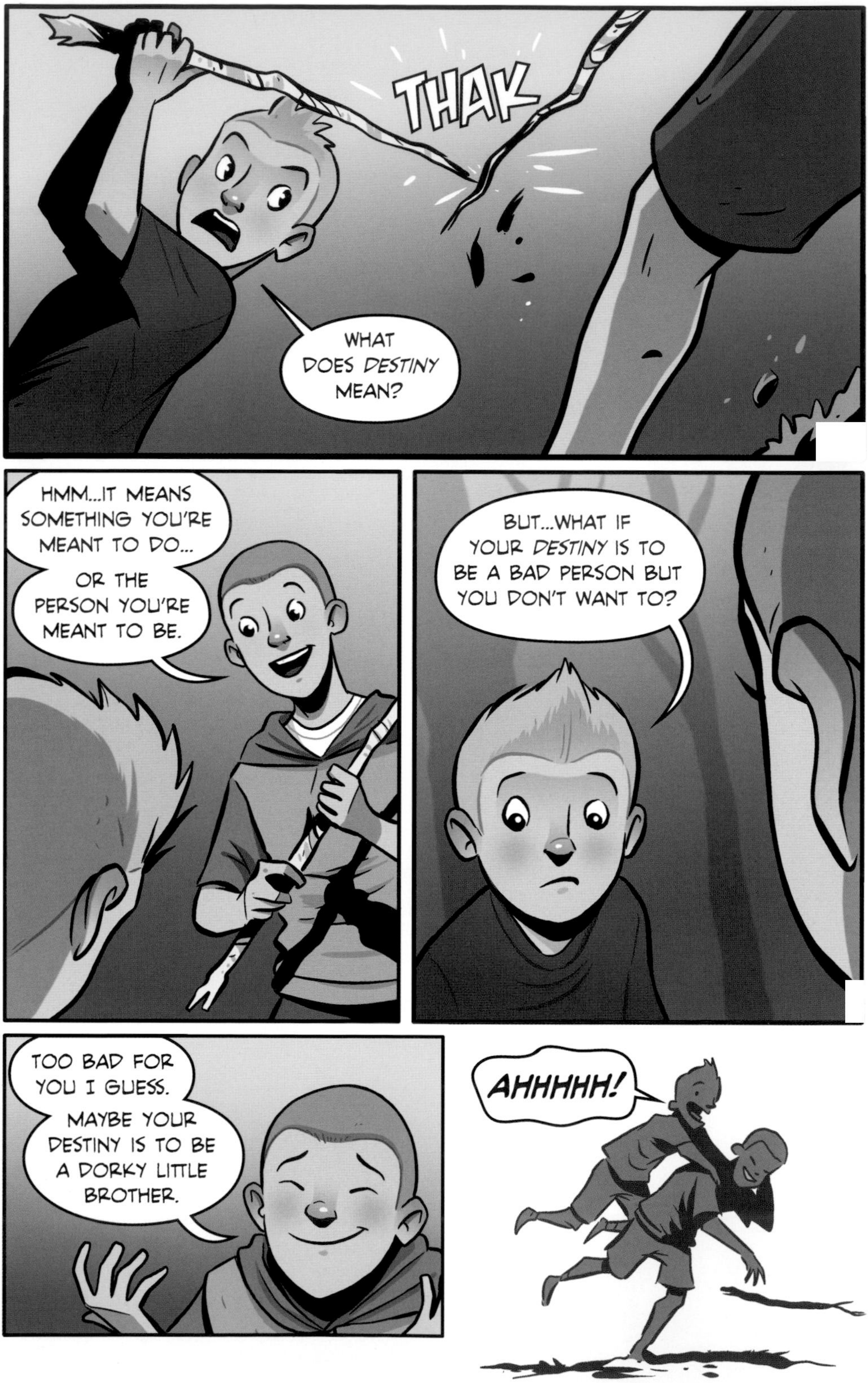
THAK
WHAT DOES *DESTINY* MEAN?
HMM...IT MEANS SOMETHING YOU'RE MEANT TO DO...
OR THE PERSON YOU'RE MEANT TO BE.
BUT...WHAT IF YOUR *DESTINY* IS TO BE A BAD PERSON BUT YOU DON'T WANT TO?
TOO BAD FOR YOU I GUESS.
MAYBE YOUR DESTINY IS TO BE A DORKY LITTLE BROTHER.
AHHHHH!

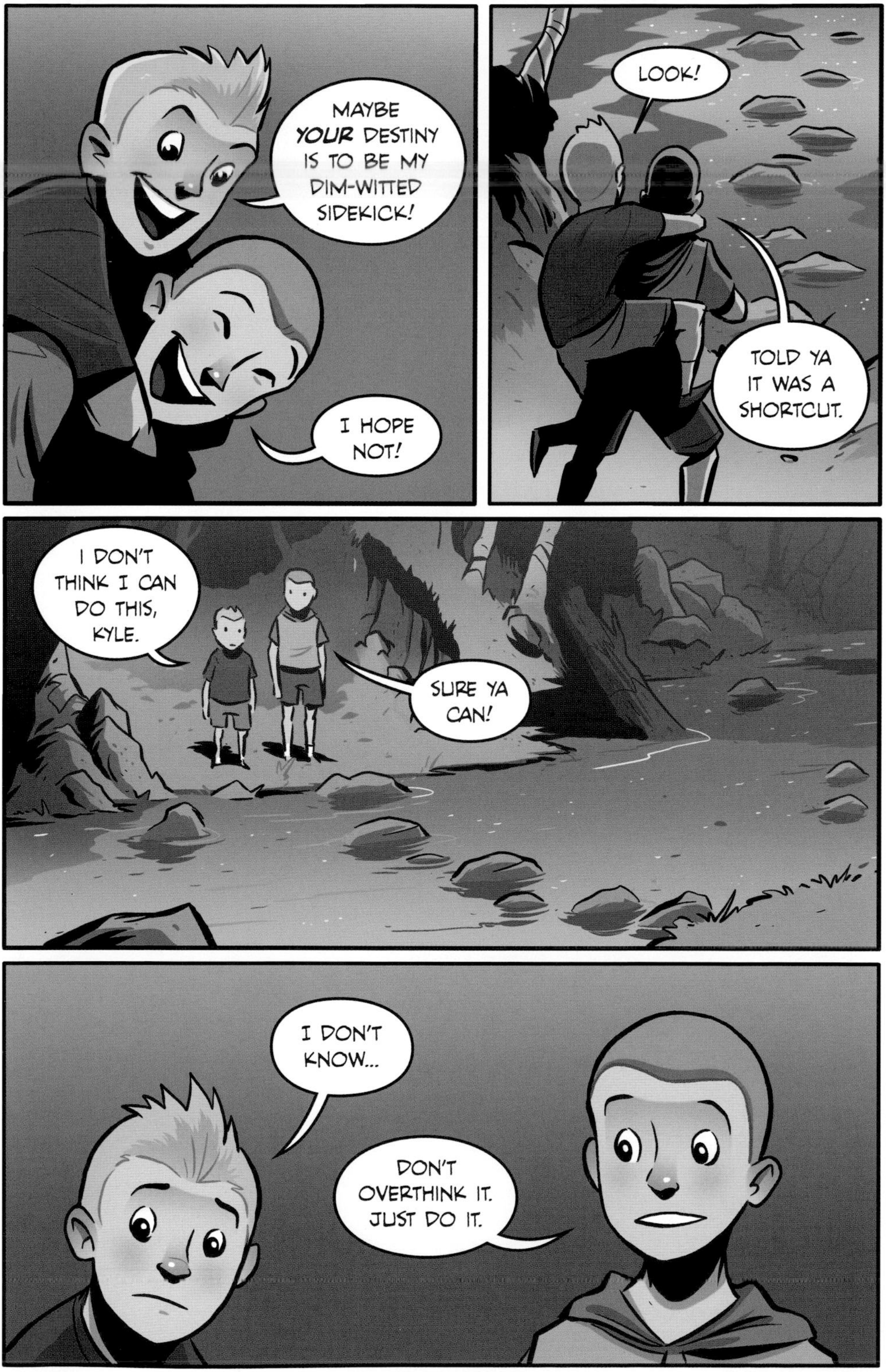
MAYBE YOUR DESTINY IS TO BE MY DIM-WITTED SIDEKICK!
I HOPE NOT!
LOOK!
TOLD YA IT WAS A SHORTCUT.
I DON'T THINK I CAN DO THIS, KYLE.
SURE YA CAN!
I DON'T KNOW...
DON'T OVERTHINK IT. JUST DO IT.

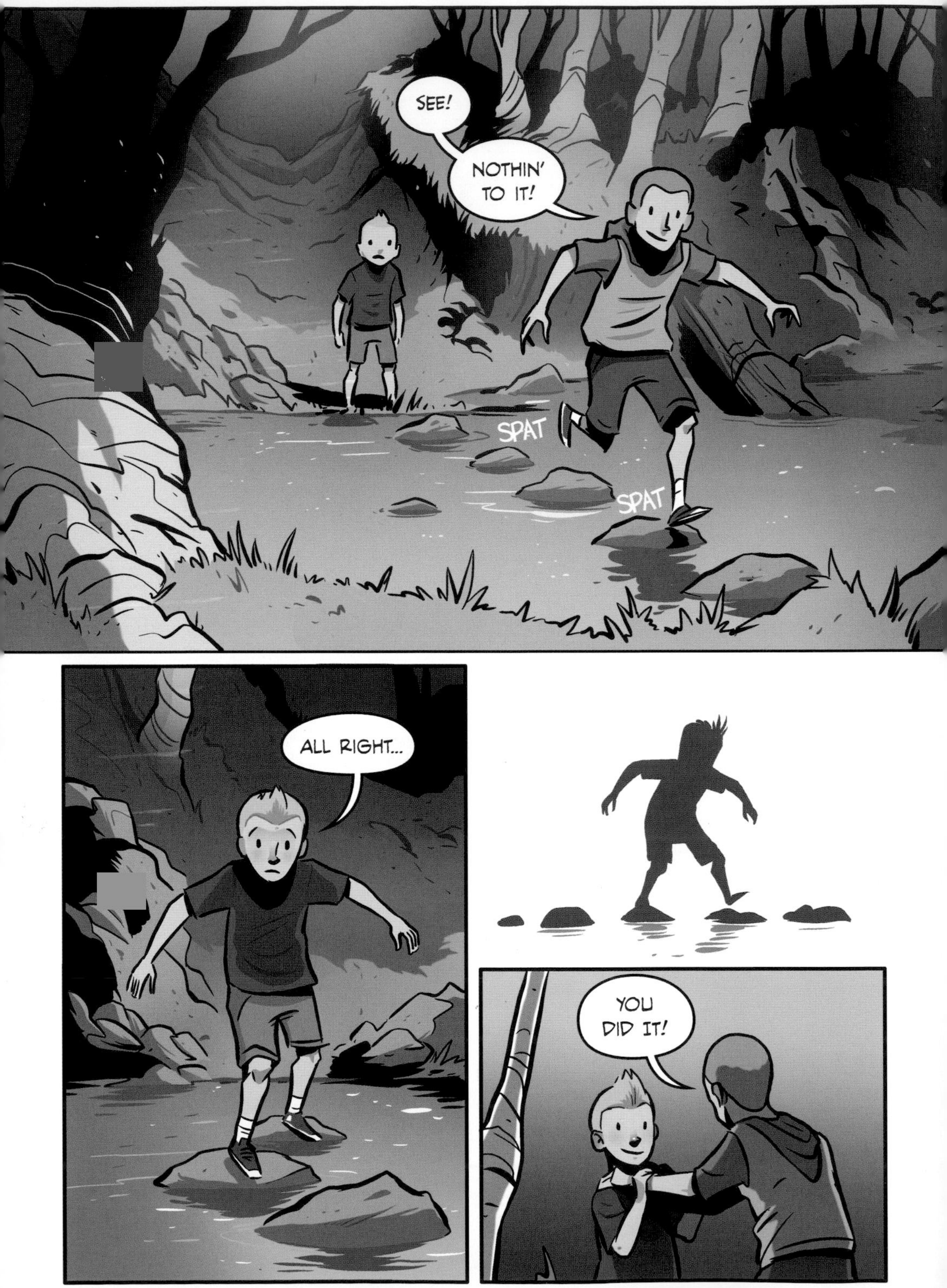
SEE!
NOTHIN' TO IT!
SPAT
SPAT
ALL RIGHT...
YOU DID IT!

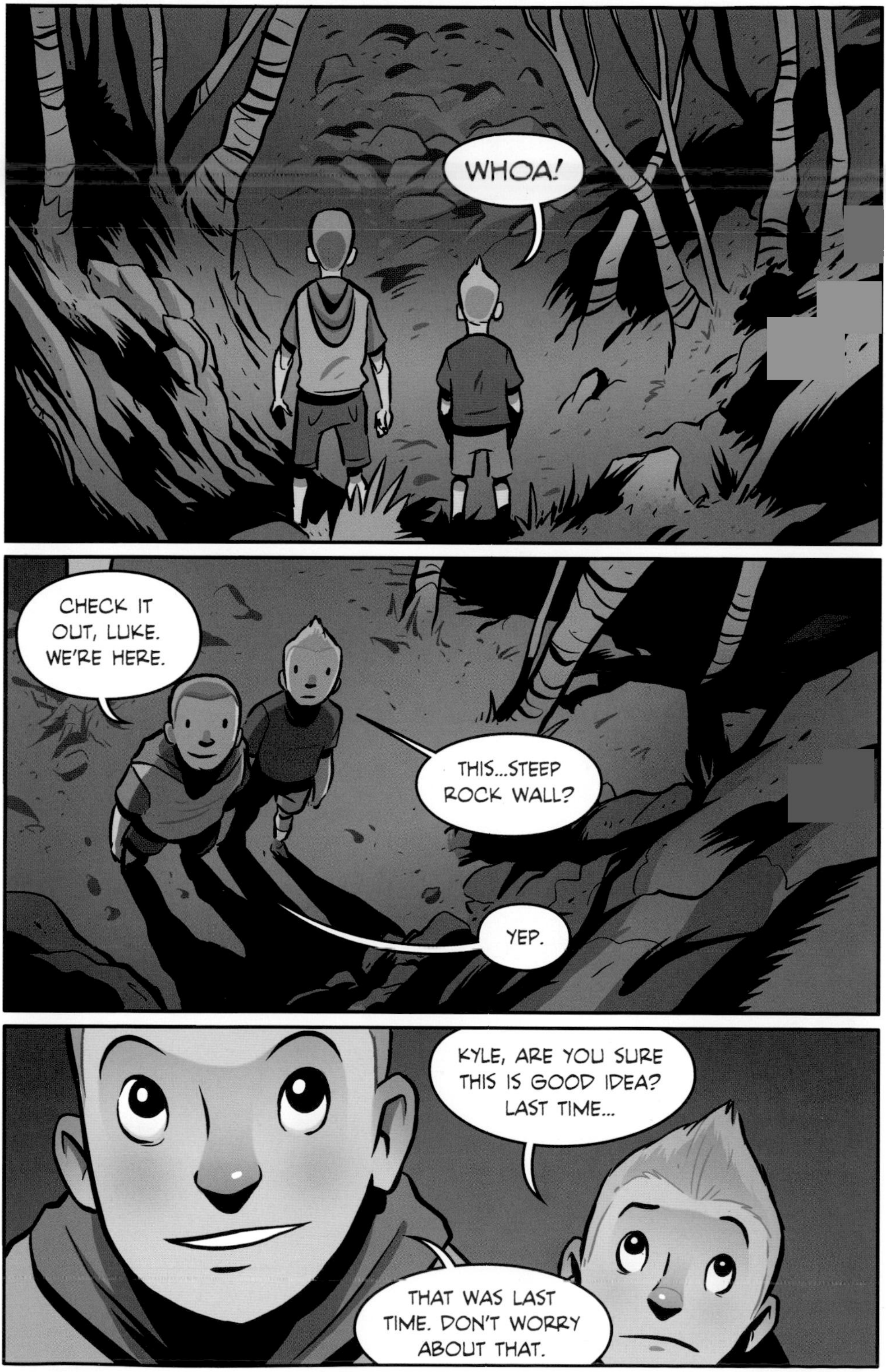
WHOA!
CHECK IT OUT, LUKE. WE'RE HERE.
THIS...STEEP ROCK WALL?
YEP.
KYLE, ARE YOU SURE THIS IS GOOD IDEA? LAST TIME...
THAT WAS LAST TIME. DON'T WORRY ABOUT THAT.

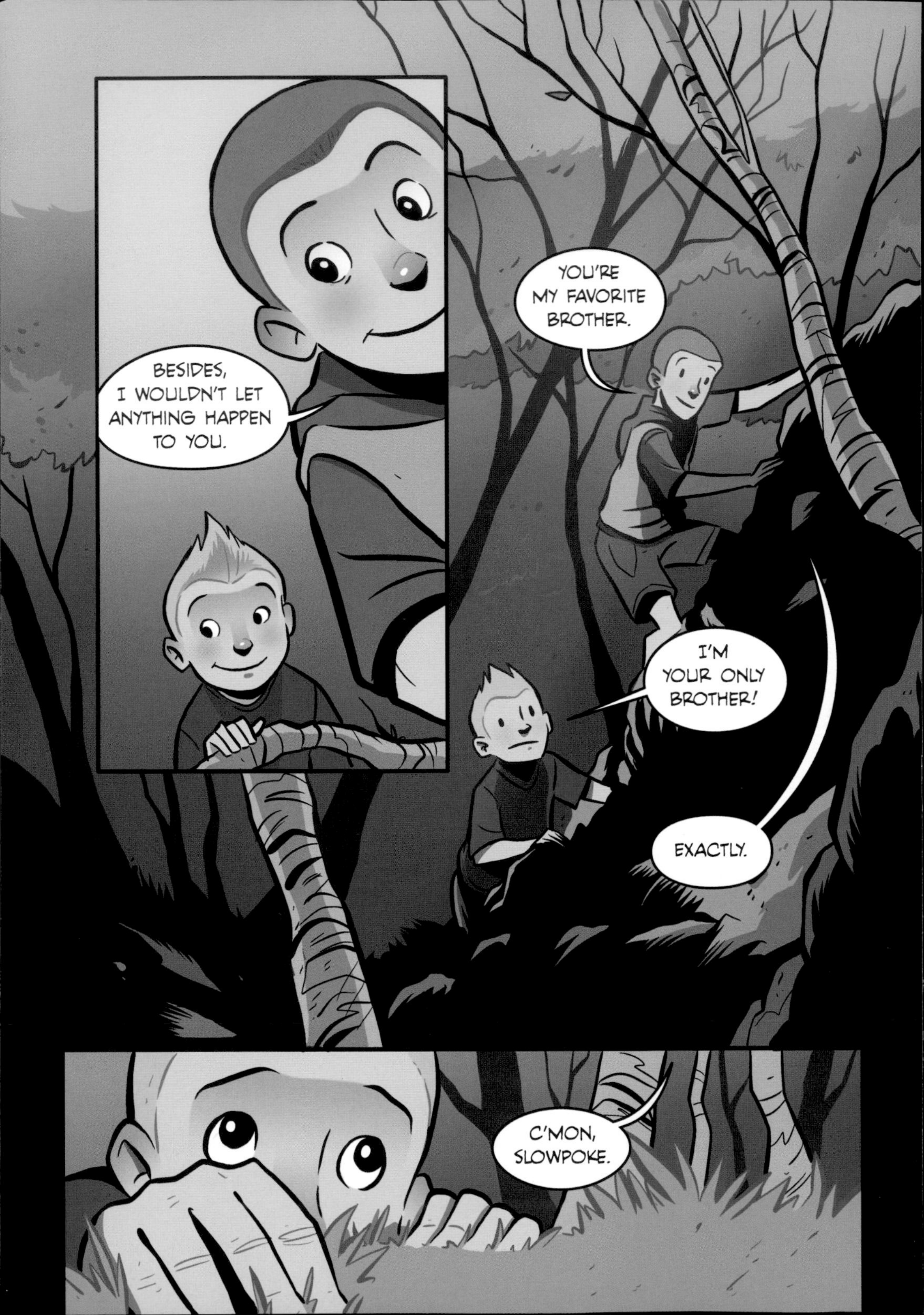
BESIDES, I WOULDN'T LET ANYTHING HAPPEN TO YOU.
YOU'RE MY FAVORITE BROTHER.
I'M YOUR ONLY BROTHER!
EXACTLY.
C'MON, SLOWPOKE.

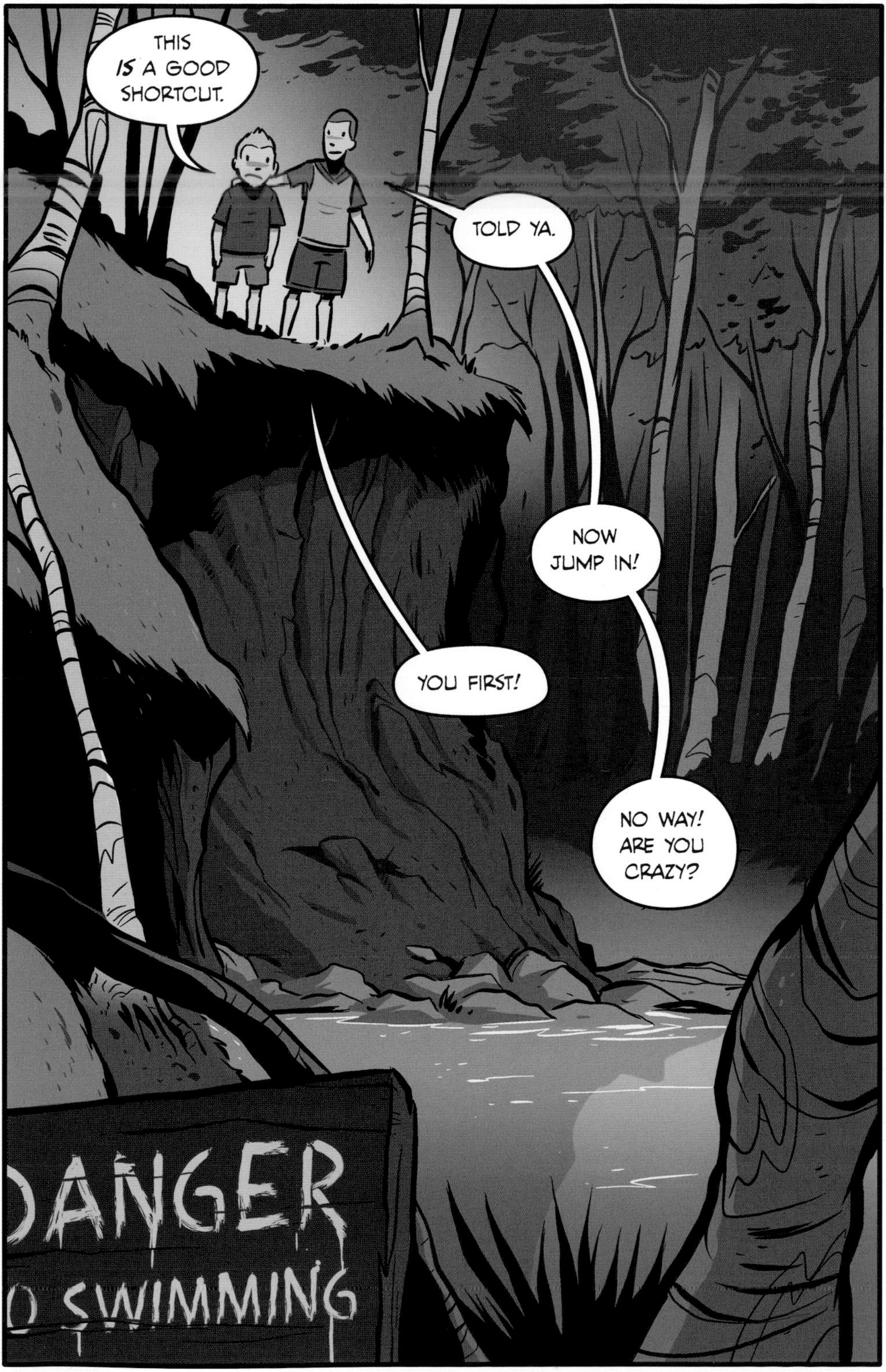
THIS IS A GOOD SHORTCUT.
TOLD YA.
NOW JUMP IN!
YOU FIRST!
NO WAY! ARE YOU CRAZY?
DANGER
O SWIMMING

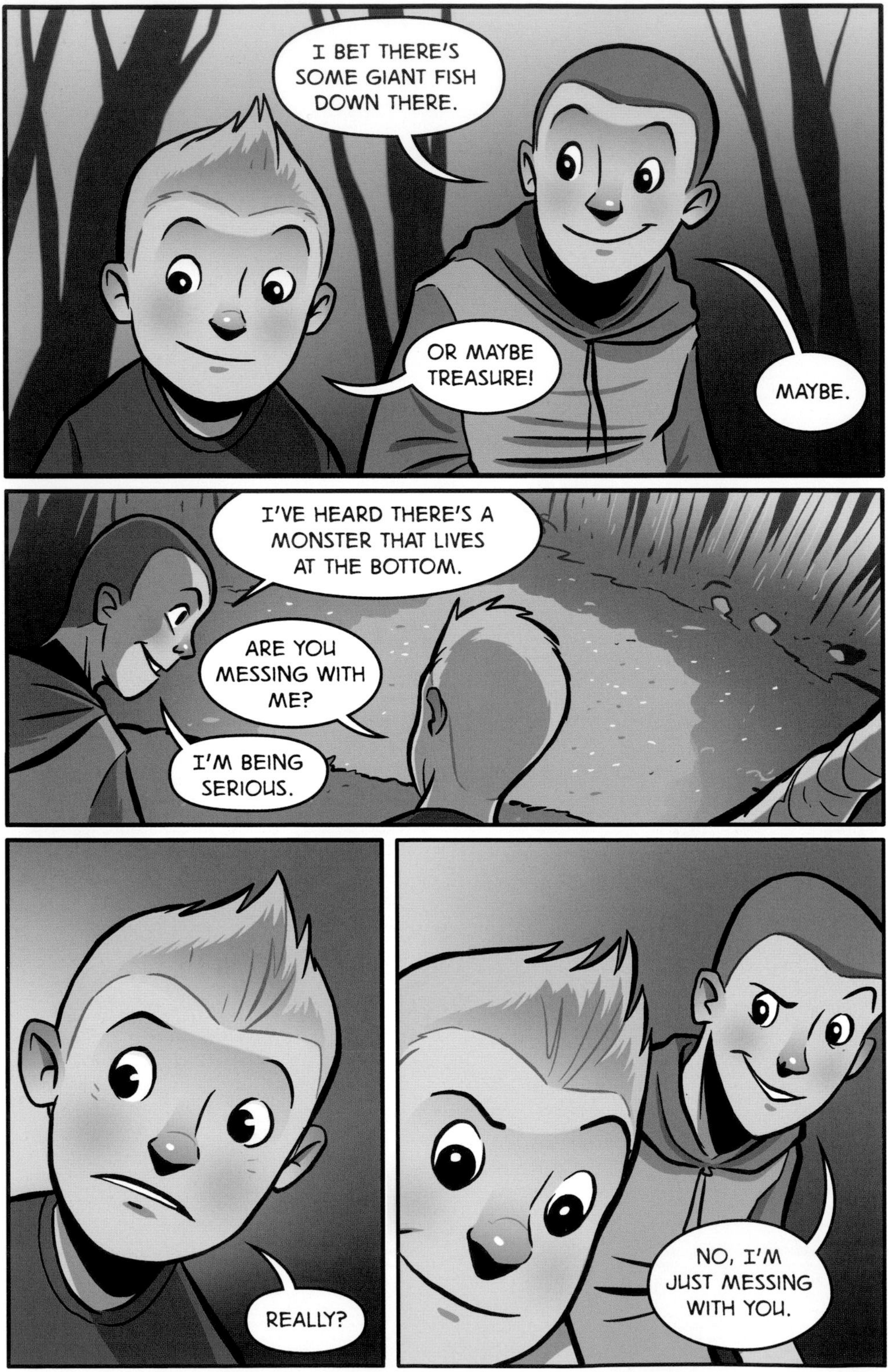
I BET THERE'S SOME GIANT FISH DOWN THERE.
OR MAYBE TREASURE!
MAYBE.
I'VE HEARD THERE'S A MONSTER THAT LIVES AT THE BOTTOM.
ARE YOU MESSING WITH ME?
I'M BEING SERIOUS.
REALLY?
NO, I'M JUST MESSING WITH YOU.

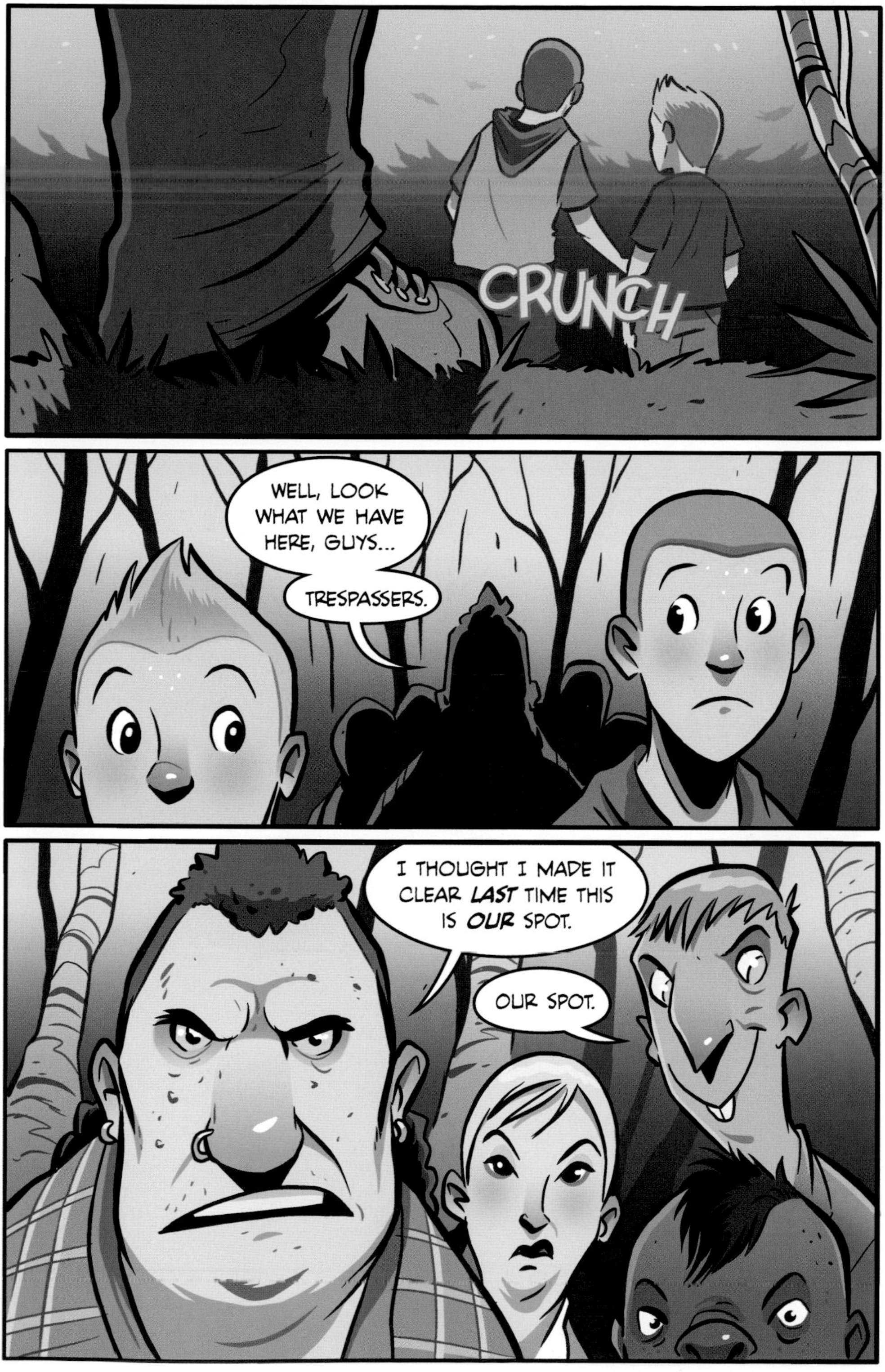
CRUNCH
WELL, LOOK WHAT WE HAVE HERE, GUYS...
TRESPASSERS.
I THOUGHT I MADE IT CLEAR *LAST* TIME THIS IS *OUR* SPOT.
OUR SPOT.

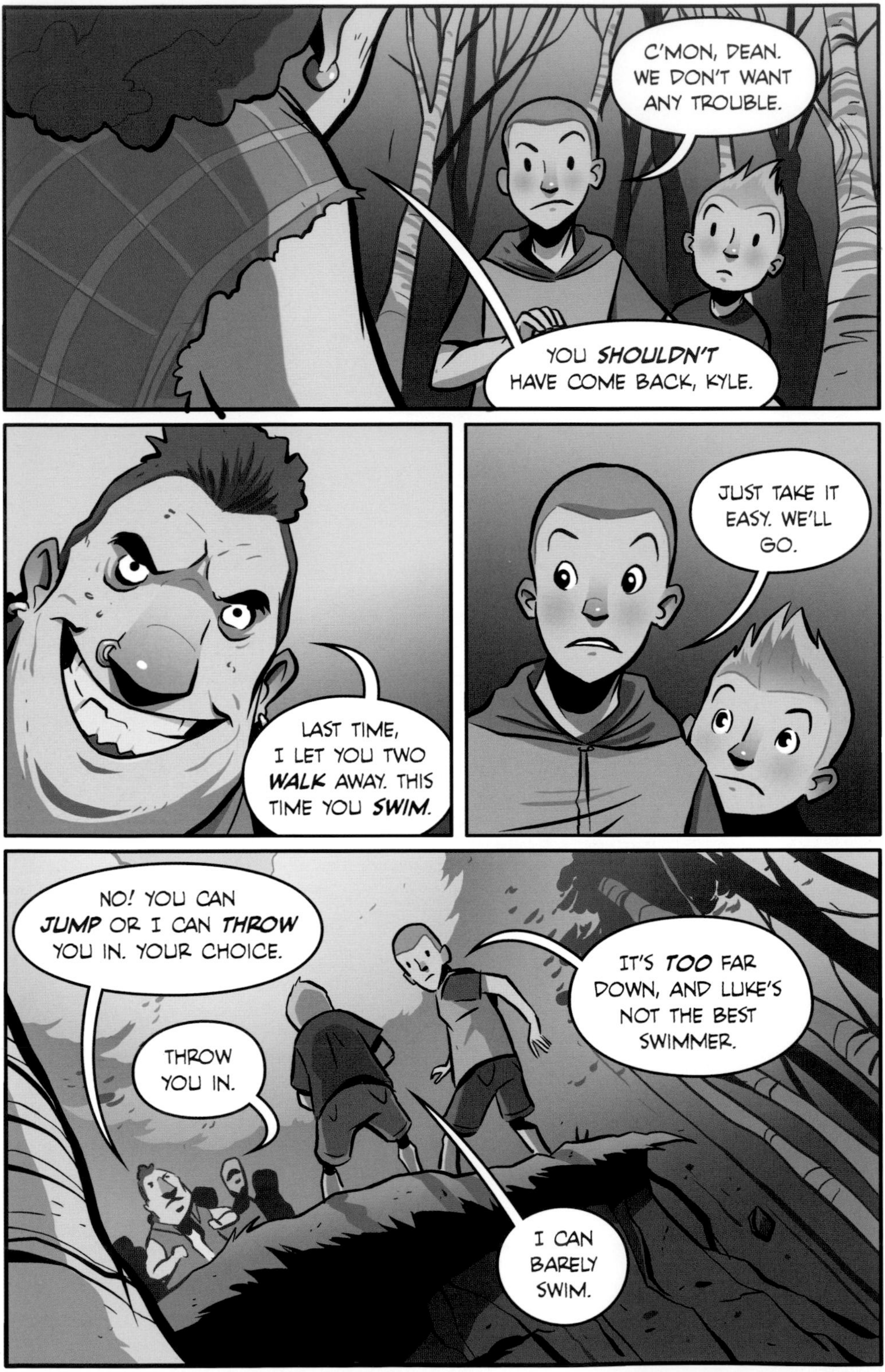
C'MON, DEAN. WE DON'T WANT ANY TROUBLE.
YOU *SHOULDN'T* HAVE COME BACK, KYLE.
LAST TIME, I LET YOU TWO *WALK* AWAY. THIS TIME YOU *SWIM*.
JUST TAKE IT EASY. WE'LL GO.
NO! YOU CAN *JUMP* OR I CAN *THROW* YOU IN. YOUR CHOICE.
THROW YOU IN.
IT'S *TOO* FAR DOWN, AND LUKE'S NOT THE BEST SWIMMER.
I CAN BARELY SWIM.

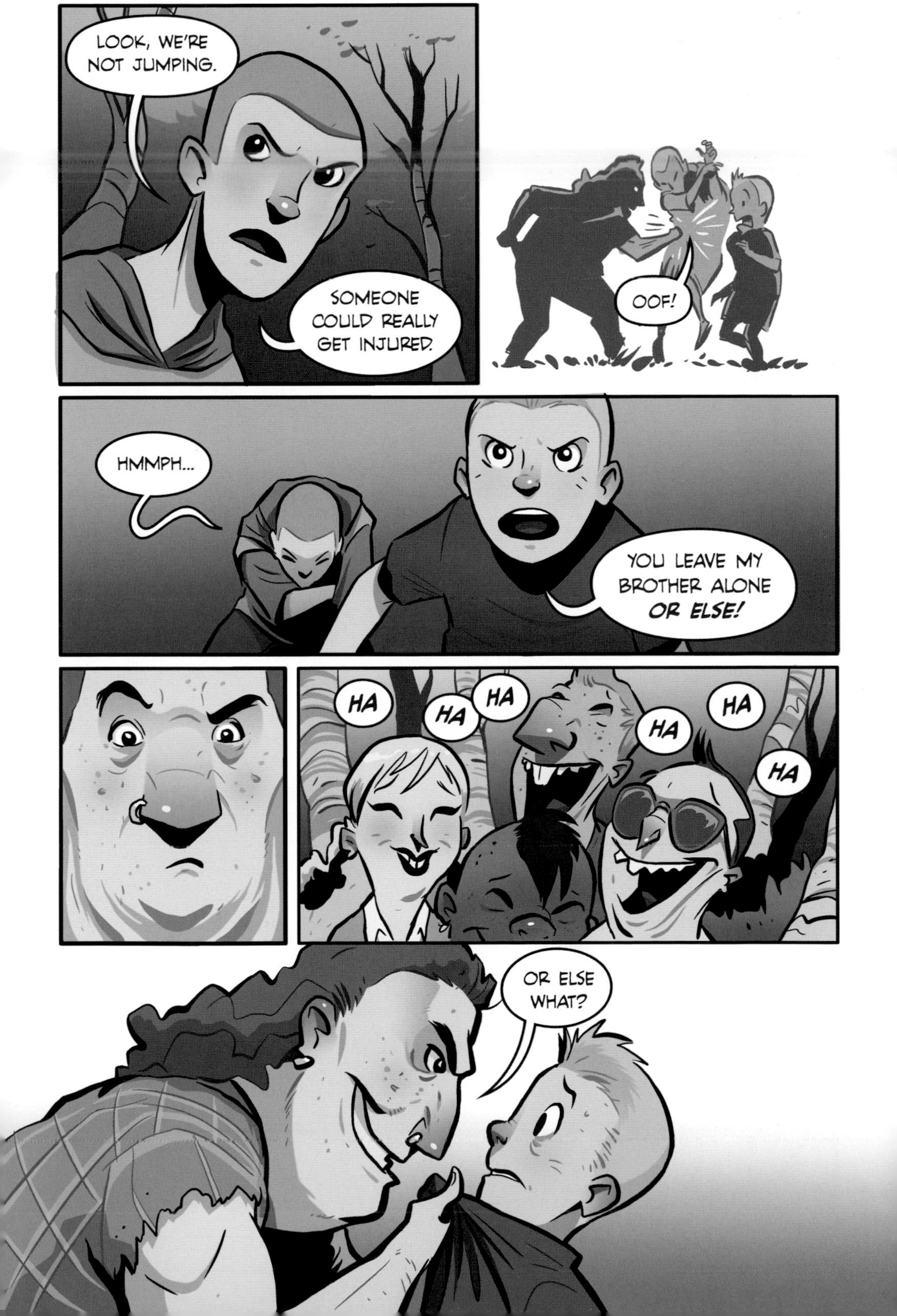
LOOK, WE'RE NOT JUMPING.
SOMEONE COULD REALLY GET INJURED.
OOF!
HMMPH...
YOU LEAVE MY BROTHER ALONE OR ELSE!
HA
HA
HA
HA
HA
HA
OR ELSE WHAT?

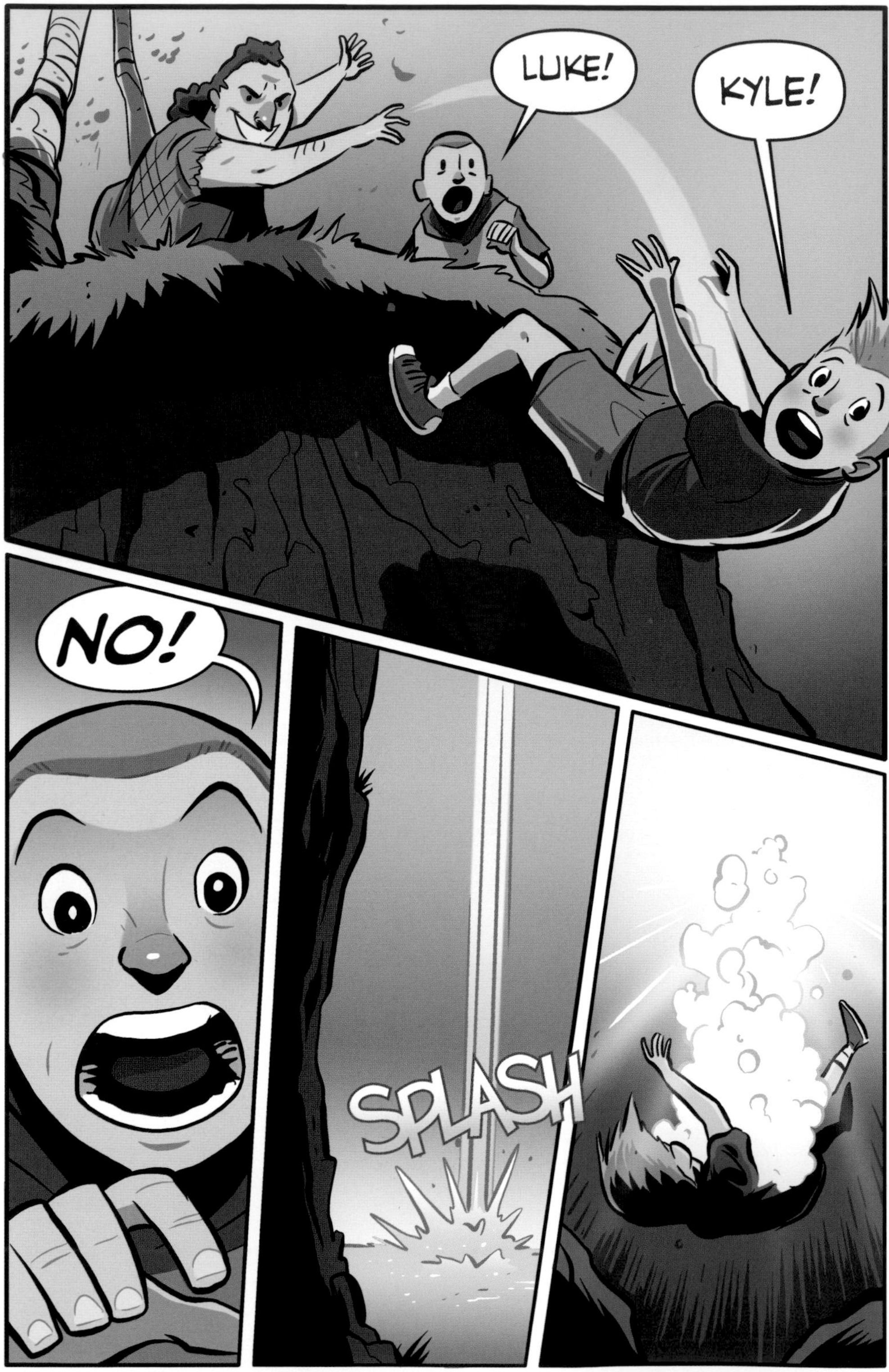
LUKE!
KYLE!
NO!
SPLASH

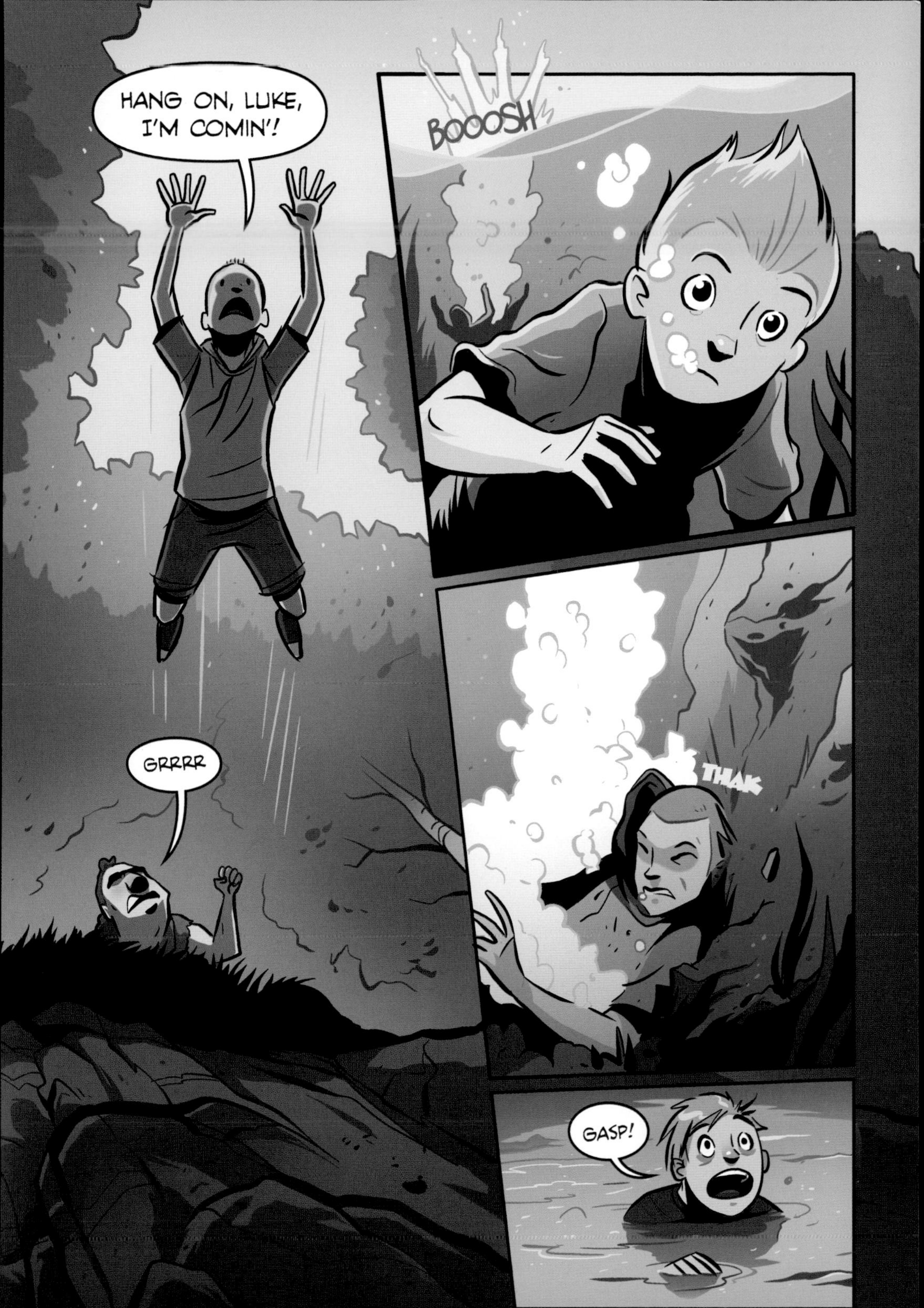
HANG ON, LUKE, I'M COMIN'!
BOOOSH
GRRRR
THAK
GASP!

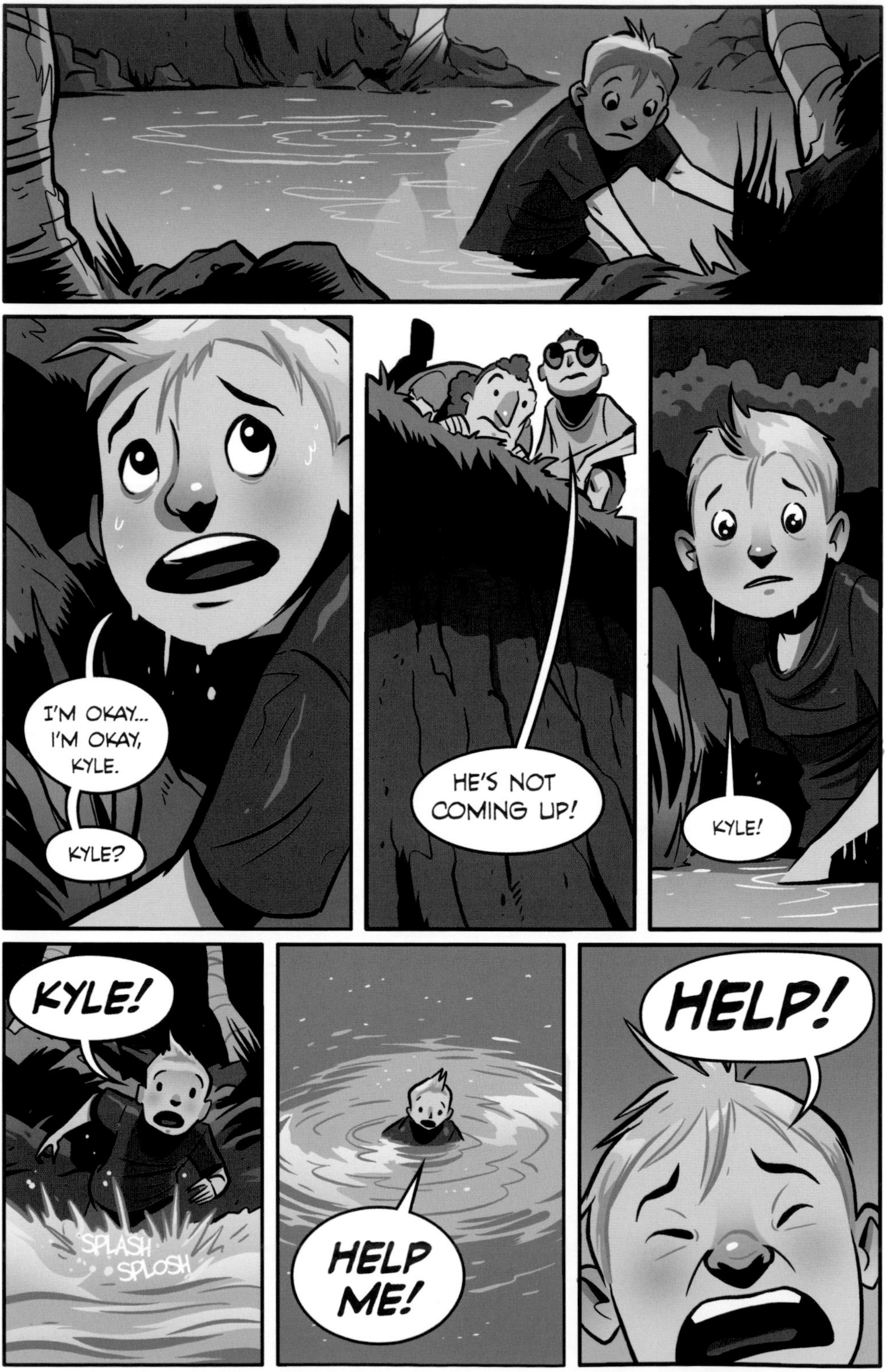
I'M OKAY... I'M OKAY, KYLE.
KYLE?
HE'S NOT COMING UP!
KYLE!
KYLE!
SPLASH
SPLOSH
HELP ME!
HELP!

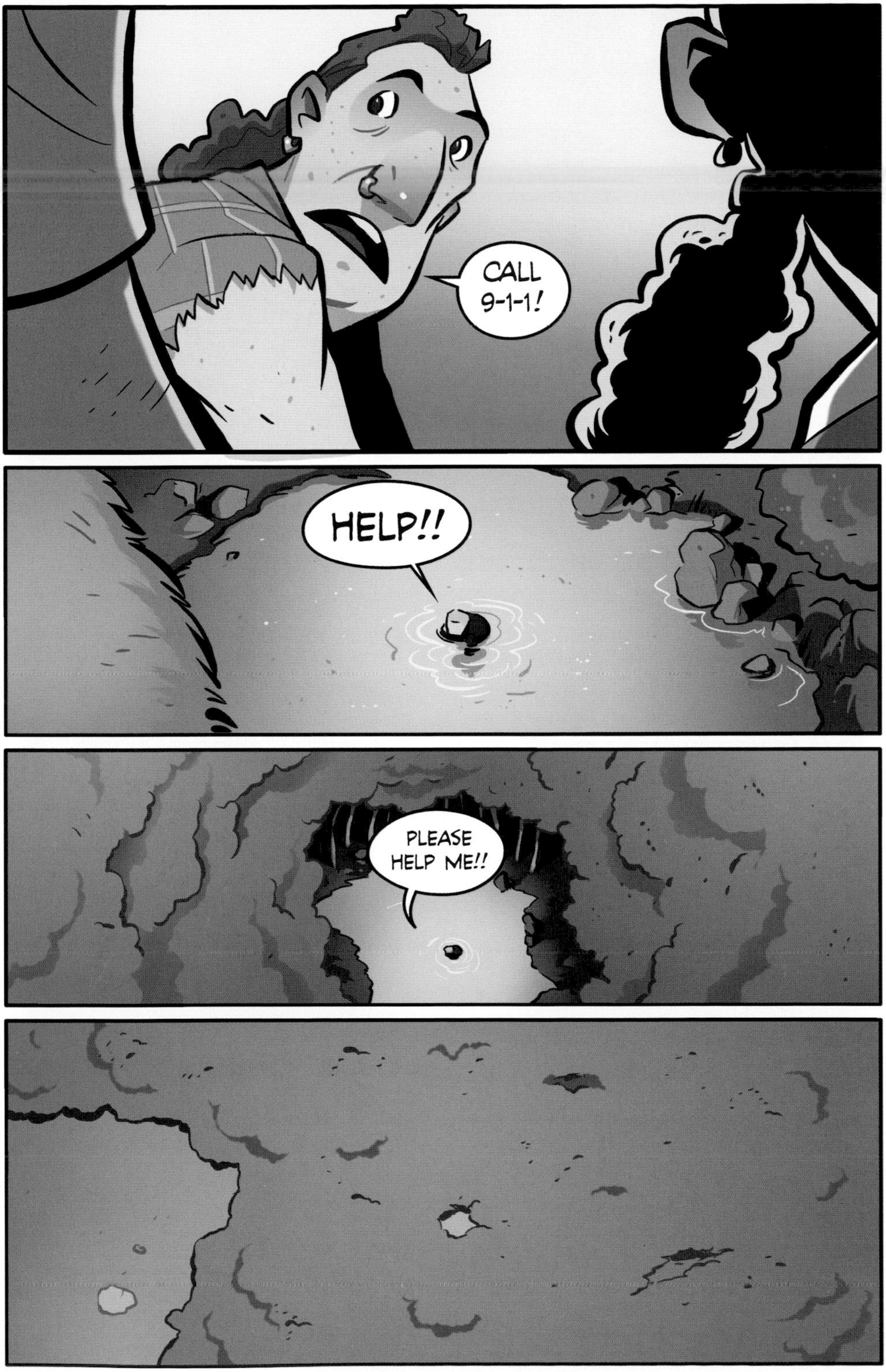
CALL 9-1-1!
HELP!!
PLEASE HELP ME!!

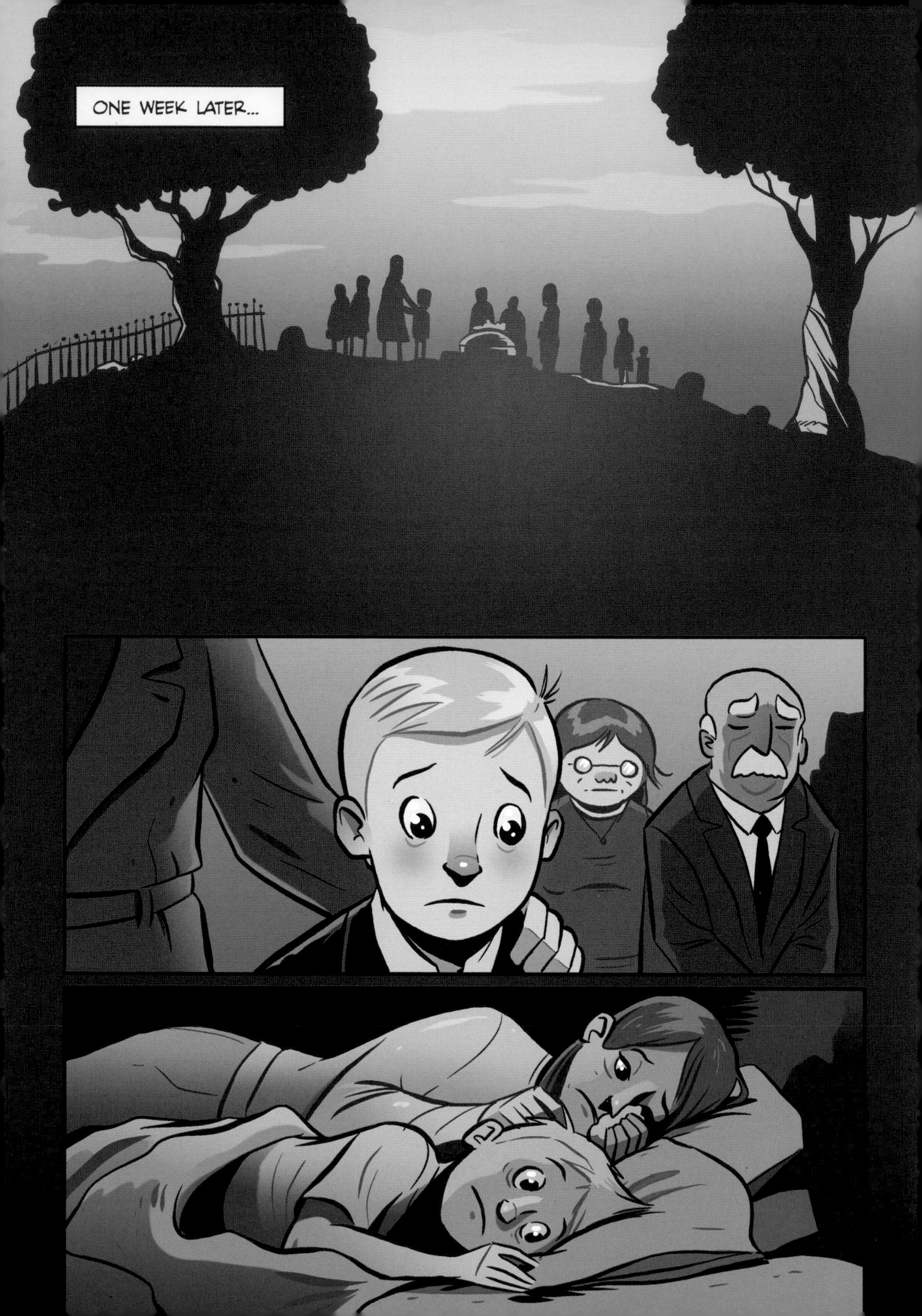
ONE WEEK LATER...

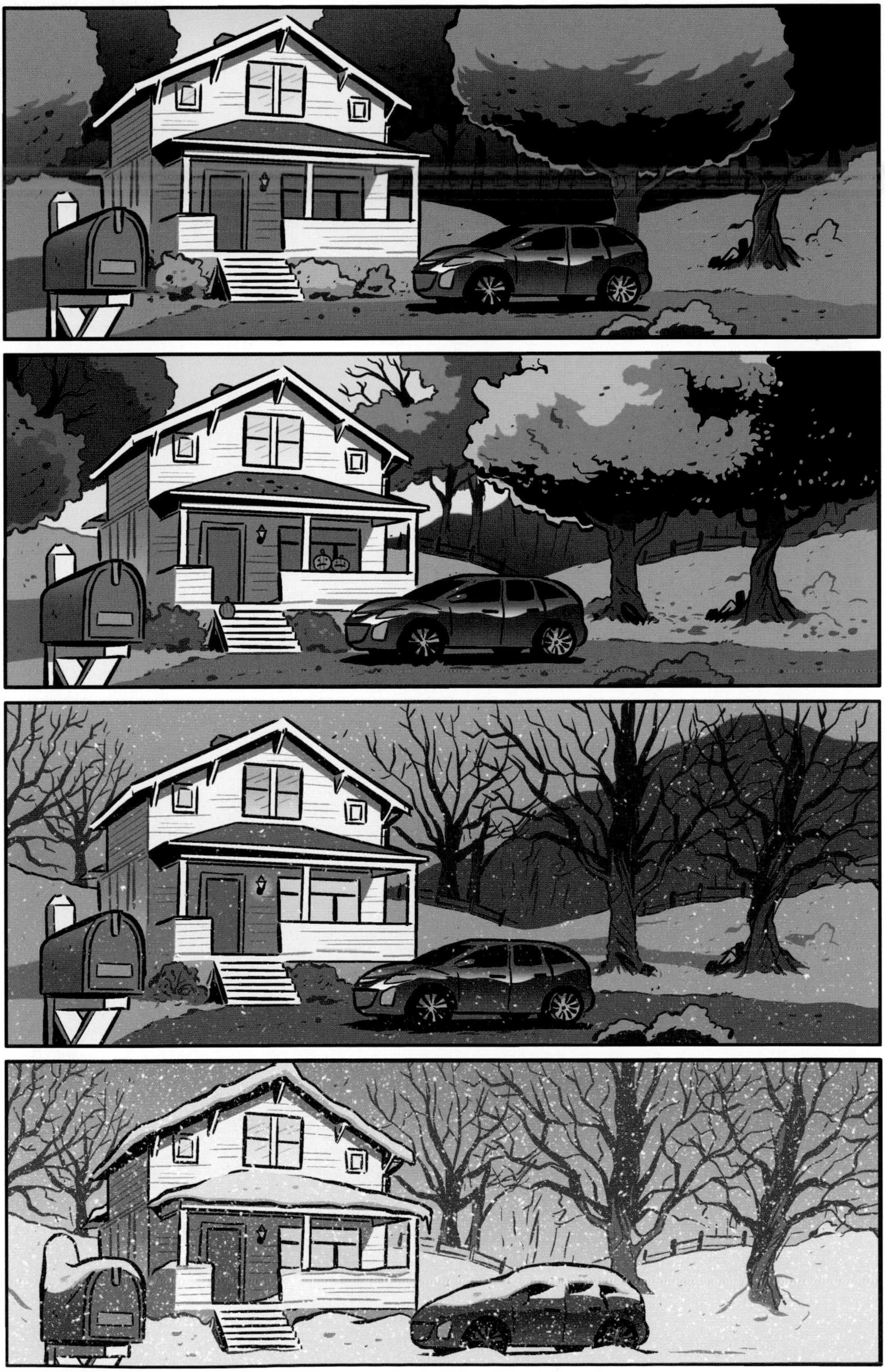

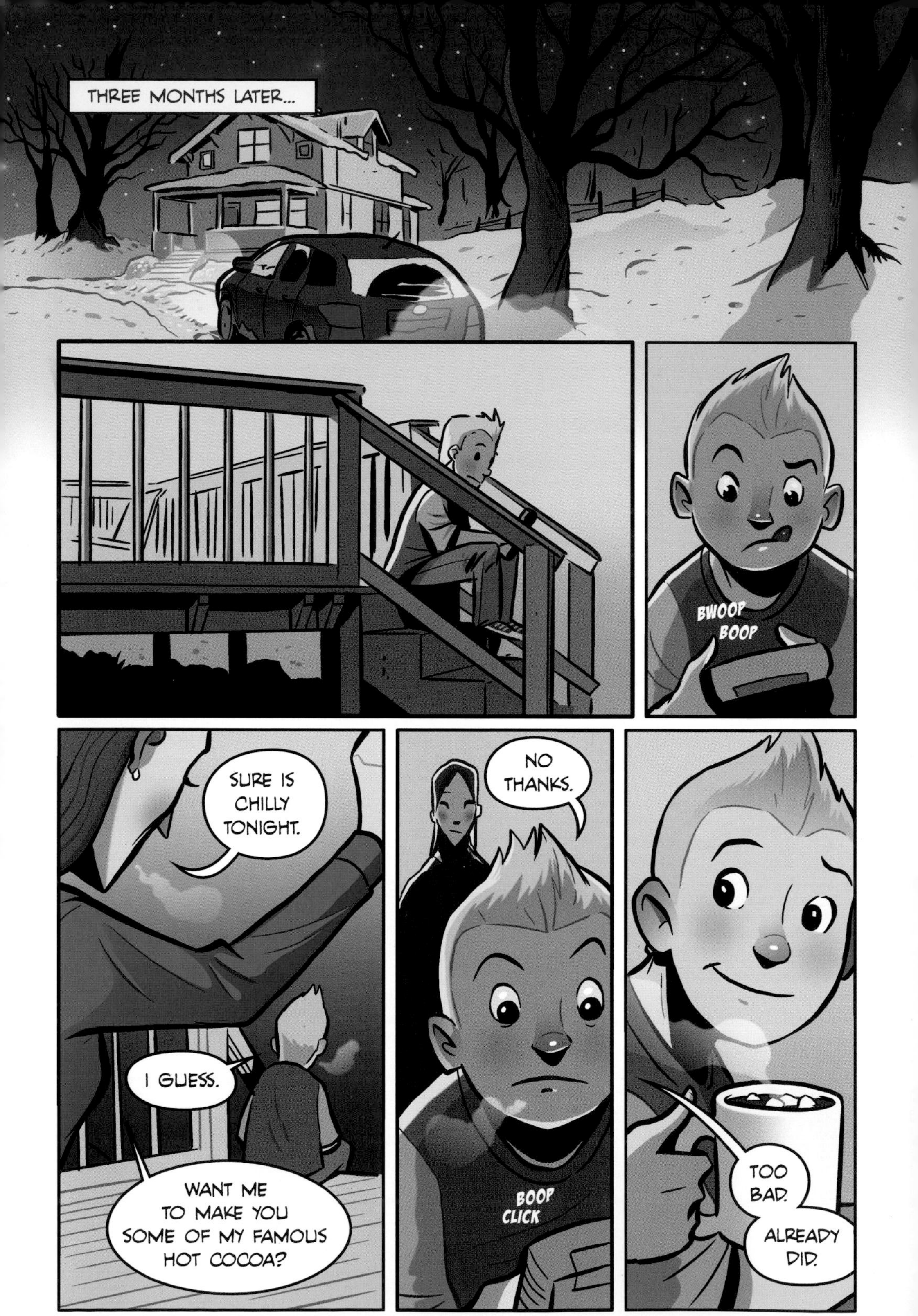
THREE MONTHS LATER...
BWOOP
BOOP
SURE IS CHILLY TONIGHT.
I GUESS.
WANT ME TO MAKE YOU SOME OF MY FAMOUS HOT COCOA?
NO THANKS.
BOOP
CLICK
TOO BAD.
ALREADY DID.

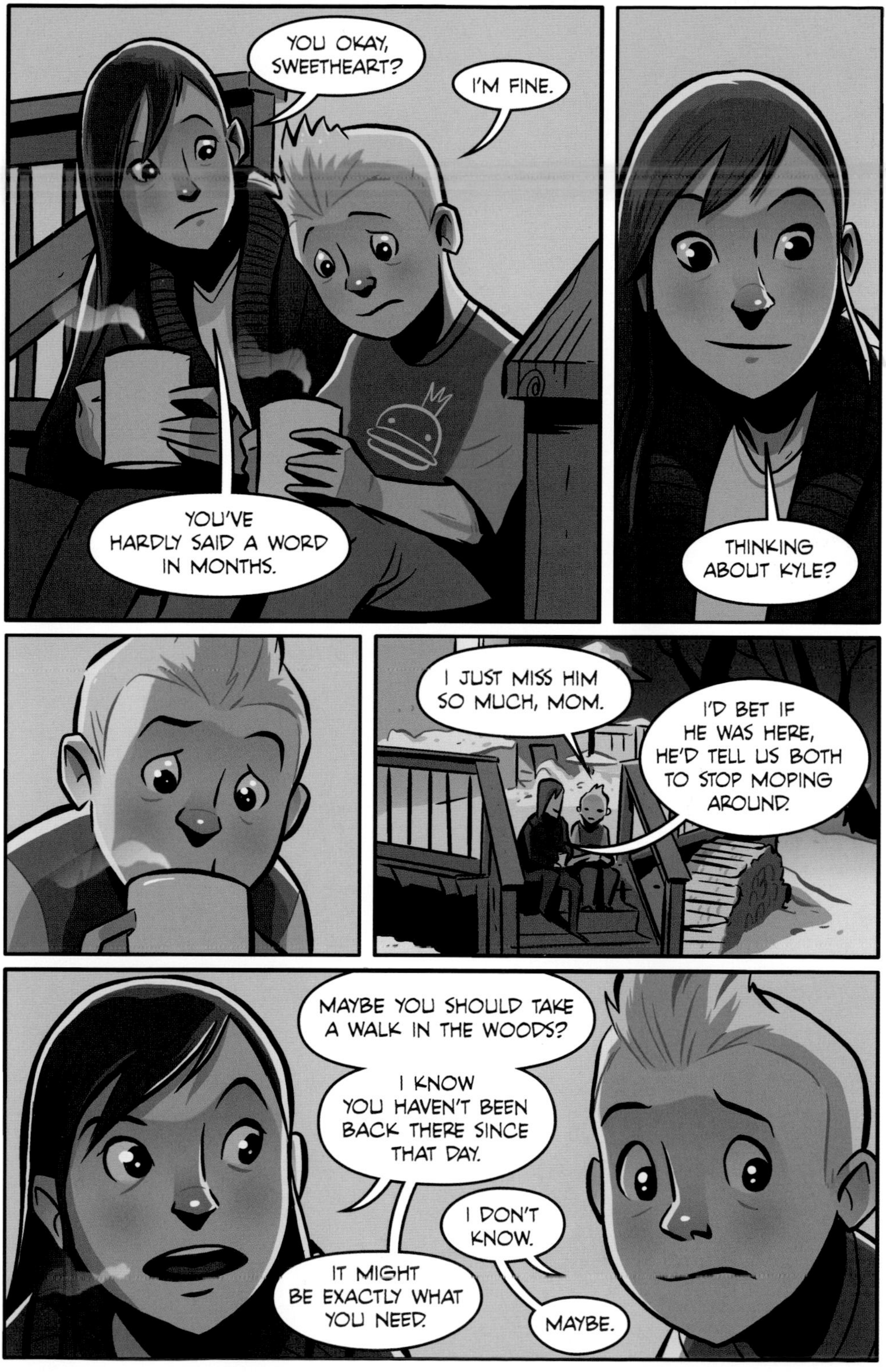
YOU OKAY, SWEETHEART?
I'M FINE.
YOU'VE HARDLY SAID A WORD IN MONTHS.
THINKING ABOUT KYLE?
I JUST MISS HIM SO MUCH, MOM.
I'D BET IF HE WAS HERE, HE'D TELL US BOTH TO STOP MOPING AROUND.
MAYBE YOU SHOULD TAKE A WALK IN THE WOODS?
I KNOW YOU HAVEN'T BEEN BACK THERE SINCE THAT DAY.
IT MIGHT BE EXACTLY WHAT YOU NEED.
I DON'T KNOW.
MAYBE.

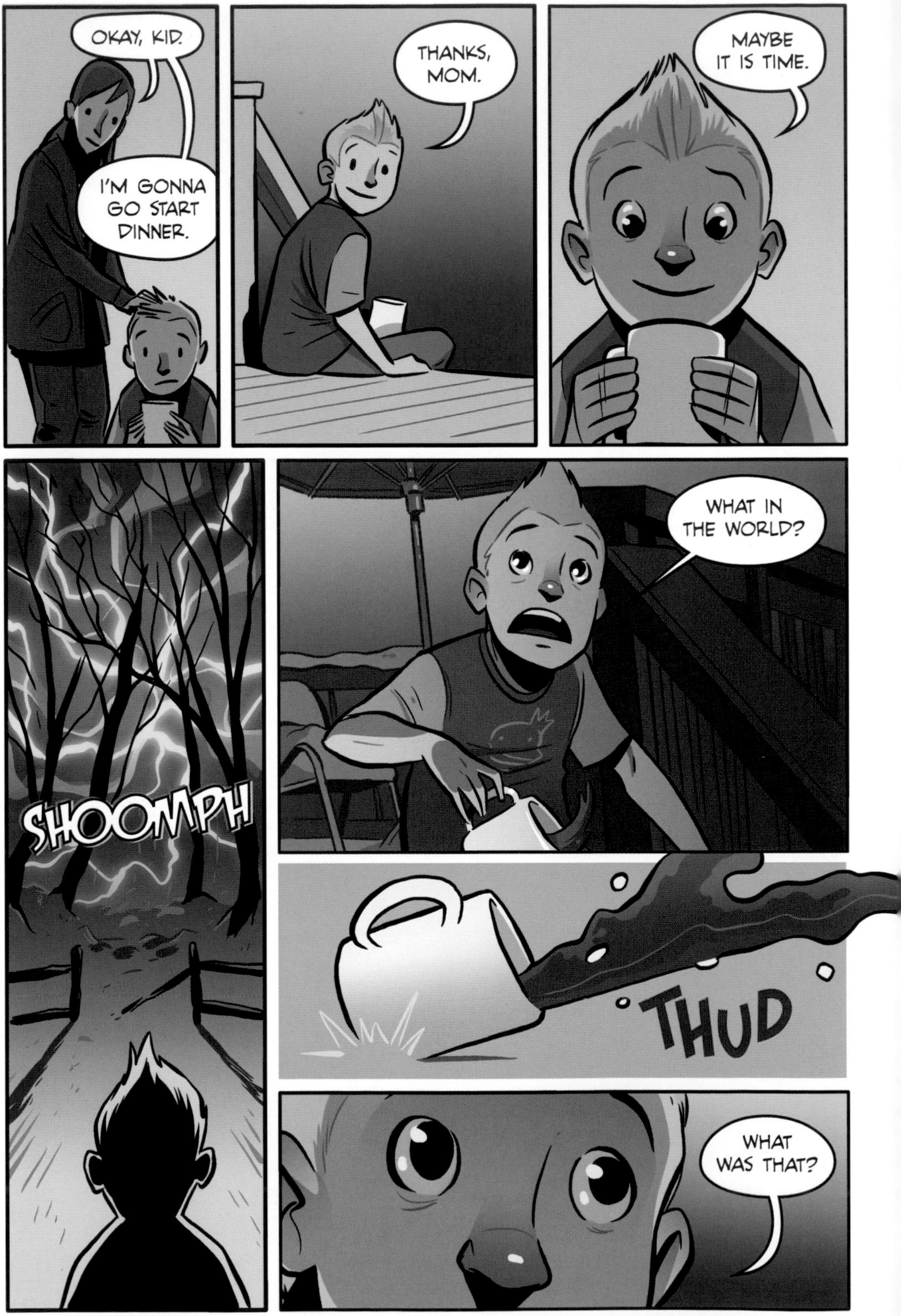
OKAY, KID.
I'M GONNA GO START DINNER.
THANKS, MOM.
MAYBE IT IS TIME.
SHOOMPH
WHAT IN THE WORLD?
THUD
WHAT WAS THAT?

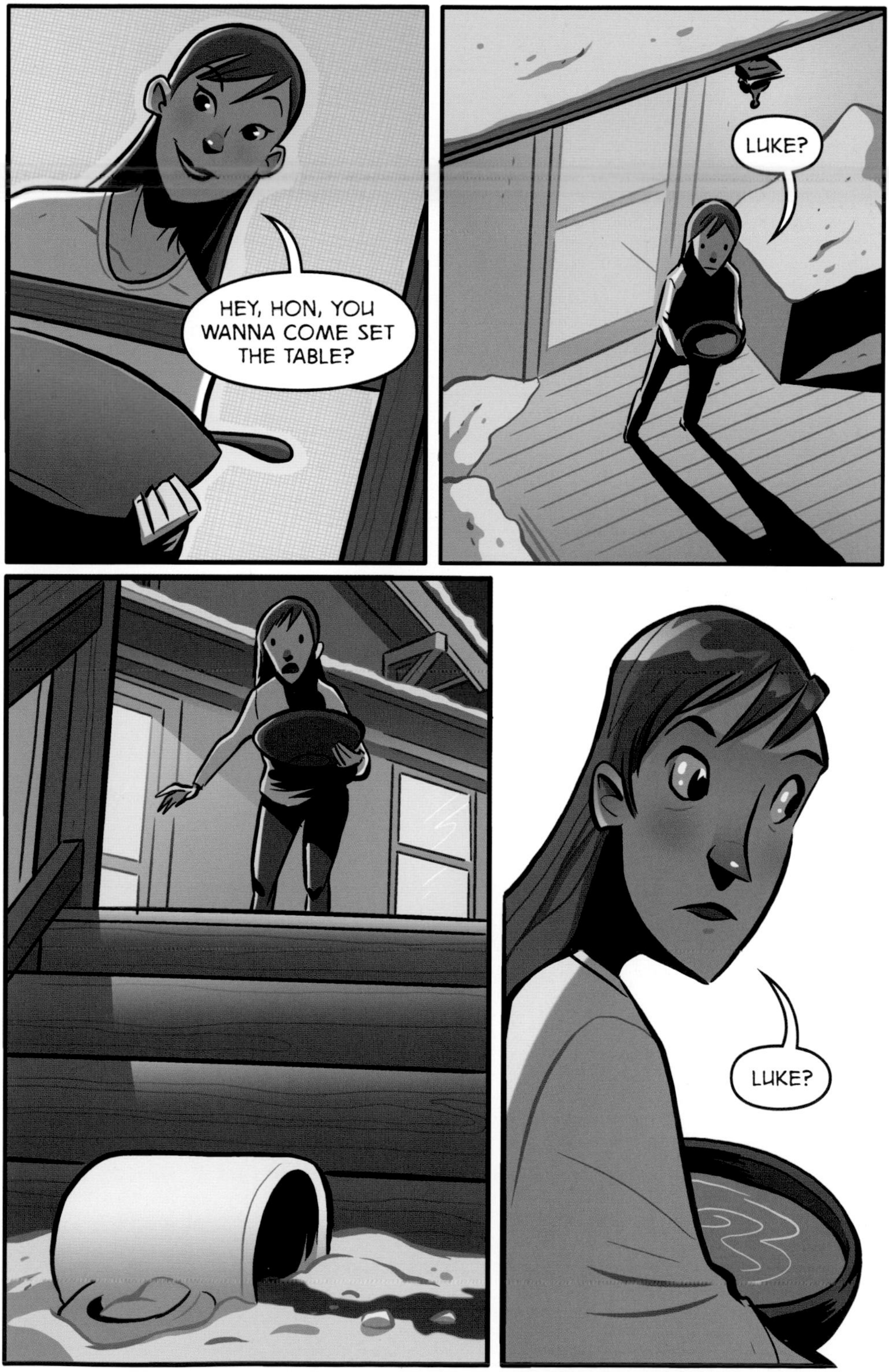
HEY, HON, YOU WANNA COME SET THE TABLE?
LUKE?
LUKE?

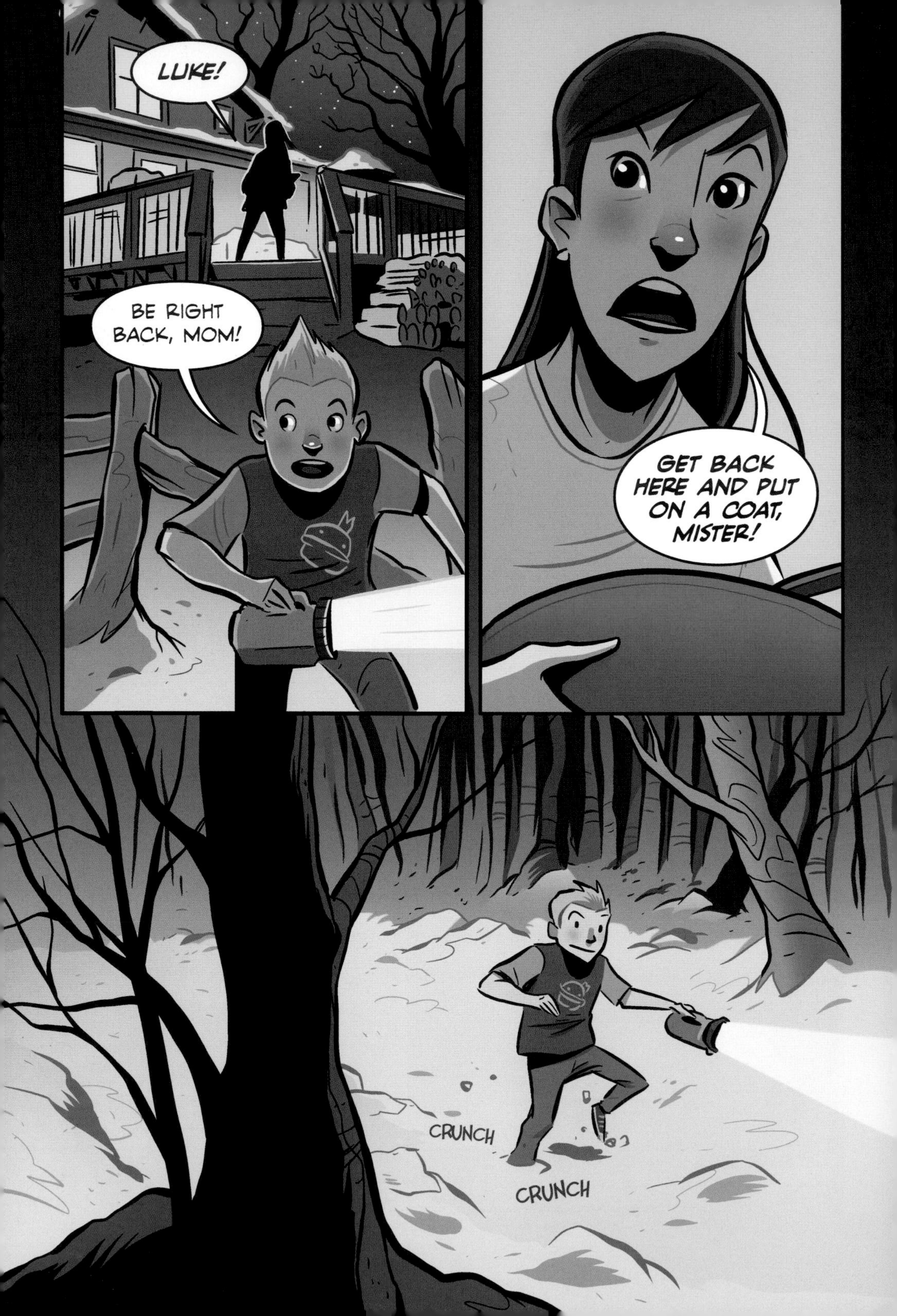
LUKE!
BE RIGHT BACK, MOM!
GET BACK HERE AND PUT ON A COAT, MISTER!
CRUNCH
CRUNCH

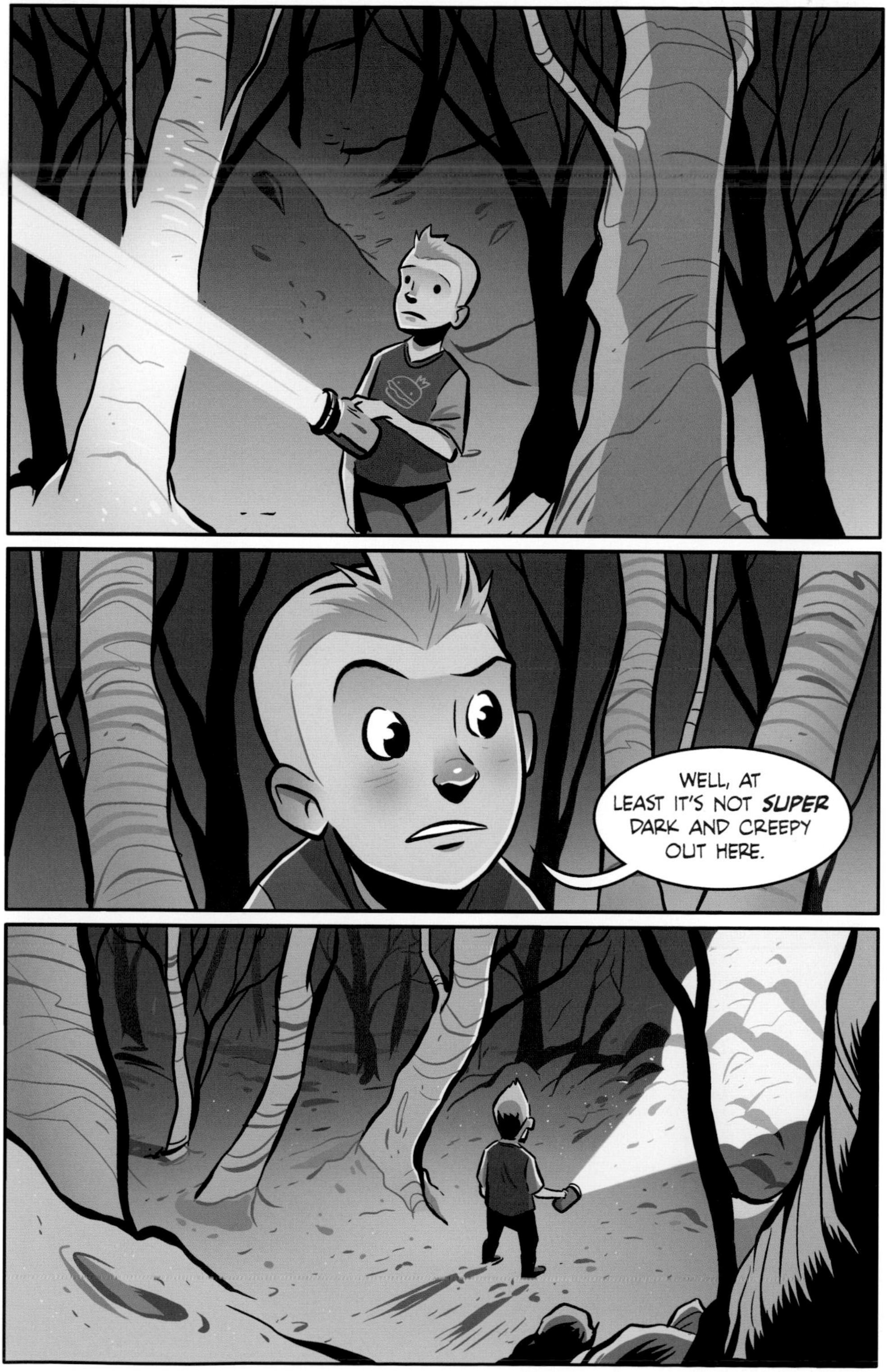
WELL, AT LEAST IT'S NOT SUPER DARK AND CREEPY OUT HERE.

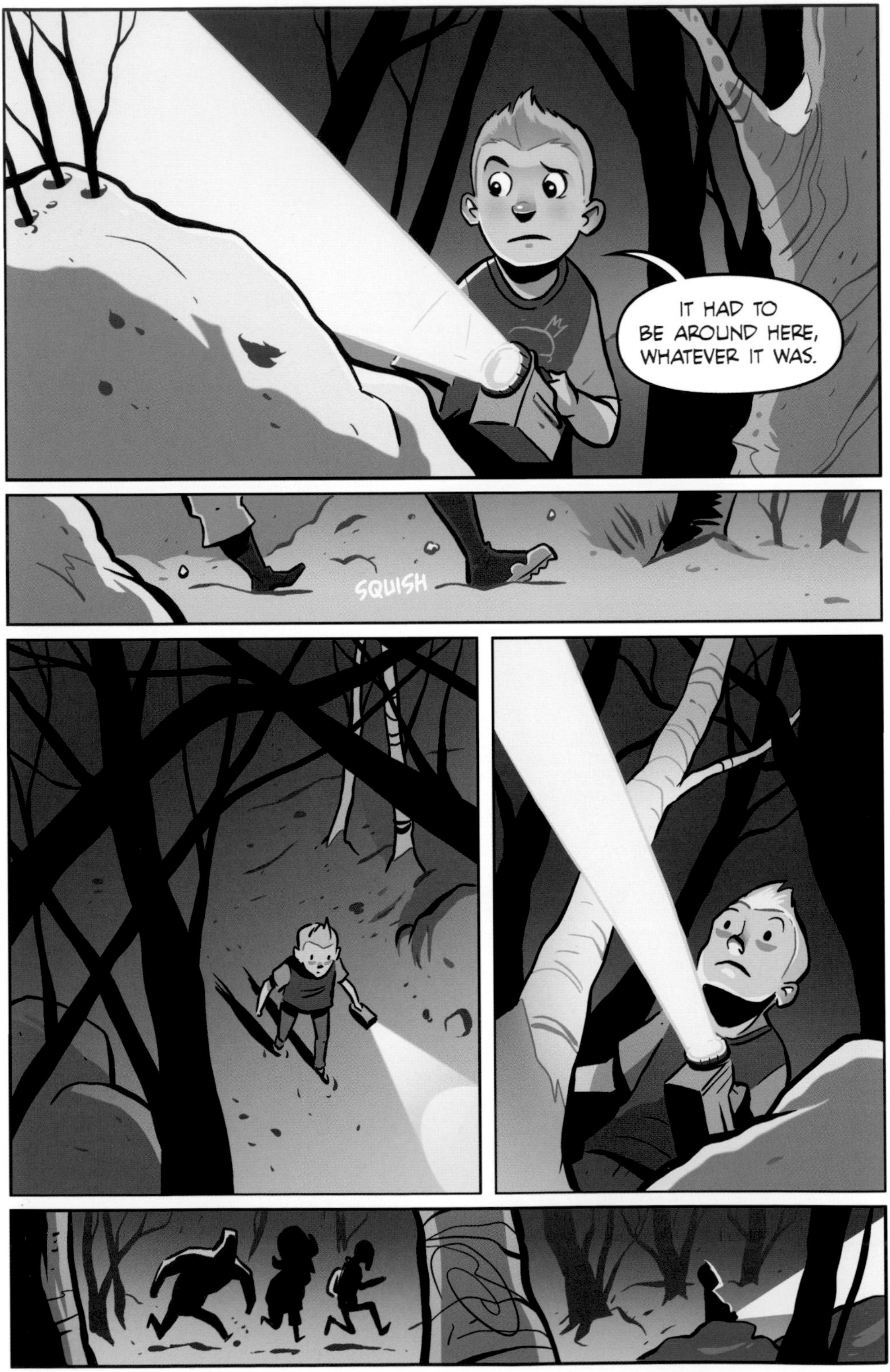
IT HAD TO BE AROUND HERE, WHATEVER IT WAS.
SQUISH

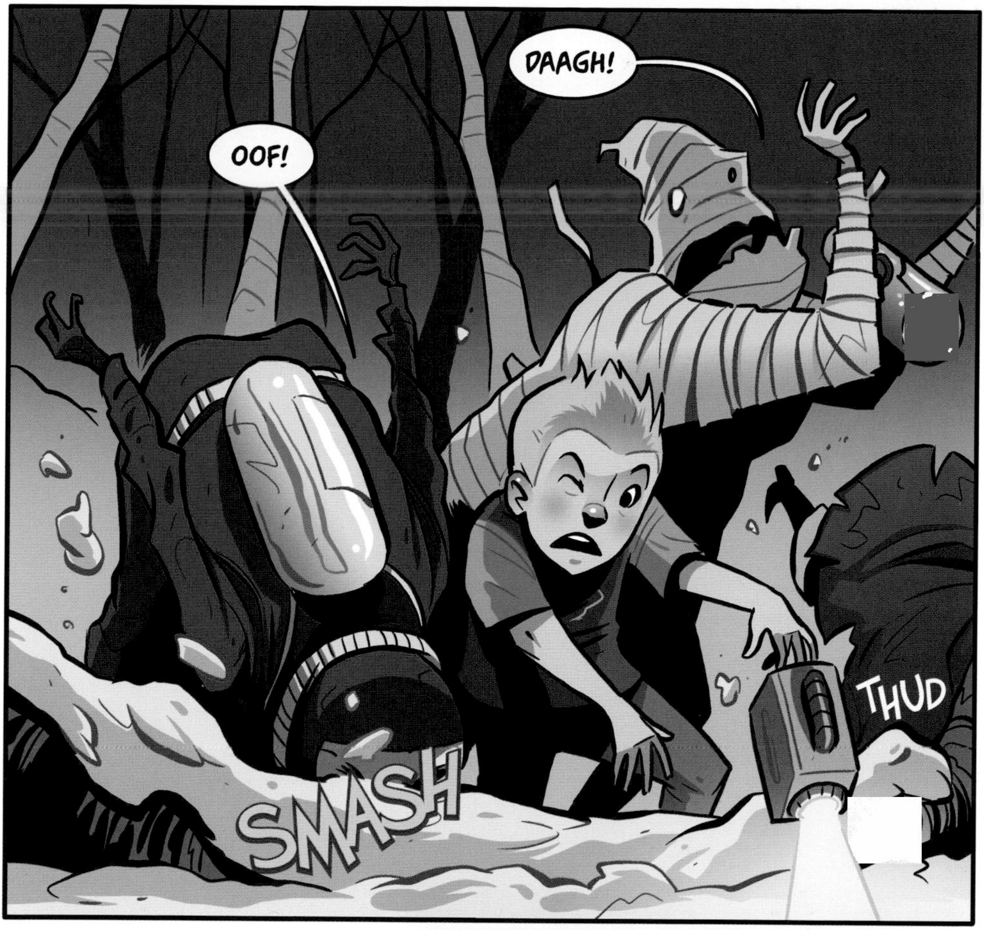
OOF!
DAAGH!
SMASH
THUD

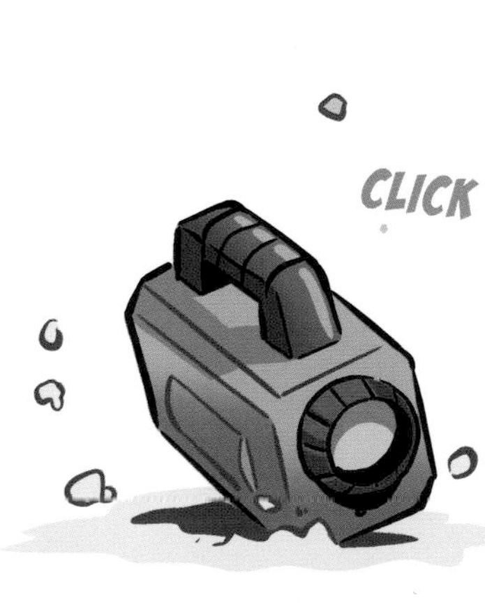
CLICK

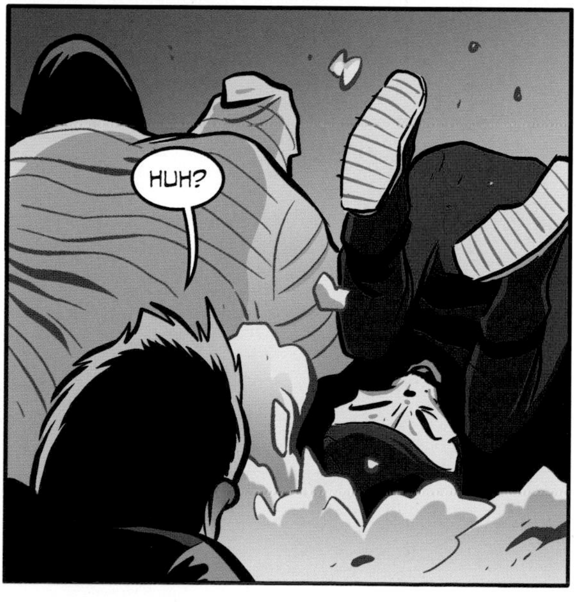
HUH?

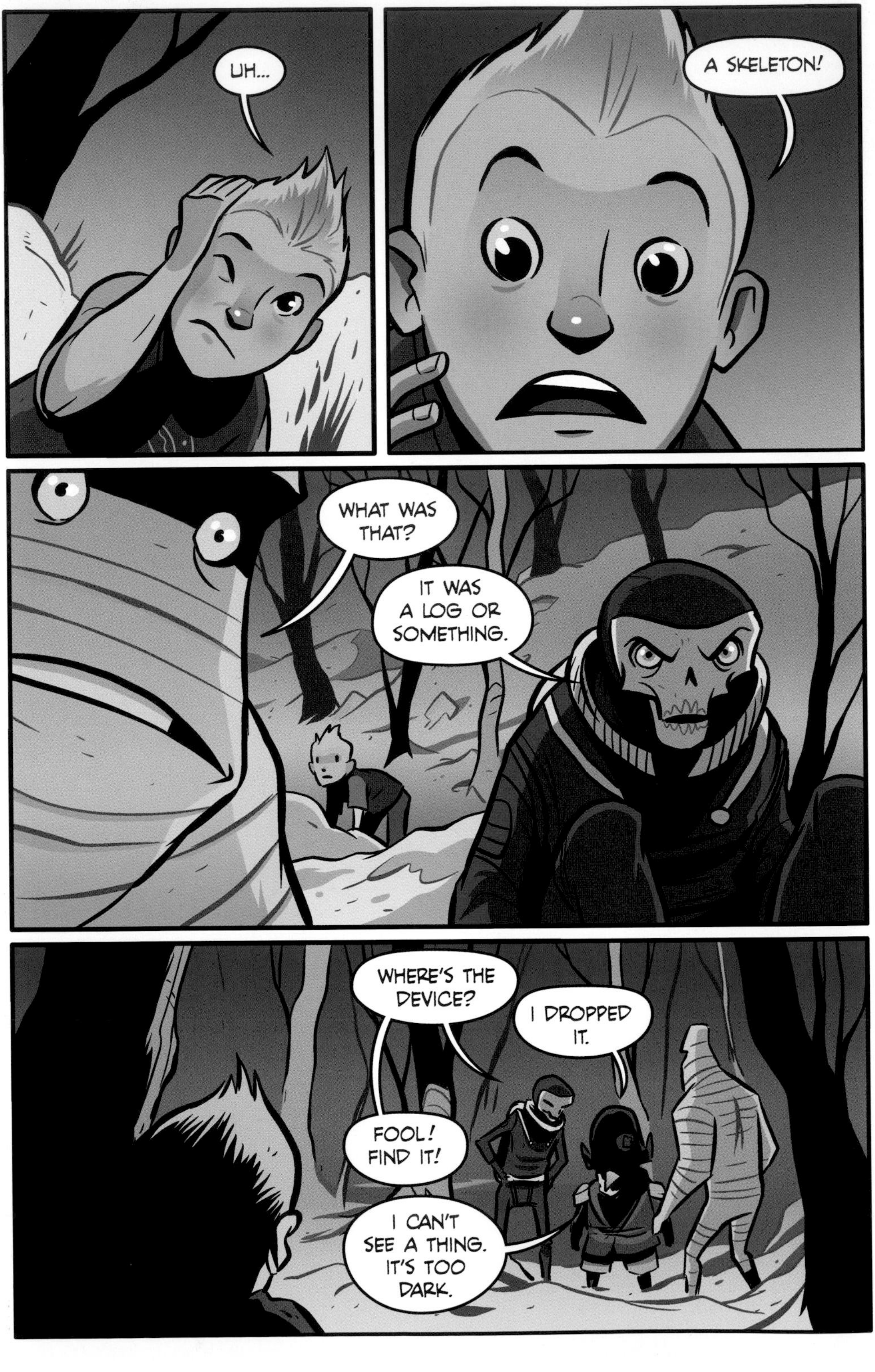
UH...
A SKELETON!
WHAT WAS THAT?
IT WAS A LOG OR SOMETHING.
WHERE'S THE DEVICE?
I DROPPED IT.
FOOL! FIND IT!
I CAN'T SEE A THING. IT'S TOO DARK.

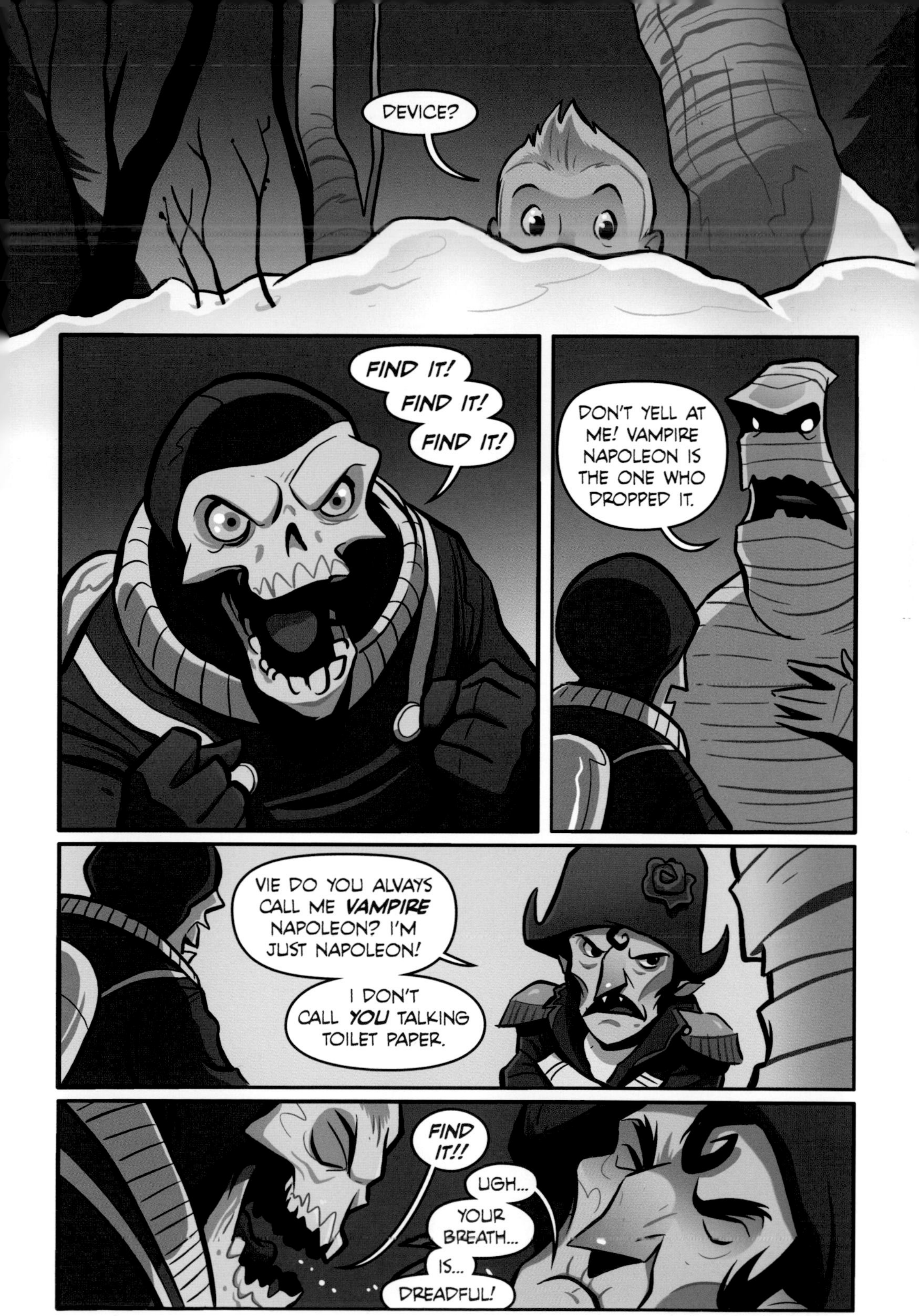
DEVICE?
FIND IT!
FIND IT!
FIND IT!
DON'T YELL AT ME! VAMPIRE NAPOLEON IS THE ONE WHO DROPPED IT.
VIE DO YOU ALVAYS CALL ME VAMPIRE NAPOLEON? I'M JUST NAPOLEON!
I DON'T CALL YOU TALKING TOILET PAPER.
FIND IT!!
UGH...
YOUR BREATH...
IS...
DREADFUL!

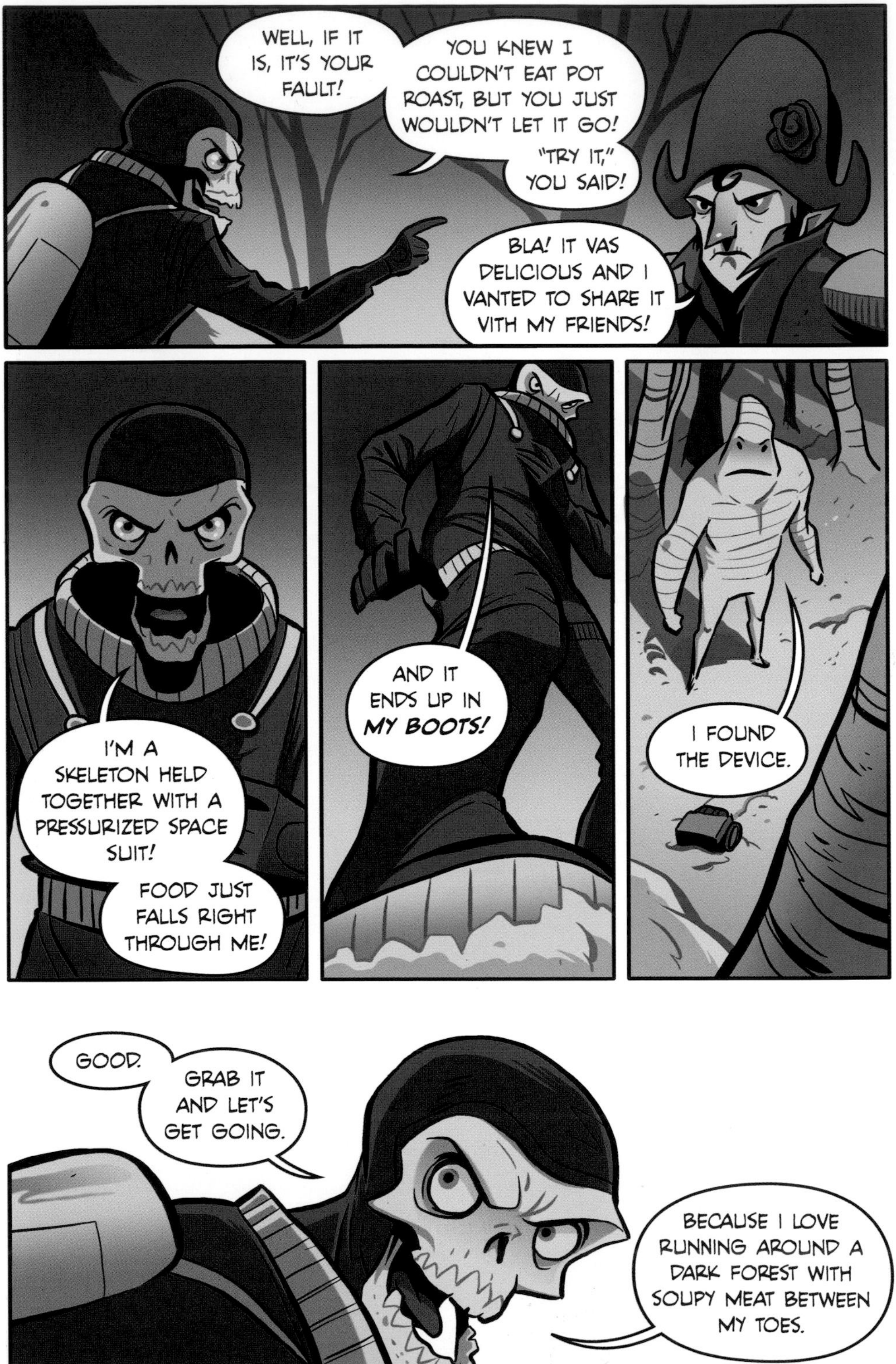
WELL, IF IT IS, IT'S YOUR FAULT!
YOU KNEW I COULDN'T EAT POT ROAST, BUT YOU JUST WOULDN'T LET IT GO!
"TRY IT," YOU SAID!
BLA! IT VAS DELICIOUS AND I VANTED TO SHARE IT VITH MY FRIENDS!
I'M A SKELETON HELD TOGETHER WITH A PRESSURIZED SPACE SUIT!
FOOD JUST FALLS RIGHT THROUGH ME!
AND IT ENDS UP IN *MY BOOTS!*
I FOUND THE DEVICE.
GOOD.
GRAB IT AND LET'S GET GOING.
BECAUSE I LOVE RUNNING AROUND A DARK FOREST WITH SOUPY MEAT BETWEEN MY TOES.

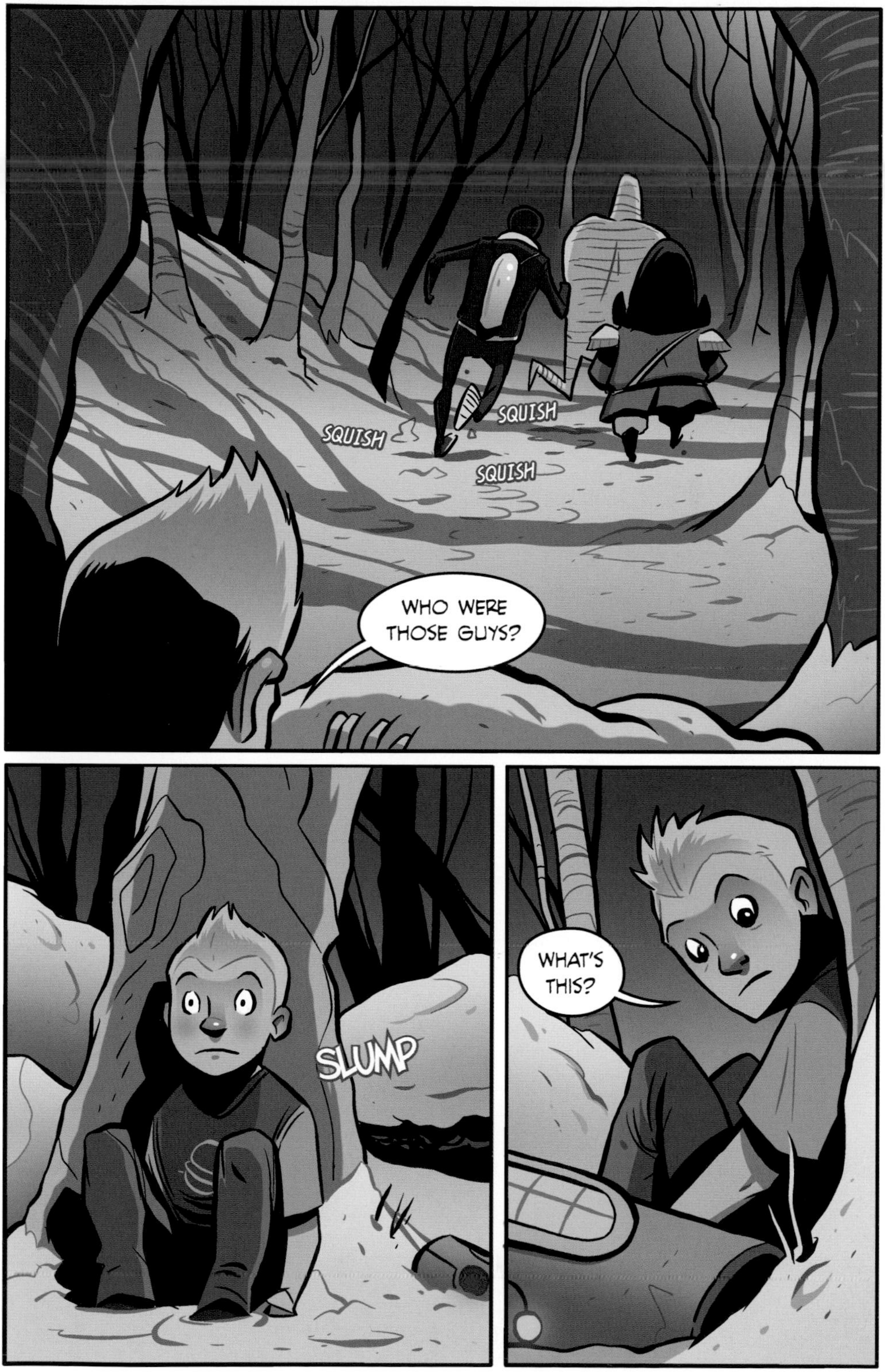
SQUISH
SQUISH
SQUISH
WHO WERE THOSE GUYS?
SLUMP
WHAT'S THIS?

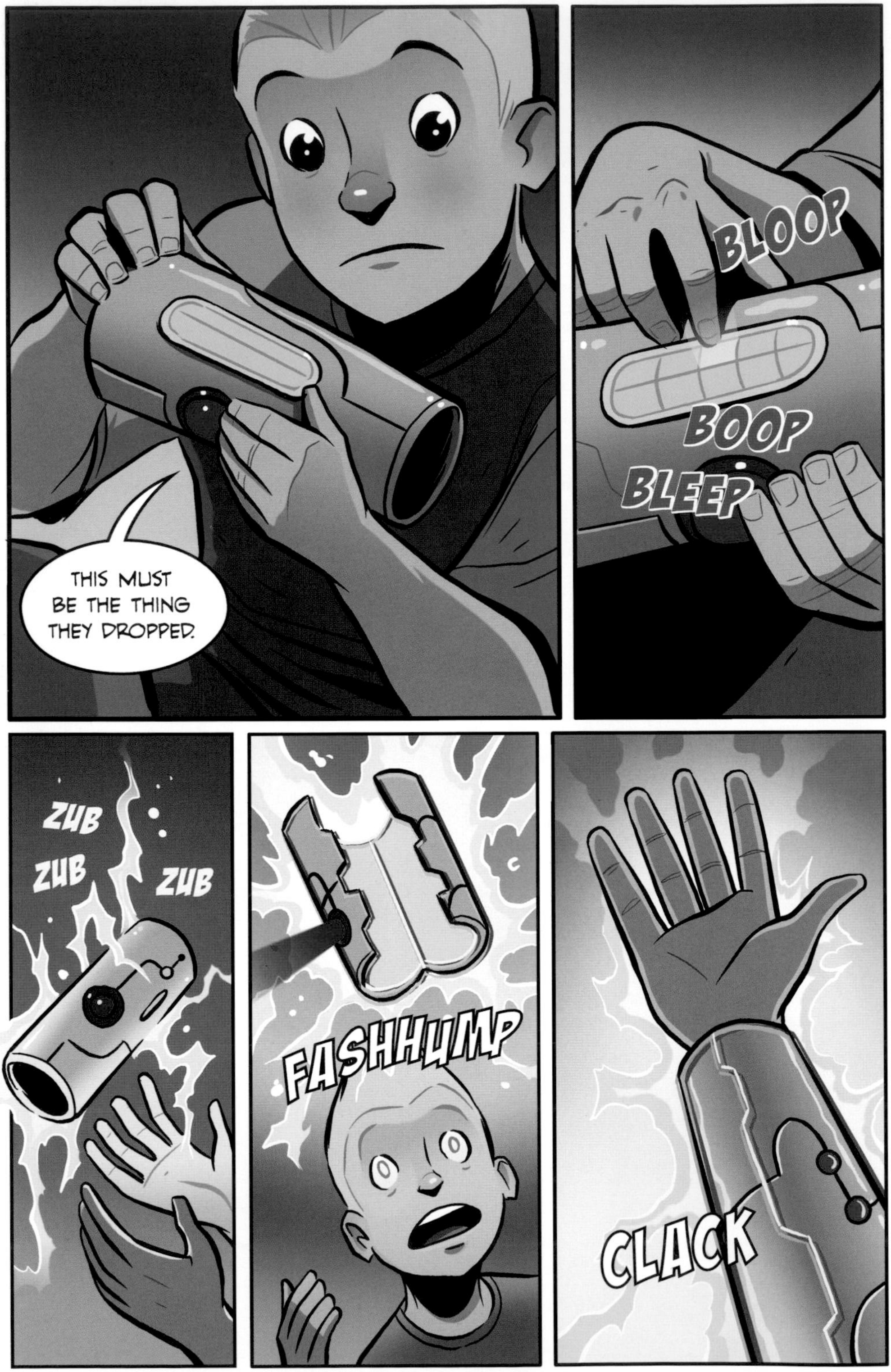
THIS MUST BE THE THING THEY DROPPED.
BLOOP
BOOP
BLEEP
ZUB
ZUB
ZUB
FASHHUMP
CLACK

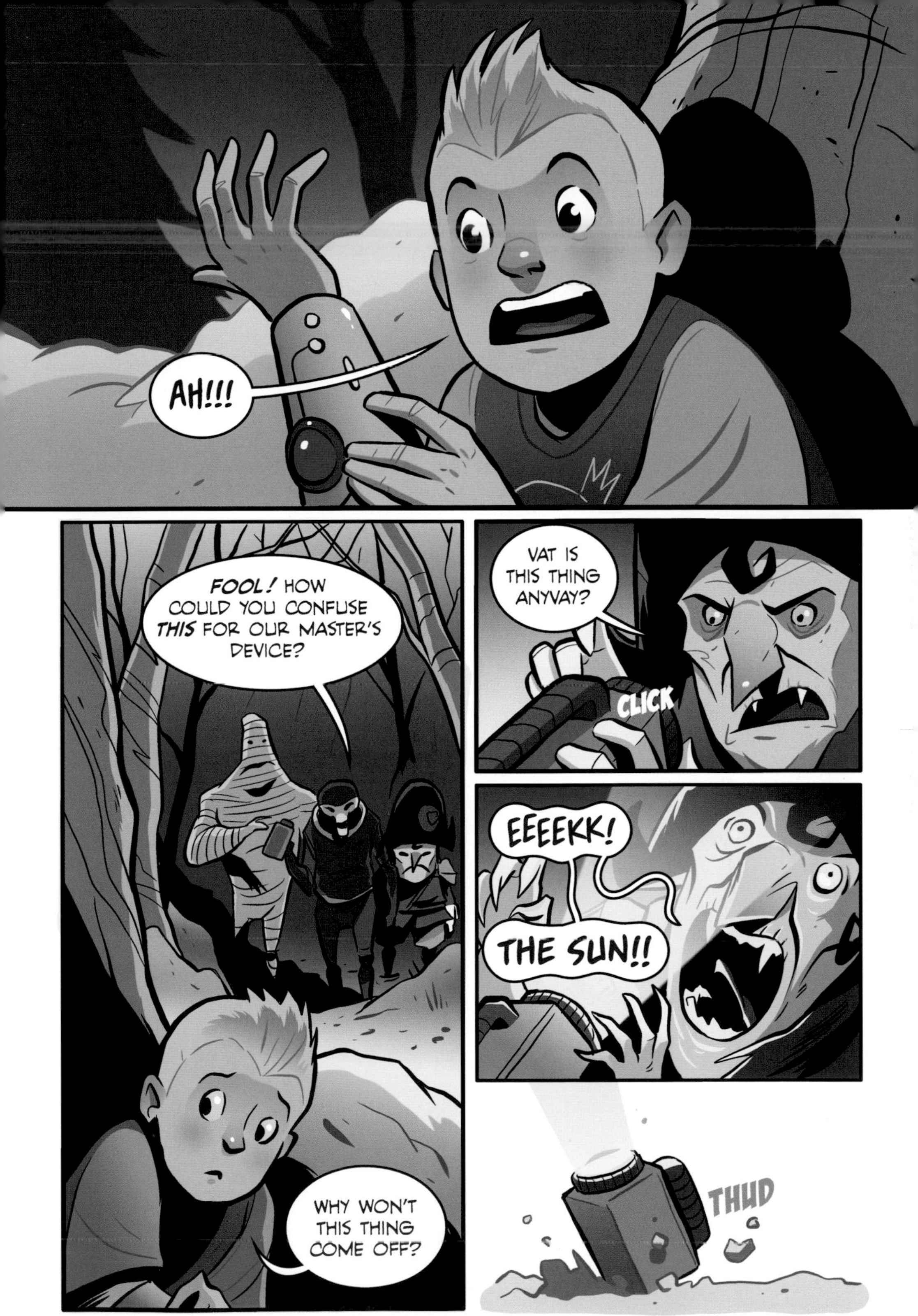
AH!!!
FOOL! HOW COULD YOU CONFUSE THIS FOR OUR MASTER'S DEVICE?
WHY WON'T THIS THING COME OFF?
VAT IS THIS THING ANYVAY?
CLICK
EEEEKK!
THE SUN!!
THUD

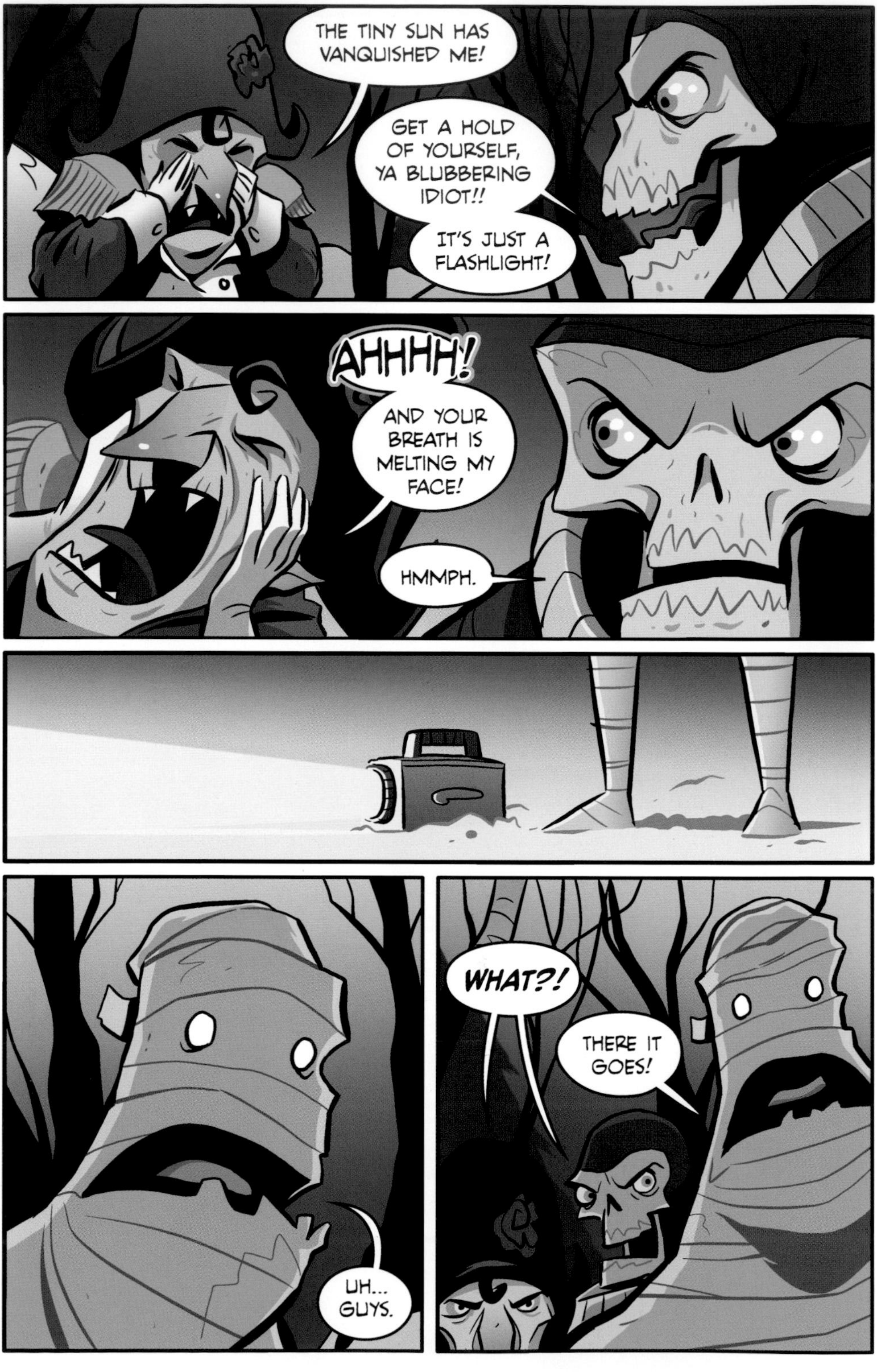
THE TINY SUN HAS VANQUISHED ME!
GET A HOLD OF YOURSELF, YA BLUBBERING IDIOT!!
IT'S JUST A FLASHLIGHT!
AHHHH!
AND YOUR BREATH IS MELTING MY FACE!
HMMPH.
UH... GUYS.
WHAT?!
THERE IT GOES!

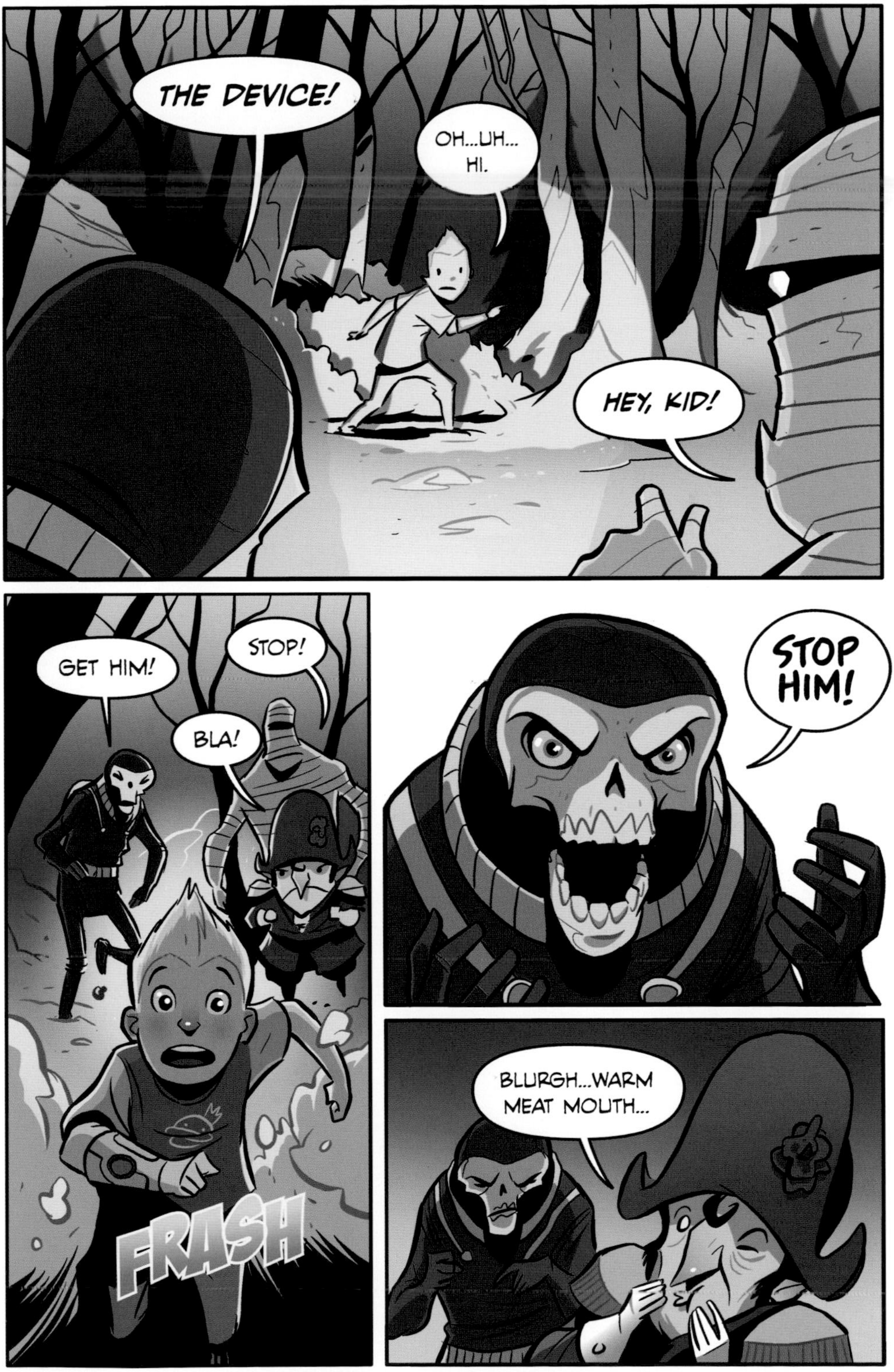
THE DEVICE!
OH...UH... HI.
HEY, KID!
GET HIM!
STOP!
BLA!
FRASH
STOP HIM!
BLURGH...WARM MEAT MOUTH...

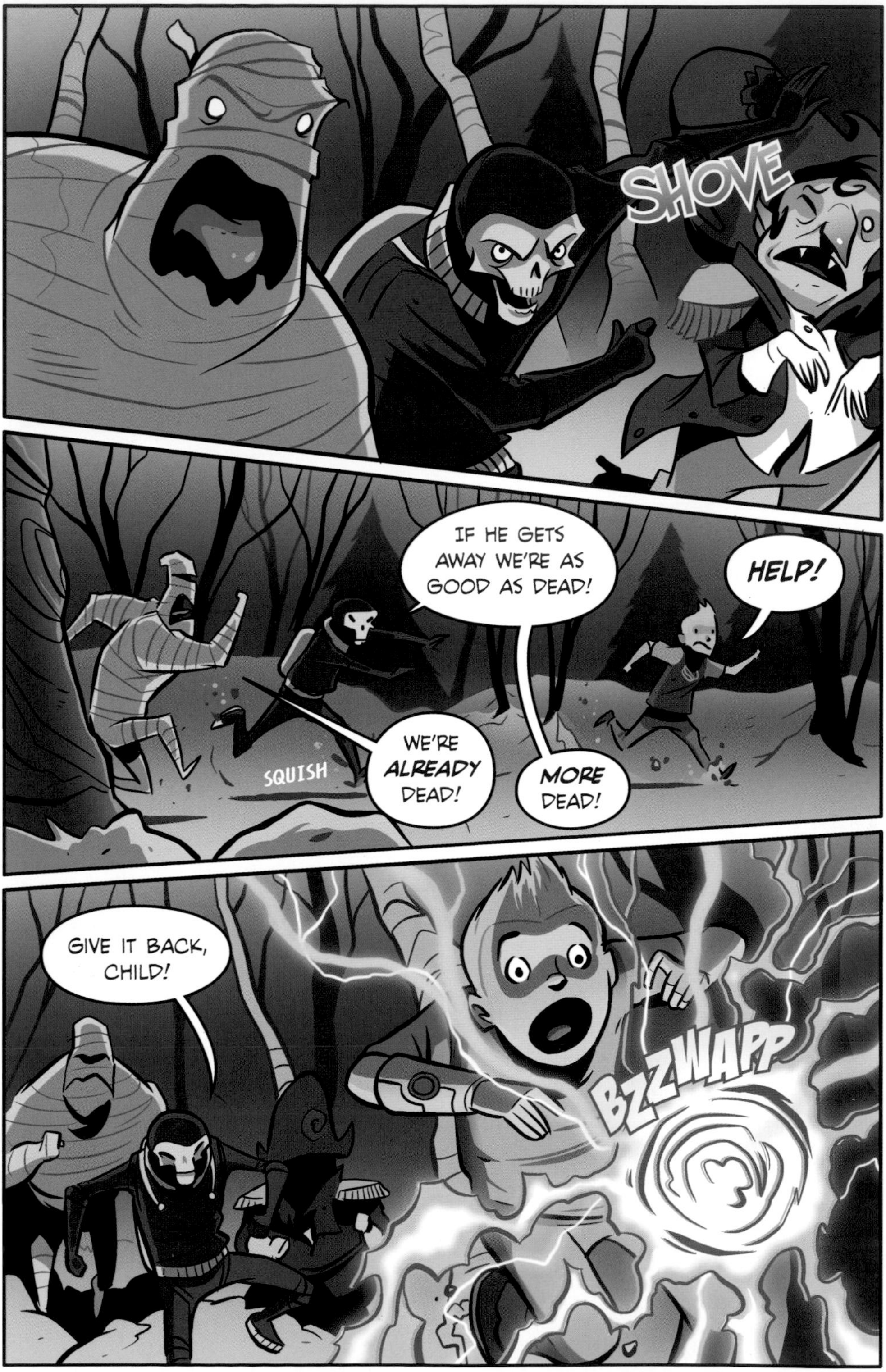
SHOVE
IF HE GETS AWAY WE'RE AS GOOD AS DEAD!
HELP!
SQUISH
WE'RE ALREADY DEAD!
MORE DEAD!
GIVE IT BACK, CHILD!
BZZWAPP

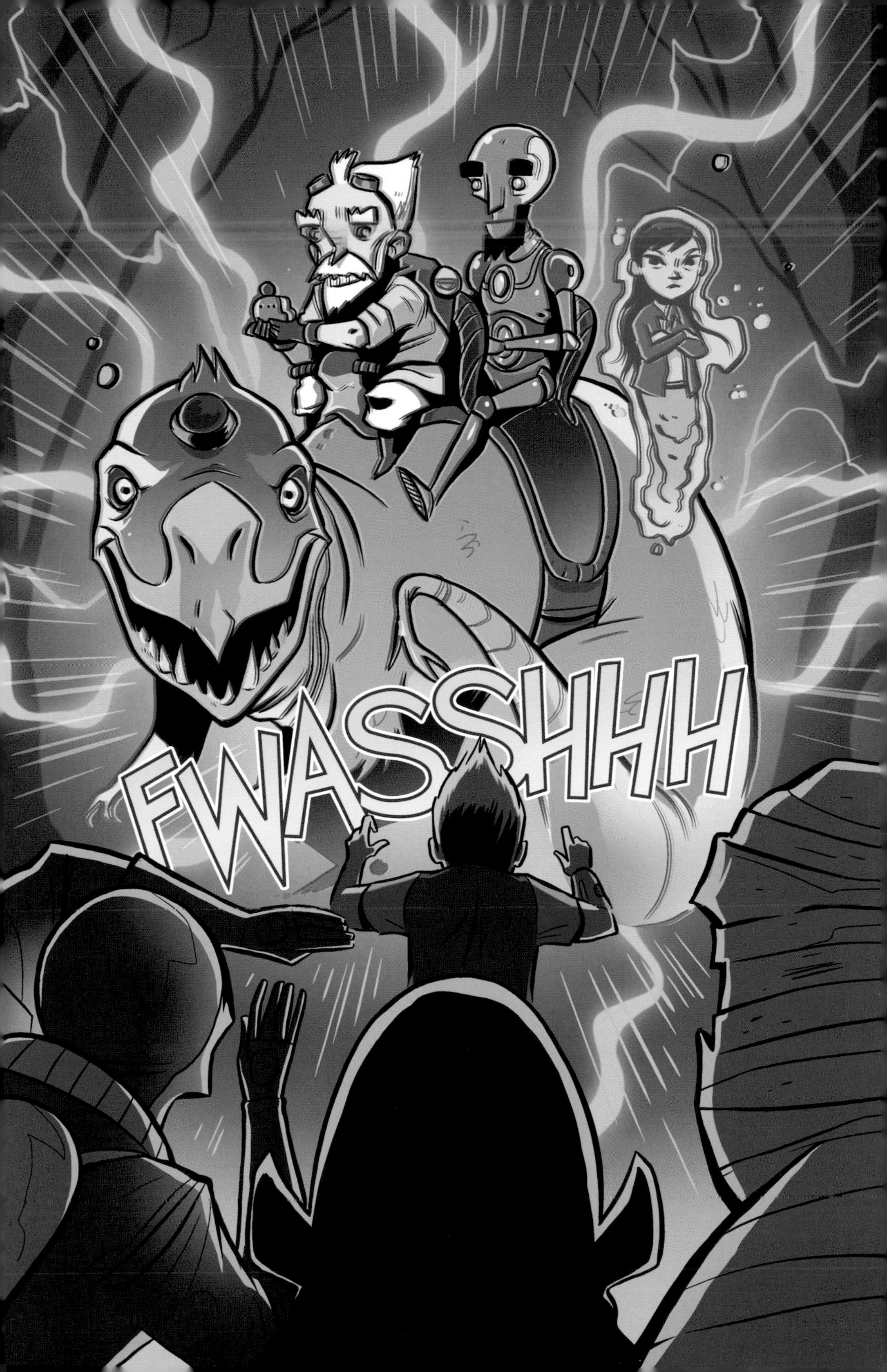
FWASSHHH

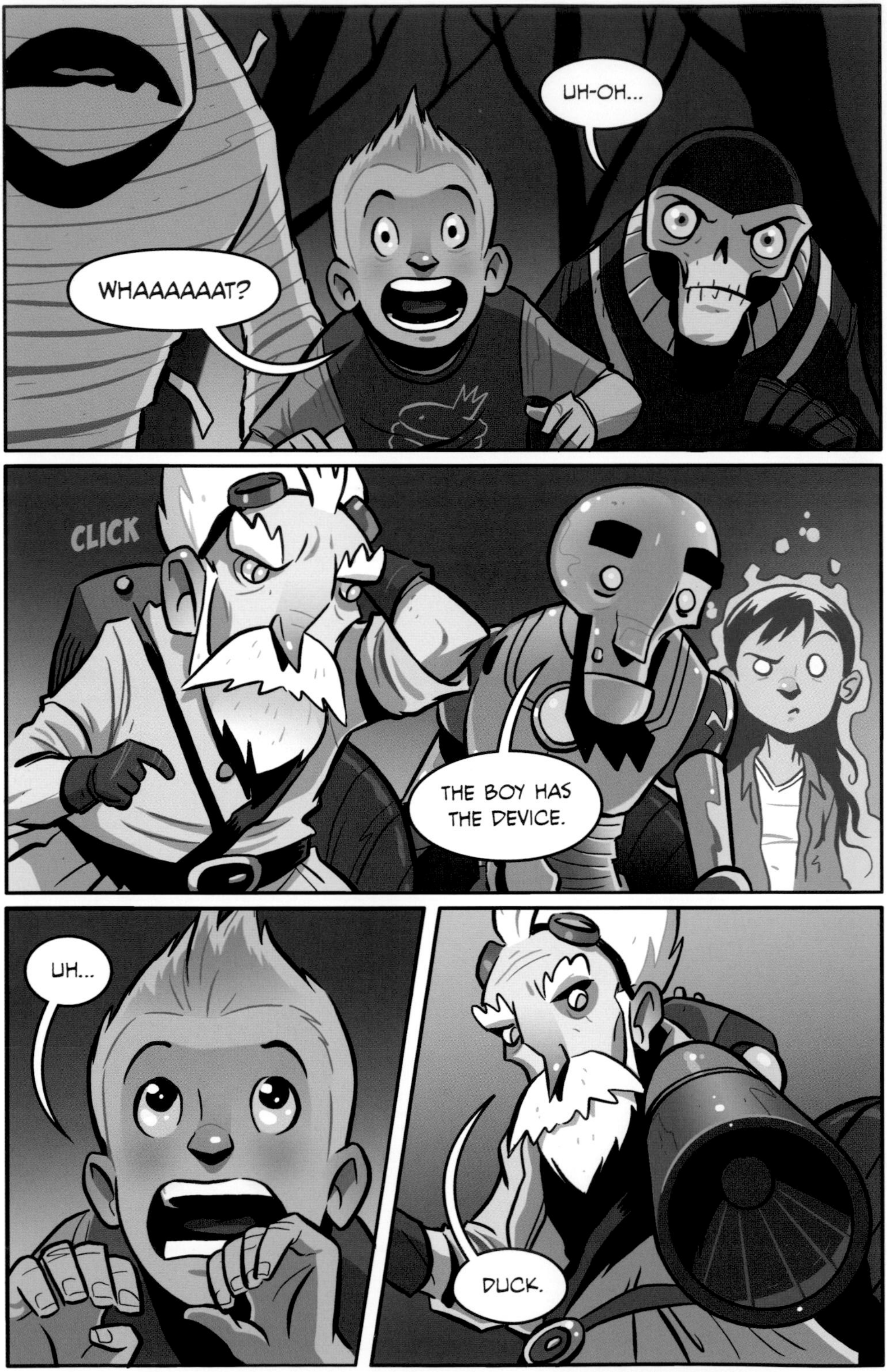
UH-OH...
WHAAAAAAT?
CLICK
THE BOY HAS THE DEVICE.
UH...
DUCK.

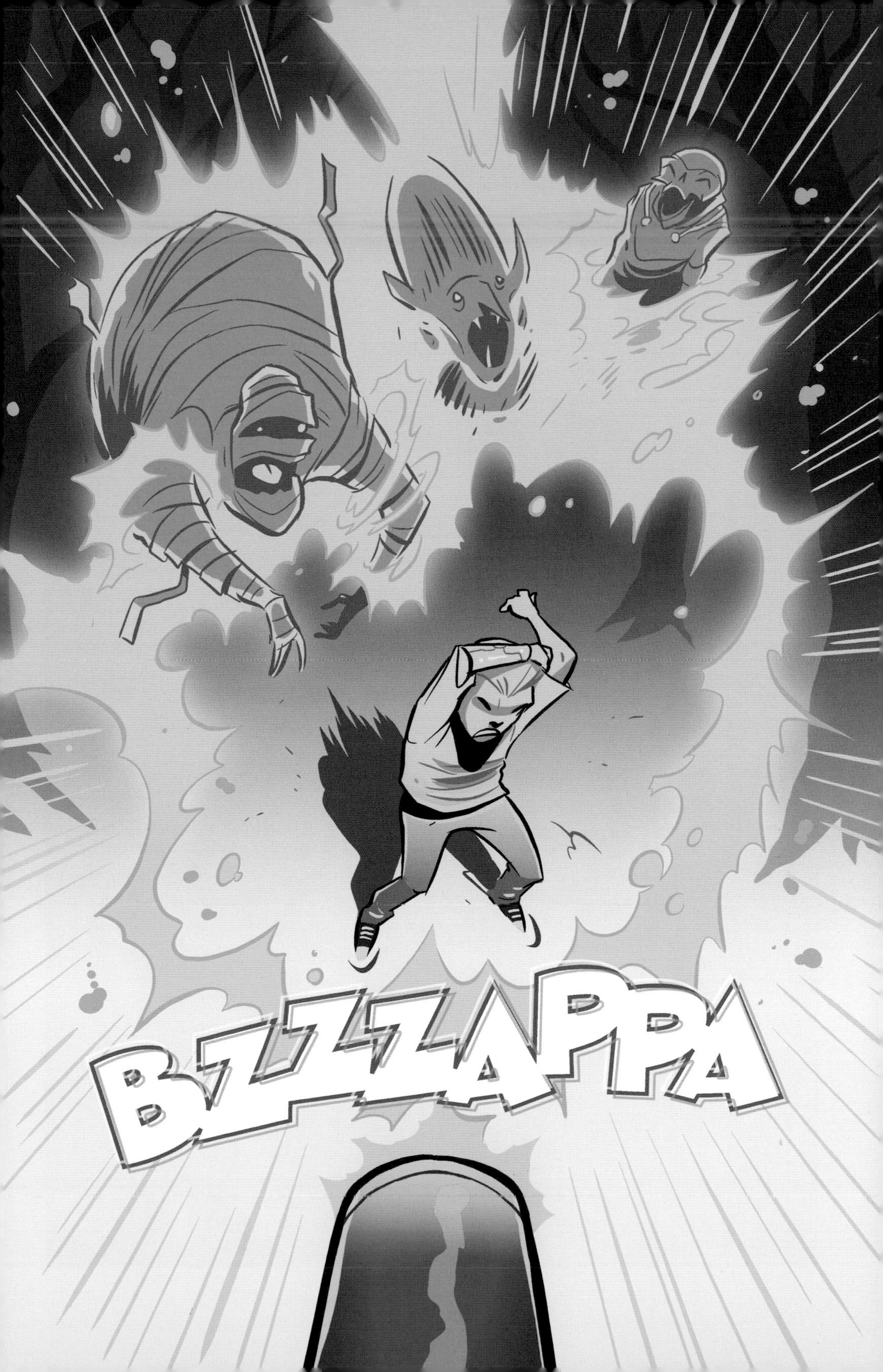
BZZZAPPA

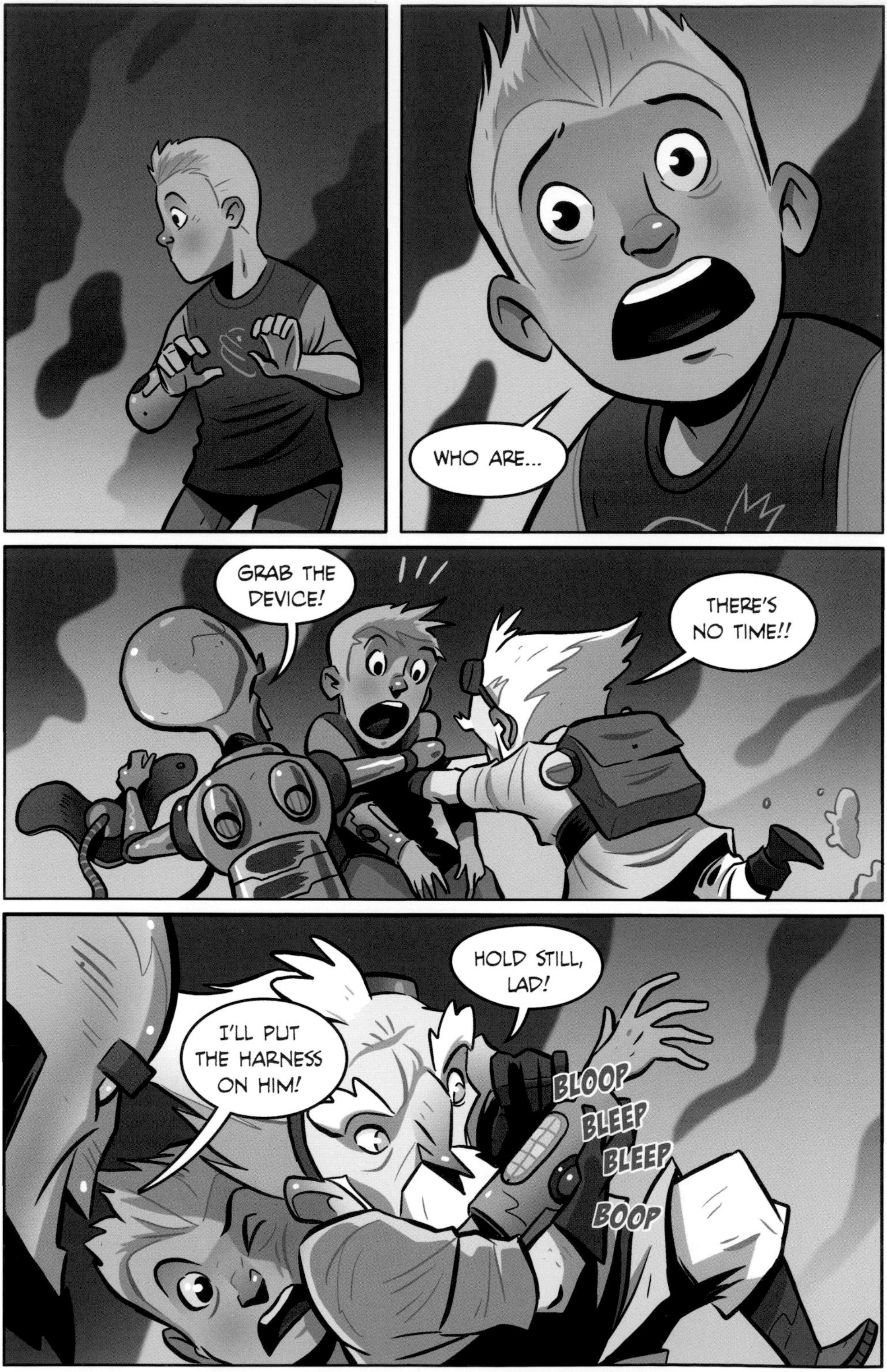
WHO ARE...
GRAB THE DEVICE!
THERE'S NO TIME!!
HOLD STILL, LAD!
I'LL PUT THE HARNESS ON HIM!
BLOOP
BLEEP
BLEEP
BOOP

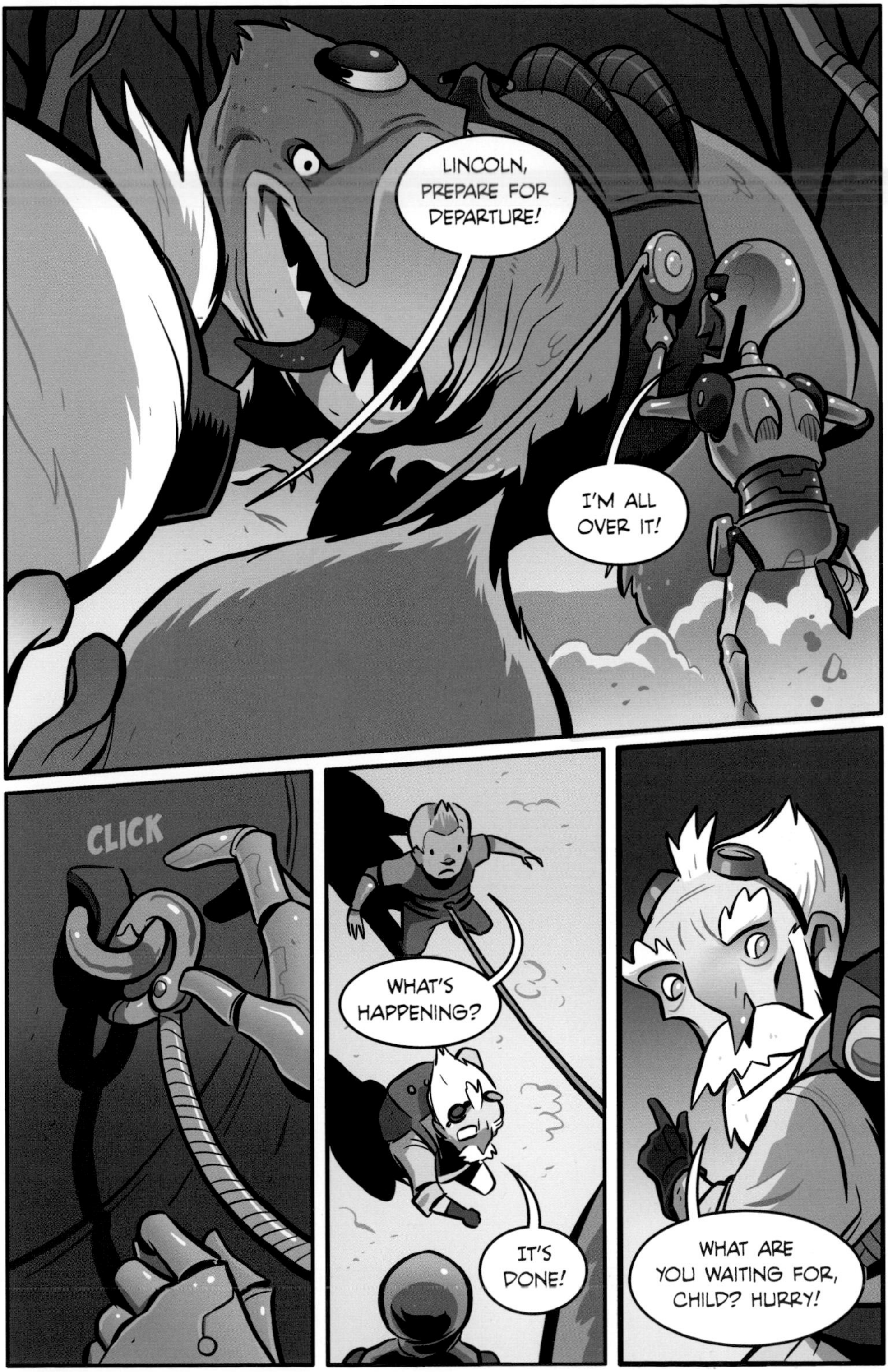
LINCOLN, PREPARE FOR DEPARTURE!
I'M ALL OVER IT!
CLICK
WHAT'S HAPPENING?
IT'S DONE!
WHAT ARE YOU WAITING FOR, CHILD? HURRY!

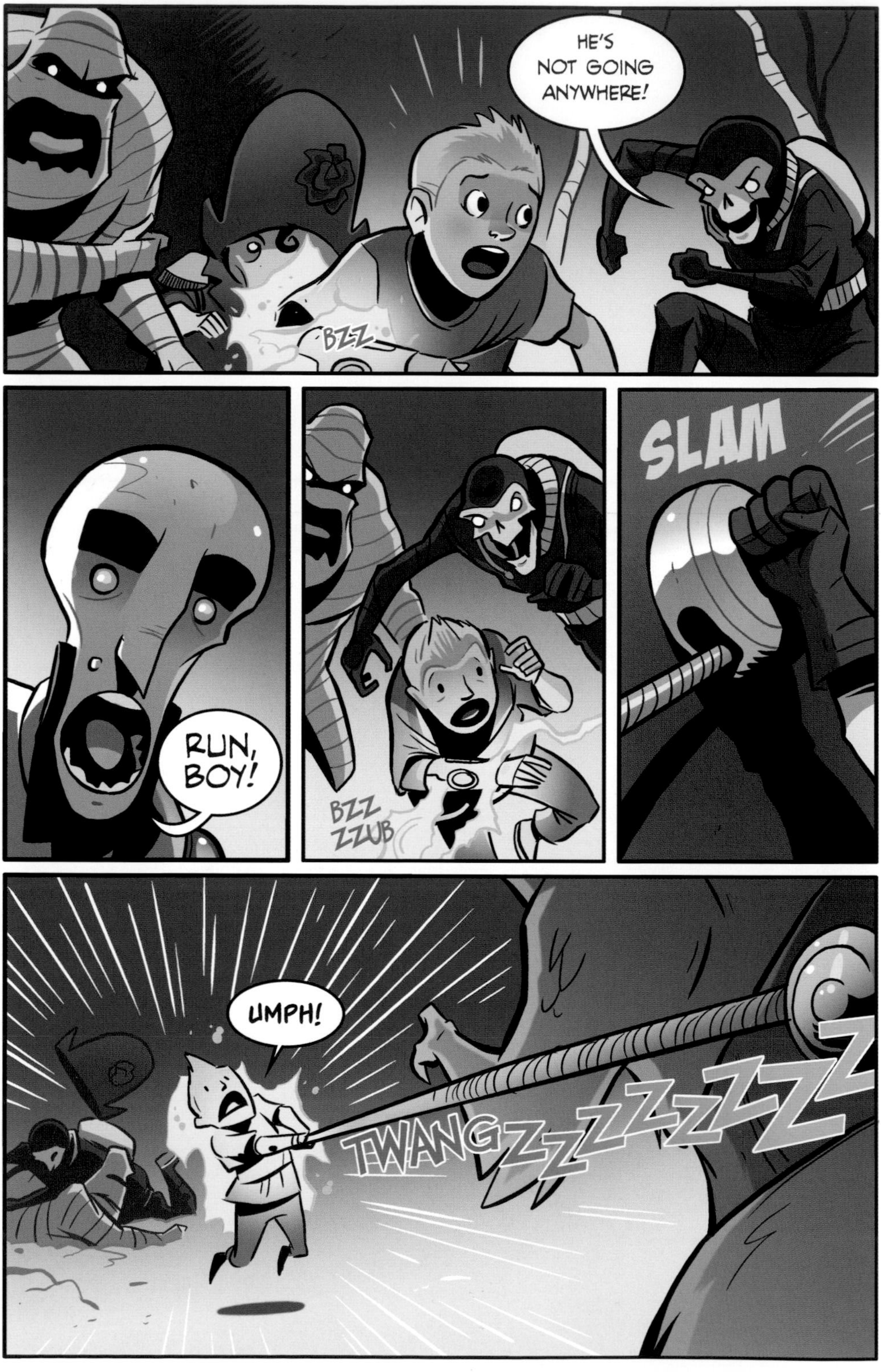
HE'S NOT GOING ANYWHERE!
BZZ
RUN, BOY!
BZZ ZZUB
SLAM
UMPH!
TWANGZZZZZZZZ

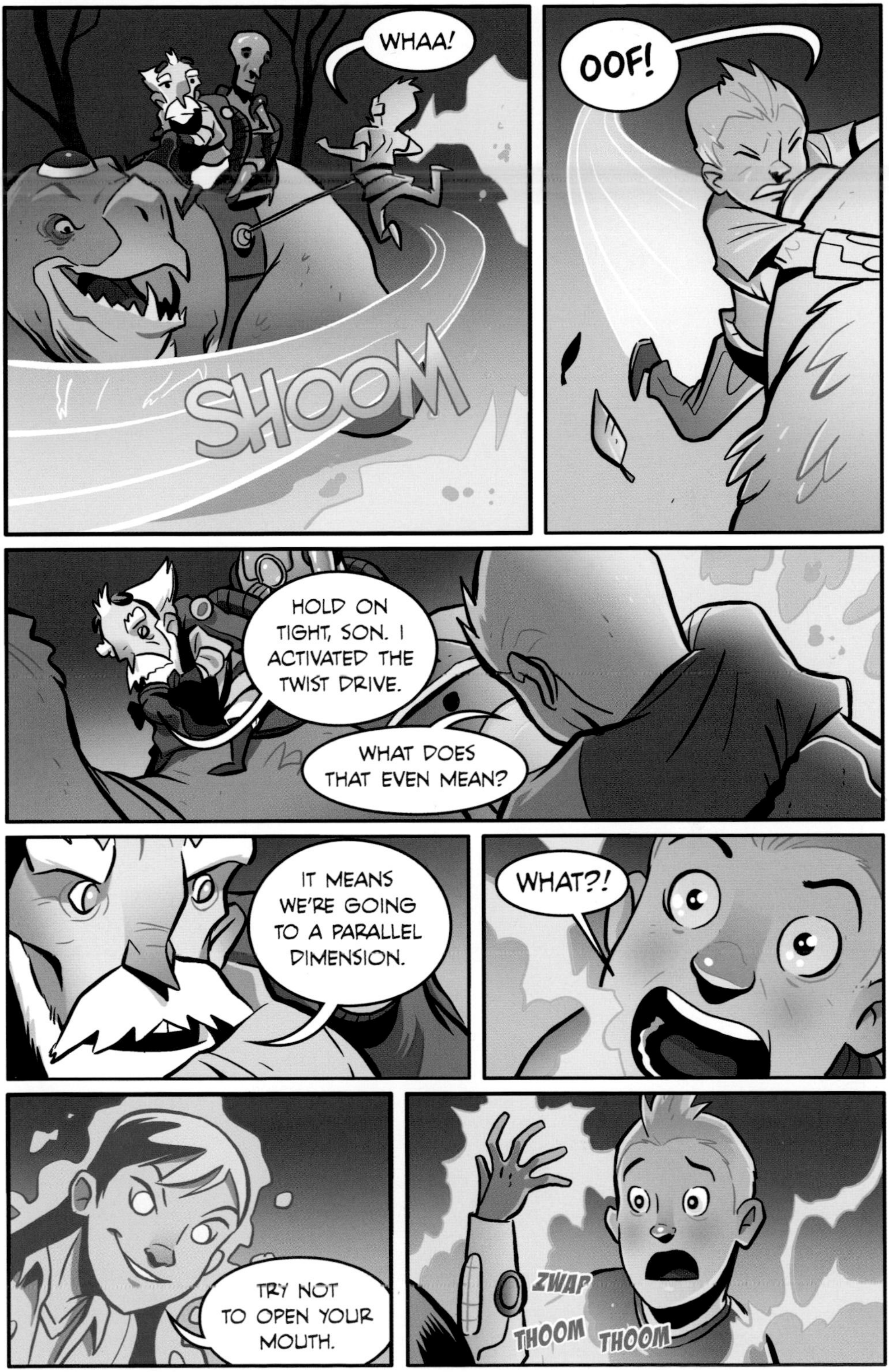
WHAA!
SHOOM
OOF!
HOLD ON TIGHT, SON. I ACTIVATED THE TWIST DRIVE.
WHAT DOES THAT EVEN MEAN?
IT MEANS WE'RE GOING TO A PARALLEL DIMENSION.
WHAT?!
TRY NOT TO OPEN YOUR MOUTH.
ZWAP
THOOM
THOOM

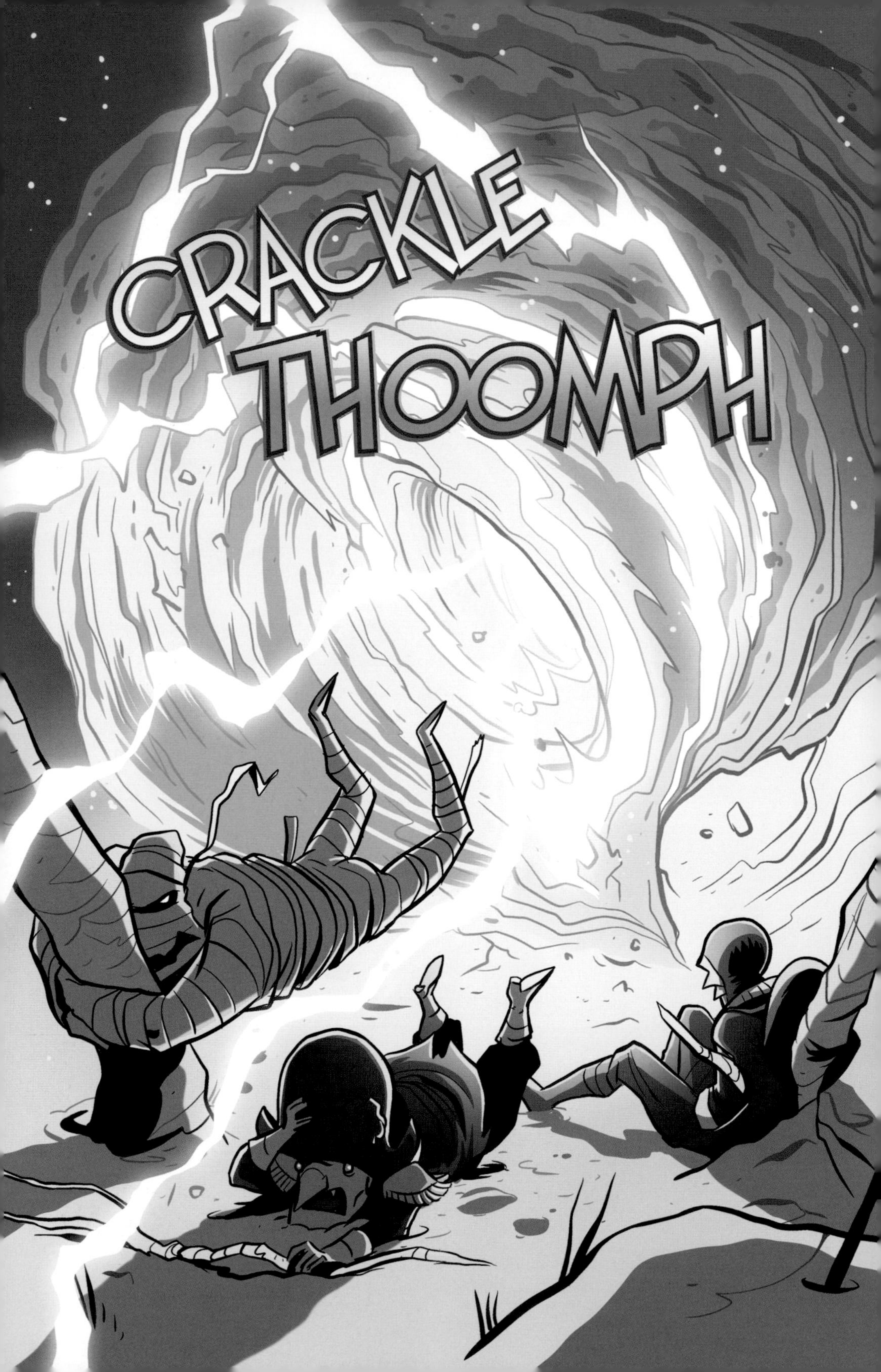
CRACKLE
THOOMPH

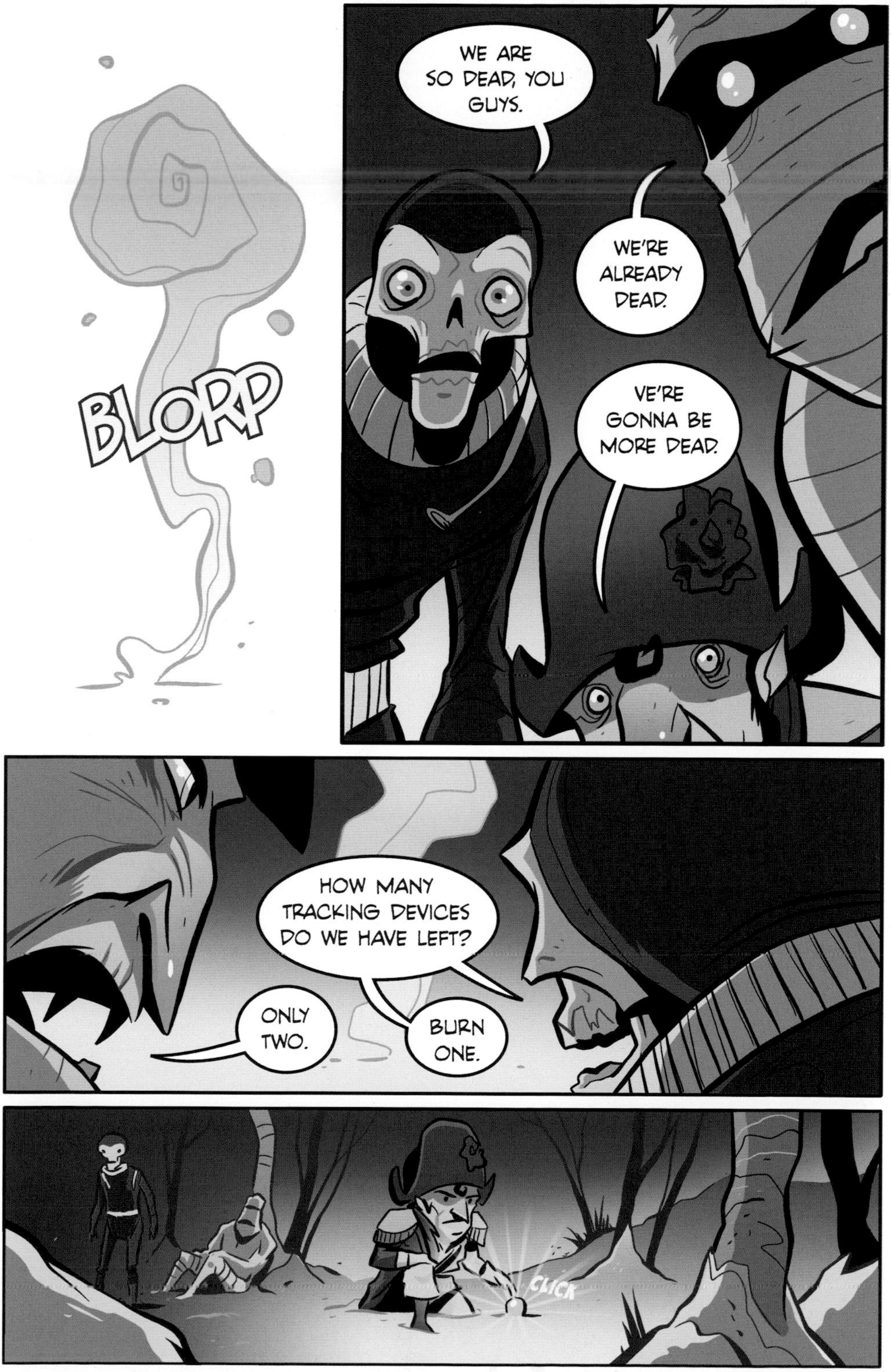
BLORP
WE ARE SO DEAD, YOU GUYS.
WE'RE ALREADY DEAD.
VE'RE GONNA BE MORE DEAD.
HOW MANY TRACKING DEVICES DO WE HAVE LEFT?
ONLY TWO.
BURN ONE.
CLICK

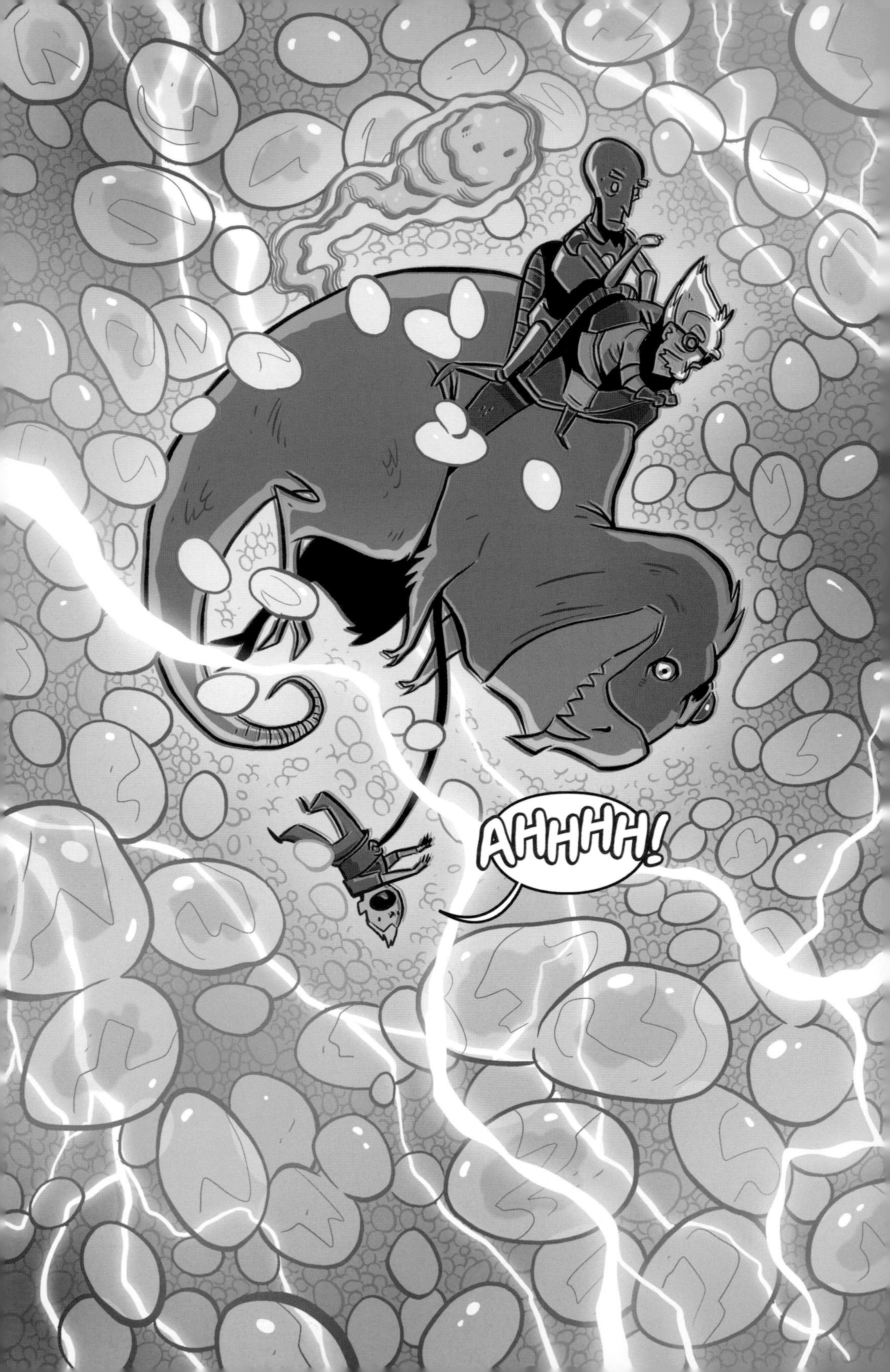
AHHHH!

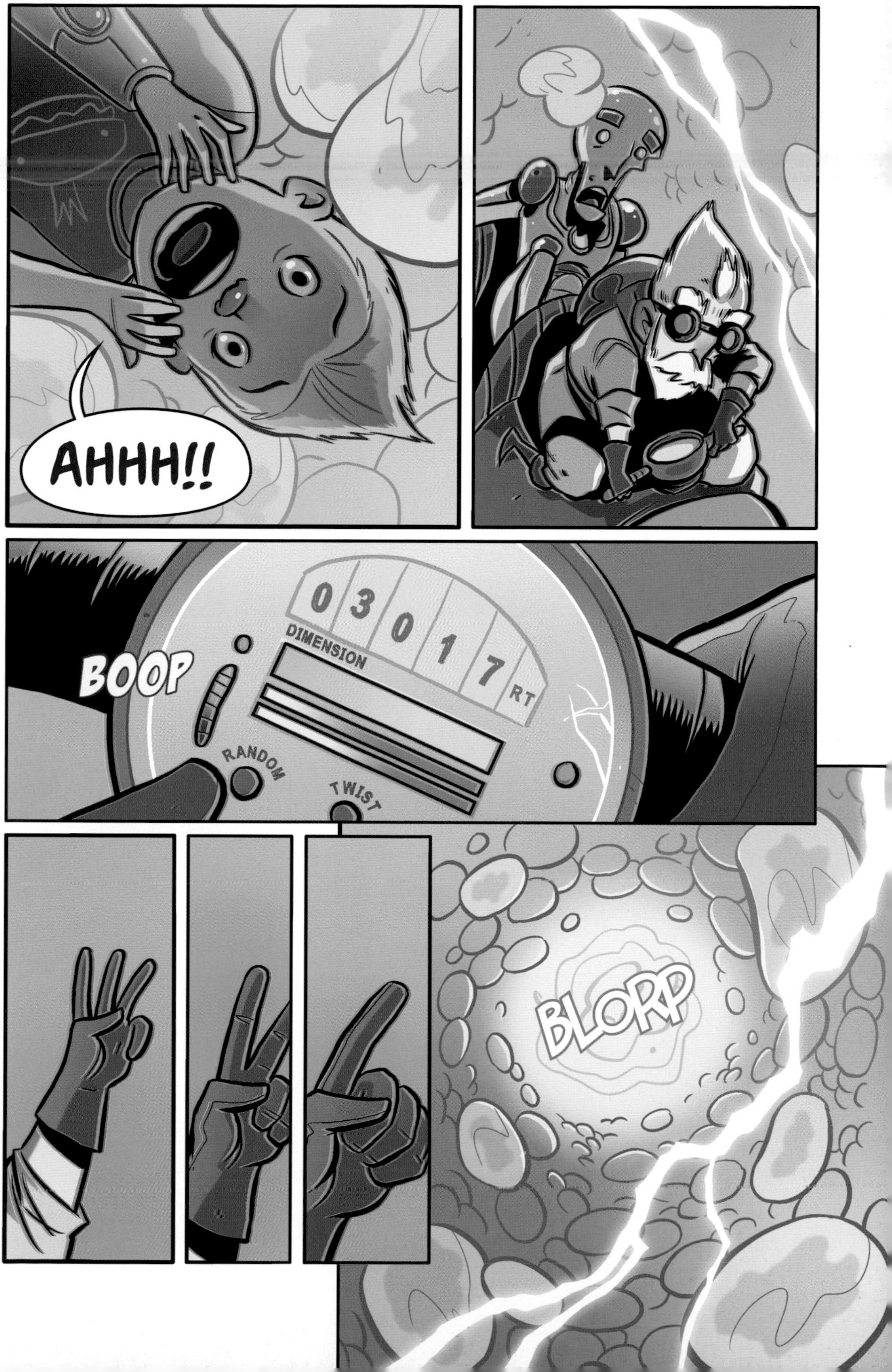
AHHH!!
BOOP
03017 RT
DIMENSION
RANDOM
TWIST
BLORP

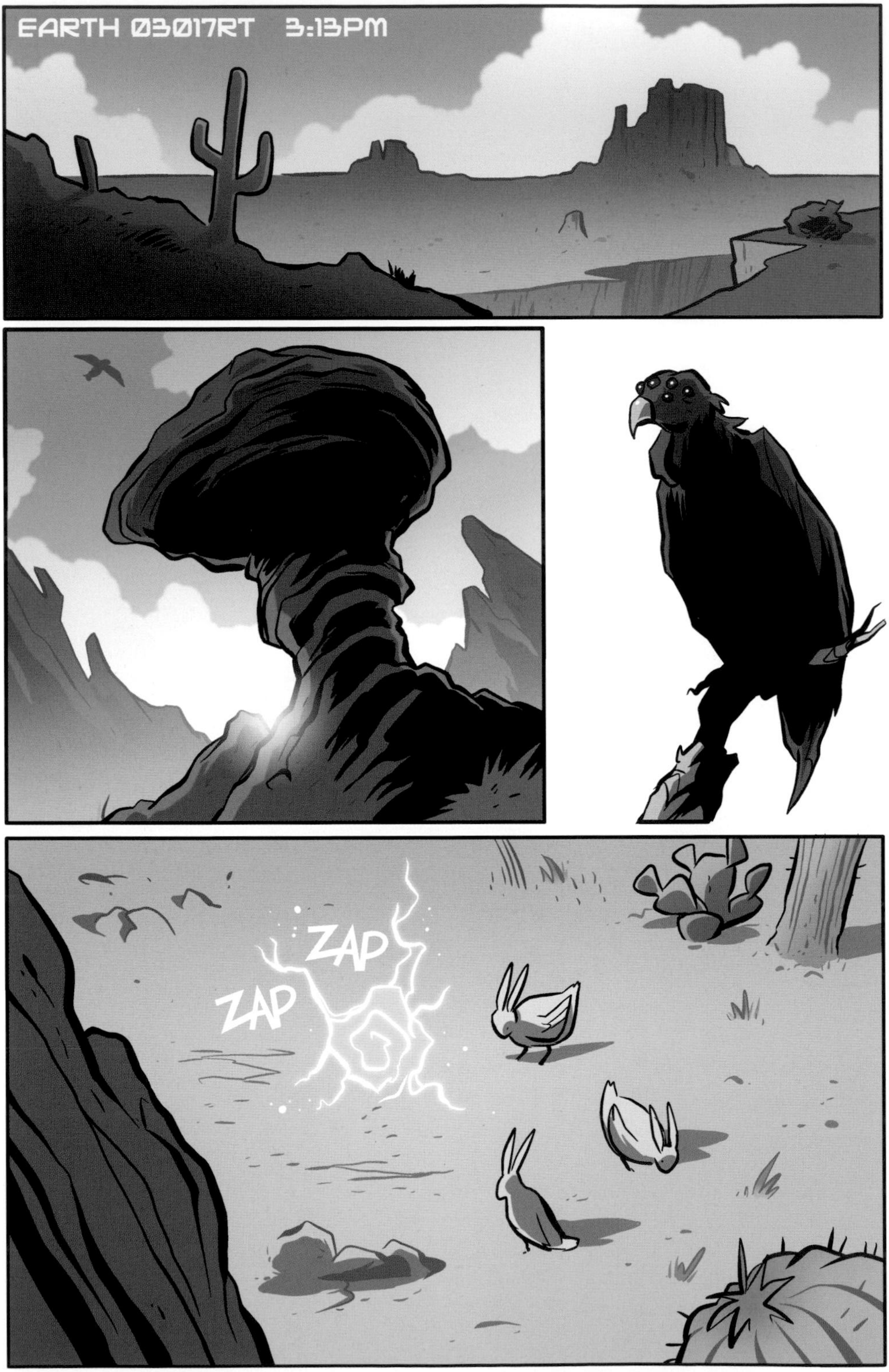
EARTH 03017RT 3:13PM
ZAP
ZAP

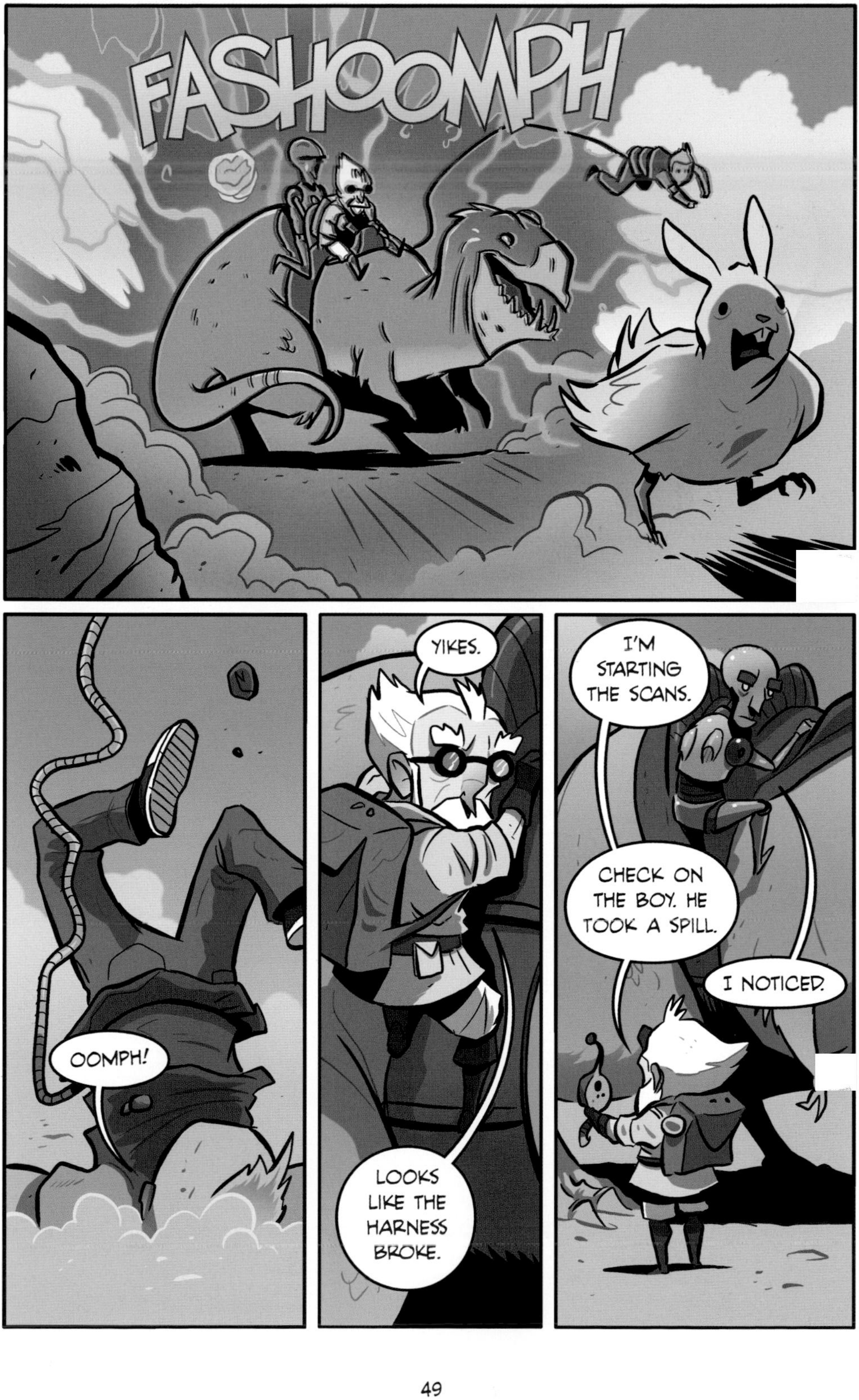
FASHOOMPH
OOMPH!
YIKES.
LOOKS LIKE THE HARNESS BROKE.
I'M STARTING THE SCANS.
CHECK ON THE BOY. HE TOOK A SPILL.
I NOTICED.

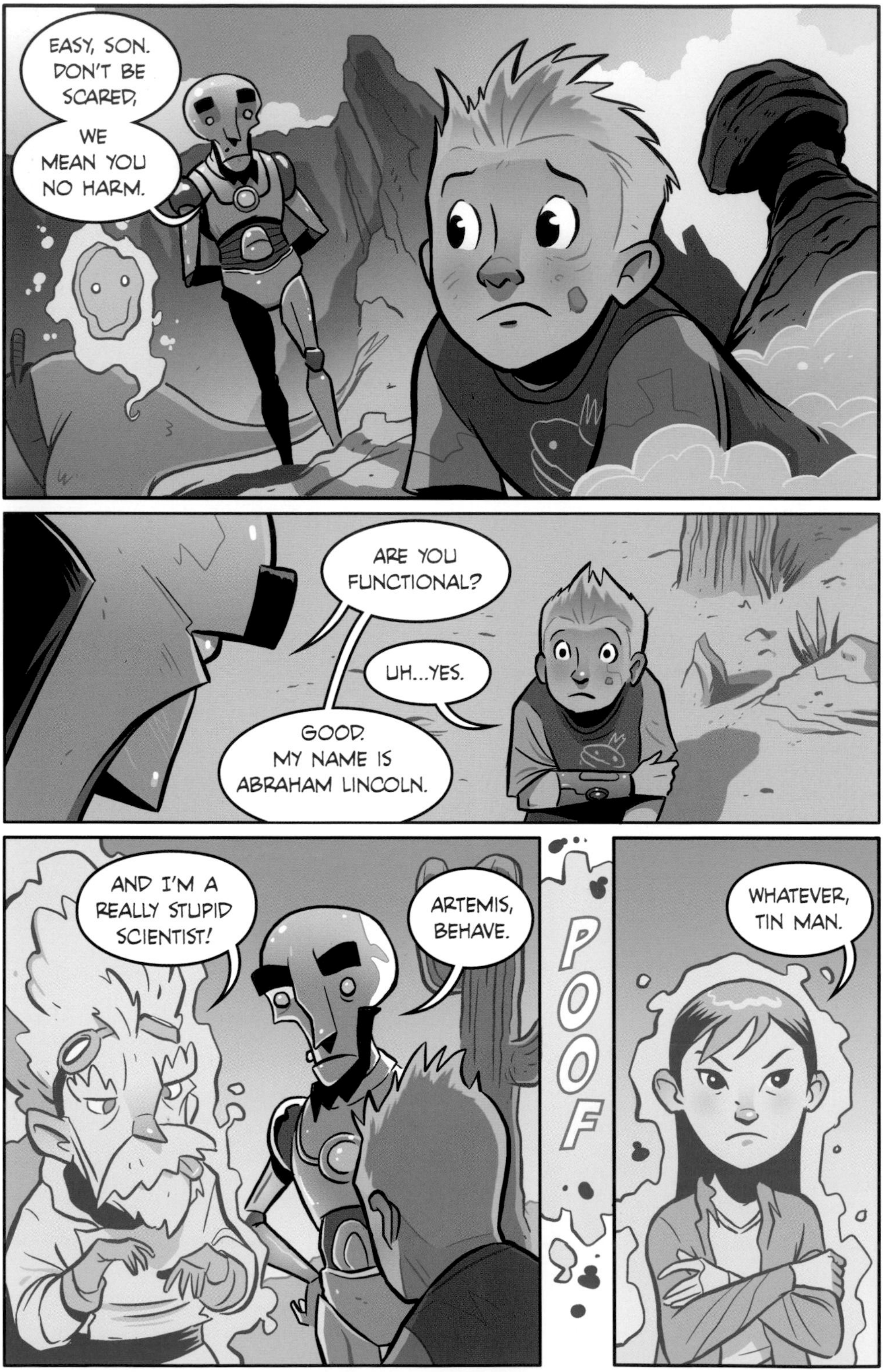
EASY, SON. DON'T BE SCARED,
WE MEAN YOU NO HARM.
ARE YOU FUNCTIONAL?
UH...YES.
GOOD. MY NAME IS ABRAHAM LINCOLN.
AND I'M A REALLY STUPID SCIENTIST!
ARTEMIS, BEHAVE.
POOF
WHATEVER, TIN MAN.

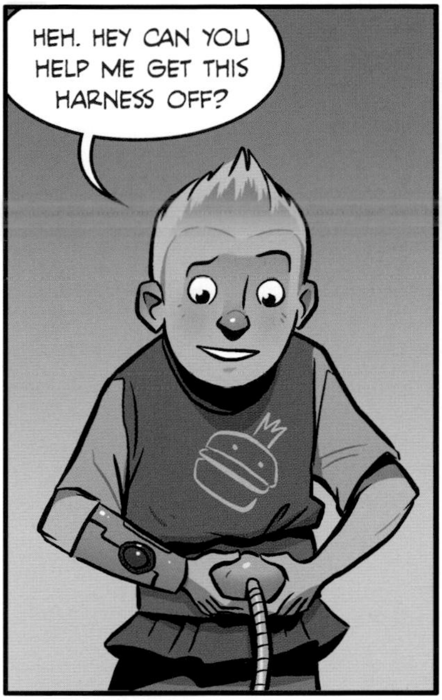
HEH. HEY CAN YOU HELP ME GET THIS HARNESS OFF?

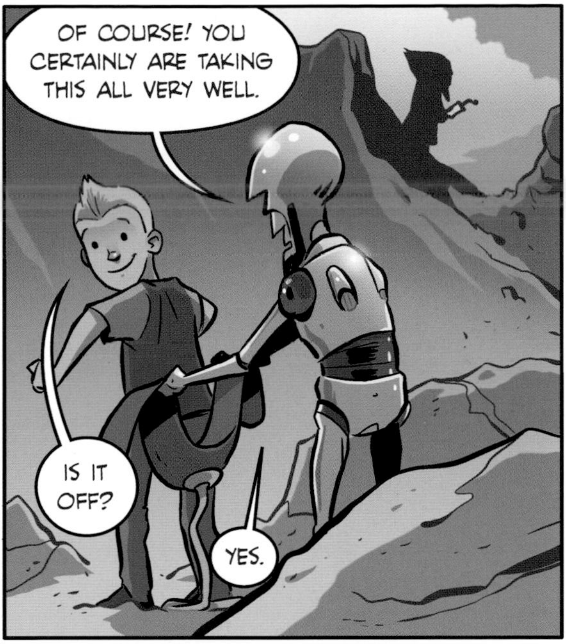
OF COURSE! YOU CERTAINLY ARE TAKING THIS ALL VERY WELL.
IS IT OFF?
YES.

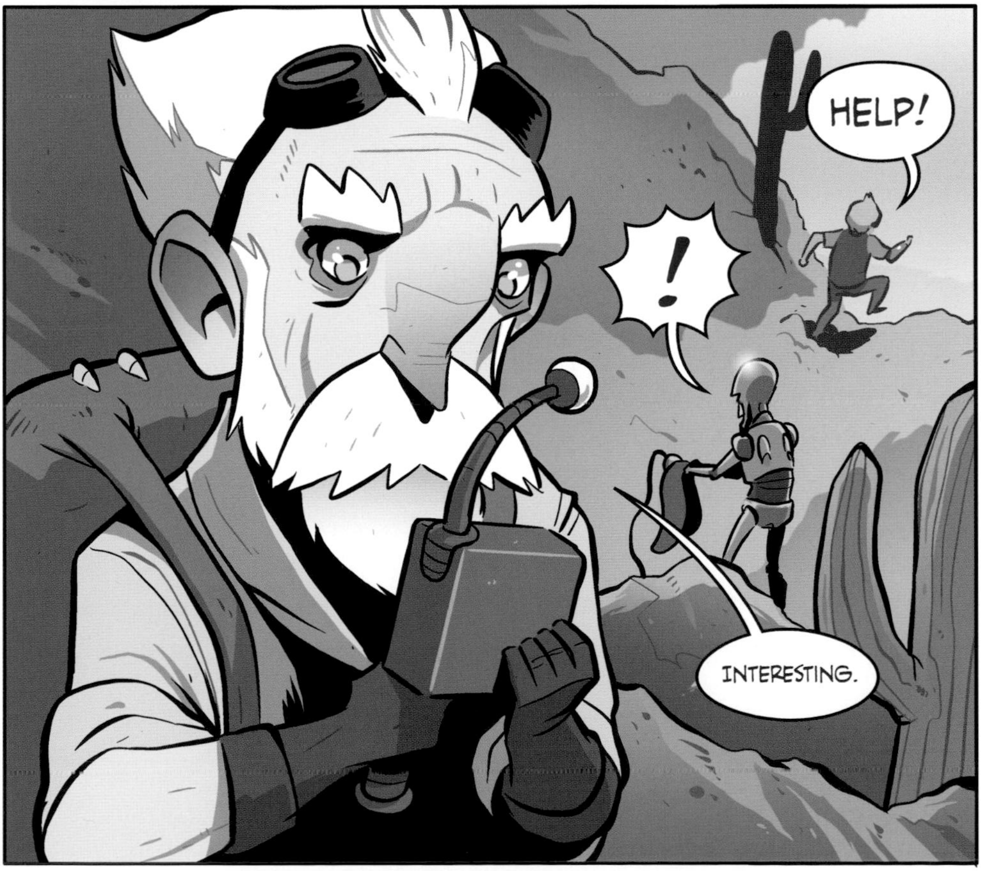
HELP!
!
INTERESTING.

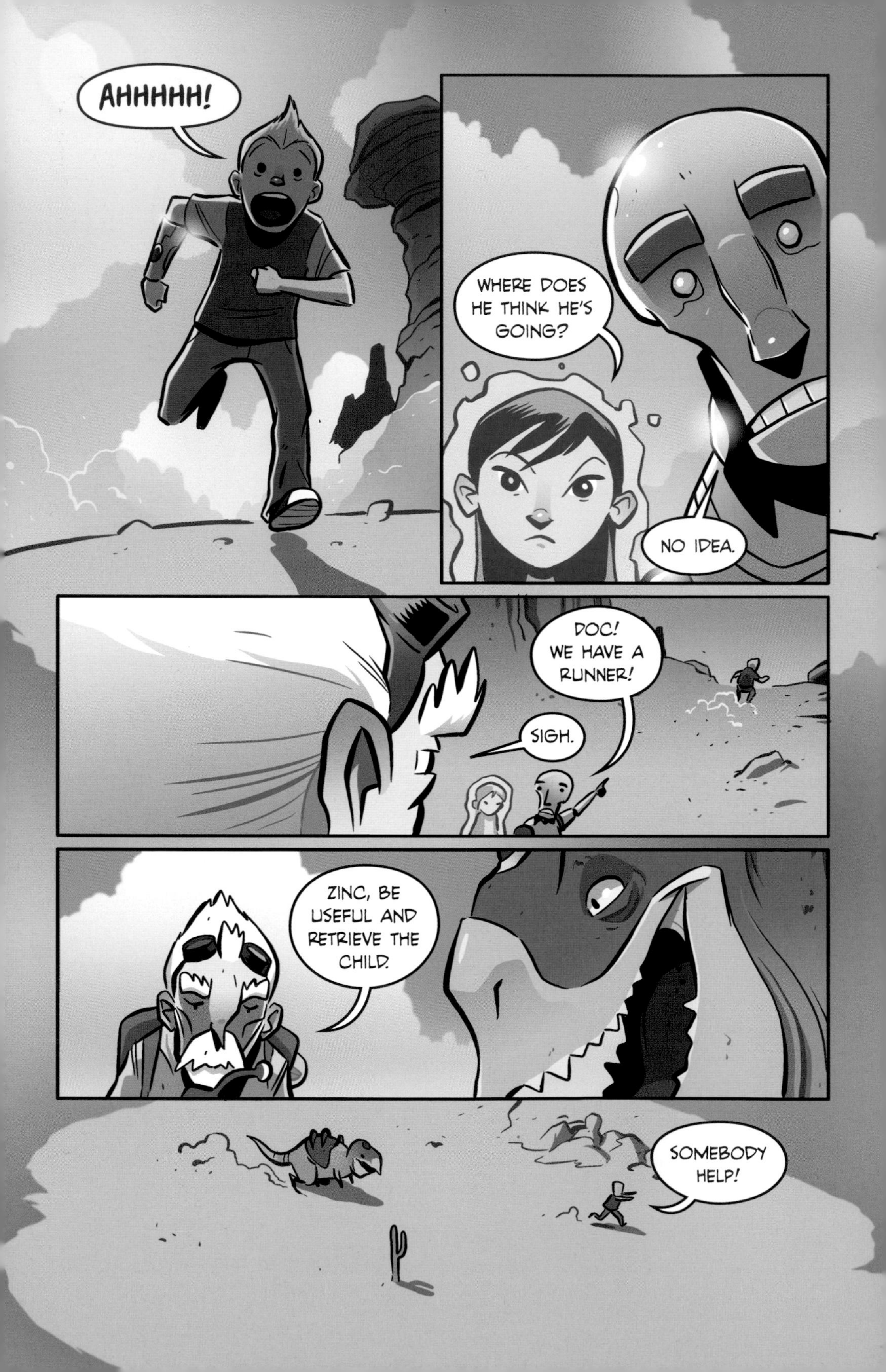
AHHHHH!
WHERE DOES HE THINK HE'S GOING?
NO IDEA.
DOC! WE HAVE A RUNNER!
SIGH.
ZINC, BE USEFUL AND RETRIEVE THE CHILD.
SOMEBODY HELP!

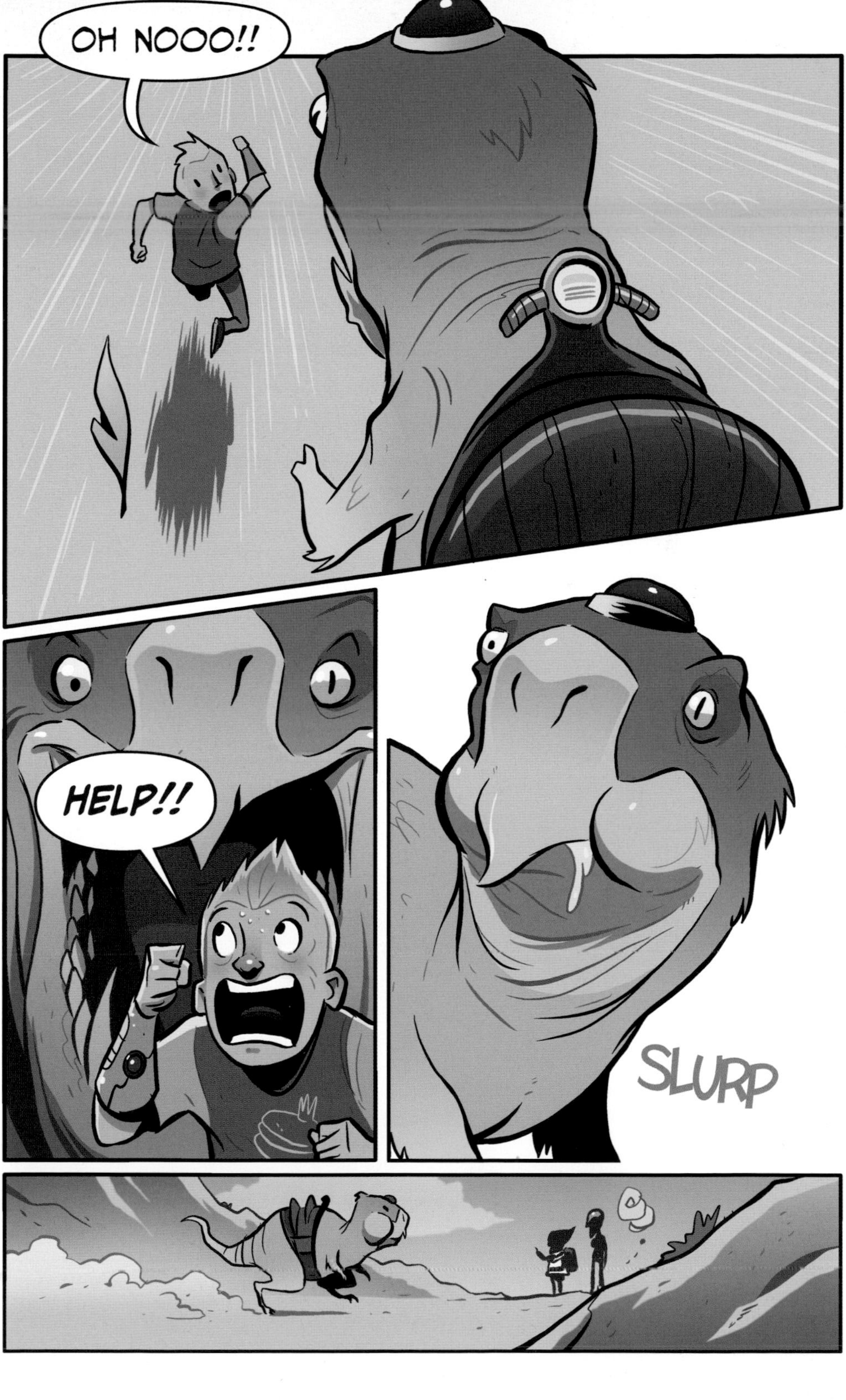
OH NOOO!!
HELP!!
SLURP

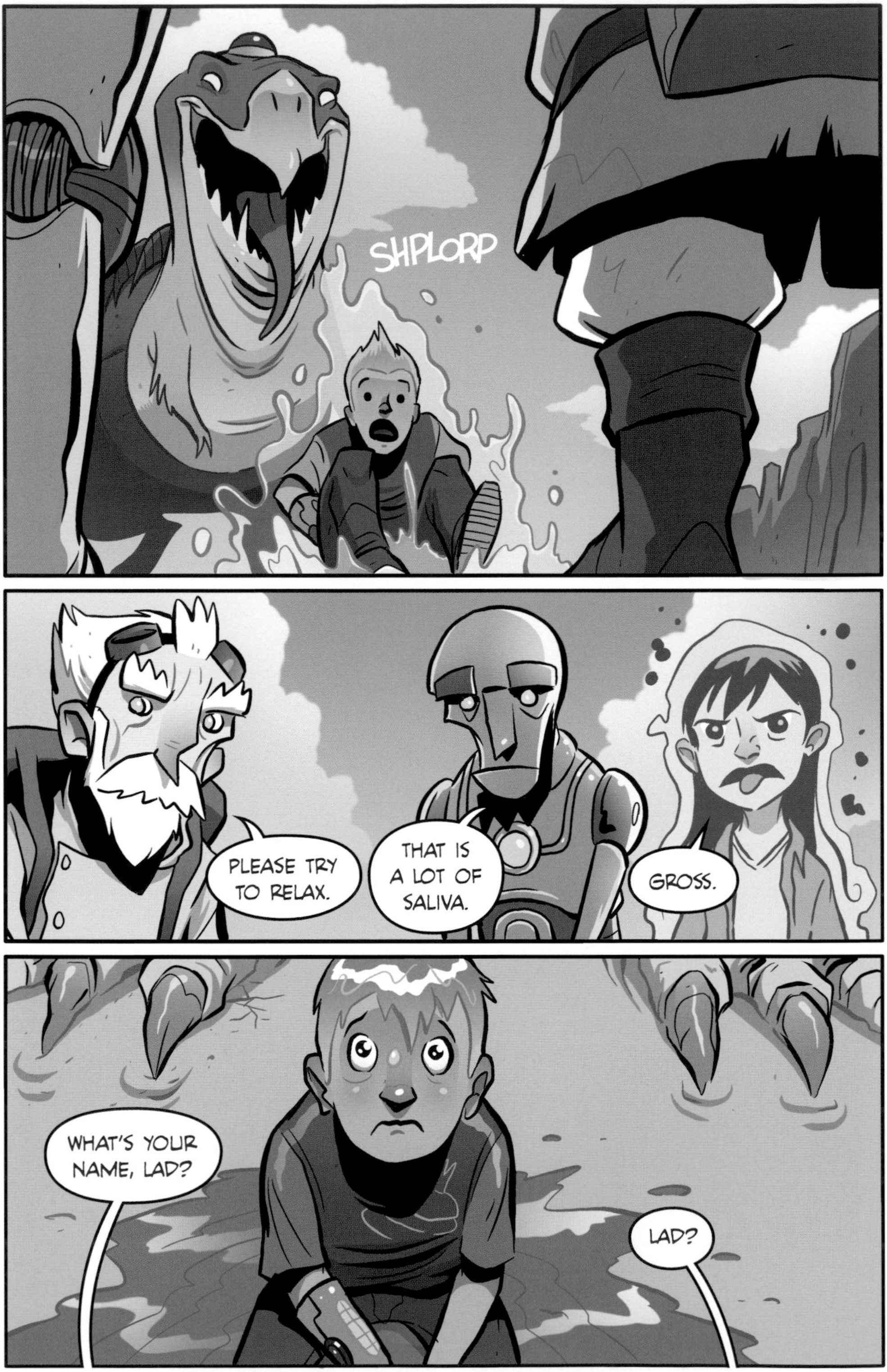
SHPLORP
PLEASE TRY TO RELAX.
THAT IS A LOT OF SALIVA.
GROSS.
WHAT'S YOUR NAME, LAD?
LAD?

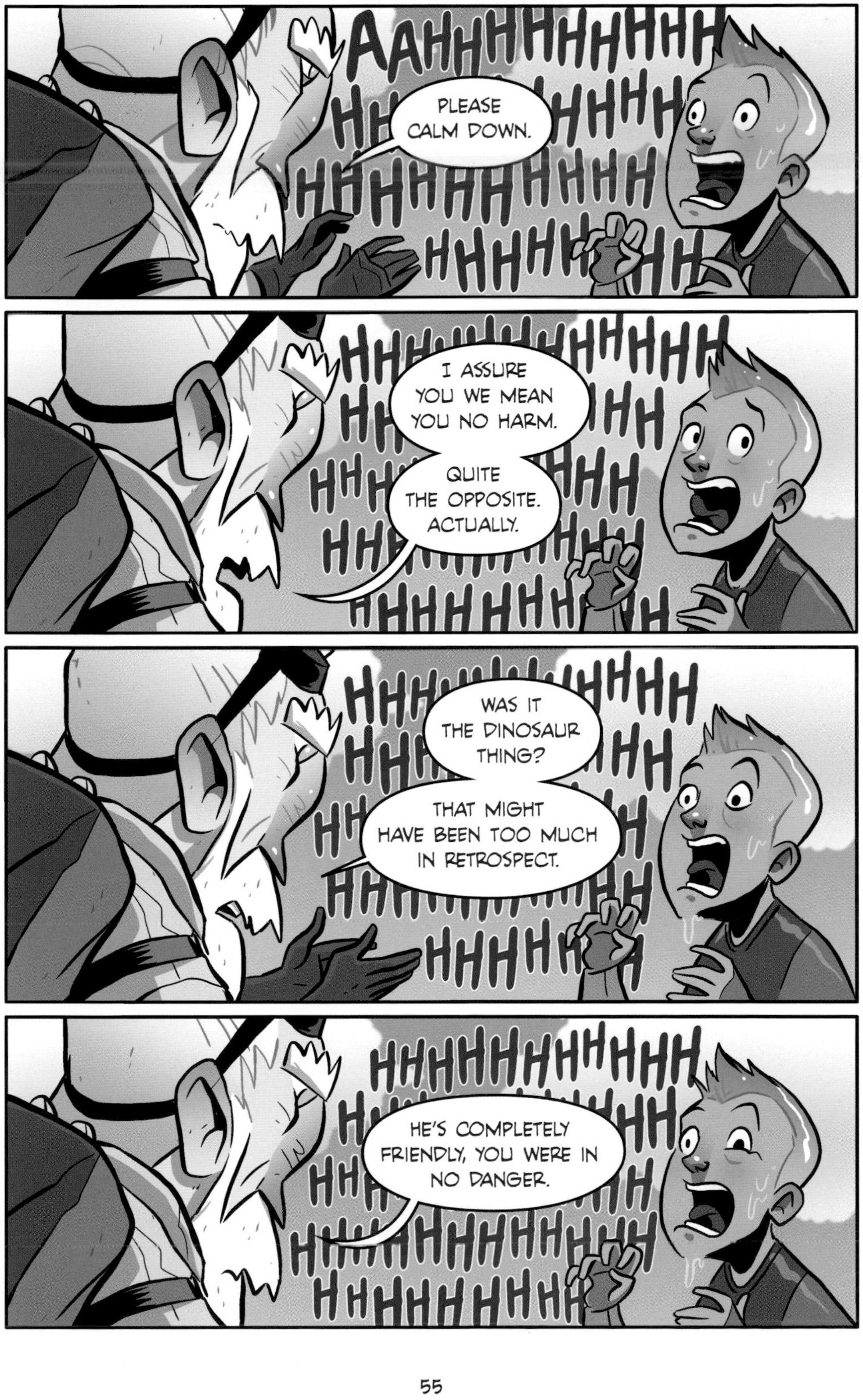
PLEASE CALM DOWN.
I ASSURE YOU WE MEAN YOU NO HARM.
QUITE THE OPPOSITE. ACTUALLY.
WAS IT THE DINOSAUR THING?
THAT MIGHT HAVE BEEN TOO MUCH IN RETROSPECT.
HE'S COMPLETELY FRIENDLY, YOU WERE IN NO DANGER.

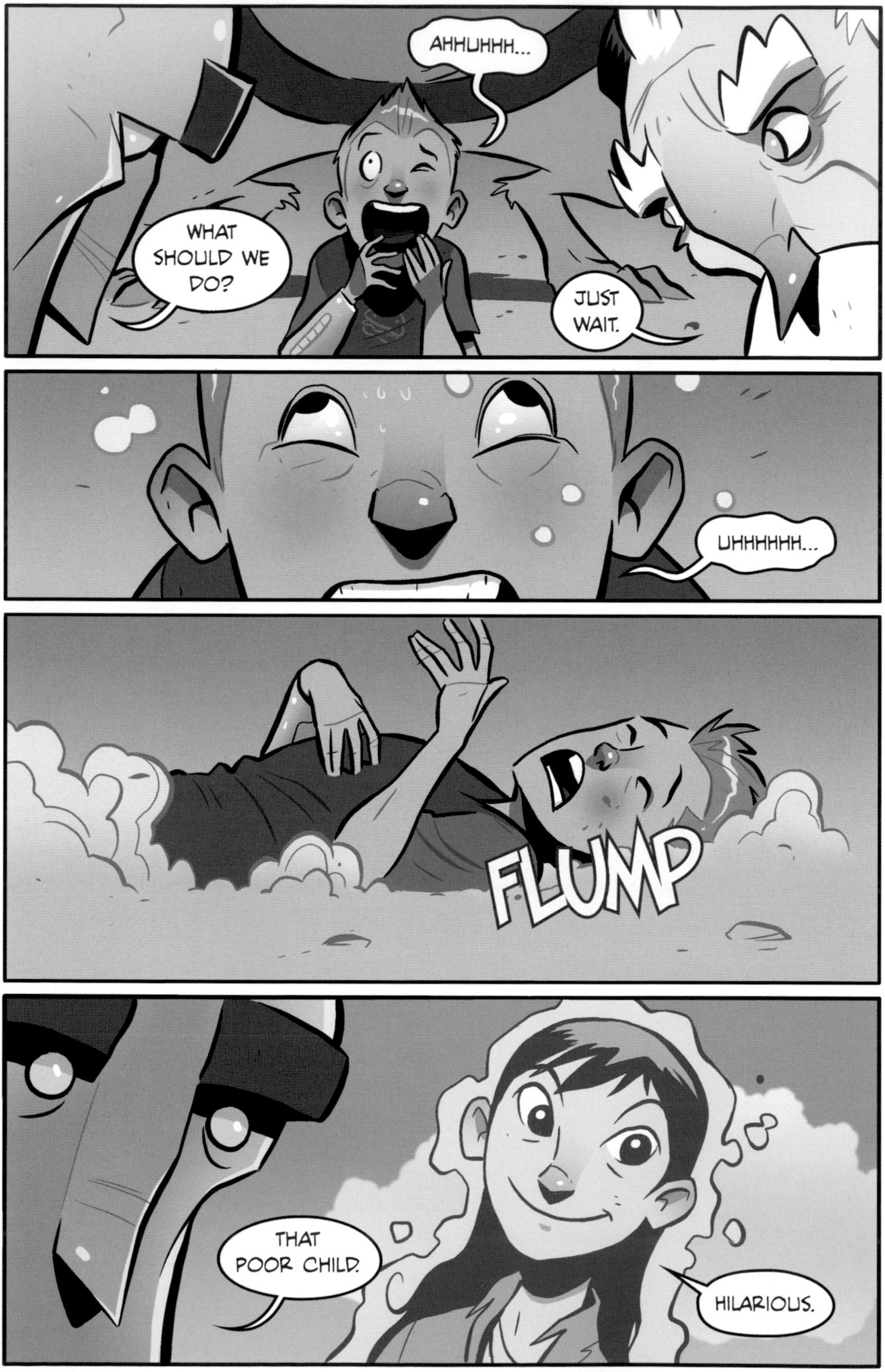
AHHUHHH...
WHAT SHOULD WE DO?
JUST WAIT.
UHHHHHH...
FLUMP
THAT POOR CHILD.
HILARIOUS.

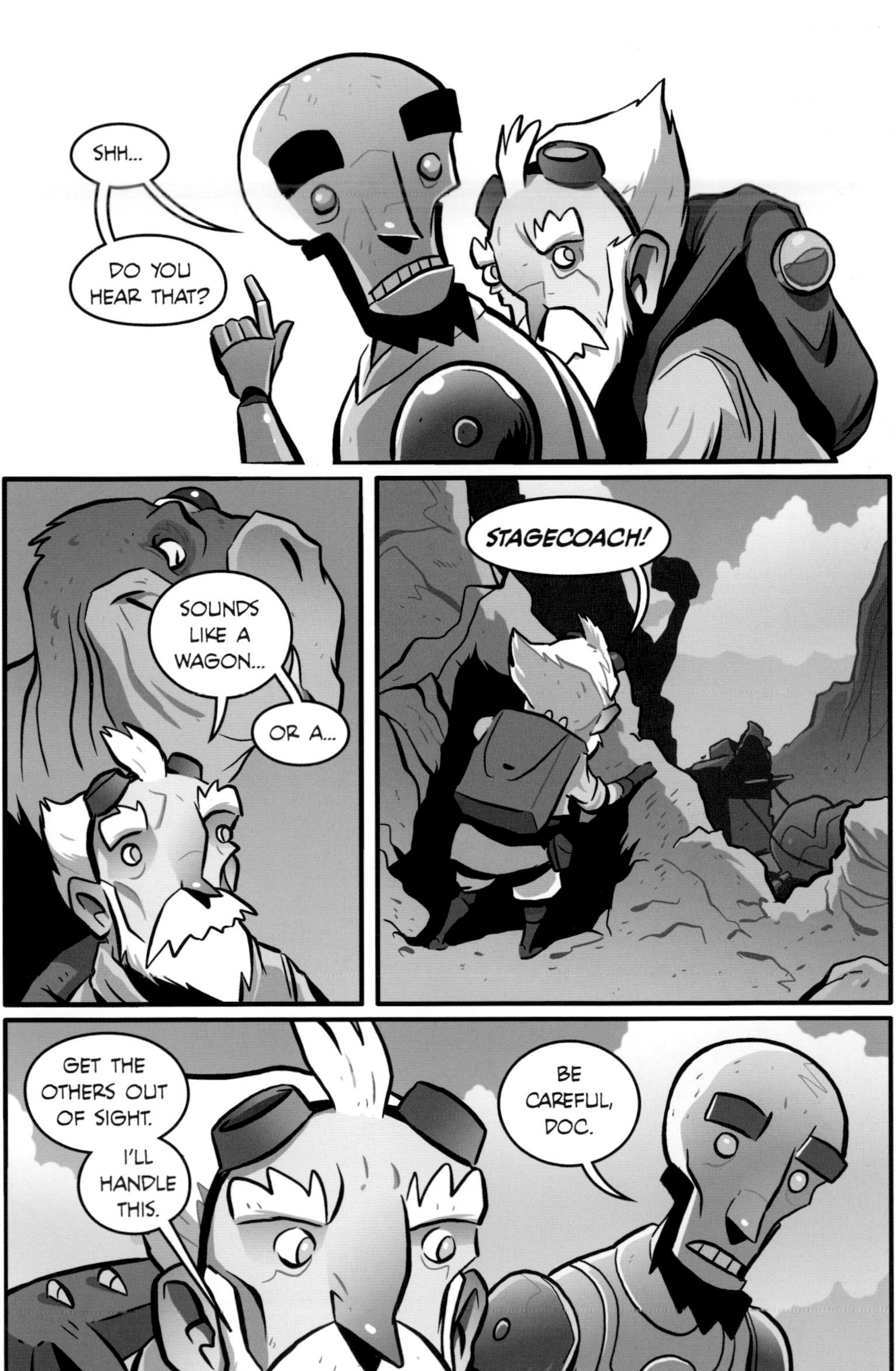
SHH...
DO YOU HEAR THAT?
SOUNDS LIKE A WAGON...
OR A...
STAGECOACH!
GET THE OTHERS OUT OF SIGHT.
I'LL HANDLE THIS.
BE CAREFUL, DOC.

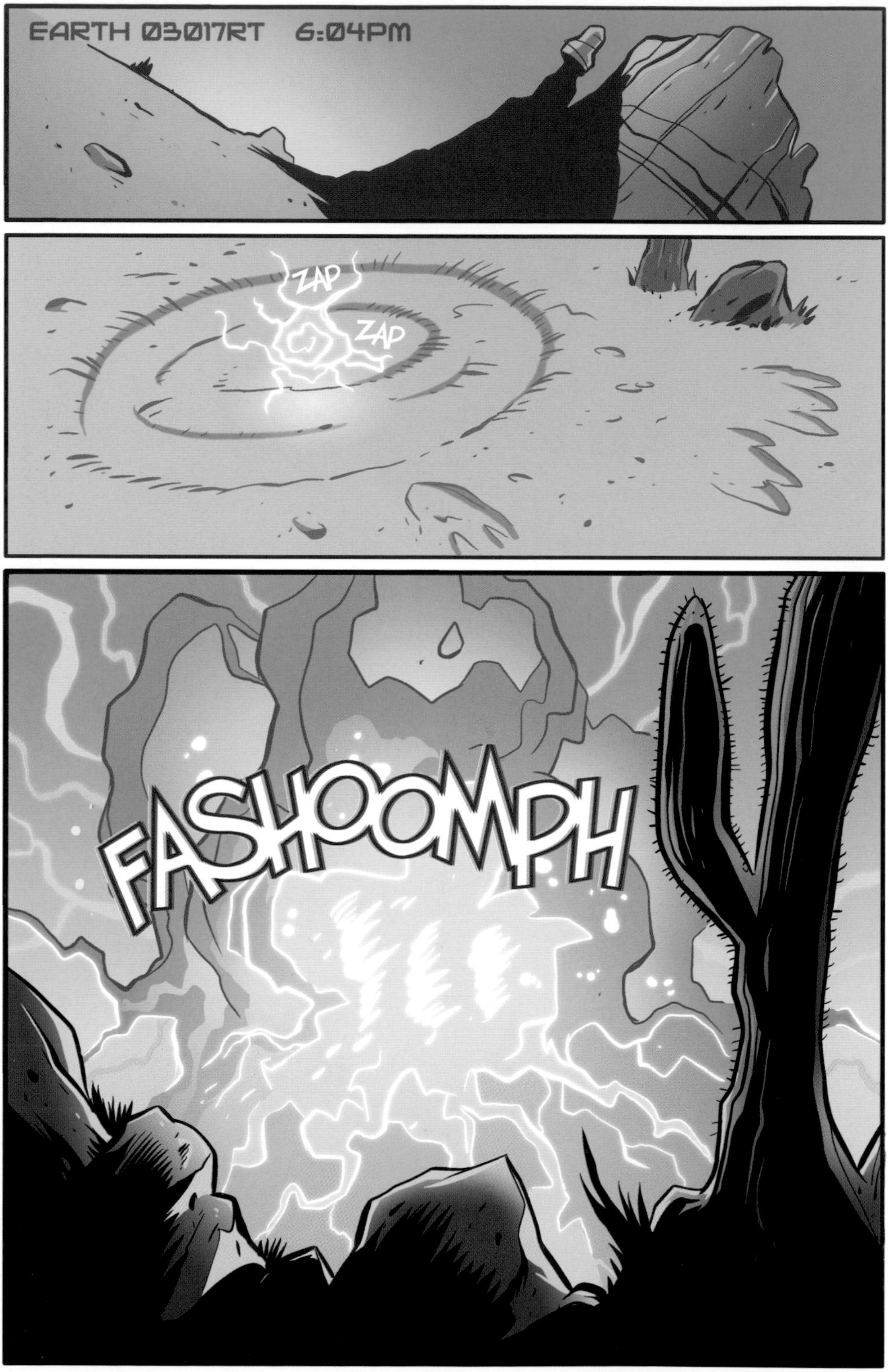
EARTH 03017RT 6:04PM
ZAP
ZAP
FASHOOMPH

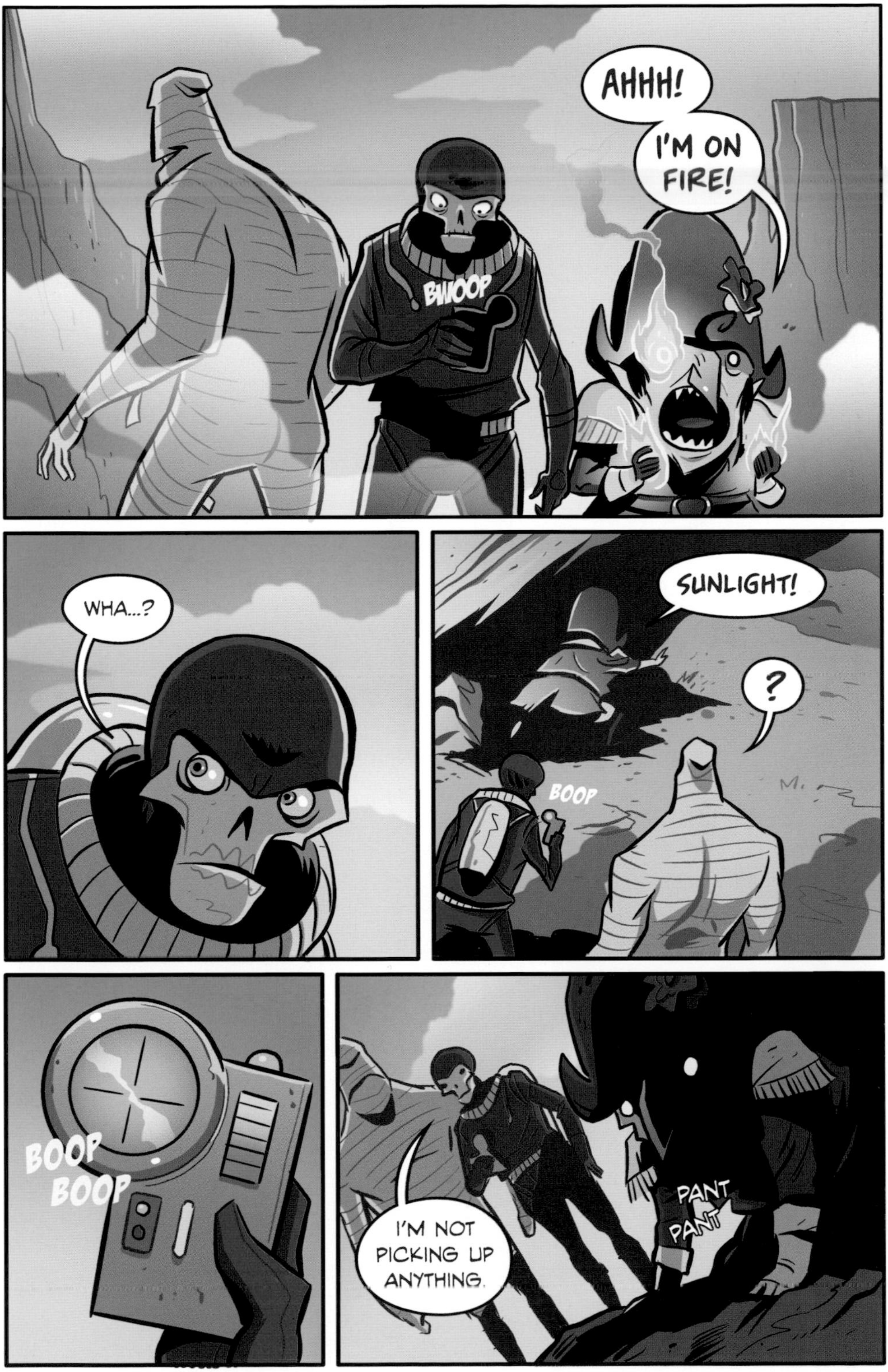
AHHH!
I'M ON FIRE!
BWOOP
WHA...?
SUNLIGHT!
?
BOOP
BOOP BOOP
I'M NOT PICKING UP ANYTHING.
PANT PANT

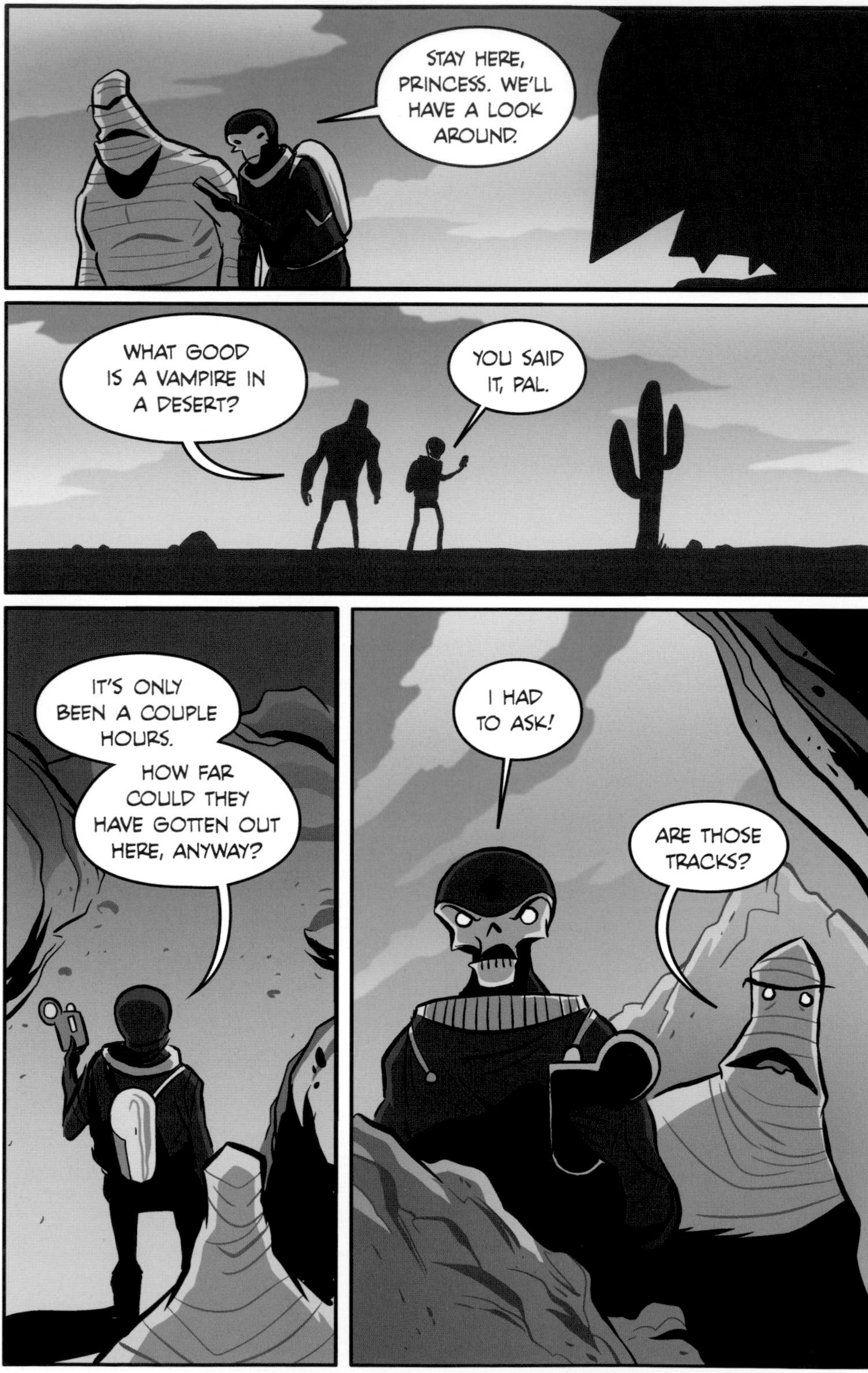
STAY HERE, PRINCESS. WE'LL HAVE A LOOK AROUND.
WHAT GOOD IS A VAMPIRE IN A DESERT?
YOU SAID IT, PAL.
IT'S ONLY BEEN A COUPLE HOURS.
HOW FAR COULD THEY HAVE GOTTEN OUT HERE, ANYWAY?
I HAD TO ASK!
ARE THOSE TRACKS?

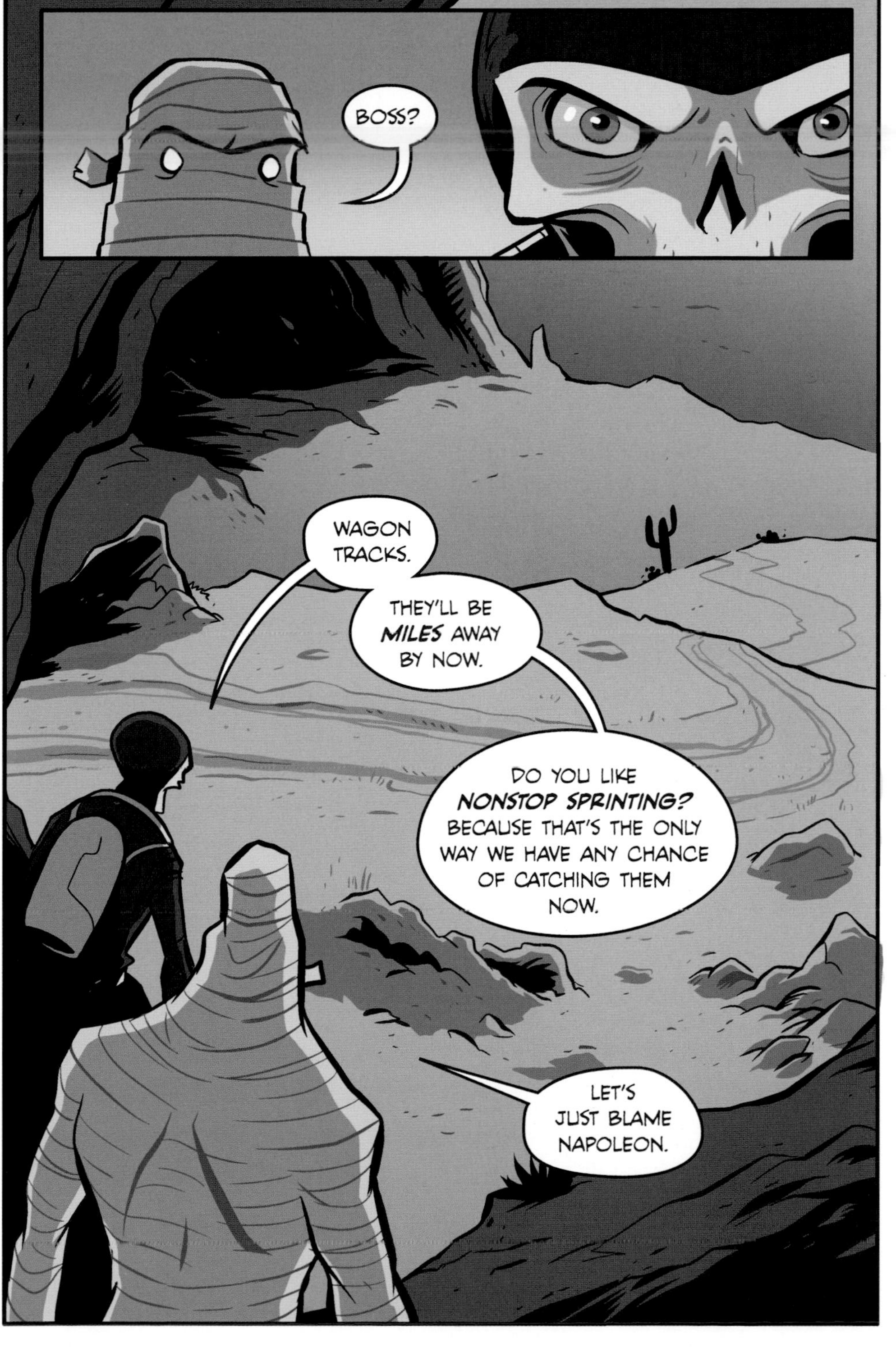
BOSS?
WAGON TRACKS.
THEY'LL BE MILES AWAY BY NOW.
DO YOU LIKE NONSTOP SPRINTING? BECAUSE THAT'S THE ONLY WAY WE HAVE ANY CHANCE OF CATCHING THEM NOW.
LET'S JUST BLAME NAPOLEON.

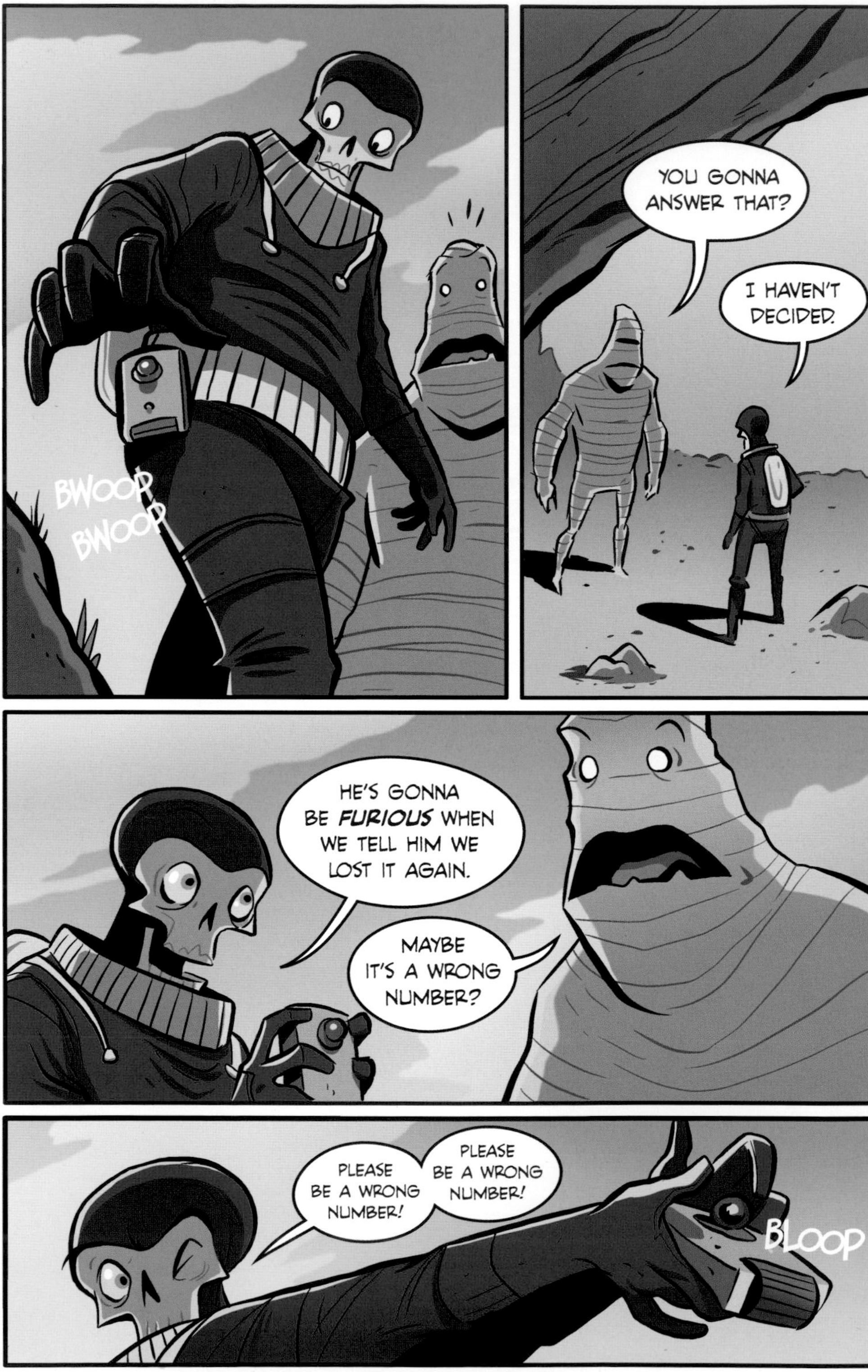
BWOOP
BWOOP
YOU GONNA ANSWER THAT?
I HAVEN'T DECIDED.
HE'S GONNA BE *FURIOUS* WHEN WE TELL HIM WE LOST IT AGAIN.
MAYBE IT'S A WRONG NUMBER?
PLEASE BE A WRONG NUMBER!
PLEASE BE A WRONG NUMBER!
BLOOP

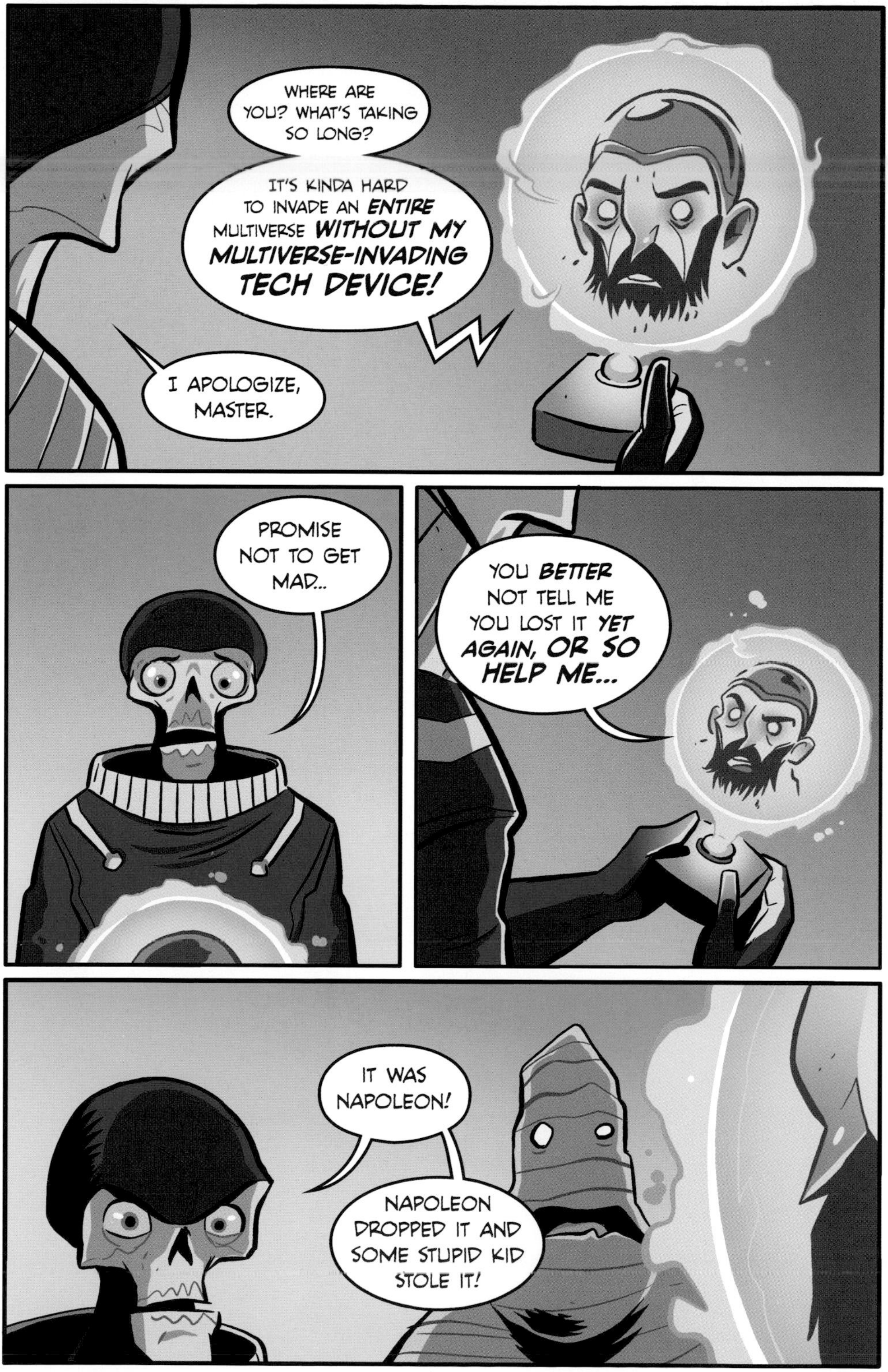
WHERE ARE YOU? WHAT'S TAKING SO LONG?
IT'S KINDA HARD TO INVADE AN ENTIRE MULTIVERSE WITHOUT MY MULTIVERSE-INVADING TECH DEVICE!
I APOLOGIZE, MASTER.
PROMISE NOT TO GET MAD...
YOU BETTER NOT TELL ME YOU LOST IT YET AGAIN, OR SO HELP ME...
IT WAS NAPOLEON!
NAPOLEON DROPPED IT AND SOME STUPID KID STOLE IT!

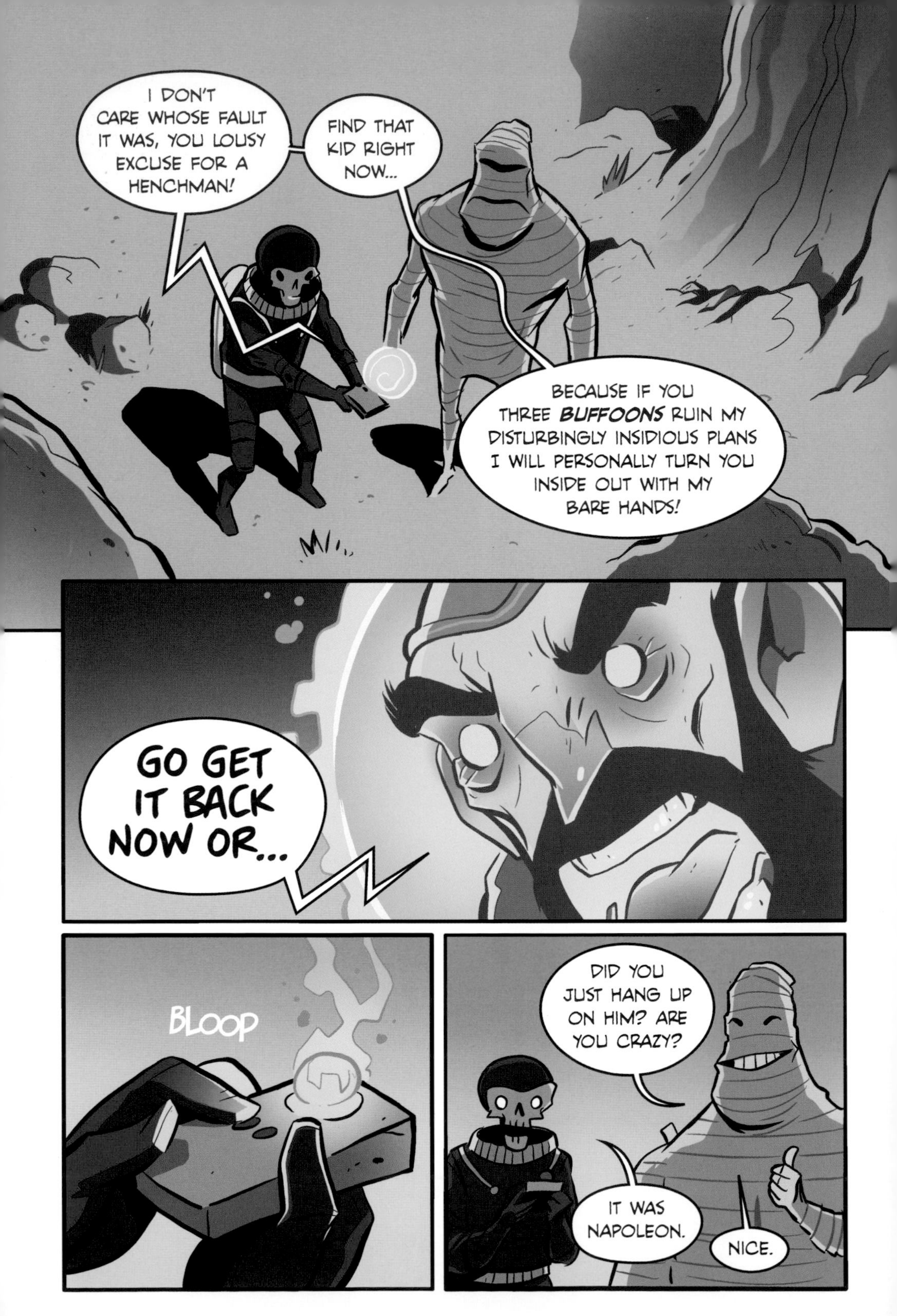
I DON'T CARE WHOSE FAULT IT WAS, YOU LOUSY EXCUSE FOR A HENCHMAN!
FIND THAT KID RIGHT NOW...
BECAUSE IF YOU THREE **BUFFOONS** RUIN MY DISTURBINGLY INSIDIOUS PLANS I WILL PERSONALLY TURN YOU INSIDE OUT WITH MY BARE HANDS!
GO GET IT BACK NOW OR...
BLOOP
DID YOU JUST HANG UP ON HIM? ARE YOU CRAZY?
IT WAS NAPOLEON.
NICE.

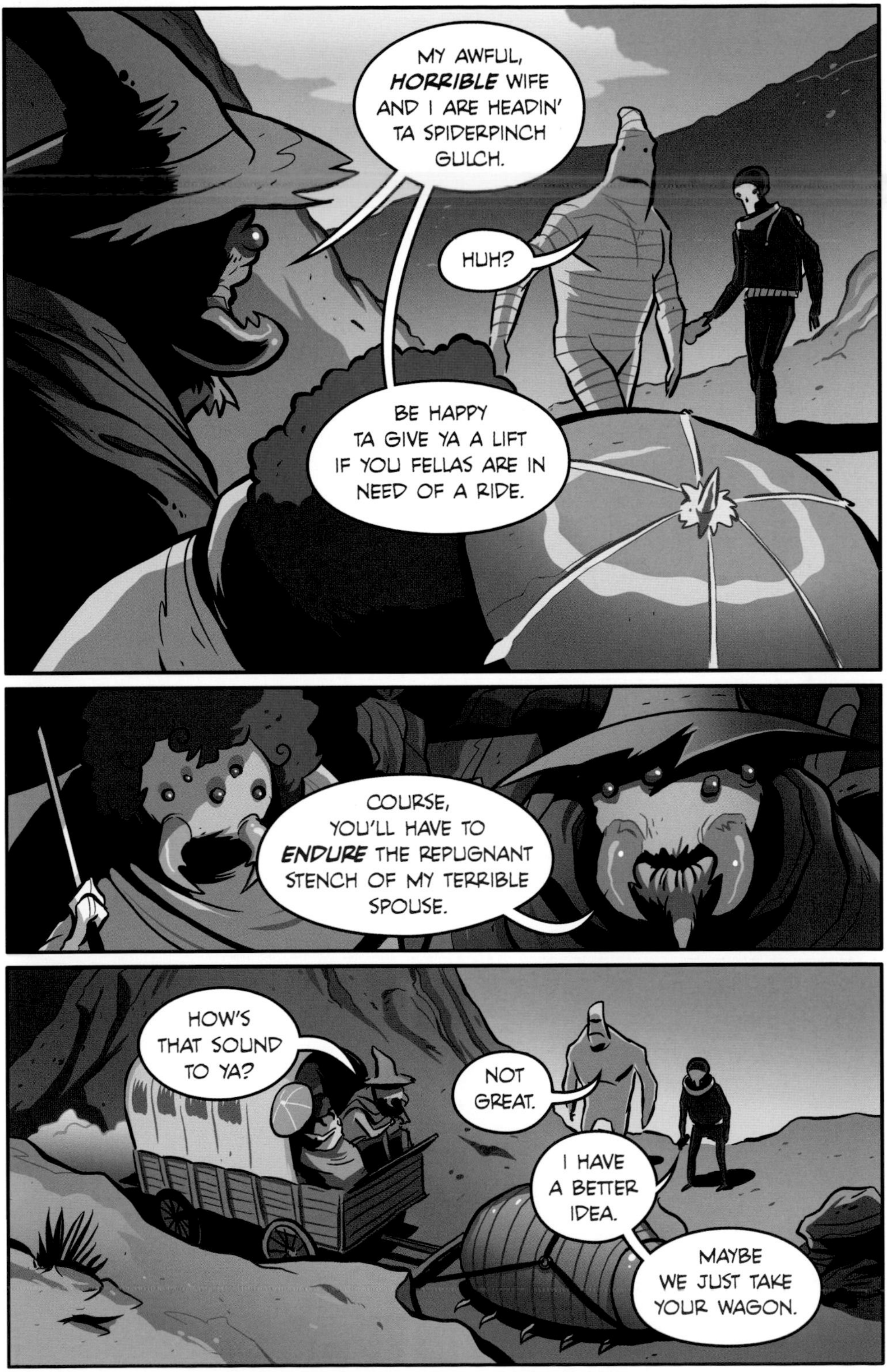
MY AWFUL, HORRIBLE WIFE AND I ARE HEADIN' TA SPIDERPINCH GULCH.
HUH?
BE HAPPY TA GIVE YA A LIFT IF YOU FELLAS ARE IN NEED OF A RIDE.
COURSE, YOU'LL HAVE TO ENDURE THE REPUGNANT STENCH OF MY TERRIBLE SPOUSE.
HOW'S THAT SOUND TO YA?
NOT GREAT.
I HAVE A BETTER IDEA.
MAYBE WE JUST TAKE YOUR WAGON.

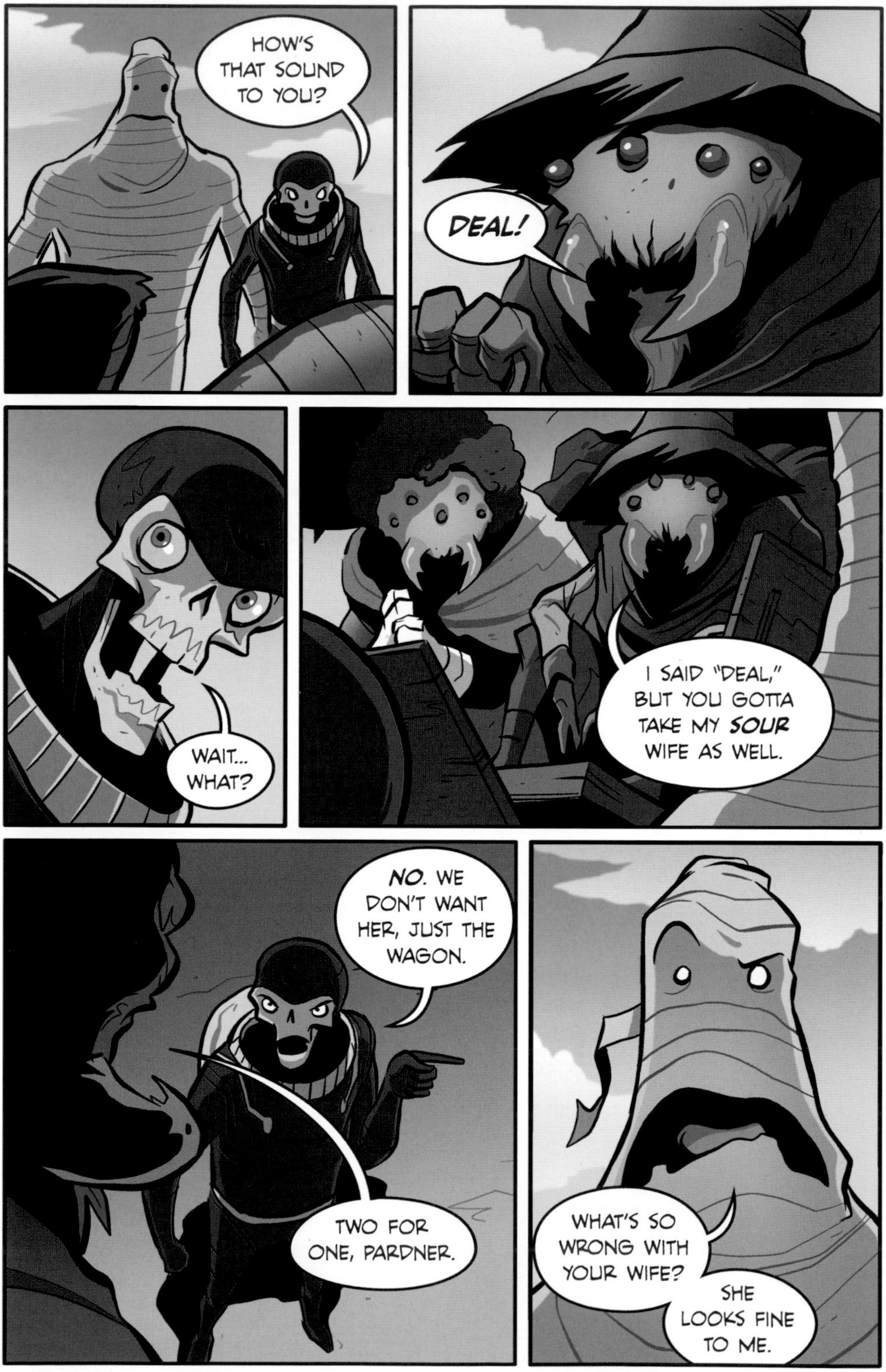
HOW'S THAT SOUND TO YOU?
DEAL!
WAIT... WHAT?
I SAID "DEAL," BUT YOU GOTTA TAKE MY SOUR WIFE AS WELL.
NO. WE DON'T WANT HER, JUST THE WAGON.
TWO FOR ONE, PARDNER.
WHAT'S SO WRONG WITH YOUR WIFE?
SHE LOOKS FINE TO ME.

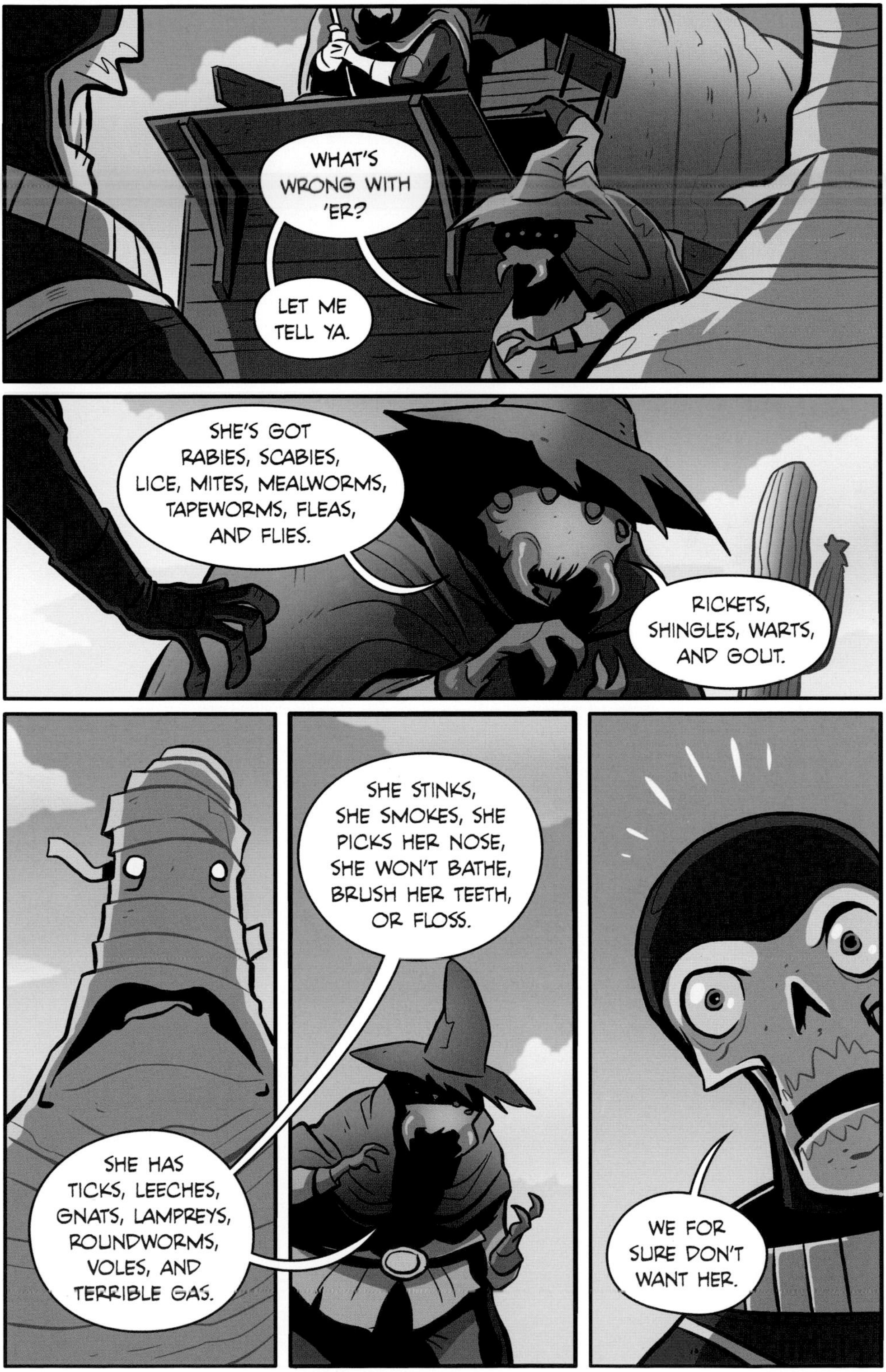
WHAT'S WRONG WITH 'ER?
LET ME TELL YA.
SHE'S GOT RABIES, SCABIES, LICE, MITES, MEALWORMS, TAPEWORMS, FLEAS, AND FLIES.
RICKETS, SHINGLES, WARTS, AND GOUT.
SHE HAS TICKS, LEECHES, GNATS, LAMPREYS, ROUNDWORMS, VOLES, AND TERRIBLE GAS.
SHE STINKS, SHE SMOKES, SHE PICKS HER NOSE, SHE WON'T BATHE, BRUSH HER TEETH, OR FLOSS.
WE FOR SURE DON'T WANT HER.

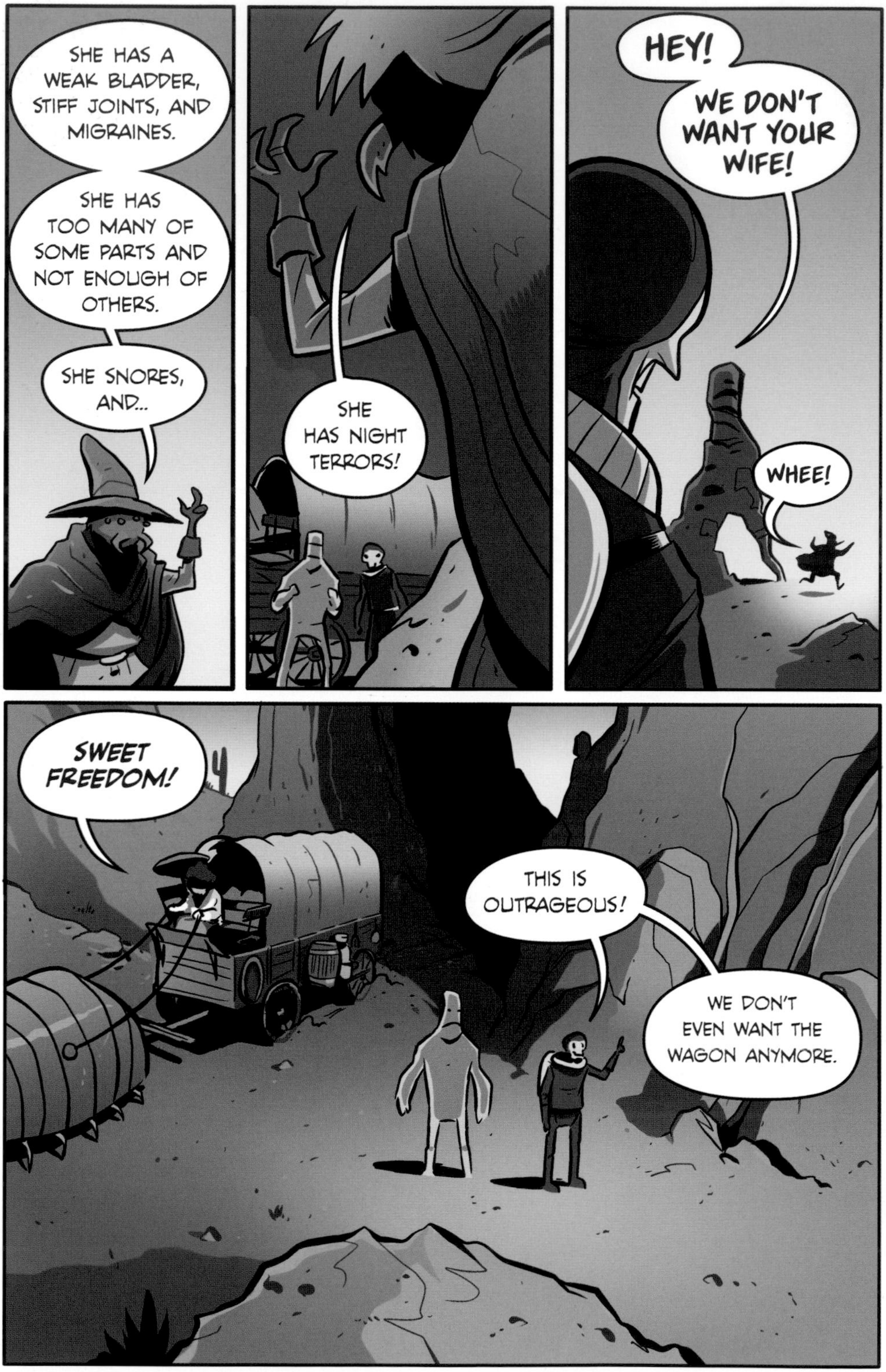
SHE HAS A WEAK BLADDER, STIFF JOINTS, AND MIGRAINES.
SHE HAS TOO MANY OF SOME PARTS AND NOT ENOUGH OF OTHERS.
SHE SNORES, AND...
SHE HAS NIGHT TERRORS!
HEY!
WE DON'T WANT YOUR WIFE!
WHEE!
SWEET FREEDOM!
THIS IS OUTRAGEOUS!
WE DON'T EVEN WANT THE WAGON ANYMORE.

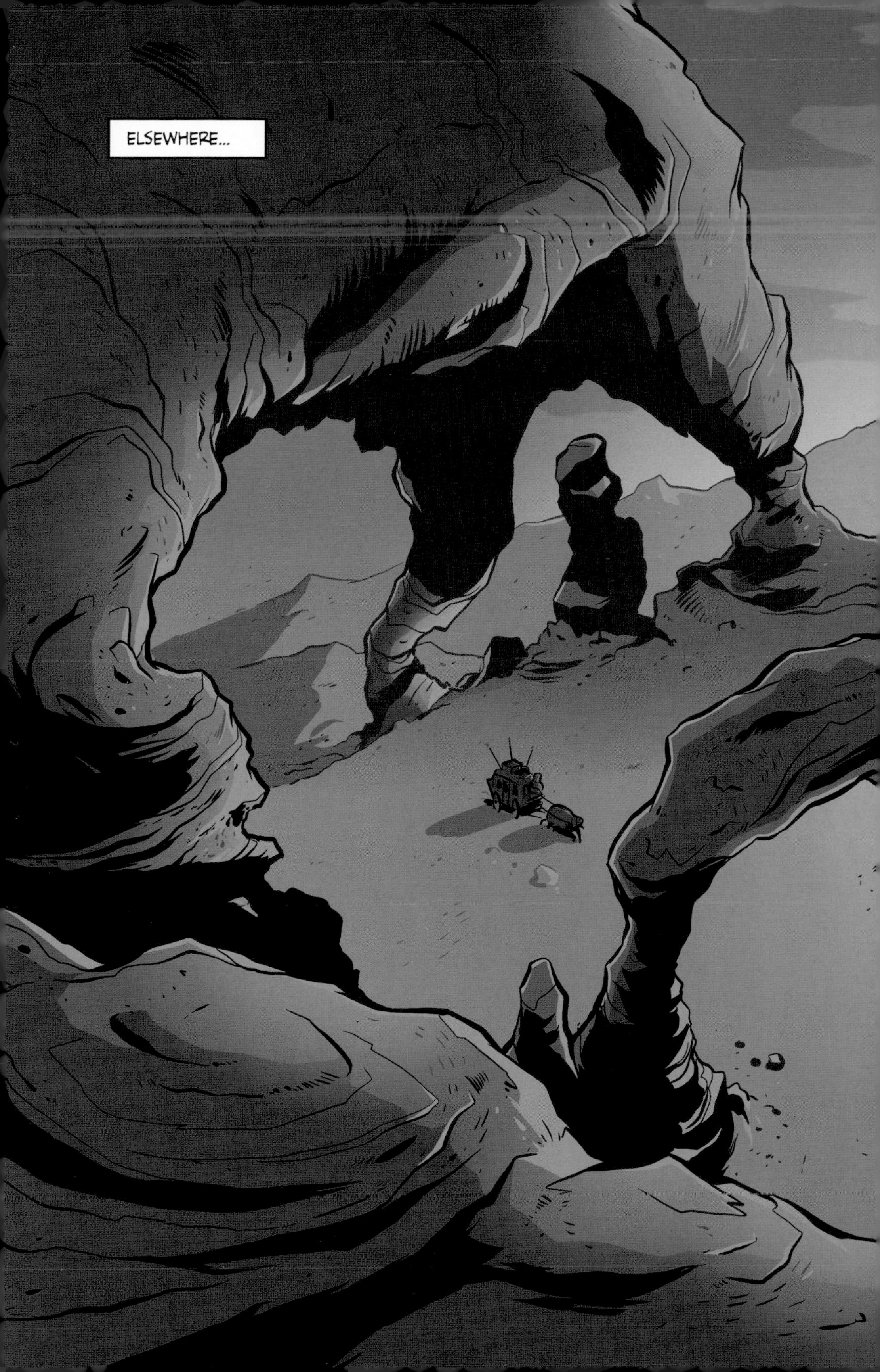
ELSEWHERE...

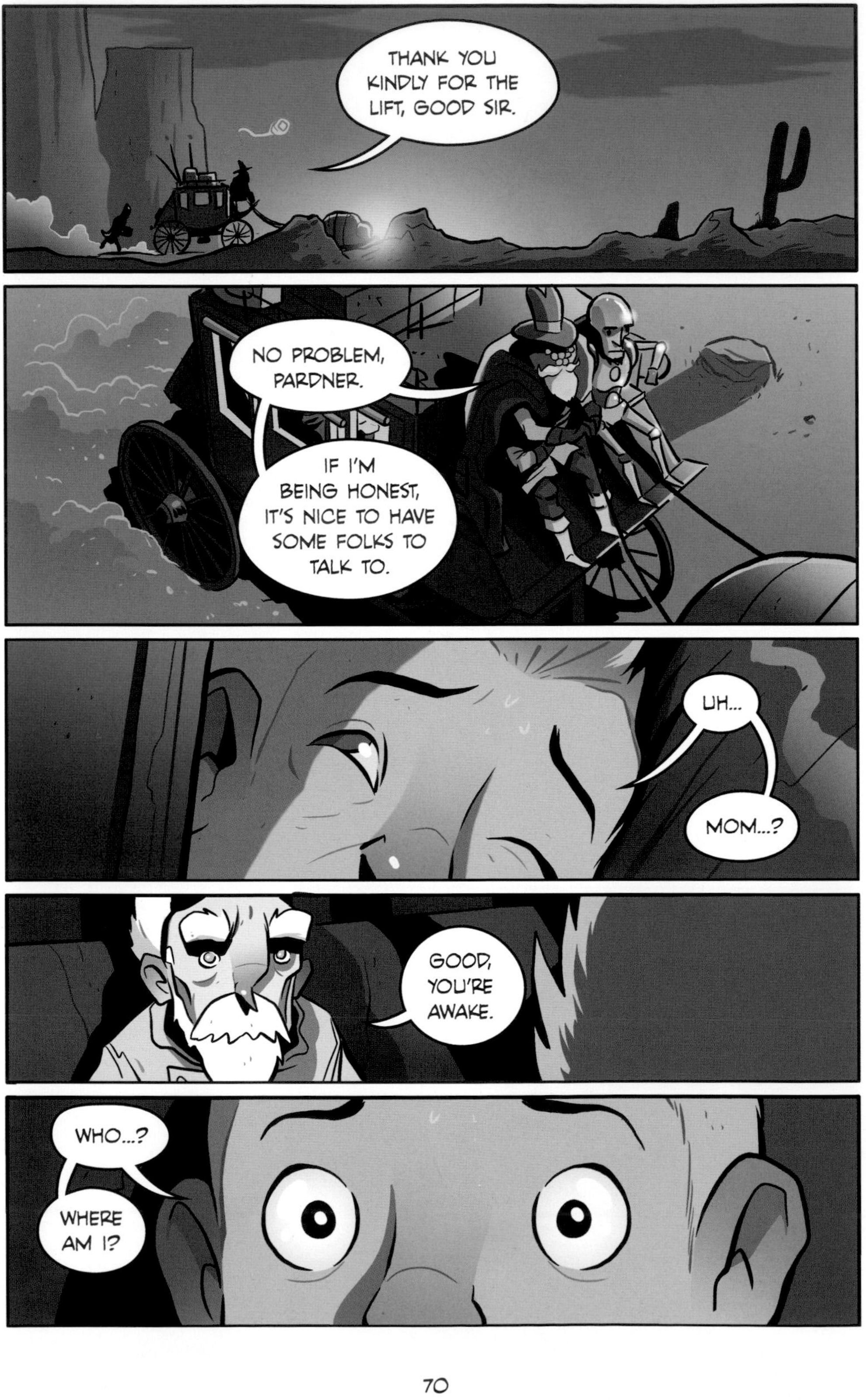
THANK YOU KINDLY FOR THE LIFT, GOOD SIR.
NO PROBLEM, PARDNER.
IF I'M BEING HONEST, IT'S NICE TO HAVE SOME FOLKS TO TALK TO.
UH...
MOM...?
GOOD, YOU'RE AWAKE.
WHO...?
WHERE AM I?

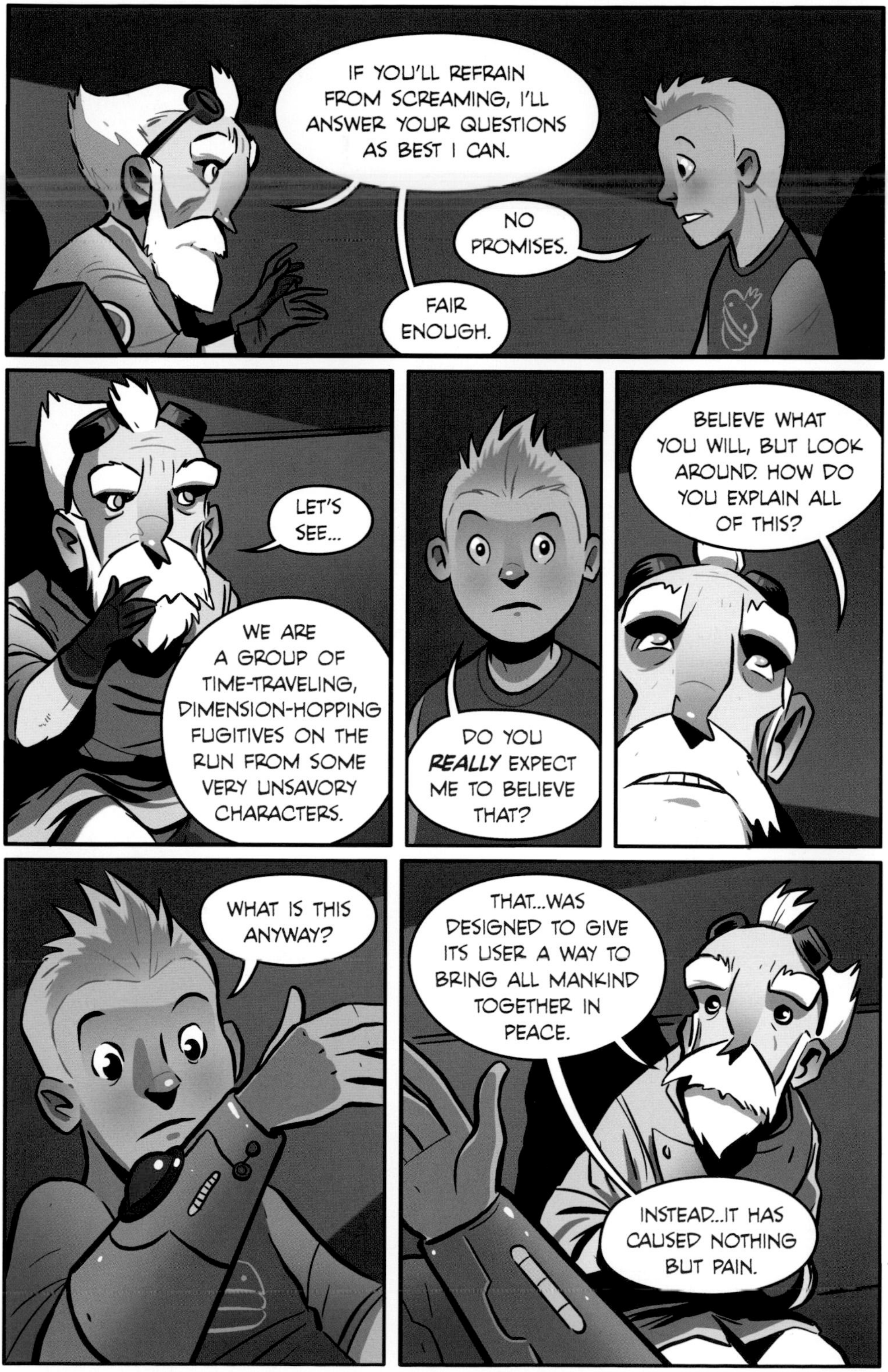
IF YOU'LL REFRAIN FROM SCREAMING, I'LL ANSWER YOUR QUESTIONS AS BEST I CAN.
NO PROMISES.
FAIR ENOUGH.
LET'S SEE...
WE ARE A GROUP OF TIME-TRAVELING, DIMENSION-HOPPING FUGITIVES ON THE RUN FROM SOME VERY UNSAVORY CHARACTERS.
DO YOU *REALLY* EXPECT ME TO BELIEVE THAT?
BELIEVE WHAT YOU WILL, BUT LOOK AROUND. HOW DO YOU EXPLAIN ALL OF THIS?
WHAT IS THIS ANYWAY?
THAT...WAS DESIGNED TO GIVE ITS USER A WAY TO BRING ALL MANKIND TOGETHER IN PEACE.
INSTEAD...IT HAS CAUSED NOTHING BUT PAIN.

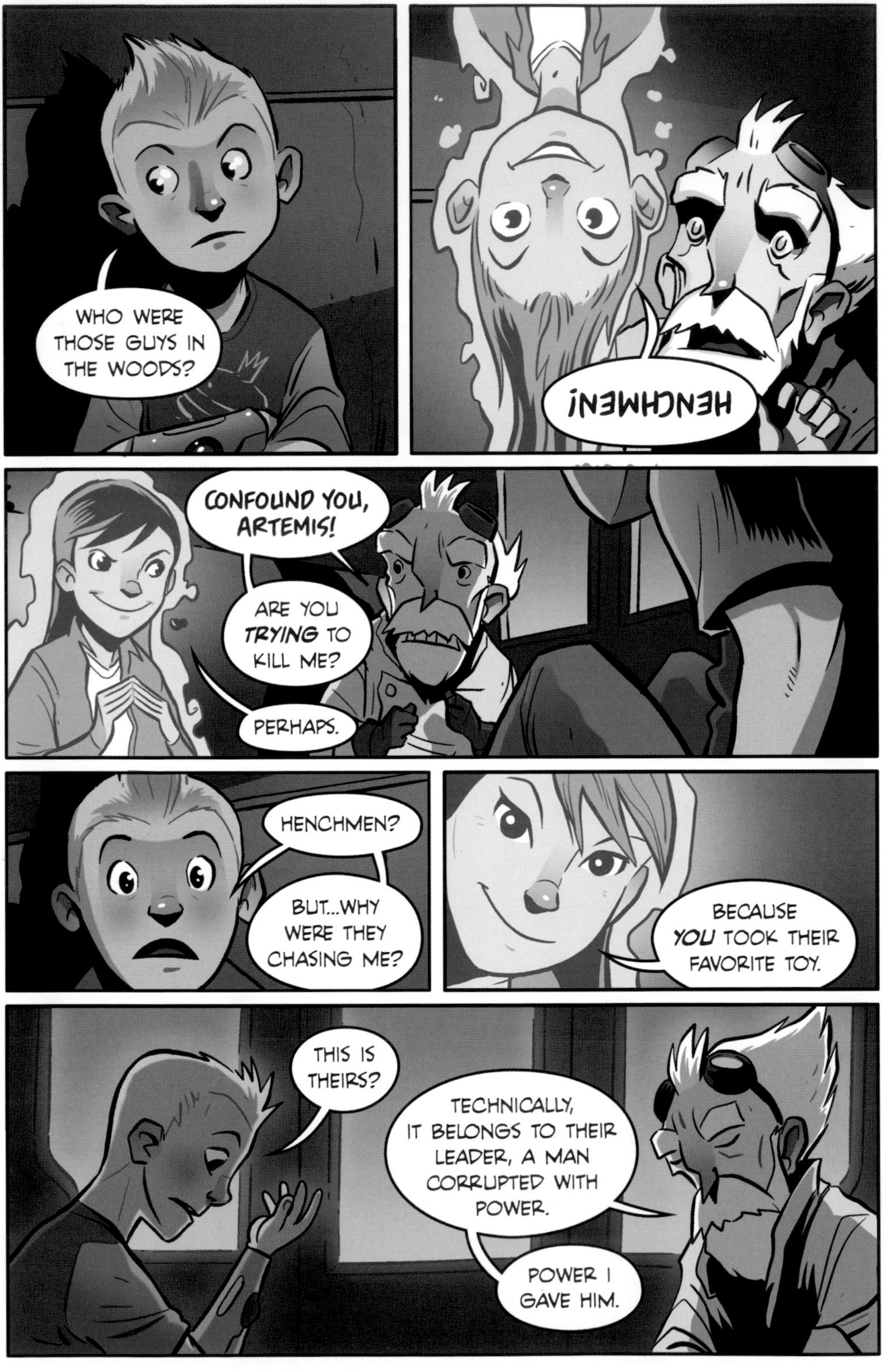
WHO WERE THOSE GUYS IN THE WOODS?
HENCHMEN!
CONFOUND YOU, ARTEMIS!
ARE YOU TRYING TO KILL ME?
PERHAPS.
HENCHMEN?
BUT...WHY WERE THEY CHASING ME?
BECAUSE YOU TOOK THEIR FAVORITE TOY.
THIS IS THEIRS?
TECHNICALLY, IT BELONGS TO THEIR LEADER, A MAN CORRUPTED WITH POWER.
POWER I GAVE HIM.

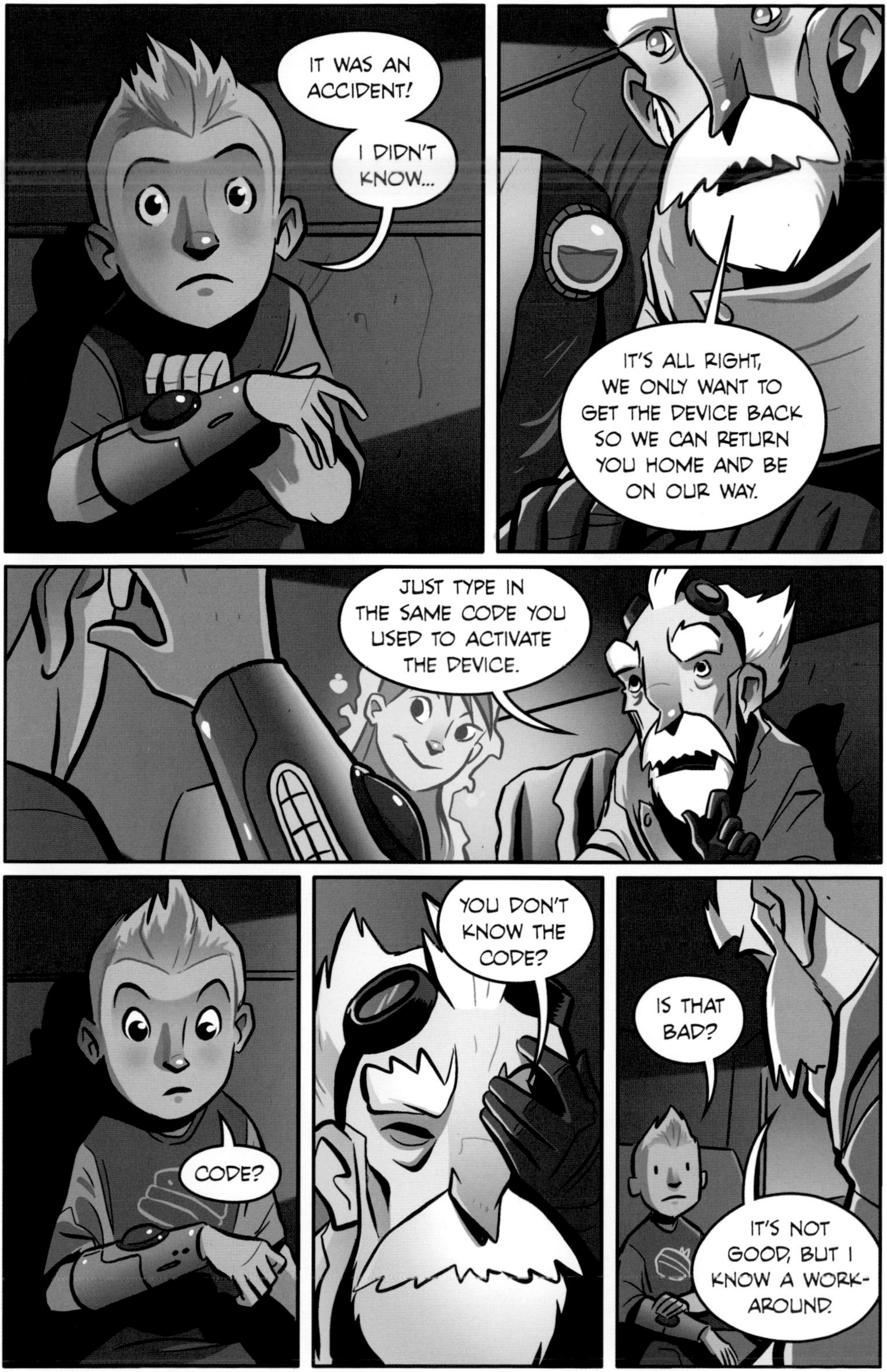
IT WAS AN ACCIDENT!
I DIDN'T KNOW...
IT'S ALL RIGHT, WE ONLY WANT TO GET THE DEVICE BACK SO WE CAN RETURN YOU HOME AND BE ON OUR WAY.
JUST TYPE IN THE SAME CODE YOU USED TO ACTIVATE THE DEVICE.
CODE?
YOU DON'T KNOW THE CODE?
IS THAT BAD?
IT'S NOT GOOD, BUT I KNOW A WORK-AROUND.

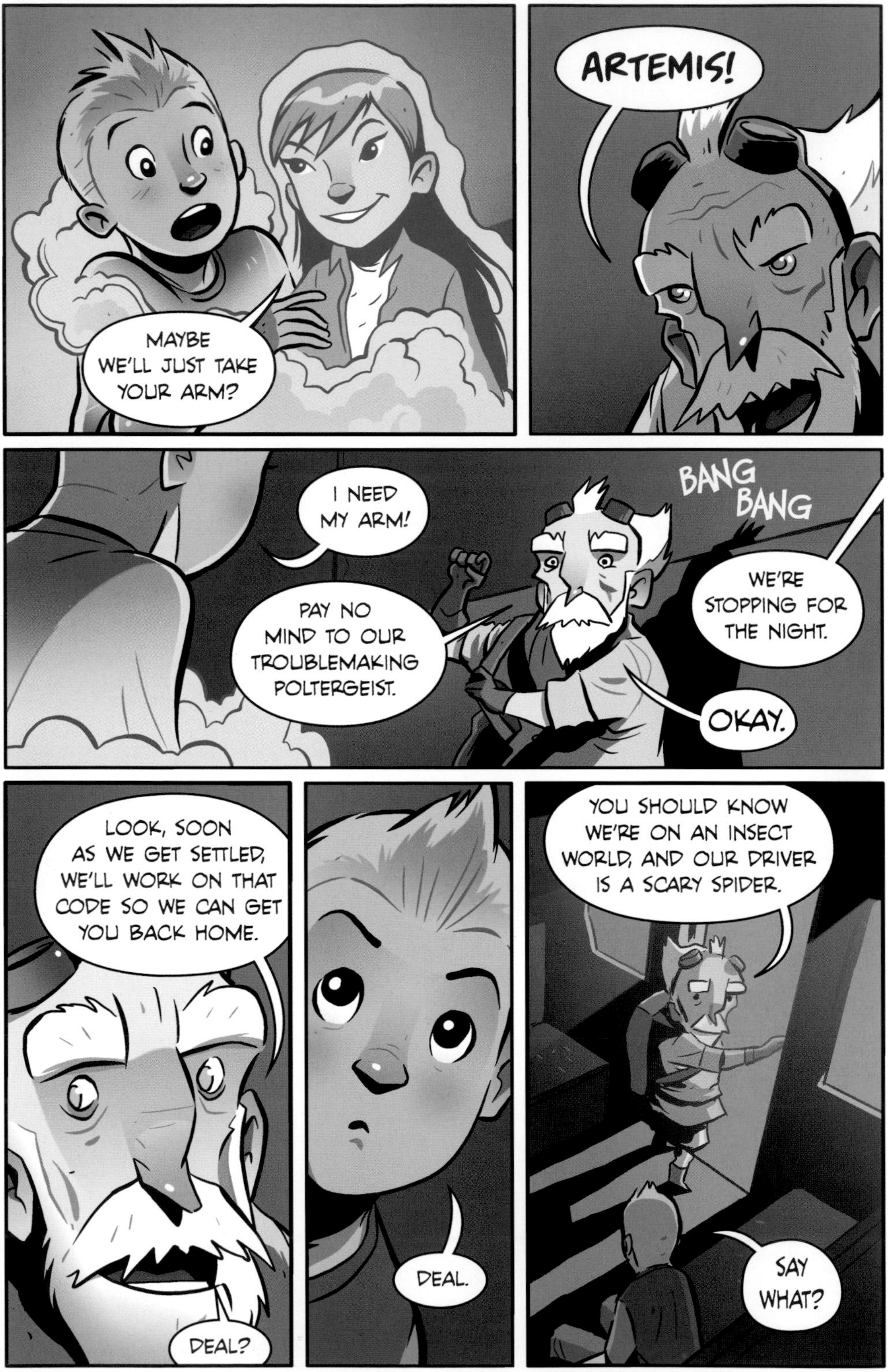
MAYBE WE'LL JUST TAKE YOUR ARM?
ARTEMIS!
I NEED MY ARM!
PAY NO MIND TO OUR TROUBLEMAKING POLTERGEIST.
BANG BANG
WE'RE STOPPING FOR THE NIGHT.
OKAY.
LOOK, SOON AS WE GET SETTLED, WE'LL WORK ON THAT CODE SO WE CAN GET YOU BACK HOME.
DEAL?
DEAL.
YOU SHOULD KNOW WE'RE ON AN INSECT WORLD, AND OUR DRIVER IS A SCARY SPIDER.
SAY WHAT?

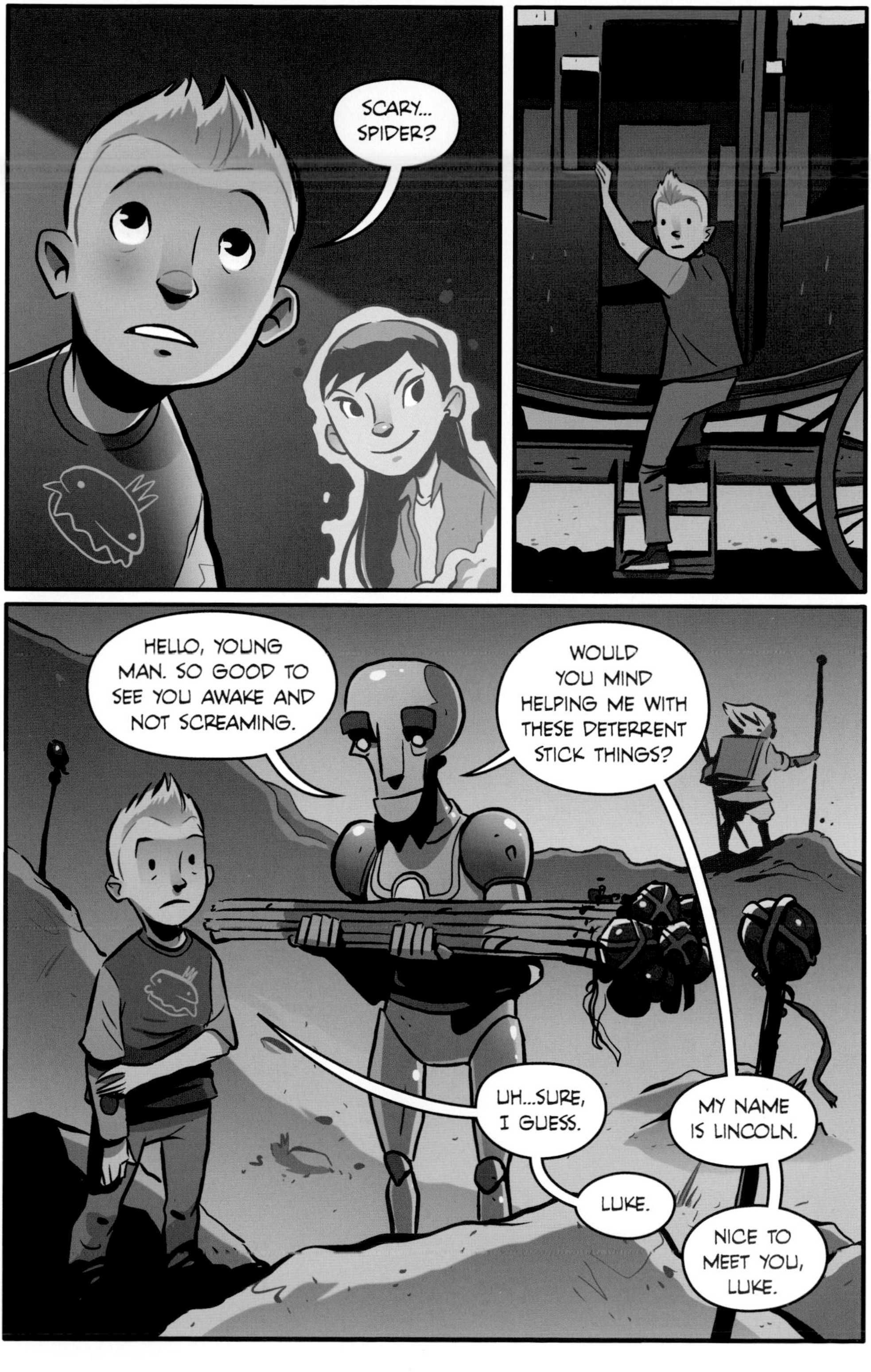
SCARY... SPIDER?
HELLO, YOUNG MAN. SO GOOD TO SEE YOU AWAKE AND NOT SCREAMING.
WOULD YOU MIND HELPING ME WITH THESE DETERRENT STICK THINGS?
UH...SURE, I GUESS.
MY NAME IS LINCOLN.
LUKE.
NICE TO MEET YOU, LUKE.

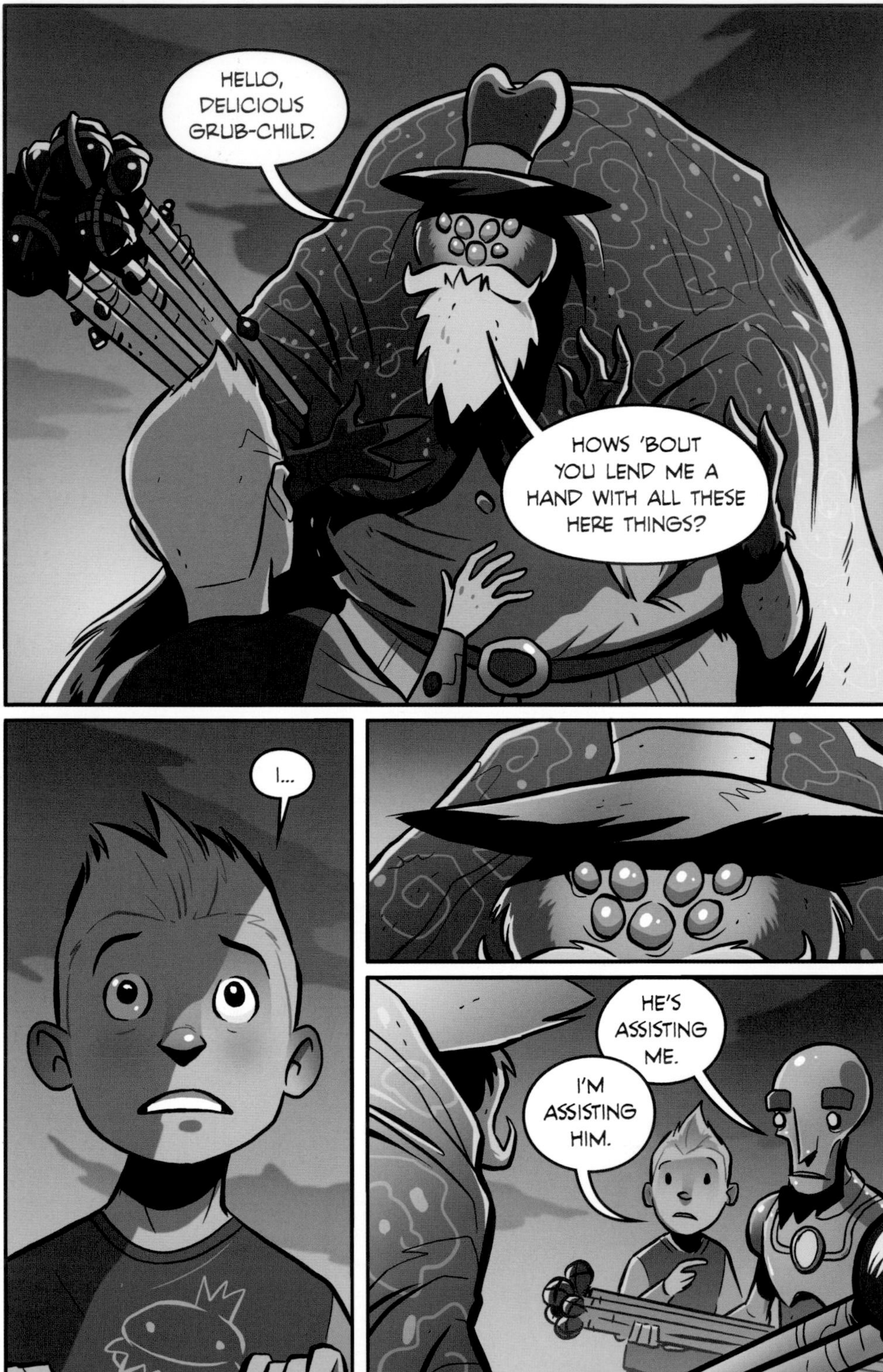
HELLO, DELICIOUS GRUB-CHILD.
HOWS 'BOUT YOU LEND ME A HAND WITH ALL THESE HERE THINGS?
I...
HE'S ASSISTING ME.
I'M ASSISTING HIM.

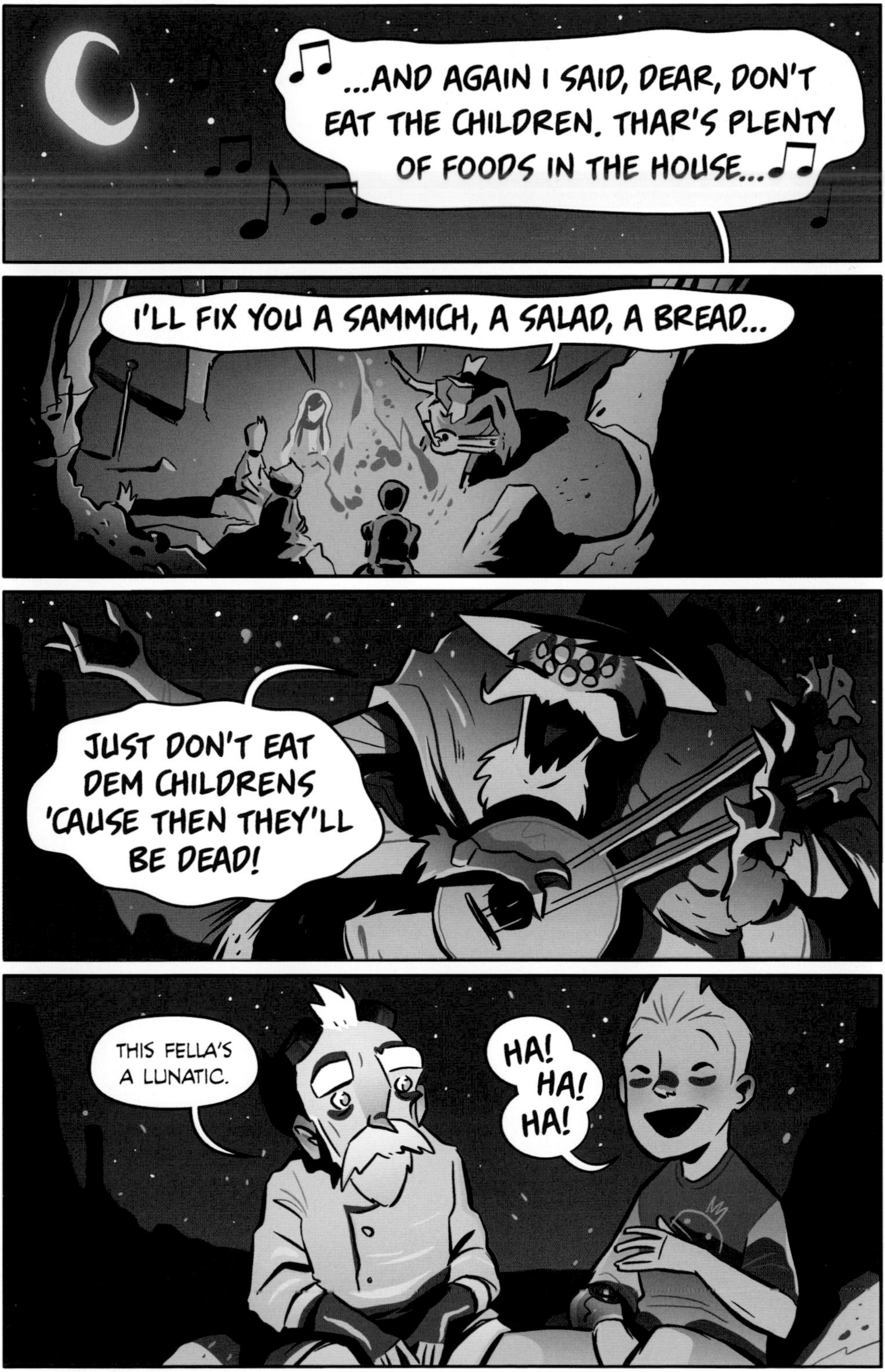
...AND AGAIN I SAID, DEAR, DON'T EAT THE CHILDREN. THAR'S PLENTY OF FOODS IN THE HOUSE...
I'LL FIX YOU A SAMMICH, A SALAD, A BREAD...
JUST DON'T EAT DEM CHILDRENS 'CAUSE THEN THEY'LL BE DEAD!
THIS FELLA'S A LUNATIC.
HA! HA! HA!

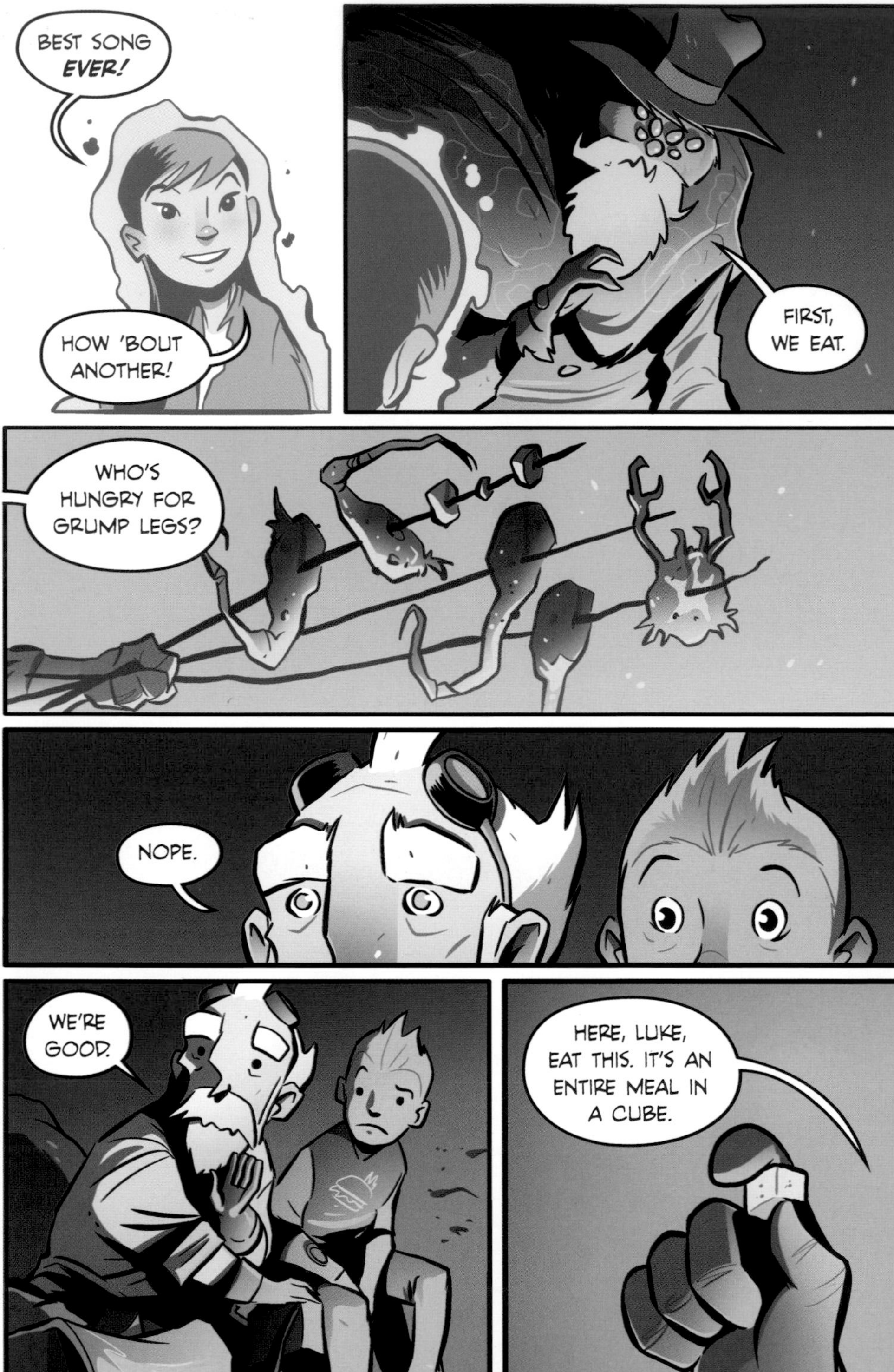
BEST SONG EVER!
HOW 'BOUT ANOTHER!
FIRST, WE EAT.
WHO'S HUNGRY FOR GRUMP LEGS?
NOPE.
WE'RE GOOD.
HERE, LUKE, EAT THIS. IT'S AN ENTIRE MEAL IN A CUBE.

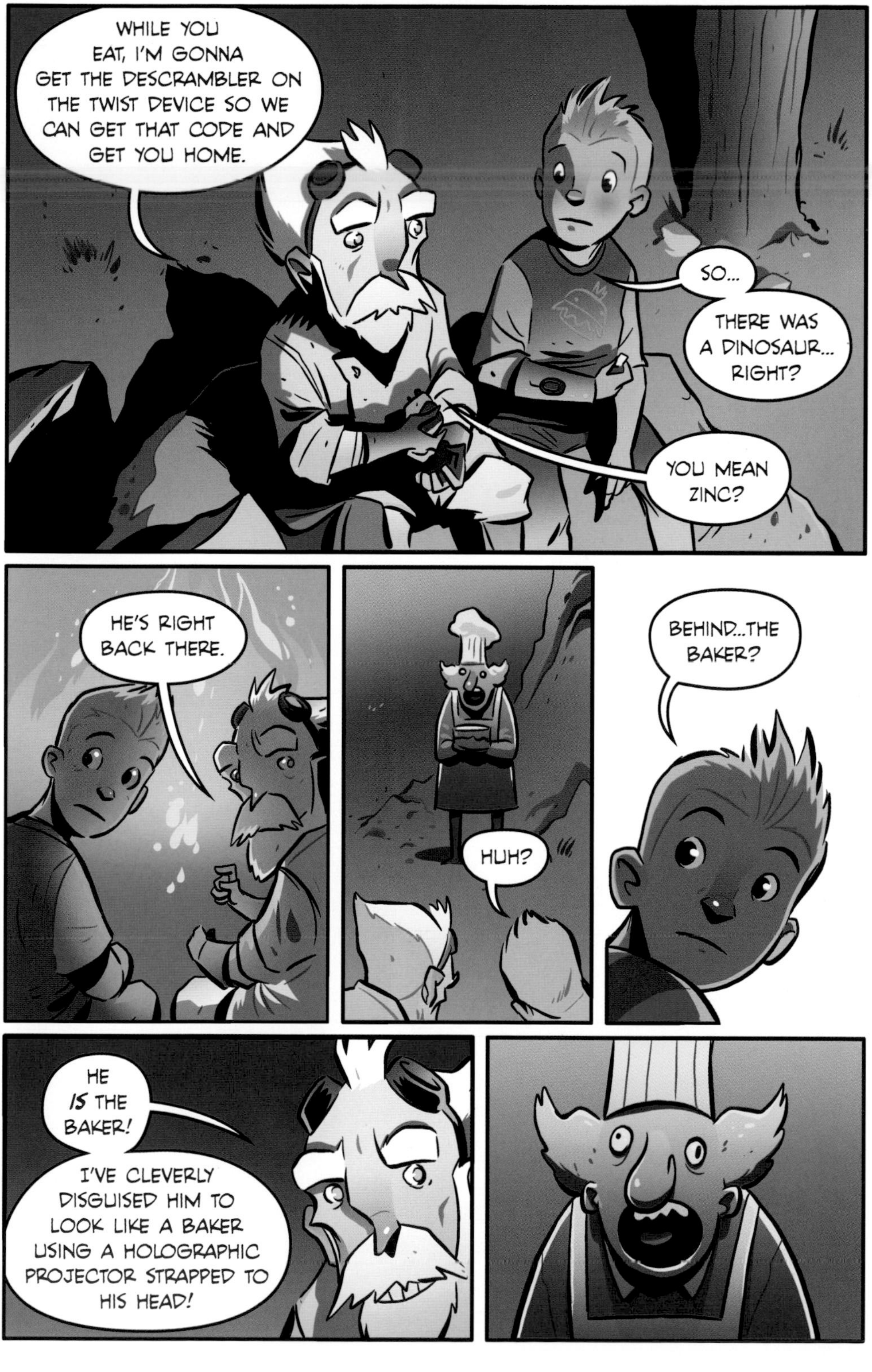
WHILE YOU EAT, I'M GONNA GET THE DESCRAMBLER ON THE TWIST DEVICE SO WE CAN GET THAT CODE AND GET YOU HOME.
SO...
THERE WAS A DINOSAUR... RIGHT?
YOU MEAN ZINC?
HE'S RIGHT BACK THERE.
HUH?
BEHIND...THE BAKER?
HE *IS* THE BAKER!
I'VE CLEVERLY DISGUISED HIM TO LOOK LIKE A BAKER USING A HOLOGRAPHIC PROJECTOR STRAPPED TO HIS HEAD!

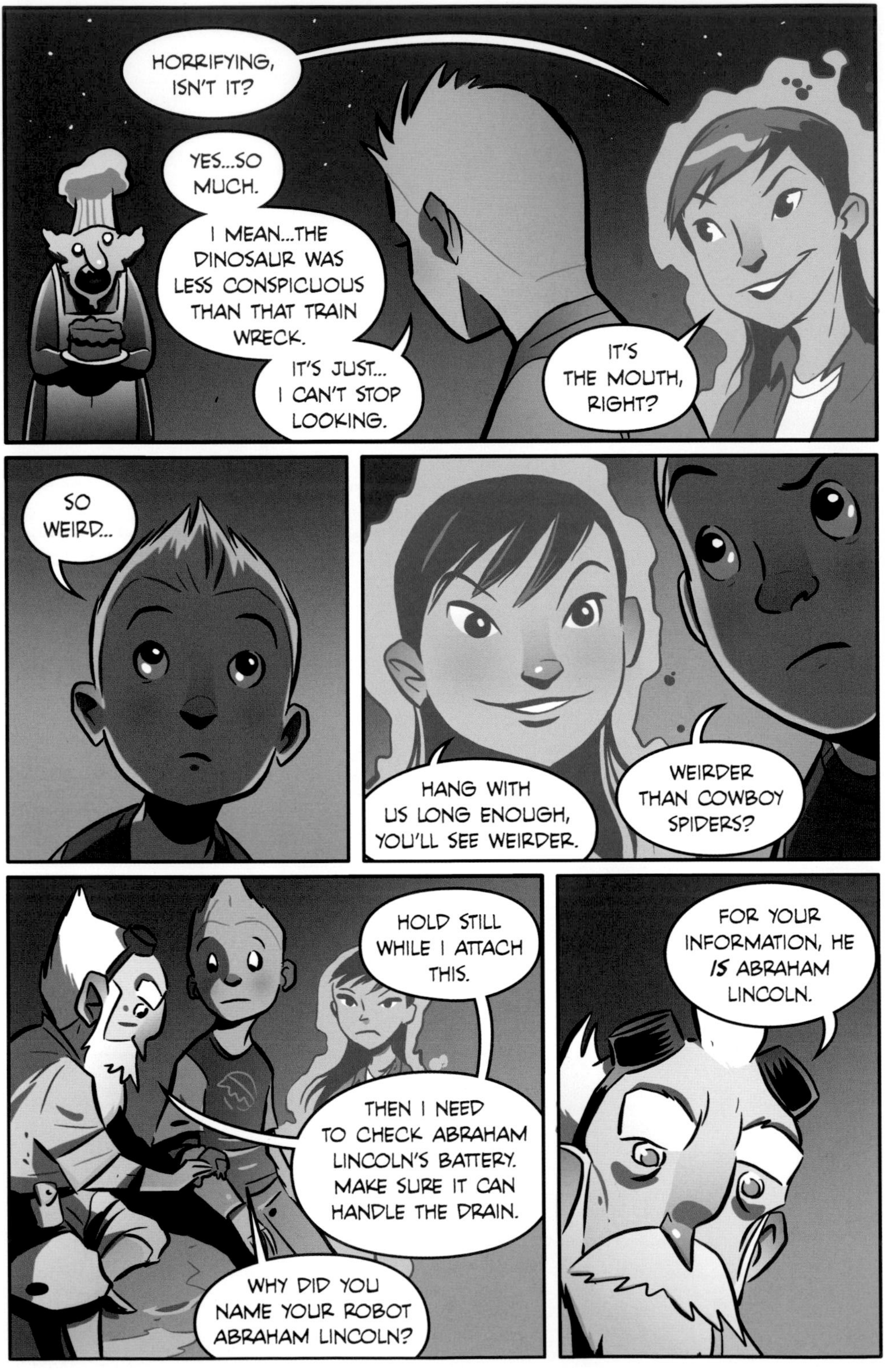
HORRIFYING, ISN'T IT?
YES...SO MUCH.
I MEAN...THE DINOSAUR WAS LESS CONSPICUOUS THAN THAT TRAIN WRECK.
IT'S JUST... I CAN'T STOP LOOKING.
IT'S THE MOUTH, RIGHT?
SO WEIRD...
HANG WITH US LONG ENOUGH, YOU'LL SEE WEIRDER.
WEIRDER THAN COWBOY SPIDERS?
HOLD STILL WHILE I ATTACH THIS.
THEN I NEED TO CHECK ABRAHAM LINCOLN'S BATTERY. MAKE SURE IT CAN HANDLE THE DRAIN.
WHY DID YOU NAME YOUR ROBOT ABRAHAM LINCOLN?
FOR YOUR INFORMATION, HE *IS* ABRAHAM LINCOLN.

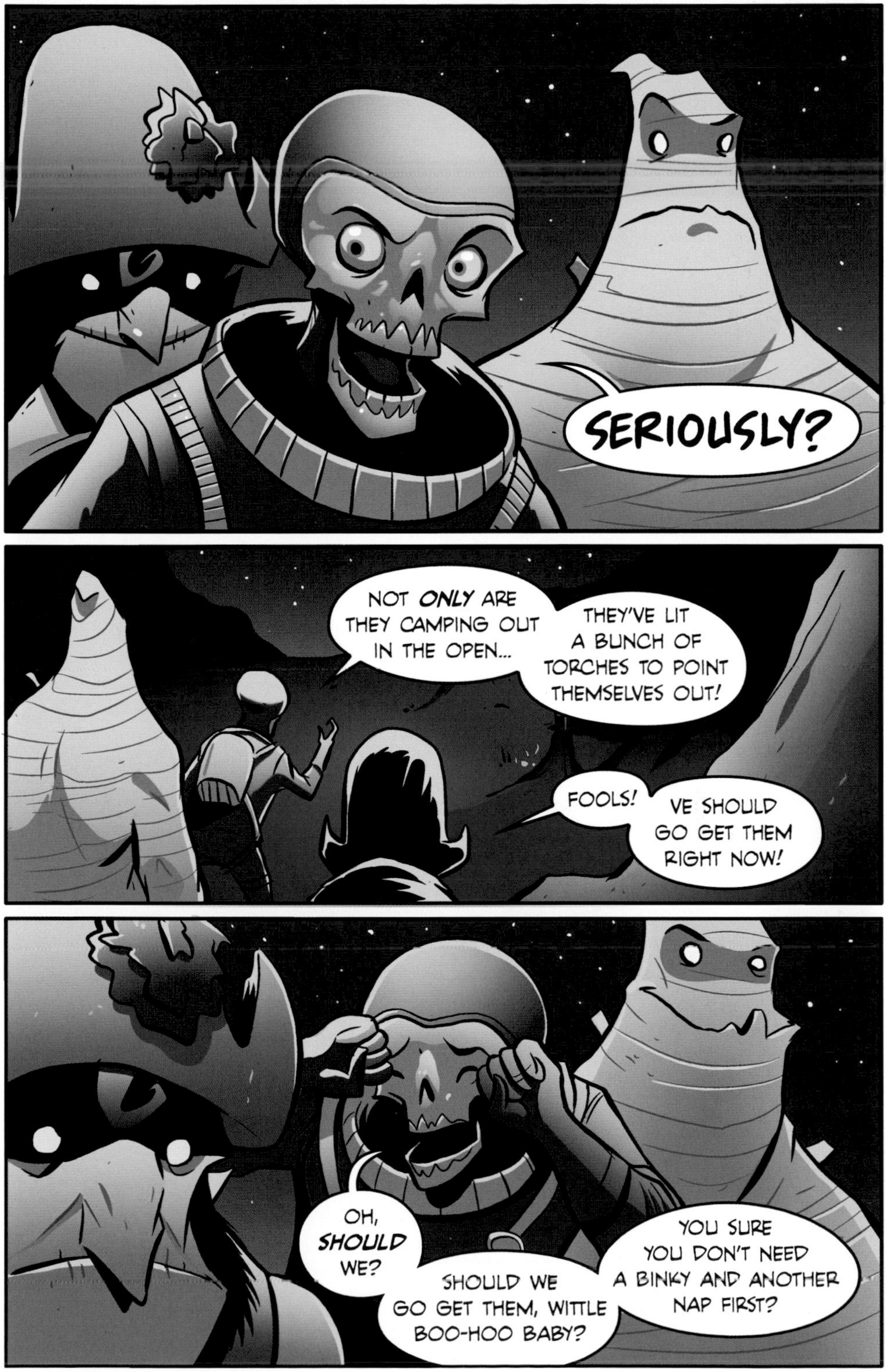
SERIOUSLY?
NOT *ONLY* ARE THEY CAMPING OUT IN THE OPEN...
THEY'VE LIT A BUNCH OF TORCHES TO POINT THEMSELVES OUT!
FOOLS!
VE SHOULD GO GET THEM RIGHT NOW!
OH, *SHOULD* WE?
SHOULD WE GO GET THEM, WITTLE BOO-HOO BABY?
YOU SURE YOU DON'T NEED A BINKY AND ANOTHER NAP FIRST?

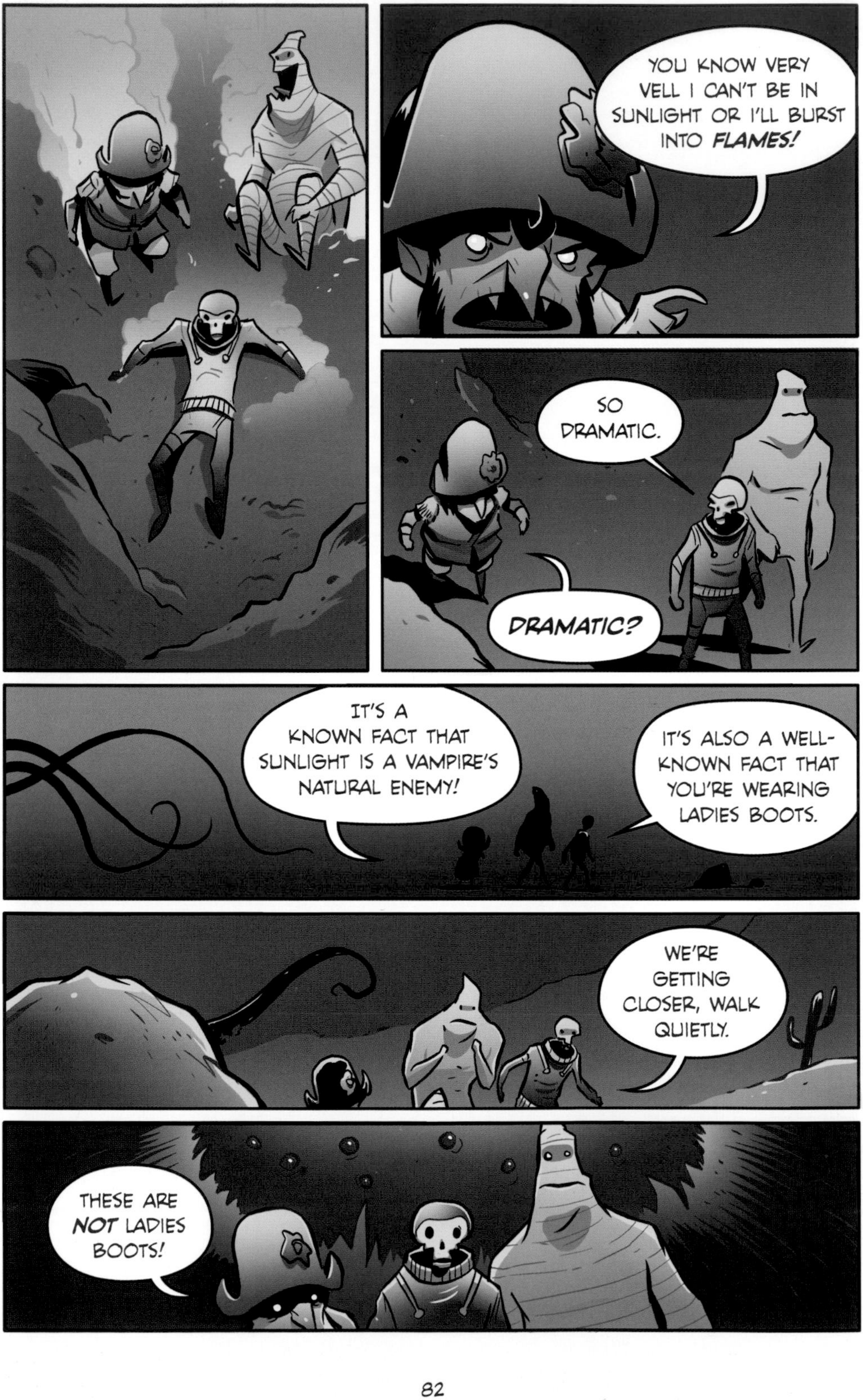
YOU KNOW VERY VELL I CAN'T BE IN SUNLIGHT OR I'LL BURST INTO *FLAMES!*
SO DRAMATIC.
DRAMATIC?
IT'S A KNOWN FACT THAT SUNLIGHT IS A VAMPIRE'S NATURAL ENEMY!
IT'S ALSO A WELL-KNOWN FACT THAT YOU'RE WEARING LADIES BOOTS.
WE'RE GETTING CLOSER, WALK QUIETLY.
THESE ARE *NOT* LADIES BOOTS!

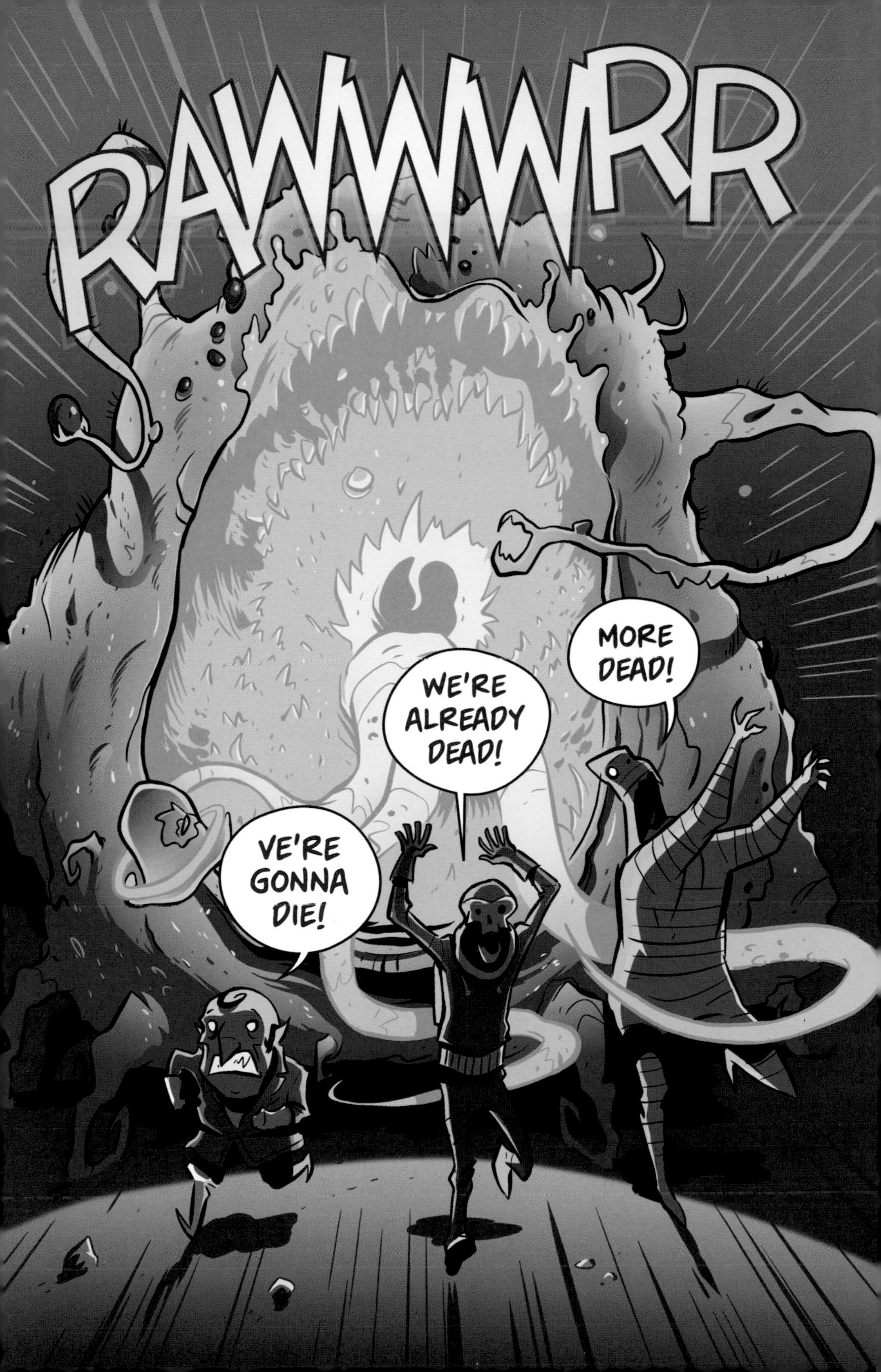
RAWWWRR
VE'RE GONNA DIE!
WE'RE ALREADY DEAD!
MORE DEAD!

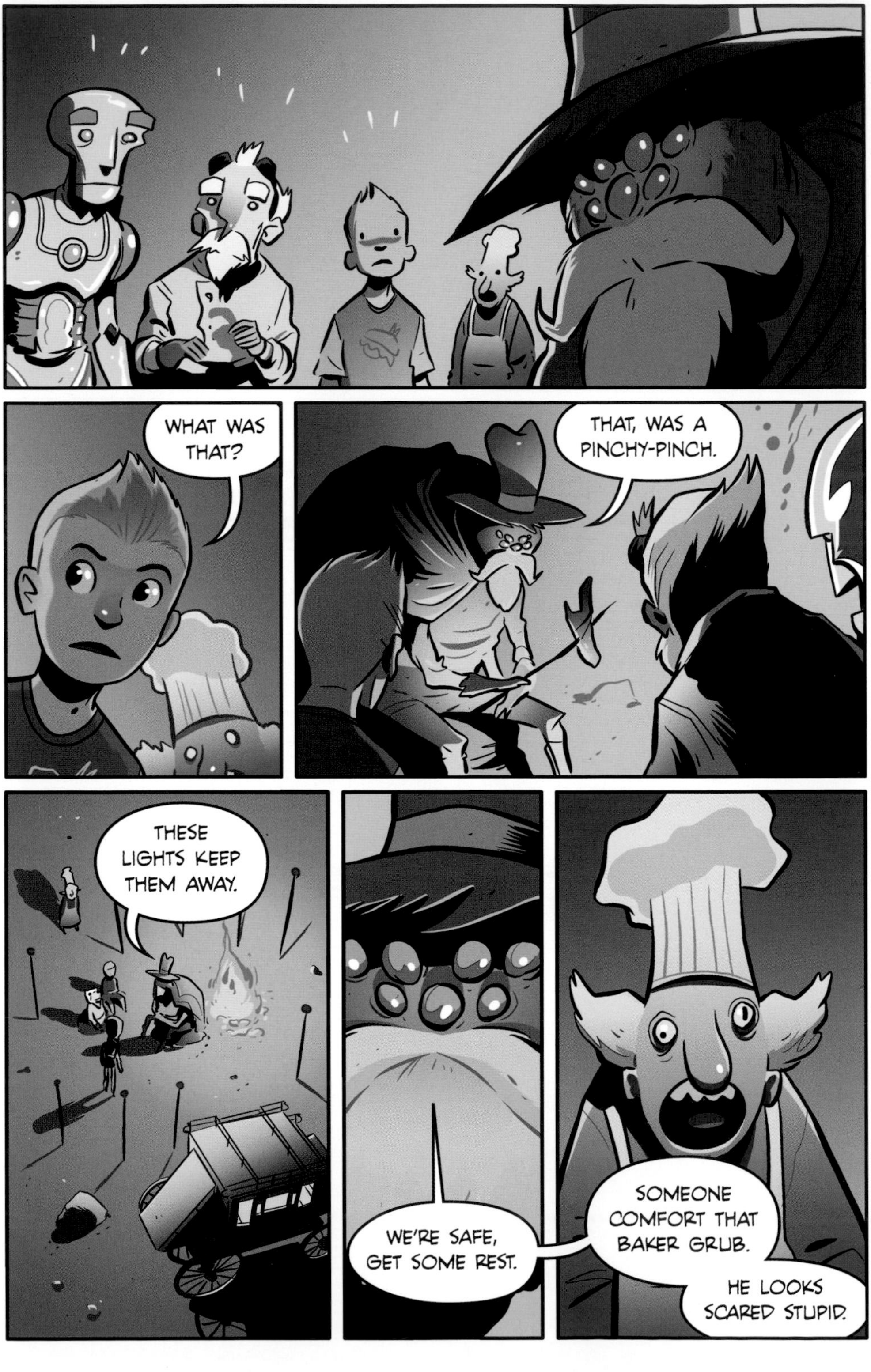
WHAT WAS THAT?
THAT, WAS A PINCHY-PINCH.
THESE LIGHTS KEEP THEM AWAY.
WE'RE SAFE, GET SOME REST.
SOMEONE COMFORT THAT BAKER GRUB.
HE LOOKS SCARED STUPID.

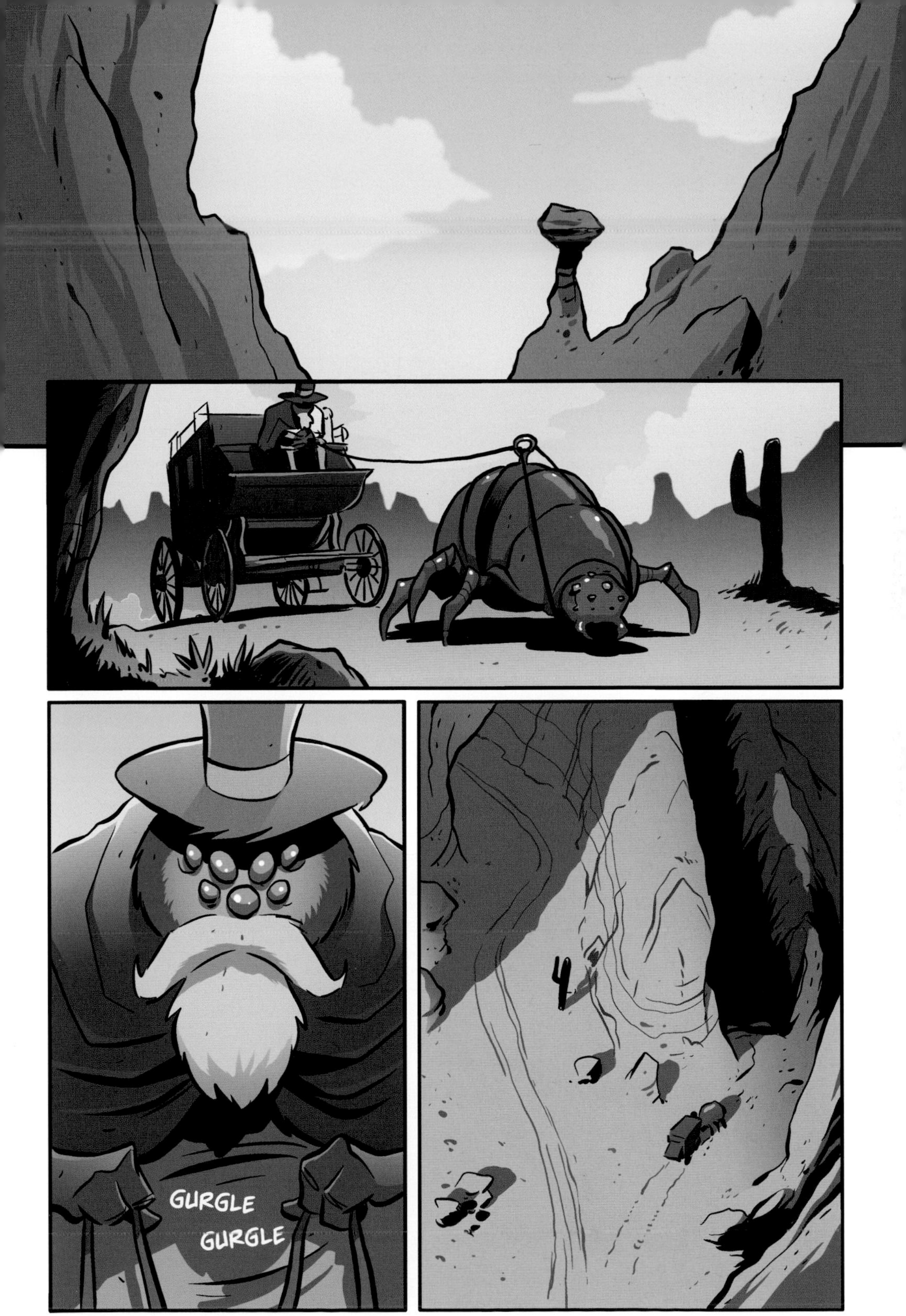
GURGLE
GURGLE

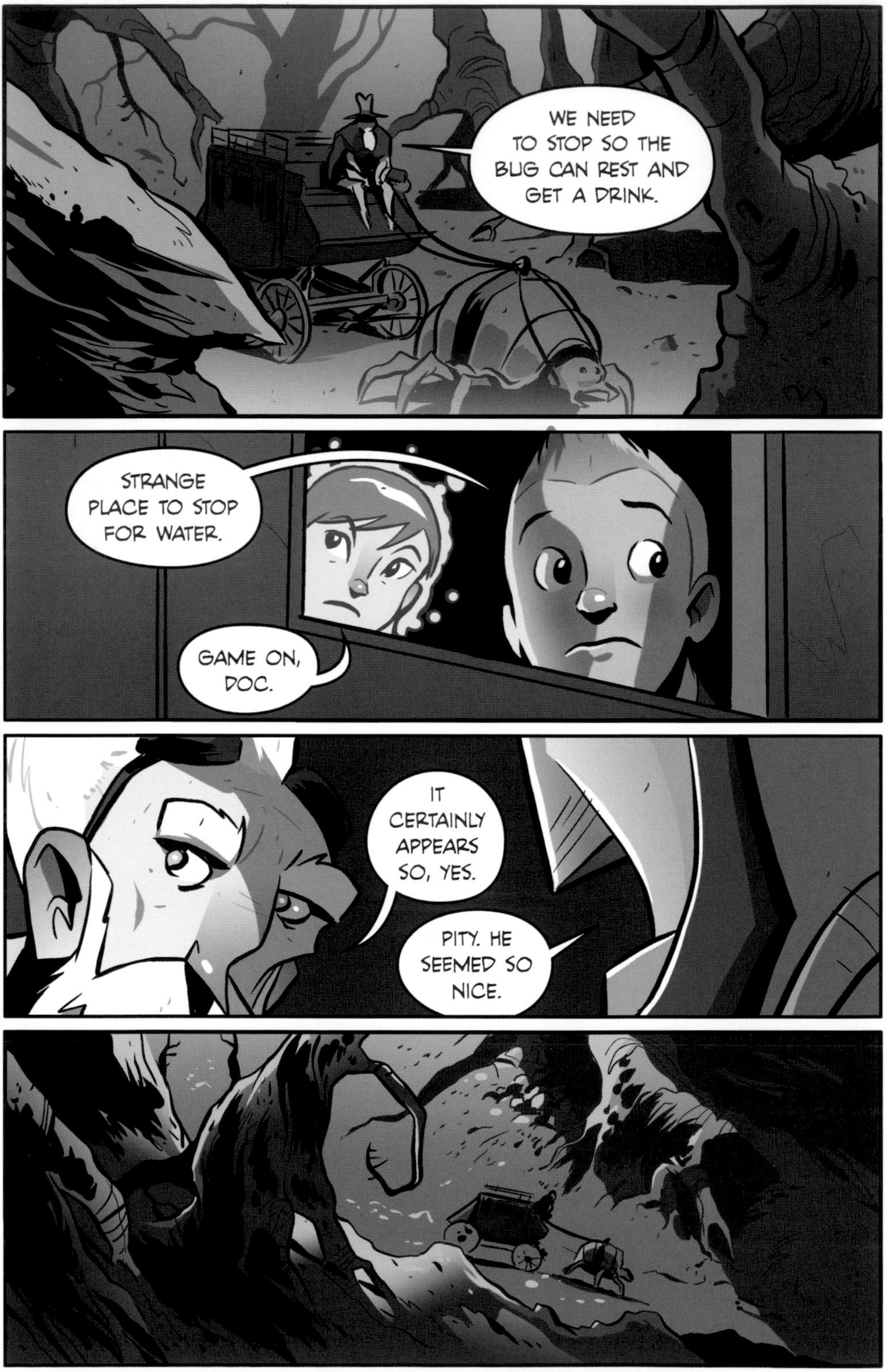
WE NEED TO STOP SO THE BUG CAN REST AND GET A DRINK.
STRANGE PLACE TO STOP FOR WATER.
GAME ON, DOC.
IT CERTAINLY APPEARS SO, YES.
PITY. HE SEEMED SO NICE.

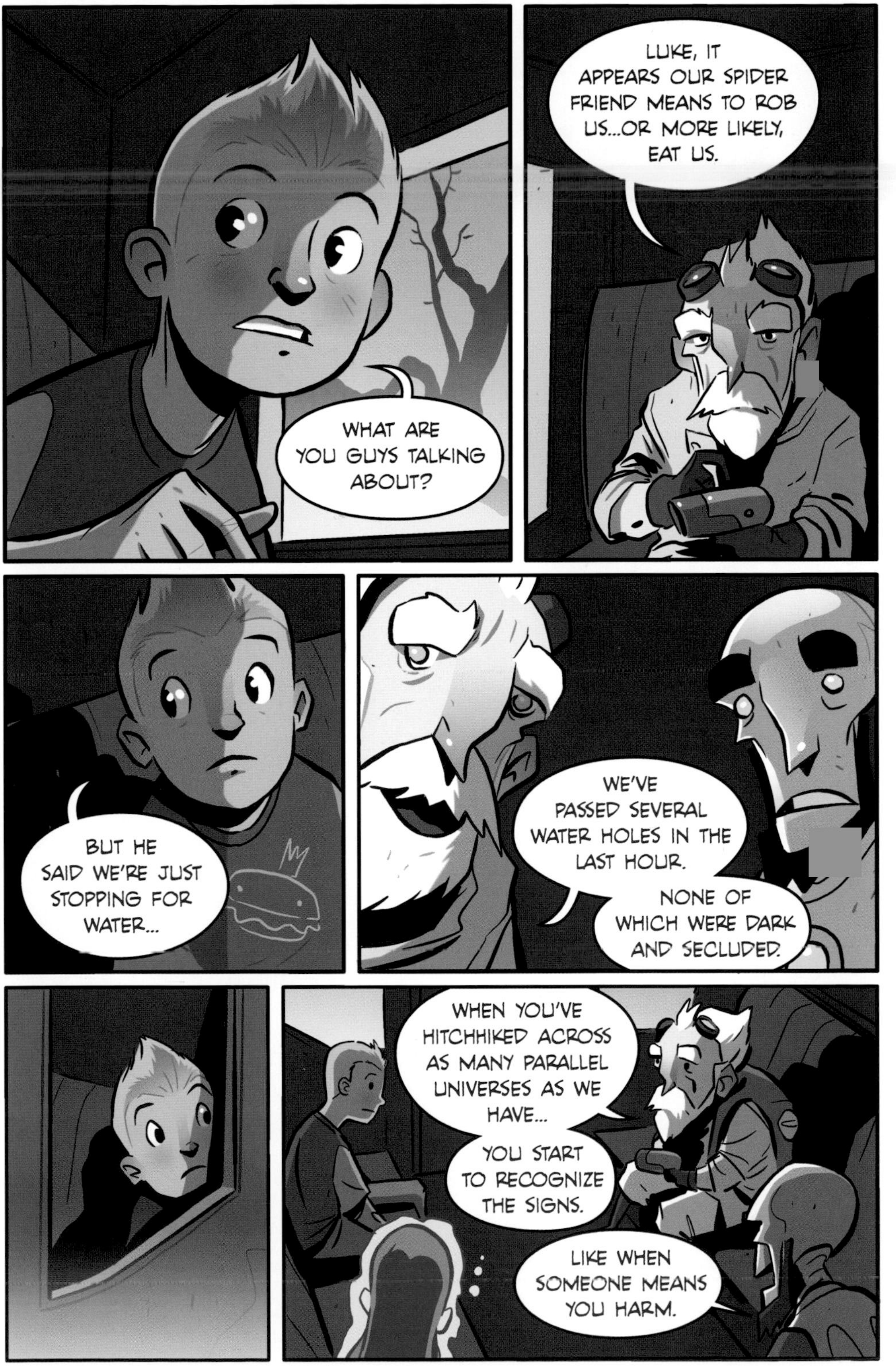
LUKE, IT APPEARS OUR SPIDER FRIEND MEANS TO ROB US...OR MORE LIKELY, EAT US.
WHAT ARE YOU GUYS TALKING ABOUT?
BUT HE SAID WE'RE JUST STOPPING FOR WATER...
WE'VE PASSED SEVERAL WATER HOLES IN THE LAST HOUR.
NONE OF WHICH WERE DARK AND SECLUDED.
WHEN YOU'VE HITCHHIKED ACROSS AS MANY PARALLEL UNIVERSES AS WE HAVE...
YOU START TO RECOGNIZE THE SIGNS.
LIKE WHEN SOMEONE MEANS YOU HARM.

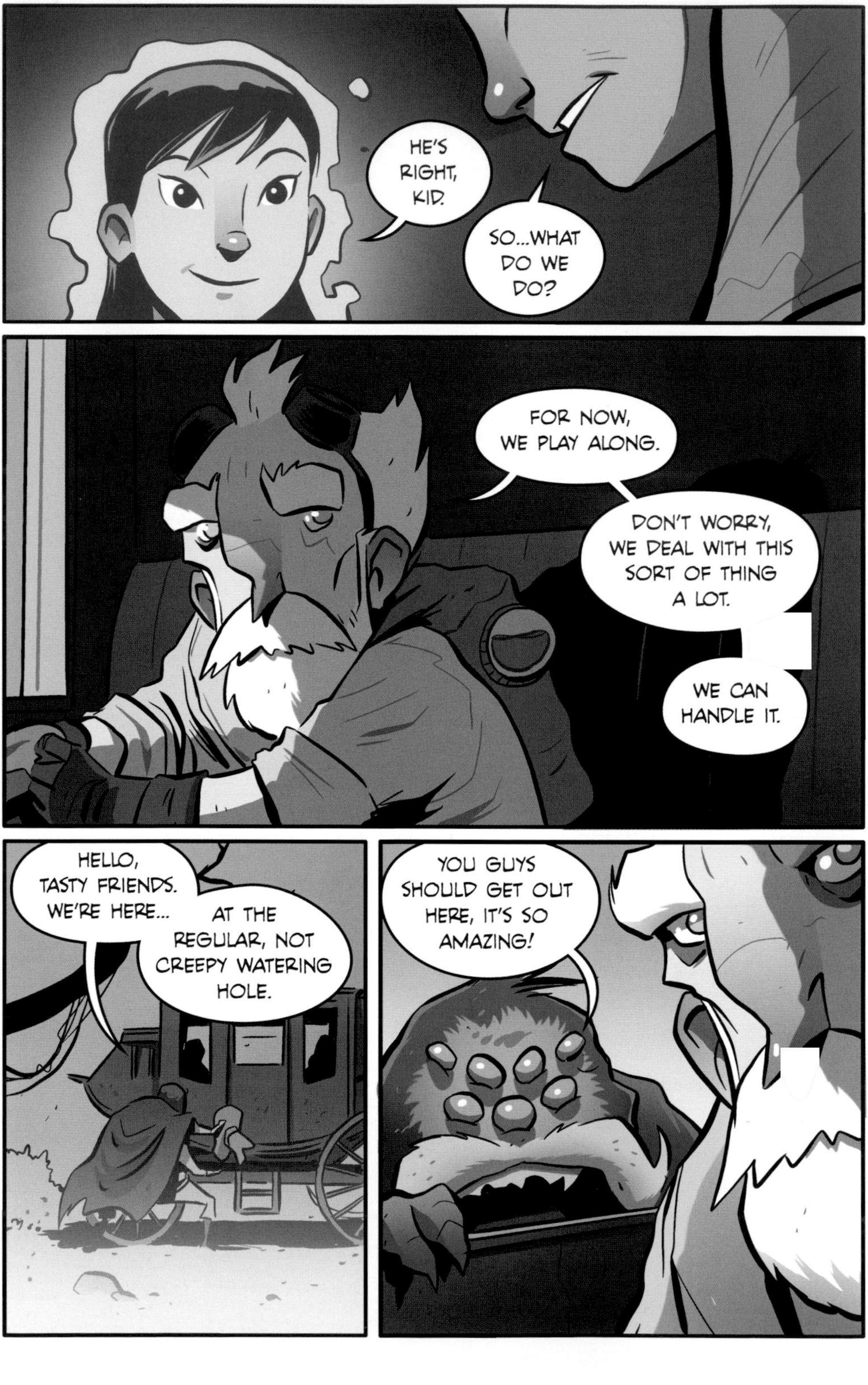
HE'S RIGHT, KID.
SO...WHAT DO WE DO?
FOR NOW, WE PLAY ALONG.
DON'T WORRY, WE DEAL WITH THIS SORT OF THING A LOT.
WE CAN HANDLE IT.
HELLO, TASTY FRIENDS. WE'RE HERE...
AT THE REGULAR, NOT CREEPY WATERING HOLE.
YOU GUYS SHOULD GET OUT HERE, IT'S SO AMAZING!

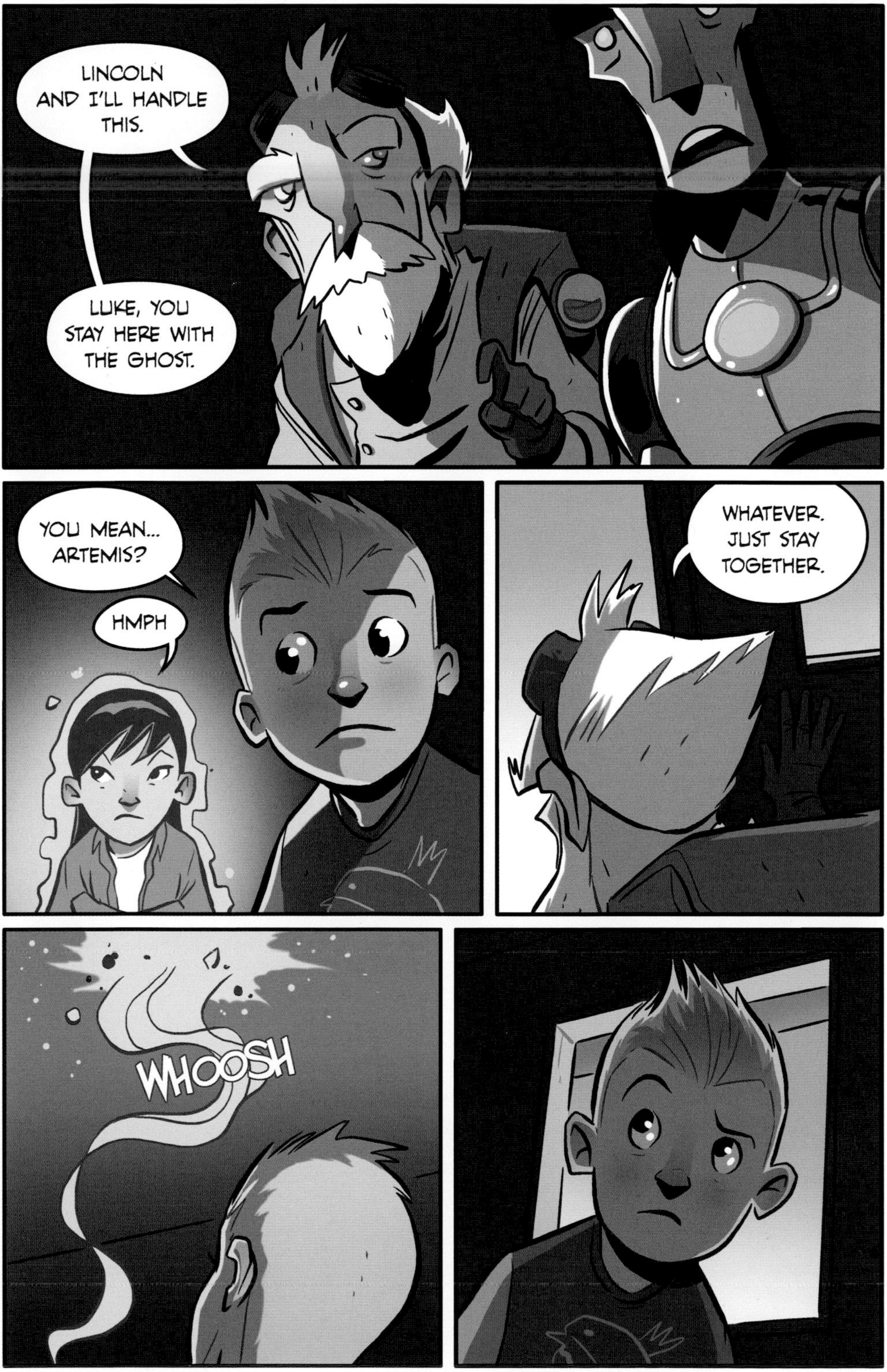
LINCOLN AND I'LL HANDLE THIS.
LUKE, YOU STAY HERE WITH THE GHOST.
YOU MEAN... ARTEMIS?
HMPH
WHATEVER. JUST STAY TOGETHER.
WHOOSH

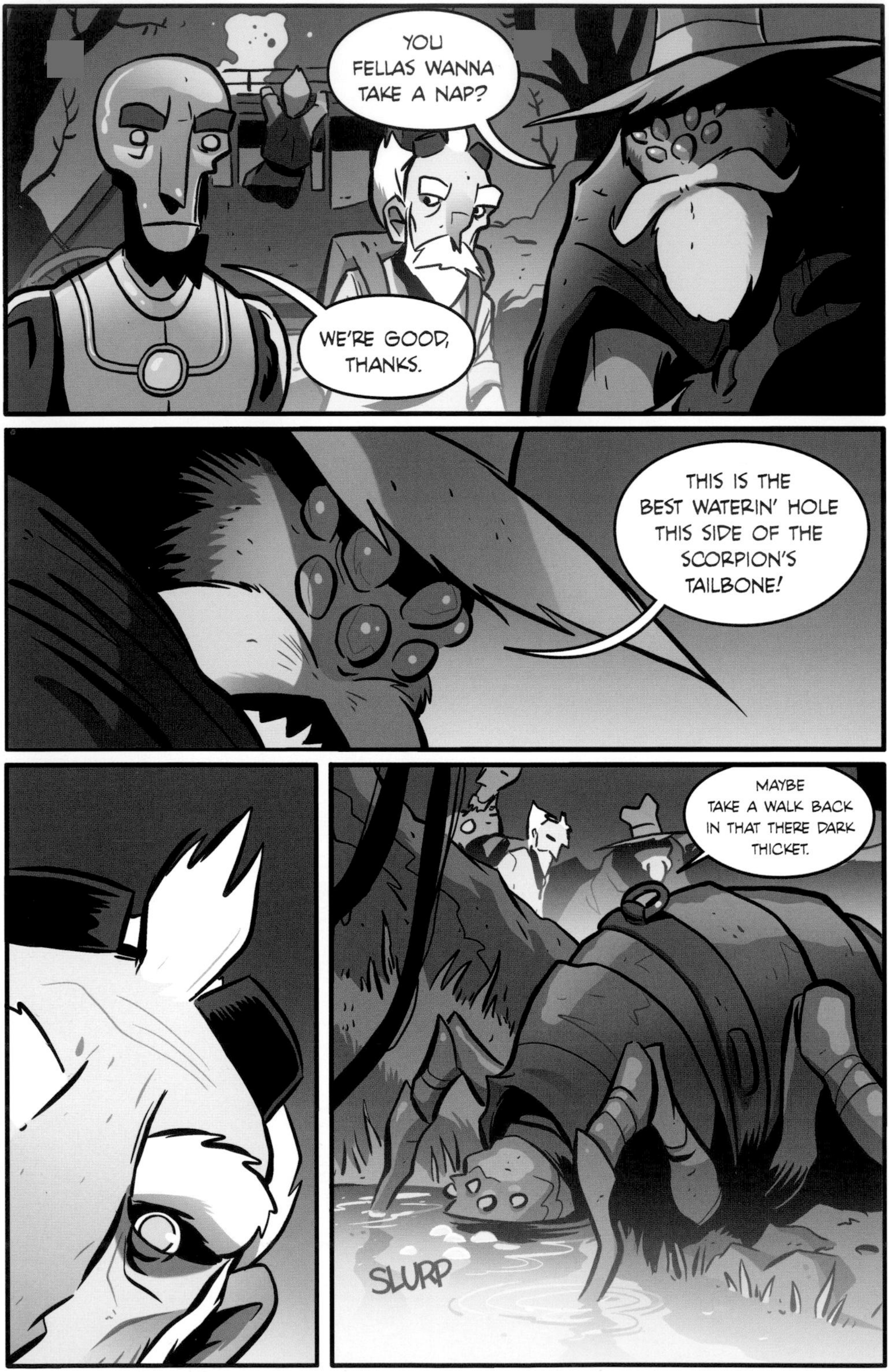
YOU FELLAS WANNA TAKE A NAP?
WE'RE GOOD, THANKS.
THIS IS THE BEST WATERIN' HOLE THIS SIDE OF THE SCORPION'S TAILBONE!
MAYBE TAKE A WALK BACK IN THAT THERE DARK THICKET.
SLURP

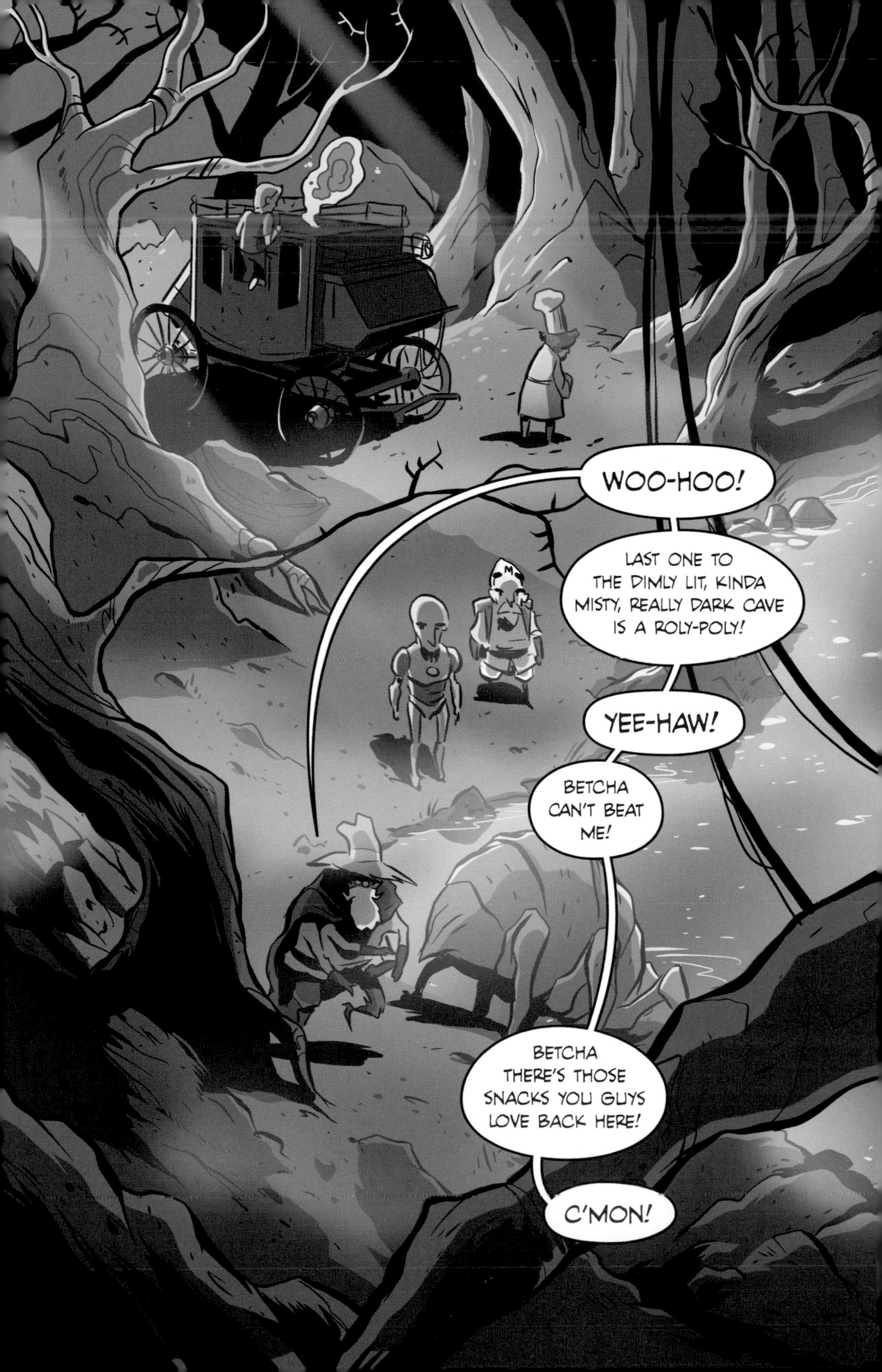
WOO-HOO!
LAST ONE TO THE DIMLY LIT, KINDA MISTY, REALLY DARK CAVE IS A ROLY-POLY!
YEE-HAW!
BETCHA CAN'T BEAT ME!
BETCHA THERE'S THOSE SNACKS YOU GUYS LOVE BACK HERE!
C'MON!

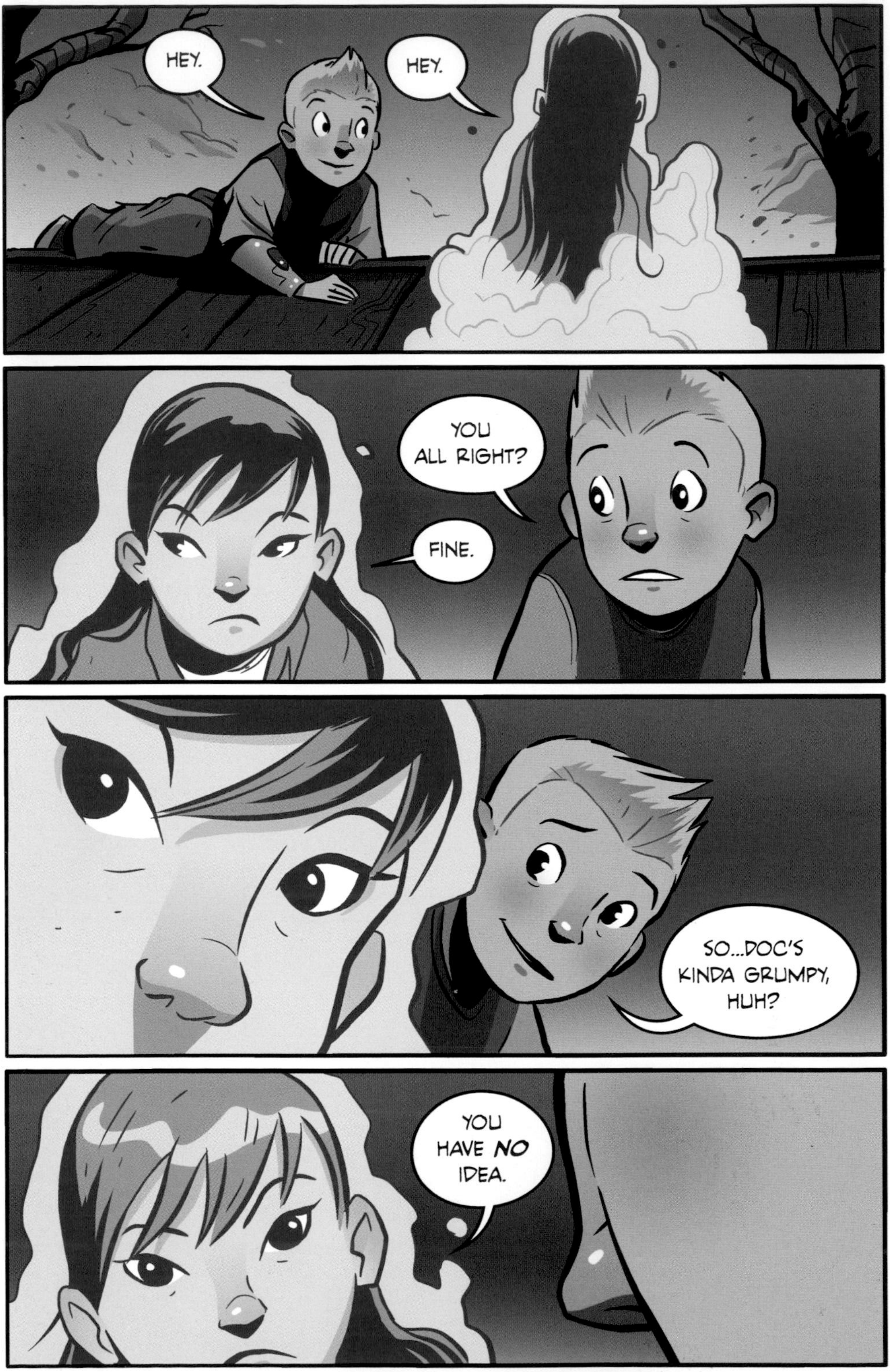
HEY.
HEY.
YOU ALL RIGHT?
FINE.
SO...DOC'S KINDA GRUMPY, HUH?
YOU HAVE **NO** IDEA.

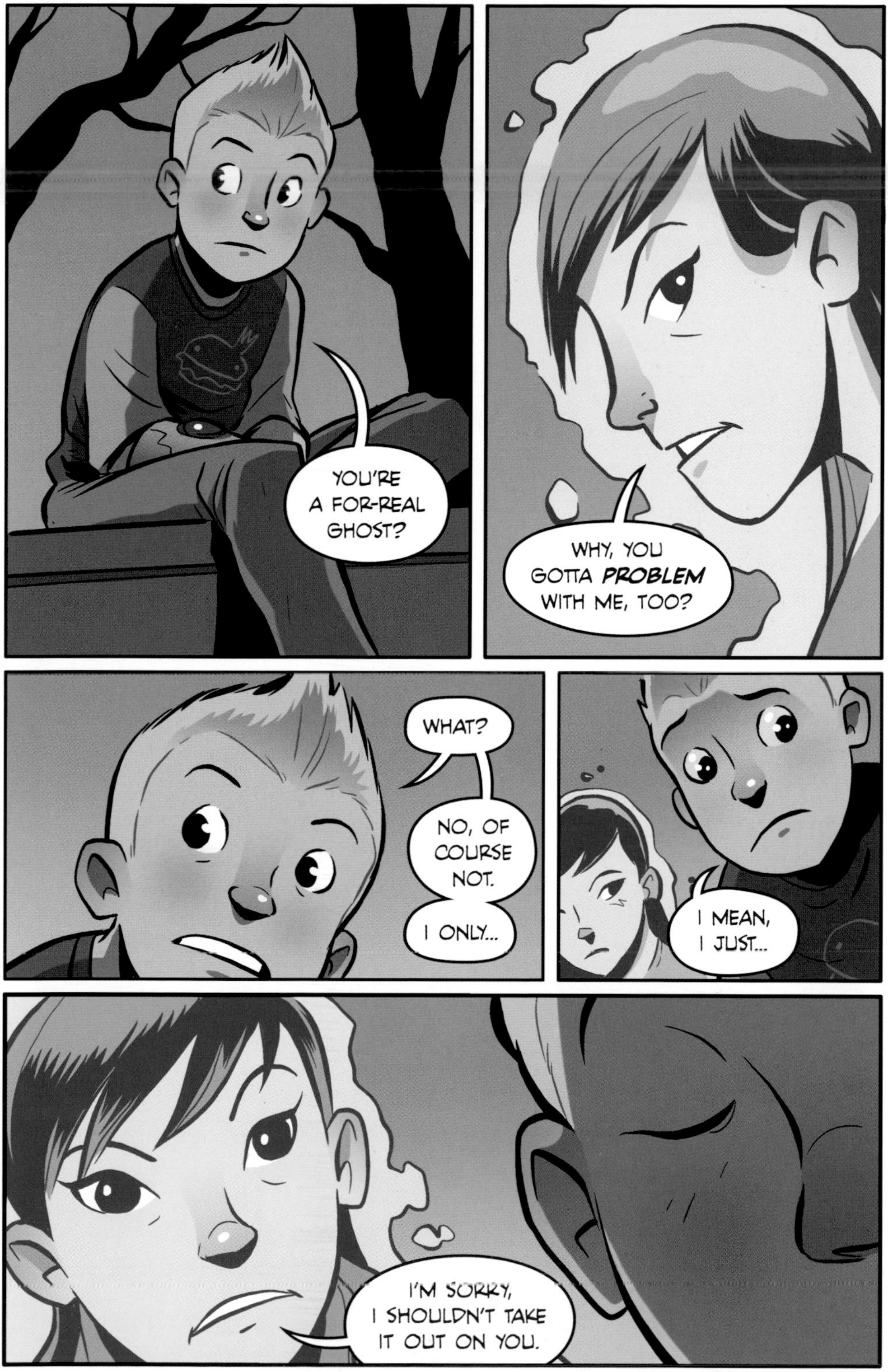
YOU'RE A FOR-REAL GHOST?
WHY, YOU GOTTA **PROBLEM** WITH ME, TOO?
WHAT?
NO, OF COURSE NOT.
I ONLY...
I MEAN, I JUST...
I'M SORRY, I SHOULDN'T TAKE IT OUT ON YOU.

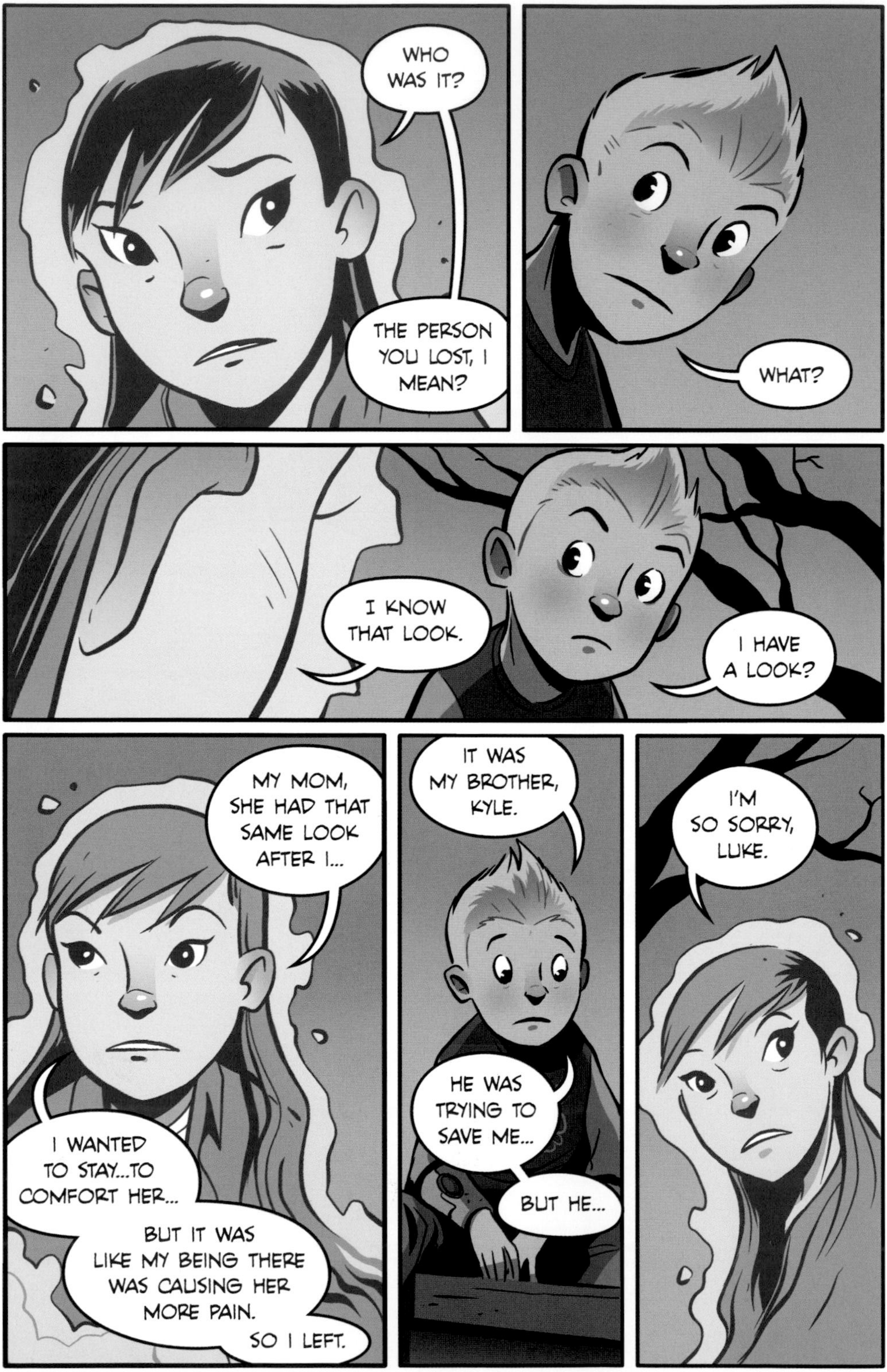
WHO WAS IT?
THE PERSON YOU LOST, I MEAN?
WHAT?
I KNOW THAT LOOK.
I HAVE A LOOK?
MY MOM, SHE HAD THAT SAME LOOK AFTER I...
I WANTED TO STAY...TO COMFORT HER...
BUT IT WAS LIKE MY BEING THERE WAS CAUSING HER MORE PAIN.
SO I LEFT.
IT WAS MY BROTHER, KYLE.
HE WAS TRYING TO SAVE ME...
BUT HE...
I'M SO SORRY, LUKE.

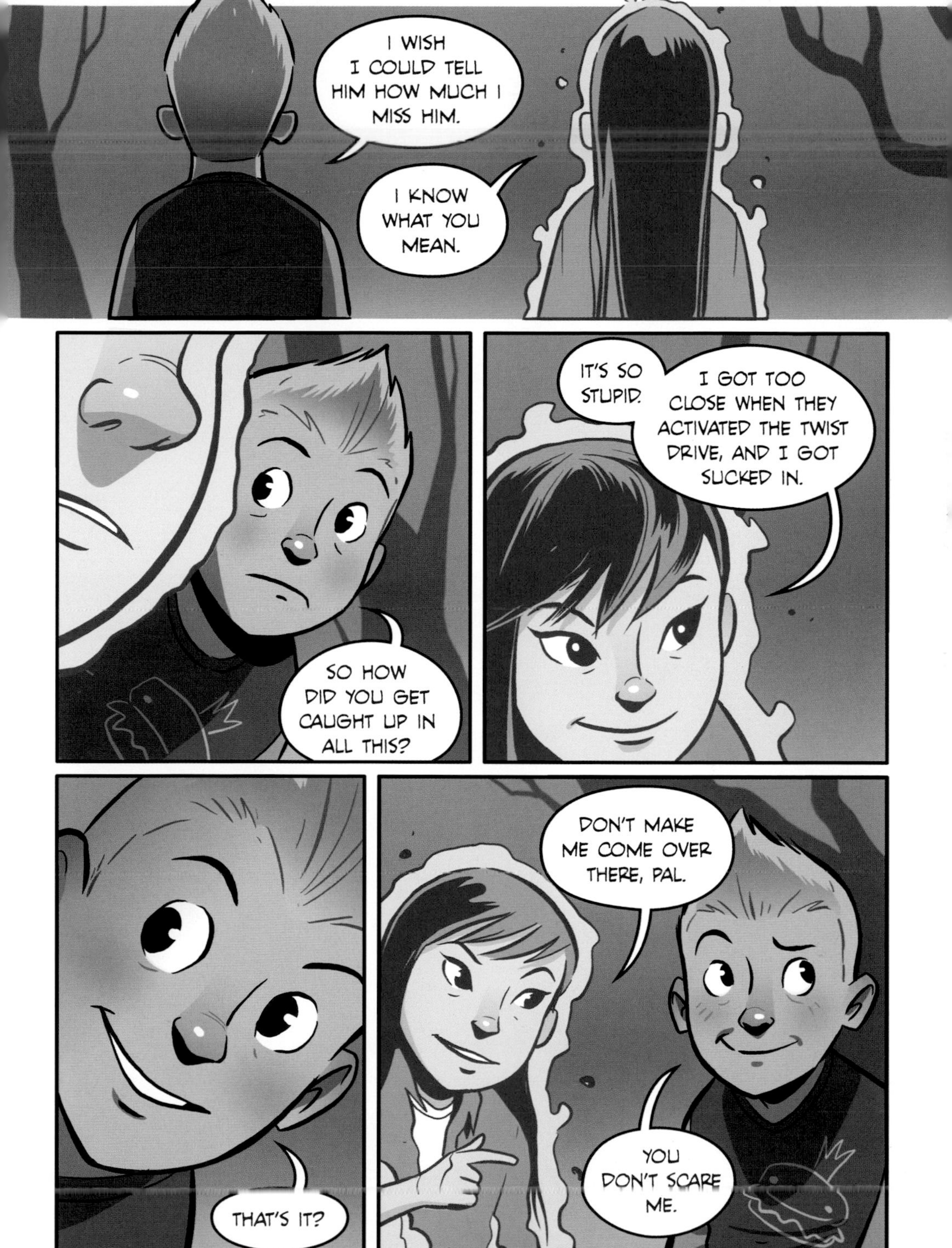
I WISH I COULD TELL HIM HOW MUCH I MISS HIM.
I KNOW WHAT YOU MEAN.
SO HOW DID YOU GET CAUGHT UP IN ALL THIS?
IT'S SO STUPID.
I GOT TOO CLOSE WHEN THEY ACTIVATED THE TWIST DRIVE, AND I GOT SUCKED IN.
THAT'S IT?
DON'T MAKE ME COME OVER THERE, PAL.
YOU DON'T SCARE ME.

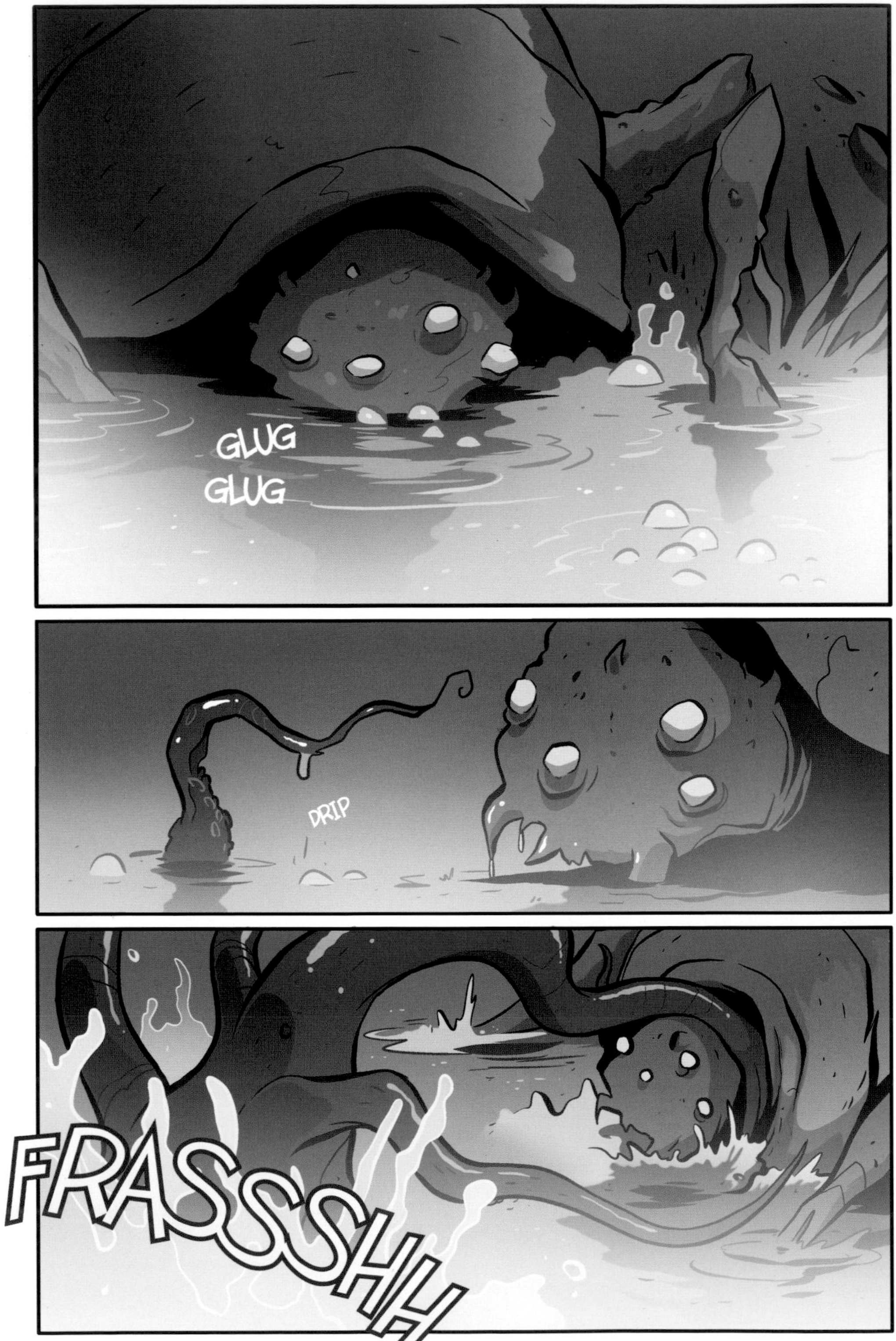
GLUG
GLUG
DRIP
FRASSSHH

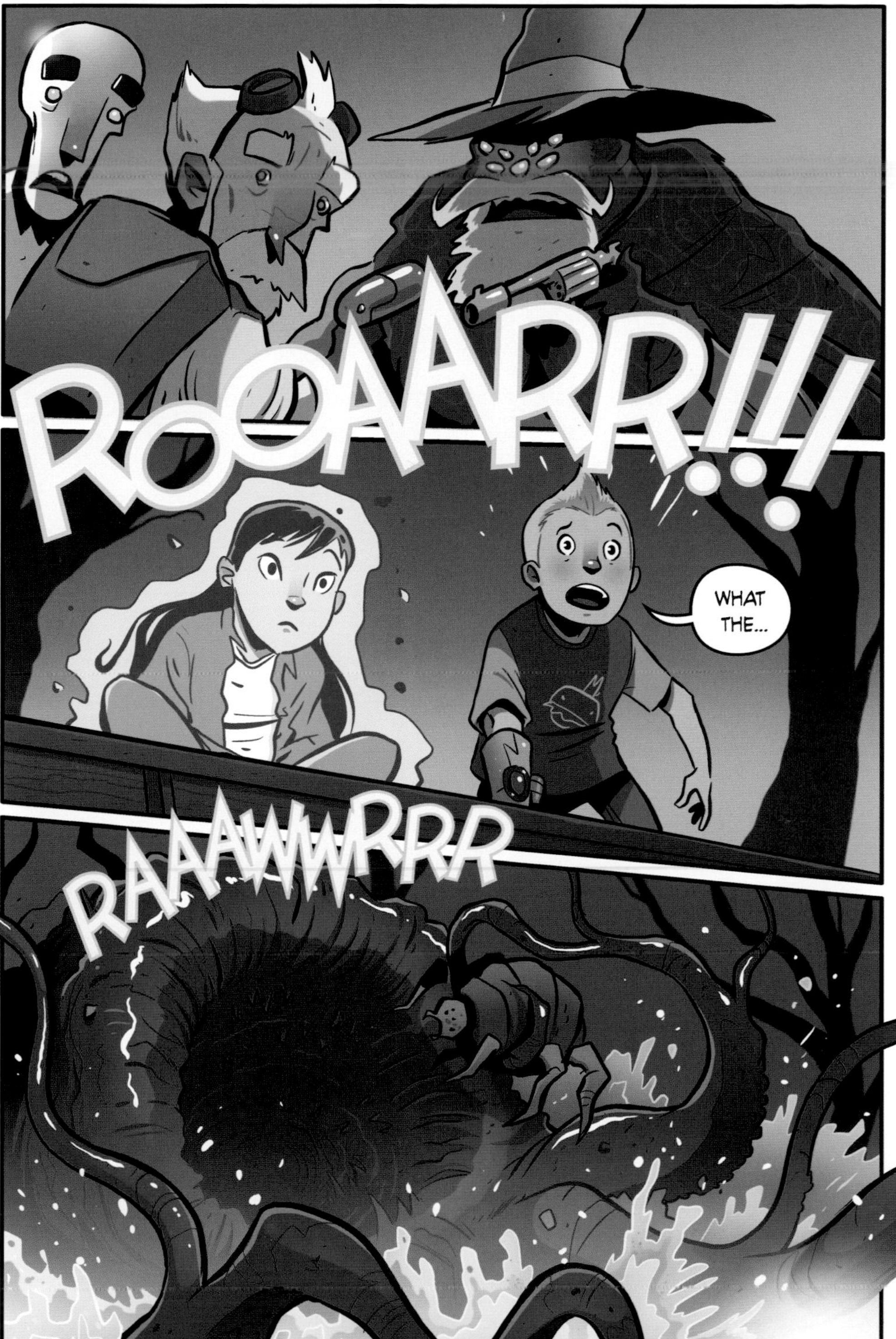
ROOAARR!!!
WHAT THE...
RAAAWWRRR

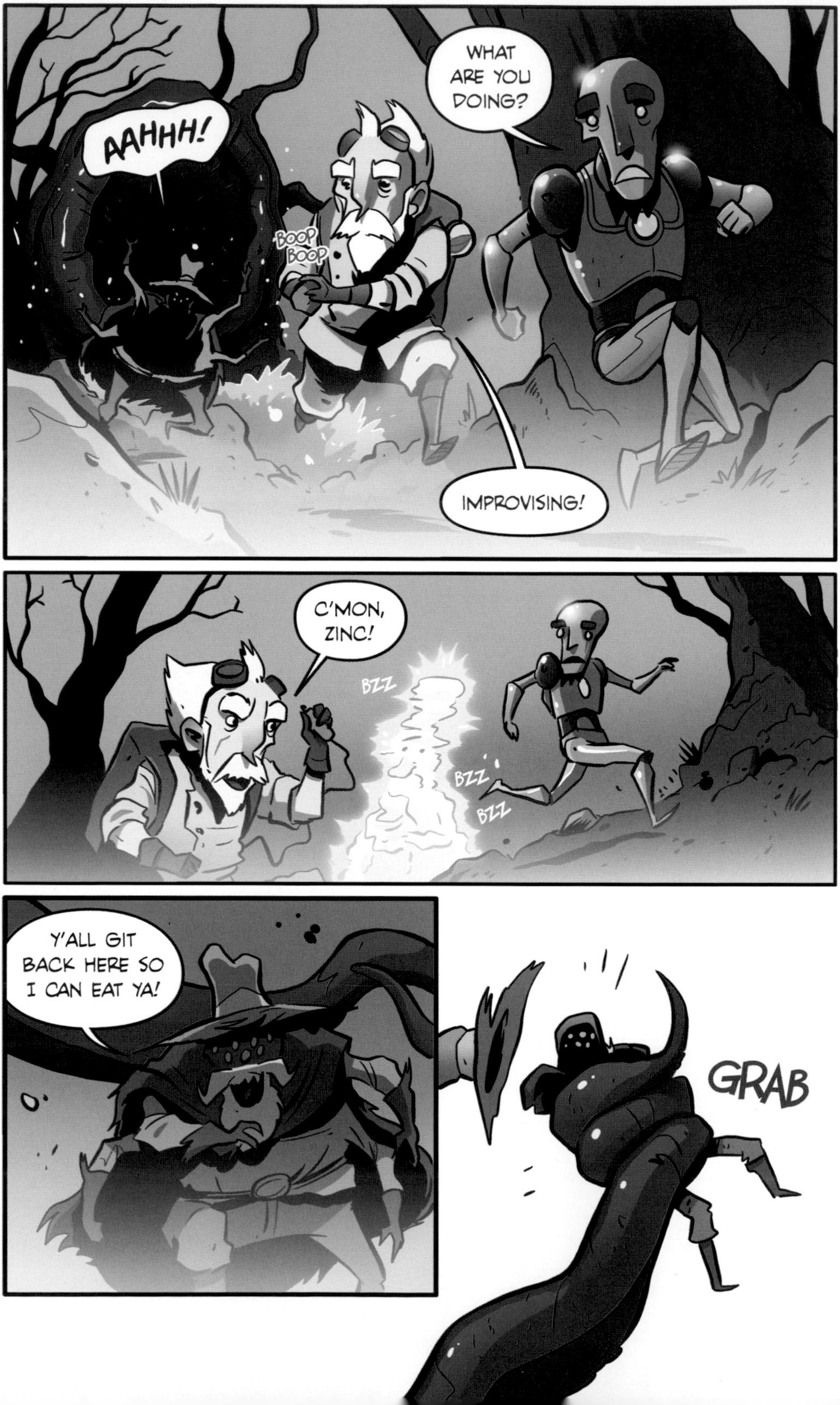
AAHHH!
BOOP BOOP
WHAT ARE YOU DOING?
IMPROVISING!
C'MON, ZINC!
BZZ
BZZ
BZZ
Y'ALL GIT BACK HERE SO I CAN EAT YA!
GRAB

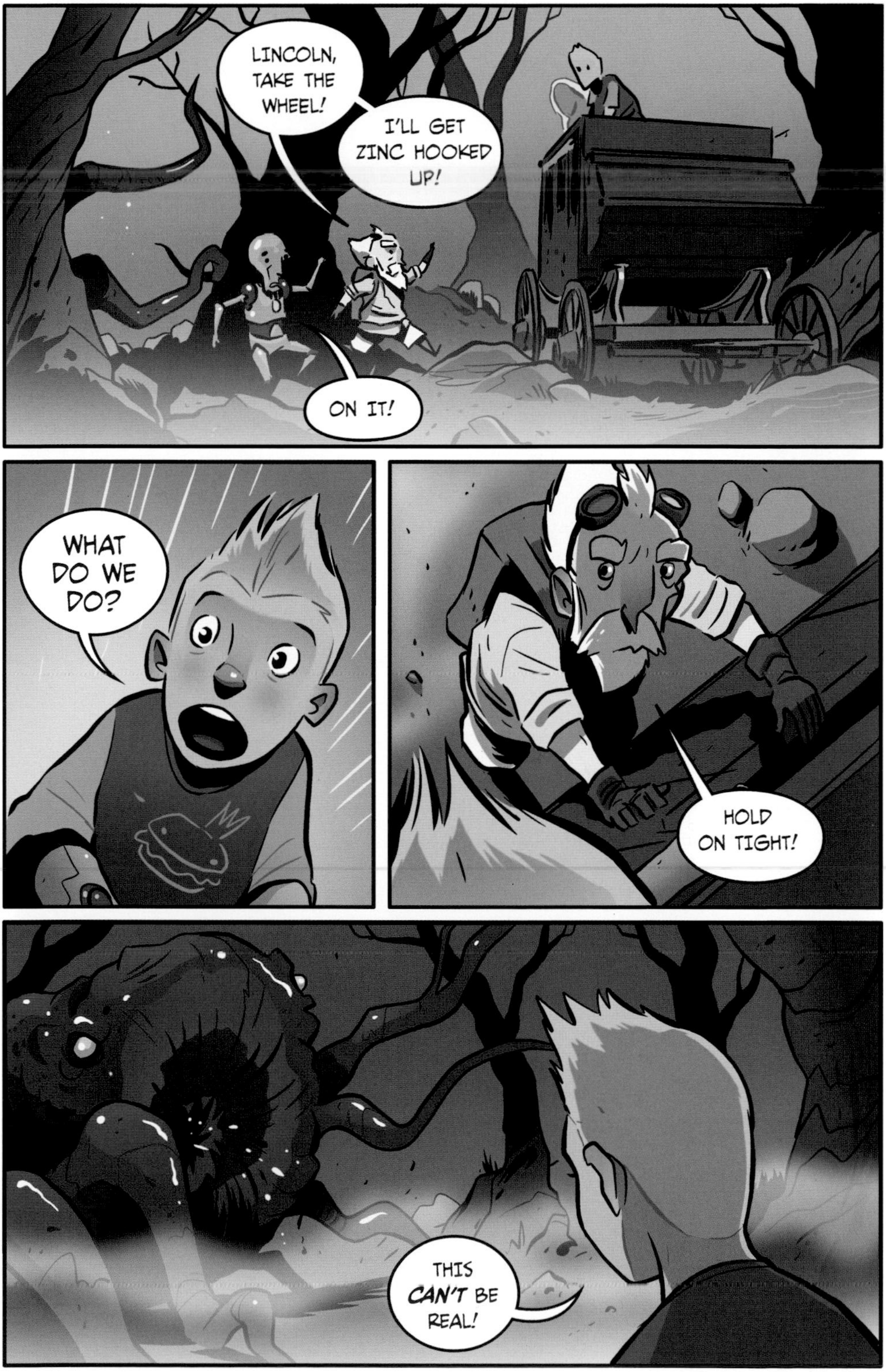
LINCOLN, TAKE THE WHEEL!
I'LL GET ZINC HOOKED UP!
ON IT!
WHAT DO WE DO?
HOLD ON TIGHT!
THIS *CAN'T* BE REAL!

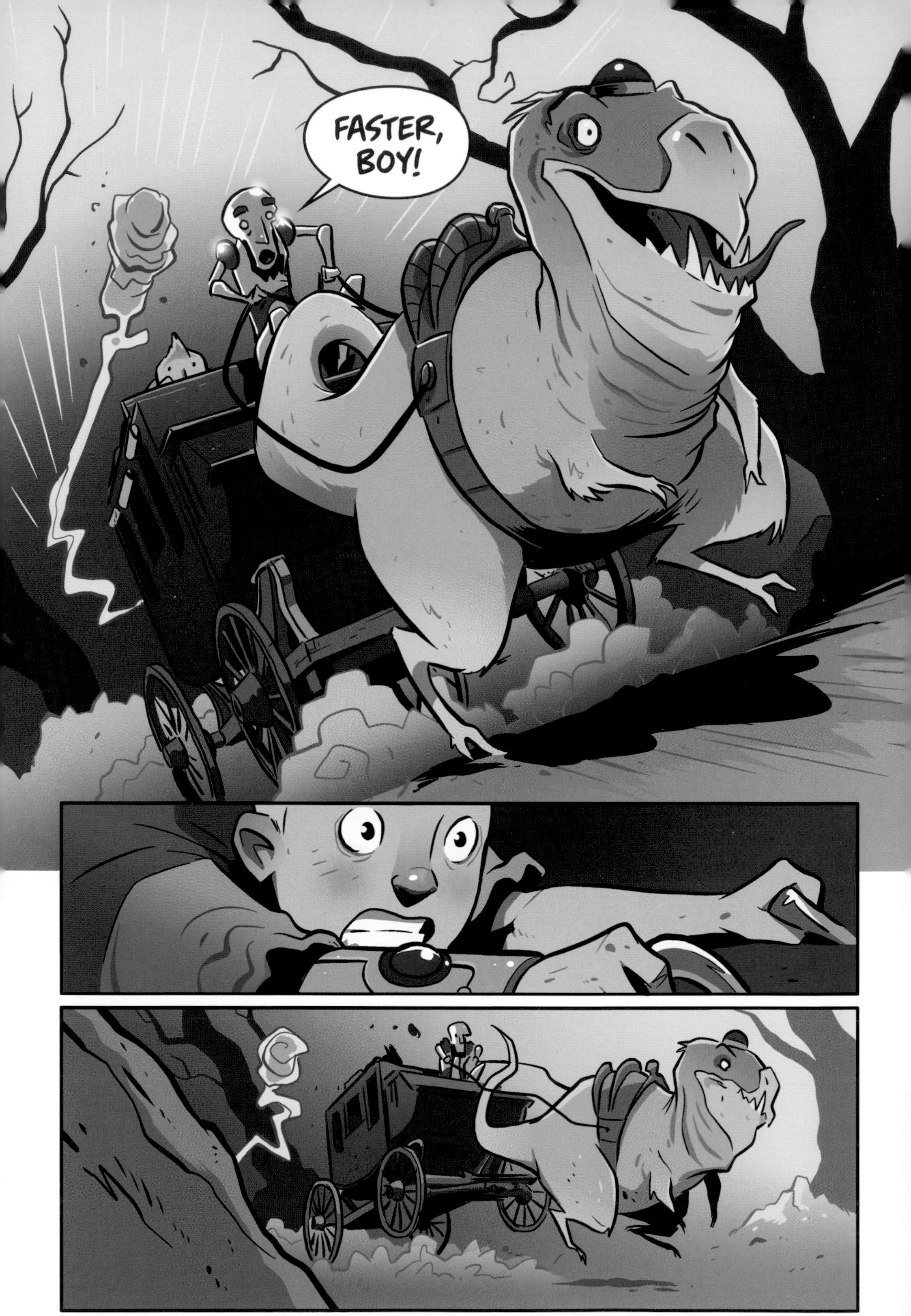
FASTER, BOY!

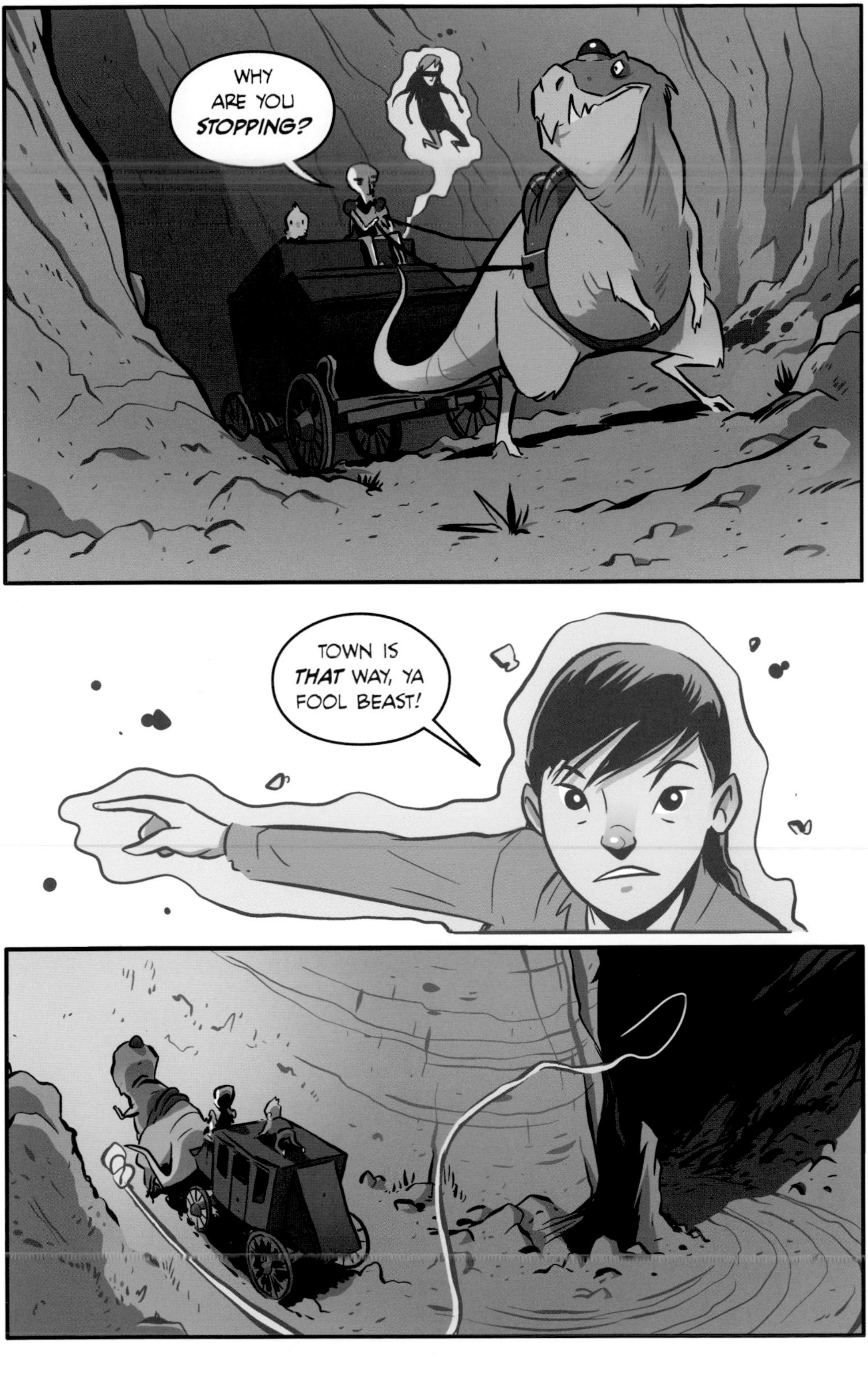

WHY ARE YOU STOPPING?
TOWN IS THAT WAY, YA FOOL BEAST!

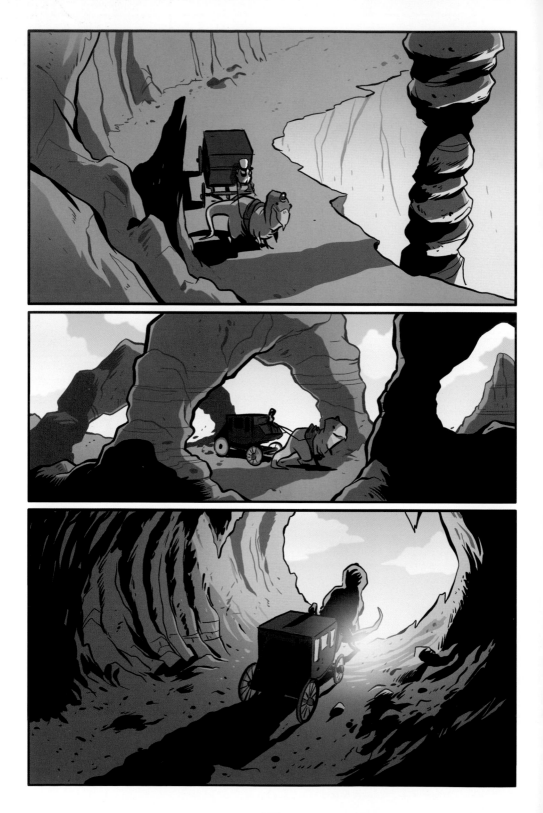

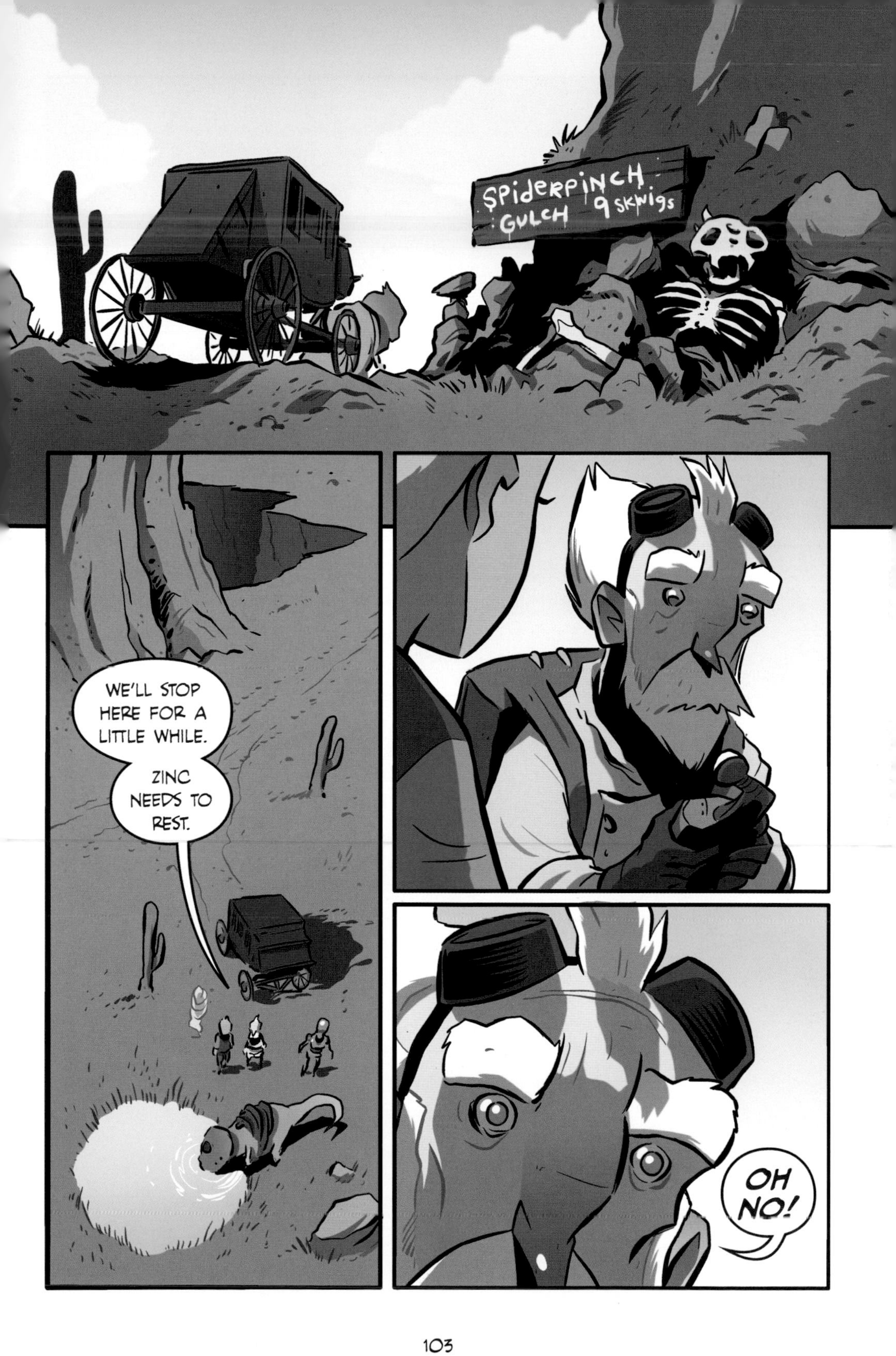
SPIDERPINCH GULCH 9 SKWIGS
WE'LL STOP HERE FOR A LITTLE WHILE.
ZINC NEEDS TO REST.
OH NO!

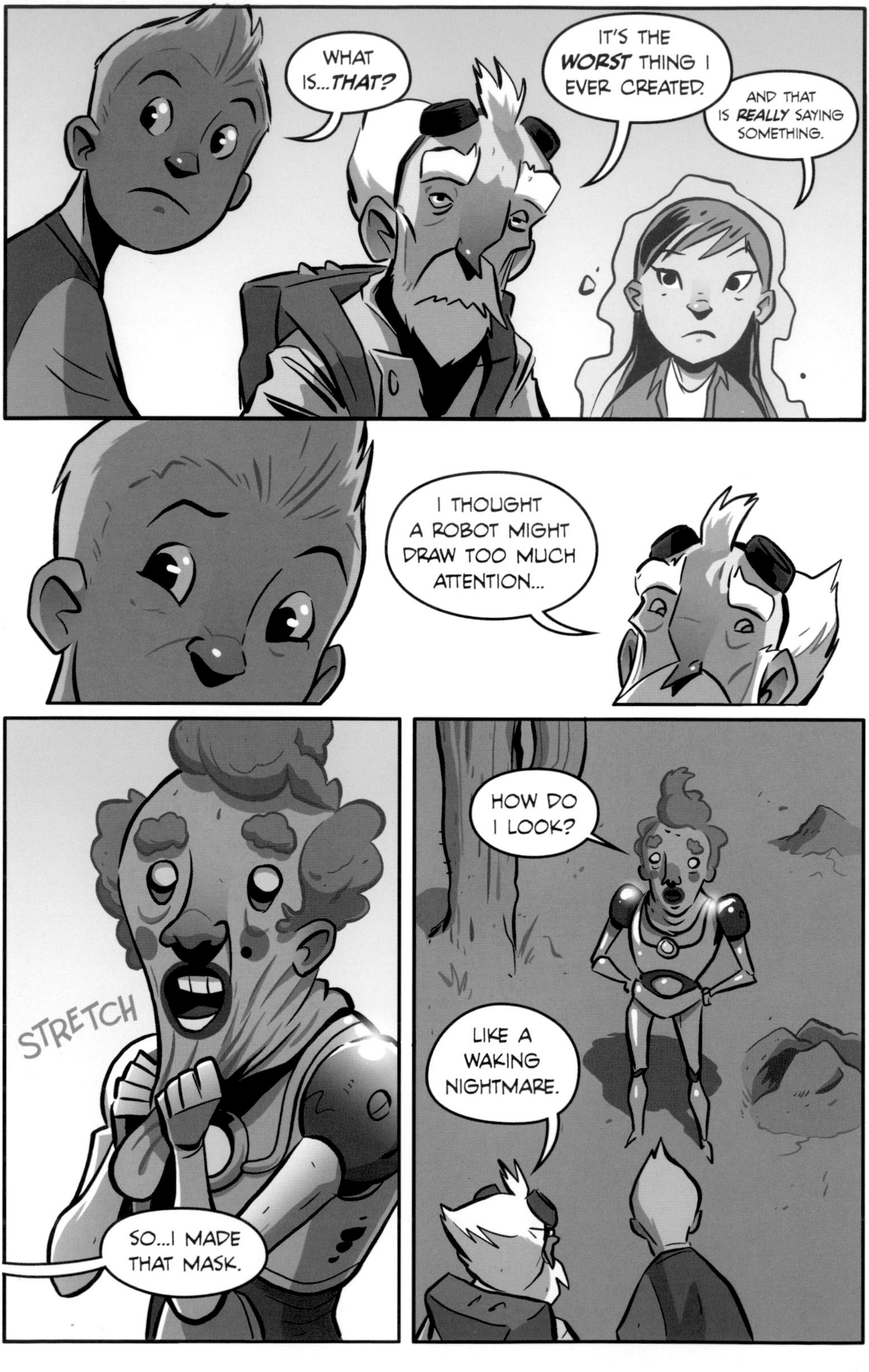
WHAT IS...THAT?
IT'S THE WORST THING I EVER CREATED.
AND THAT IS REALLY SAYING SOMETHING.
I THOUGHT A ROBOT MIGHT DRAW TOO MUCH ATTENTION...
STRETCH
SO...I MADE THAT MASK.
HOW DO I LOOK?
LIKE A WAKING NIGHTMARE.

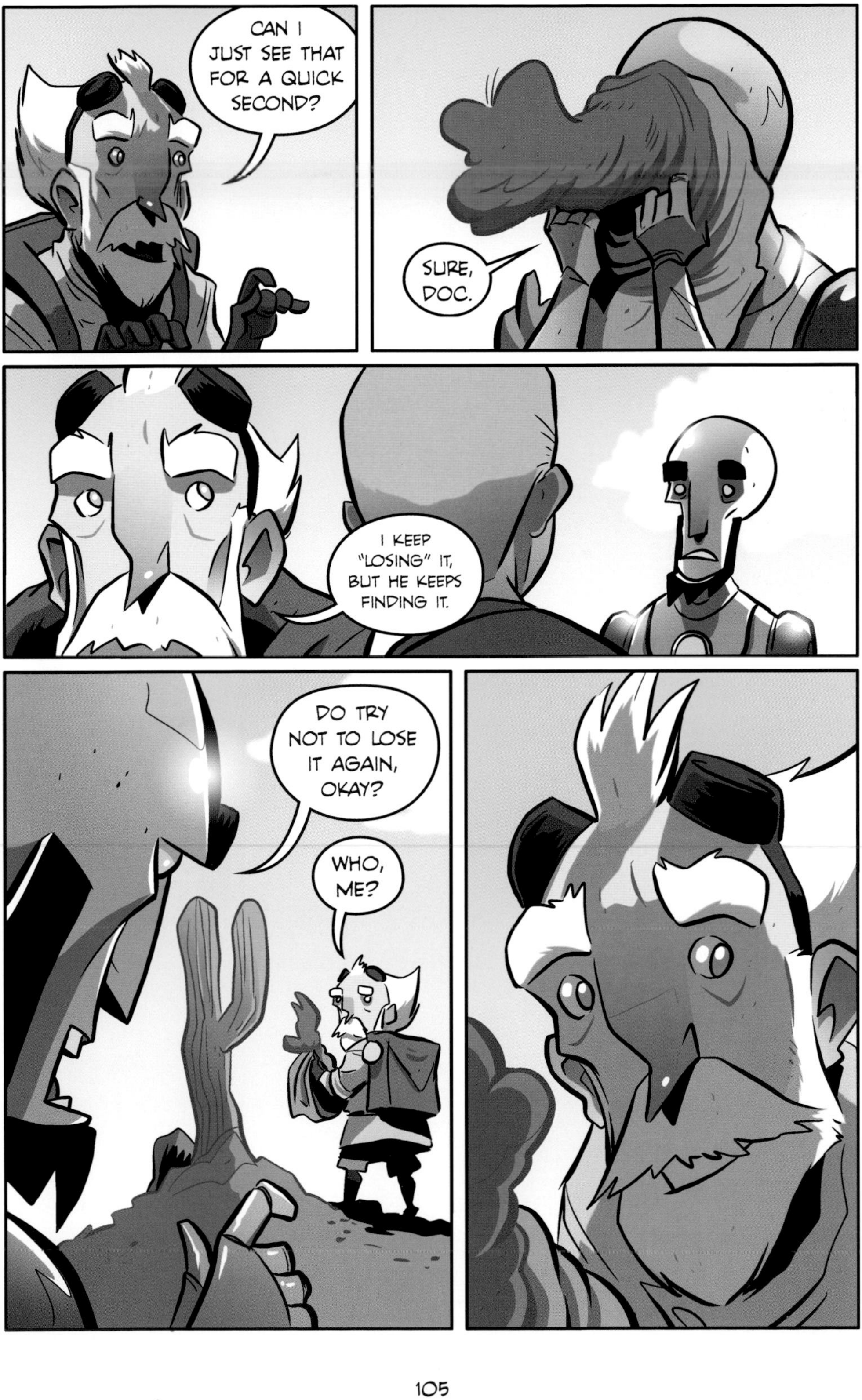
CAN I JUST SEE THAT FOR A QUICK SECOND?
SURE, DOC.
I KEEP "LOSING" IT, BUT HE KEEPS FINDING IT.
DO TRY NOT TO LOSE IT AGAIN, OKAY?
WHO, ME?

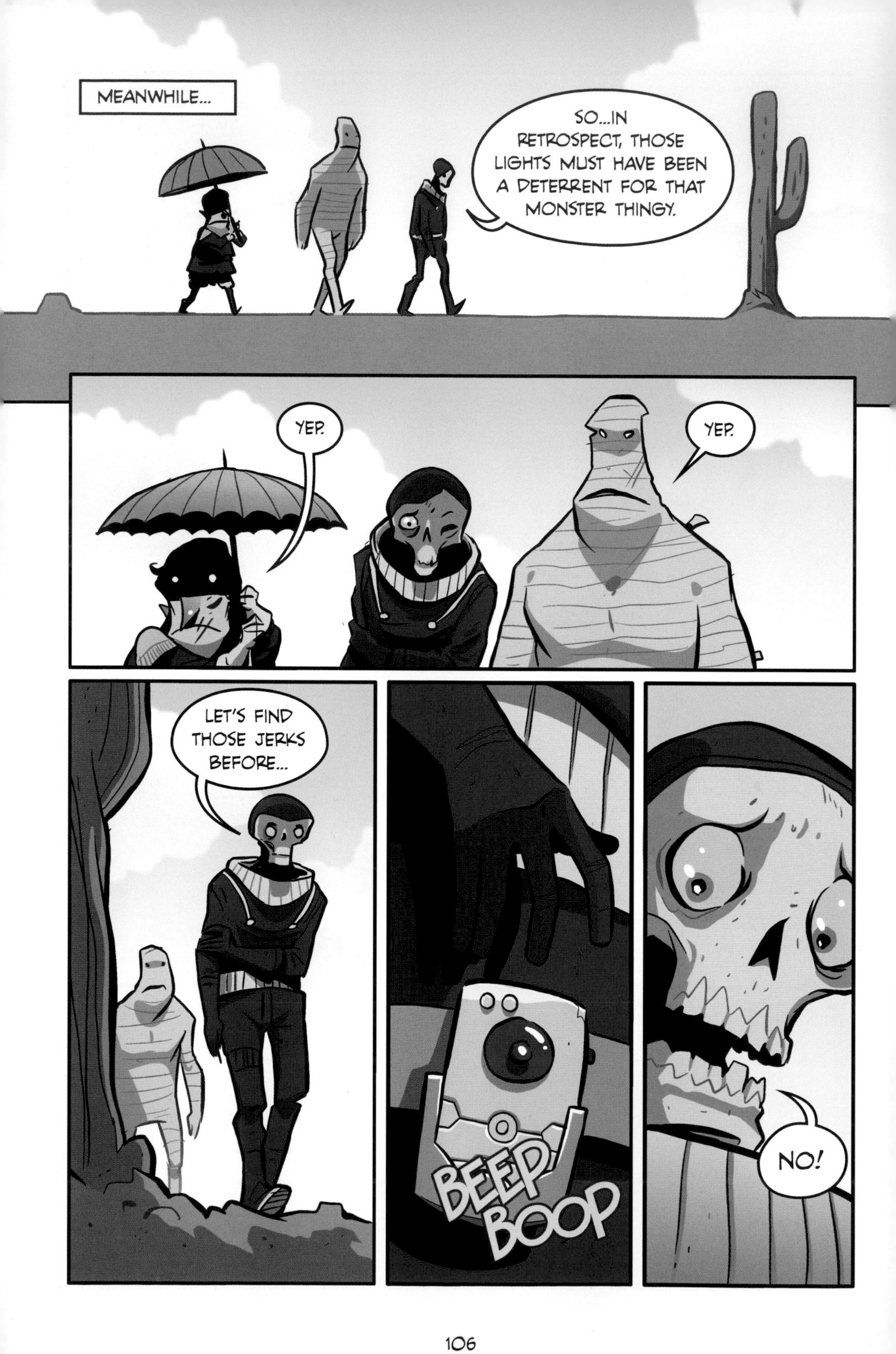

MEANWHILE...
SO...IN RETROSPECT, THOSE LIGHTS MUST HAVE BEEN A DETERRENT FOR THAT MONSTER THINGY.
YEP.
YEP.
LET'S FIND THOSE JERKS BEFORE...
BEEP BOOP
NO!

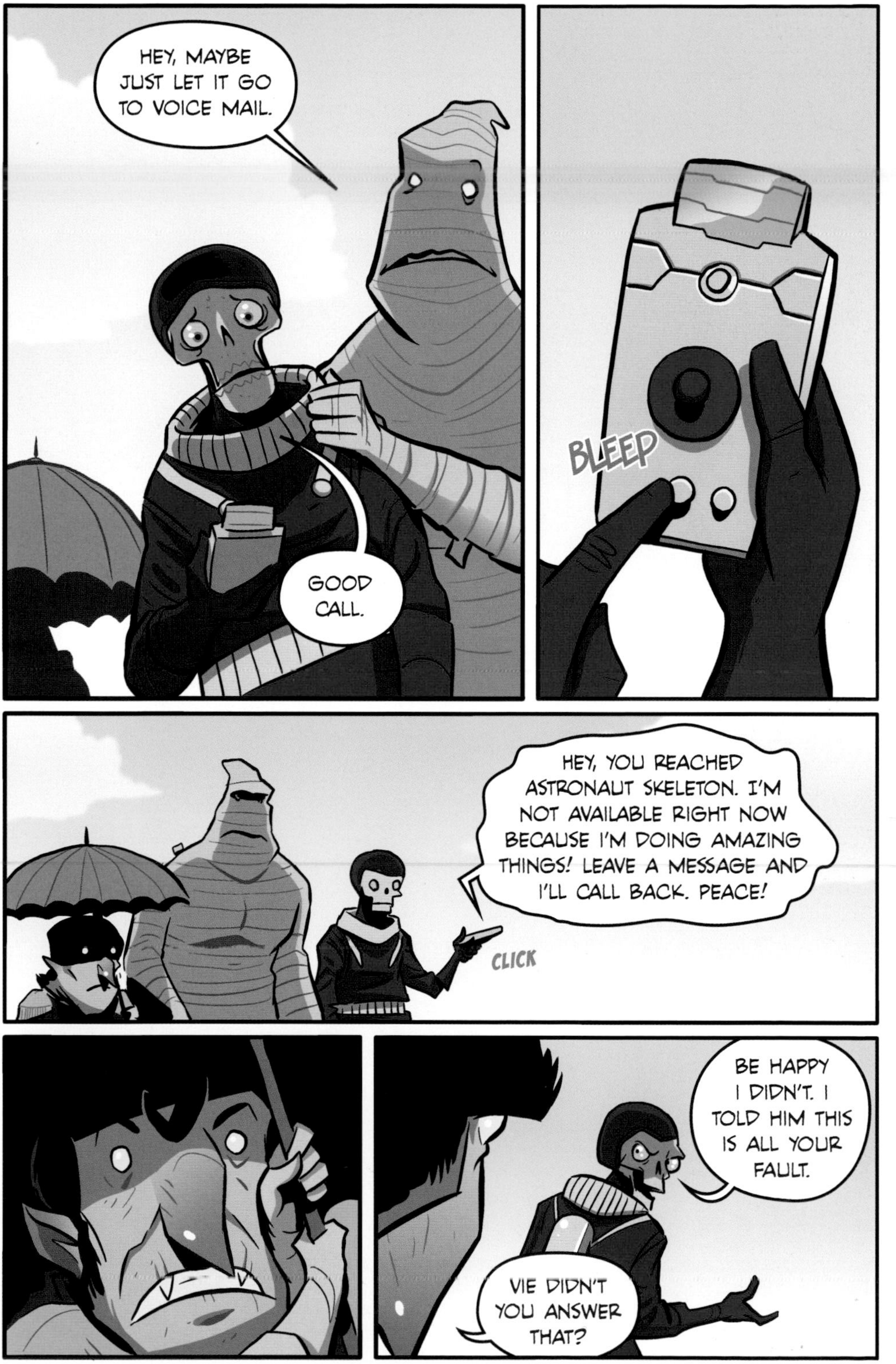
HEY, MAYBE JUST LET IT GO TO VOICE MAIL.
GOOD CALL.
BLEEP
HEY, YOU REACHED ASTRONAUT SKELETON. I'M NOT AVAILABLE RIGHT NOW BECAUSE I'M DOING AMAZING THINGS! LEAVE A MESSAGE AND I'LL CALL BACK. PEACE!
CLICK
VIE DIDN'T YOU ANSWER THAT?
BE HAPPY I DIDN'T. I TOLD HIM THIS IS ALL YOUR FAULT.

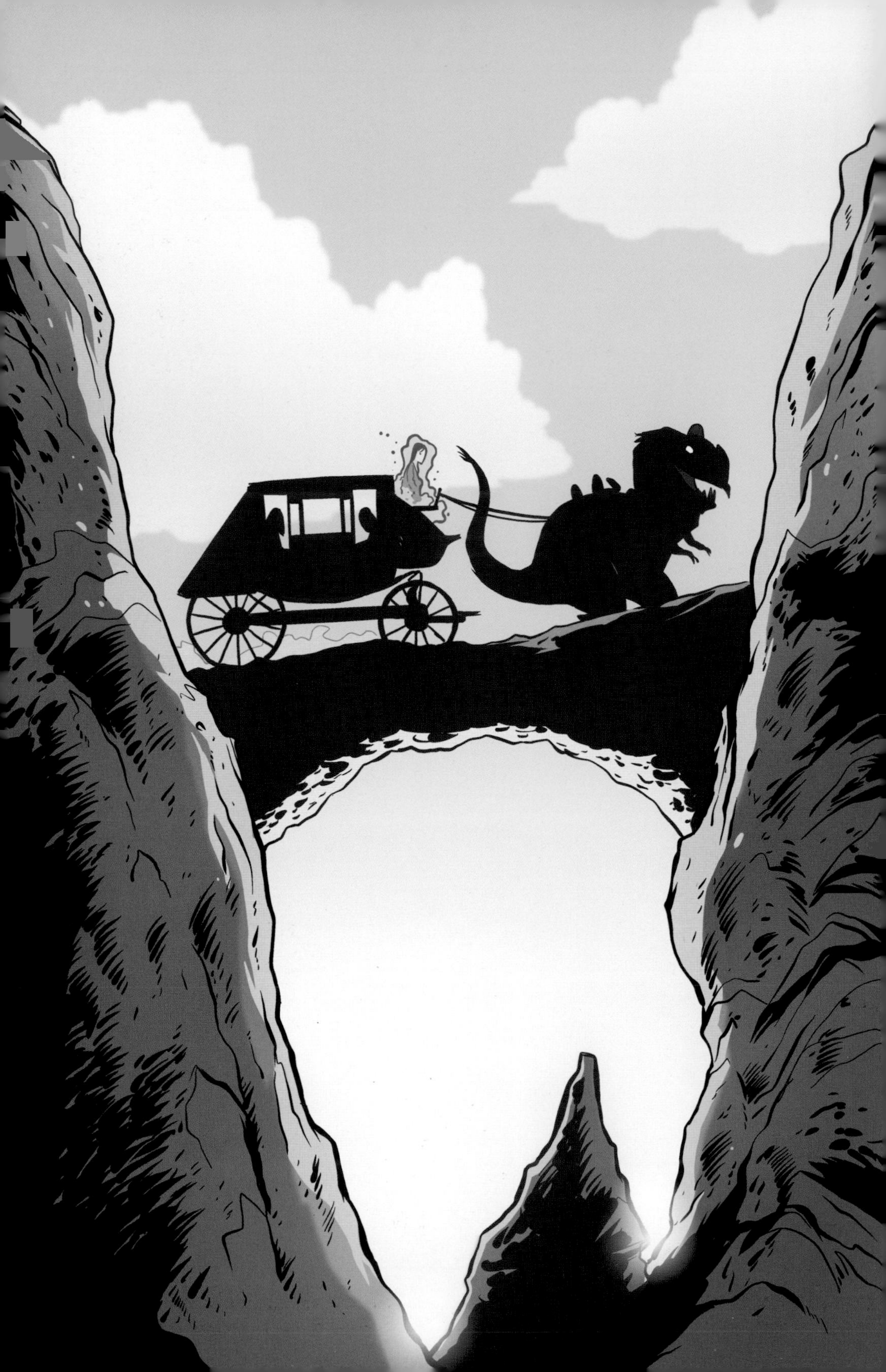

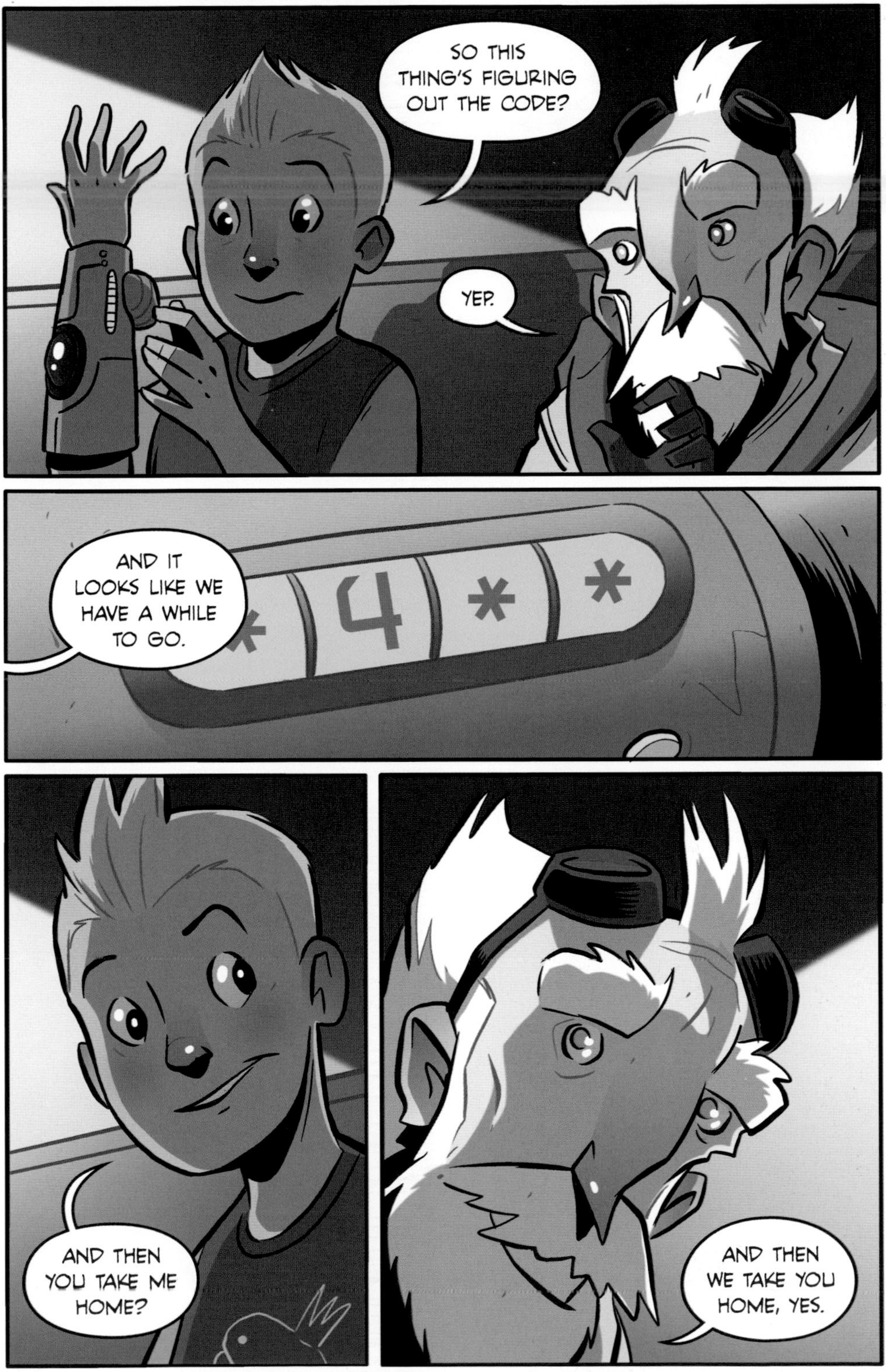
SO THIS THING'S FIGURING OUT THE CODE?
YEP.
AND IT LOOKS LIKE WE HAVE A WHILE TO GO.
*4**
AND THEN YOU TAKE ME HOME?
AND THEN WE TAKE YOU HOME, YES.

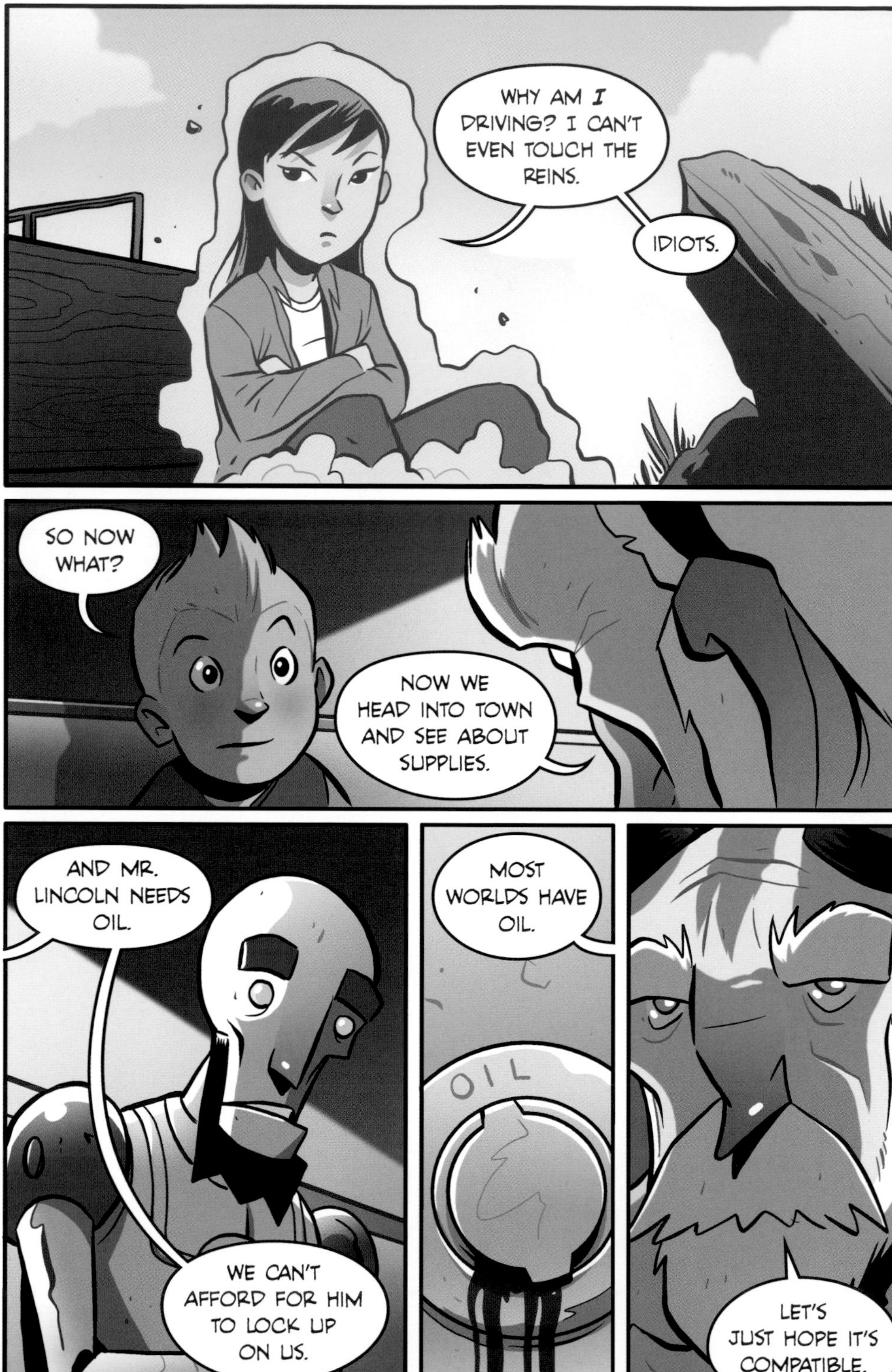
WHY AM *I* DRIVING? I CAN'T EVEN TOUCH THE REINS.
IDIOTS.
SO NOW WHAT?
NOW WE HEAD INTO TOWN AND SEE ABOUT SUPPLIES.
AND MR. LINCOLN NEEDS OIL.
WE CAN'T AFFORD FOR HIM TO LOCK UP ON US.
MOST WORLDS HAVE OIL.
OIL
LET'S JUST HOPE IT'S COMPATIBLE.

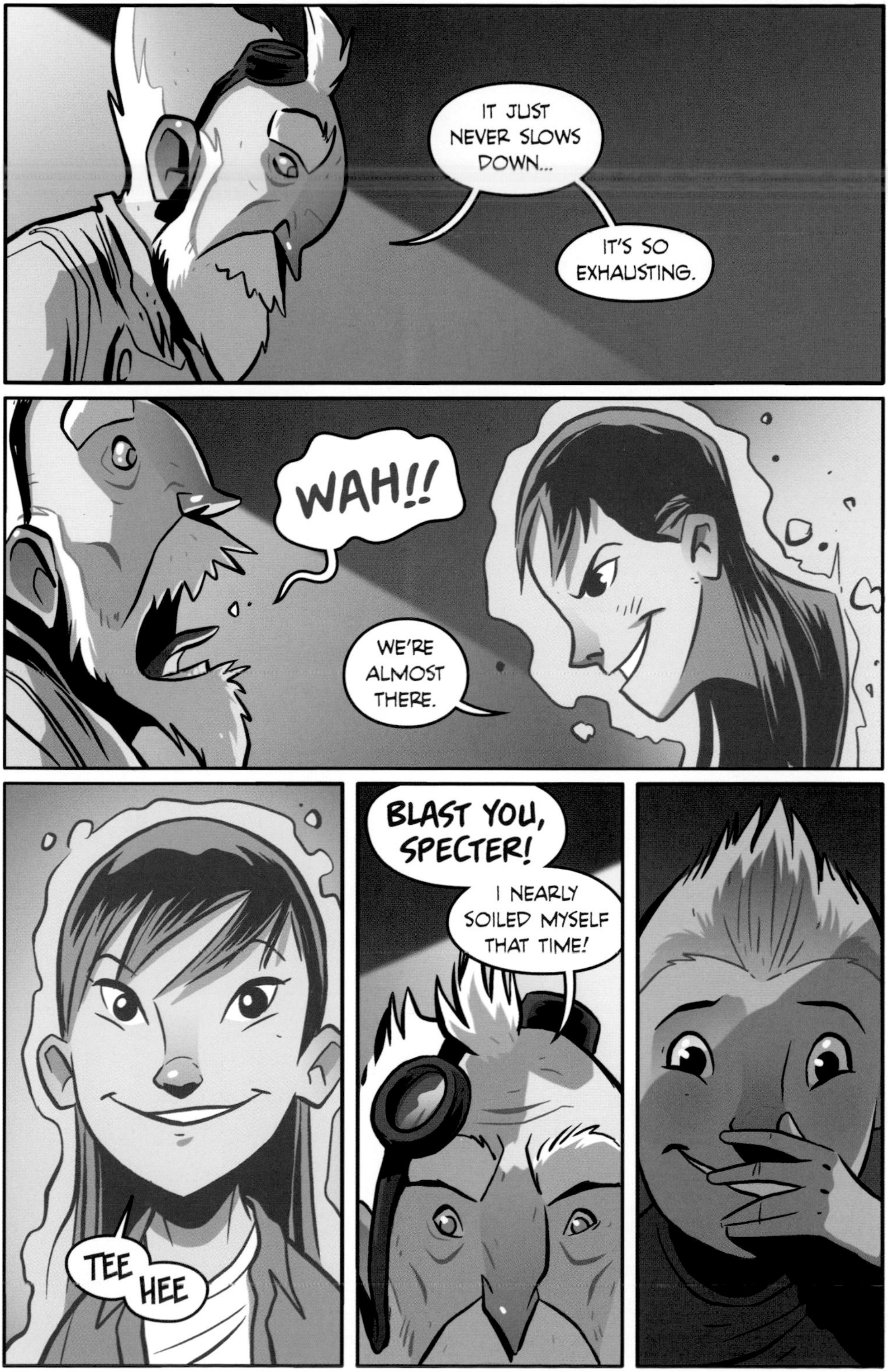
IT JUST NEVER SLOWS DOWN...
IT'S SO EXHAUSTING.
WAH!!
WE'RE ALMOST THERE.
TEE HEE
BLAST YOU, SPECTER!
I NEARLY SOILED MYSELF THAT TIME!

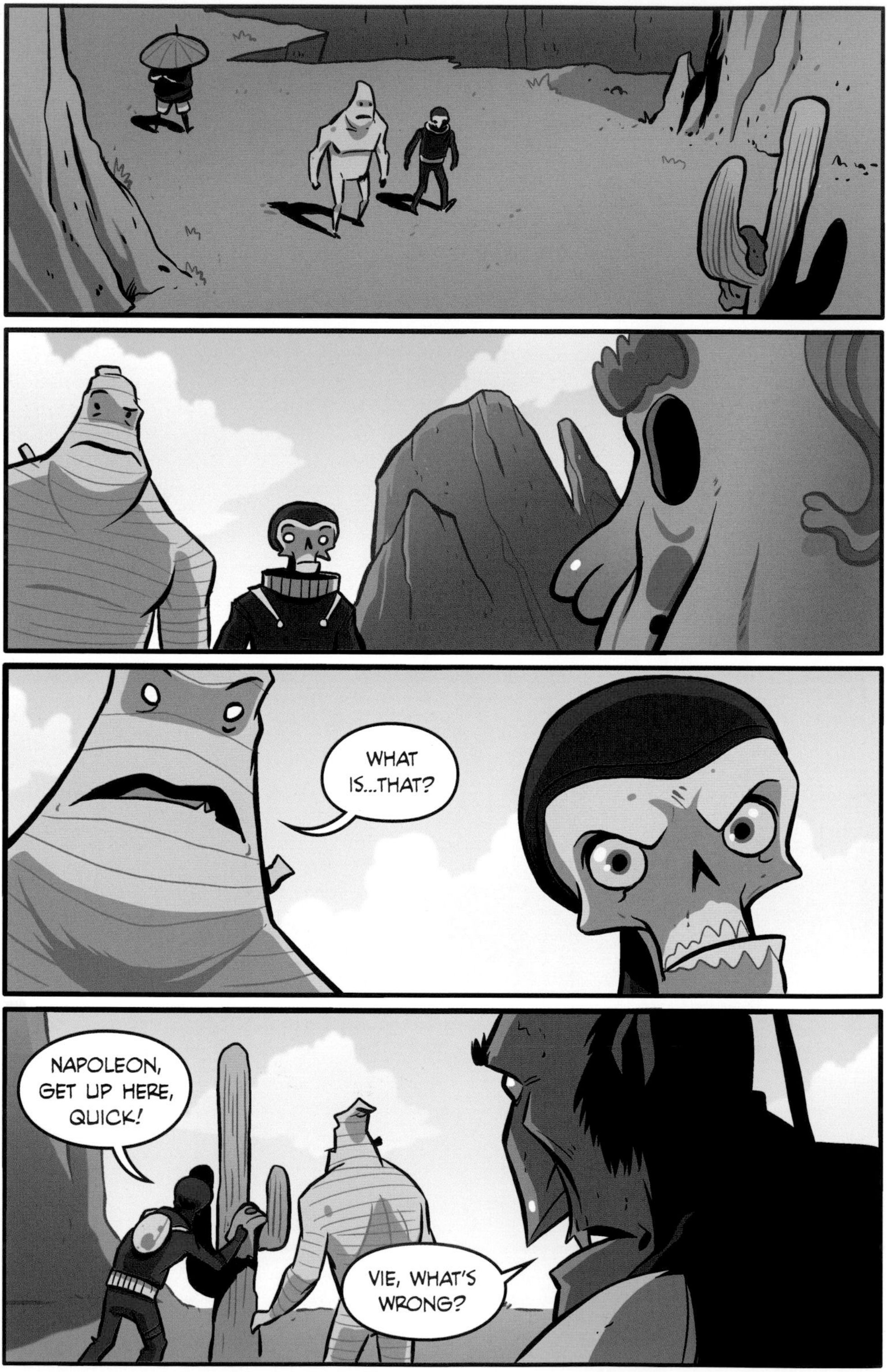
WHAT IS...THAT?
NAPOLEON, GET UP HERE, QUICK!
VIE, WHAT'S WRONG?

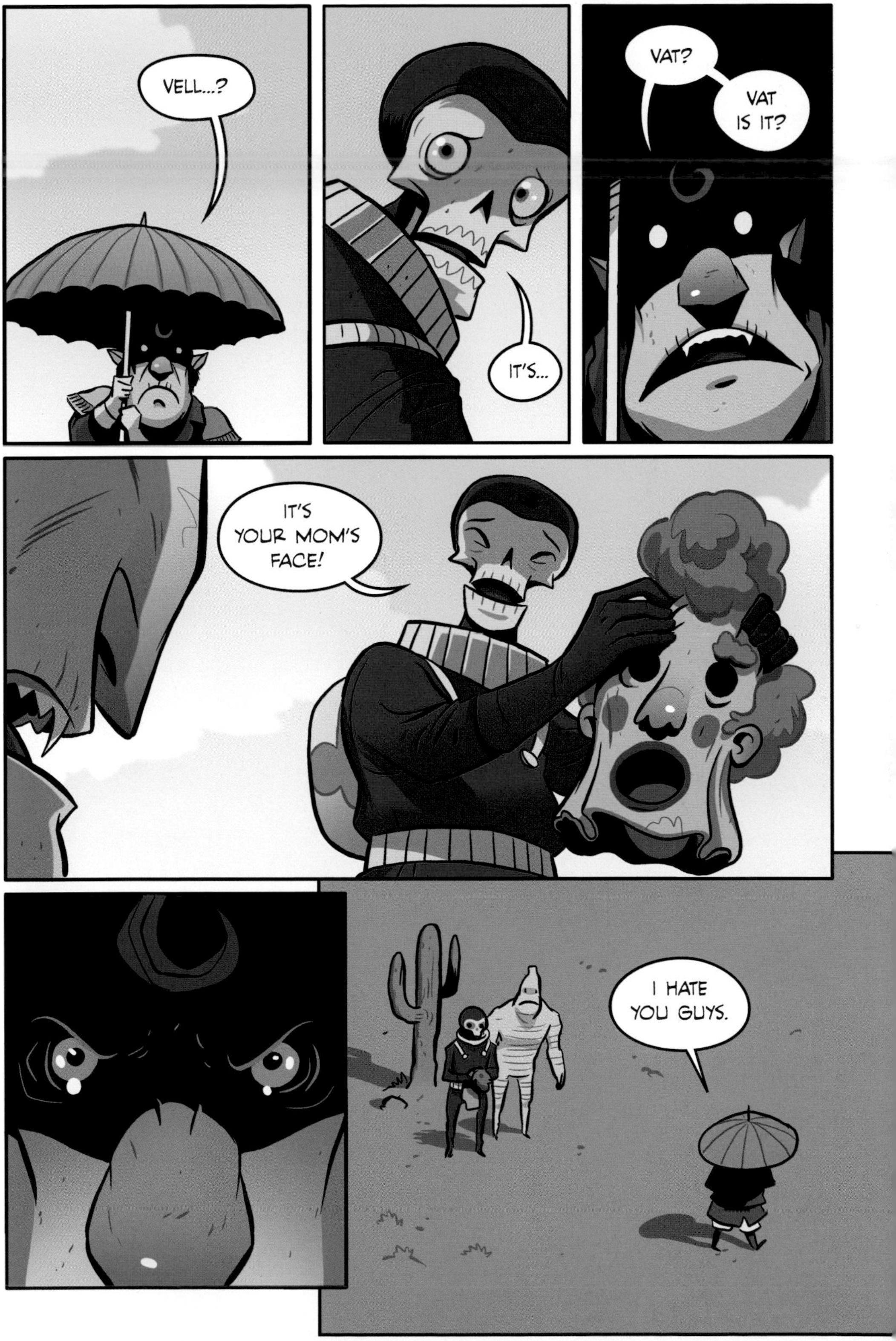
VELL...?
IT'S...
VAT?
VAT IS IT?
IT'S YOUR MOM'S FACE!
I HATE YOU GUYS.

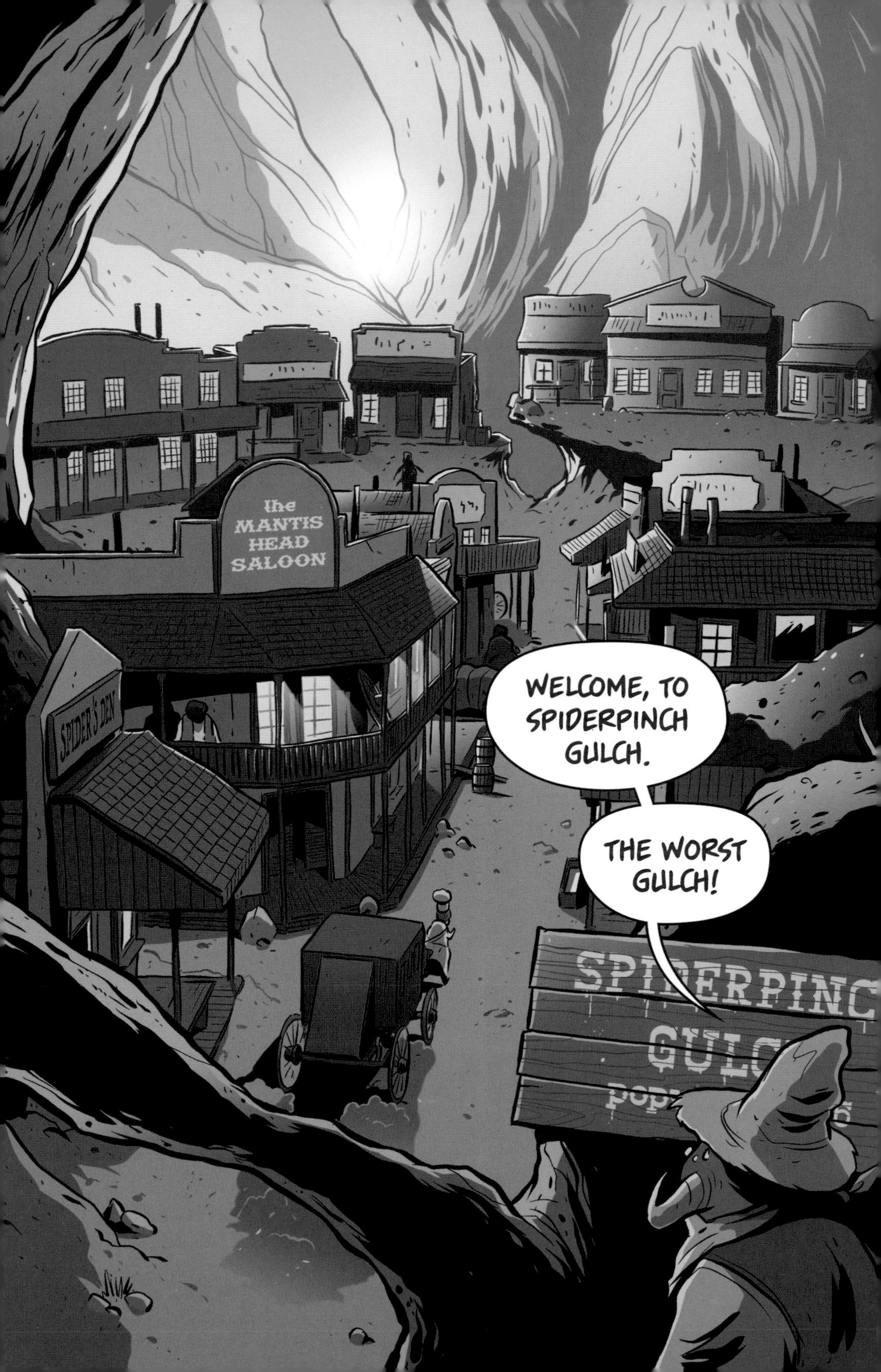
the MANTIS HEAD SALOON
SPIDER'S DEN
WELCOME, TO SPIDERPINCH GULCH.
THE WORST GULCH!

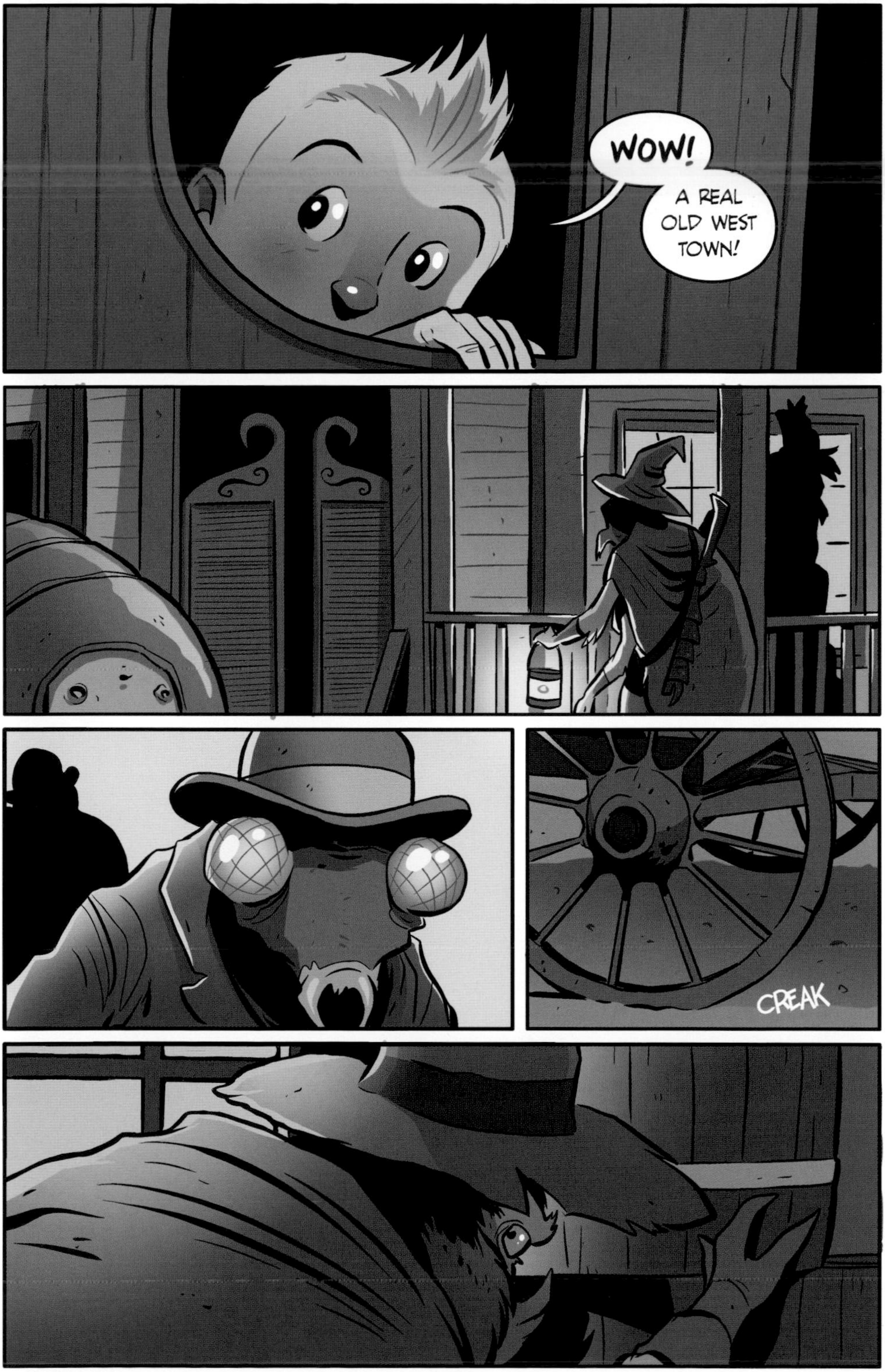
WOW!
A REAL OLD WEST TOWN!
CREAK

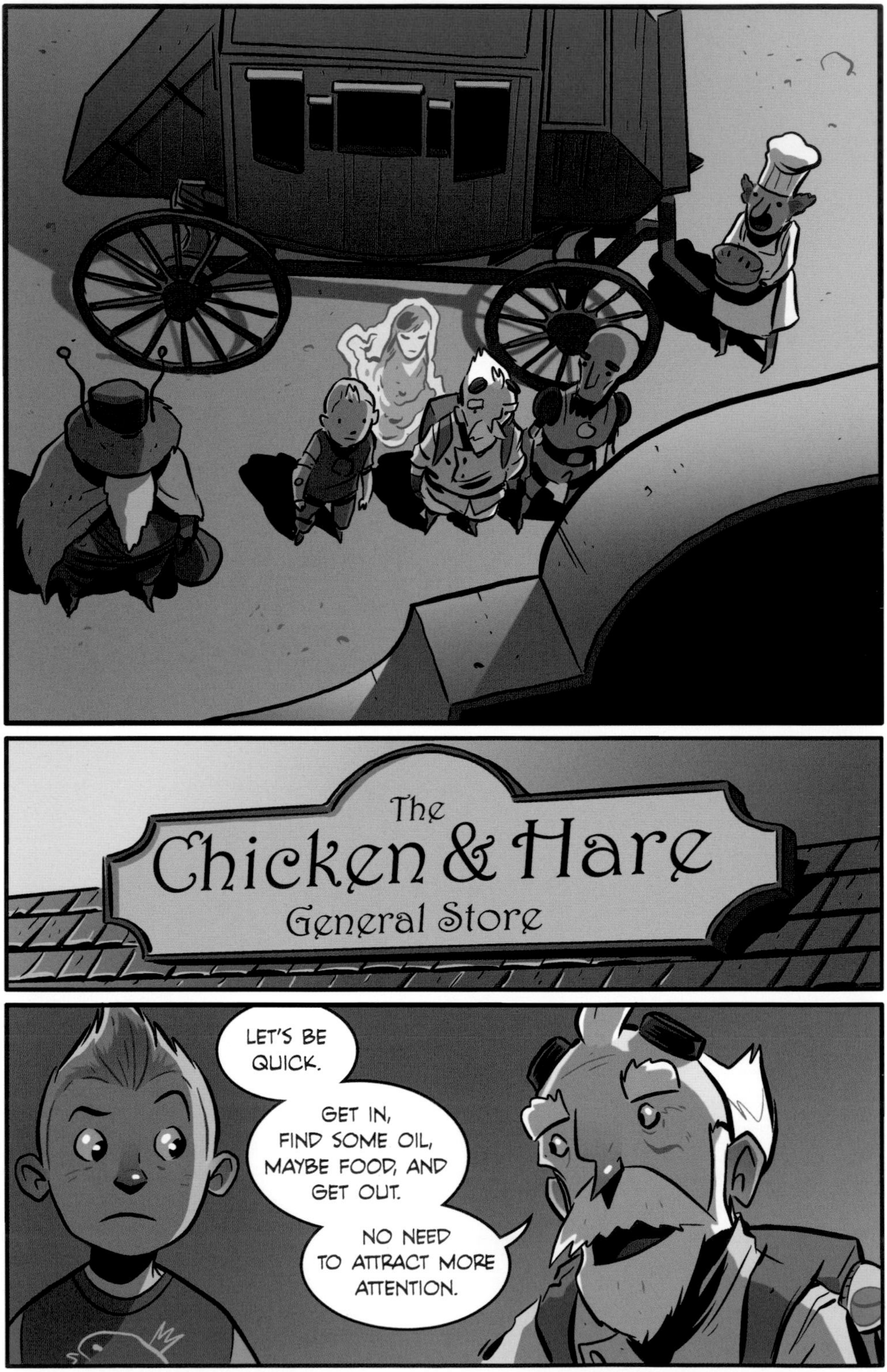
The Chicken & Hare General Store
LET'S BE QUICK.
GET IN, FIND SOME OIL, MAYBE FOOD, AND GET OUT.
NO NEED TO ATTRACT MORE ATTENTION.

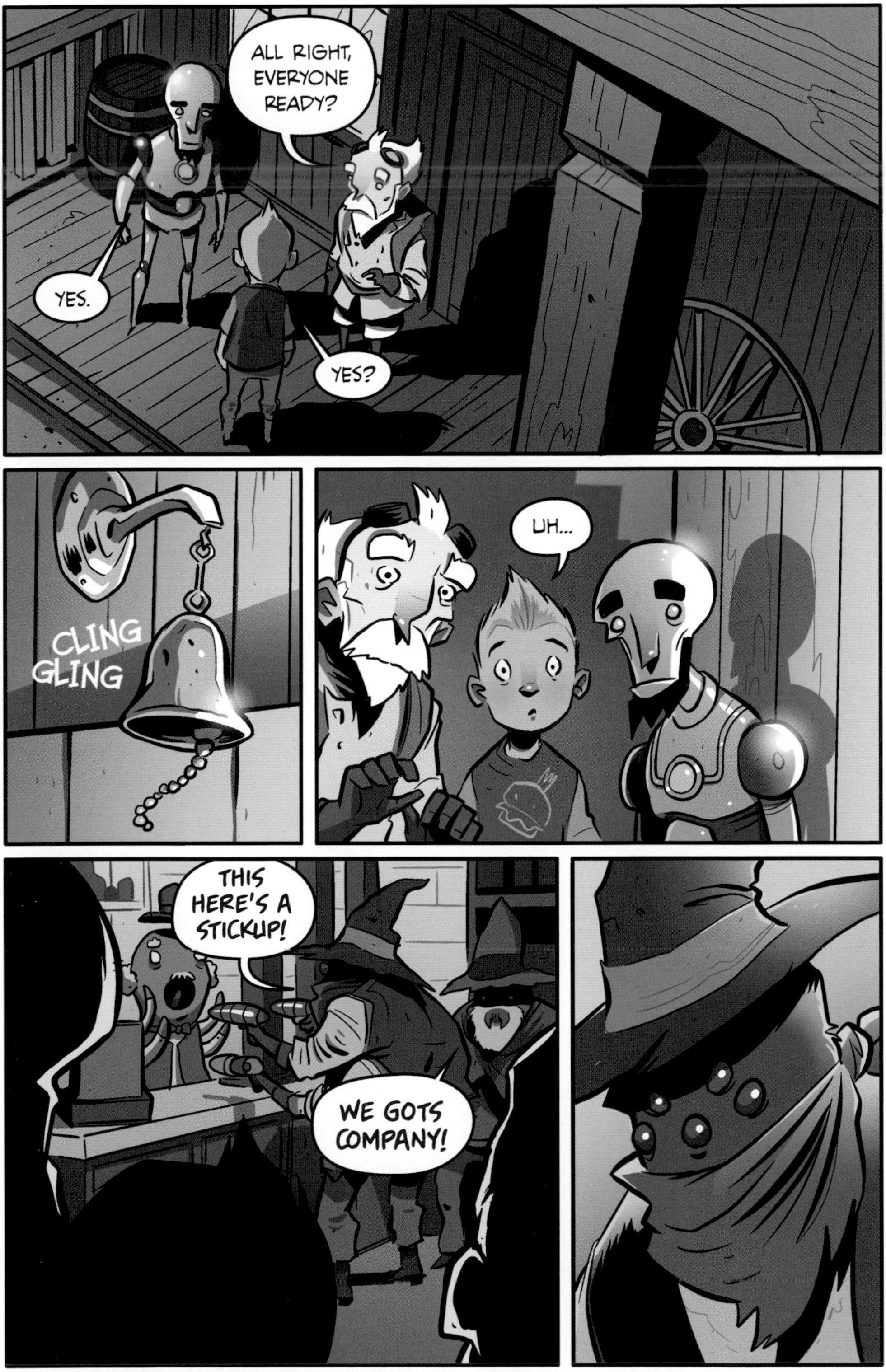
ALL RIGHT, EVERYONE READY?
YES.
YES?
CLING GLING
UH...
THIS HERE'S A STICKUP!
WE GOTS COMPANY!

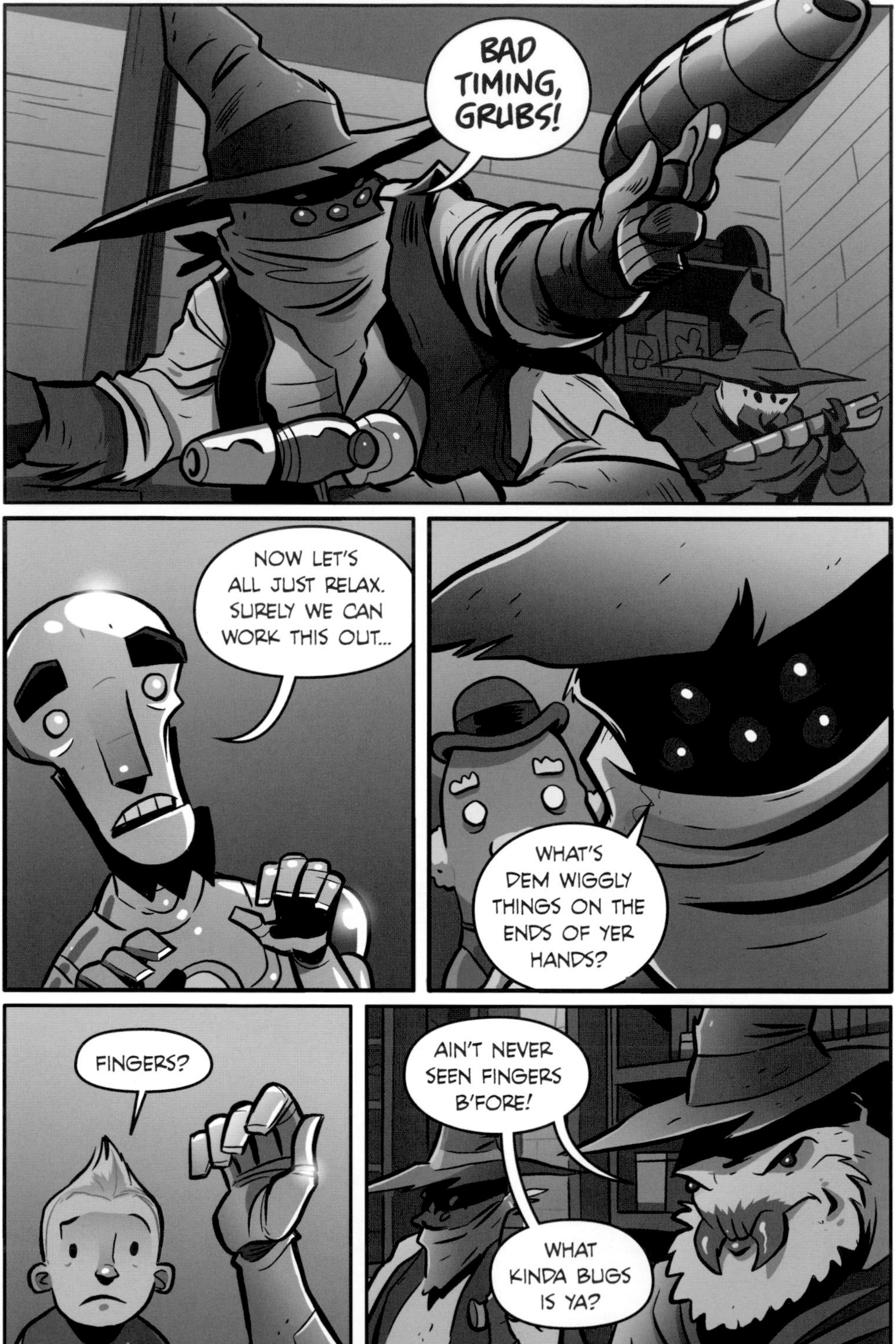
BAD TIMING, GRUBS!
NOW LET'S ALL JUST RELAX. SURELY WE CAN WORK THIS OUT...
WHAT'S DEM WIGGLY THINGS ON THE ENDS OF YER HANDS?
FINGERS?
AIN'T NEVER SEEN FINGERS B'FORE!
WHAT KINDA BUGS IS YA?

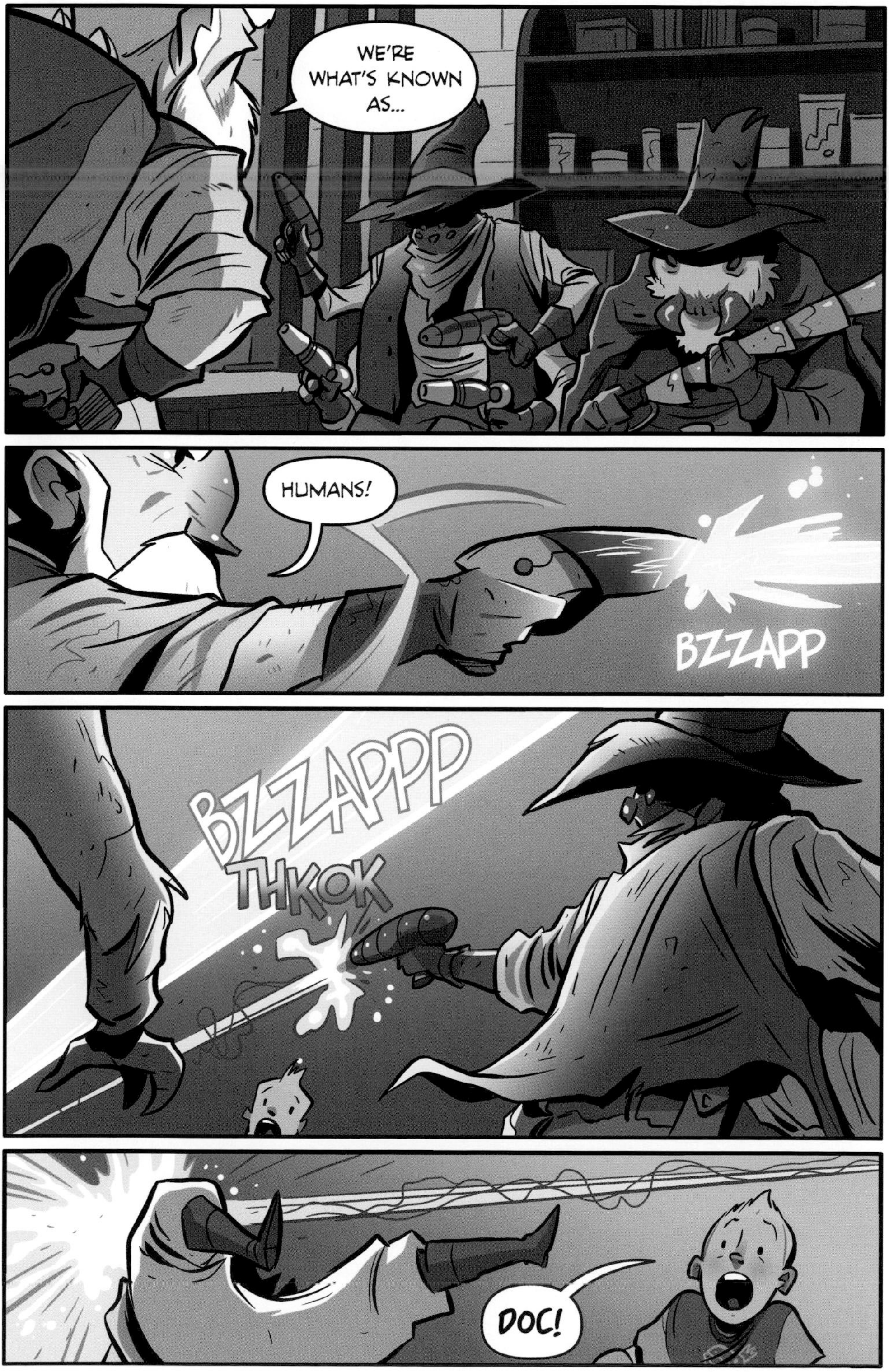
WE'RE WHAT'S KNOWN AS...
HUMANS!
BZZAPP
BZZAPPP
THKOK
DOC!

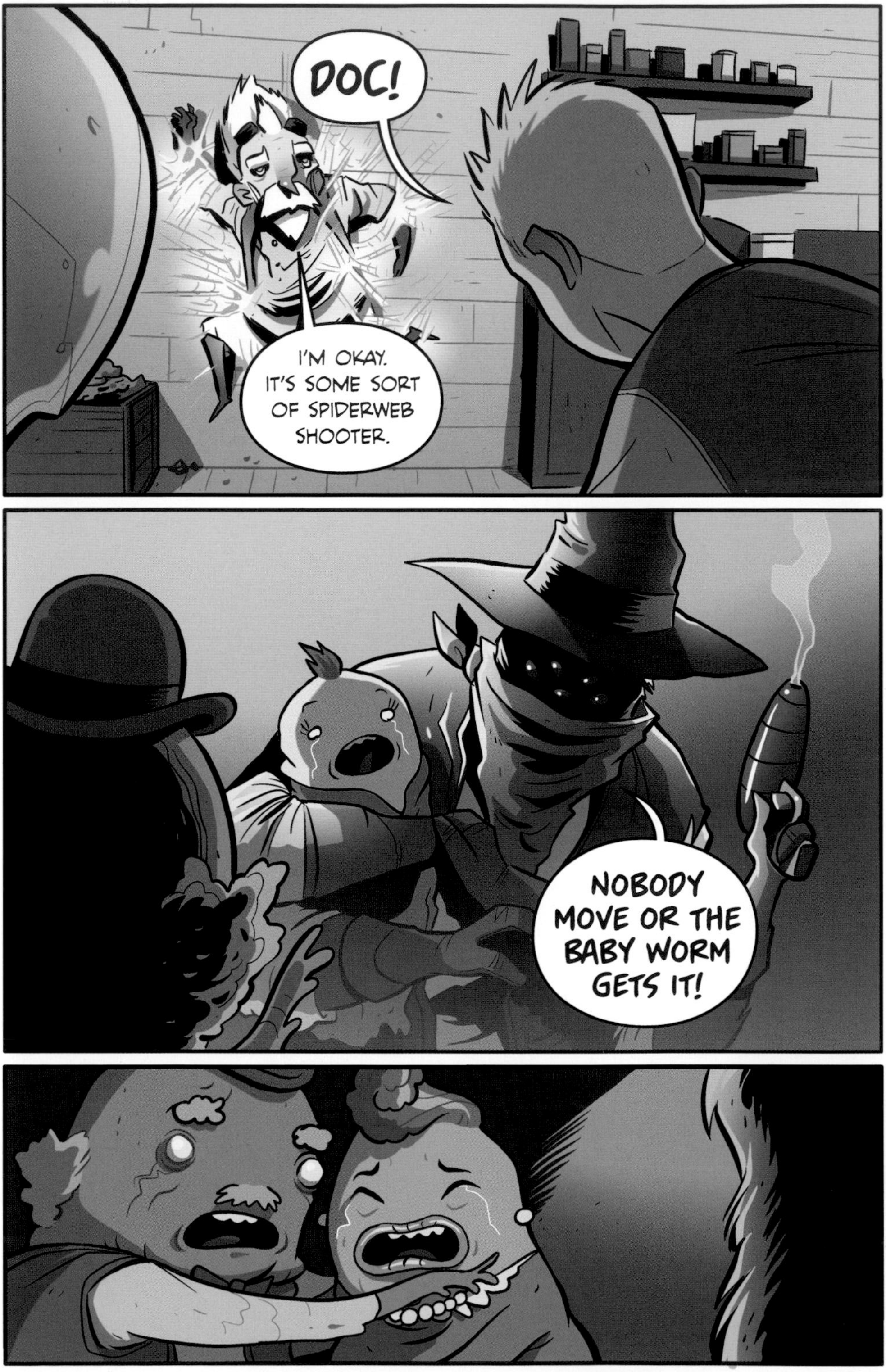
DOC!
I'M OKAY. IT'S SOME SORT OF SPIDERWEB SHOOTER.
NOBODY MOVE OR THE BABY WORM GETS IT!

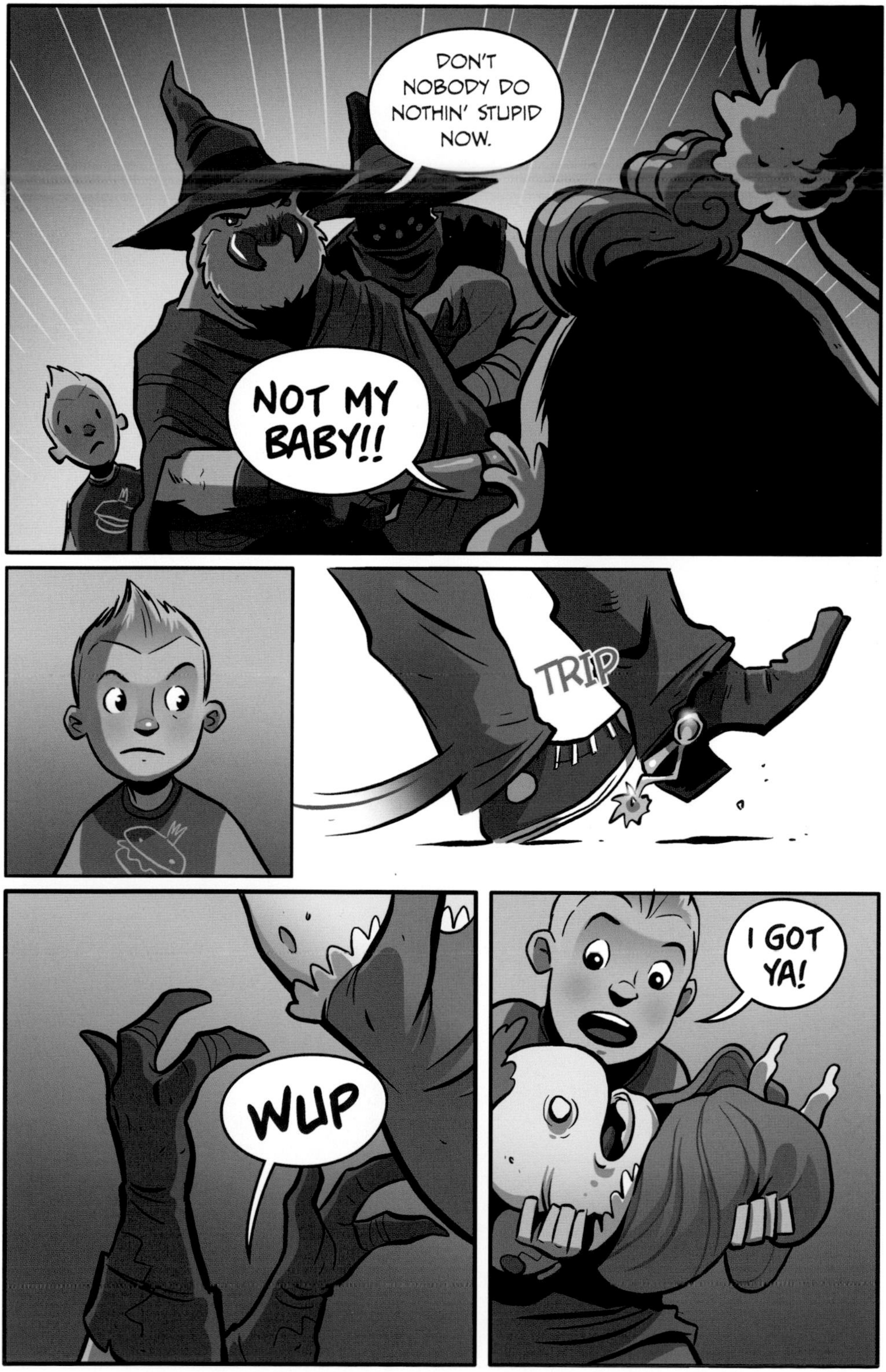
DON'T NOBODY DO NOTHIN' STUPID NOW.
NOT MY BABY!!
TRIP
WUP
I GOT YA!

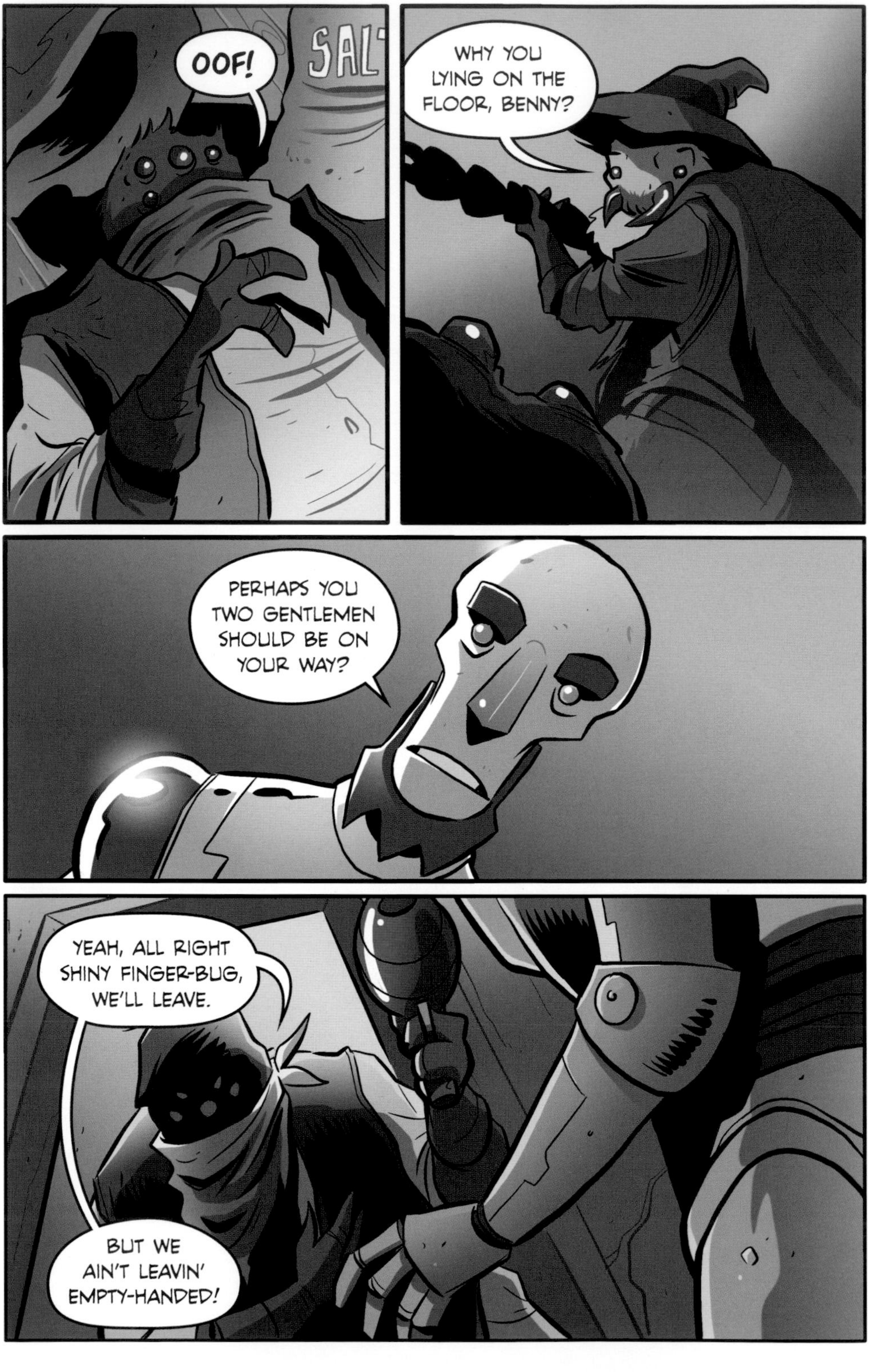
SALT
OOF!
WHY YOU LYING ON THE FLOOR, BENNY?
PERHAPS YOU TWO GENTLEMEN SHOULD BE ON YOUR WAY?
YEAH, ALL RIGHT SHINY FINGER-BUG, WE'LL LEAVE.
BUT WE AIN'T LEAVIN' EMPTY-HANDED!

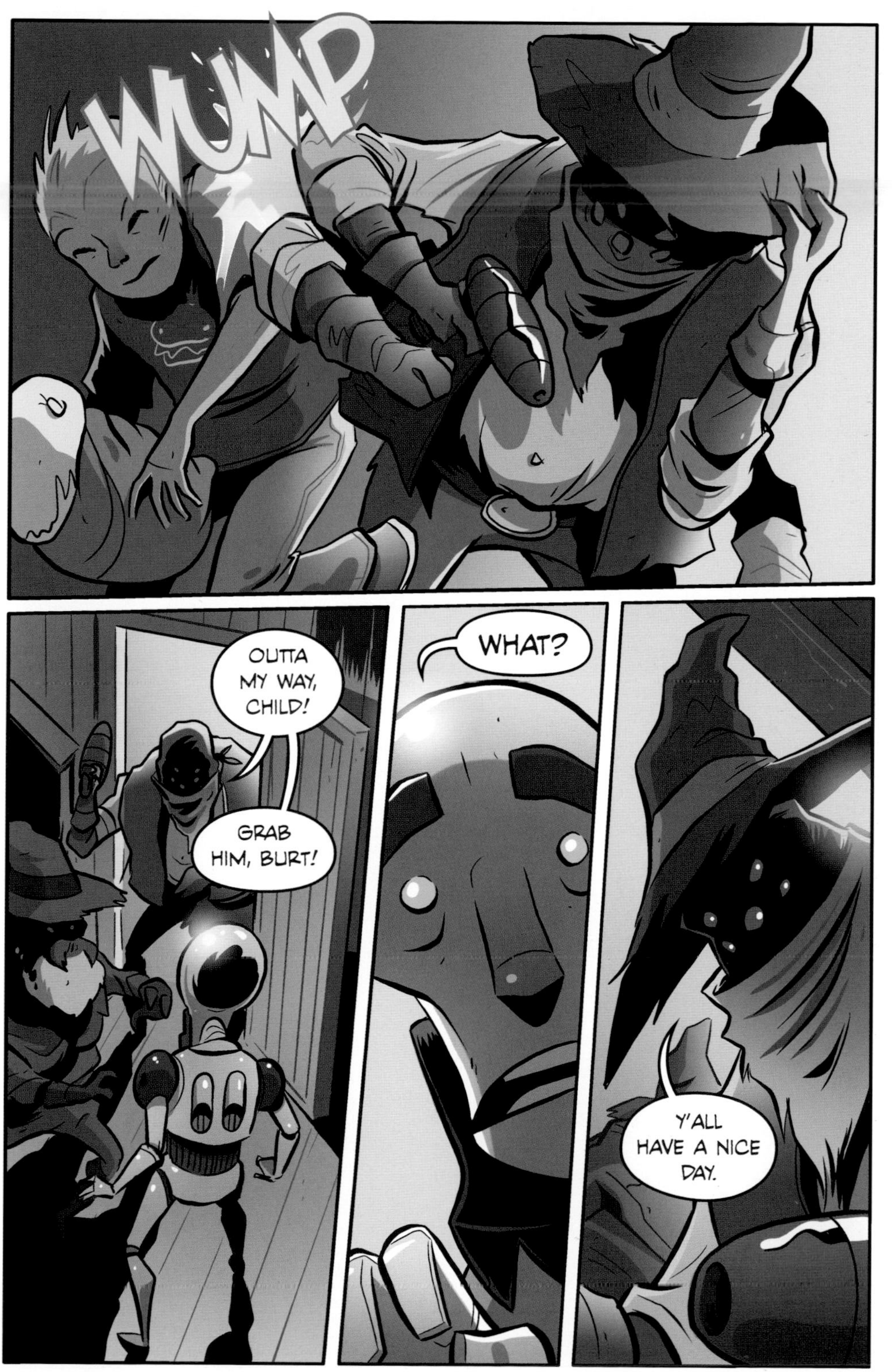
WUMP
OUTTA MY WAY, CHILD!
GRAB HIM, BURT!
WHAT?
Y'ALL HAVE A NICE DAY.

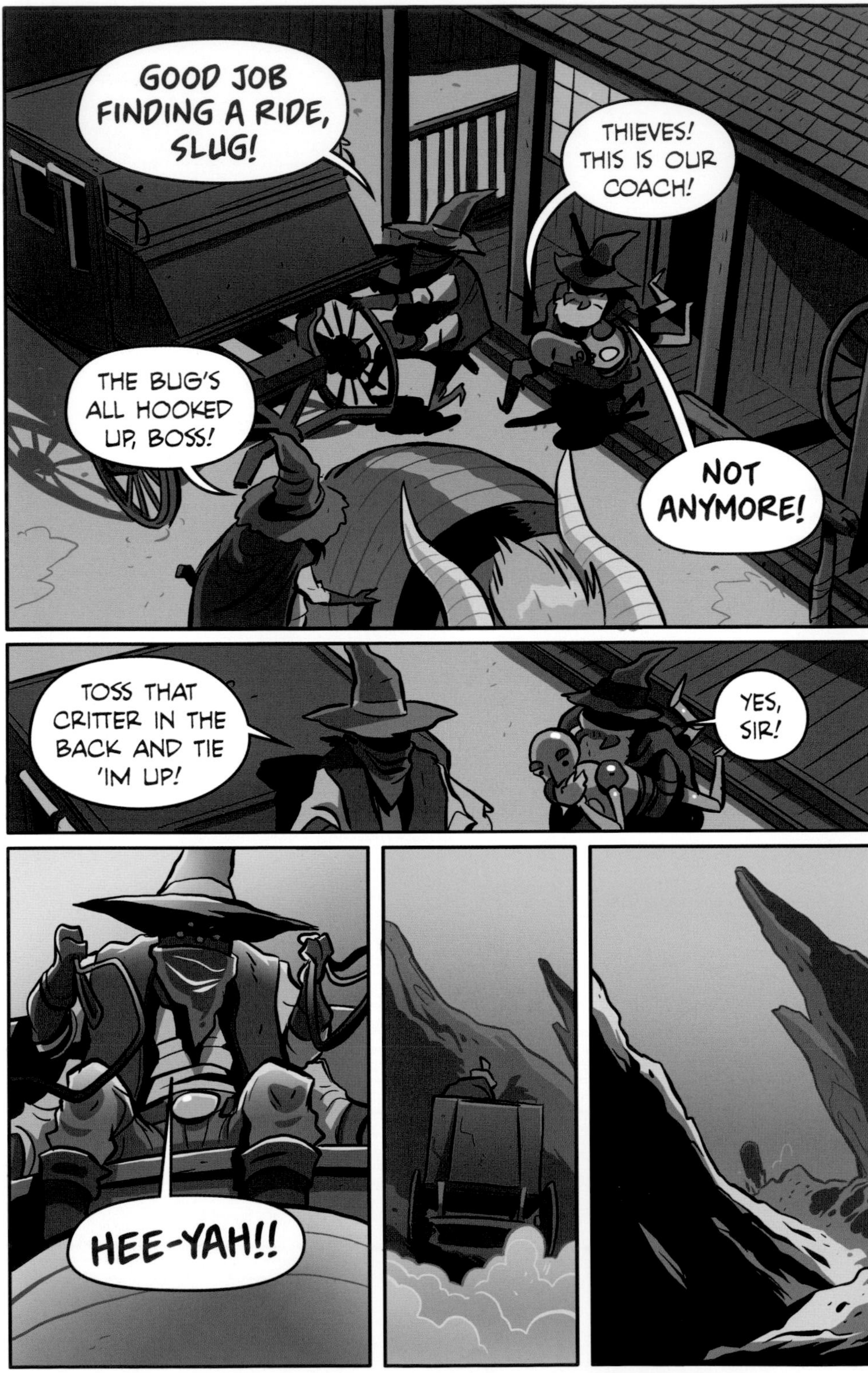
GOOD JOB FINDING A RIDE, SLUG!
THIEVES! THIS IS OUR COACH!
THE BUG'S ALL HOOKED UP, BOSS!
NOT ANYMORE!
TOSS THAT CRITTER IN THE BACK AND TIE 'IM UP!
YES, SIR!
HEE-YAH!!

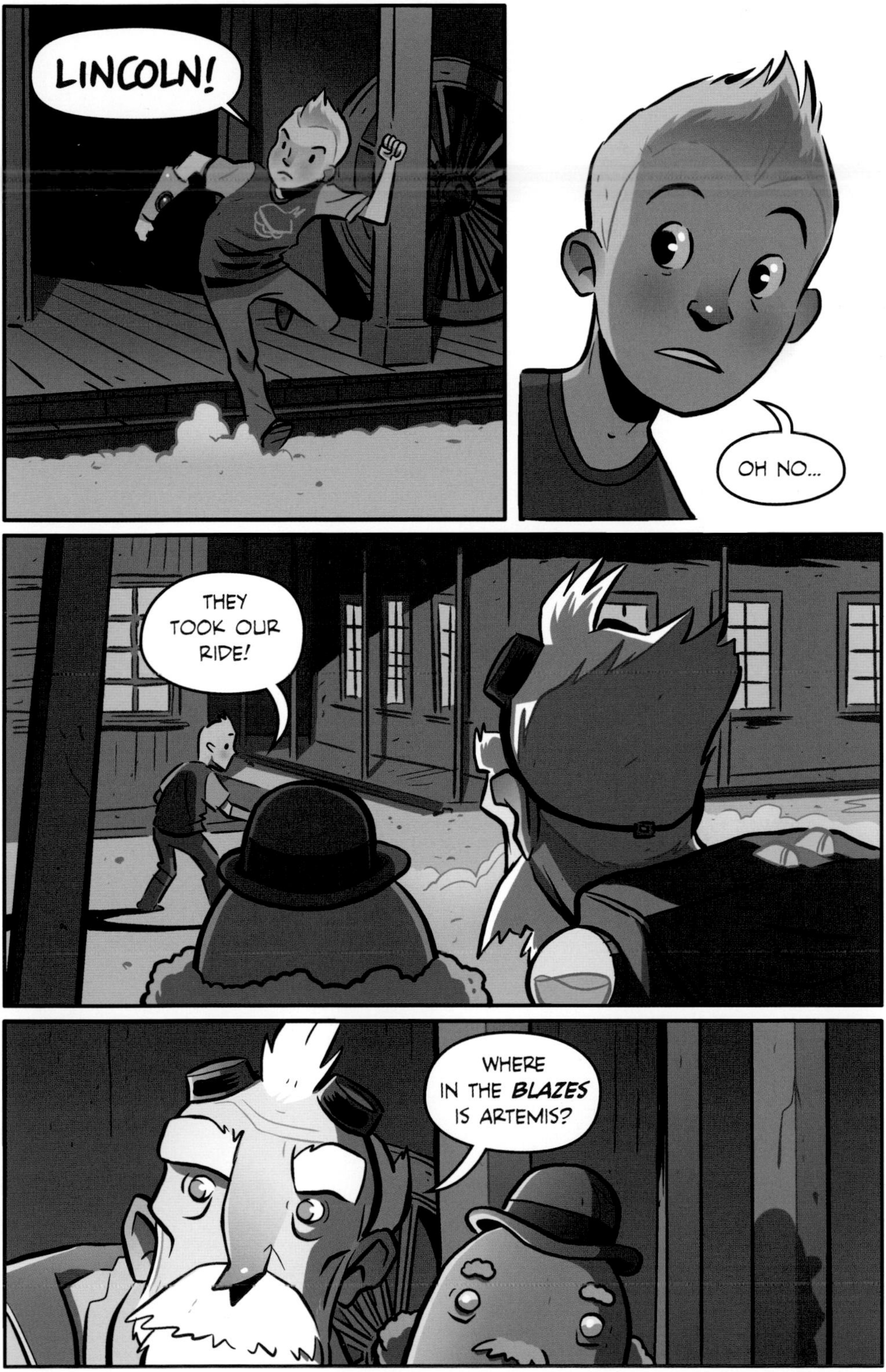
LINCOLN!
OH NO...
THEY TOOK OUR RIDE!
WHERE IN THE *BLAZES* IS ARTEMIS?

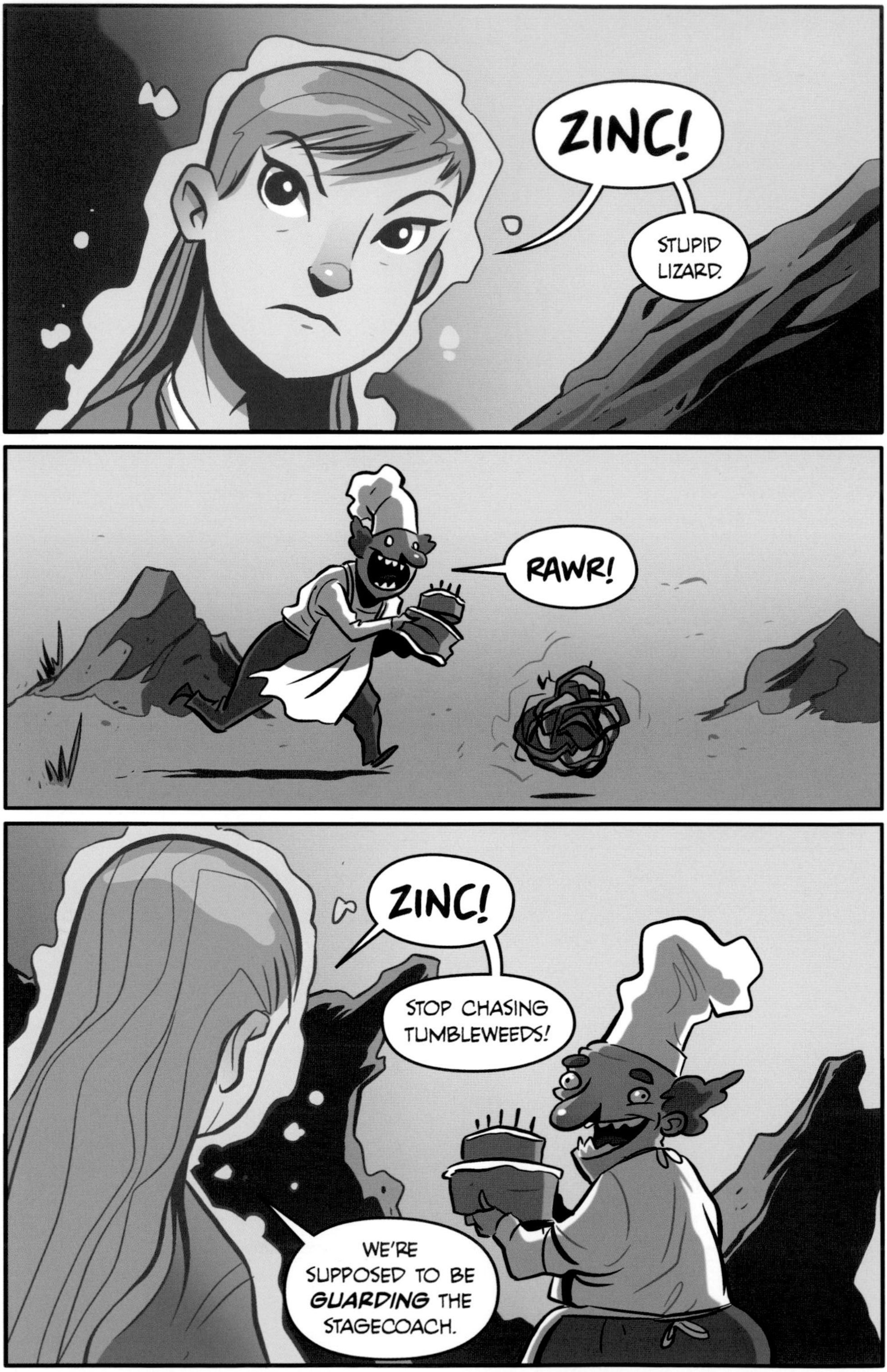
ZINC!
STUPID LIZARD.
RAWR!
ZINC!
STOP CHASING TUMBLEWEEDS!
WE'RE SUPPOSED TO BE GUARDING THE STAGECOACH.

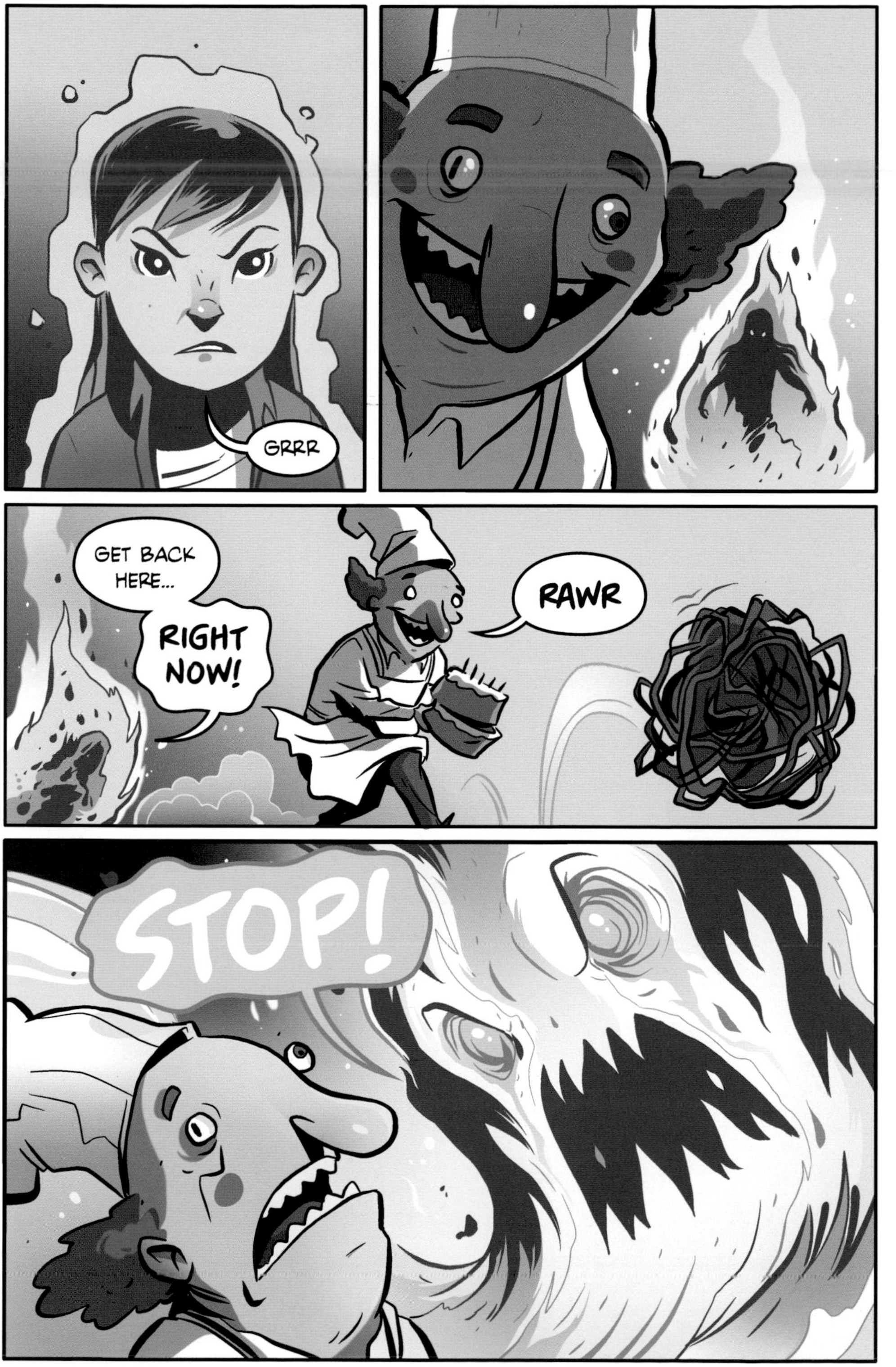
GRRR
GET BACK HERE...
RIGHT NOW!
RAWR
STOP!

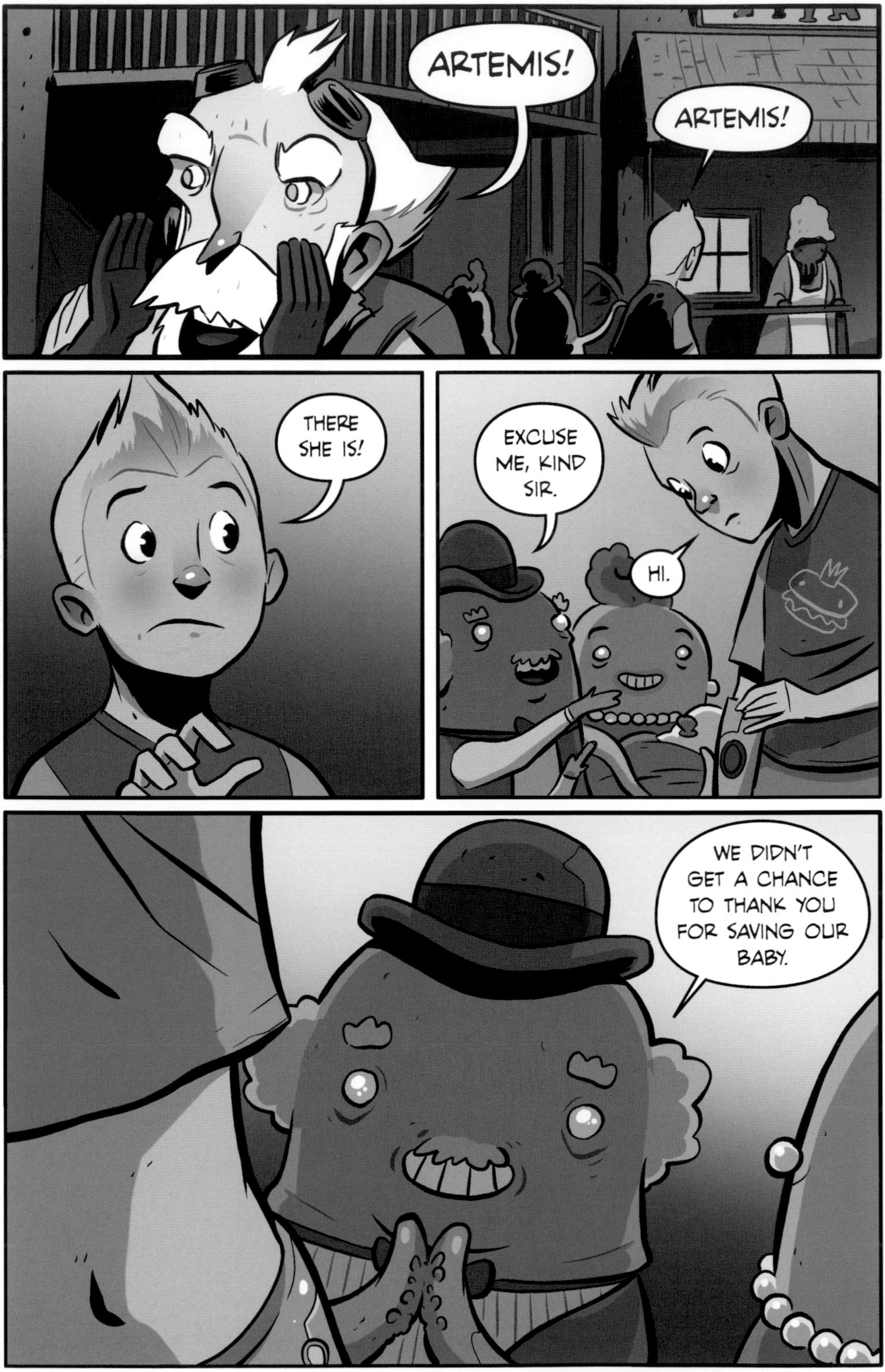
ARTEMIS!
ARTEMIS!
THERE SHE IS!
EXCUSE ME, KIND SIR.
HI.
WE DIDN'T GET A CHANCE TO THANK YOU FOR SAVING OUR BABY.

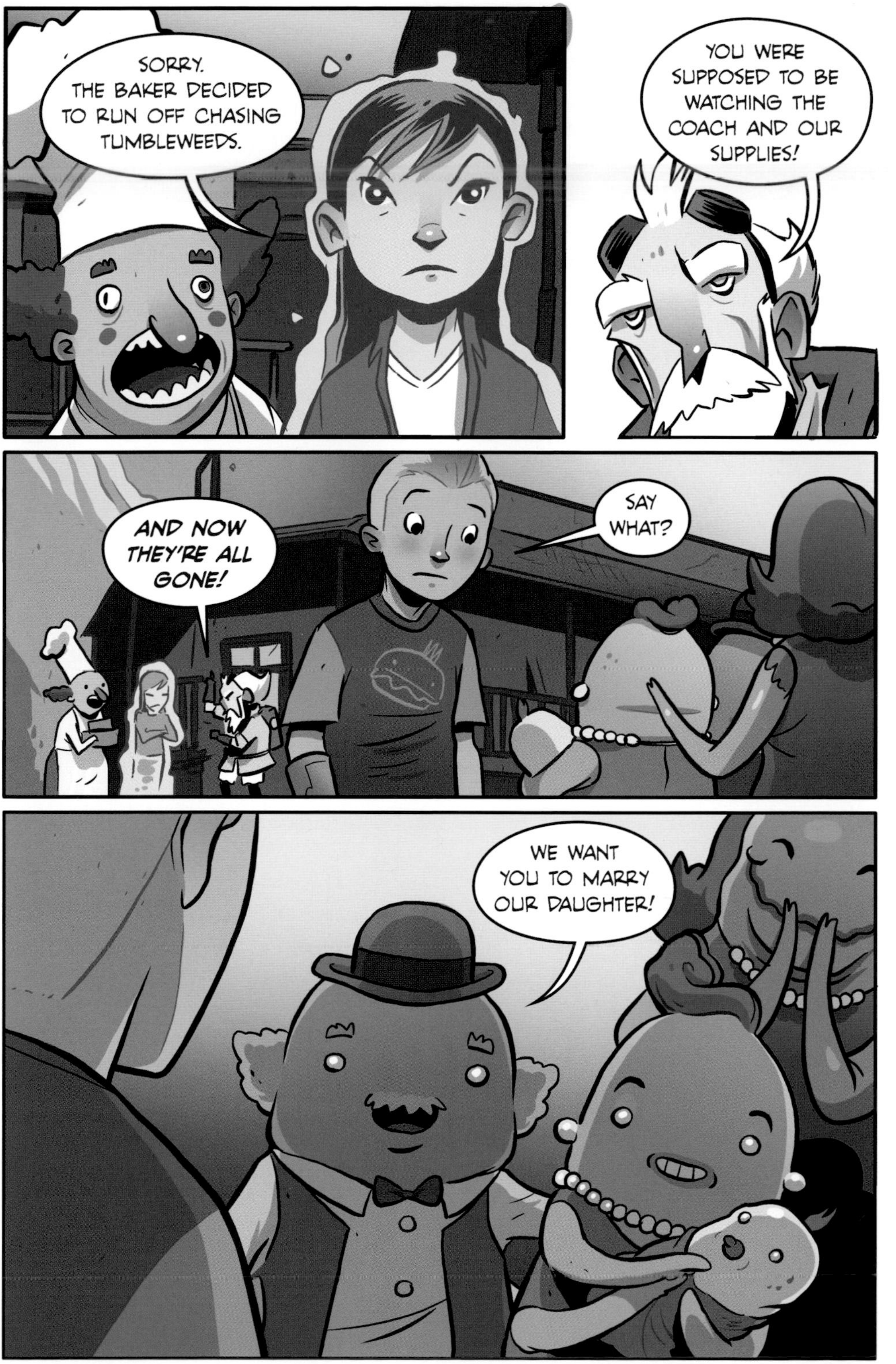
SORRY. THE BAKER DECIDED TO RUN OFF CHASING TUMBLEWEEDS.
YOU WERE SUPPOSED TO BE WATCHING THE COACH AND OUR SUPPLIES!
AND NOW THEY'RE ALL GONE!
SAY WHAT?
WE WANT YOU TO MARRY OUR DAUGHTER!

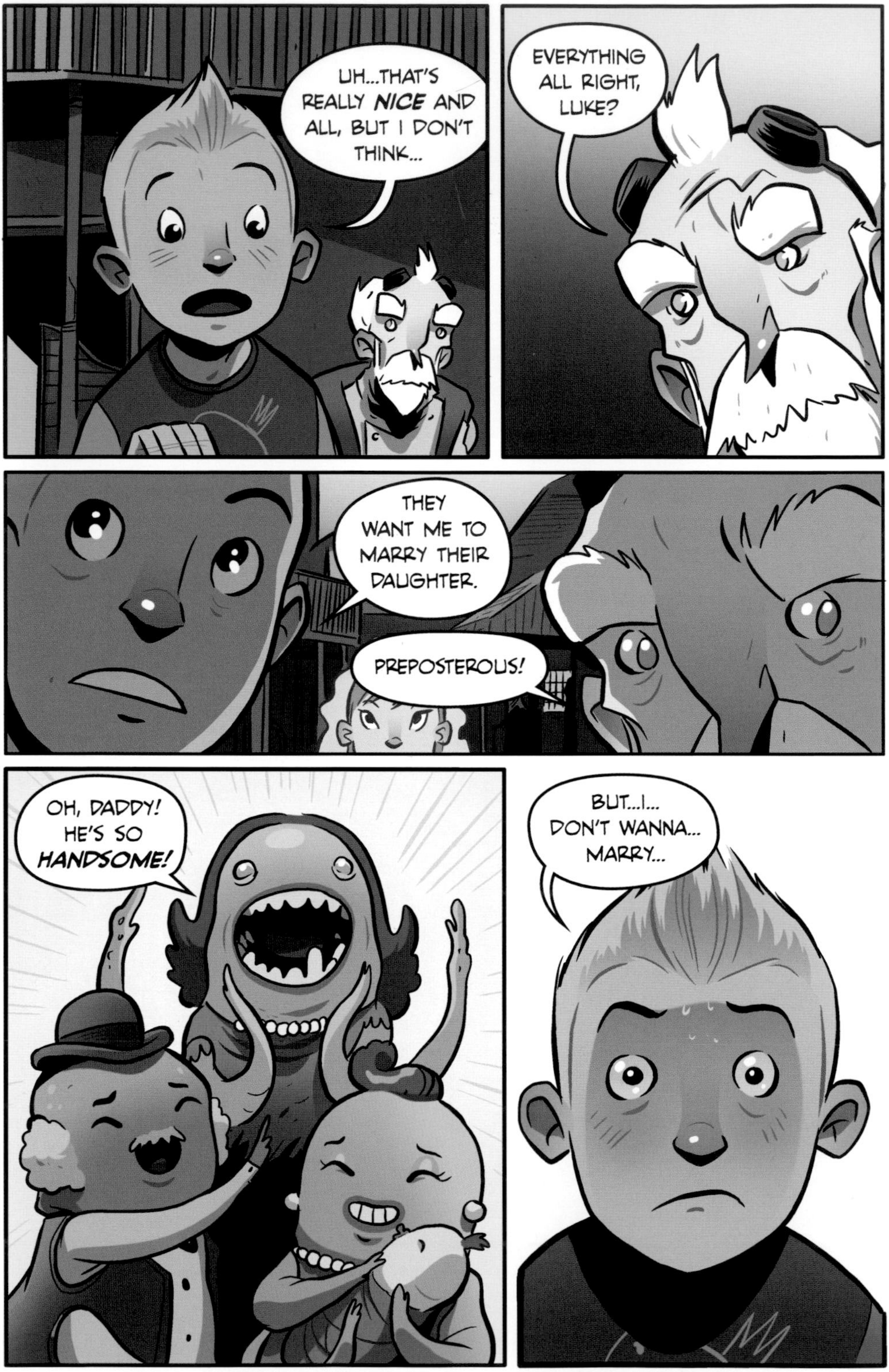
UH...THAT'S REALLY NICE AND ALL, BUT I DON'T THINK...
EVERYTHING ALL RIGHT, LUKE?
THEY WANT ME TO MARRY THEIR DAUGHTER.
PREPOSTEROUS!
OH, DADDY! HE'S SO HANDSOME!
BUT...I... DON'T WANNA... MARRY...

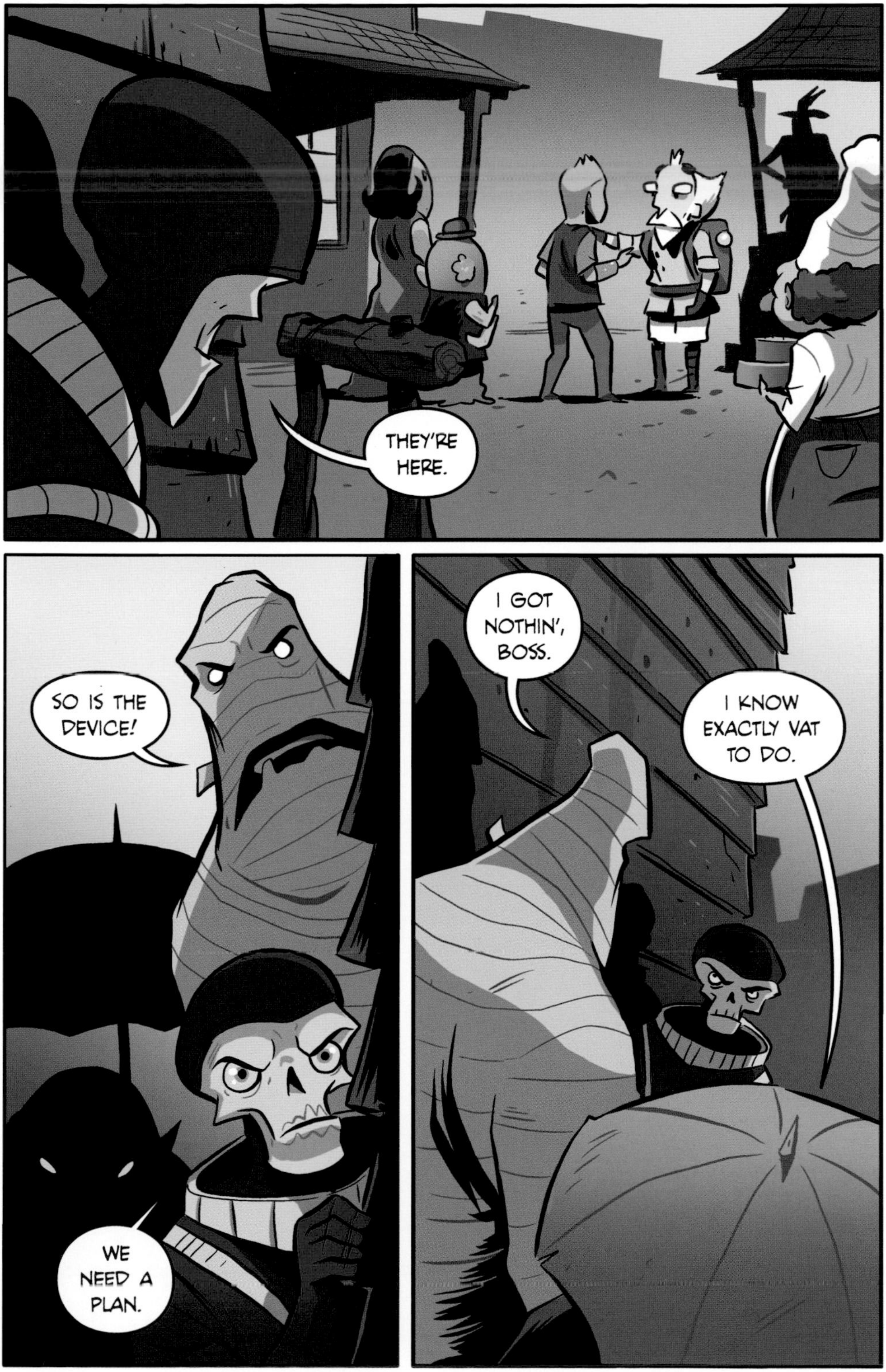
THEY'RE HERE.
SO IS THE DEVICE!
WE NEED A PLAN.
I GOT NOTHIN', BOSS.
I KNOW EXACTLY VAT TO DO.

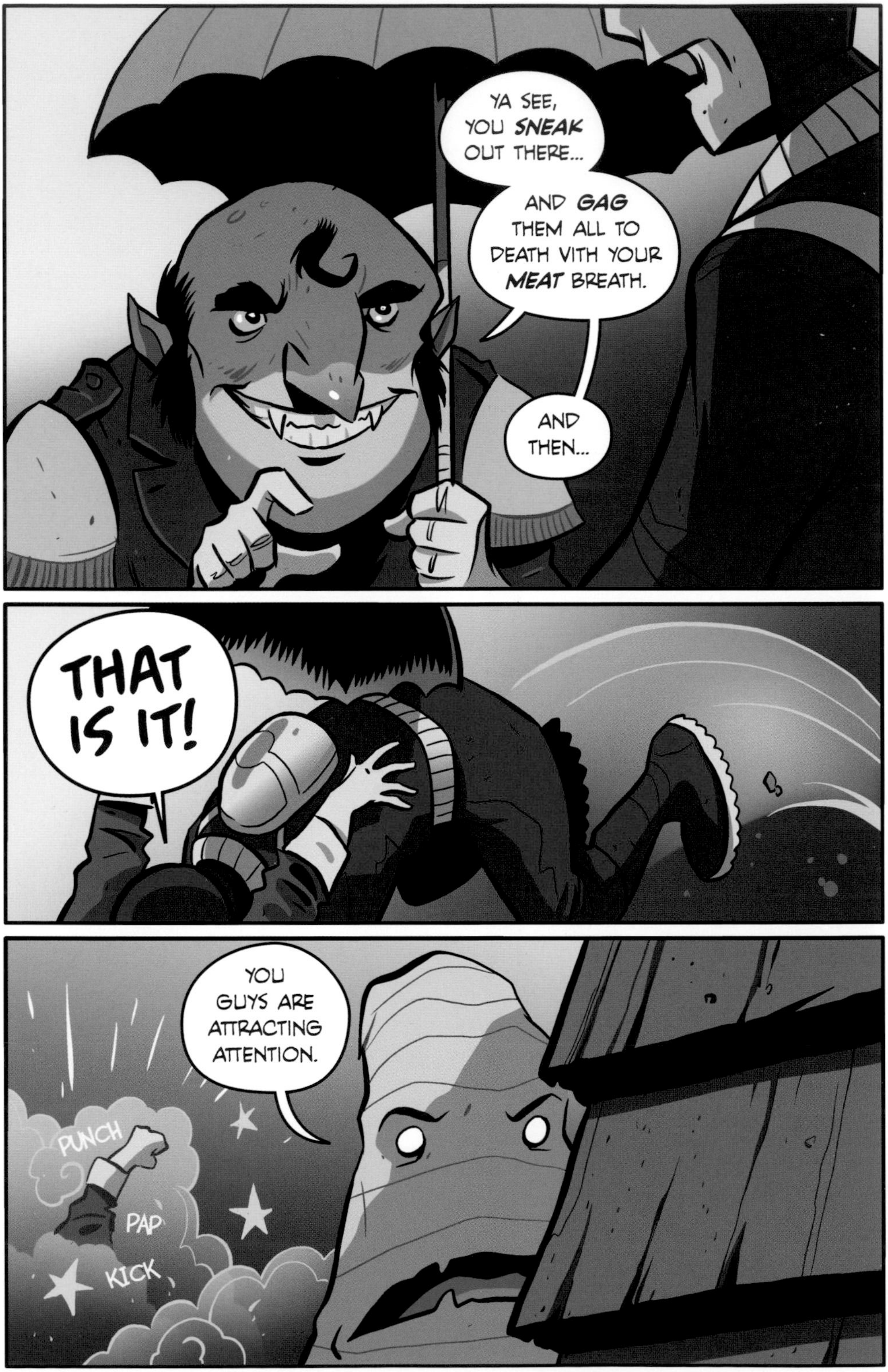
YA SEE, YOU SNEAK OUT THERE...
AND GAG THEM ALL TO DEATH VITH YOUR MEAT BREATH.
AND THEN...
THAT IS IT!
YOU GUYS ARE ATTRACTING ATTENTION.
PUNCH
PAP
KICK

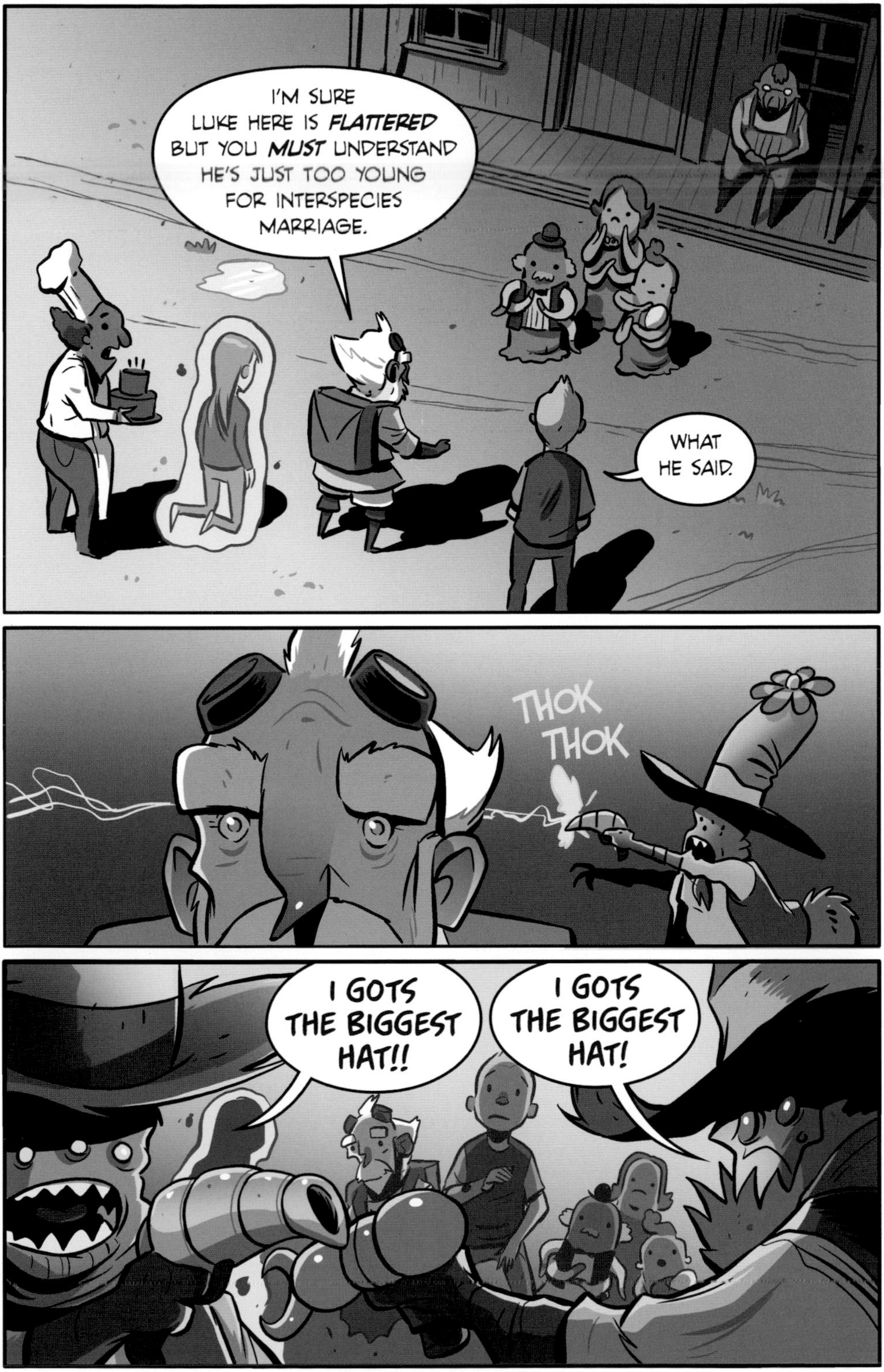
I'M SURE LUKE HERE IS FLATTERED BUT YOU MUST UNDERSTAND HE'S JUST TOO YOUNG FOR INTERSPECIES MARRIAGE.
WHAT HE SAID.
THOK THOK
I GOTS THE BIGGEST HAT!!
I GOTS THE BIGGEST HAT!

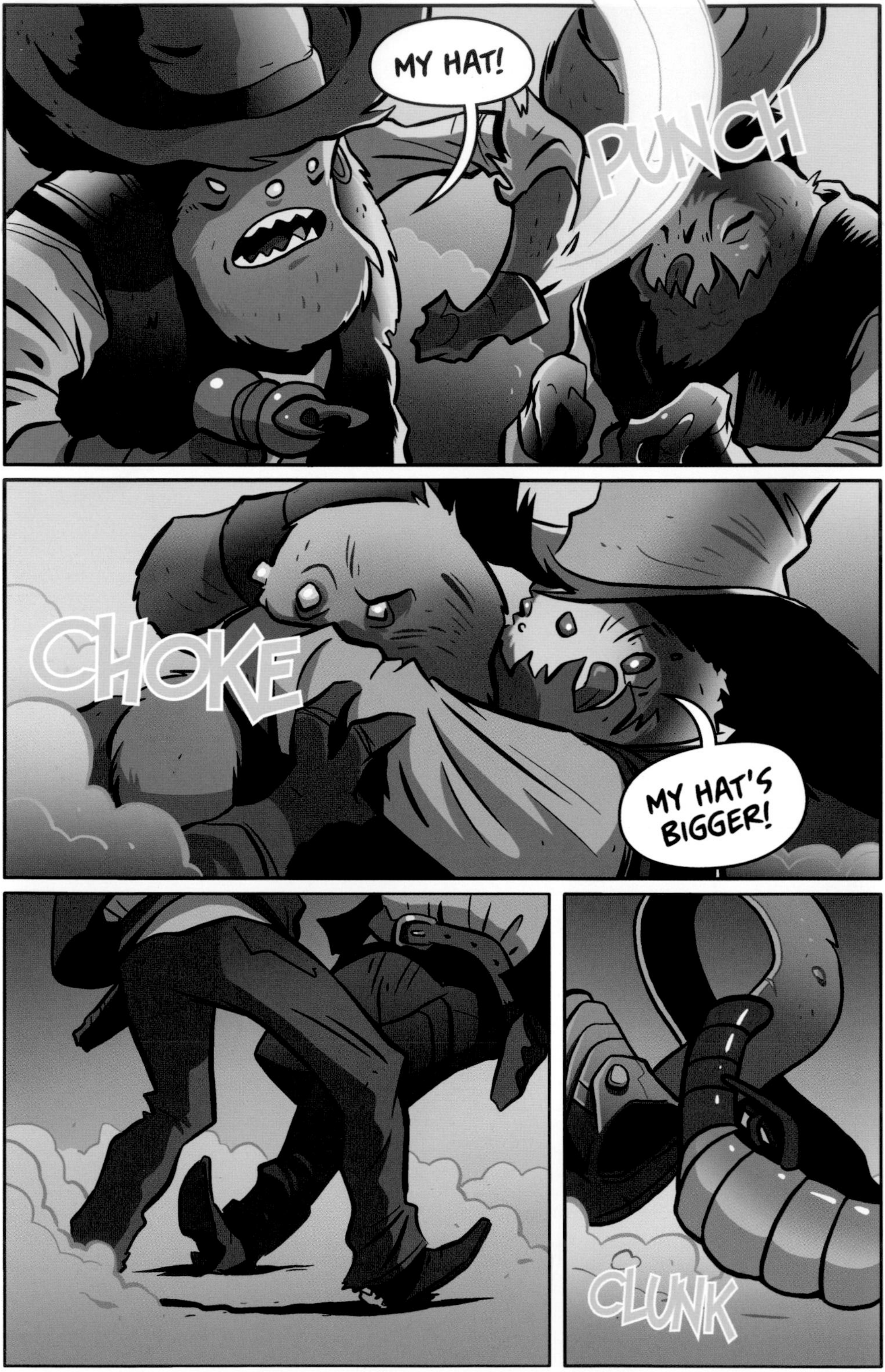
MY HAT!
PUNCH
CHOKE
MY HAT'S BIGGER!
CLUNK

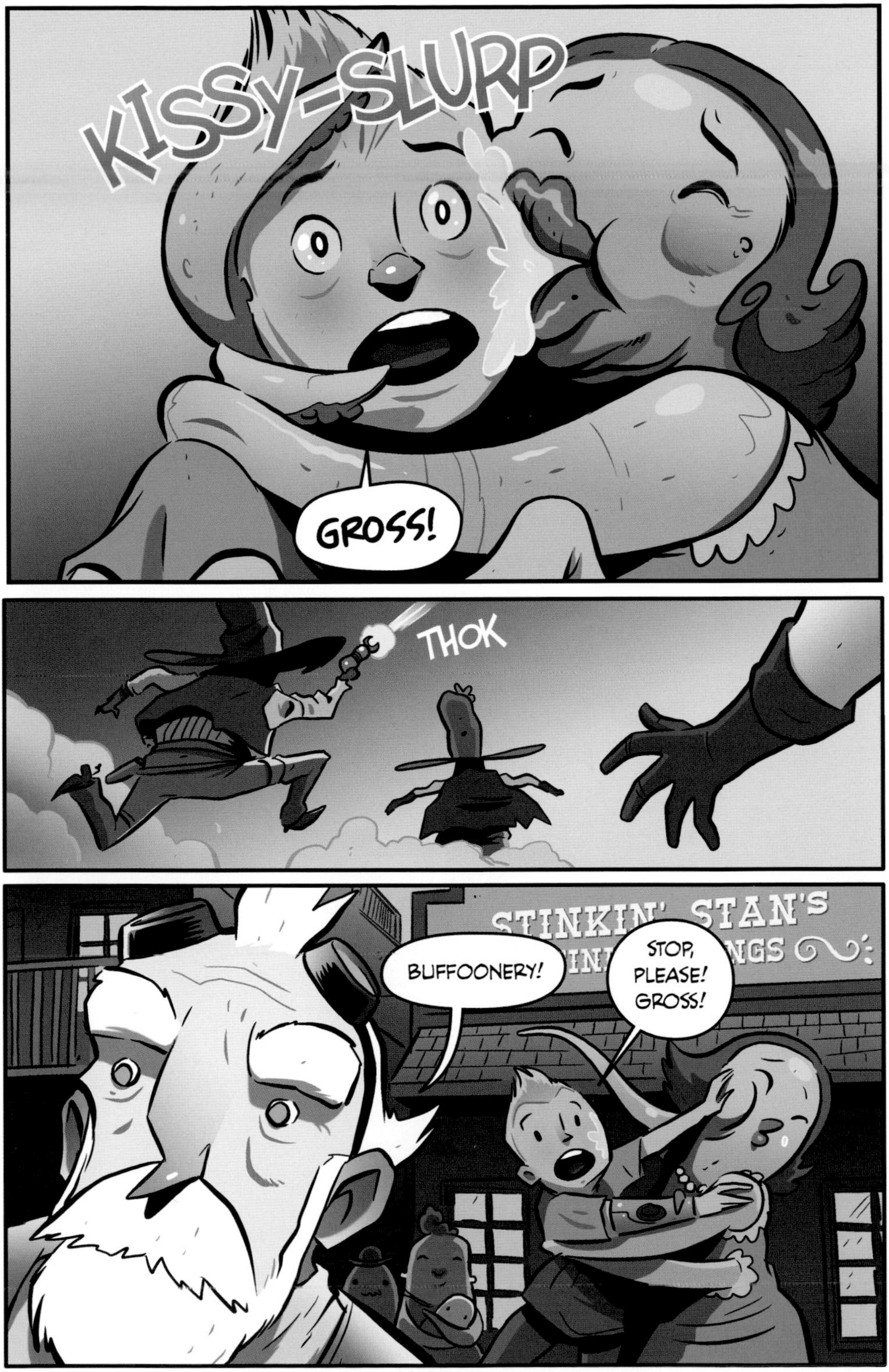
KISSY-SLURP
GROSS!
THOK
STINKIN' STAN'S
BUFFOONERY!
STOP, PLEASE! GROSS!

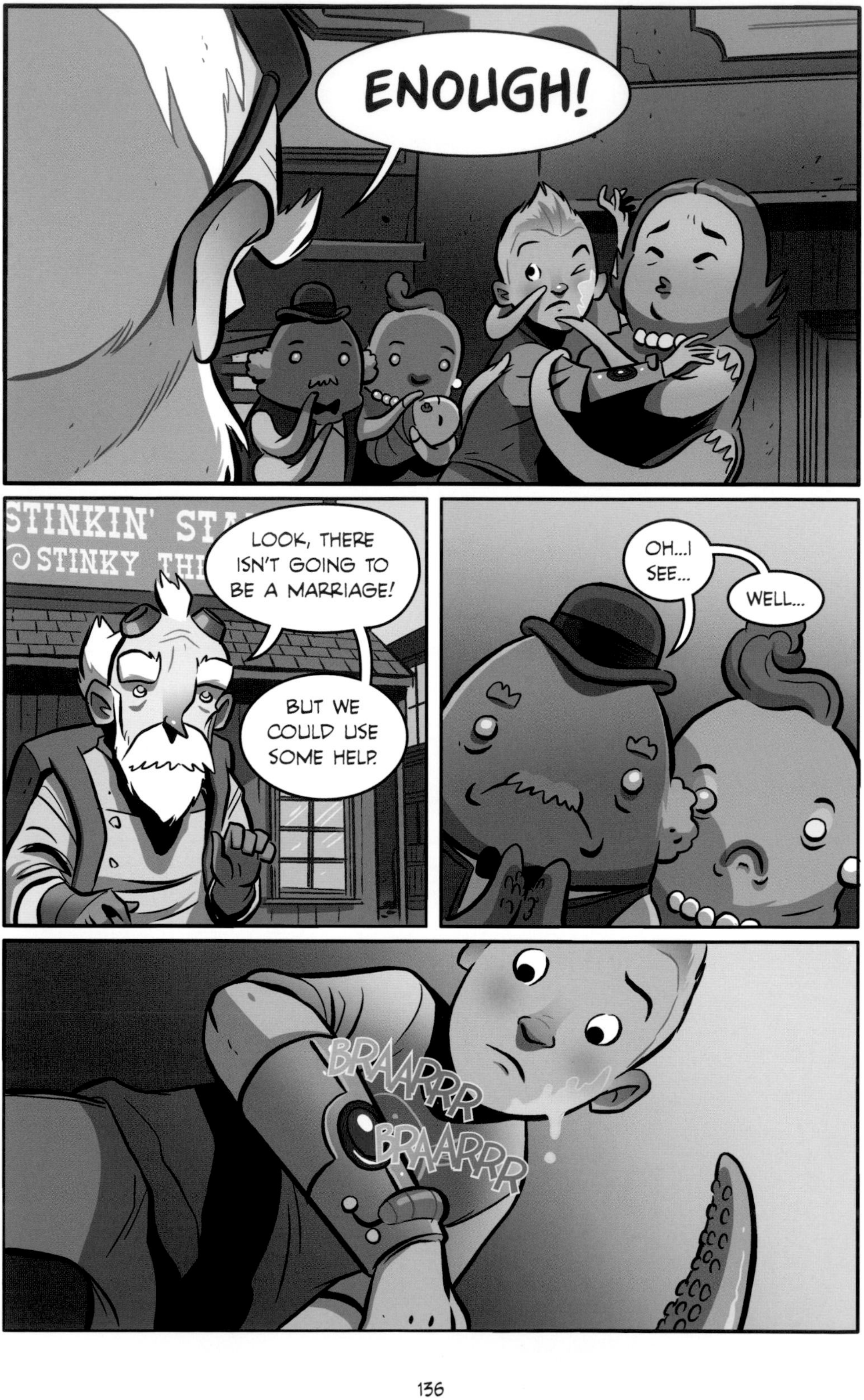
ENOUGH!
STINKIN' STA
STINKY THI
LOOK, THERE ISN'T GOING TO BE A MARRIAGE!
BUT WE COULD USE SOME HELP.
OH...I SEE...
WELL...
BRAARRRR
BRAARRRR

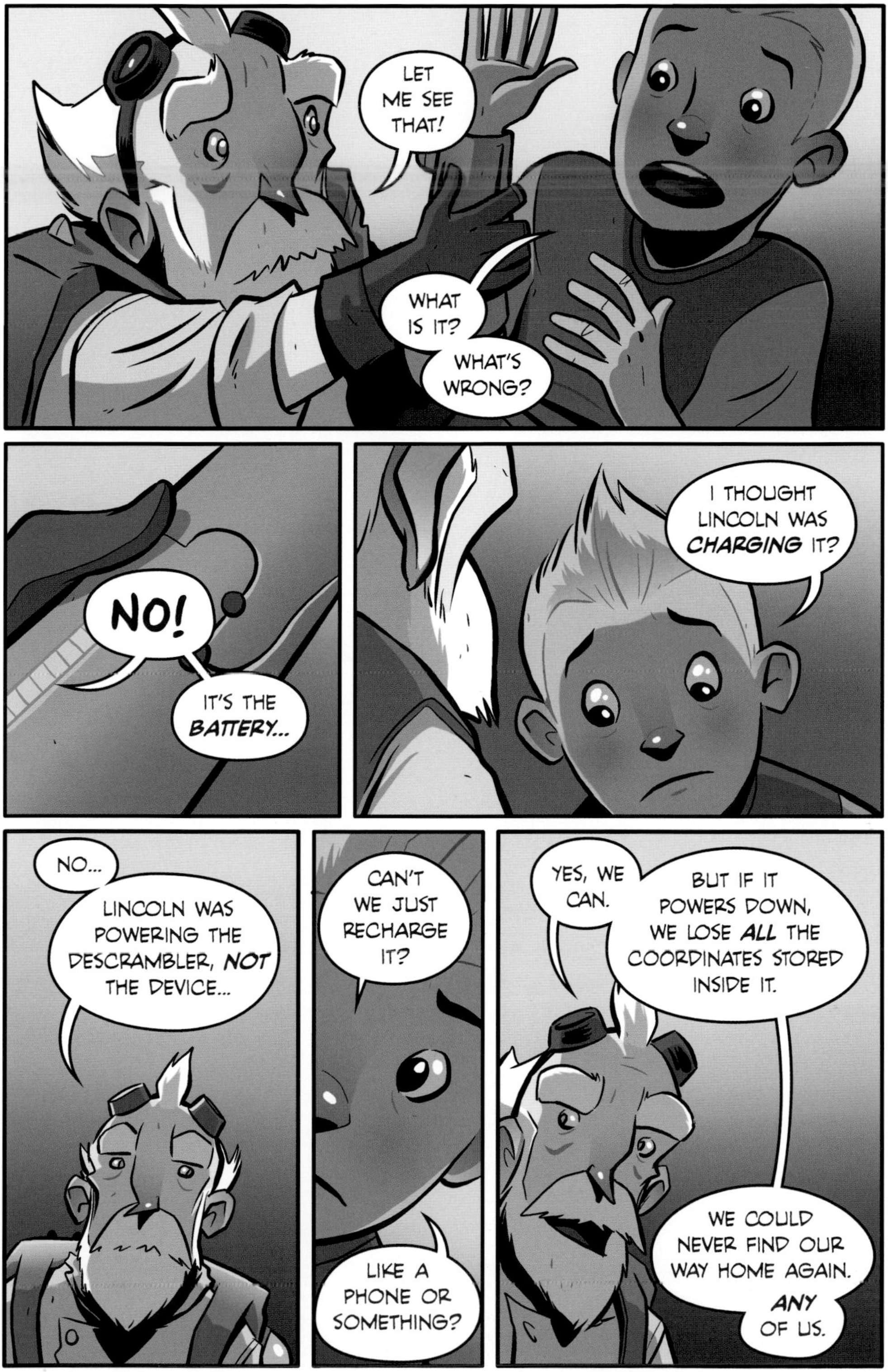
LET ME SEE THAT!
WHAT IS IT?
WHAT'S WRONG?
NO!
IT'S THE *BATTERY...*
I THOUGHT LINCOLN WAS *CHARGING* IT?
NO...
LINCOLN WAS POWERING THE DESCRAMBLER, *NOT* THE DEVICE...
CAN'T WE JUST RECHARGE IT?
LIKE A PHONE OR SOMETHING?
YES, WE CAN.
BUT IF IT POWERS DOWN, WE LOSE *ALL* THE COORDINATES STORED INSIDE IT.
WE COULD NEVER FIND OUR WAY HOME AGAIN.
ANY OF US.

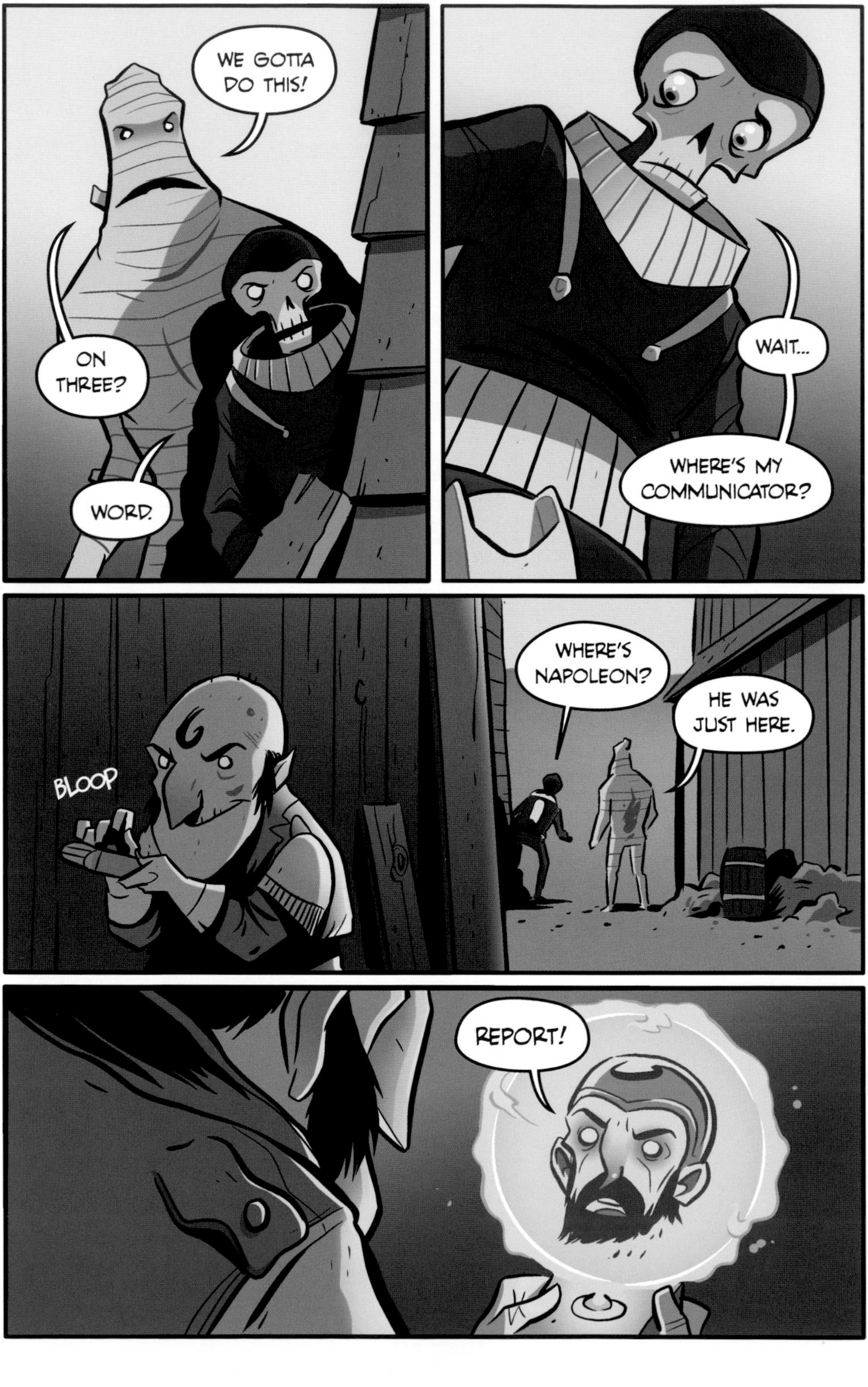
WE GOTTA DO THIS!
ON THREE?
WORD.
WAIT...
WHERE'S MY COMMUNICATOR?
BLOOP
WHERE'S NAPOLEON?
HE WAS JUST HERE.
REPORT!

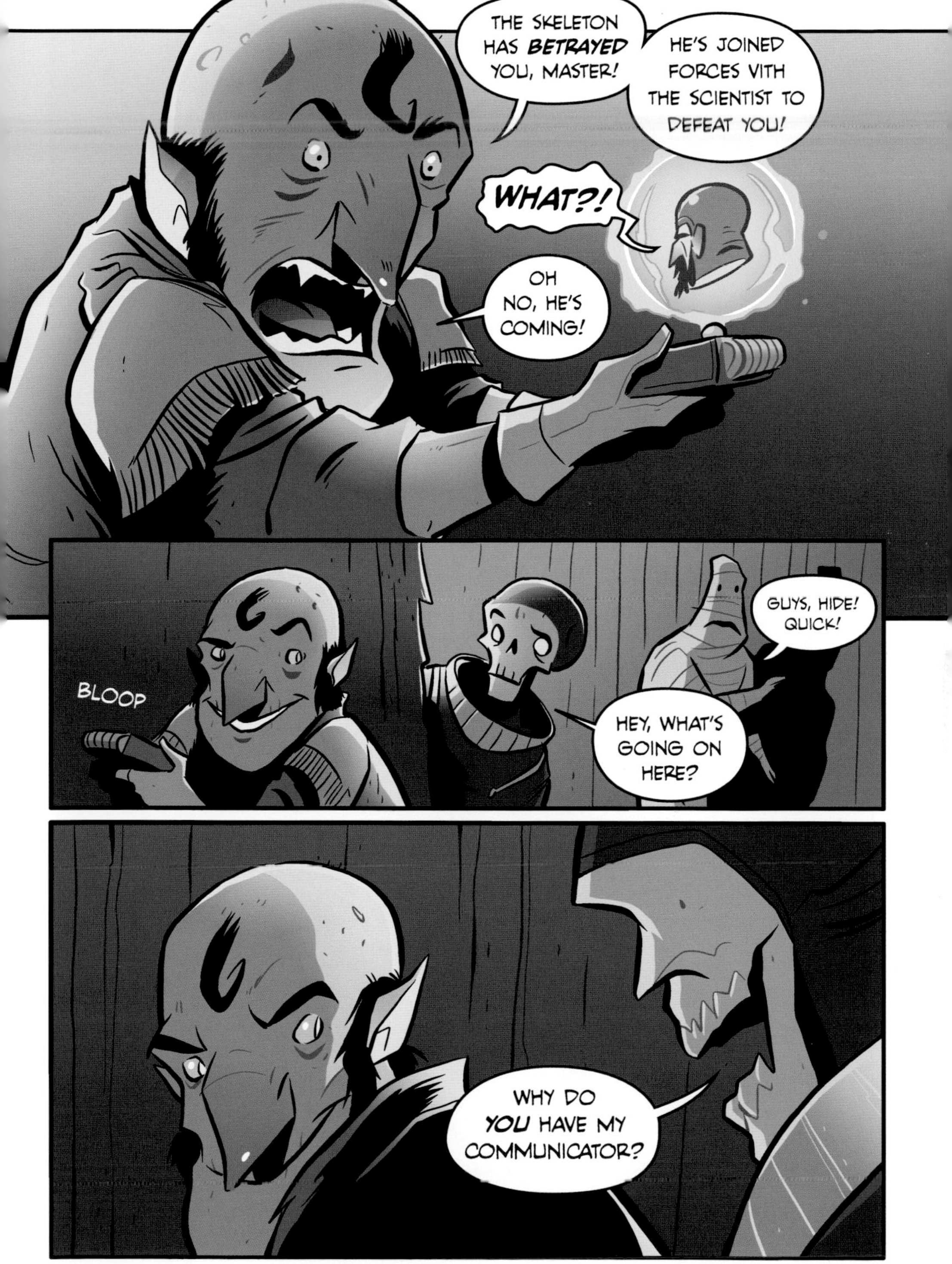
THE SKELETON HAS BETRAYED YOU, MASTER!
HE'S JOINED FORCES VITH THE SCIENTIST TO DEFEAT YOU!
WHAT?!
OH NO, HE'S COMING!
BLOOP
GUYS, HIDE! QUICK!
HEY, WHAT'S GOING ON HERE?
WHY DO YOU HAVE MY COMMUNICATOR?

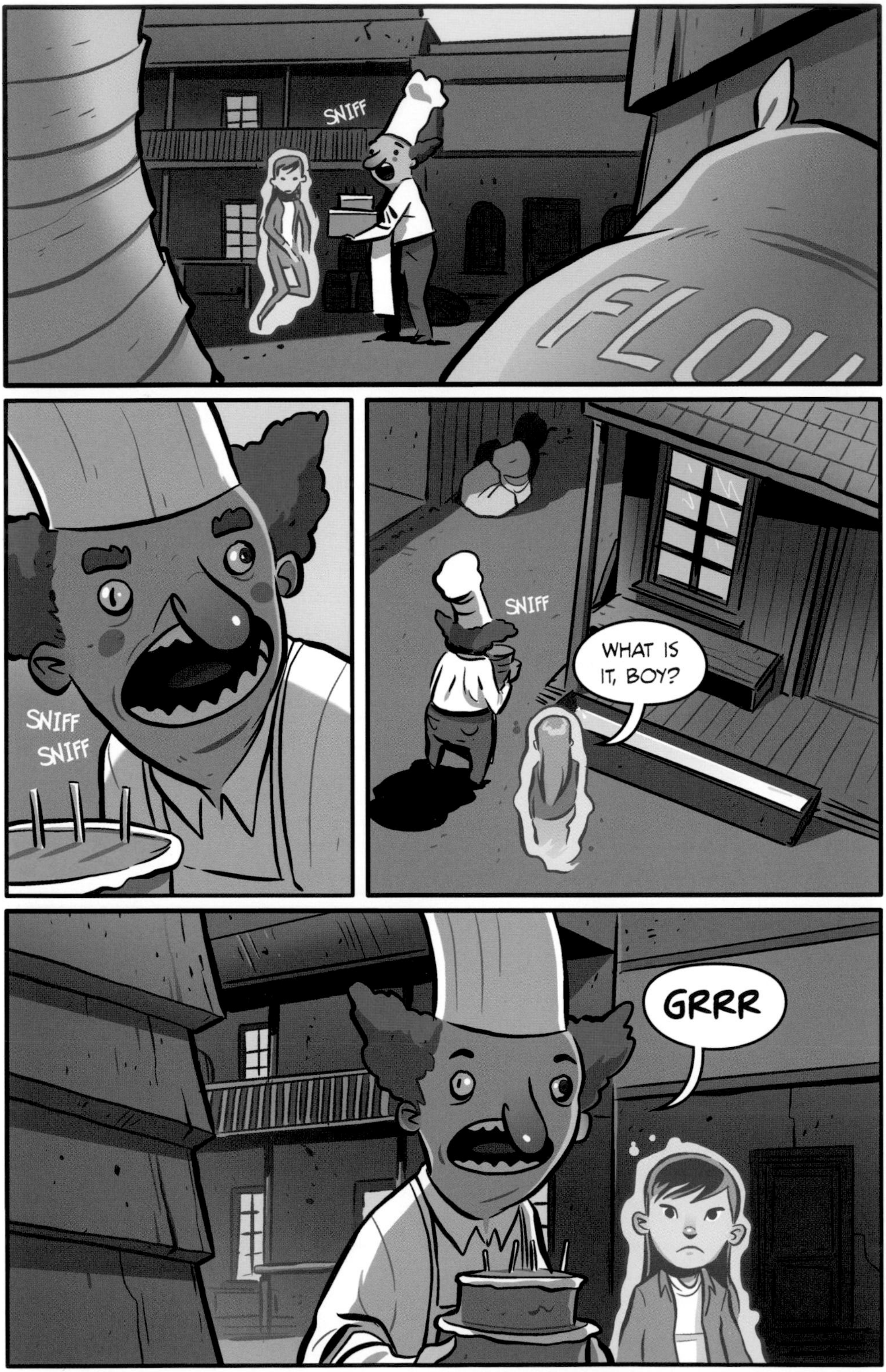
SNIFF
FLOU
SNIFF
SNIFF
SNIFF
WHAT IS IT, BOY?
GRRR

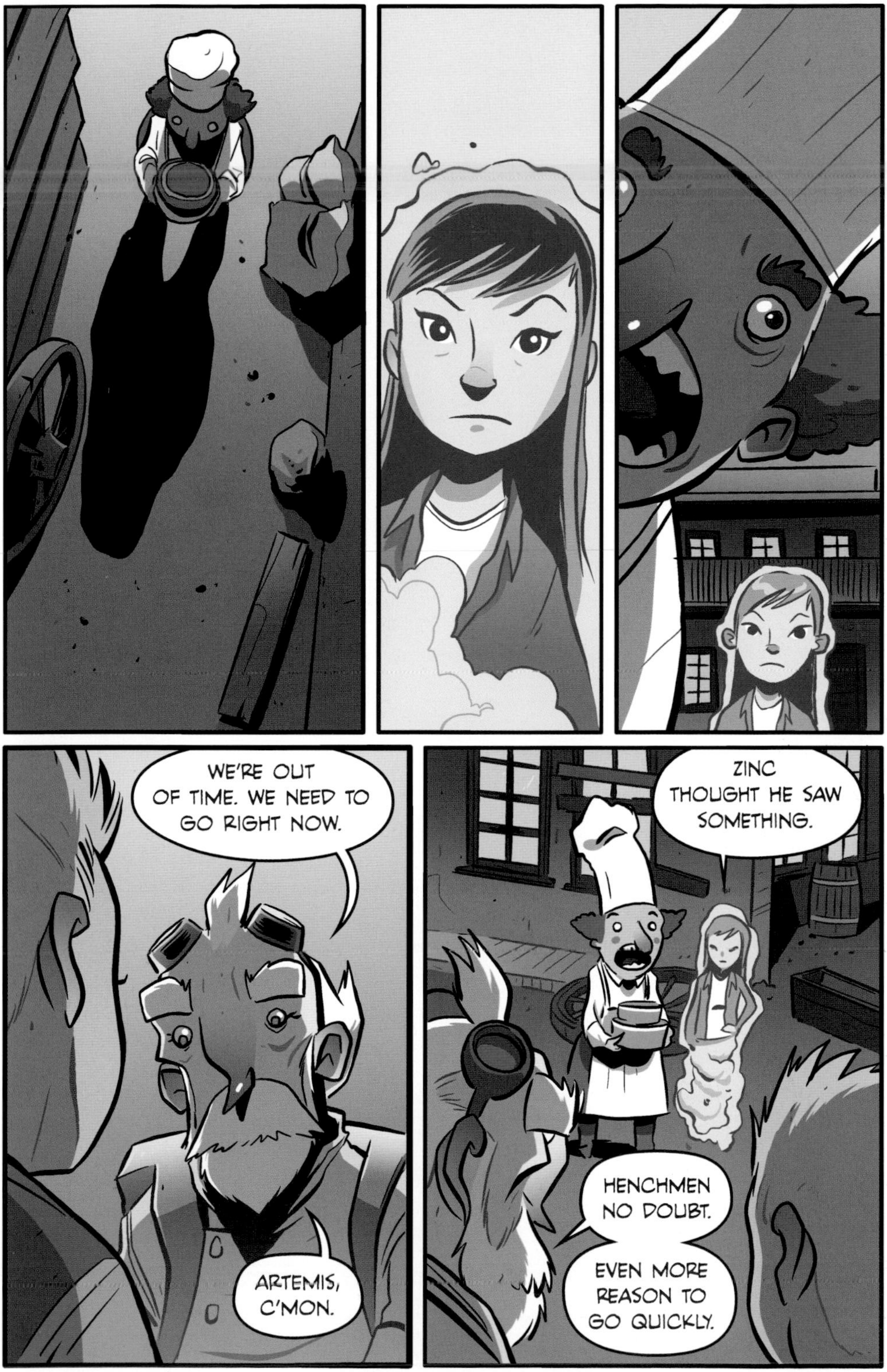
WE'RE OUT OF TIME. WE NEED TO GO RIGHT NOW.
ARTEMIS, C'MON.
ZINC THOUGHT HE SAW SOMETHING.
HENCHMEN NO DOUBT.
EVEN MORE REASON TO GO QUICKLY.

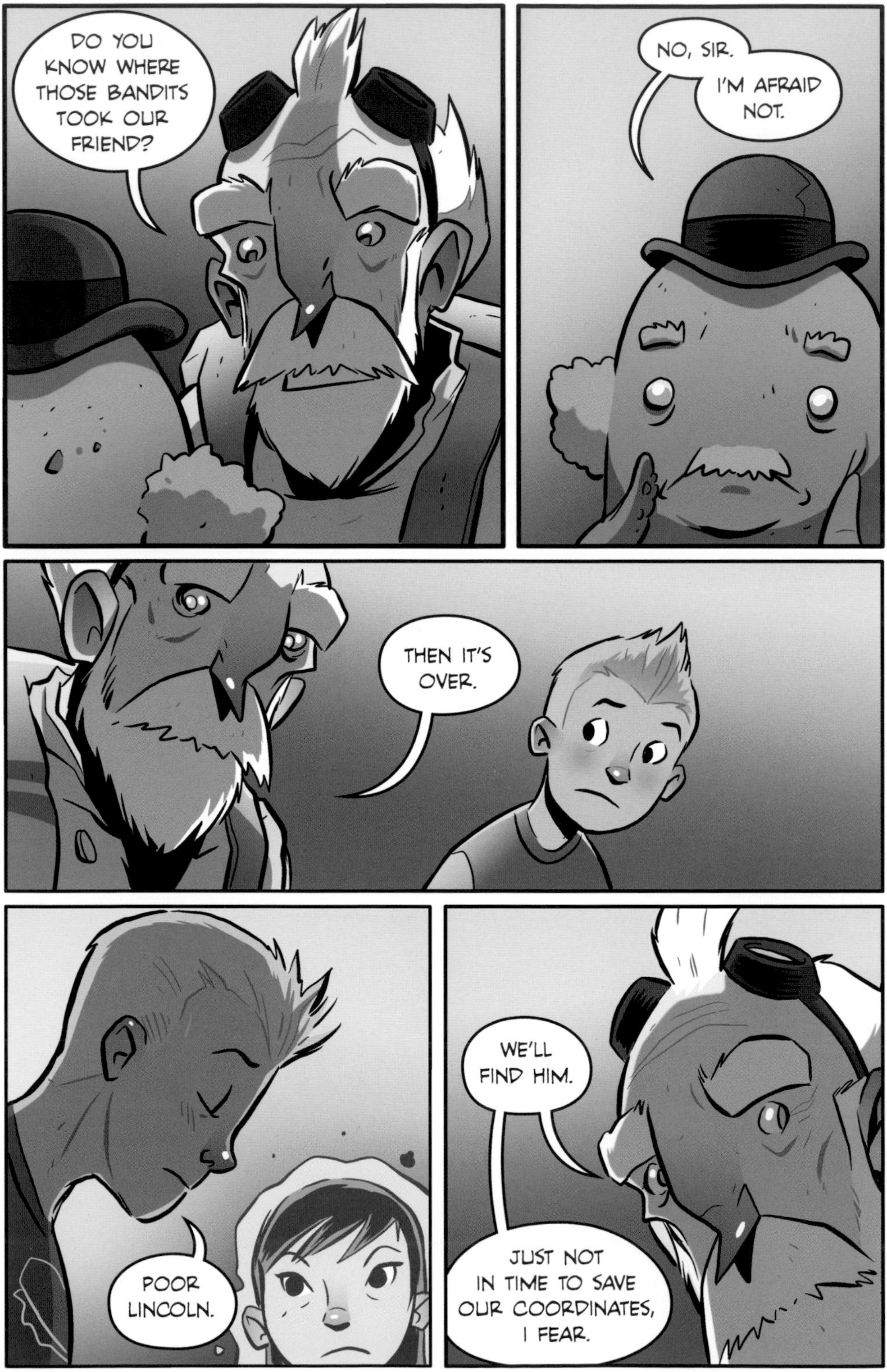
DO YOU KNOW WHERE THOSE BANDITS TOOK OUR FRIEND?
NO, SIR.
I'M AFRAID NOT.
THEN IT'S OVER.
POOR LINCOLN.
WE'LL FIND HIM.
JUST NOT IN TIME TO SAVE OUR COORDINATES, I FEAR.

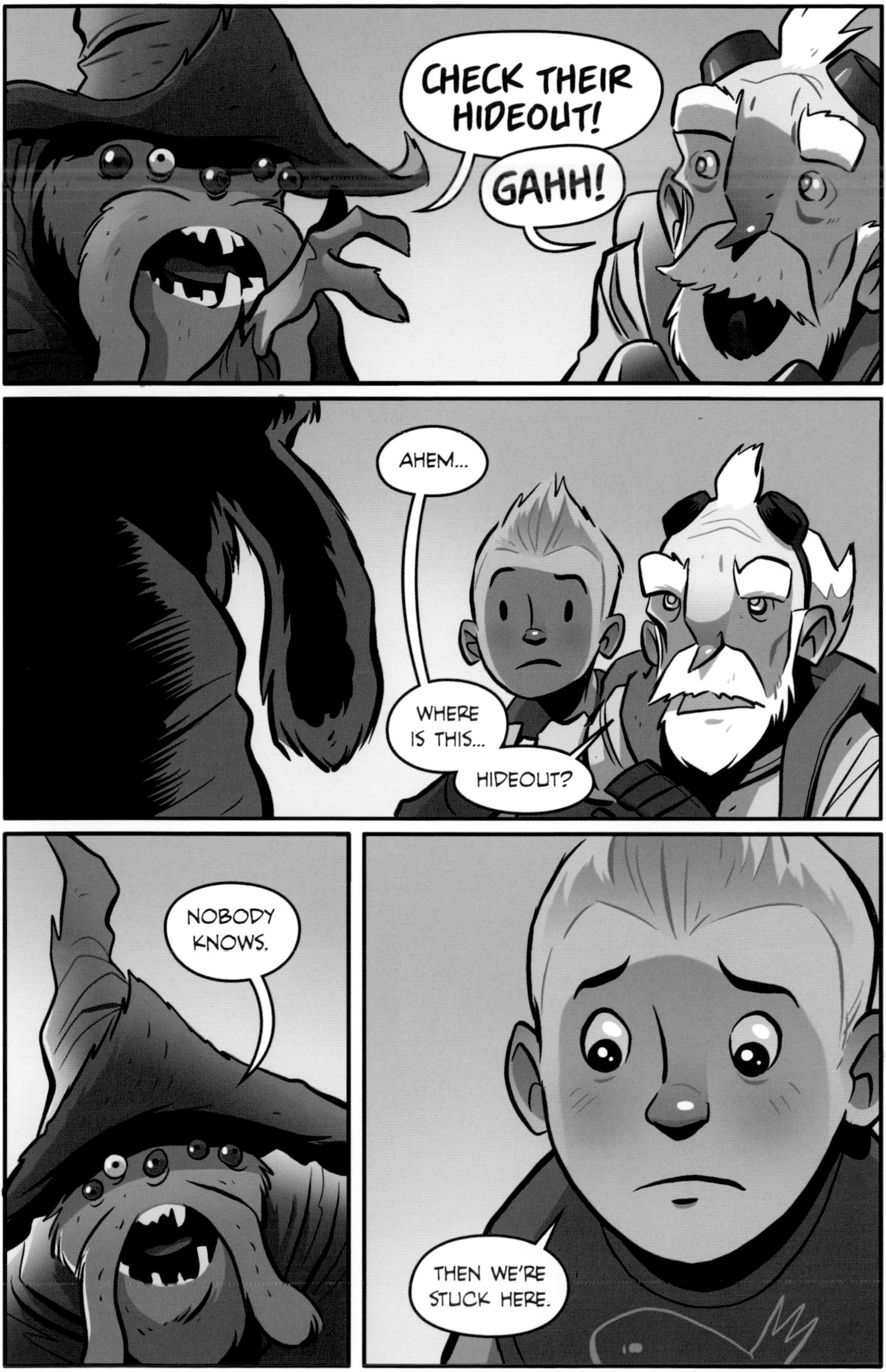
CHECK THEIR HIDEOUT!
GAHH!
AHEM...
WHERE IS THIS...
HIDEOUT?
NOBODY KNOWS.
THEN WE'RE STUCK HERE.

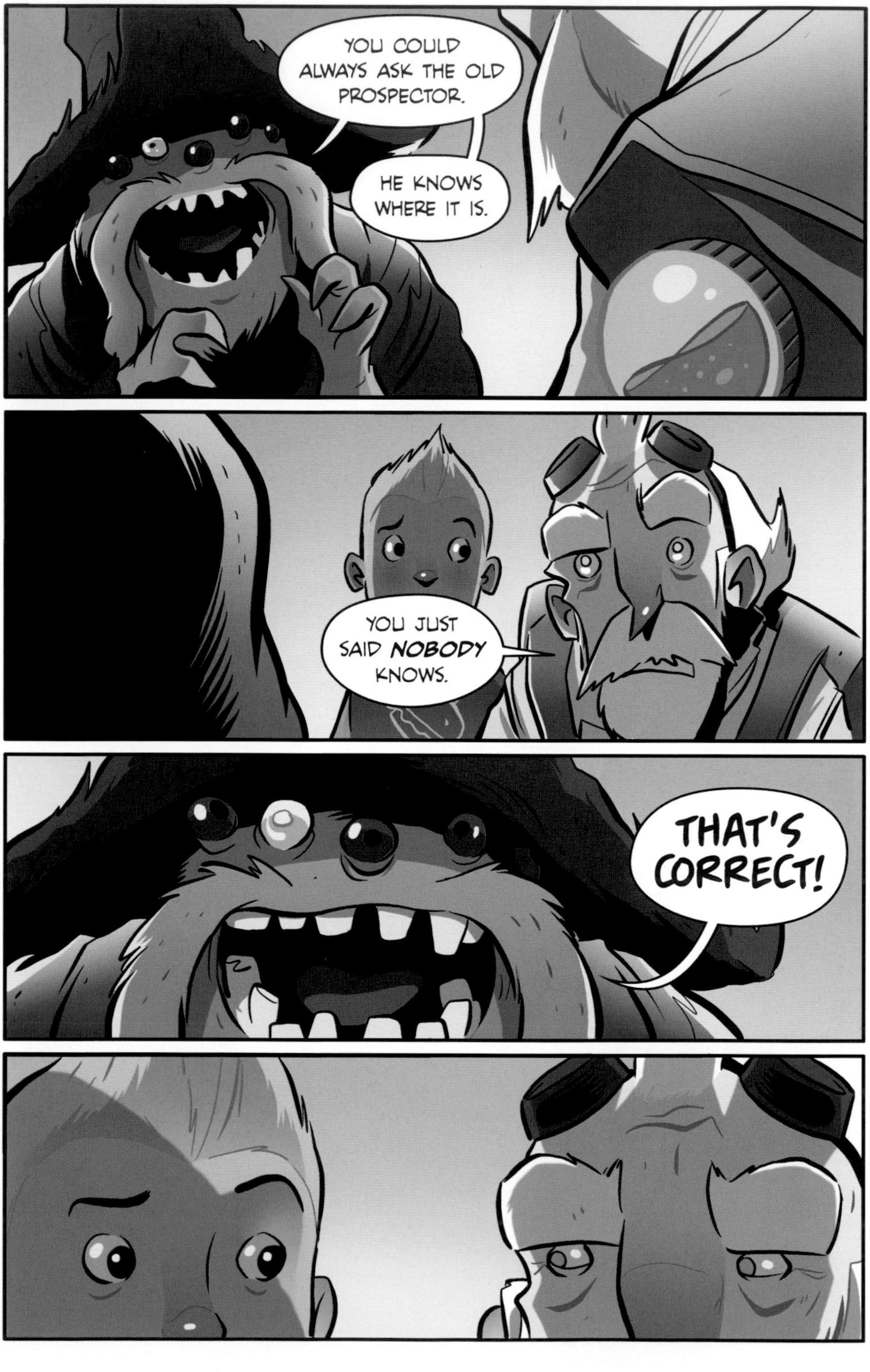
YOU COULD ALWAYS ASK THE OLD PROSPECTOR.
HE KNOWS WHERE IT IS.
YOU JUST SAID NOBODY KNOWS.
THAT'S CORRECT!

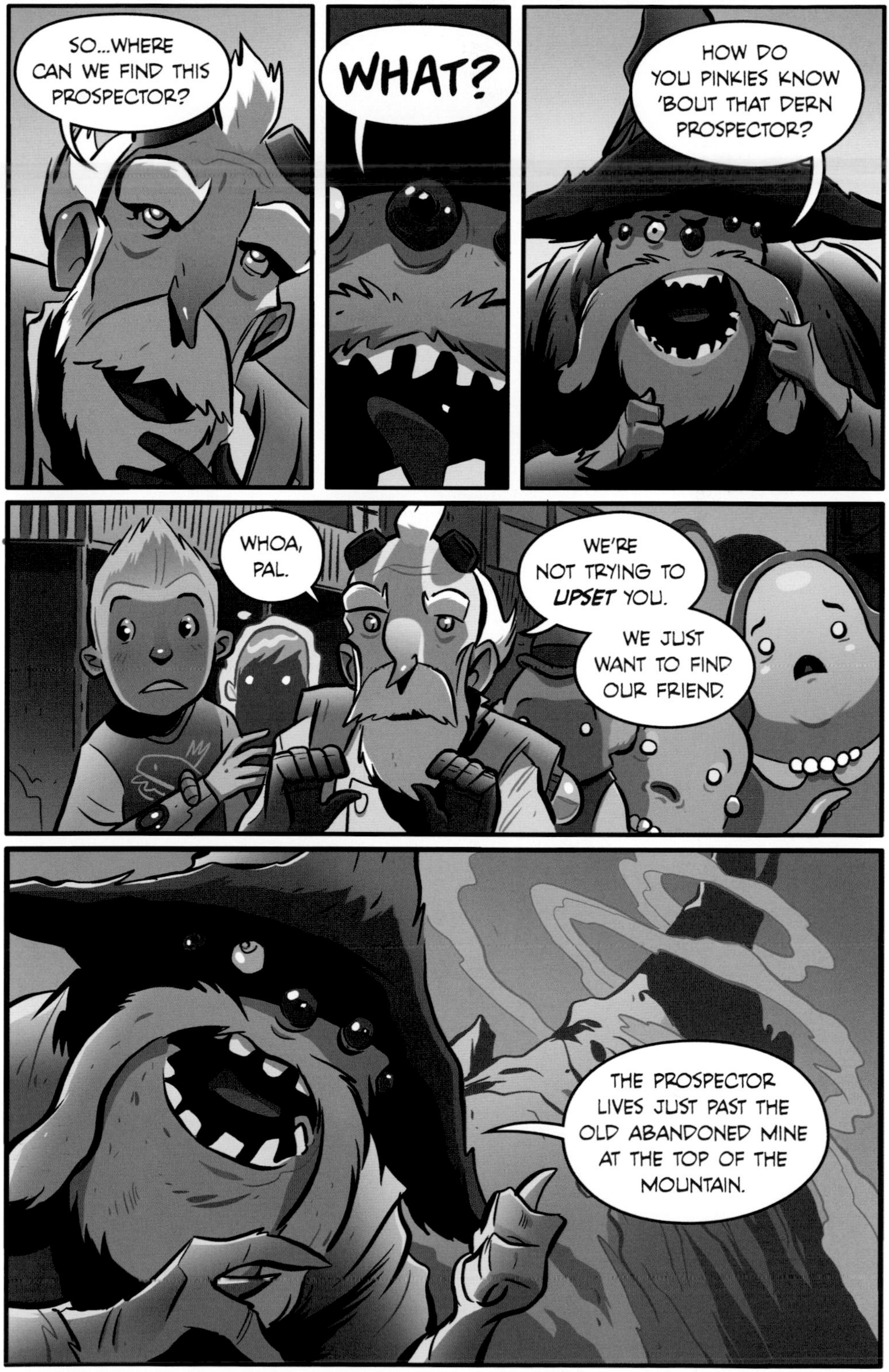
SO...WHERE CAN WE FIND THIS PROSPECTOR?
WHAT?
HOW DO YOU PINKIES KNOW 'BOUT THAT DERN PROSPECTOR?
WHOA, PAL.
WE'RE NOT TRYING TO UPSET YOU.
WE JUST WANT TO FIND OUR FRIEND.
THE PROSPECTOR LIVES JUST PAST THE OLD ABANDONED MINE AT THE TOP OF THE MOUNTAIN.

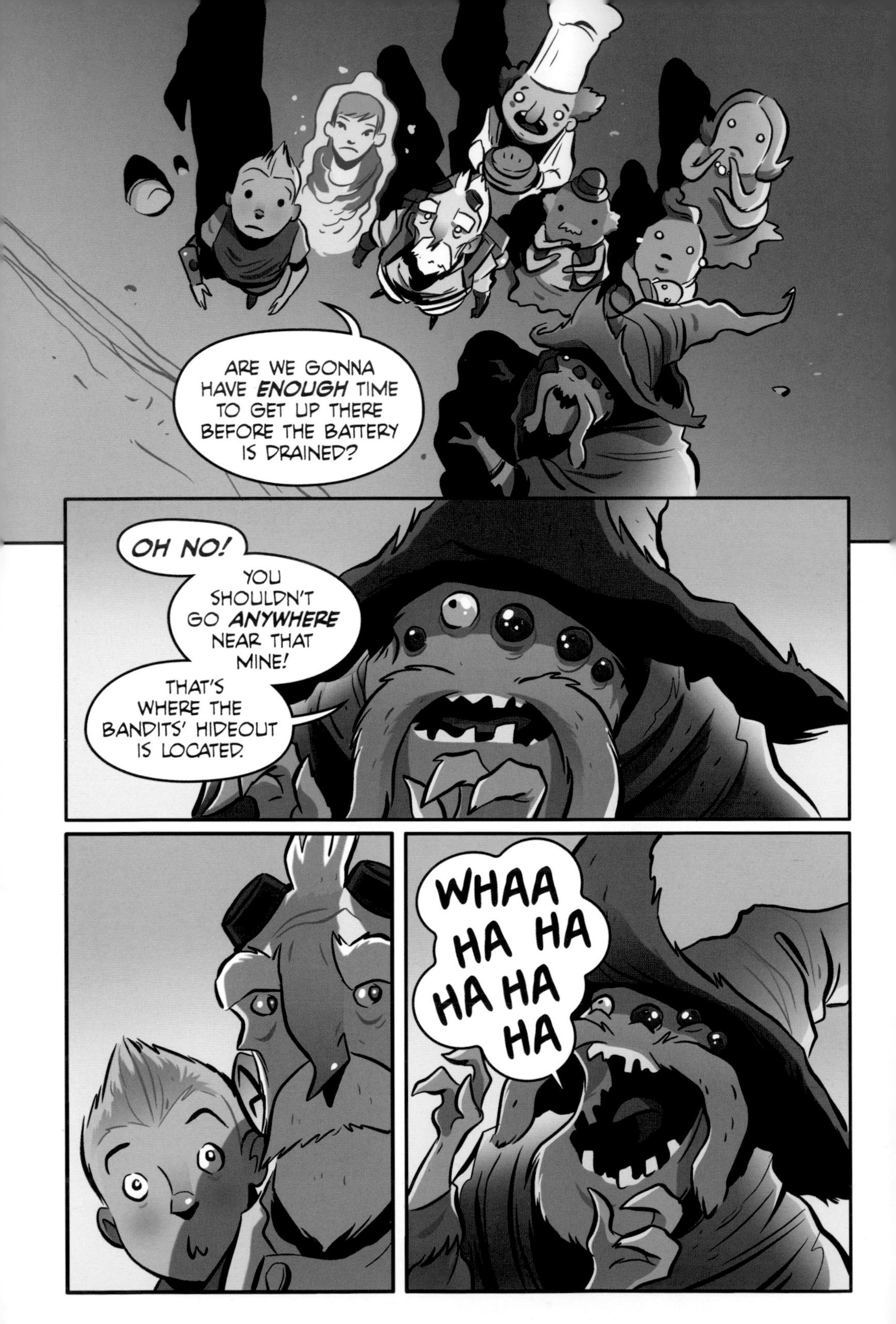
ARE WE GONNA HAVE ENOUGH TIME TO GET UP THERE BEFORE THE BATTERY IS DRAINED?
OH NO!
YOU SHOULDN'T GO ANYWHERE NEAR THAT MINE!
THAT'S WHERE THE BANDITS' HIDEOUT IS LOCATED.
WHAA HA HA HA HA HA

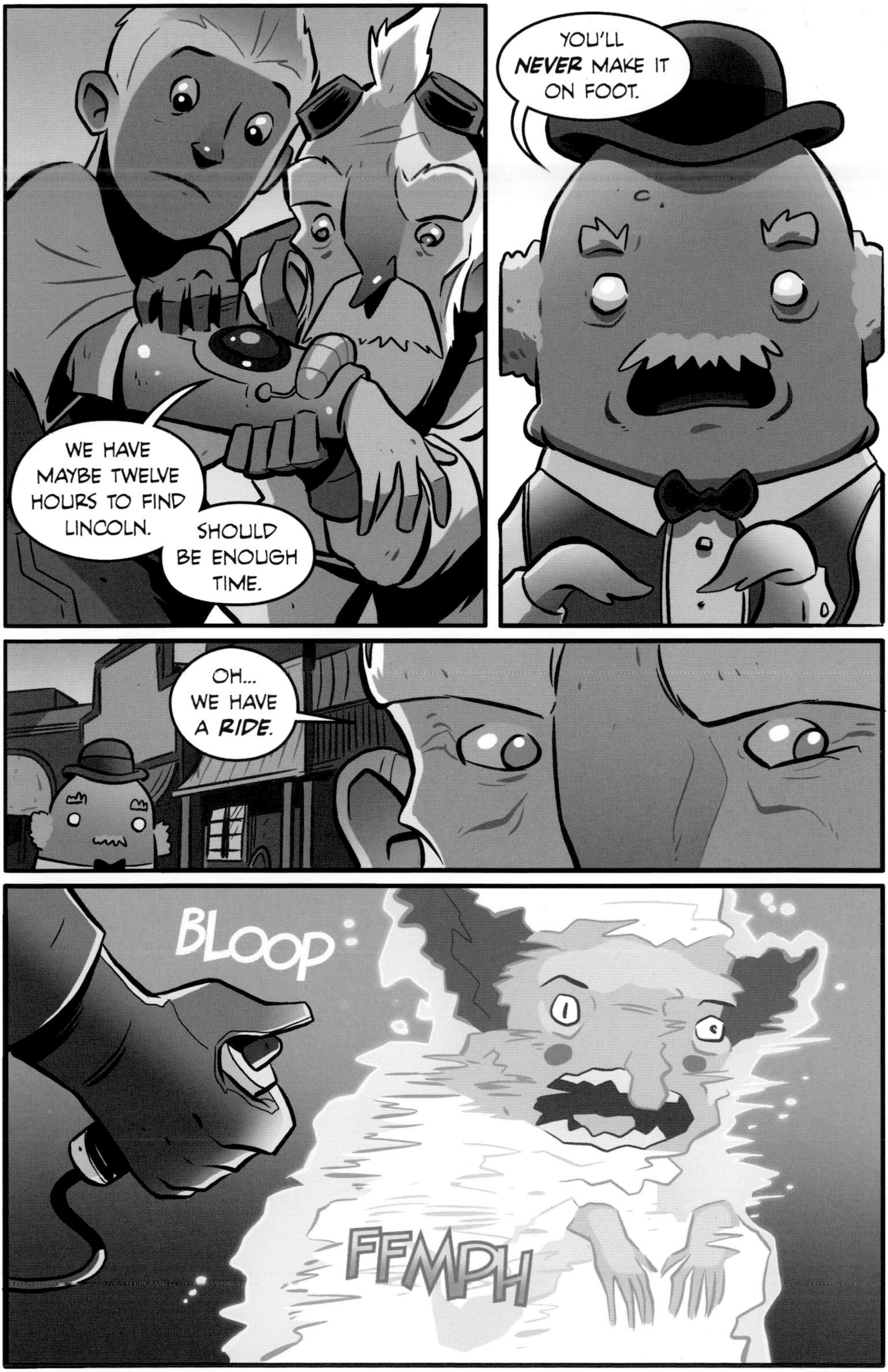
YOU'LL NEVER MAKE IT ON FOOT.
WE HAVE MAYBE TWELVE HOURS TO FIND LINCOLN.
SHOULD BE ENOUGH TIME.
OH... WE HAVE A RIDE.
BLOOP
FFMPH

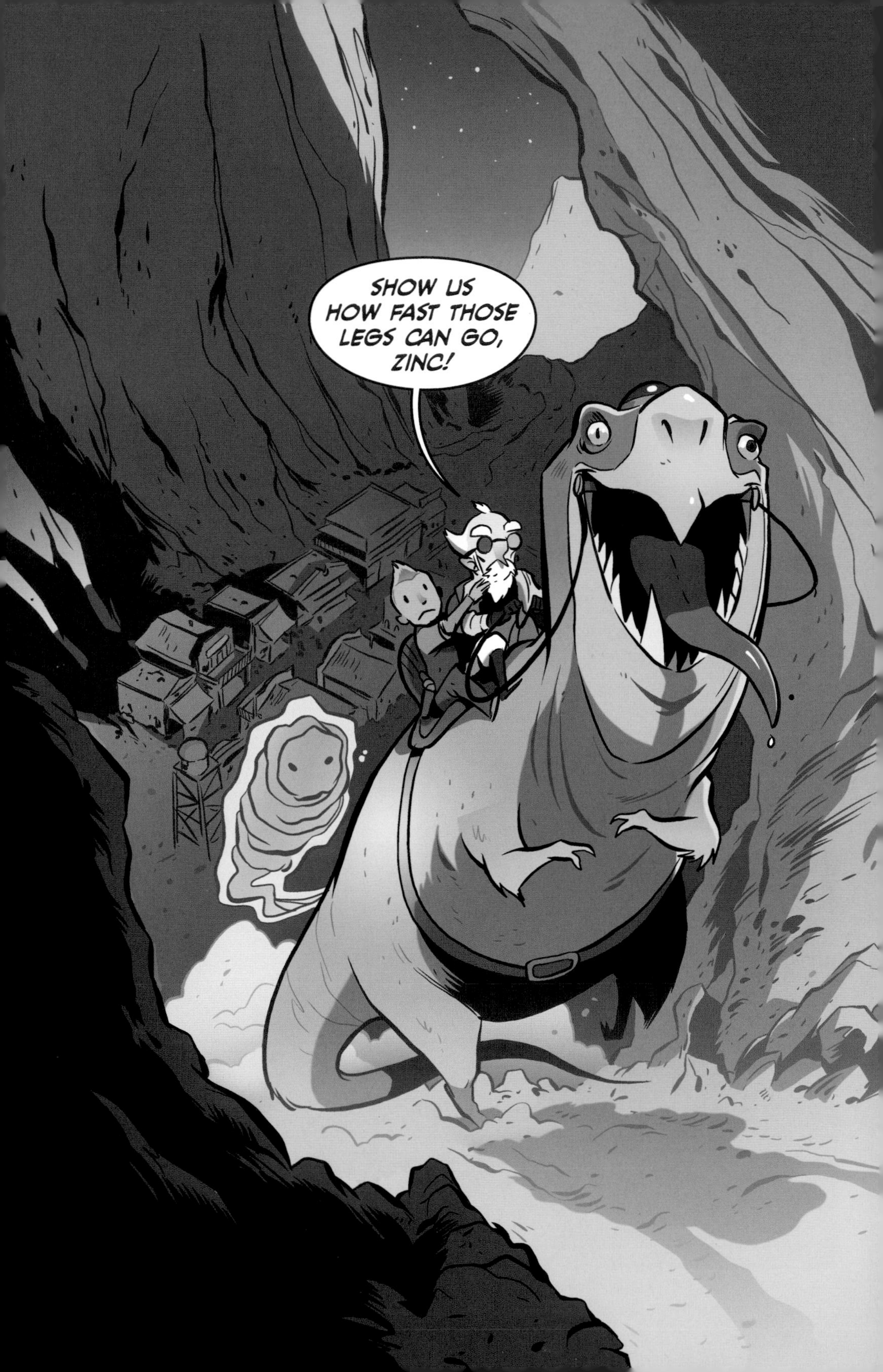
SHOW US HOW FAST THOSE LEGS CAN GO, ZINC!

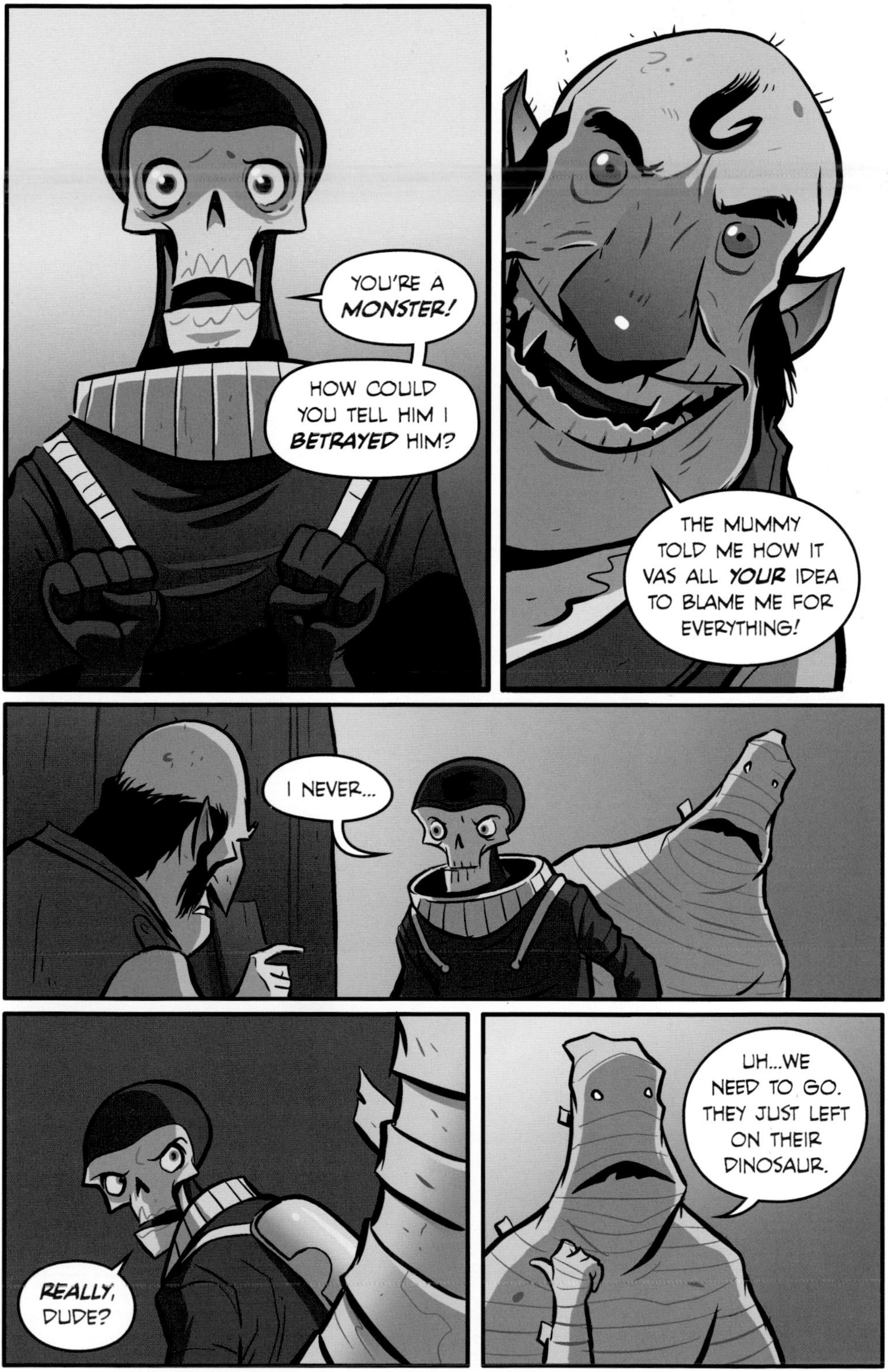
YOU'RE A MONSTER!
HOW COULD YOU TELL HIM I BETRAYED HIM?
THE MUMMY TOLD ME HOW IT VAS ALL YOUR IDEA TO BLAME ME FOR EVERYTHING!
I NEVER...
REALLY, DUDE?
UH...WE NEED TO GO. THEY JUST LEFT ON THEIR DINOSAUR.

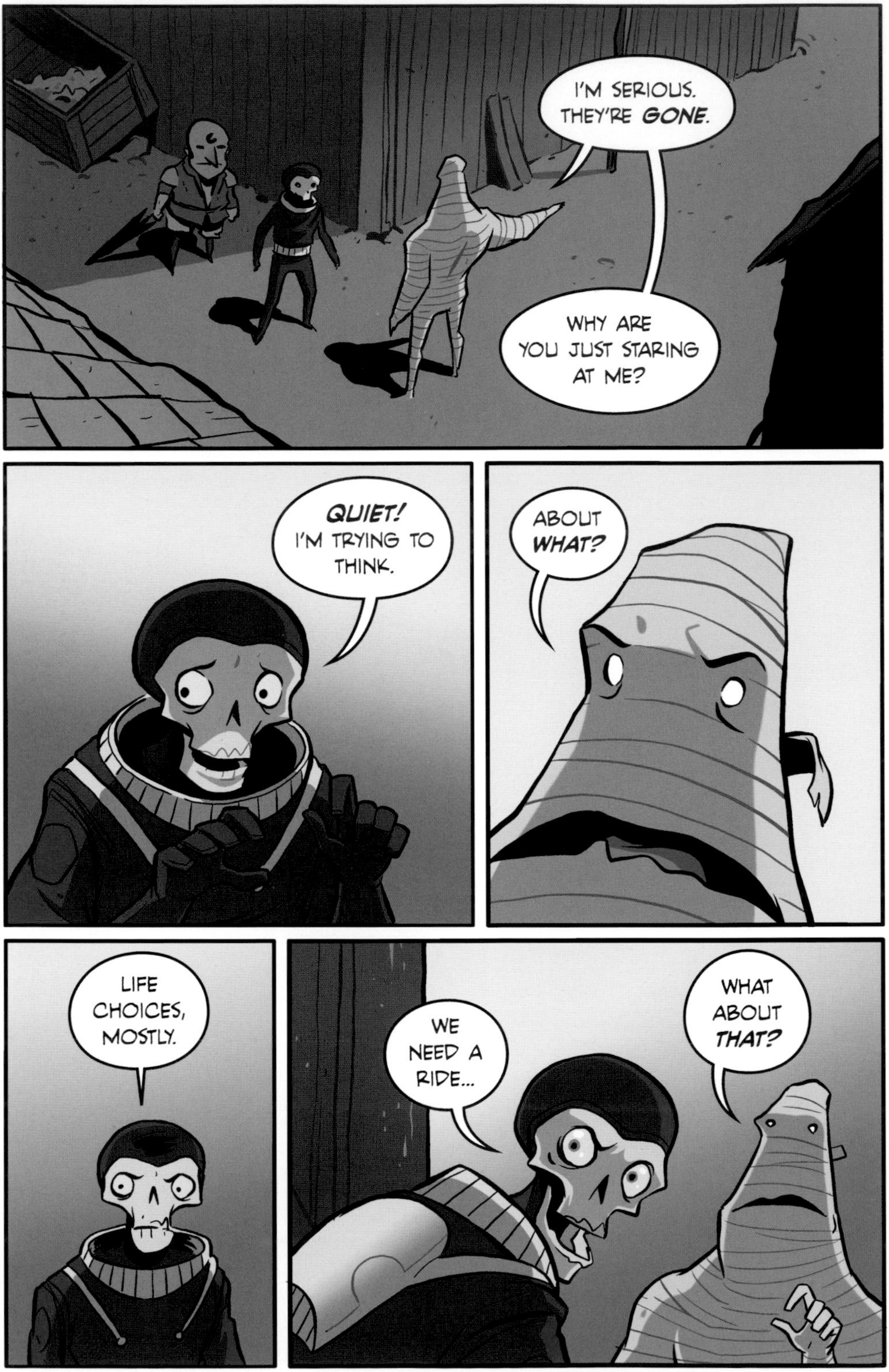
I'M SERIOUS. THEY'RE **GONE**.
WHY ARE YOU JUST STARING AT ME?
QUIET! I'M TRYING TO THINK.
ABOUT **WHAT?**
LIFE CHOICES, MOSTLY.
WE NEED A RIDE...
WHAT ABOUT **THAT?**

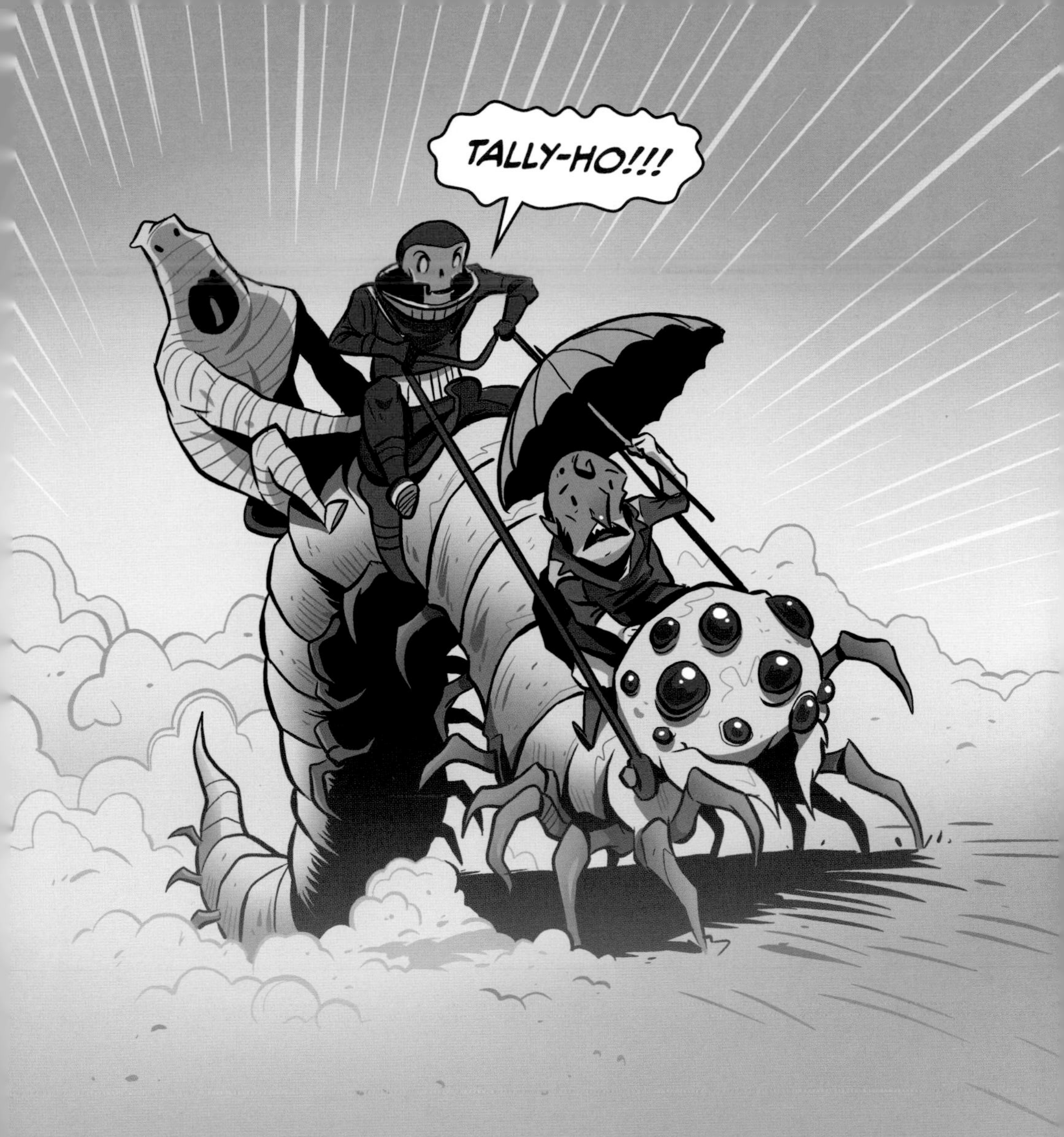
TALLY-HO!!!

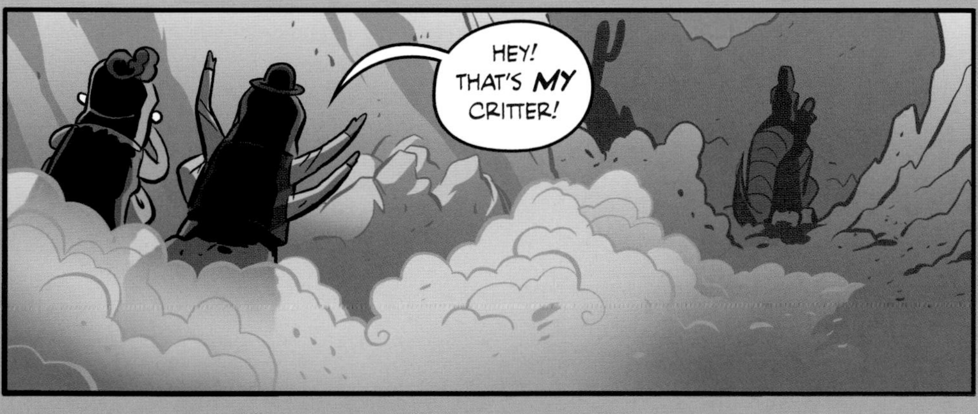
HEY! THAT'S MY CRITTER!

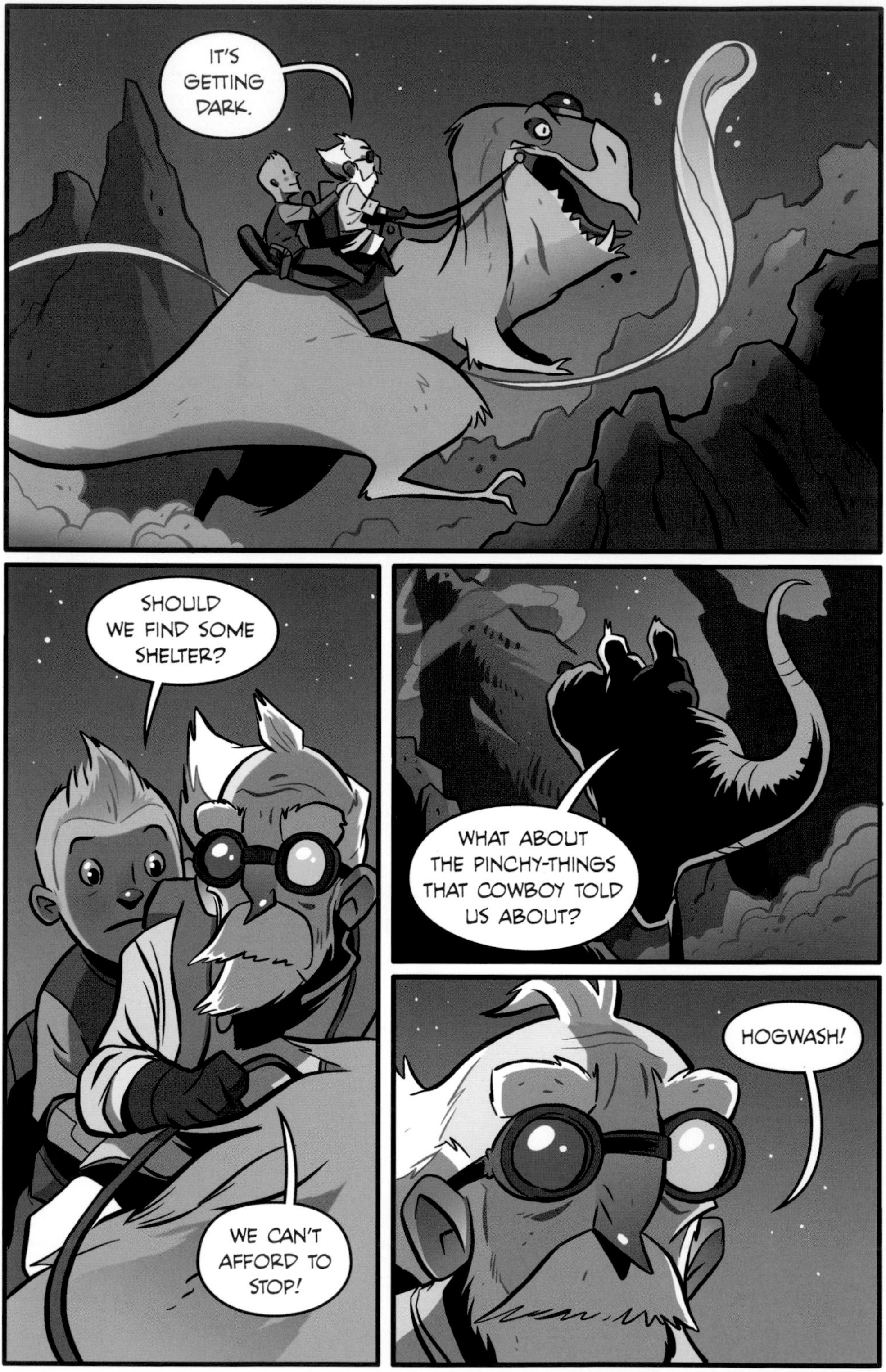
IT'S GETTING DARK.
SHOULD WE FIND SOME SHELTER?
WHAT ABOUT THE PINCHY-THINGS THAT COWBOY TOLD US ABOUT?
WE CAN'T AFFORD TO STOP!
HOGWASH!

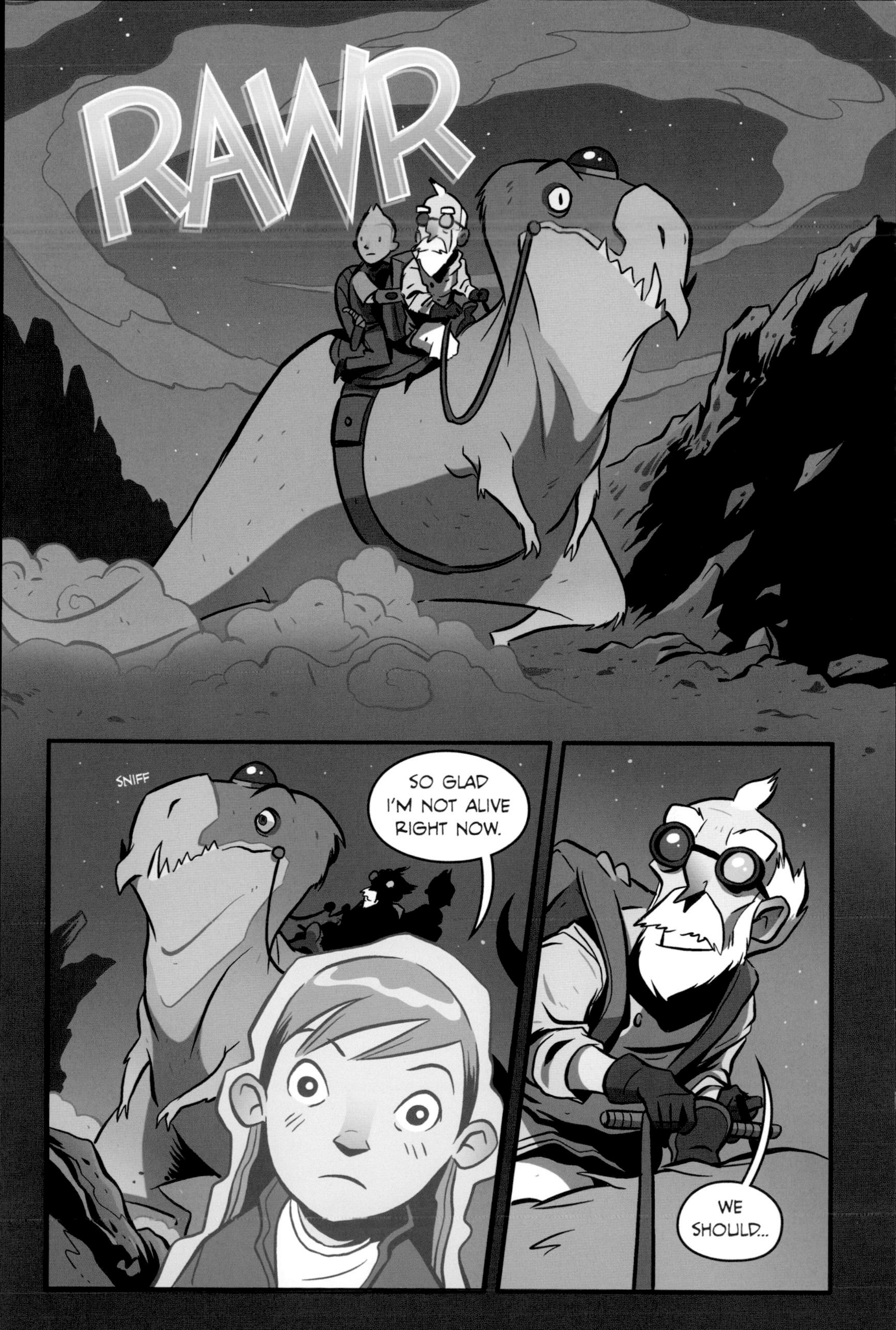
RAWR
SNIFF
SO GLAD I'M NOT ALIVE RIGHT NOW.
WE SHOULD...

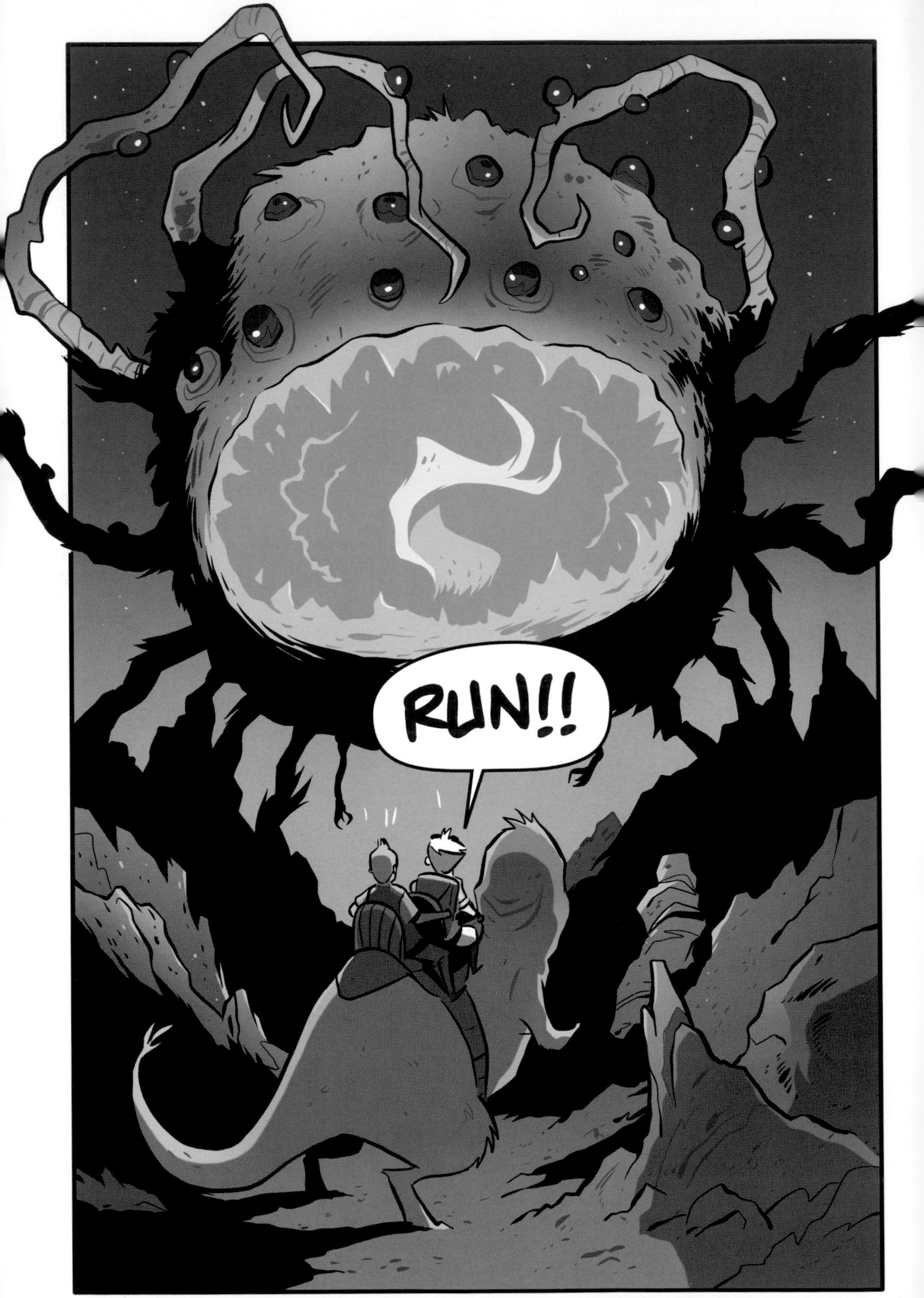
RUN!!

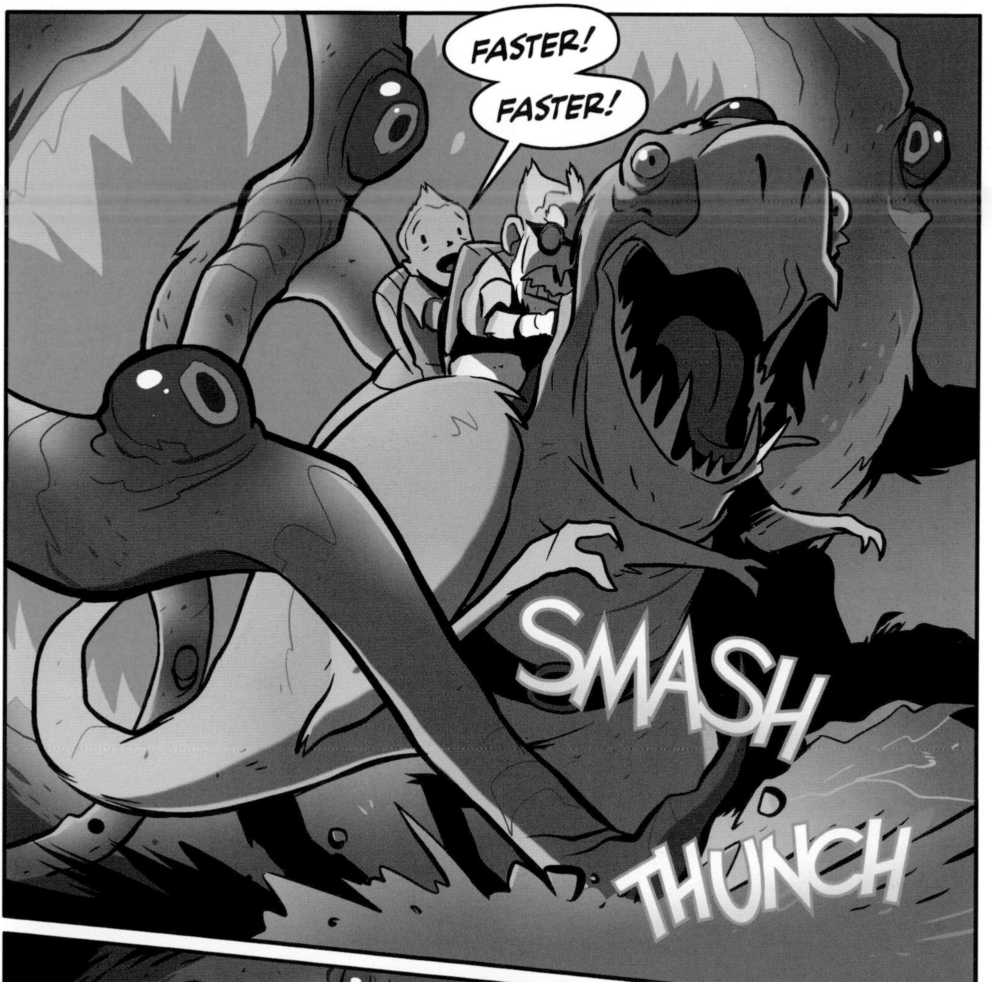
FASTER!
FASTER!
SMASH
THUNCH

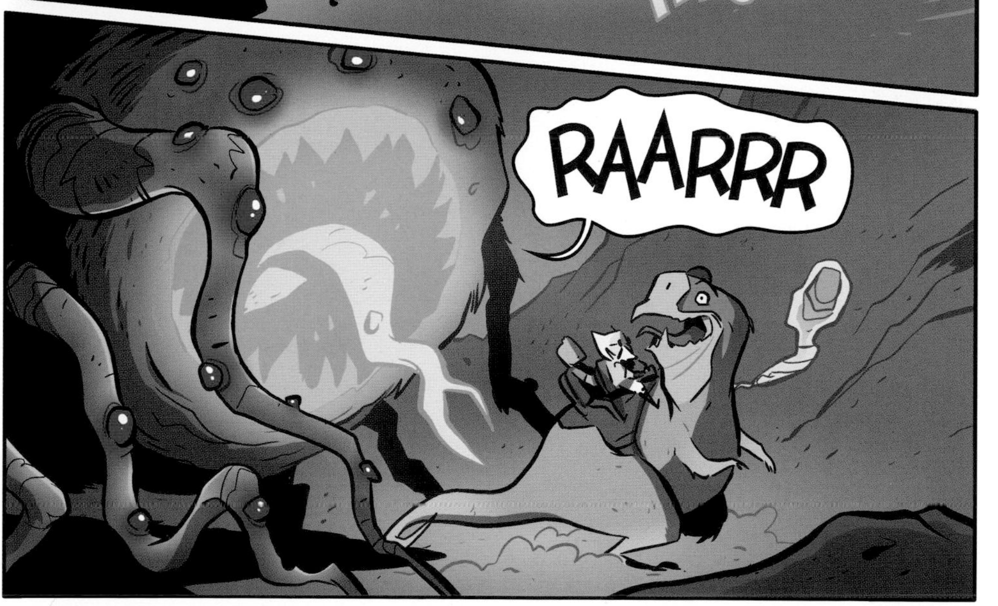
RAARRR

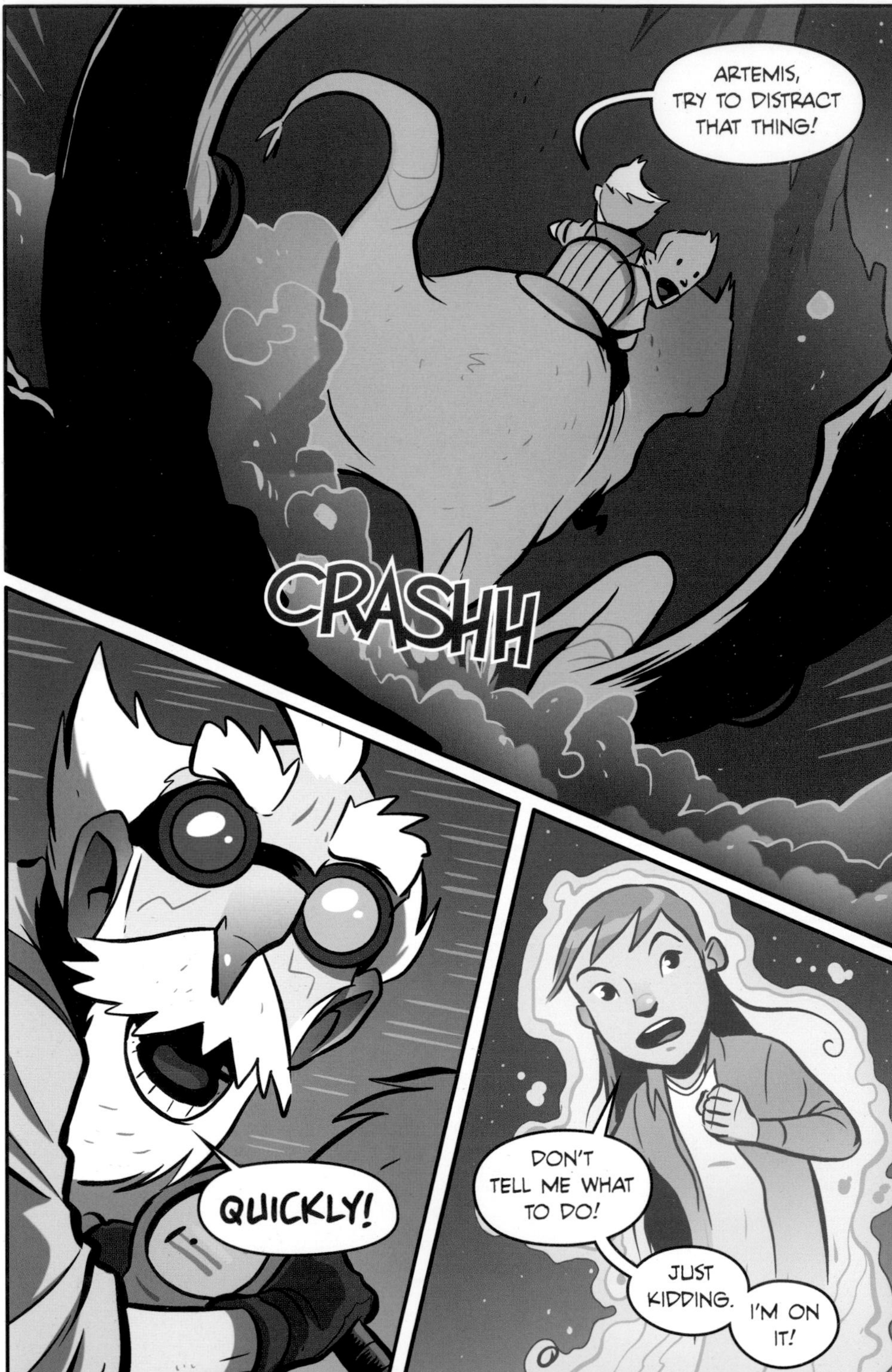
ARTEMIS, TRY TO DISTRACT THAT THING!
CRASHH
QUICKLY!
DON'T TELL ME WHAT TO DO!
JUST KIDDING.
I'M ON IT!

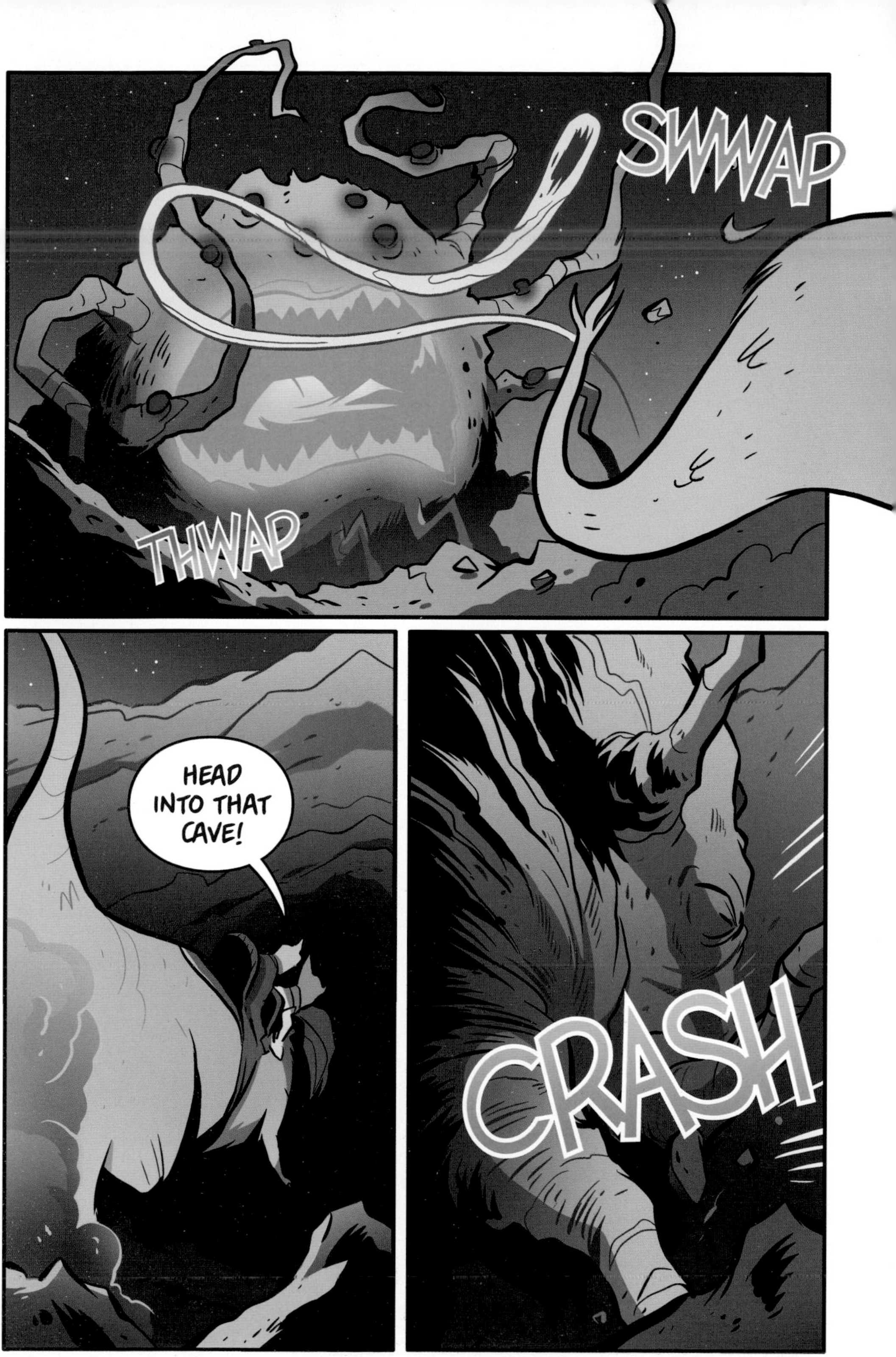
SWWAP
THWAP
HEAD INTO THAT CAVE!
CRASH

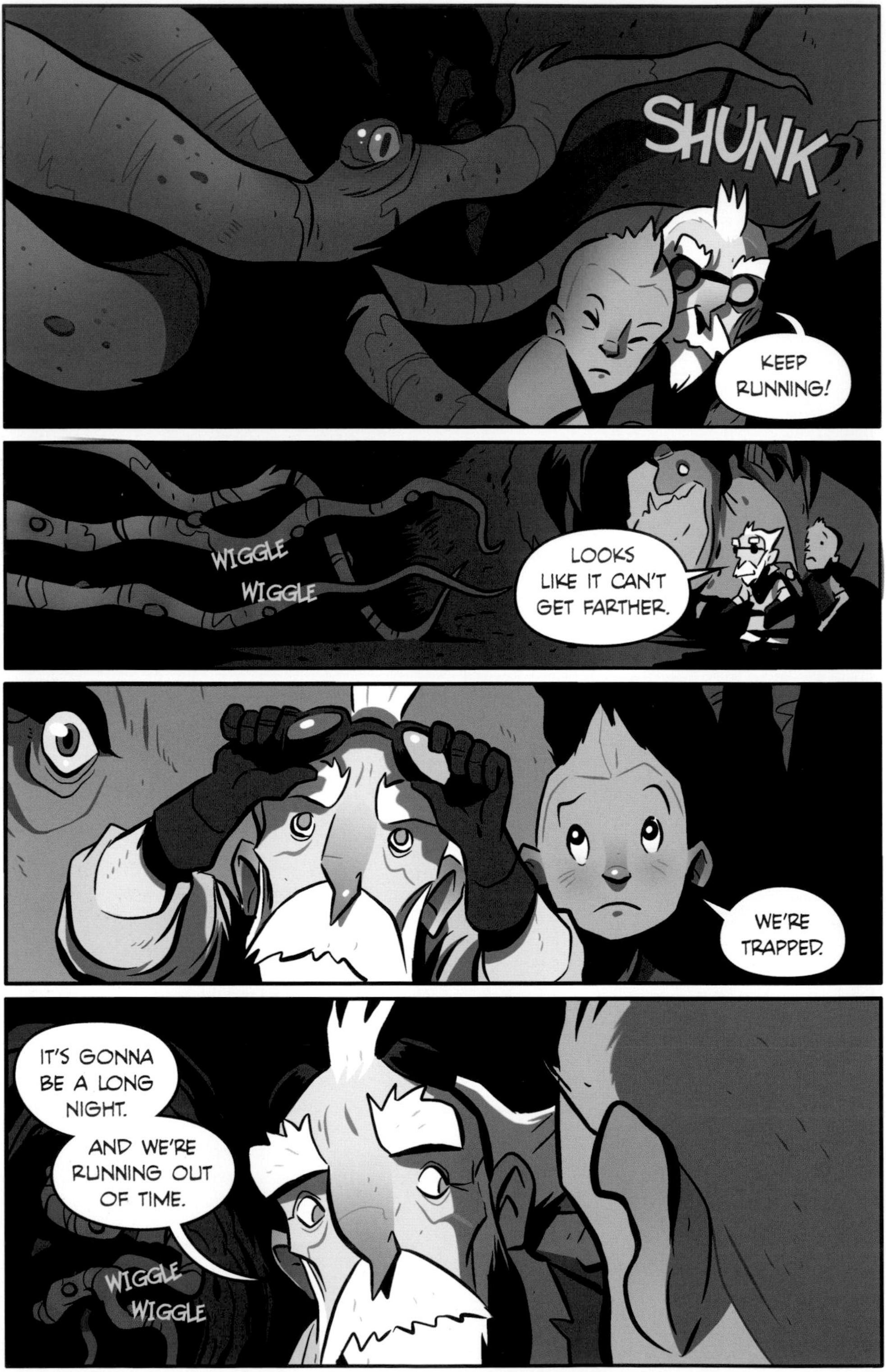
SHUNK
KEEP RUNNING!
WIGGLE
WIGGLE
LOOKS LIKE IT CAN'T GET FARTHER.
WE'RE TRAPPED.
IT'S GONNA BE A LONG NIGHT.
AND WE'RE RUNNING OUT OF TIME.
WIGGLE
WIGGLE

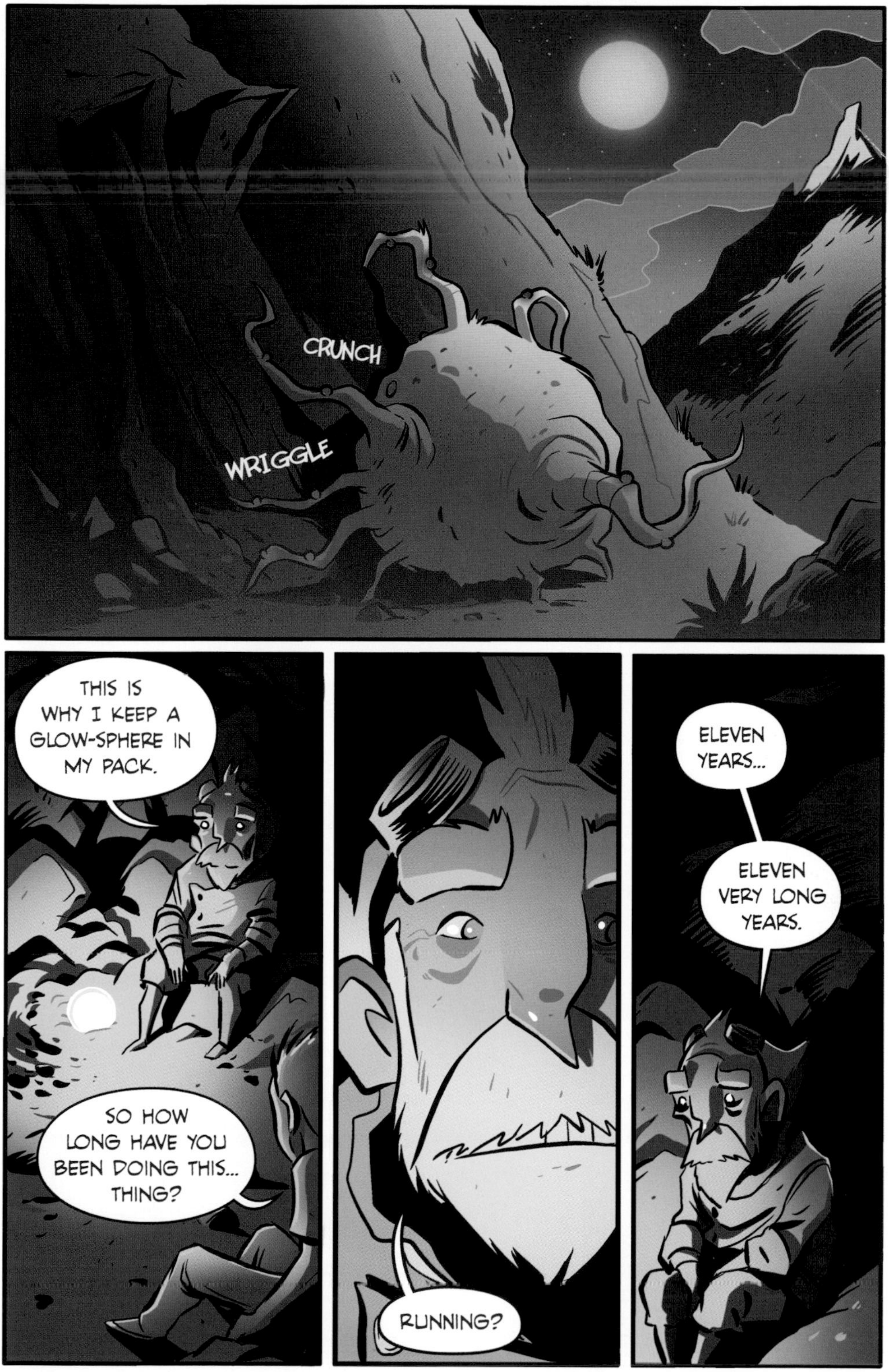
CRUNCH
WRIGGLE
THIS IS WHY I KEEP A GLOW-SPHERE IN MY PACK.
SO HOW LONG HAVE YOU BEEN DOING THIS... THING?
RUNNING?
ELEVEN YEARS...
ELEVEN VERY LONG YEARS.

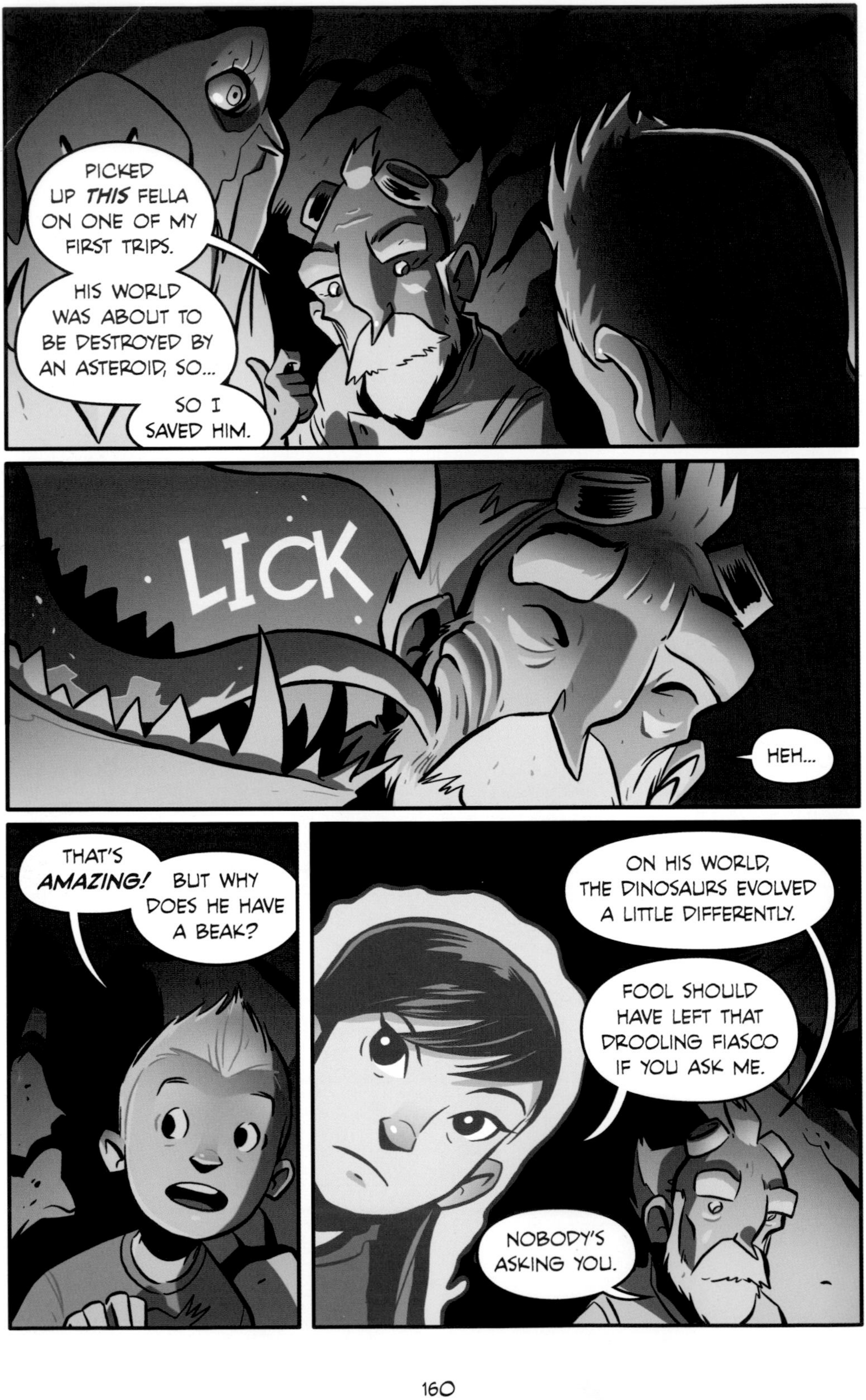
PICKED UP *THIS* FELLA ON ONE OF MY FIRST TRIPS.
HIS WORLD WAS ABOUT TO BE DESTROYED BY AN ASTEROID, SO...
SO I SAVED HIM.
LICK
HEH...
THAT'S *AMAZING!*
BUT WHY DOES HE HAVE A BEAK?
ON HIS WORLD, THE DINOSAURS EVOLVED A LITTLE DIFFERENTLY.
FOOL SHOULD HAVE LEFT THAT DROOLING FIASCO IF YOU ASK ME.
NOBODY'S ASKING YOU.

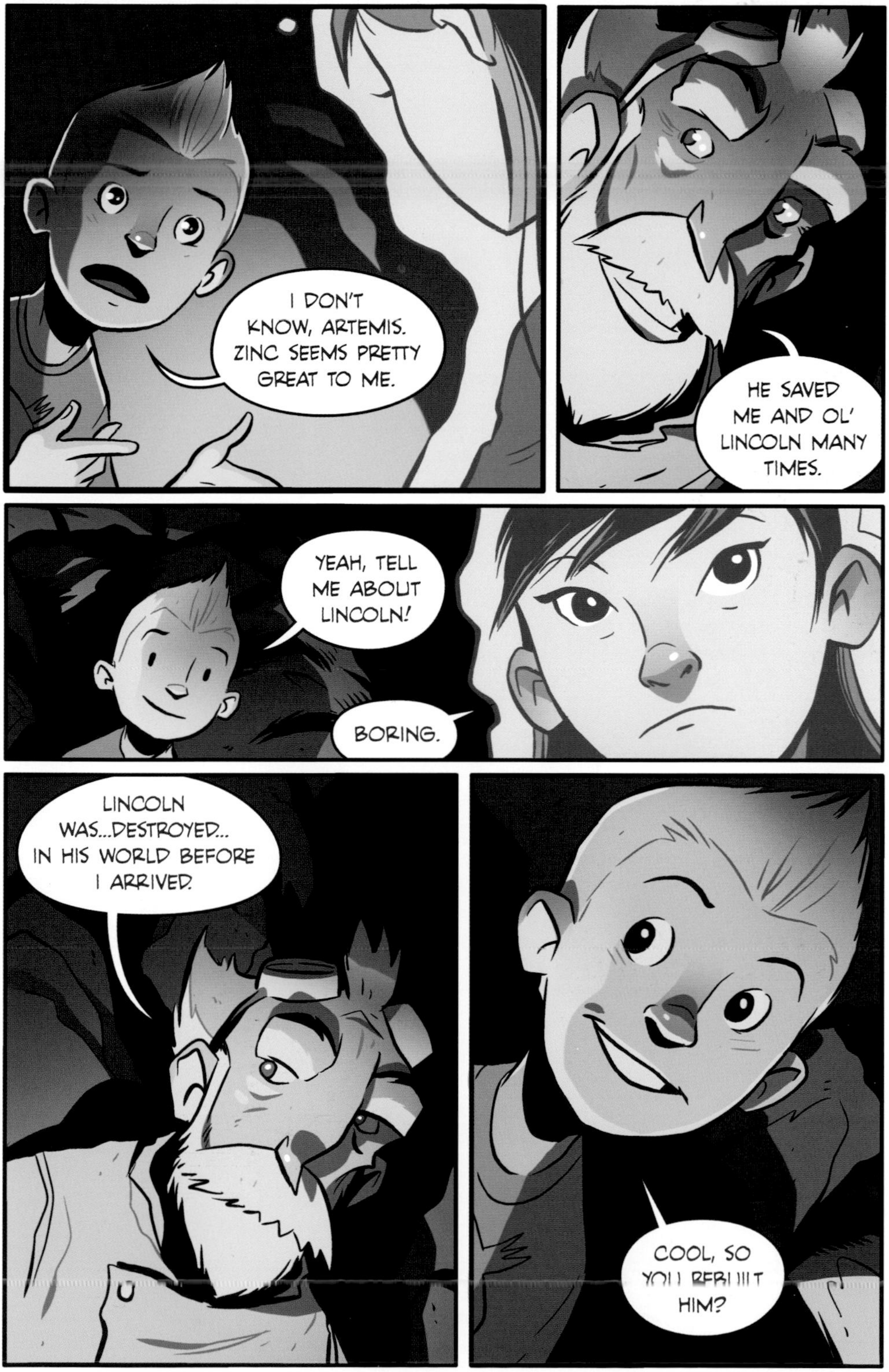
I DON'T KNOW, ARTEMIS. ZINC SEEMS PRETTY GREAT TO ME.
HE SAVED ME AND OL' LINCOLN MANY TIMES.
YEAH, TELL ME ABOUT LINCOLN!
BORING.
LINCOLN WAS...DESTROYED... IN HIS WORLD BEFORE I ARRIVED.
COOL, SO YOU REBUILT HIM?

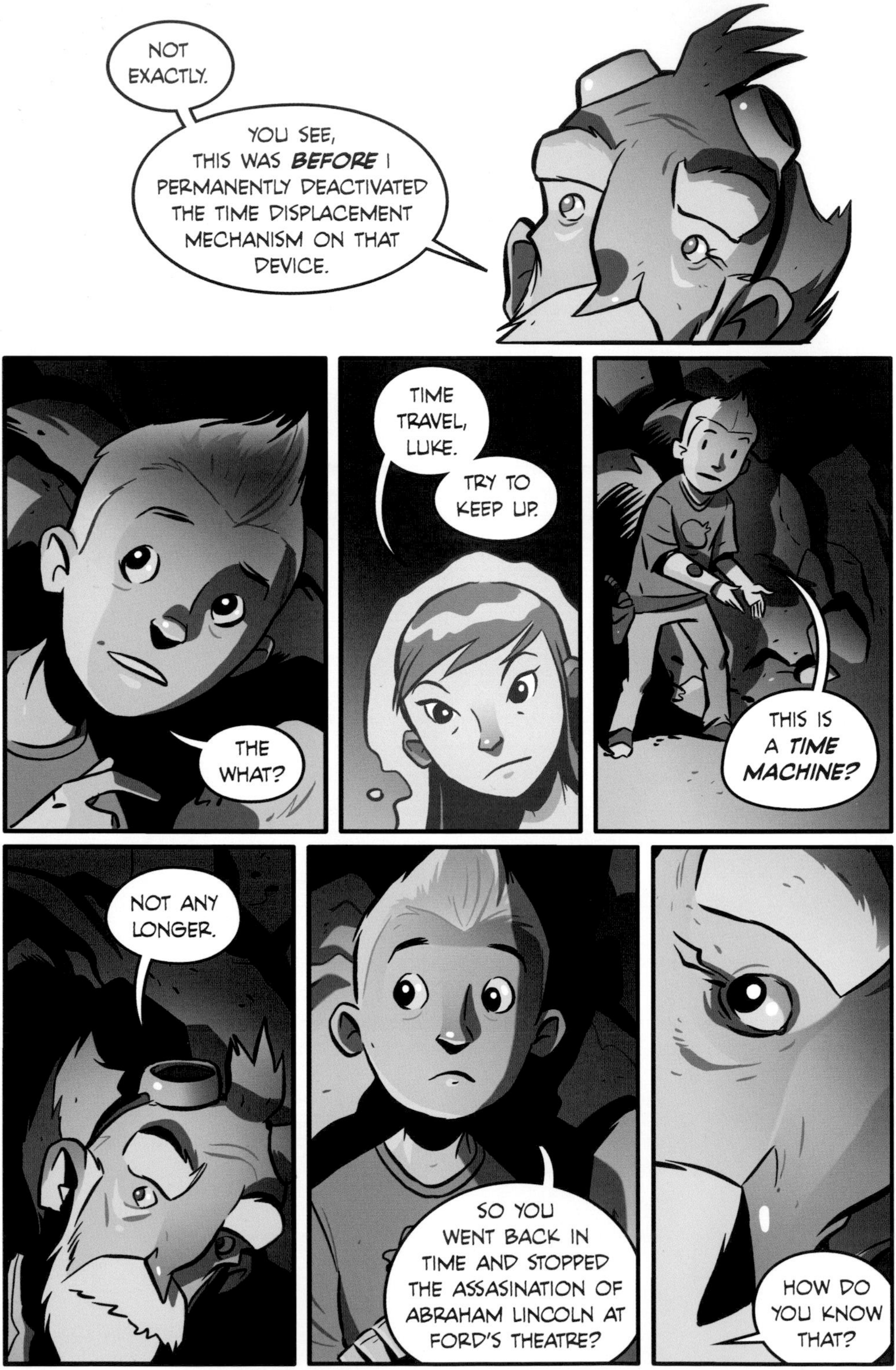
NOT EXACTLY.
YOU SEE, THIS WAS BEFORE I PERMANENTLY DEACTIVATED THE TIME DISPLACEMENT MECHANISM ON THAT DEVICE.
THE WHAT?
TIME TRAVEL, LUKE.
TRY TO KEEP UP.
THIS IS A TIME MACHINE?
NOT ANY LONGER.
SO YOU WENT BACK IN TIME AND STOPPED THE ASSASINATION OF ABRAHAM LINCOLN AT FORD'S THEATRE?
HOW DO YOU KNOW THAT?

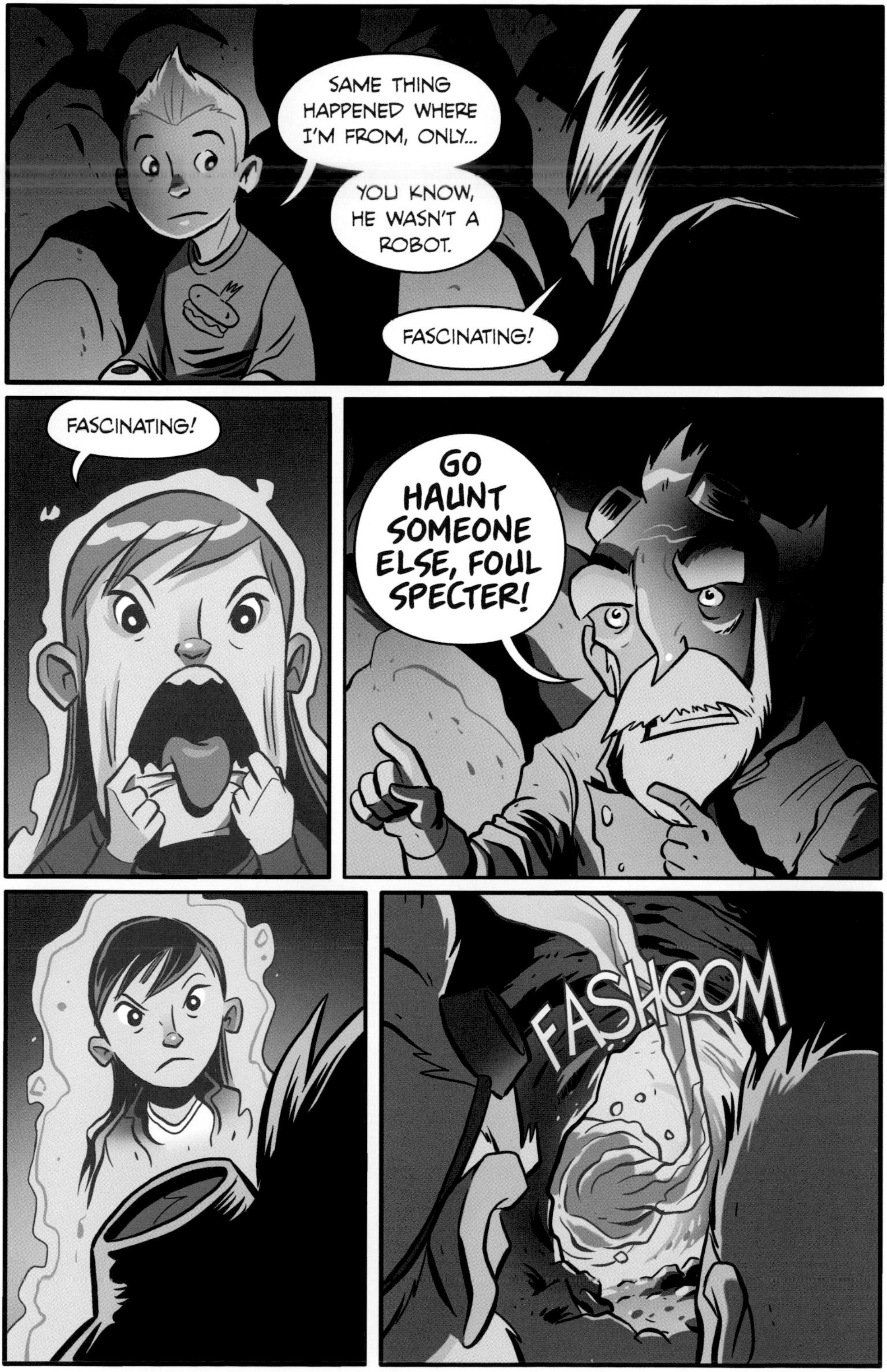
SAME THING HAPPENED WHERE I'M FROM, ONLY...
YOU KNOW, HE WASN'T A ROBOT.
FASCINATING!
FASCINATING!
GO HAUNT SOMEONE ELSE, FOUL SPECTER!
FASHOOM

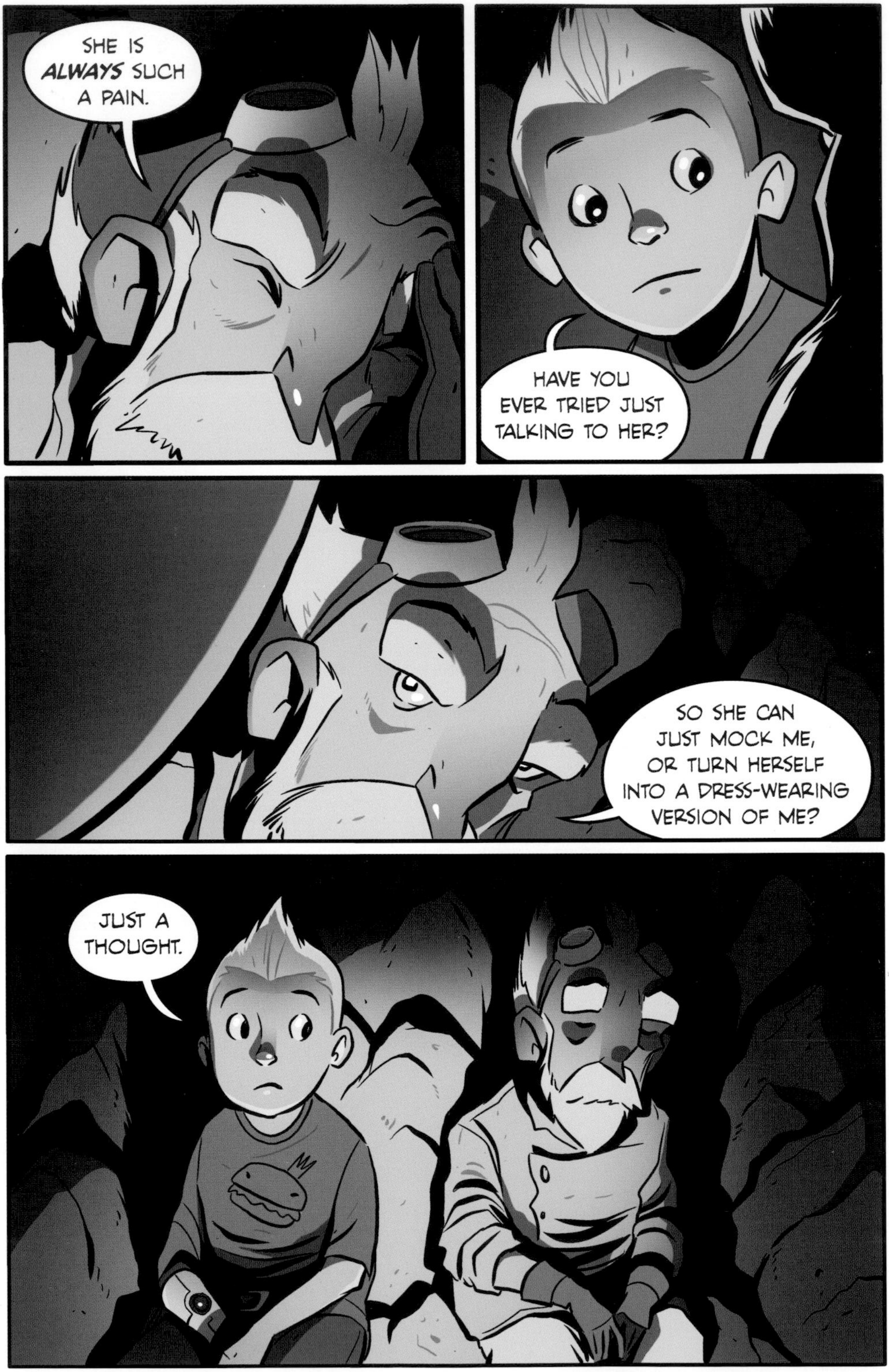
SHE IS *ALWAYS* SUCH A PAIN.
HAVE YOU EVER TRIED JUST TALKING TO HER?
SO SHE CAN JUST MOCK ME, OR TURN HERSELF INTO A DRESS-WEARING VERSION OF ME?
JUST A THOUGHT.

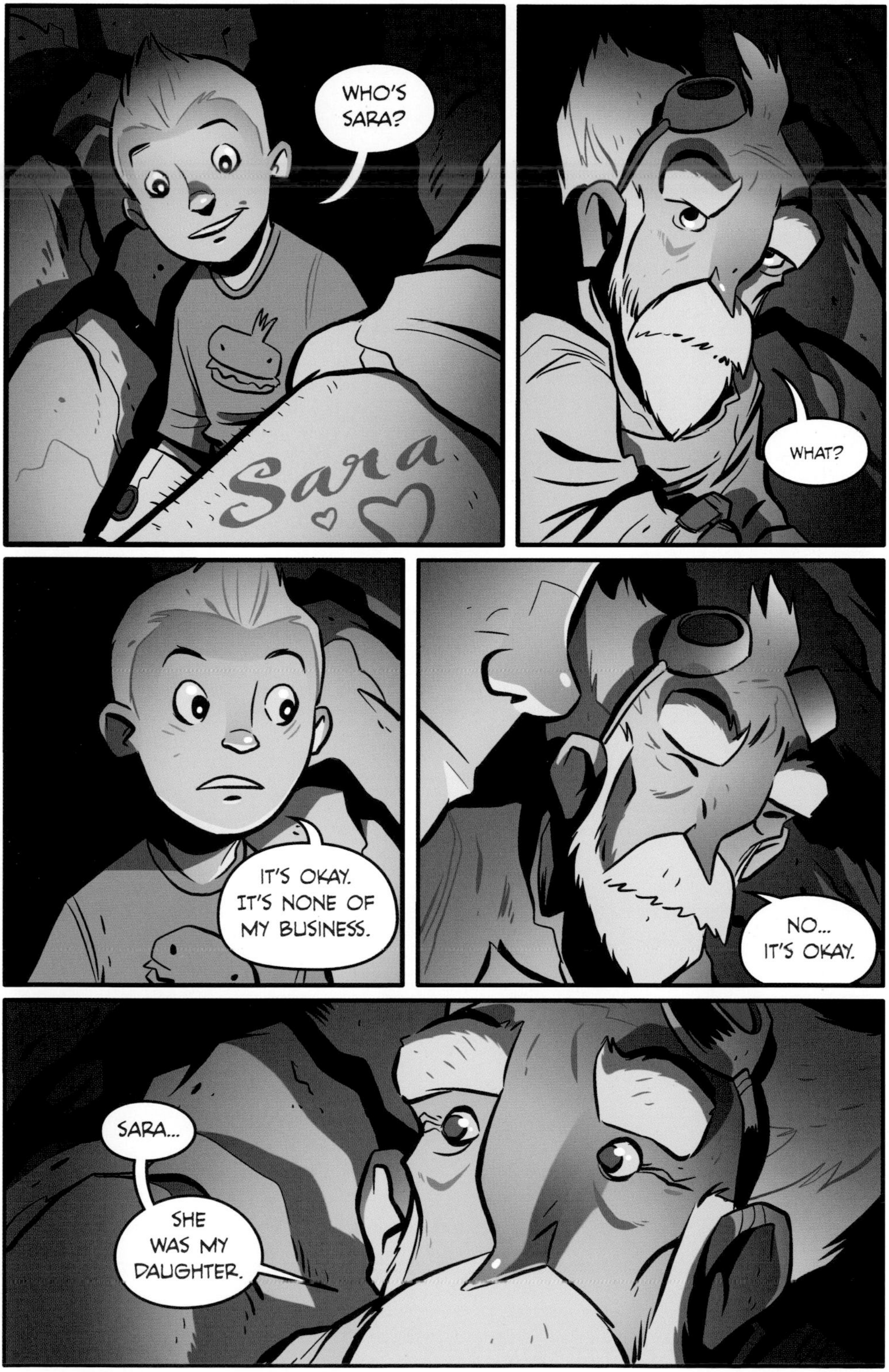
WHO'S SARA?
Sara
WHAT?
IT'S OKAY. IT'S NONE OF MY BUSINESS.
NO... IT'S OKAY.
SARA...
SHE WAS MY DAUGHTER.

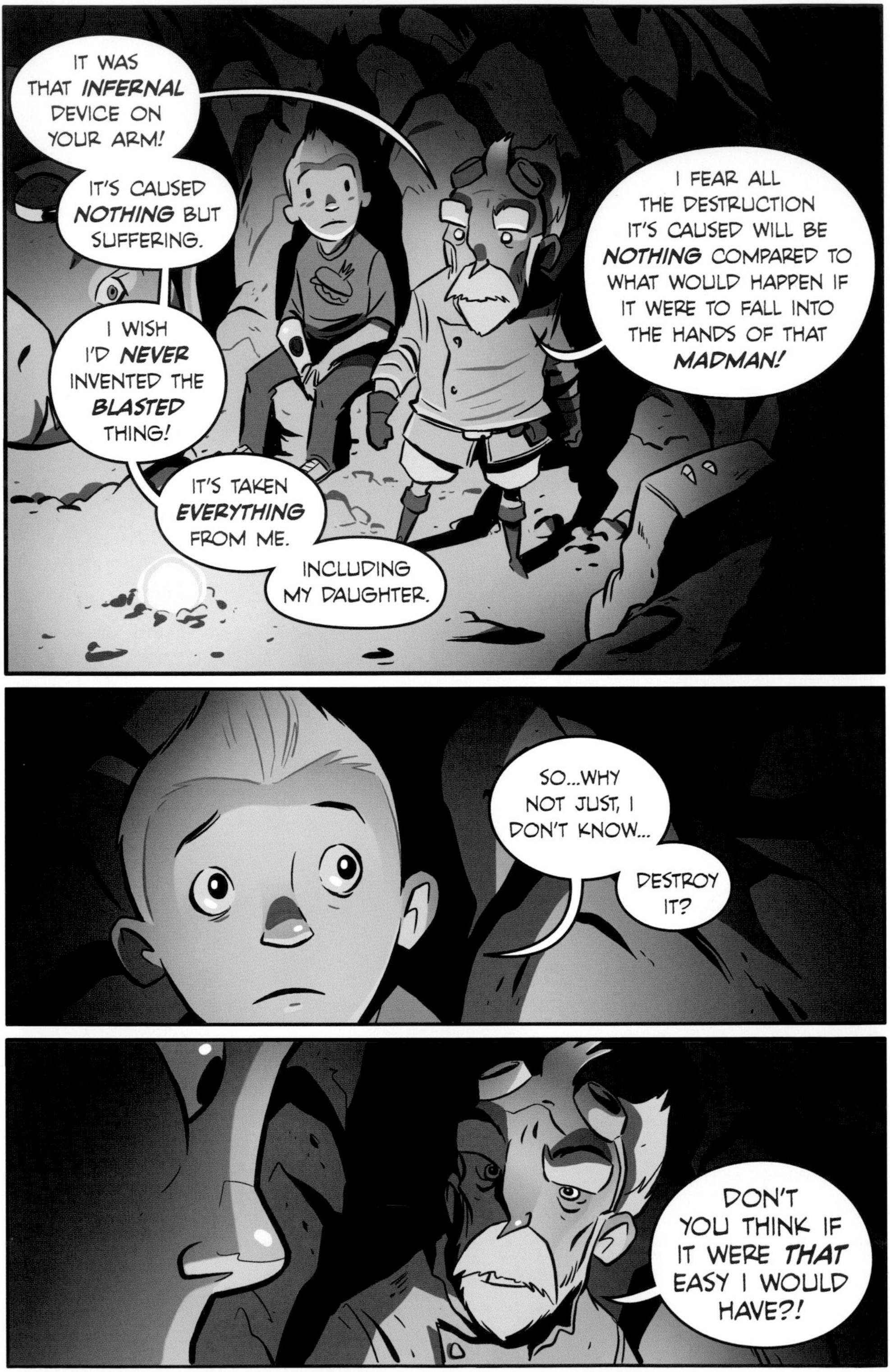
IT WAS THAT INFERNAL DEVICE ON YOUR ARM!
IT'S CAUSED NOTHING BUT SUFFERING.
I WISH I'D NEVER INVENTED THE BLASTED THING!
IT'S TAKEN EVERYTHING FROM ME.
INCLUDING MY DAUGHTER.
I FEAR ALL THE DESTRUCTION IT'S CAUSED WILL BE NOTHING COMPARED TO WHAT WOULD HAPPEN IF IT WERE TO FALL INTO THE HANDS OF THAT MADMAN!
SO...WHY NOT JUST, I DON'T KNOW...
DESTROY IT?
DON'T YOU THINK IF IT WERE THAT EASY I WOULD HAVE?!

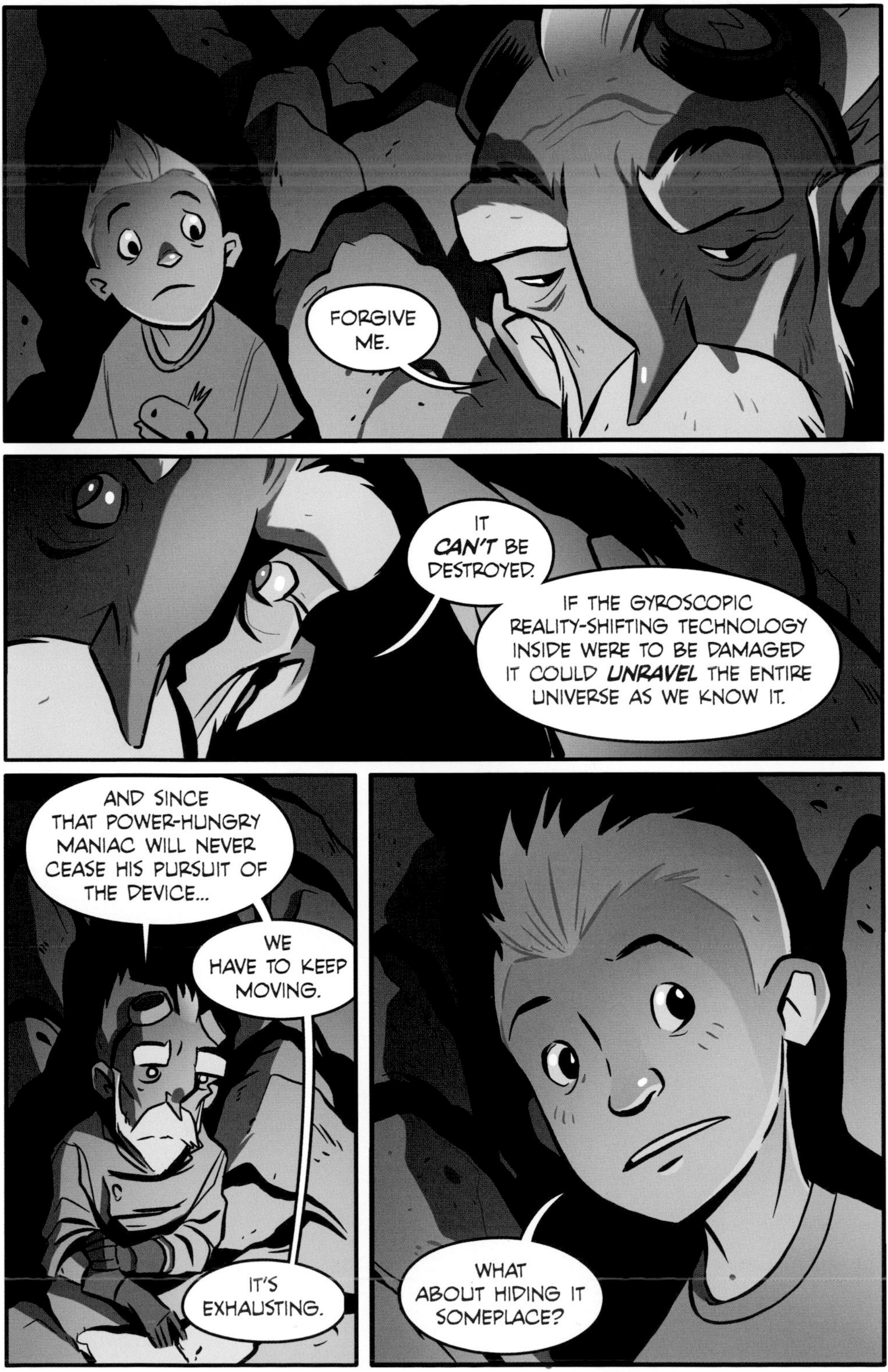
FORGIVE ME.
IT *CAN'T* BE DESTROYED.
IF THE GYROSCOPIC REALITY-SHIFTING TECHNOLOGY INSIDE WERE TO BE DAMAGED IT COULD *UNRAVEL* THE ENTIRE UNIVERSE AS WE KNOW IT.
AND SINCE THAT POWER-HUNGRY MANIAC WILL NEVER CEASE HIS PURSUIT OF THE DEVICE...
WE HAVE TO KEEP MOVING.
IT'S EXHAUSTING.
WHAT ABOUT HIDING IT SOMEPLACE?

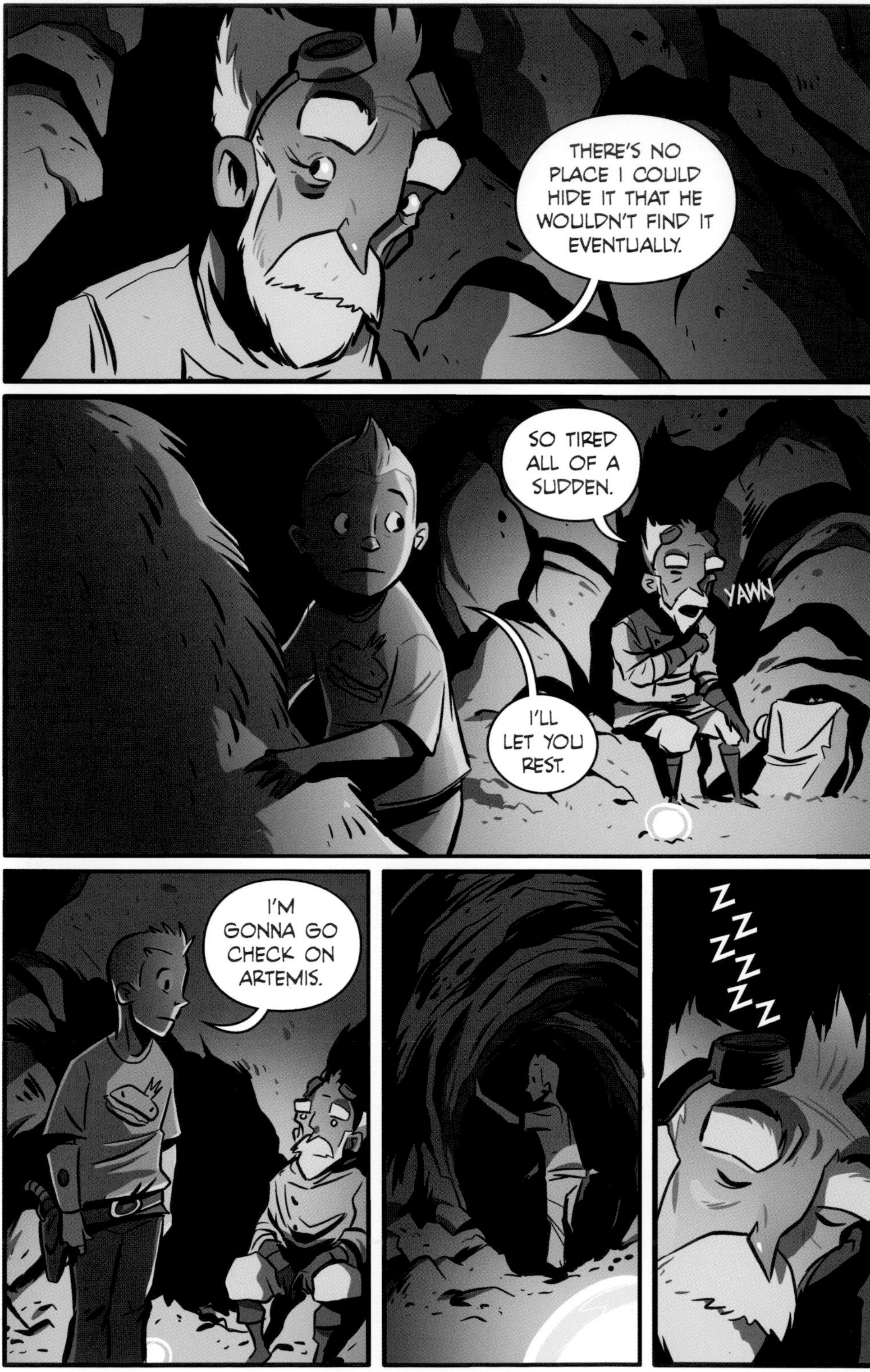
THERE'S NO PLACE I COULD HIDE IT THAT HE WOULDN'T FIND IT EVENTUALLY.
SO TIRED ALL OF A SUDDEN.
YAWN
I'LL LET YOU REST.
I'M GONNA GO CHECK ON ARTEMIS.
Z Z Z Z Z Z

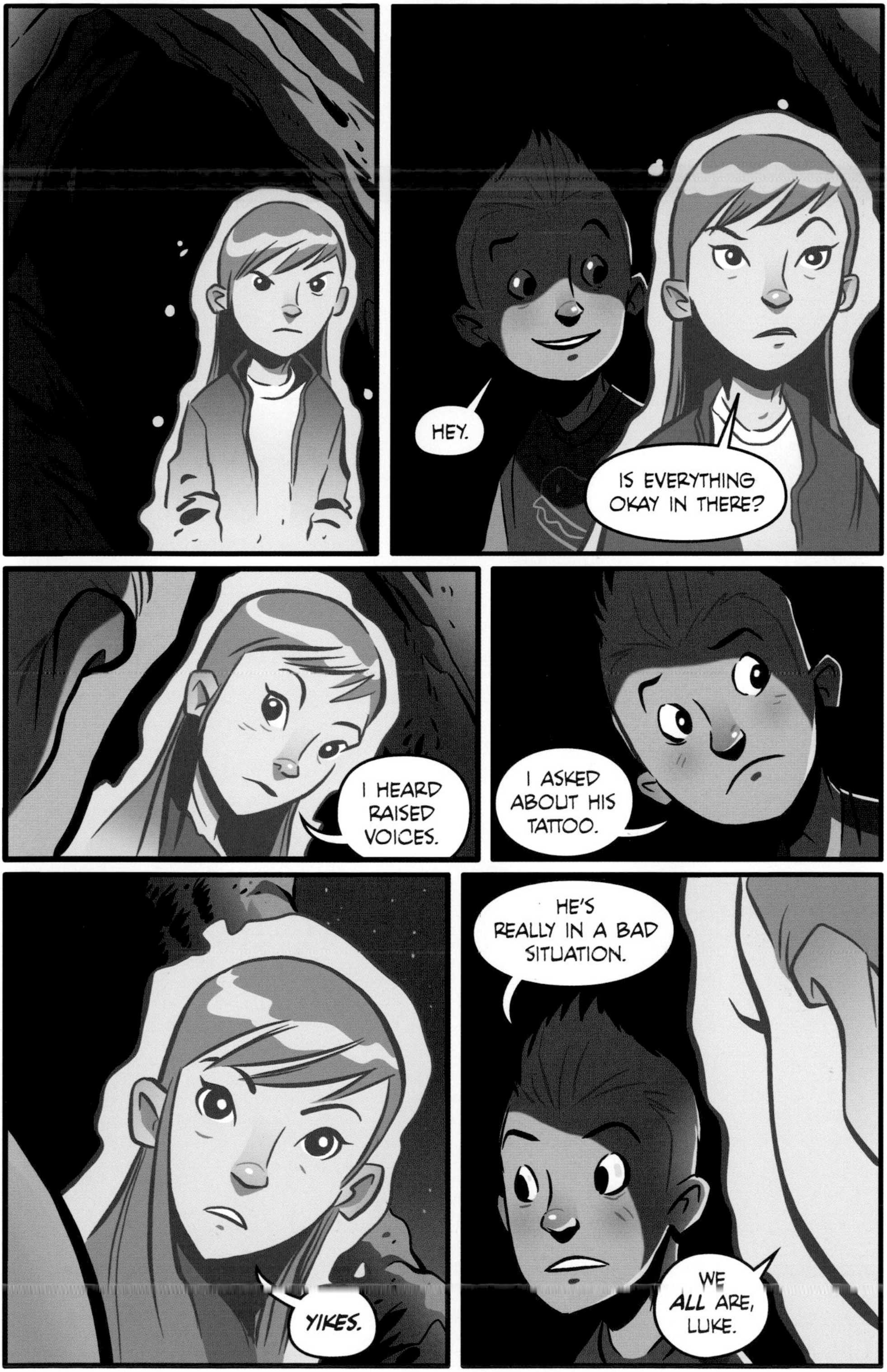
HEY.
IS EVERYTHING OKAY IN THERE?
I HEARD RAISED VOICES.
I ASKED ABOUT HIS TATTOO.
YIKES.
HE'S REALLY IN A BAD SITUATION.
WE *ALL* ARE, LUKE.

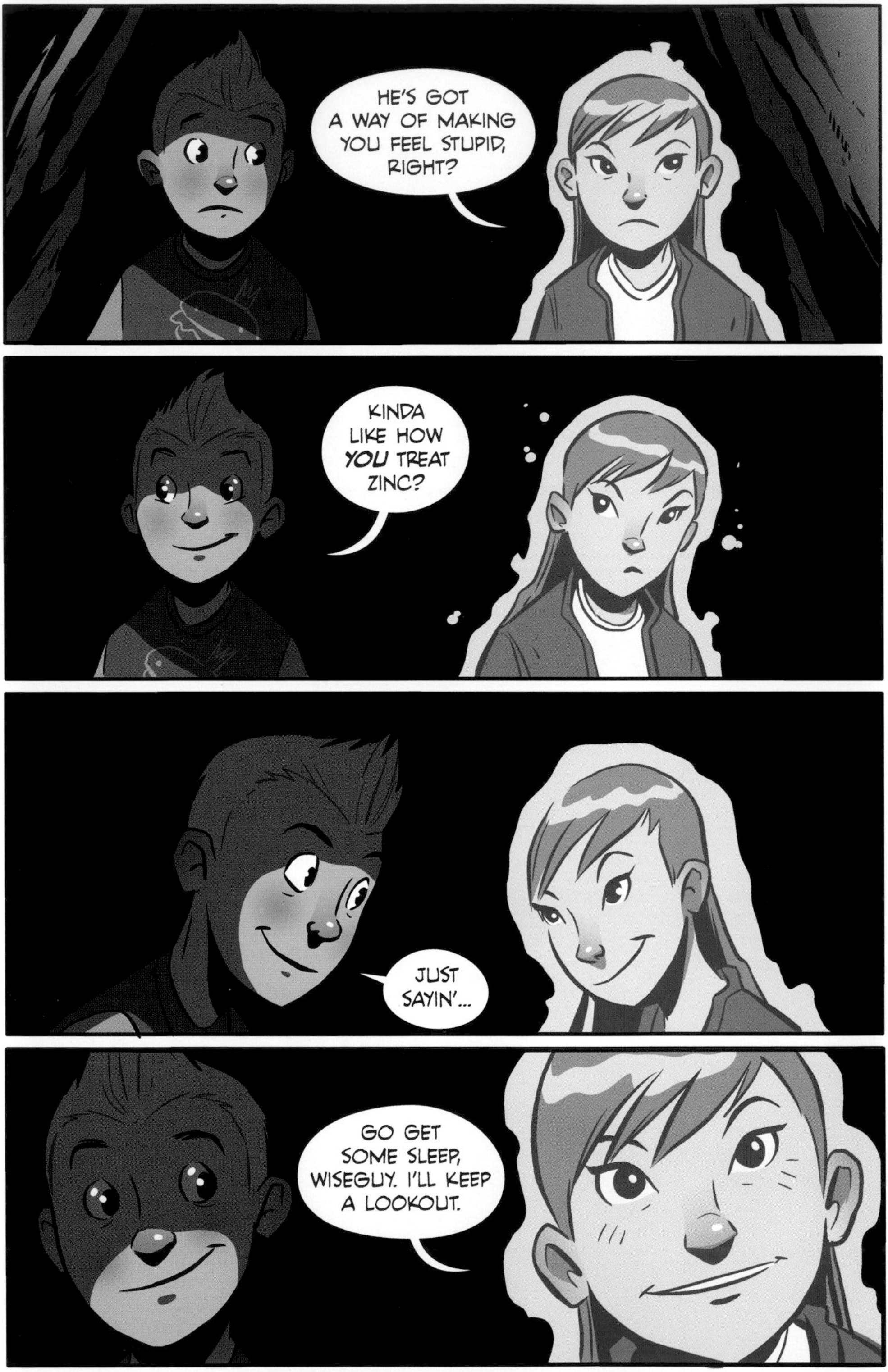
HE'S GOT A WAY OF MAKING YOU FEEL STUPID, RIGHT?
KINDA LIKE HOW YOU TREAT ZINC?
JUST SAYIN'...
GO GET SOME SLEEP, WISEGUY. I'LL KEEP A LOOKOUT.

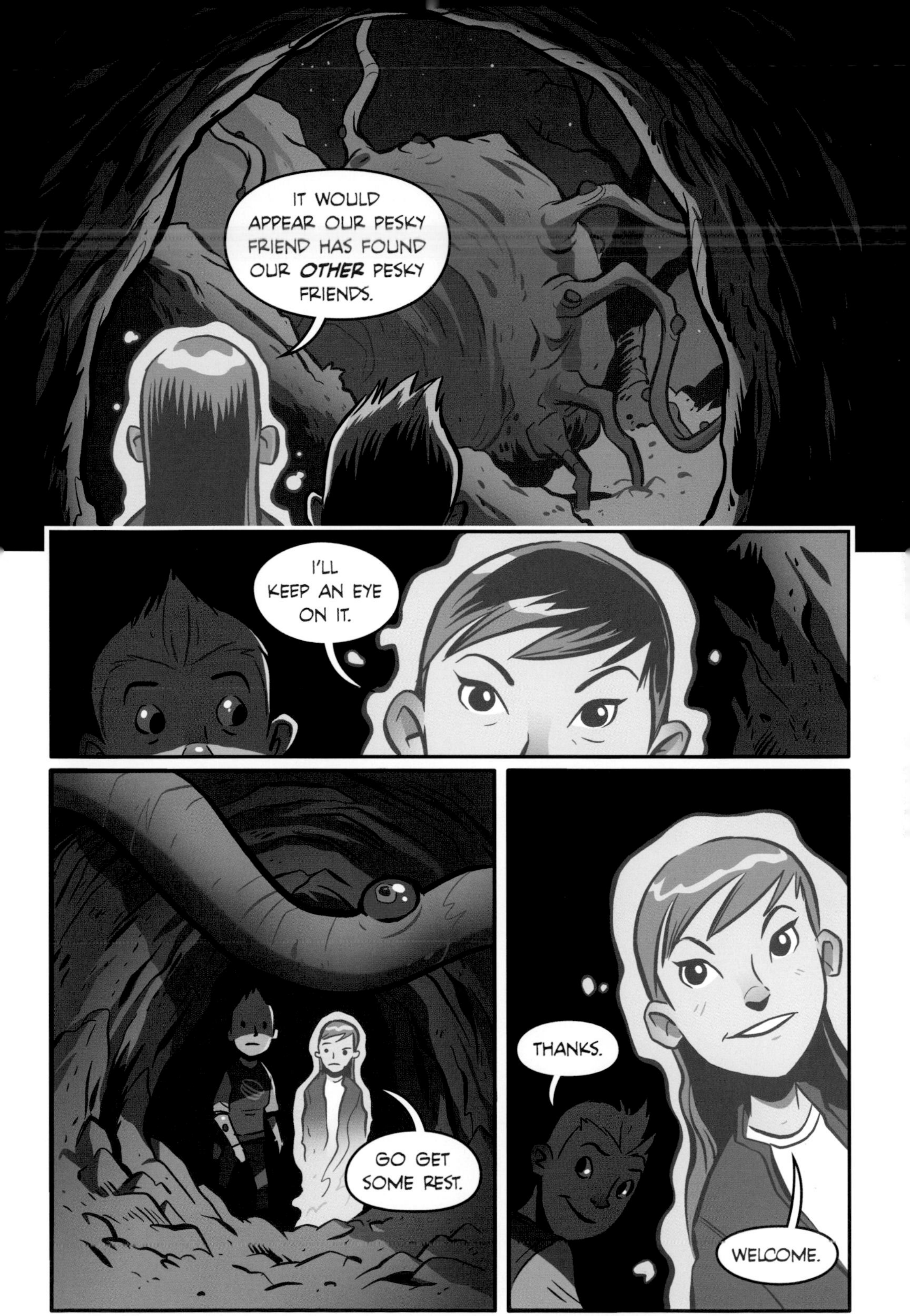
IT WOULD APPEAR OUR PESKY FRIEND HAS FOUND OUR OTHER PESKY FRIENDS.
I'LL KEEP AN EYE ON IT.
GO GET SOME REST.
THANKS.
WELCOME.

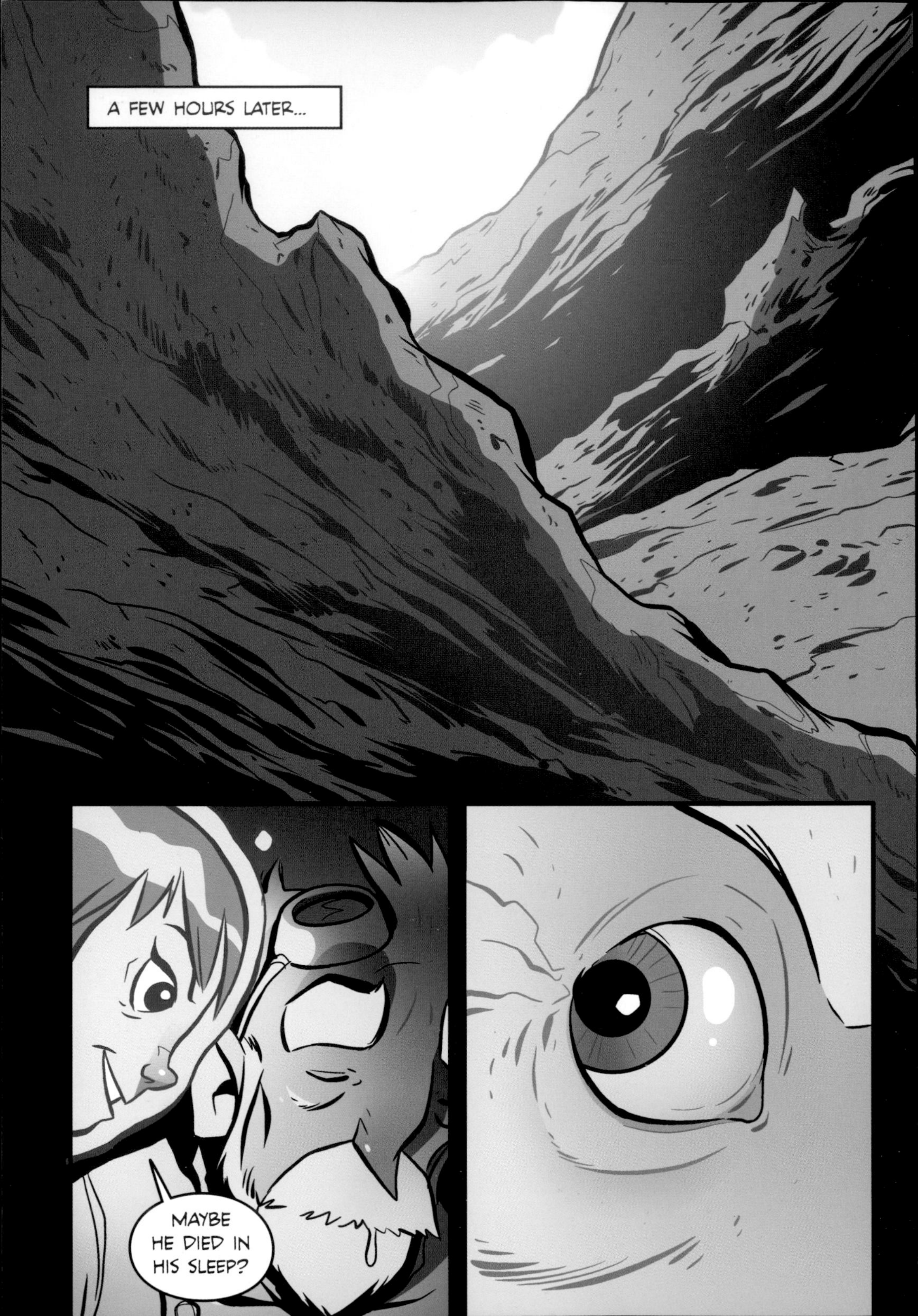
A FEW HOURS LATER...
MAYBE HE DIED IN HIS SLEEP?

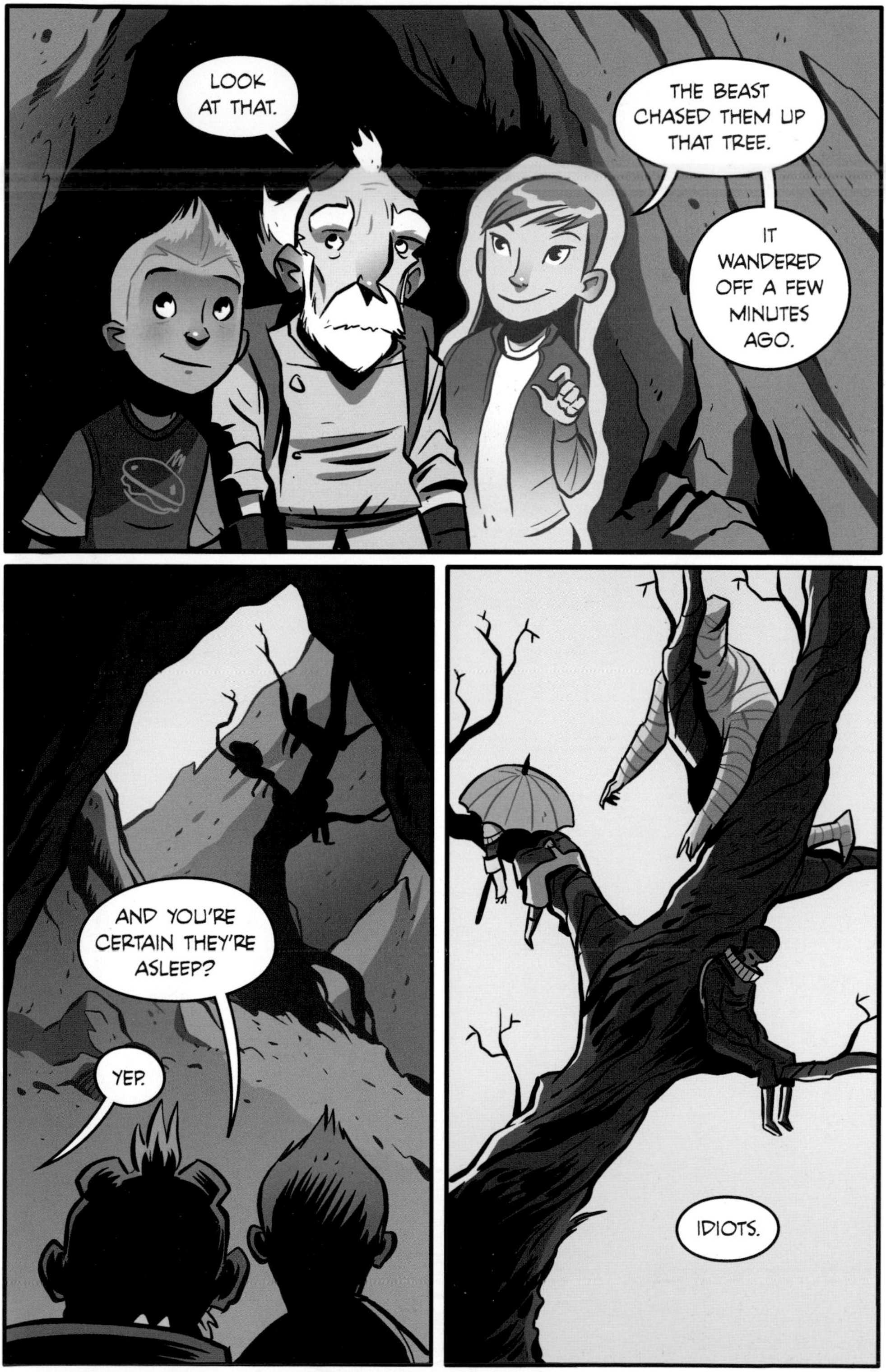
LOOK AT THAT.
THE BEAST CHASED THEM UP THAT TREE.
IT WANDERED OFF A FEW MINUTES AGO.
AND YOU'RE CERTAIN THEY'RE ASLEEP?
YEP.
IDIOTS.

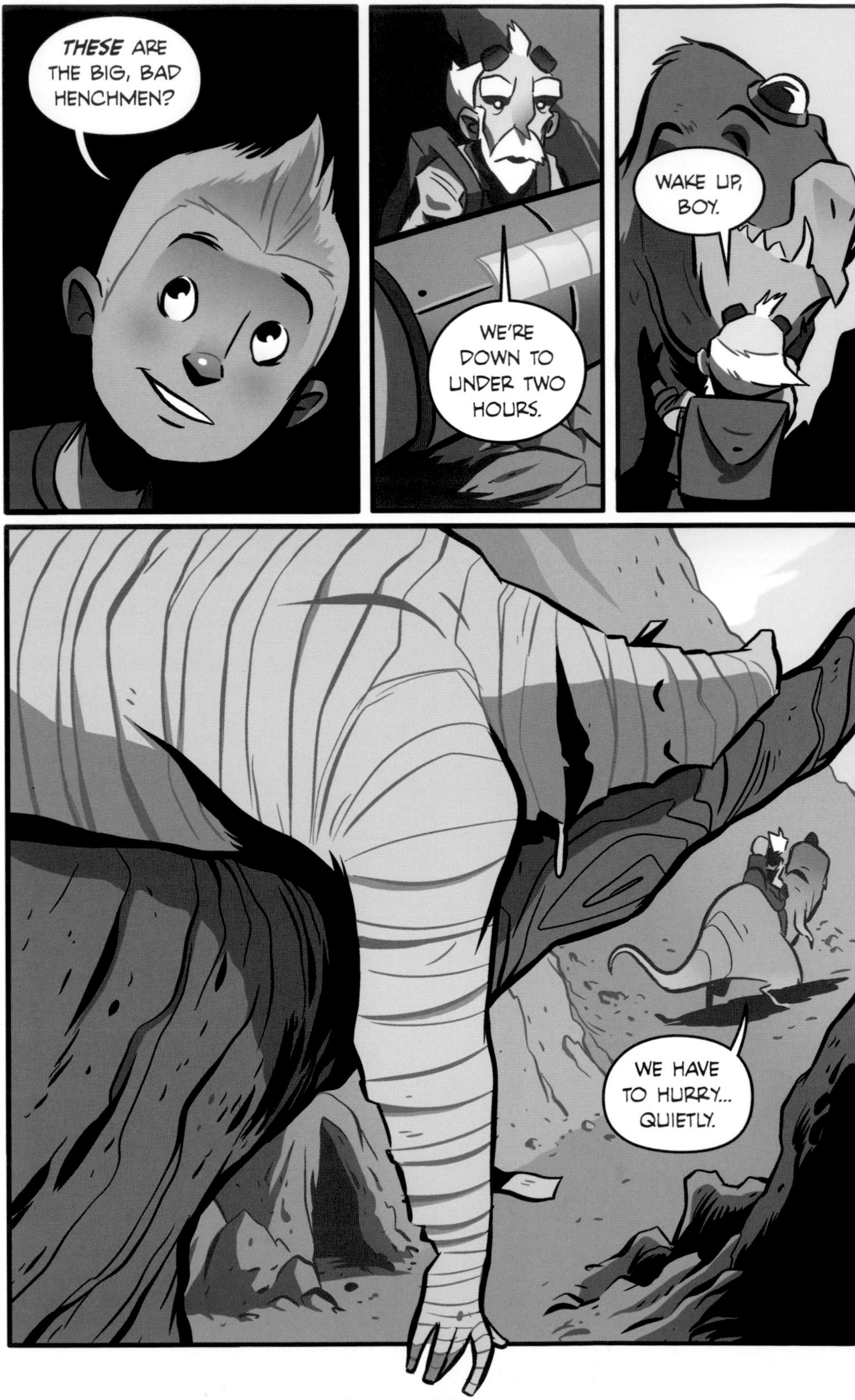
THESE ARE THE BIG, BAD HENCHMEN?
WE'RE DOWN TO UNDER TWO HOURS.
WAKE UP, BOY.
WE HAVE TO HURRY... QUIETLY.

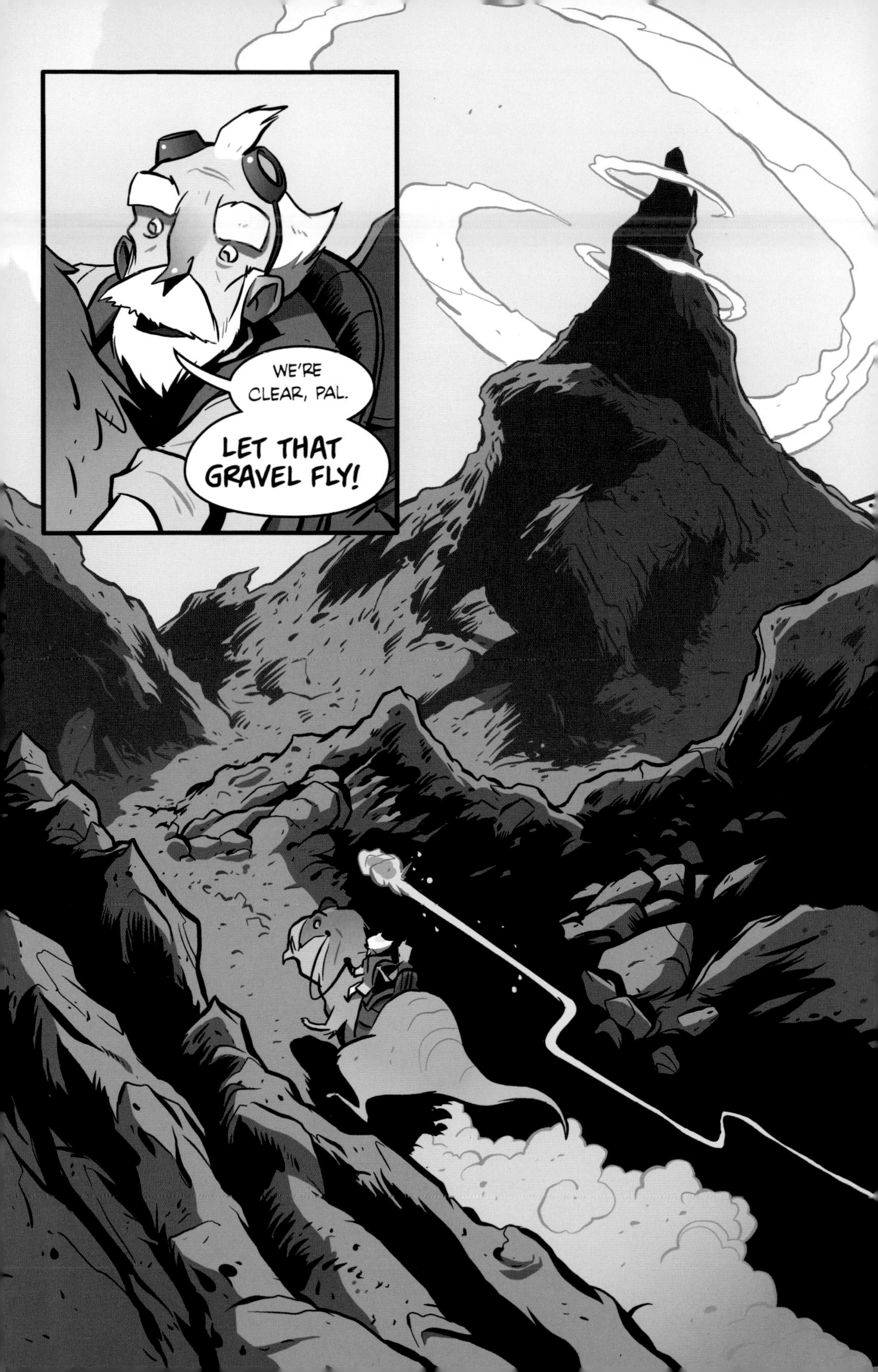
WE'RE CLEAR, PAL.
LET THAT GRAVEL FLY!

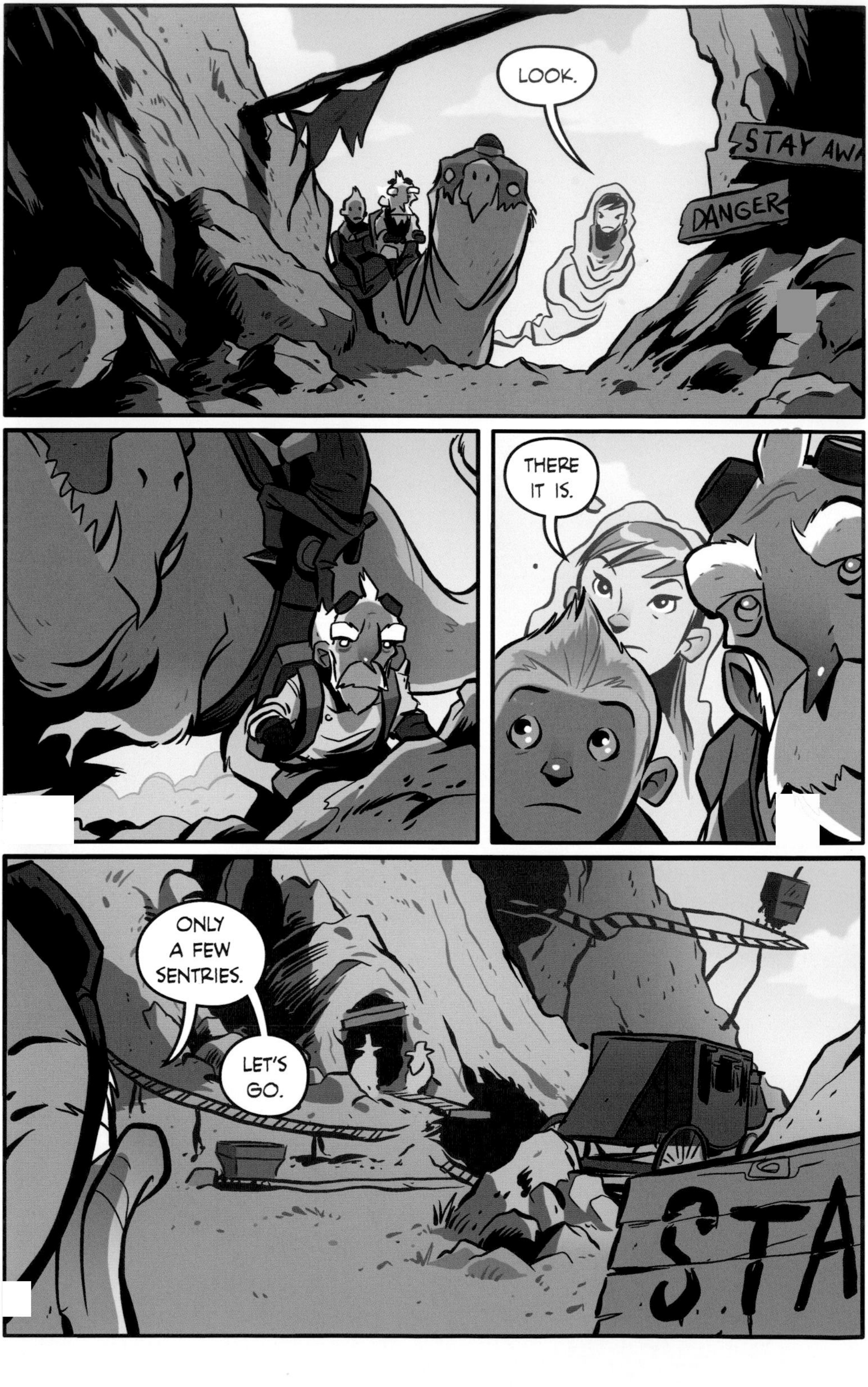
LOOK.
STAY AWA
DANGER
THERE IT IS.
ONLY A FEW SENTRIES.
LET'S GO.
STA

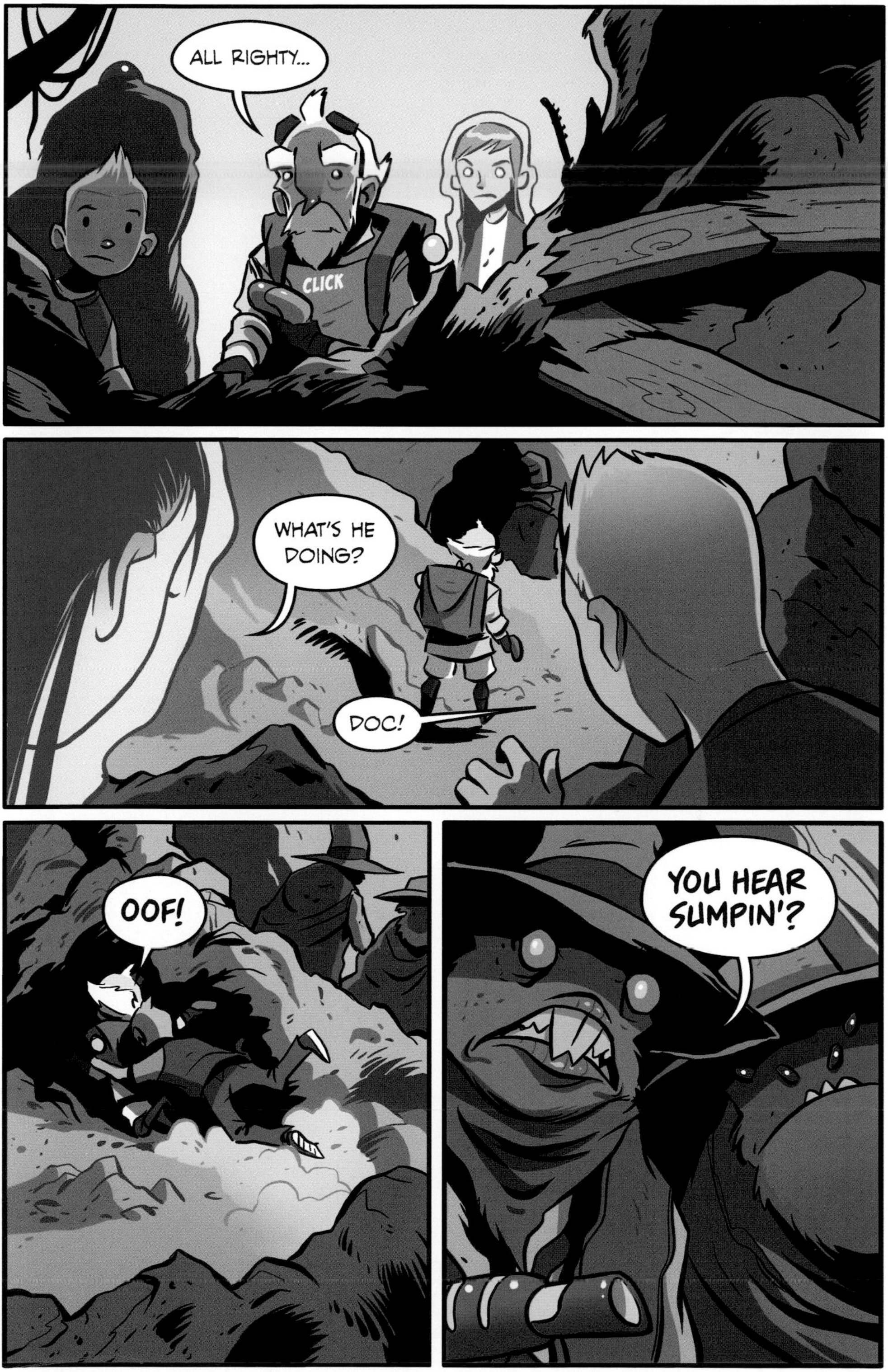
ALL RIGHTY...
CLICK
WHAT'S HE DOING?
DOC!
OOF!
YOU HEAR SUMPIN'?

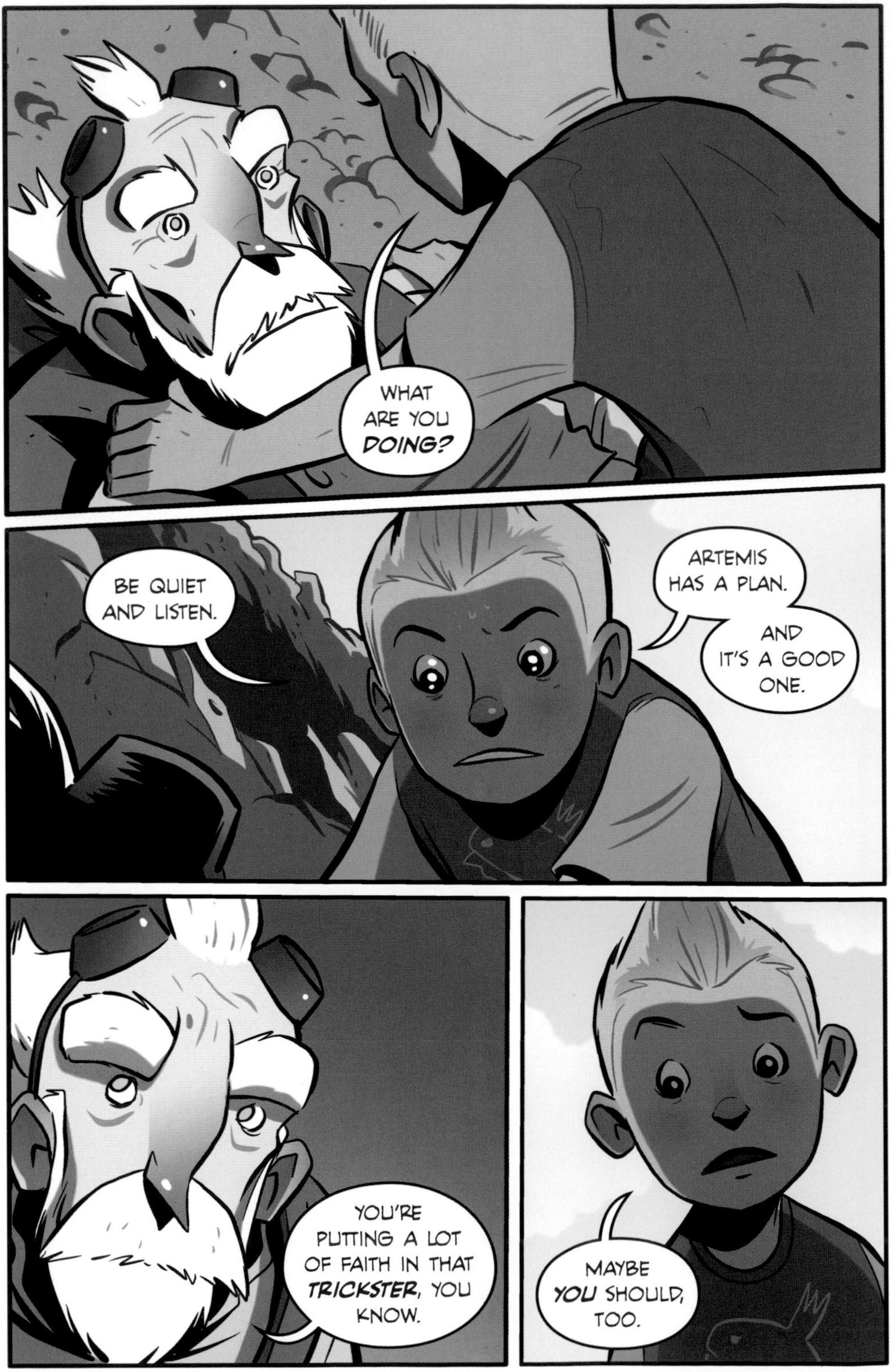
WHAT ARE YOU *DOING?*
BE QUIET AND LISTEN.
ARTEMIS HAS A PLAN.
AND IT'S A GOOD ONE.
YOU'RE PUTTING A LOT OF FAITH IN THAT *TRICKSTER*, YOU KNOW.
MAYBE *YOU* SHOULD, TOO.

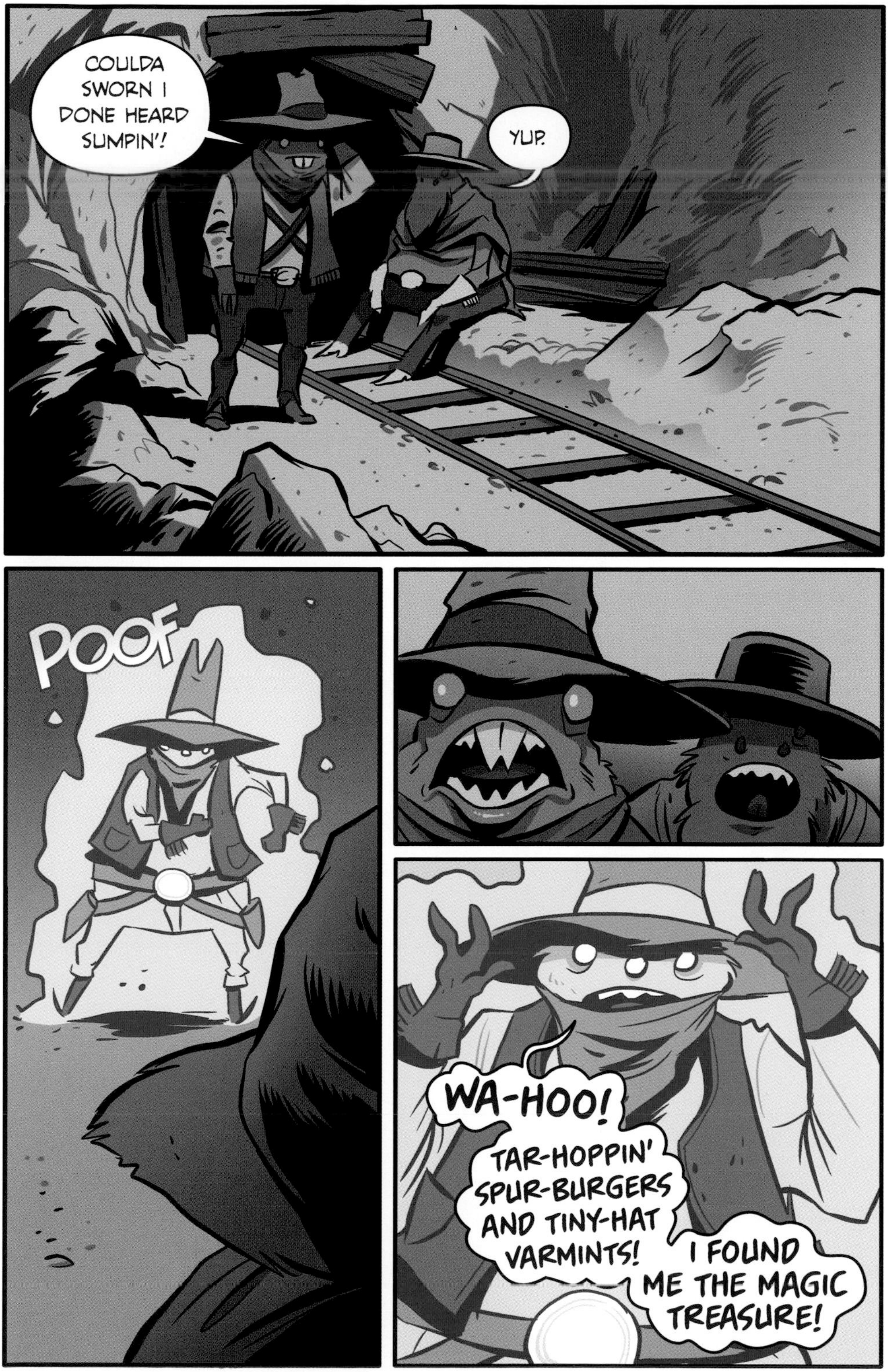
COULDA SWORN I DONE HEARD SUMPIN'!
YUP.
POOF
WA-HOO!
TAR-HOPPIN' SPUR-BURGERS AND TINY-HAT VARMINTS!
I FOUND ME THE MAGIC TREASURE!

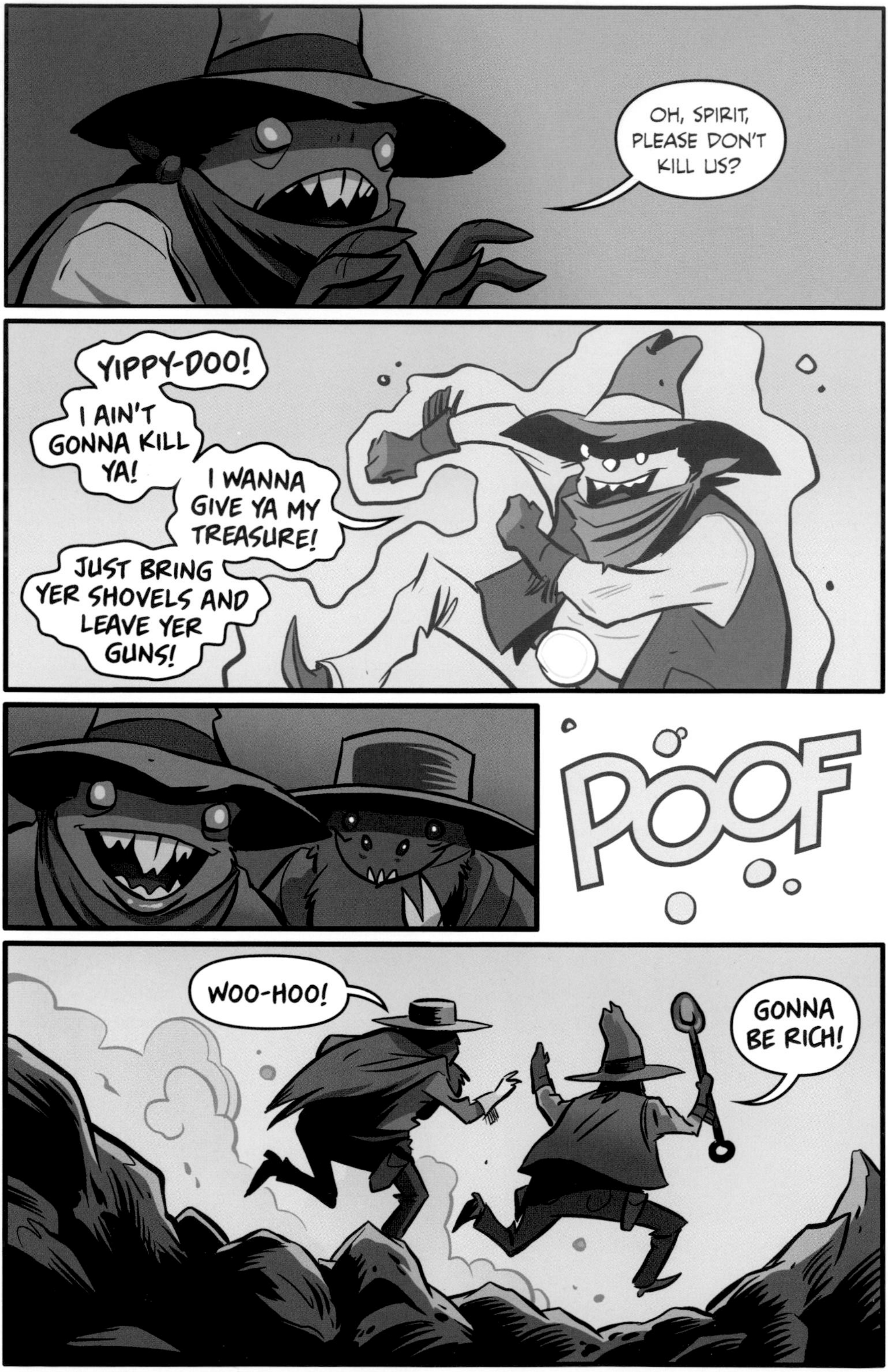
OH, SPIRIT, PLEASE DON'T KILL US?
YIPPY-DOO!
I AIN'T GONNA KILL YA!
I WANNA GIVE YA MY TREASURE!
JUST BRING YER SHOVELS AND LEAVE YER GUNS!
POOF
WOO-HOO!
GONNA BE RICH!

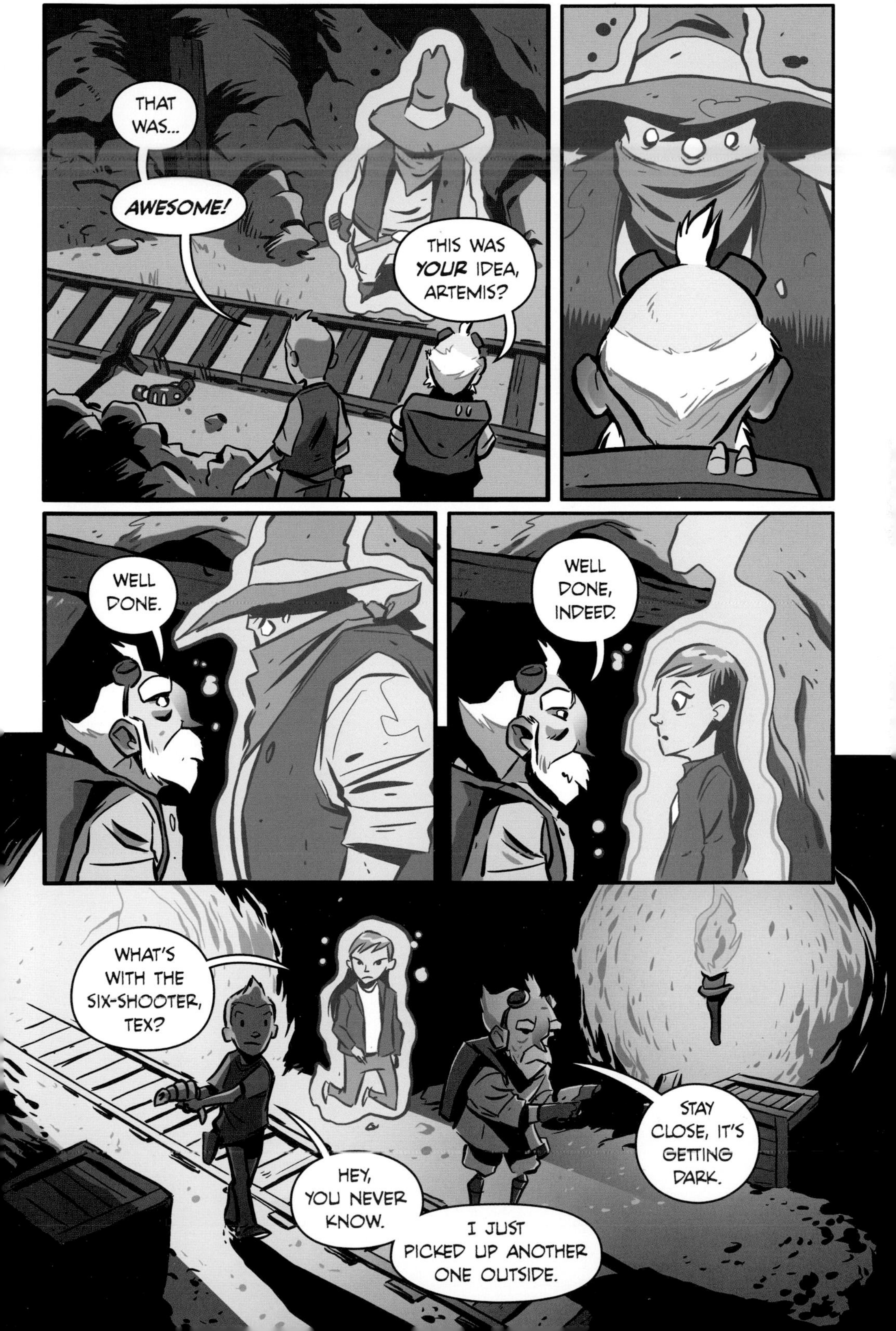
THAT WAS...
AWESOME!
THIS WAS YOUR IDEA, ARTEMIS?
WELL DONE.
WELL DONE, INDEED.
WHAT'S WITH THE SIX-SHOOTER, TEX?
HEY, YOU NEVER KNOW.
I JUST PICKED UP ANOTHER ONE OUTSIDE.
STAY CLOSE, IT'S GETTING DARK.

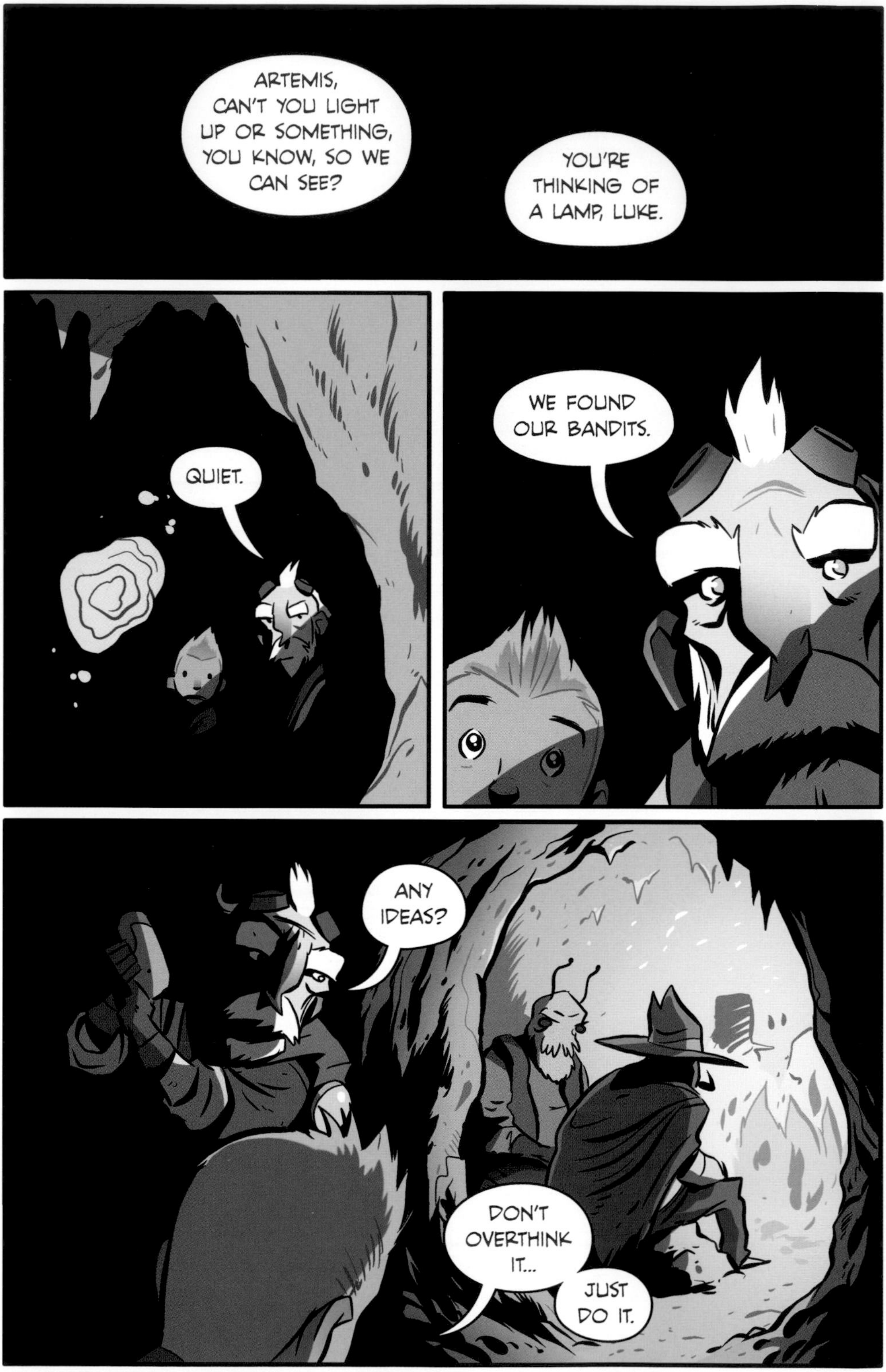
ARTEMIS, CAN'T YOU LIGHT UP OR SOMETHING, YOU KNOW, SO WE CAN SEE?
YOU'RE THINKING OF A LAMP, LUKE.
QUIET.
WE FOUND OUR BANDITS.
ANY IDEAS?
DON'T OVERTHINK IT...
JUST DO IT.

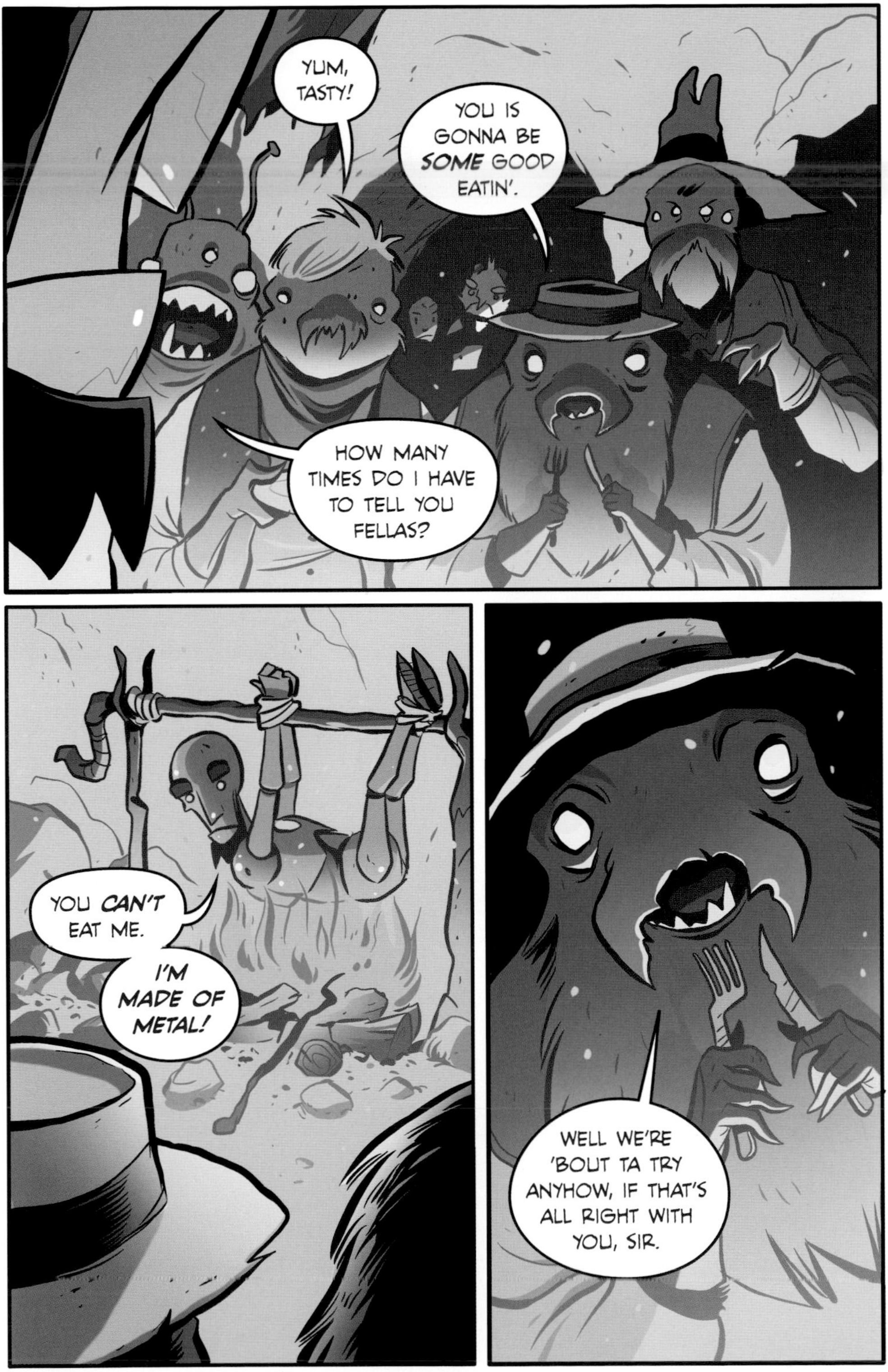
YUM, TASTY!
YOU IS GONNA BE *SOME* GOOD EATIN'.
HOW MANY TIMES DO I HAVE TO TELL YOU FELLAS?
YOU *CAN'T* EAT ME.
I'M MADE OF METAL!
WELL WE'RE 'BOUT TA TRY ANYHOW, IF THAT'S ALL RIGHT WITH YOU, SIR.

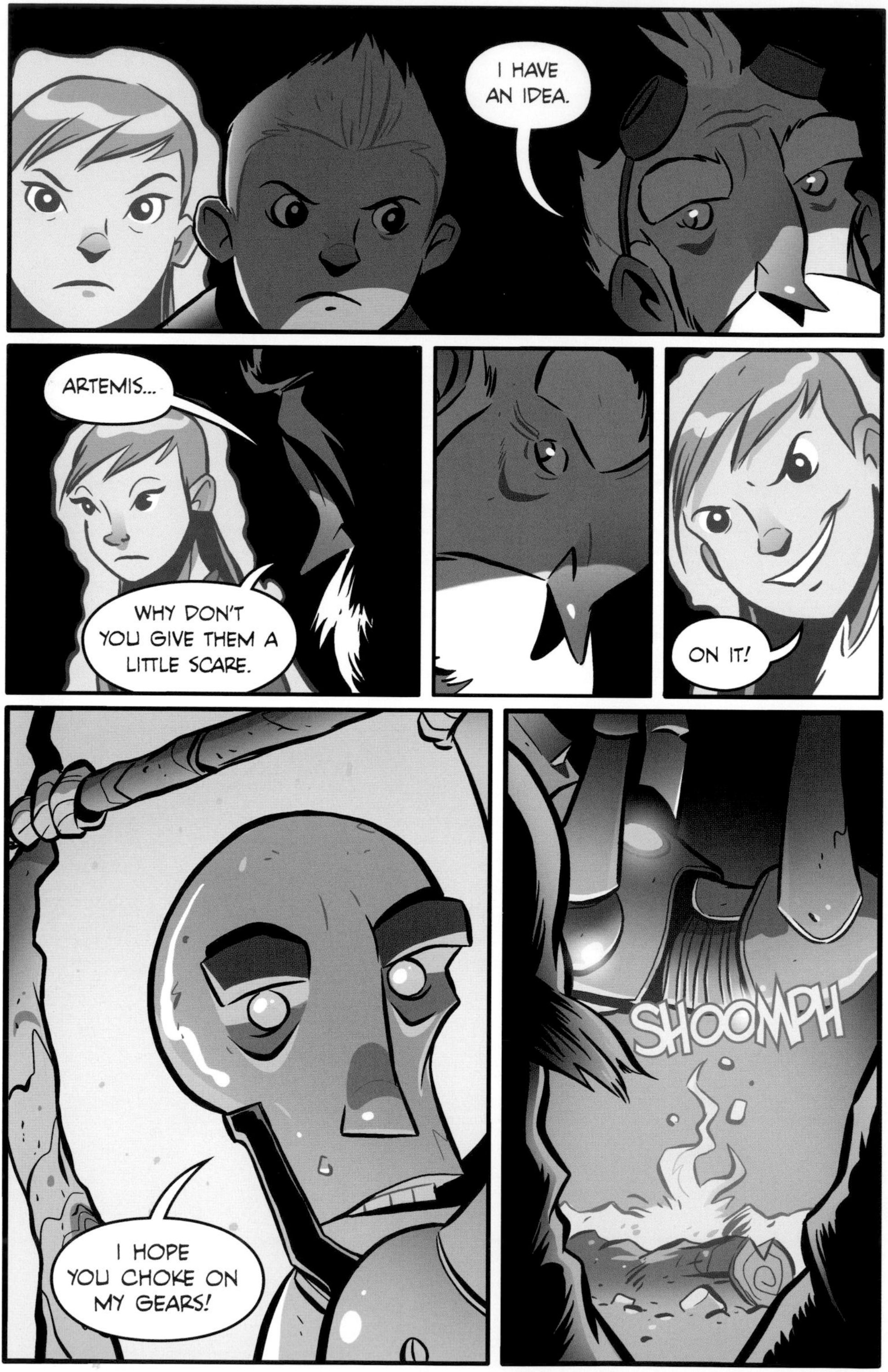
I HAVE AN IDEA.
ARTEMIS...
WHY DON'T YOU GIVE THEM A LITTLE SCARE.
ON IT!
I HOPE YOU CHOKE ON MY GEARS!
SHOOMPH

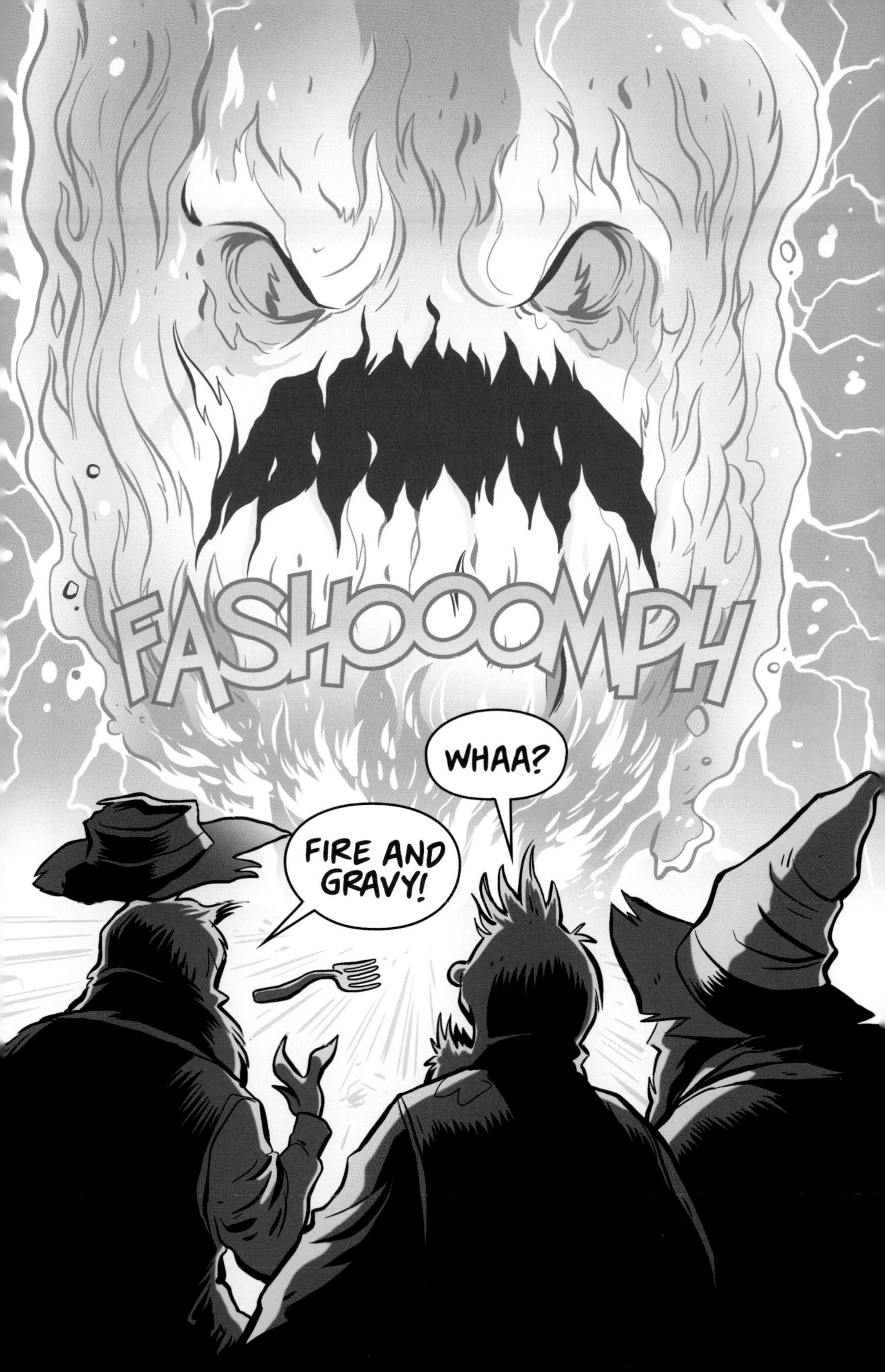
FASHOOOMPH
WHAA?
FIRE AND GRAVY!

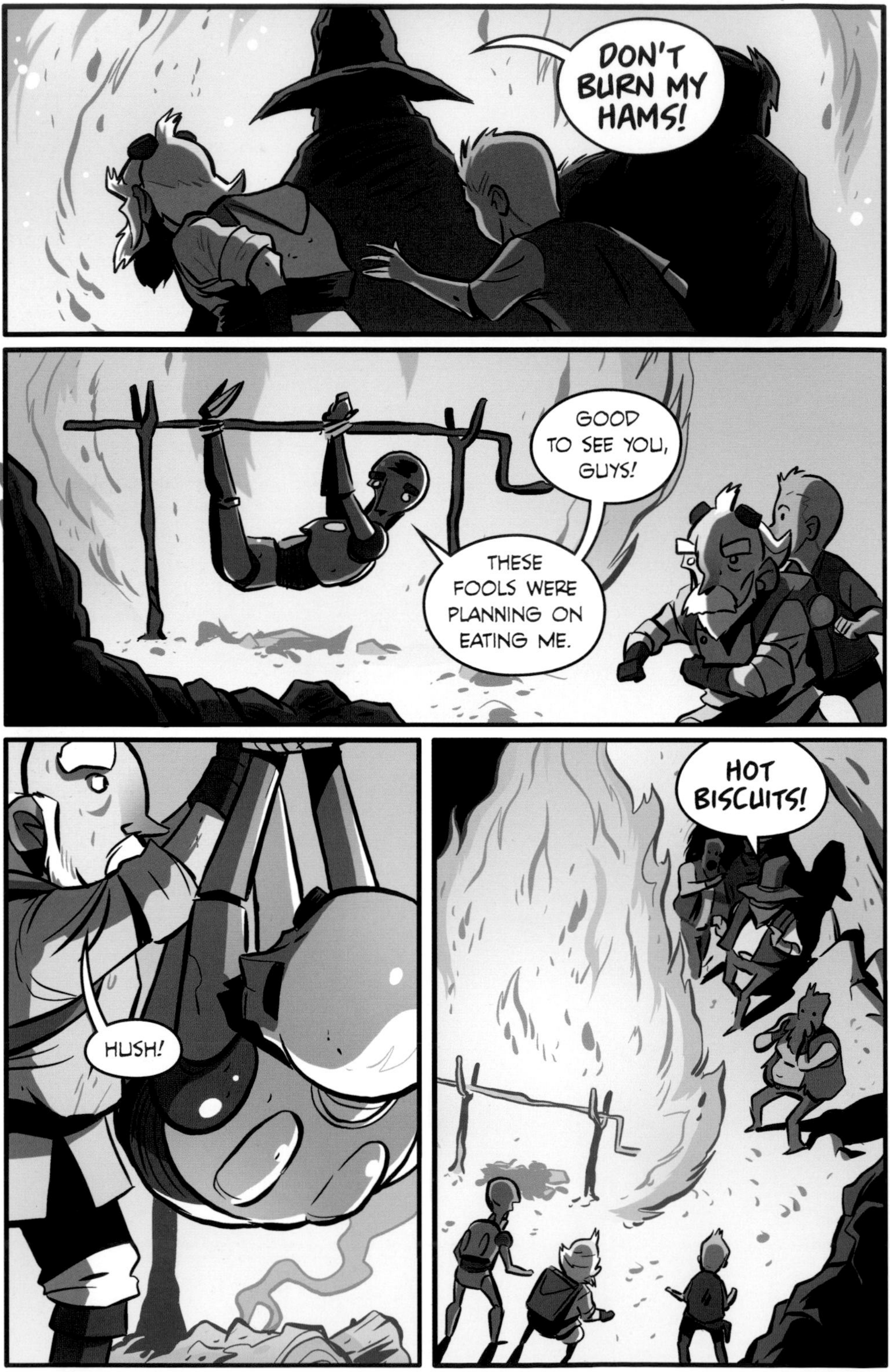
DON'T BURN MY HAMS!
GOOD TO SEE YOU, GUYS!
THESE FOOLS WERE PLANNING ON EATING ME.
HUSH!
HOT BISCUITS!

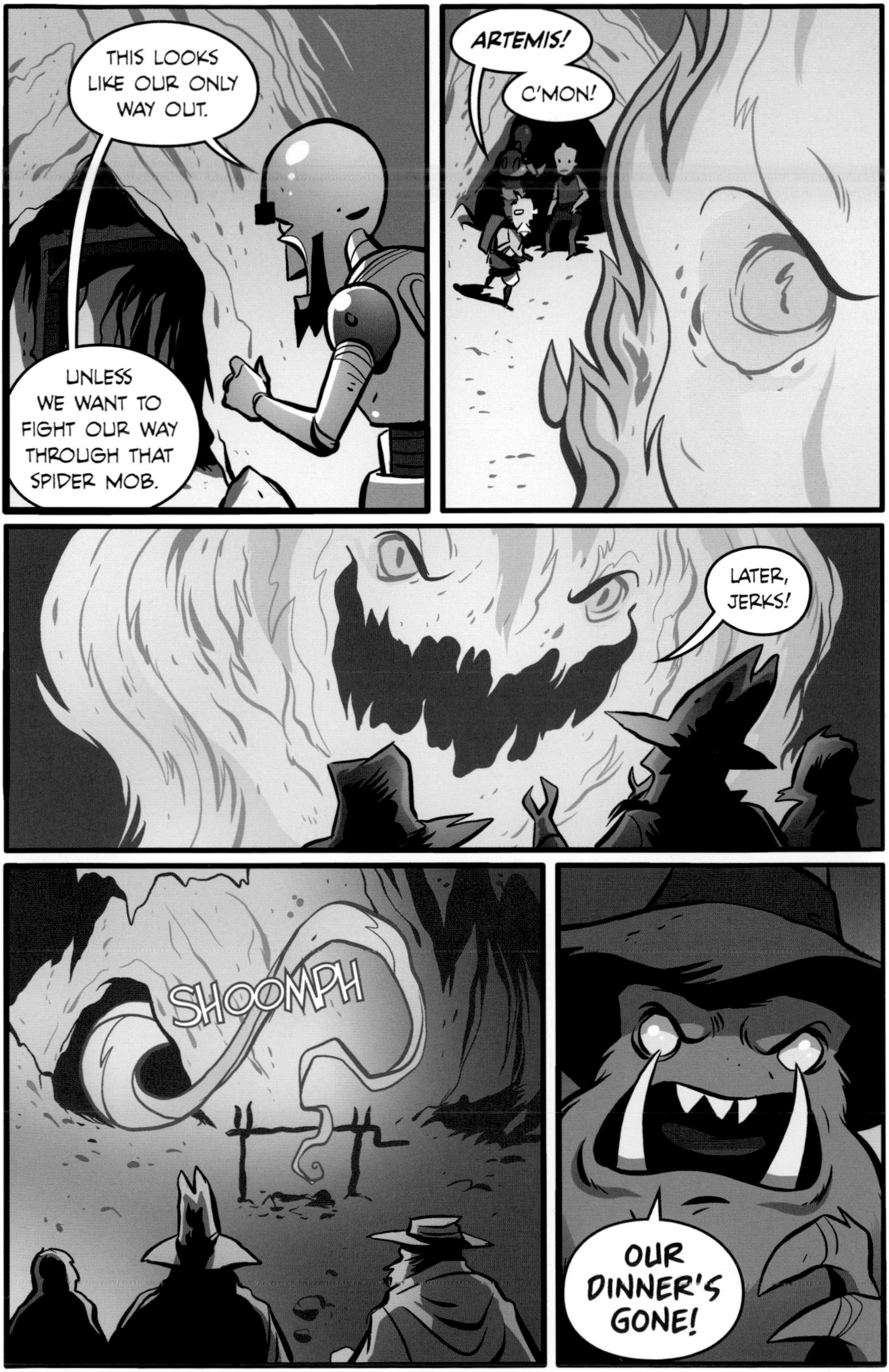
THIS LOOKS LIKE OUR ONLY WAY OUT.
UNLESS WE WANT TO FIGHT OUR WAY THROUGH THAT SPIDER MOB.
ARTEMIS!
C'MON!
LATER, JERKS!
SHOOMPH
OUR DINNER'S GONE!

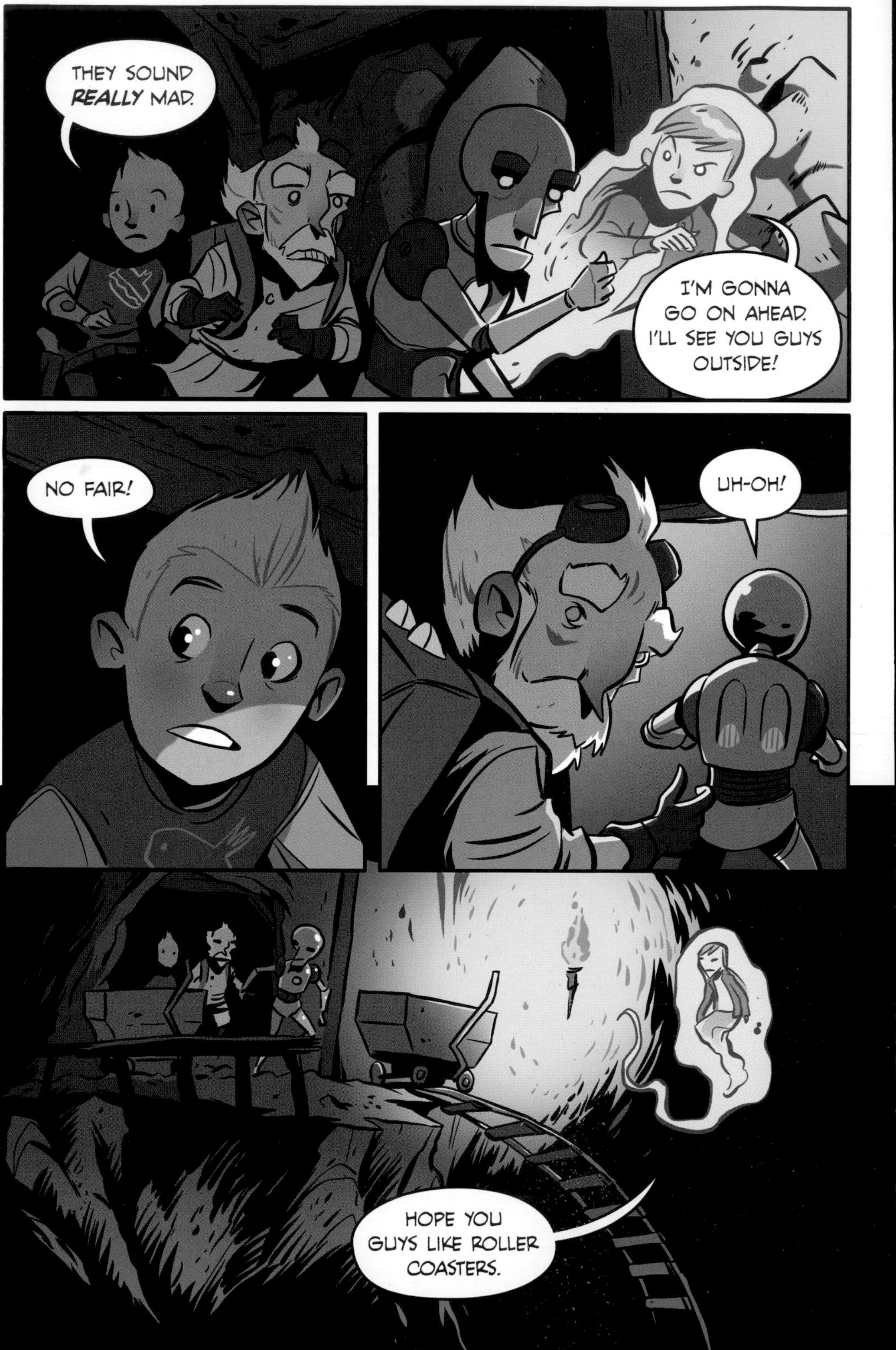
THEY SOUND *REALLY* MAD.
I'M GONNA GO ON AHEAD. I'LL SEE YOU GUYS OUTSIDE!
NO FAIR!
UH-OH!
HOPE YOU GUYS LIKE ROLLER COASTERS.

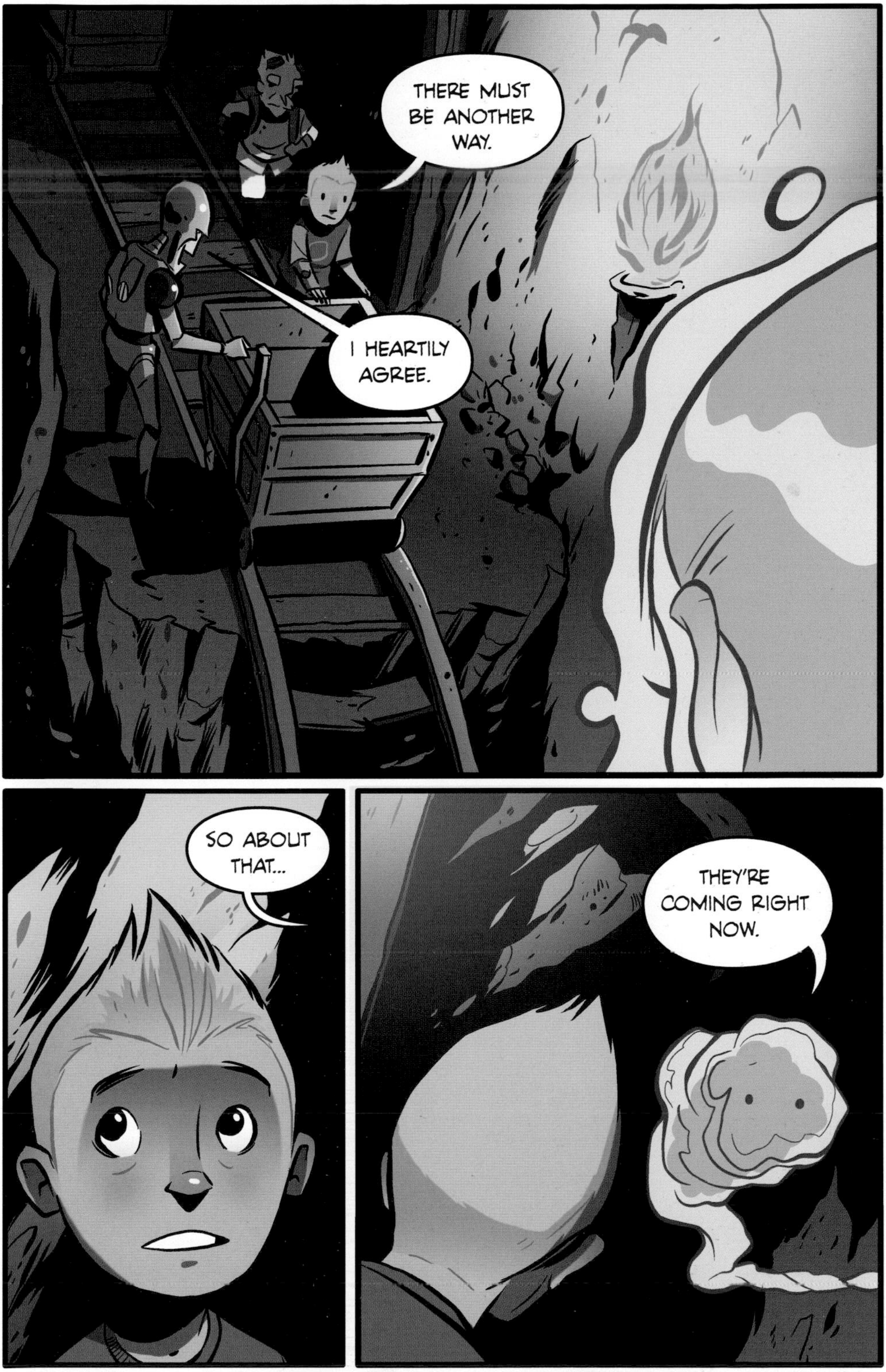
THERE MUST BE ANOTHER WAY.
I HEARTILY AGREE.
SO ABOUT THAT...
THEY'RE COMING RIGHT NOW.

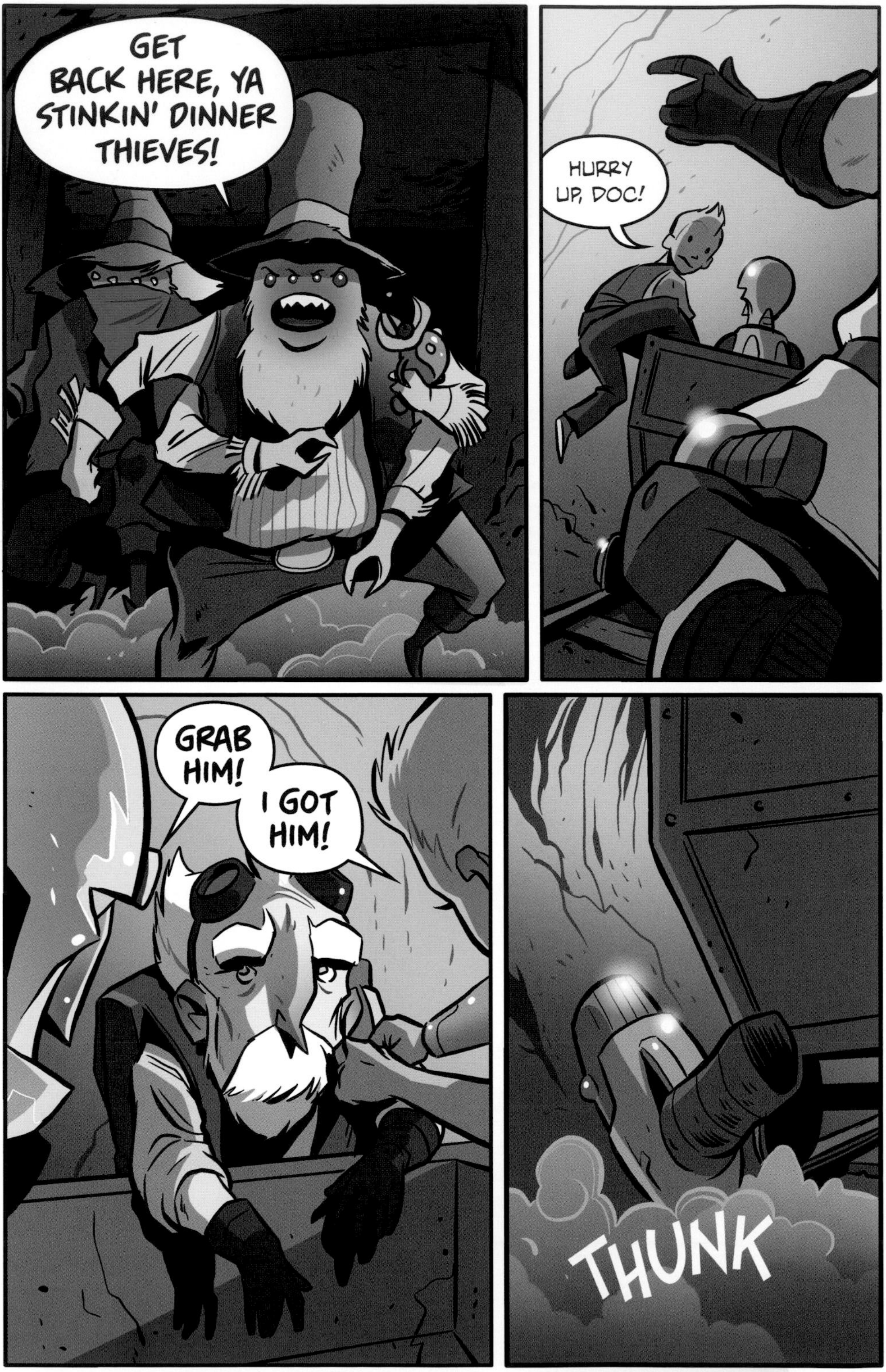
GET BACK HERE, YA STINKIN' DINNER THIEVES!
HURRY UP, DOC!
GRAB HIM!
I GOT HIM!
THUNK

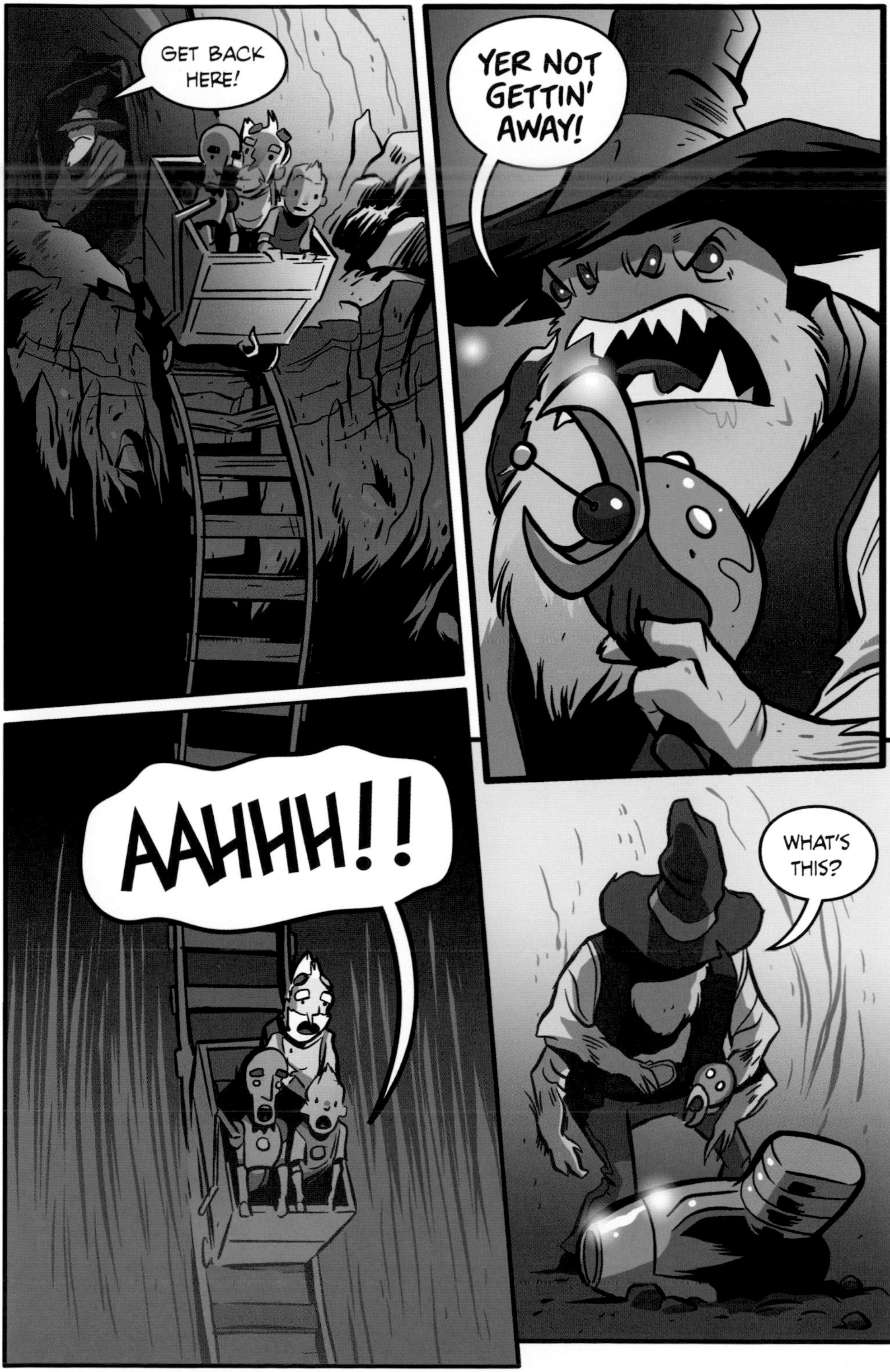
GET BACK HERE!
YER NOT GETTIN' AWAY!
AAHHH!!
WHAT'S THIS?

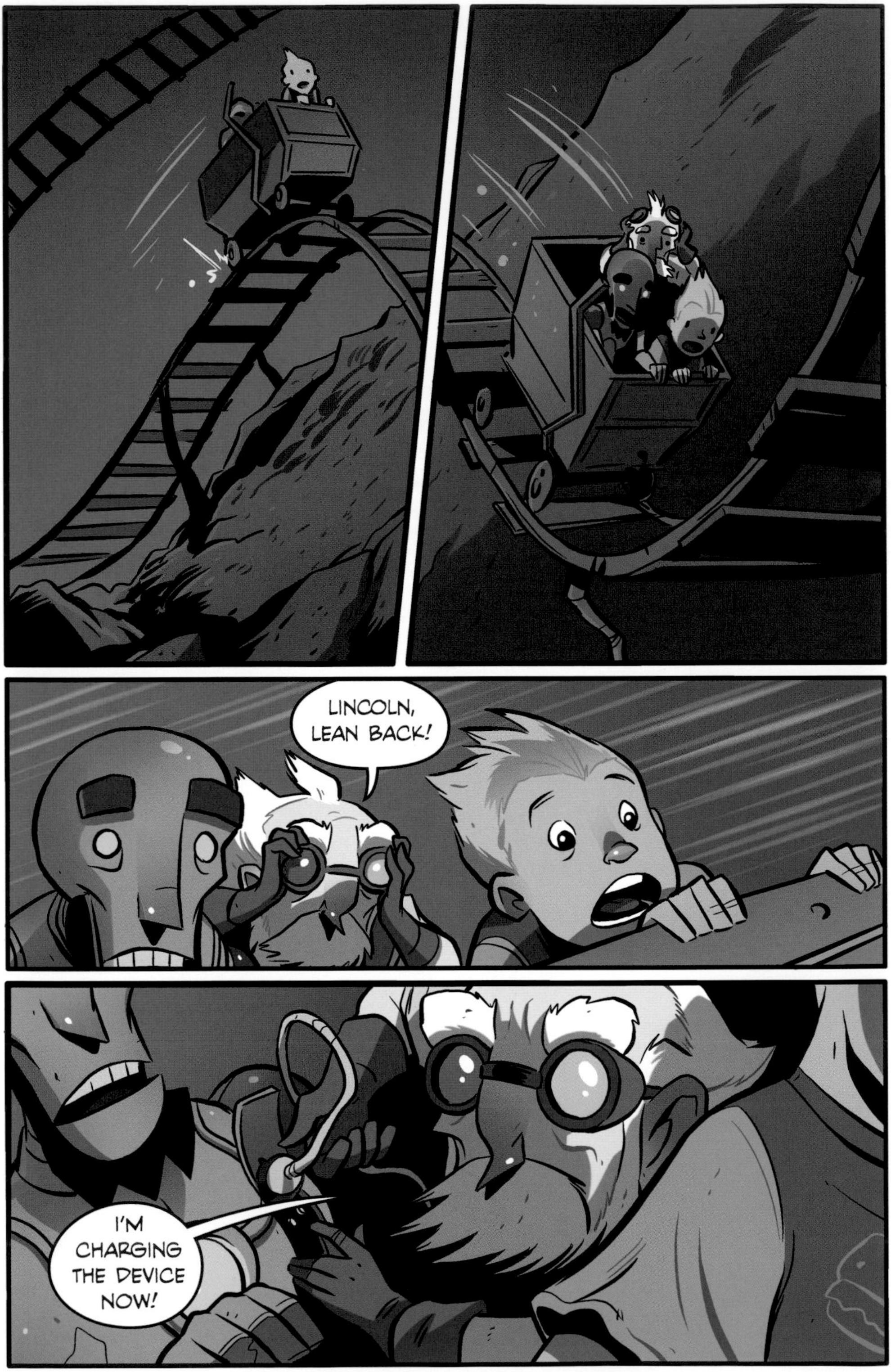
LINCOLN, LEAN BACK!
I'M CHARGING THE DEVICE NOW!

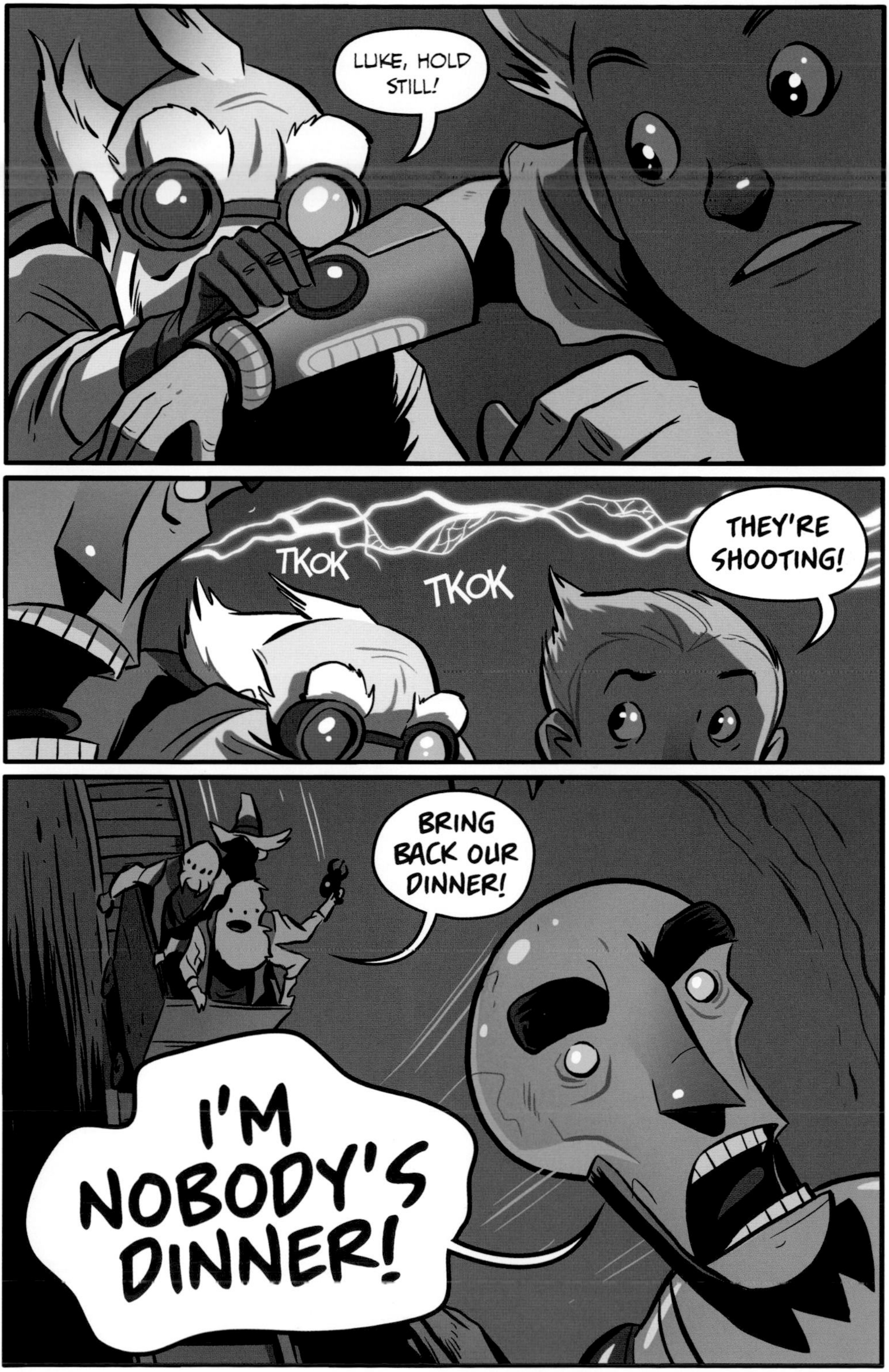
LUKE, HOLD STILL!
TKOK
TKOK
THEY'RE SHOOTING!
BRING BACK OUR DINNER!
I'M NOBODY'S DINNER!

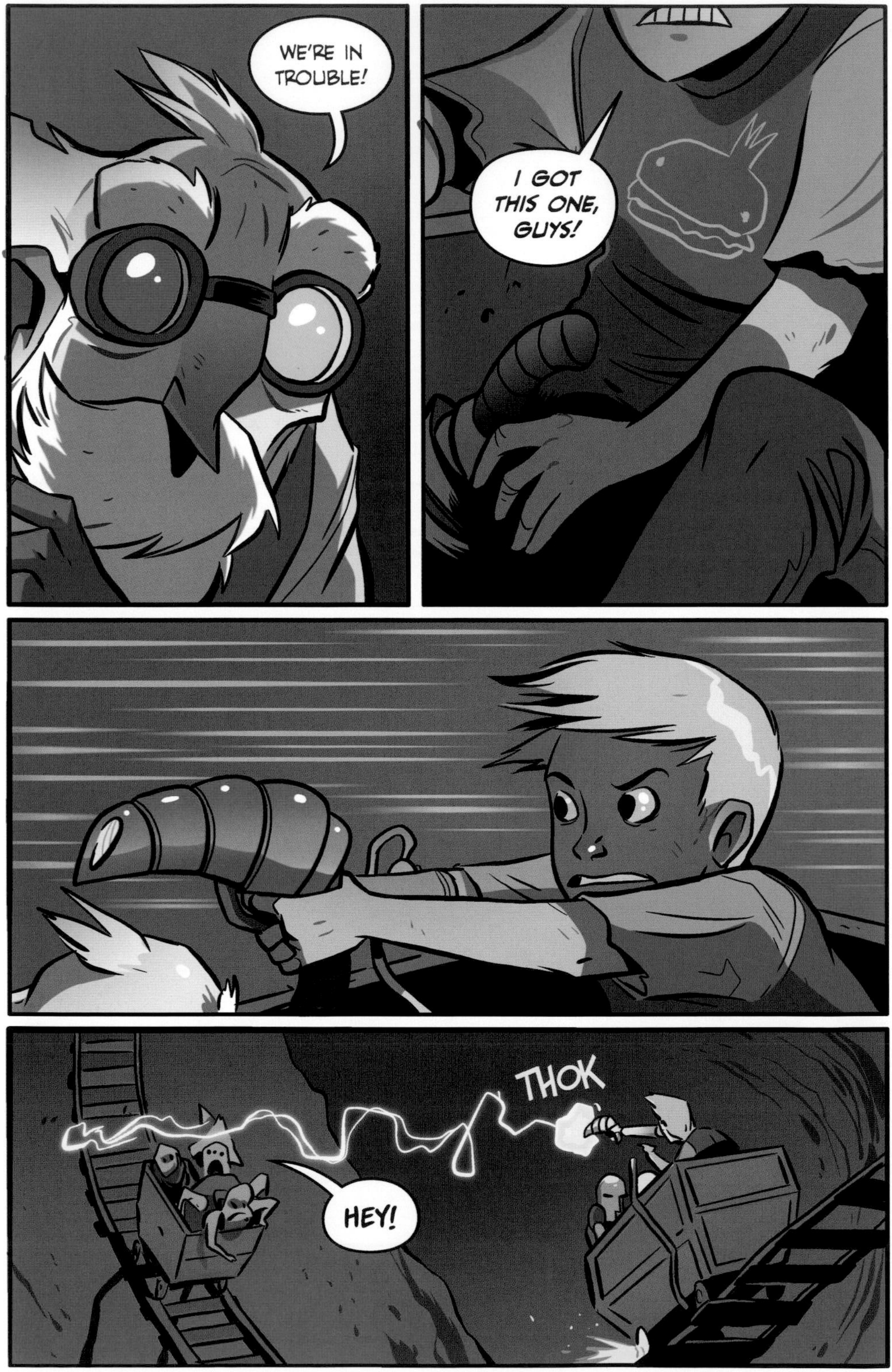
WE'RE IN TROUBLE!
I GOT THIS ONE, GUYS!
THOK
HEY!

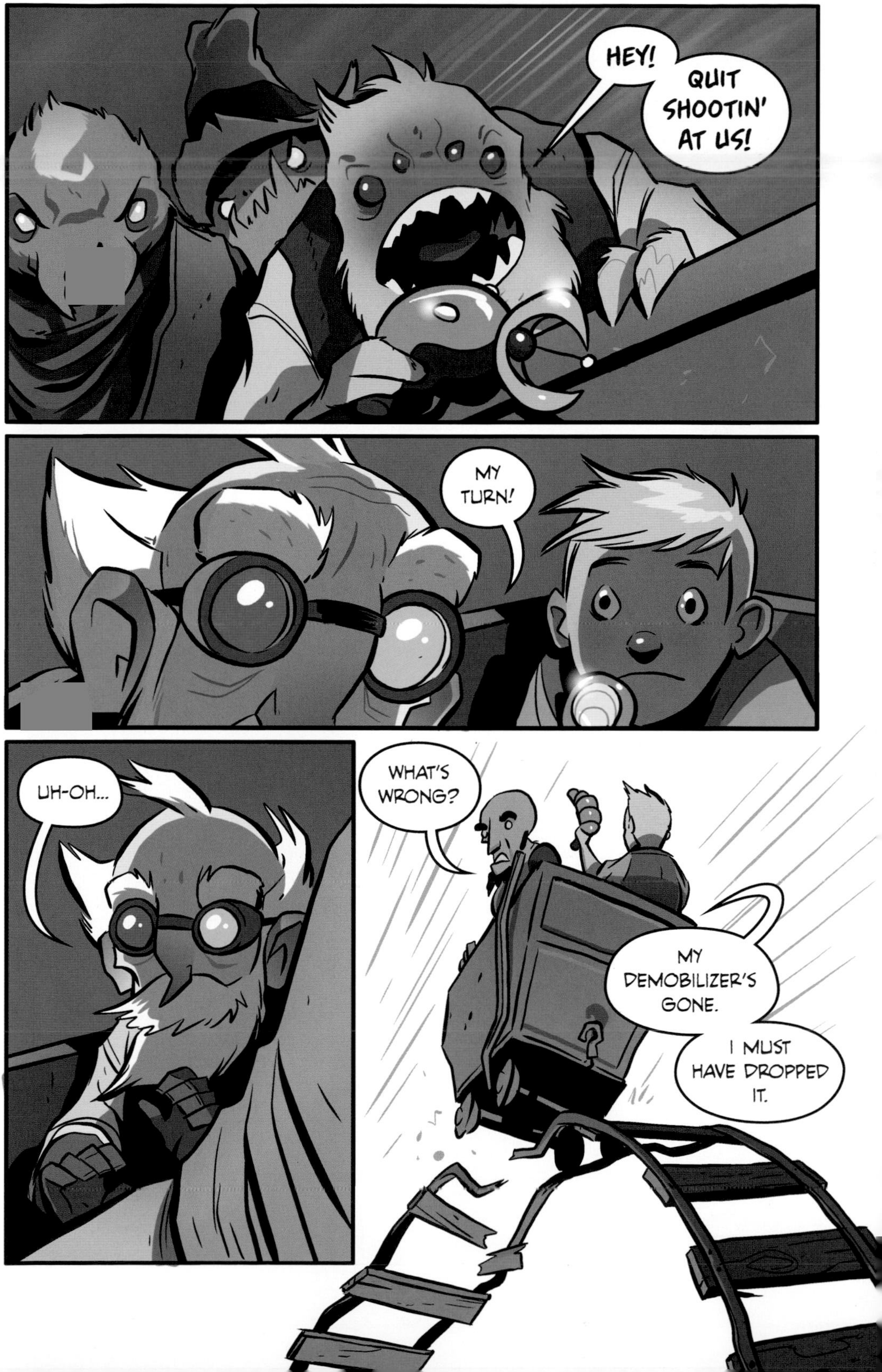
HEY!
QUIT SHOOTIN' AT US!
MY TURN!
UH-OH...
WHAT'S WRONG?
MY DEMOBILIZER'S GONE.
I MUST HAVE DROPPED IT.

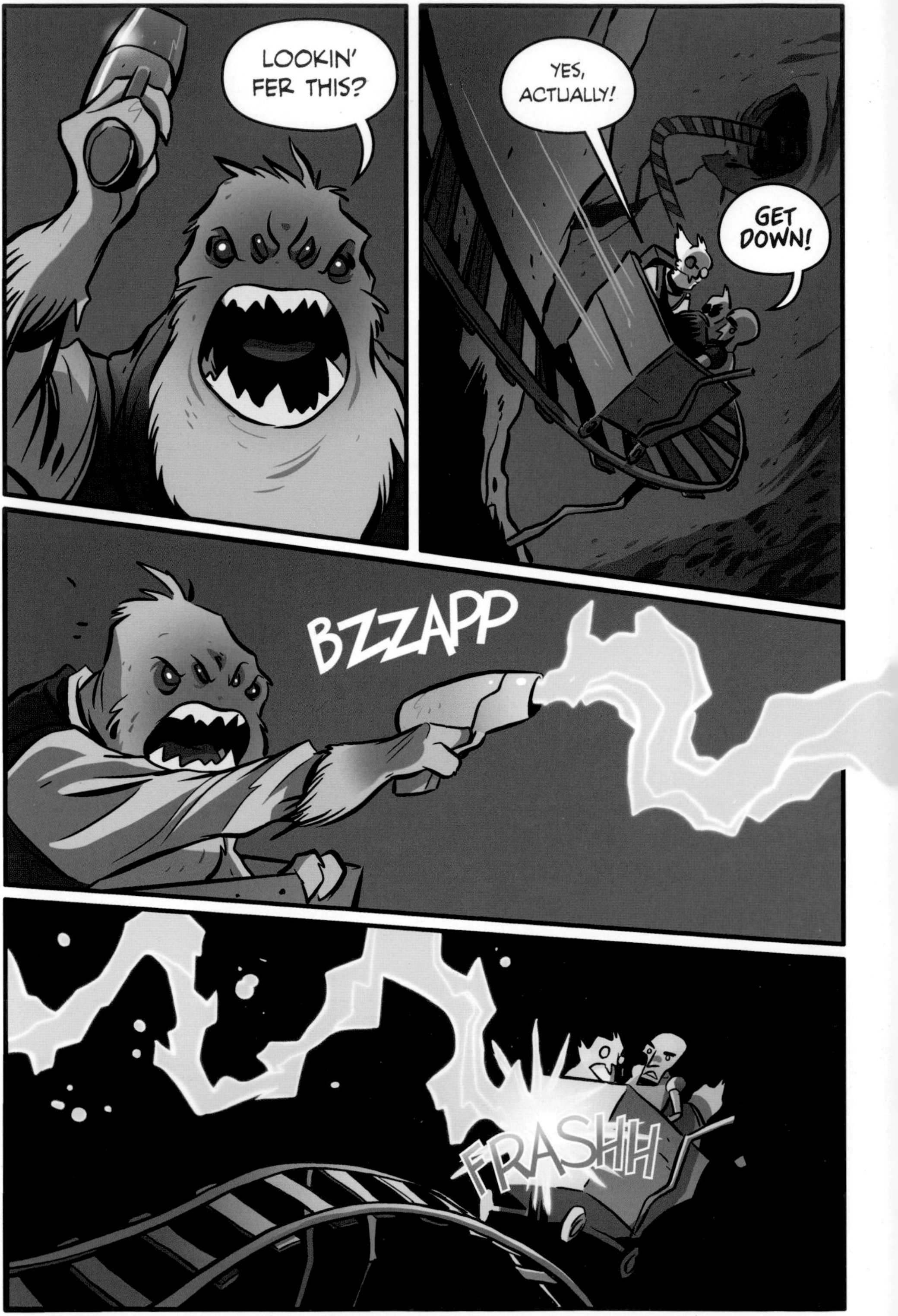
LOOKIN' FER THIS?
YES, ACTUALLY!
GET DOWN!
BZZAPP
FRASHH

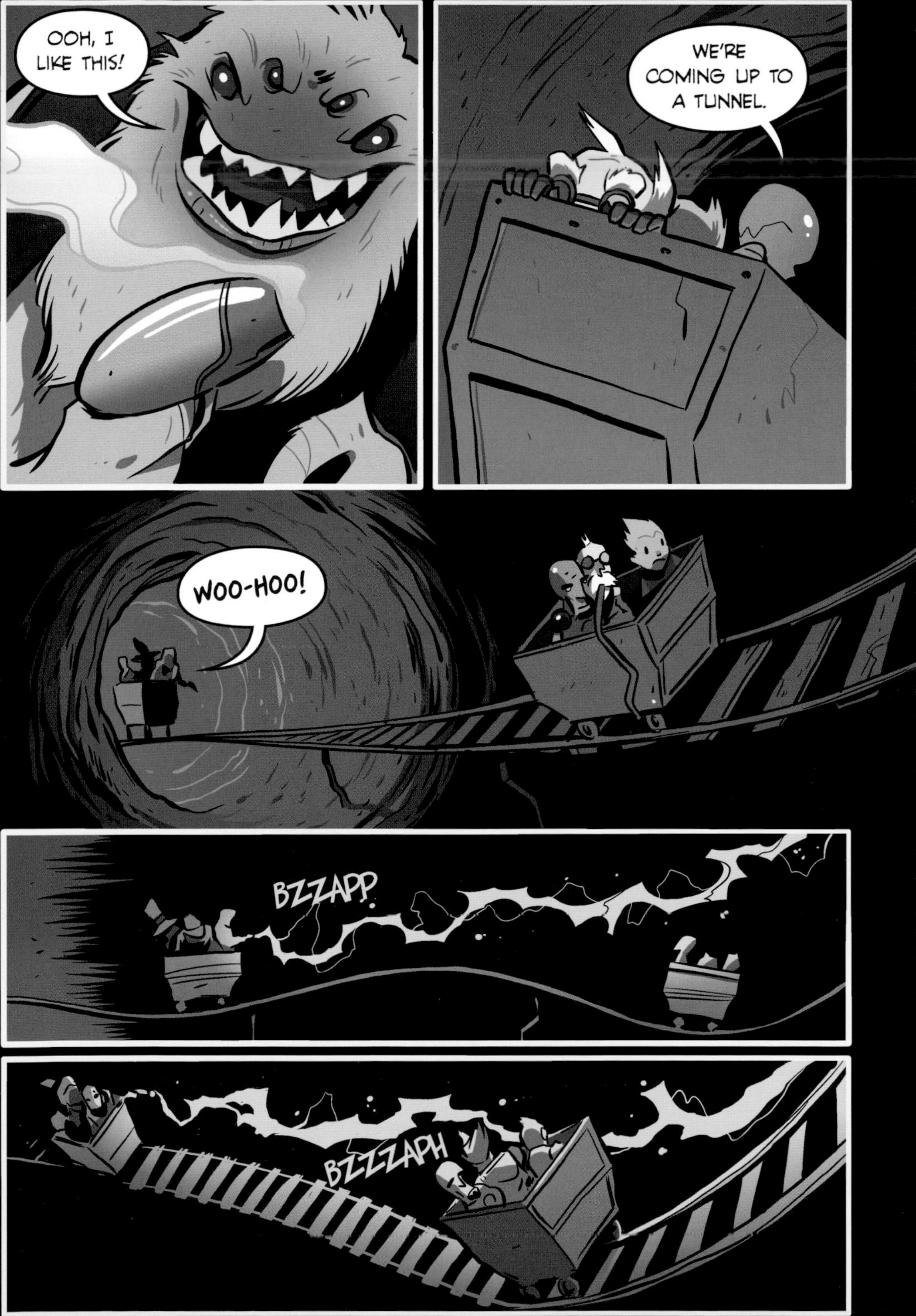
OOH, I LIKE THIS!
WE'RE COMING UP TO A TUNNEL.
WOO-HOO!
BZZAPP
BZZZAPH

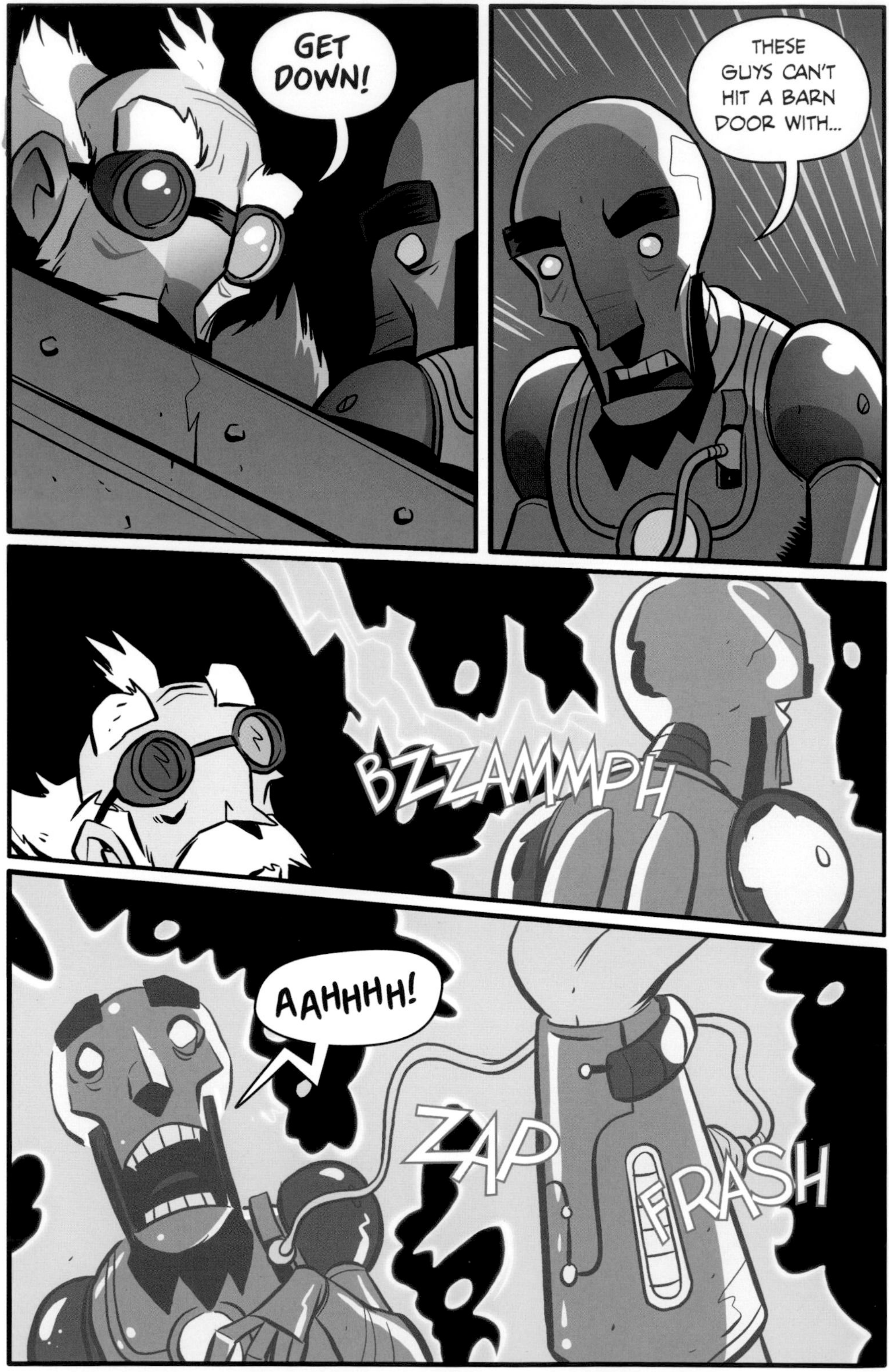
GET DOWN!
THESE GUYS CAN'T HIT A BARN DOOR WITH...
BZZAMMPH
AAHHHH!
ZAP
FRASH

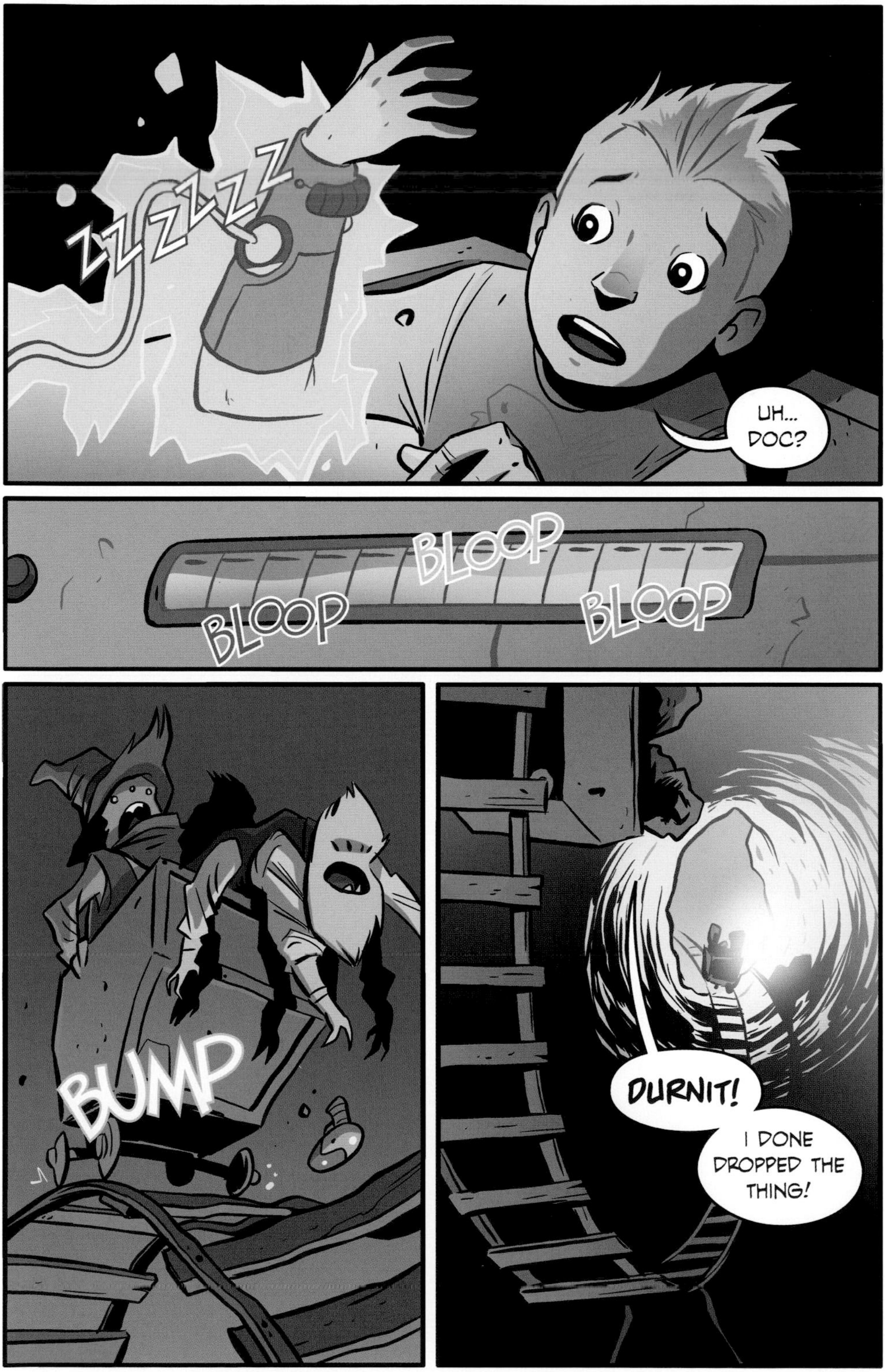
ZZZZZZ
UH... DOC?
BLOOP
BLOOP
BLOOP
BUMP
DURNIT!
I DONE DROPPED THE THING!

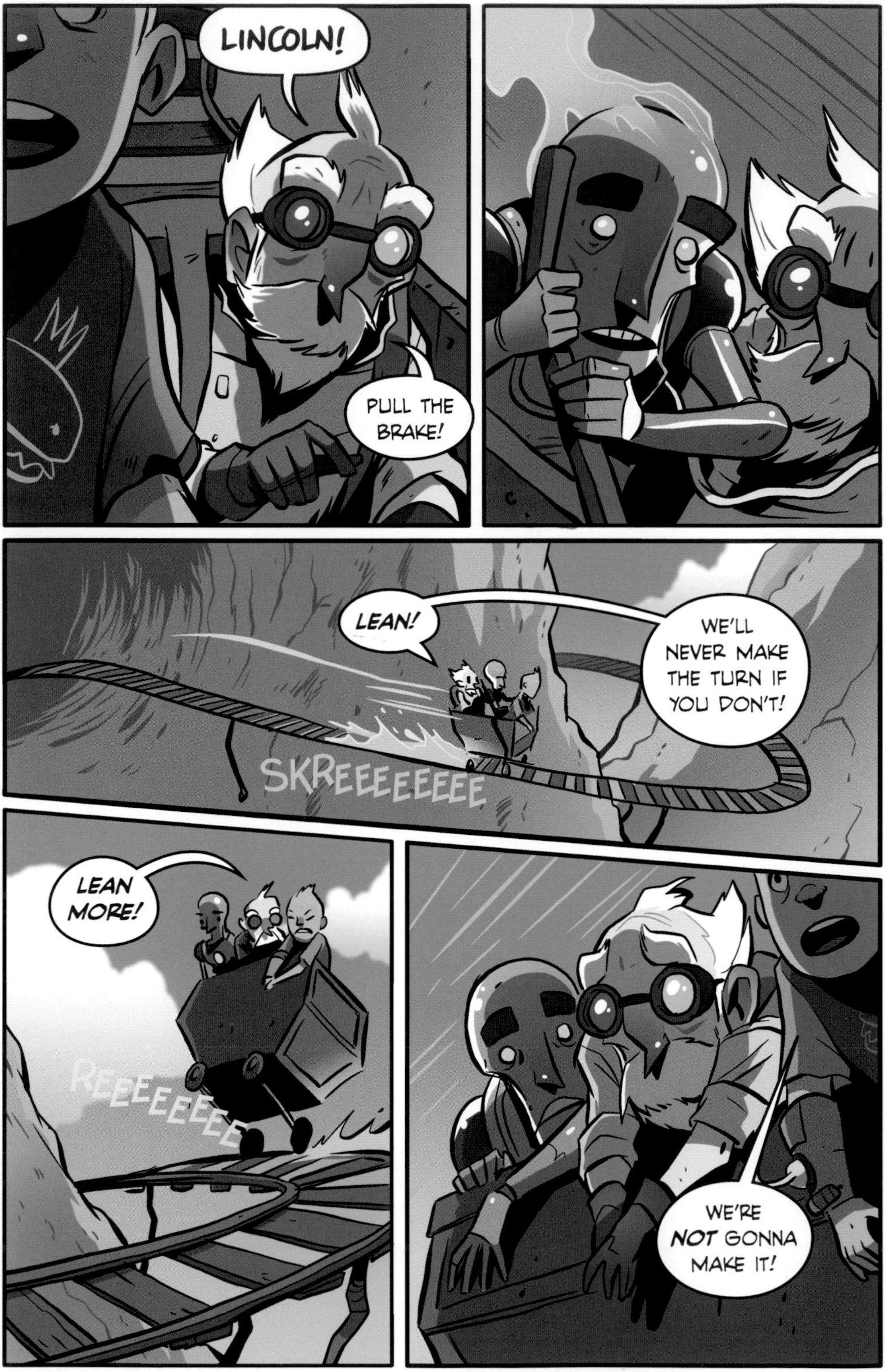
LINCOLN!
PULL THE BRAKE!
LEAN!
WE'LL NEVER MAKE THE TURN IF YOU DON'T!
SKREEEEEEEEE
LEAN MORE!
REEEEEEEEE
WE'RE NOT GONNA MAKE IT!

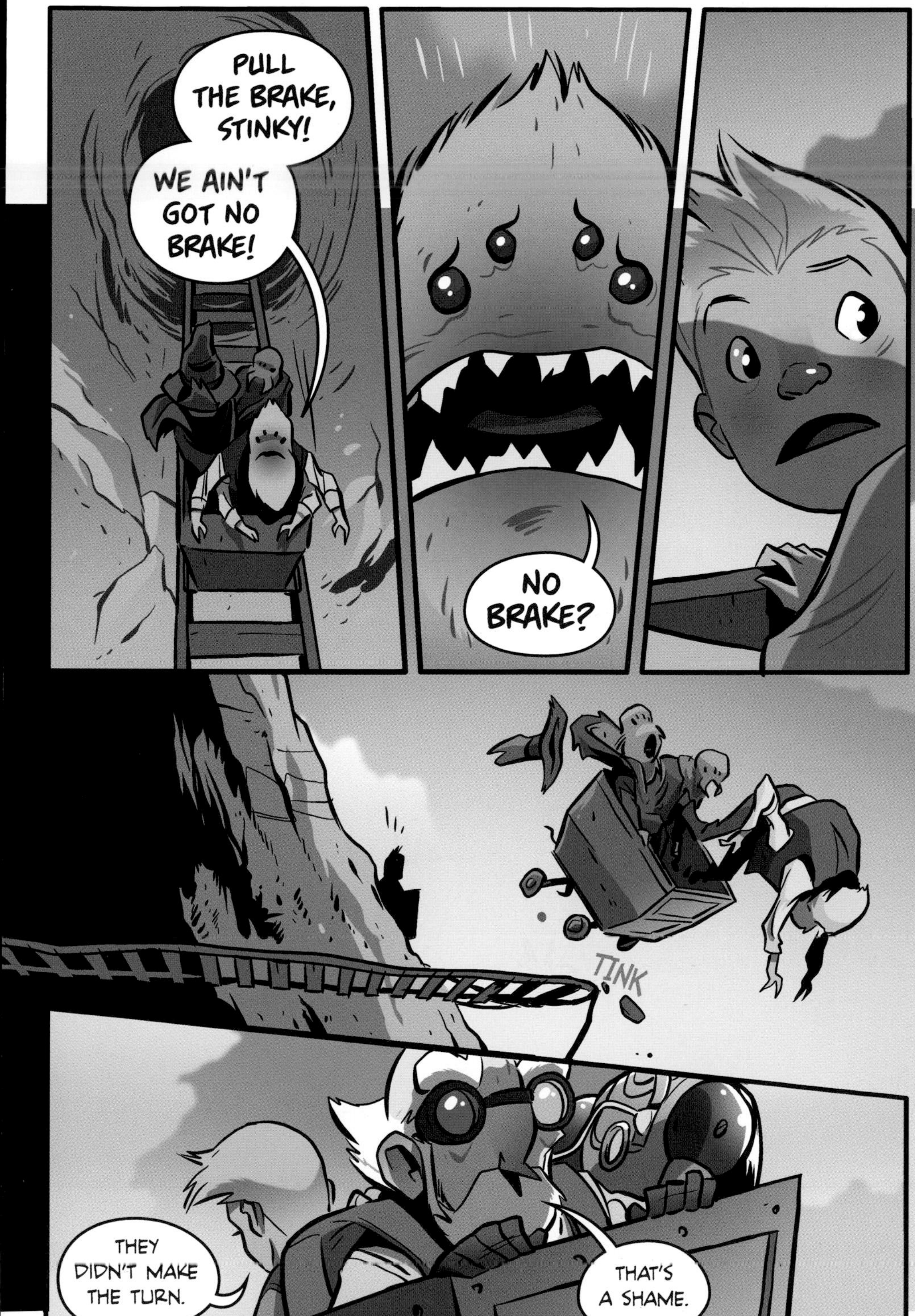
PULL THE BRAKE, STINKY!
WE AIN'T GOT NO BRAKE!
NO BRAKE?
TINK
THEY DIDN'T MAKE THE TURN.
THAT'S A SHAME.

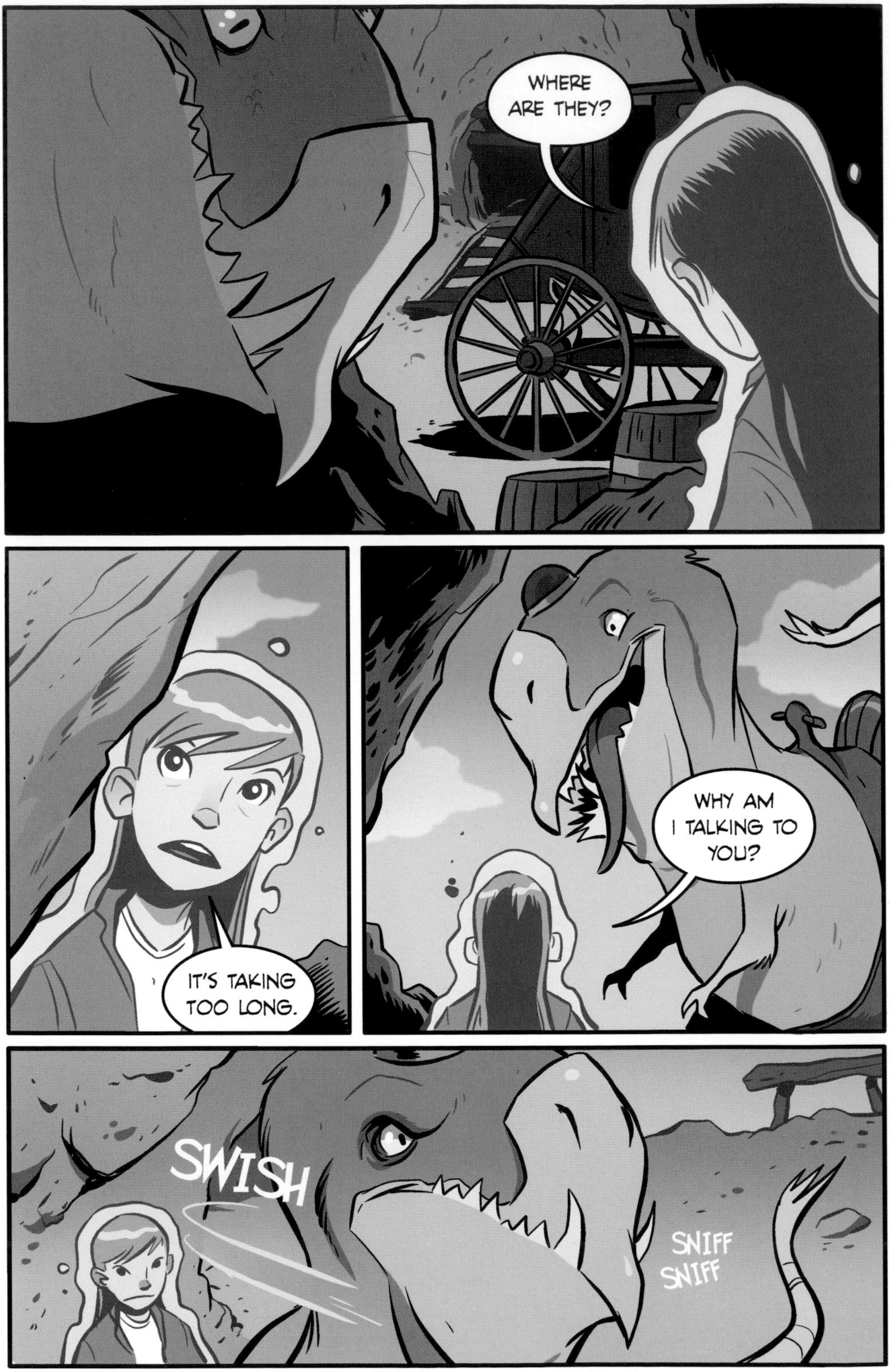
WHERE ARE THEY?
IT'S TAKING TOO LONG.
WHY AM I TALKING TO YOU?
SWISH
SNIFF SNIFF

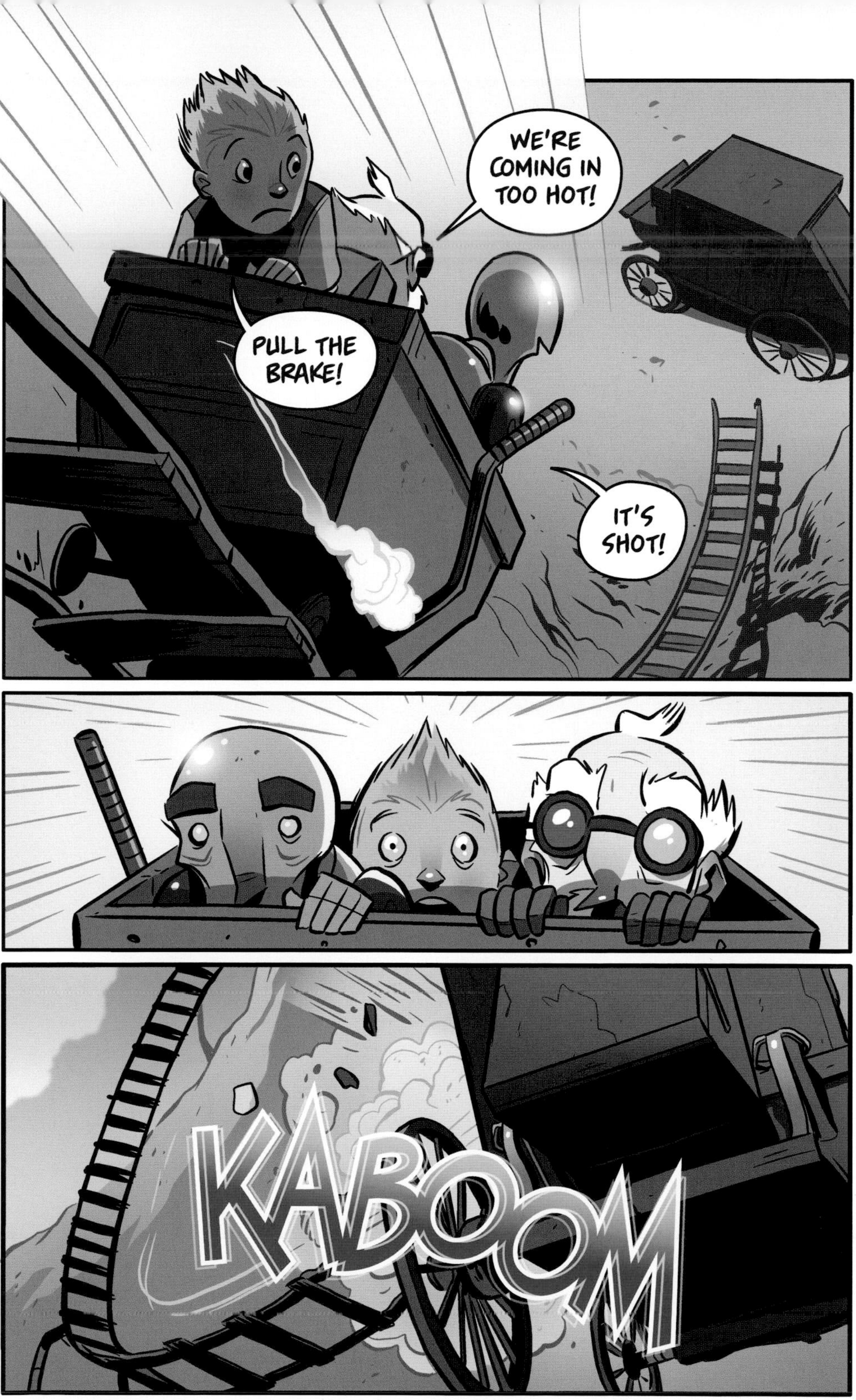
WE'RE COMING IN TOO HOT!
PULL THE BRAKE!
IT'S SHOT!
KABOOOM

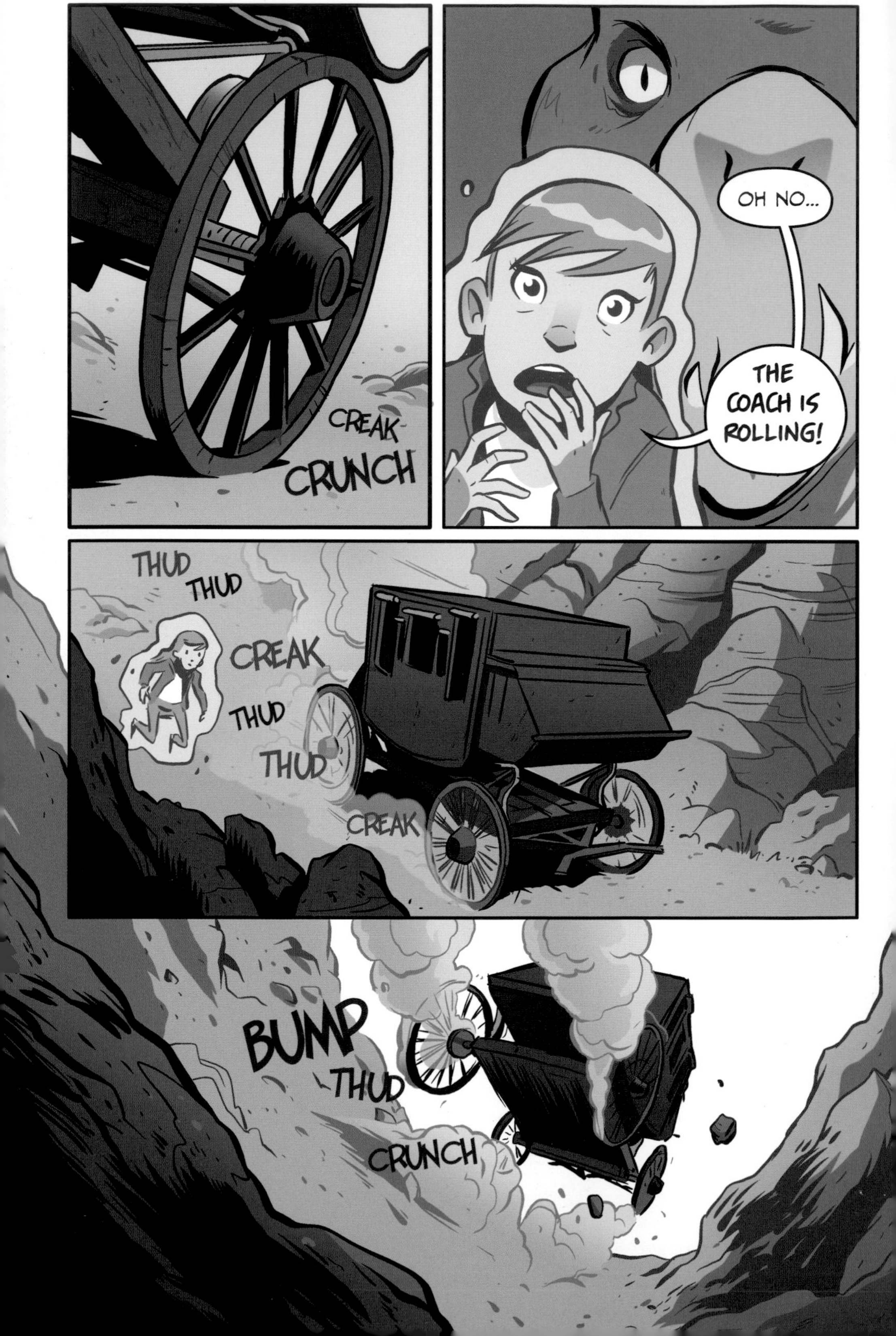
CREAK
CRUNCH
OH NO...
THE COACH IS ROLLING!
THUD
THUD
CREAK
THUD
THUD
CREAK
BUMP
THUD
CRUNCH

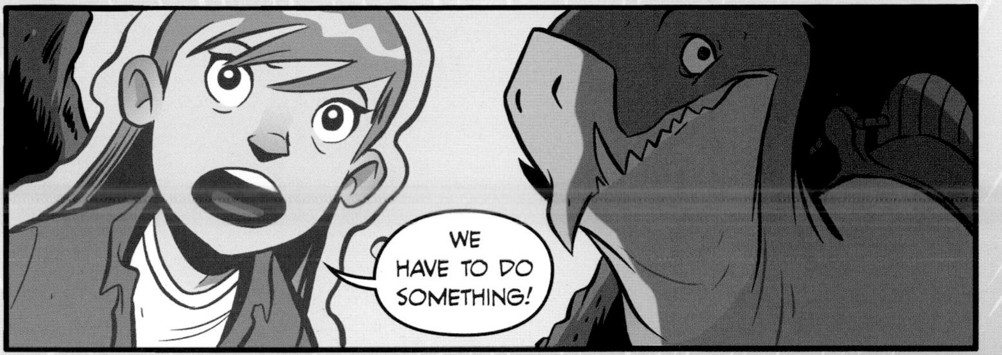
WE HAVE TO DO SOMETHING!

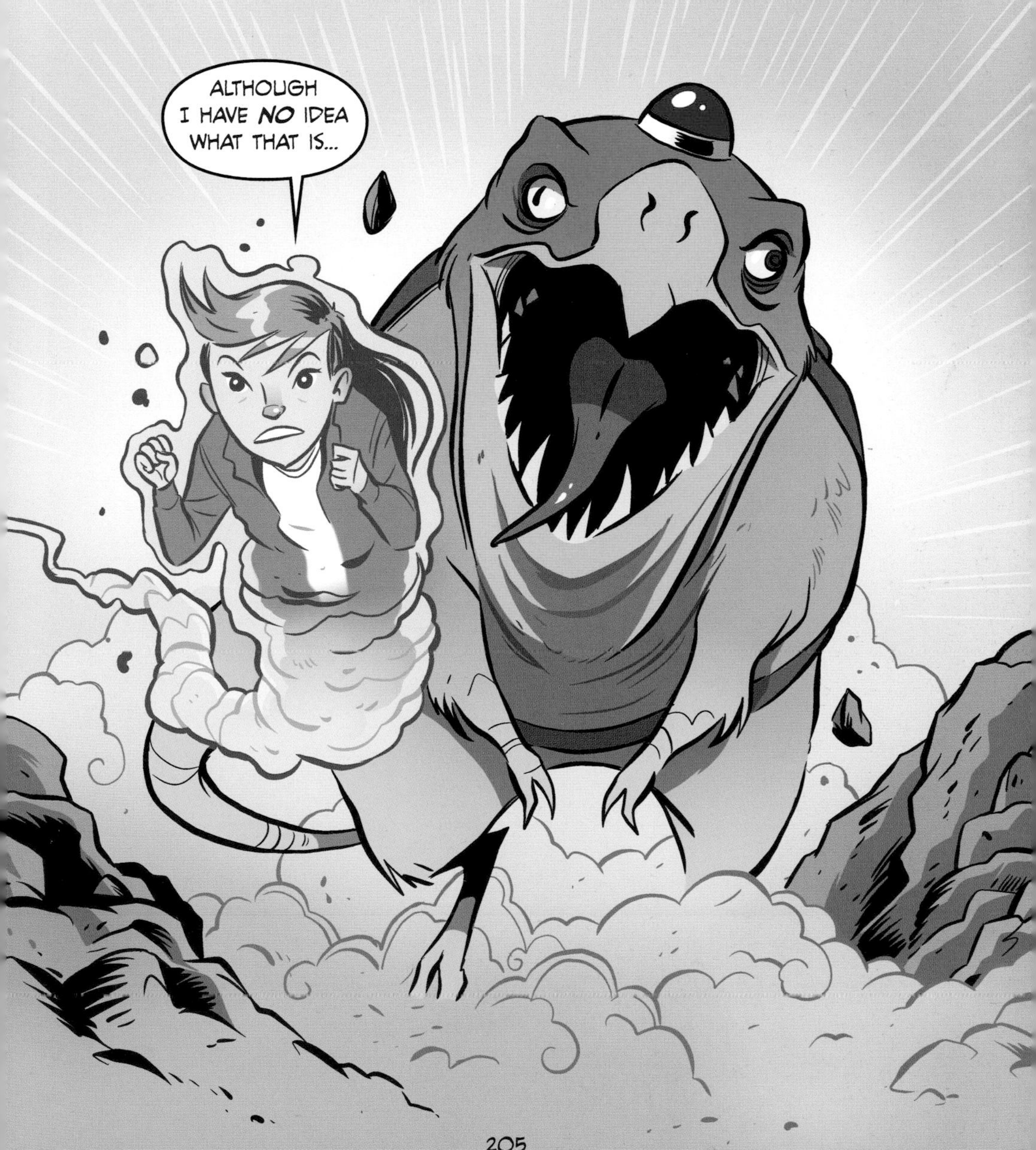
ALTHOUGH I HAVE NO IDEA WHAT THAT IS...

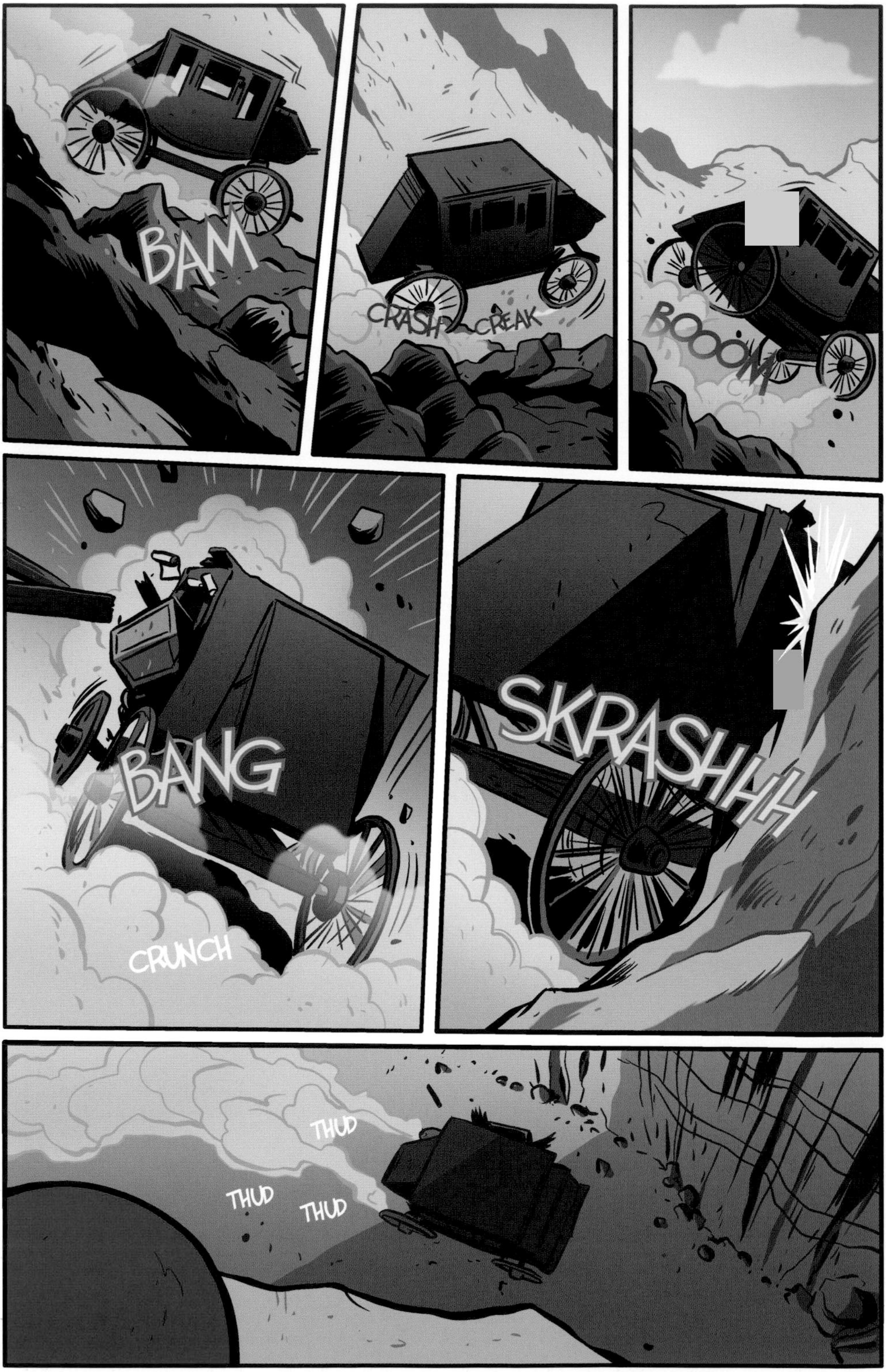
BAM
CRASH
CREAK
BOOOOM
BANG
CRUNCH
SKRASHHH
THUD
THUD
THUD

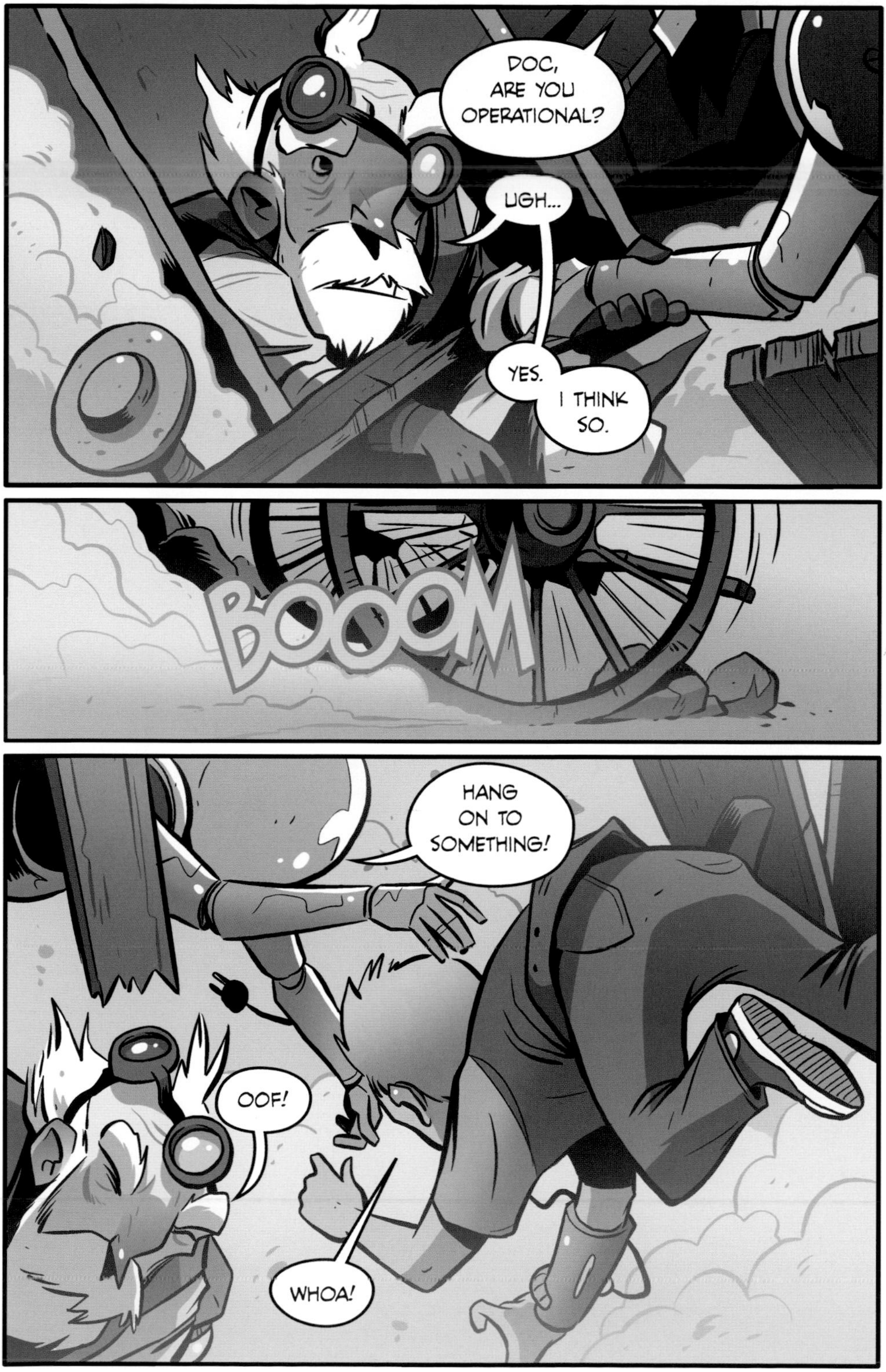
DOC, ARE YOU OPERATIONAL?
UGH...
YES.
I THINK SO.
BOOOM
HANG ON TO SOMETHING!
OOF!
WHOA!

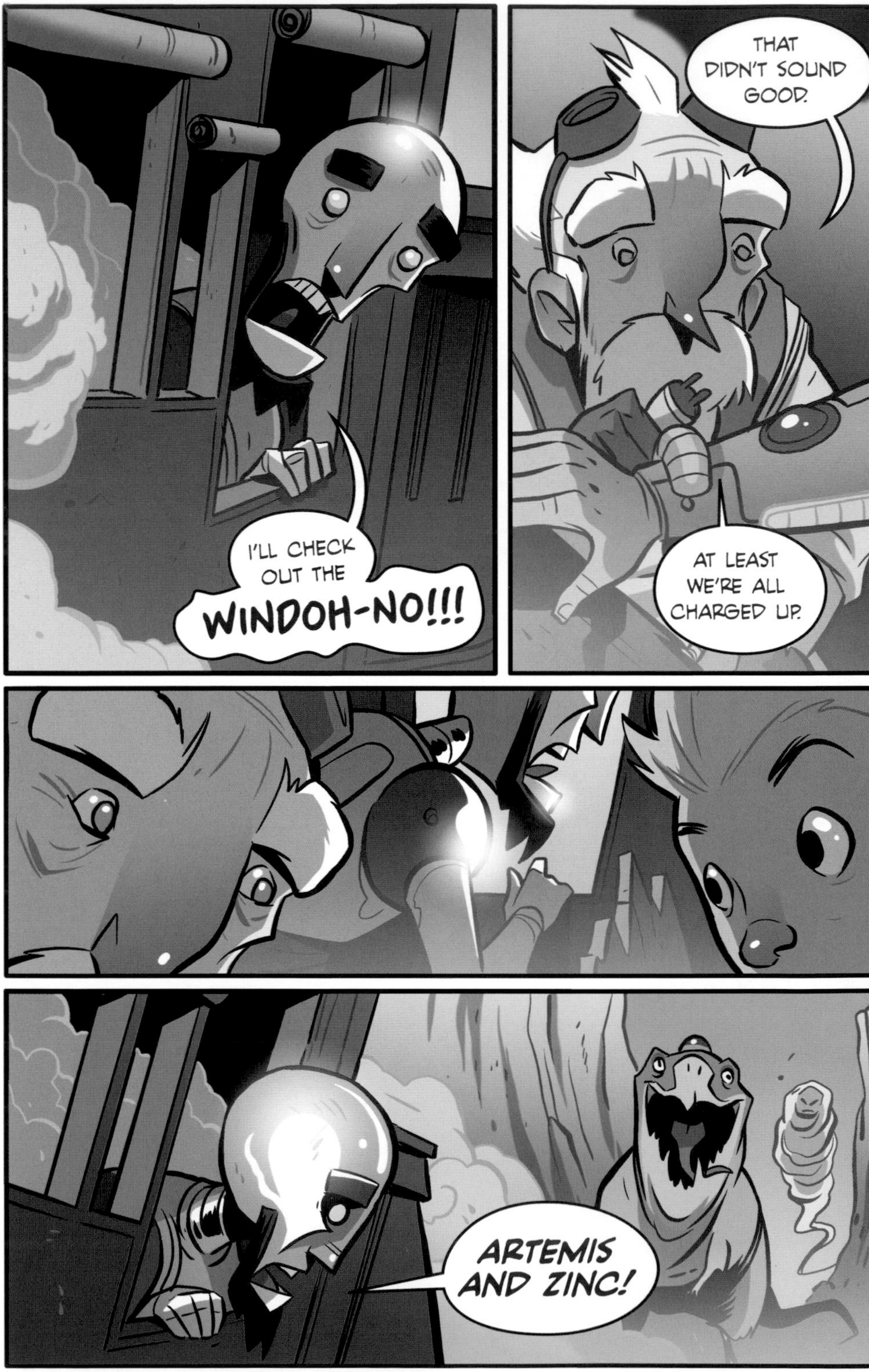
I'LL CHECK OUT THE
WINDOH-NO!!!
THAT DIDN'T SOUND GOOD.
AT LEAST WE'RE ALL CHARGED UP.
ARTEMIS AND ZINC!

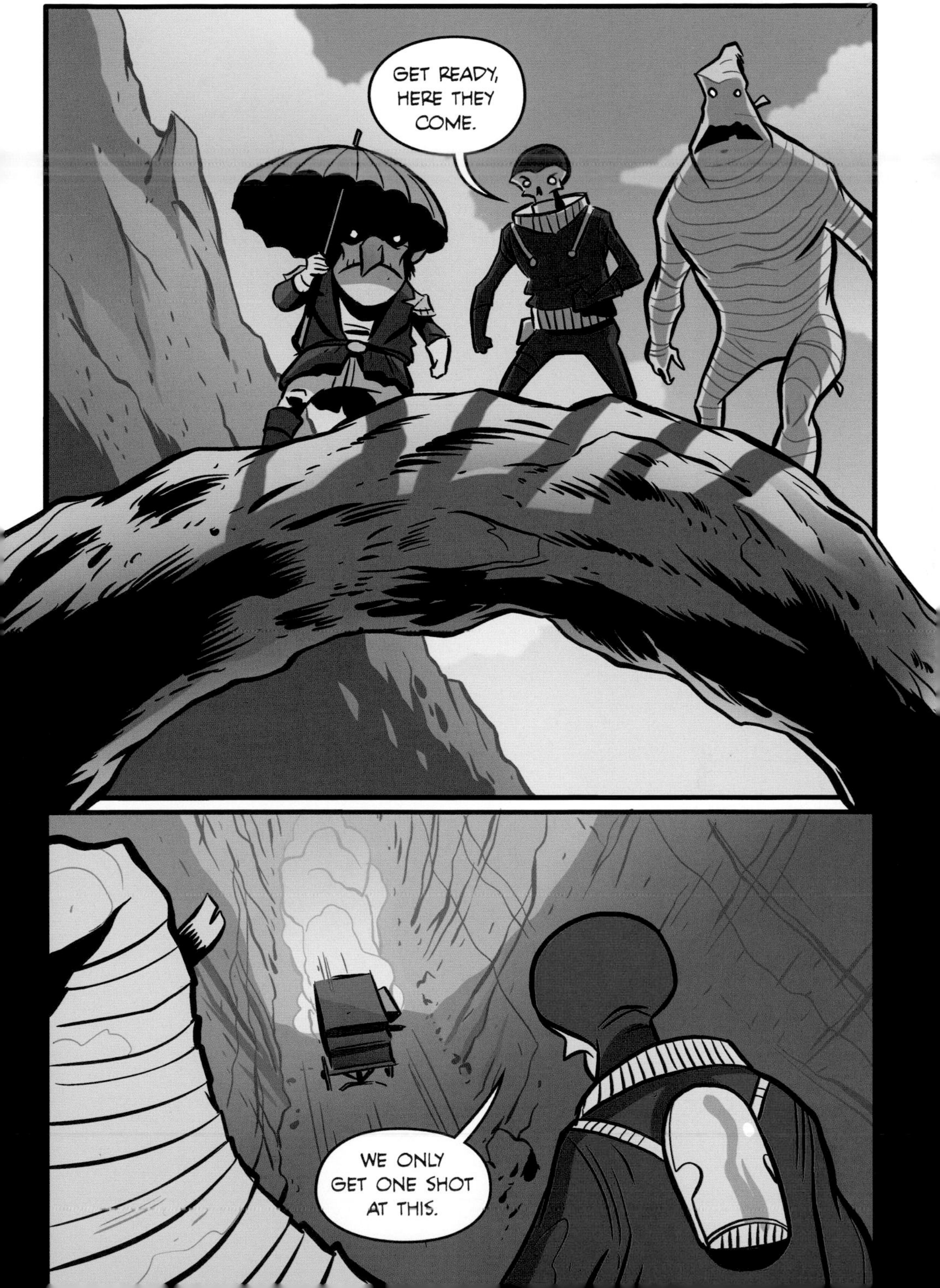
GET READY, HERE THEY COME.
WE ONLY GET ONE SHOT AT THIS.

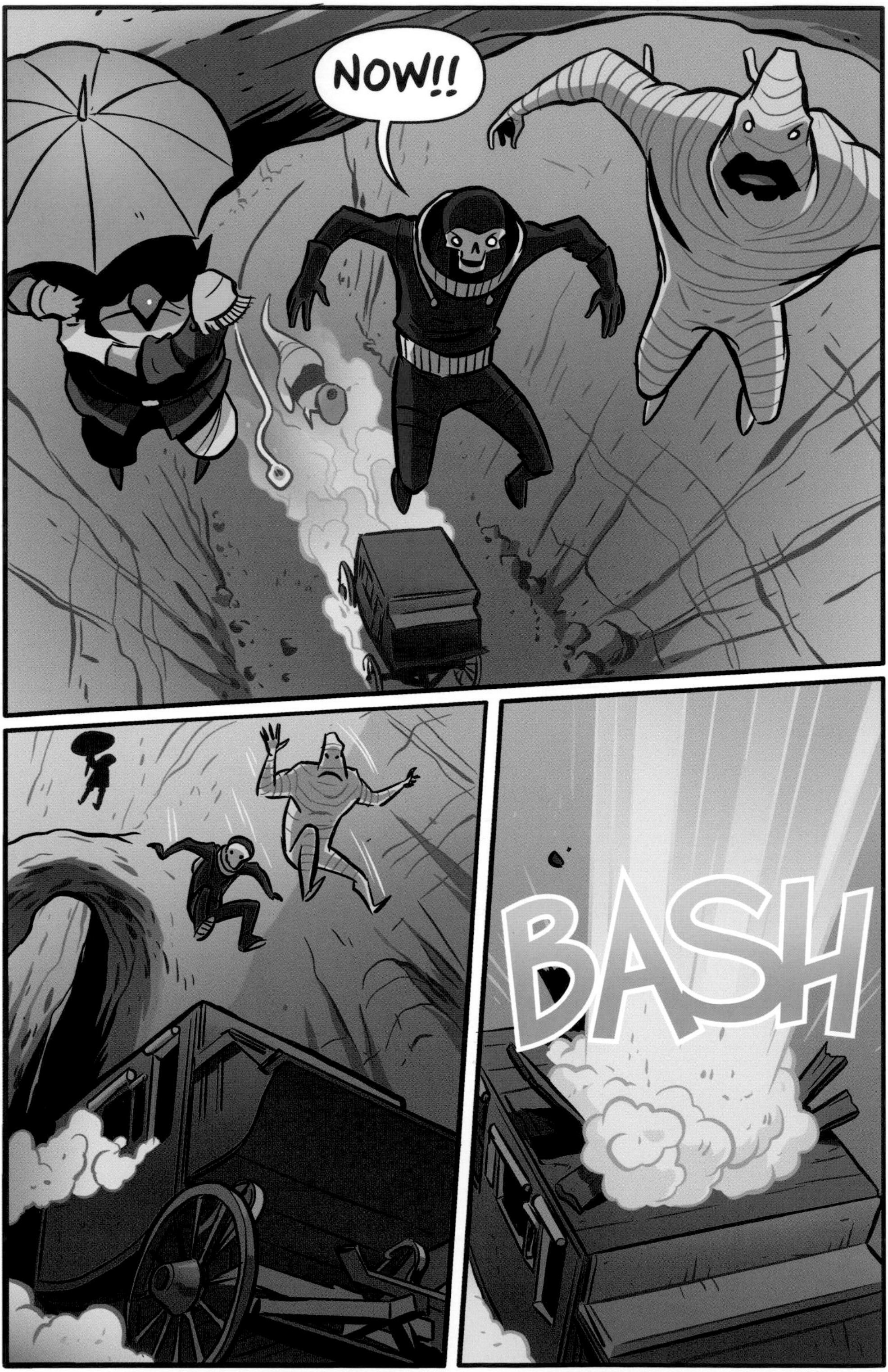
NOW!!
BASH

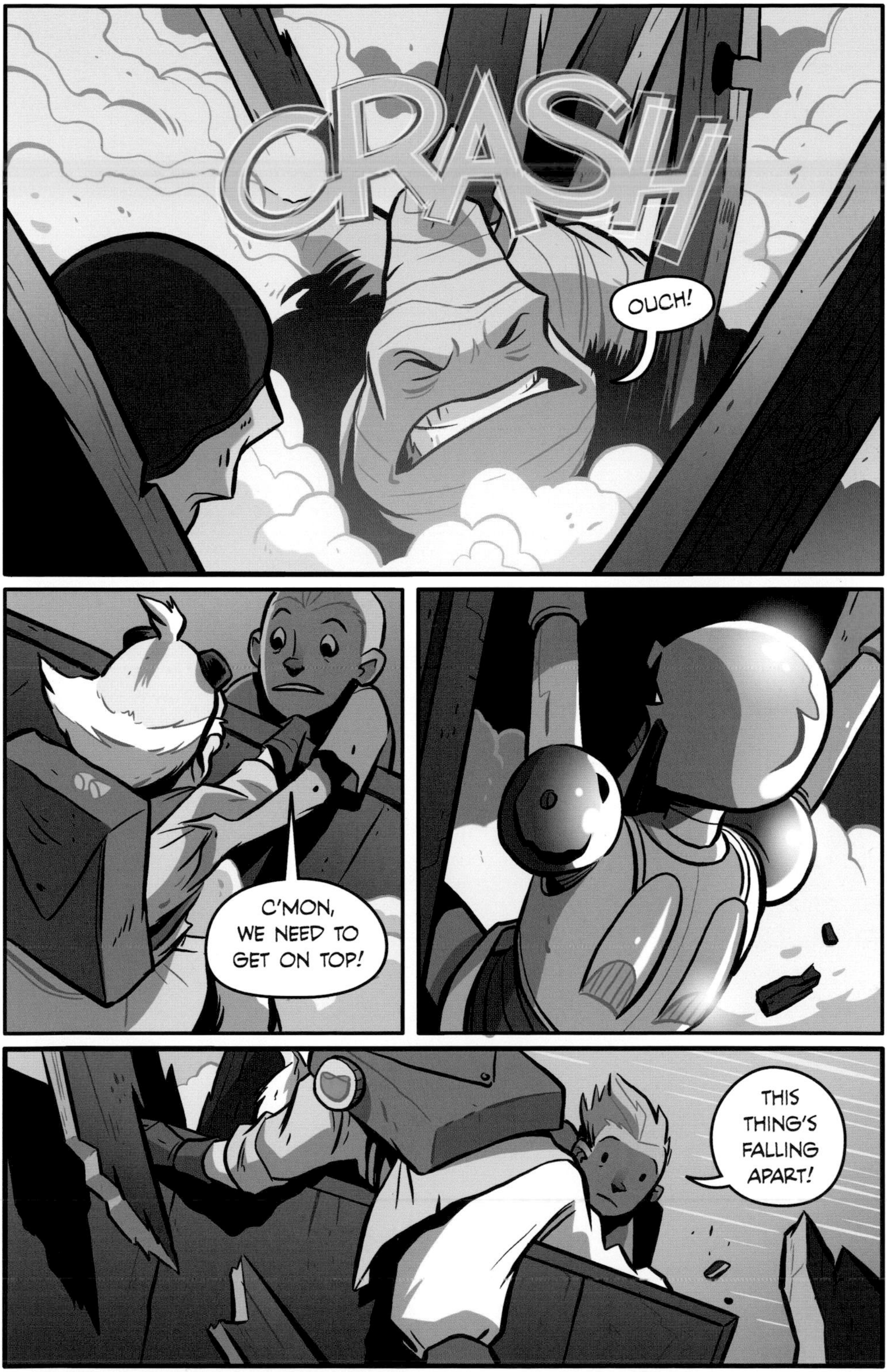
CRASH
OUCH!
C'MON, WE NEED TO GET ON TOP!
THIS THING'S FALLING APART!

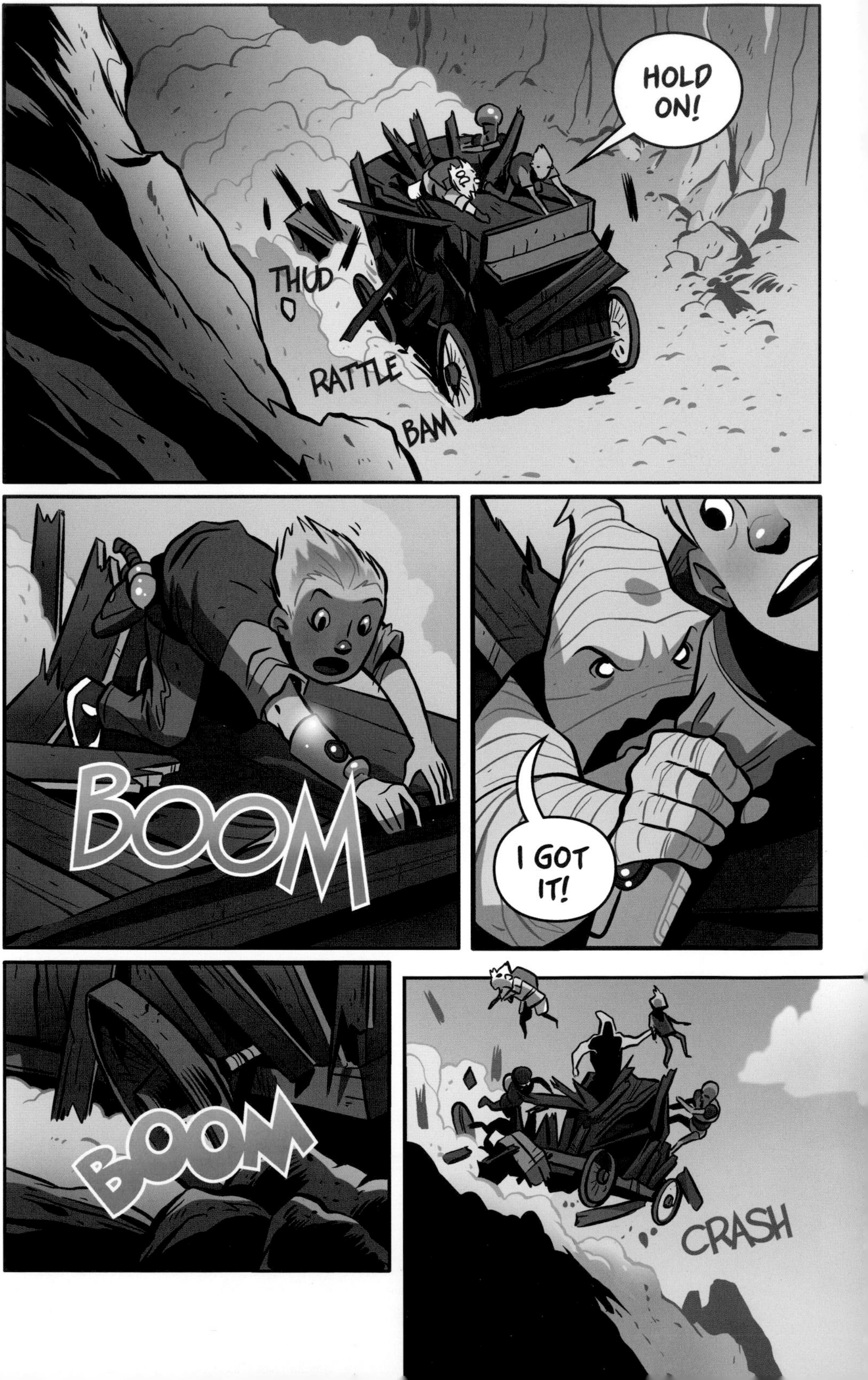
HOLD ON!
THUD
RATTLE
BAM
BOOM
I GOT IT!
BOOM
CRASH

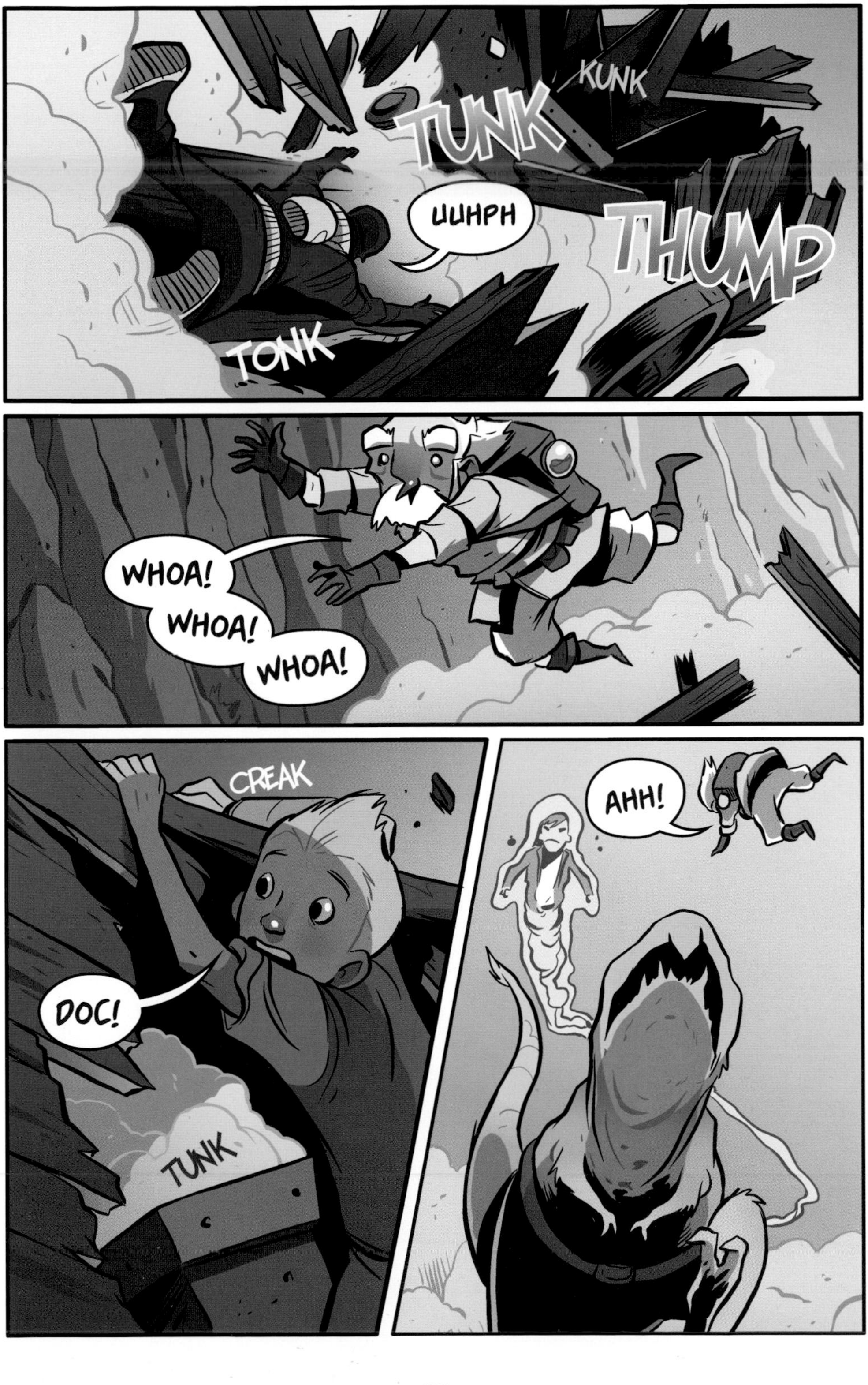
KUNK
TUNK
UUHPH
THUMP
TONK
WHOA!
WHOA!
WHOA!
CREAK
DOC!
TUNK
AHH!

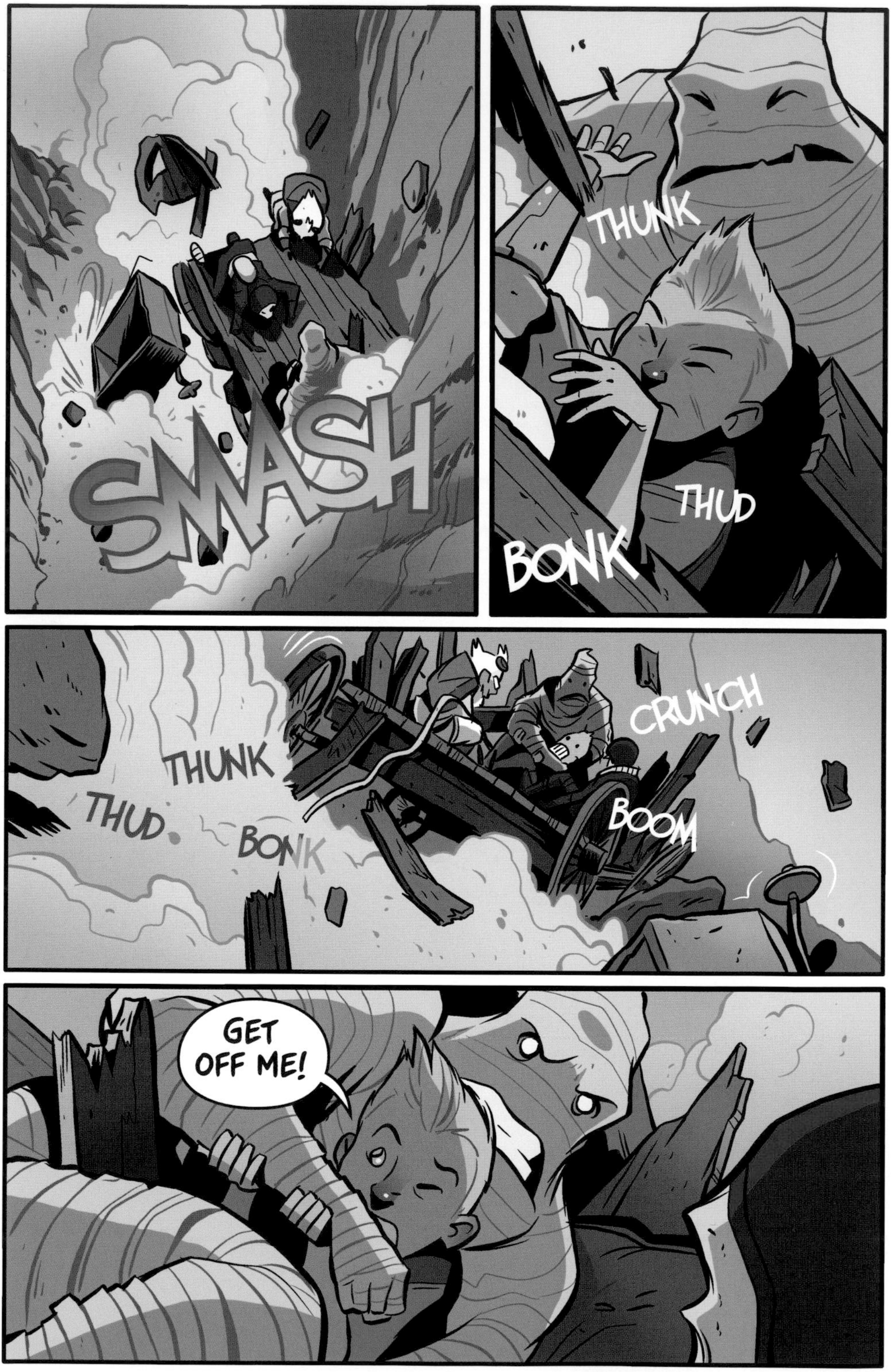
SMASH
THUNK
THUD
BONK
THUNK
THUD
BONK
CRUNCH
BOOM
GET OFF ME!

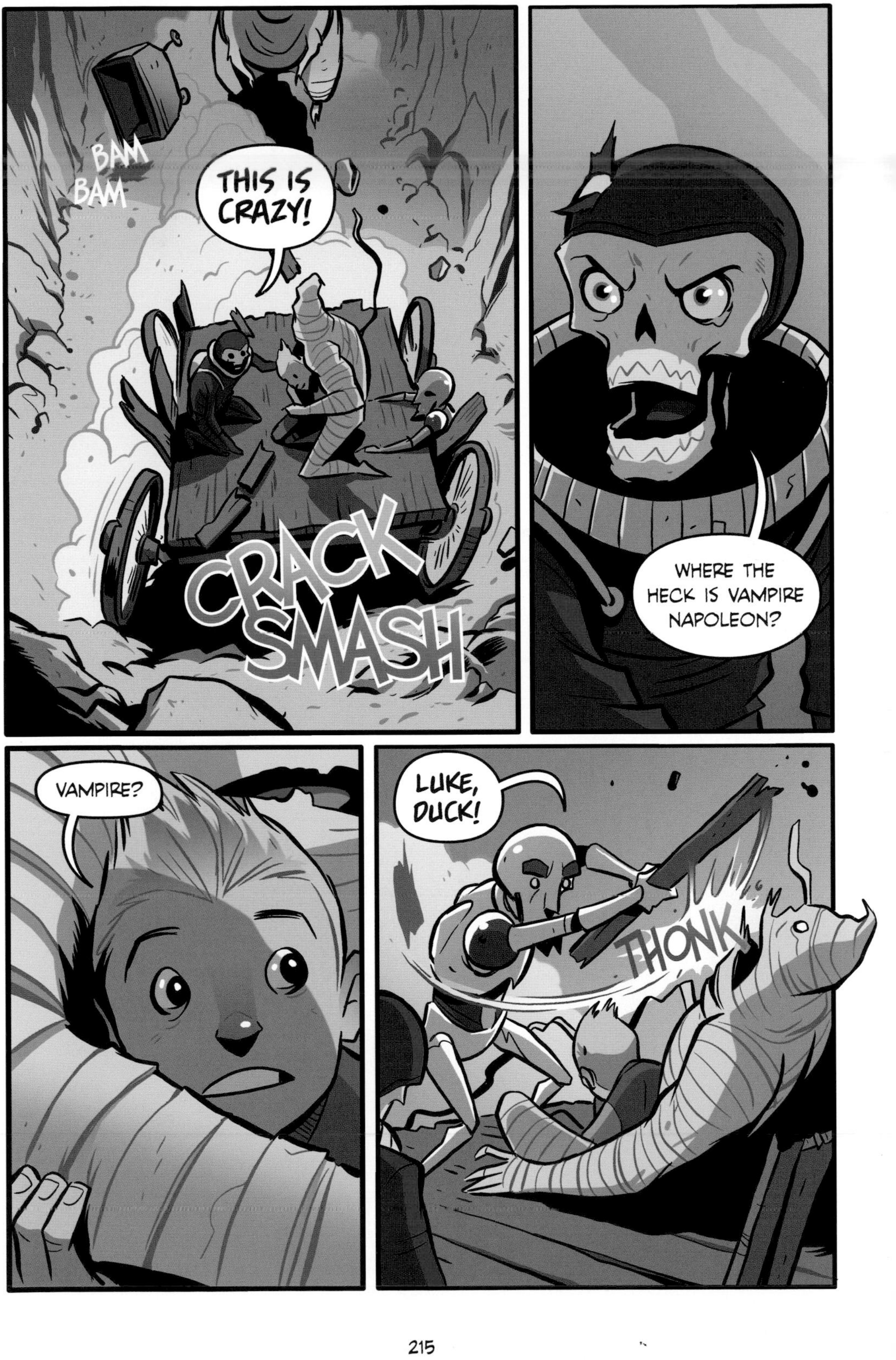
BAM
BAM
THIS IS CRAZY!
CRACK
SMASH
WHERE THE HECK IS VAMPIRE NAPOLEON?
VAMPIRE?
LUKE, DUCK!
THONK

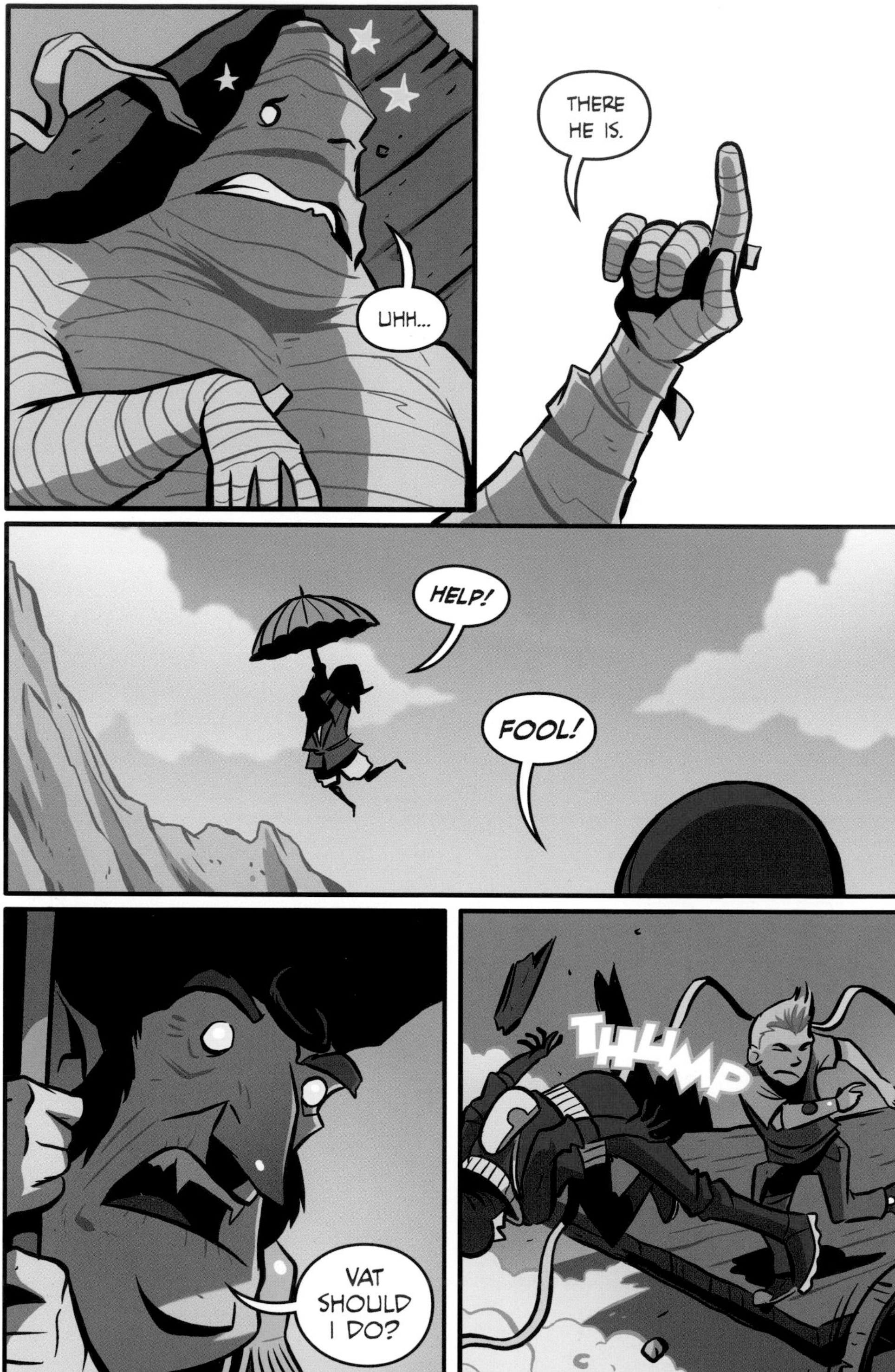
UHH...
THERE HE IS.
HELP!
FOOL!
VAT SHOULD I DO?
THUMP

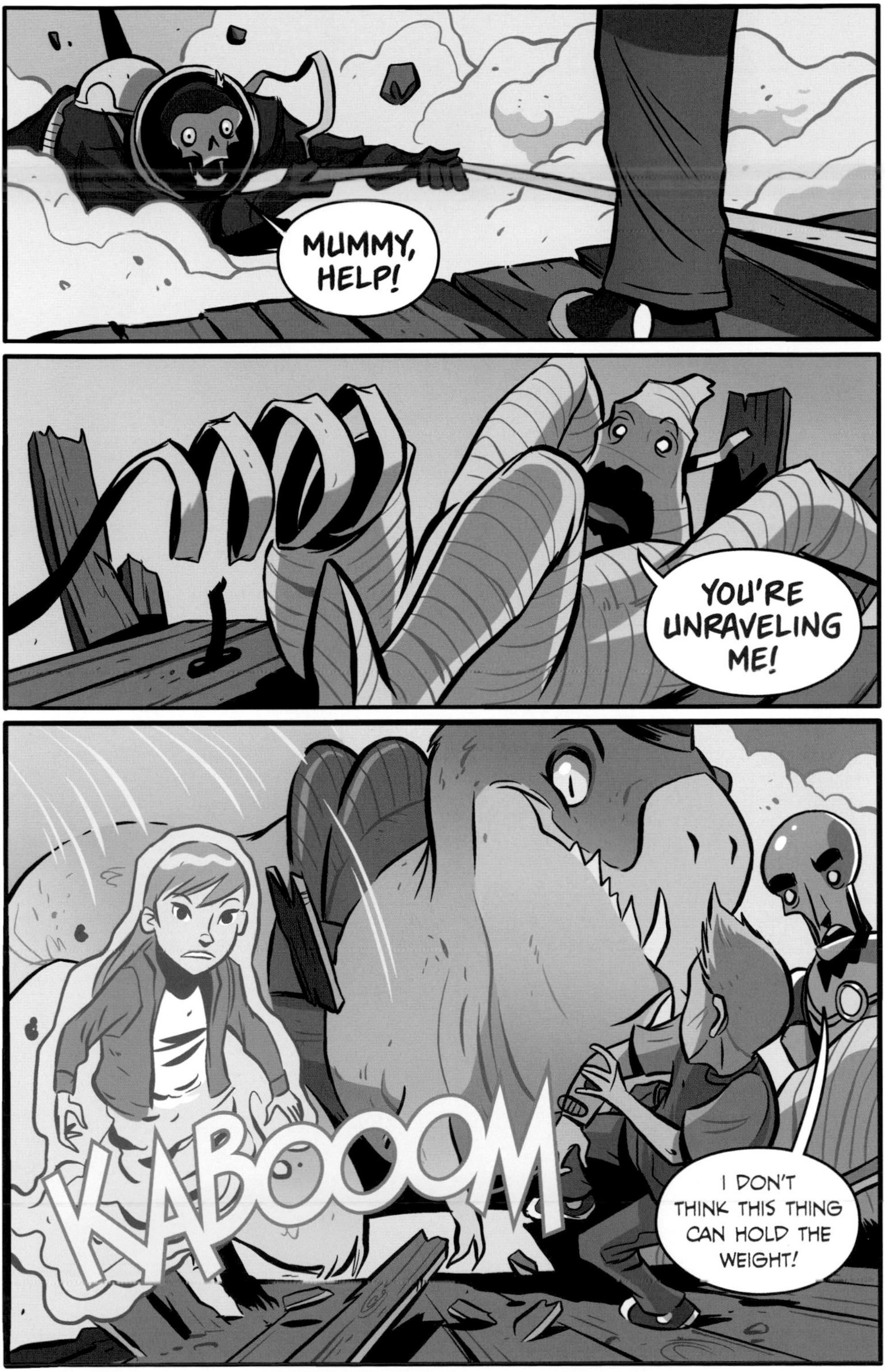
MUMMY, HELP!
YOU'RE UNRAVELING ME!
KABOOOM
I DON'T THINK THIS THING CAN HOLD THE WEIGHT!

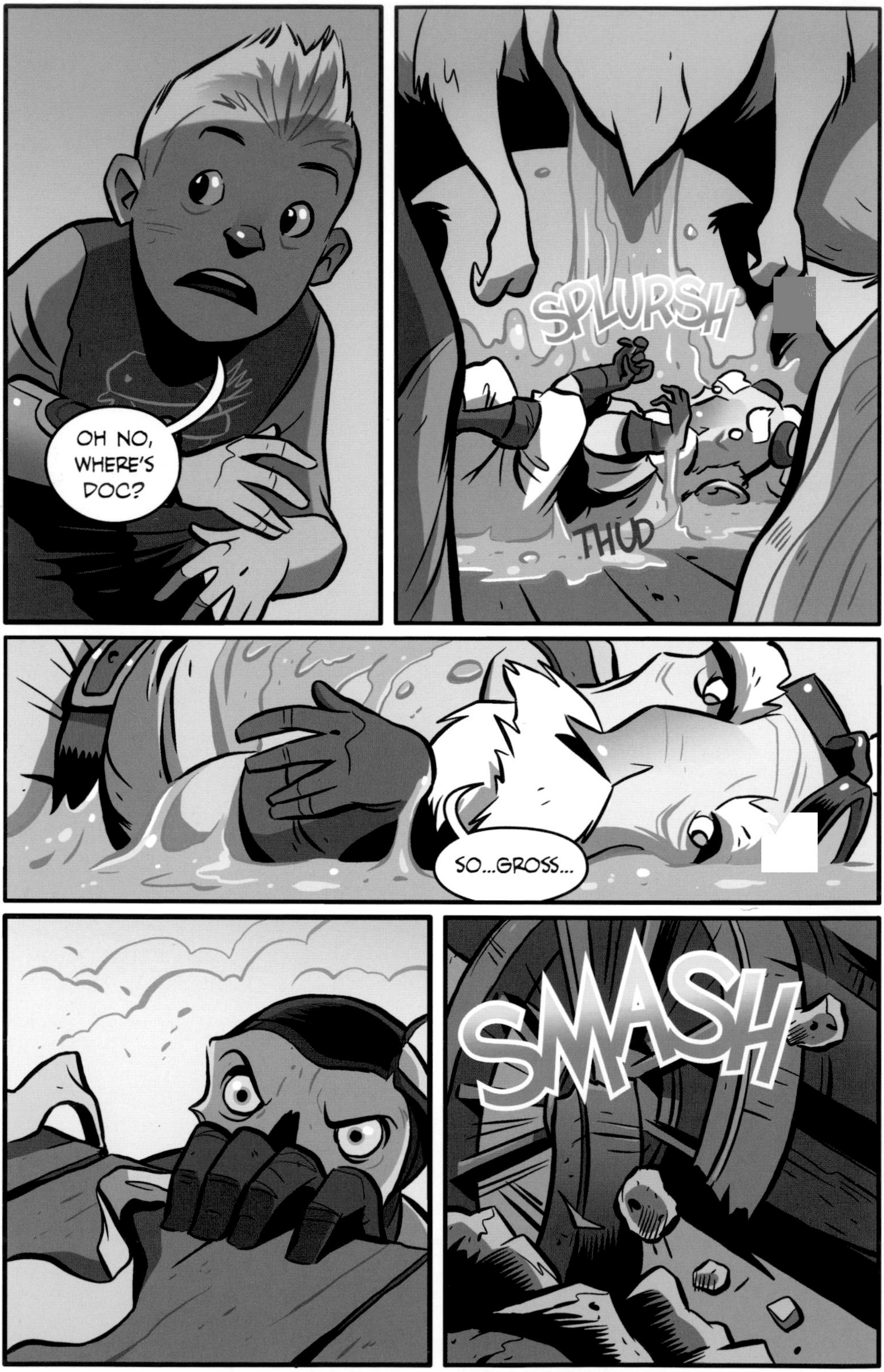
OH NO, WHERE'S DOC?
SPLURSH
THUD
SO...GROSS...
SMASH

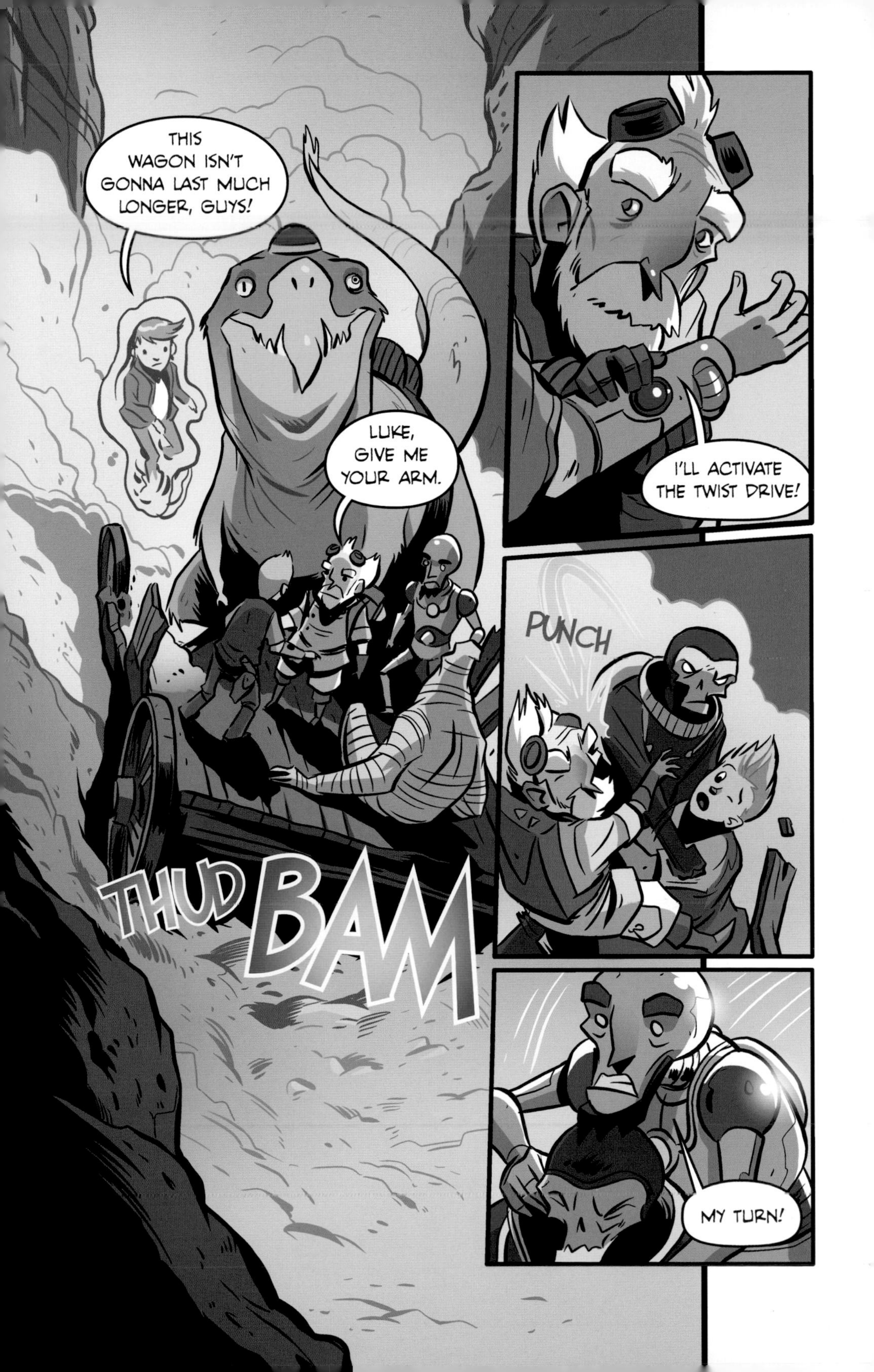
THIS WAGON ISN'T GONNA LAST MUCH LONGER, GUYS!
LUKE, GIVE ME YOUR ARM.
THUD
BAM
I'LL ACTIVATE THE TWIST DRIVE!
PUNCH
MY TURN!

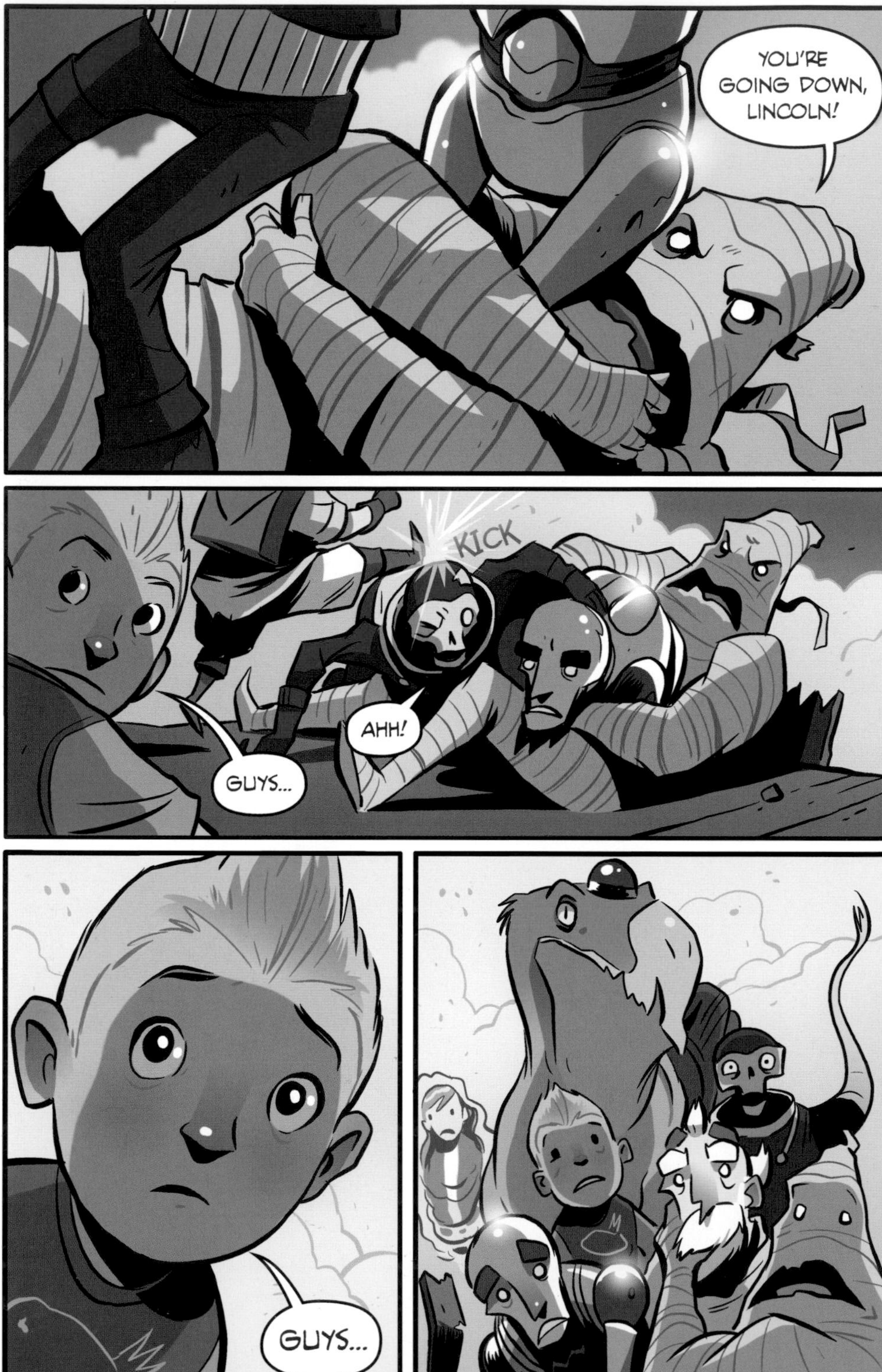
YOU'RE GOING DOWN, LINCOLN!
KICK
AHH!
GUYS...
GUYS...

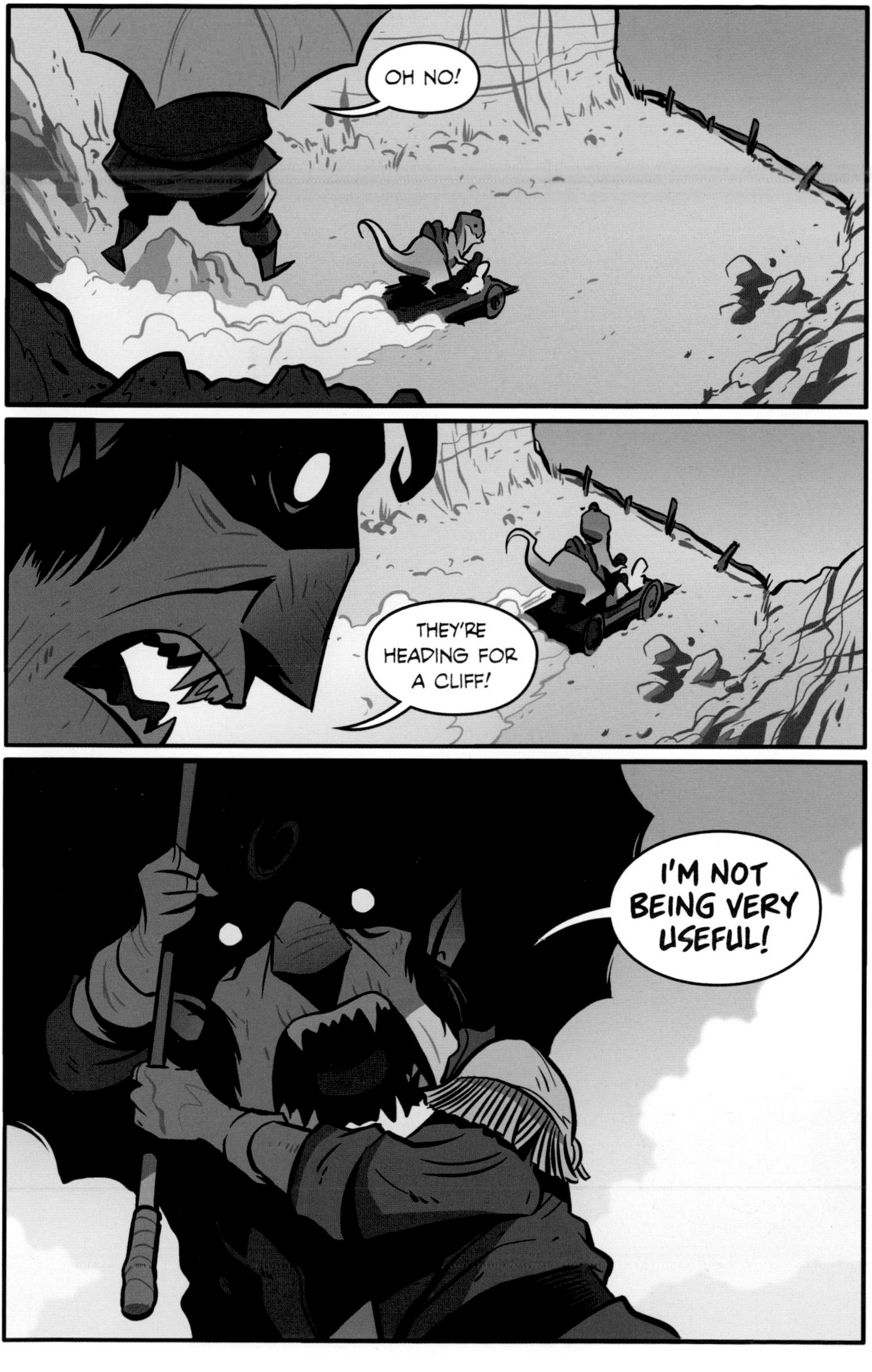
OH NO!
THEY'RE HEADING FOR A CLIFF!
I'M NOT BEING VERY USEFUL!

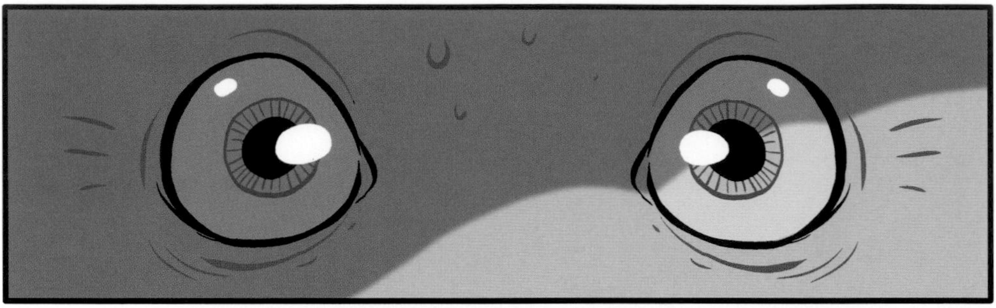

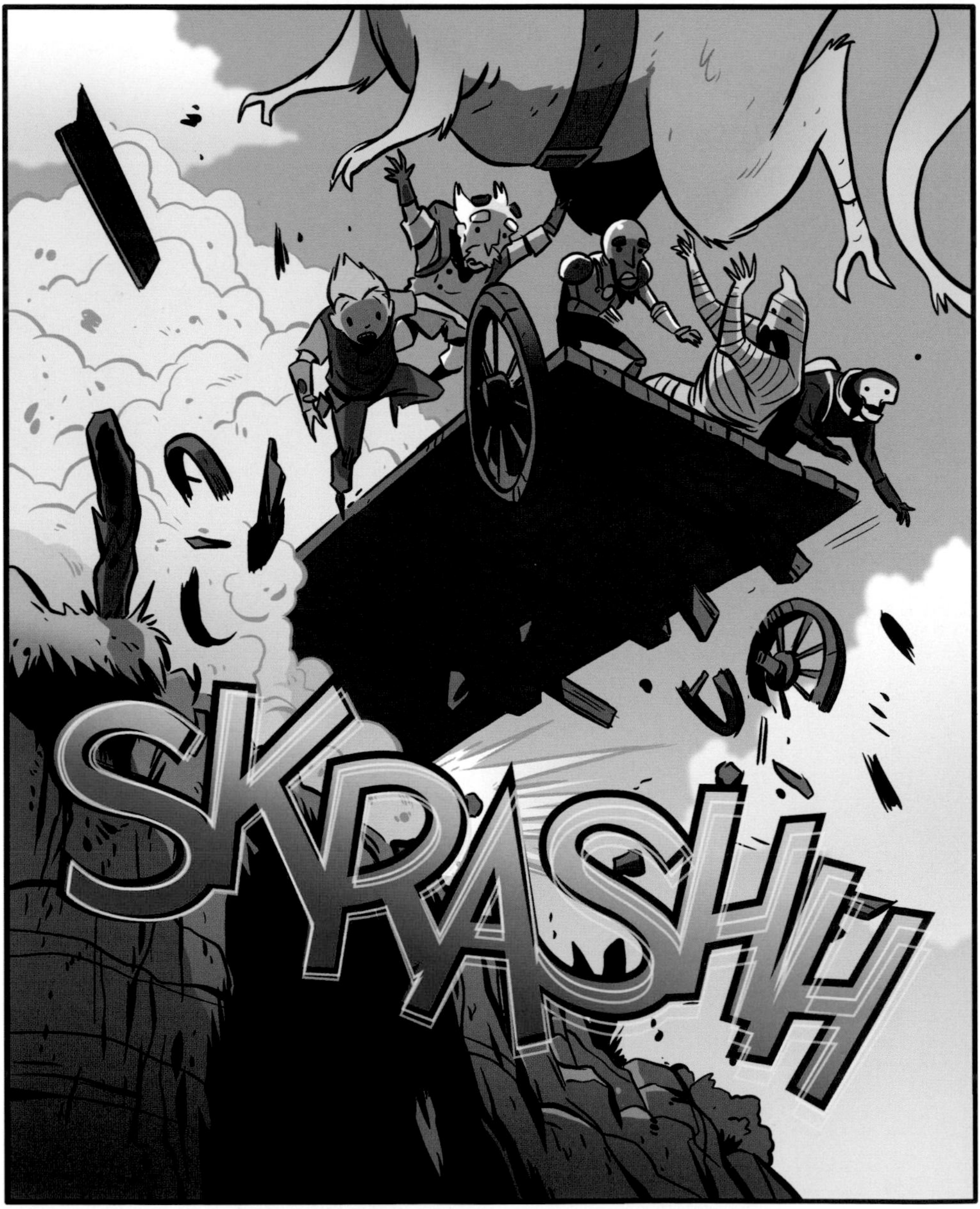
SKRASHH

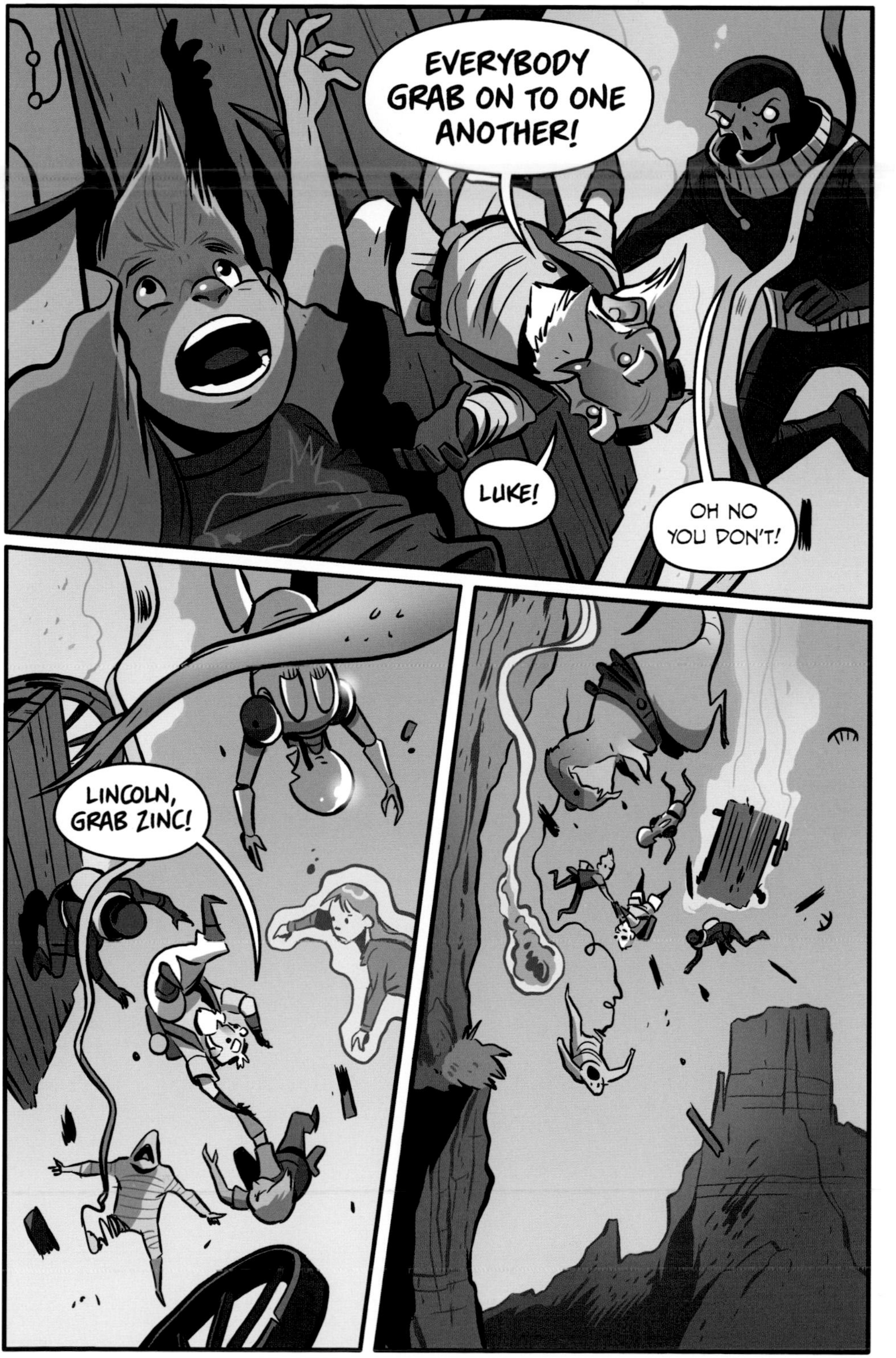

EVERYBODY GRAB ON TO ONE ANOTHER!
LUKE!
OH NO YOU DON'T!
LINCOLN, GRAB ZINC!

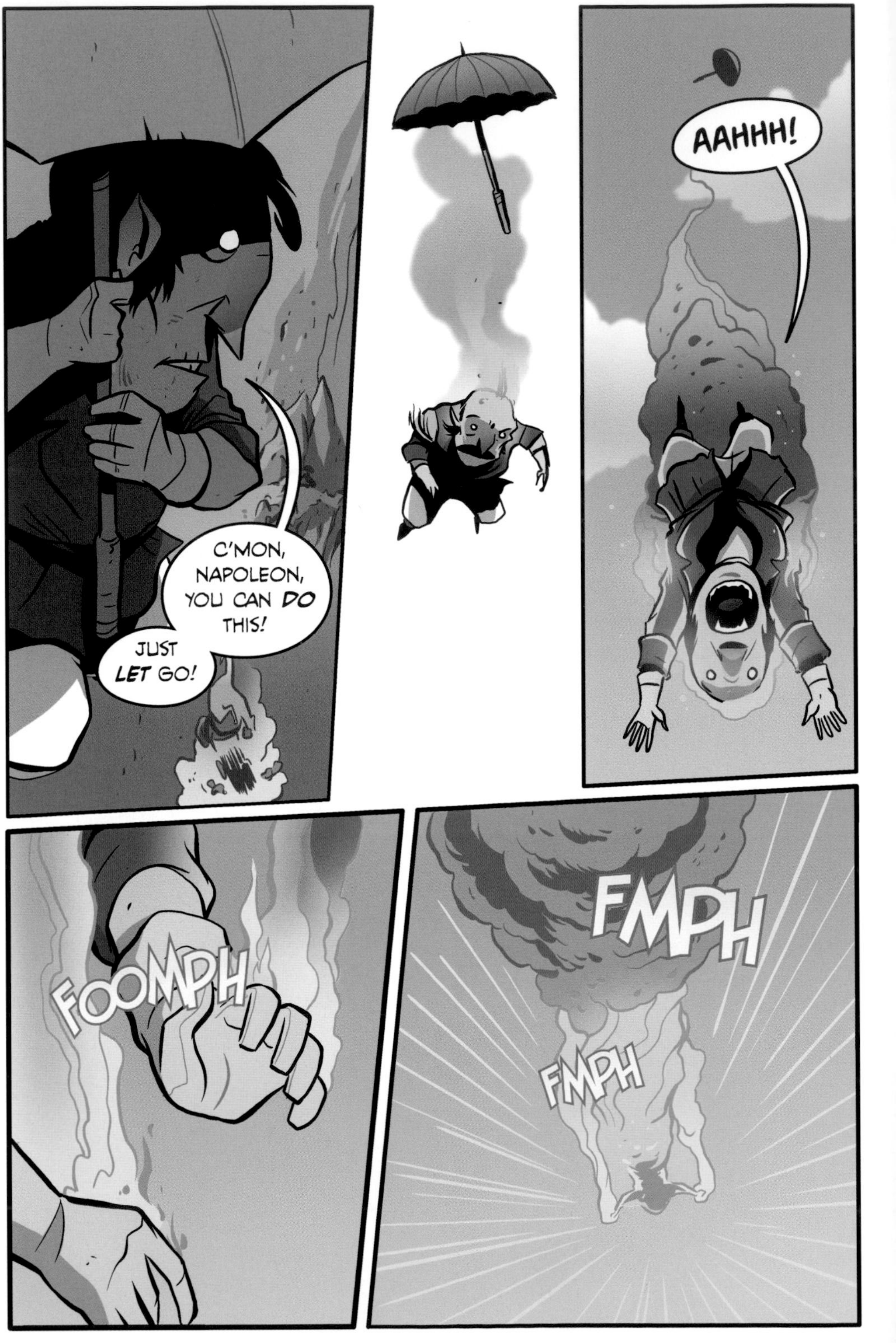
C'MON, NAPOLEON, YOU CAN DO THIS!
JUST LET GO!
AAHHH!
FOOMPH
FMPH
FMPH

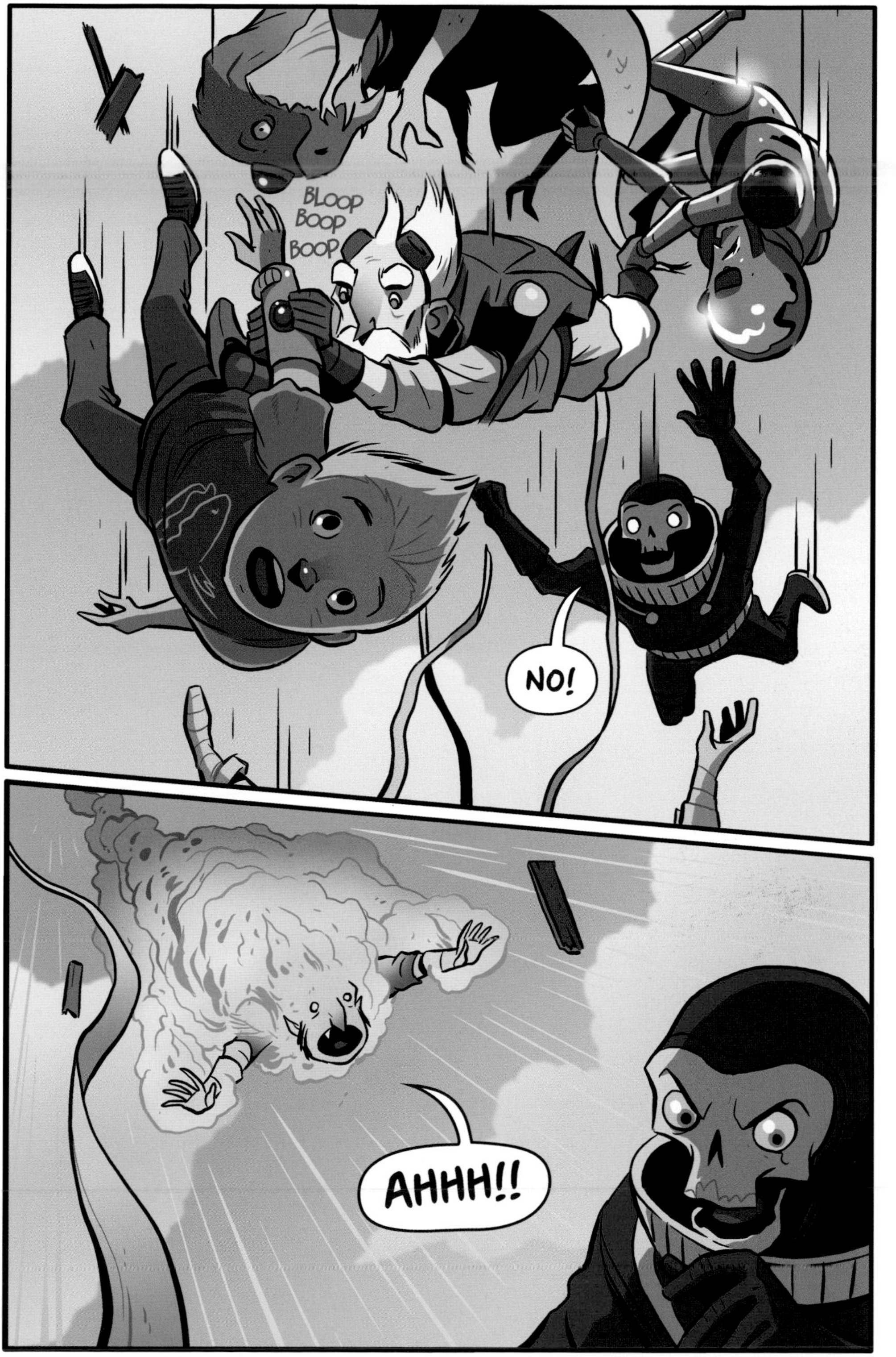
BLOOP
BOOP
BOOP
NO!
AHHH!!

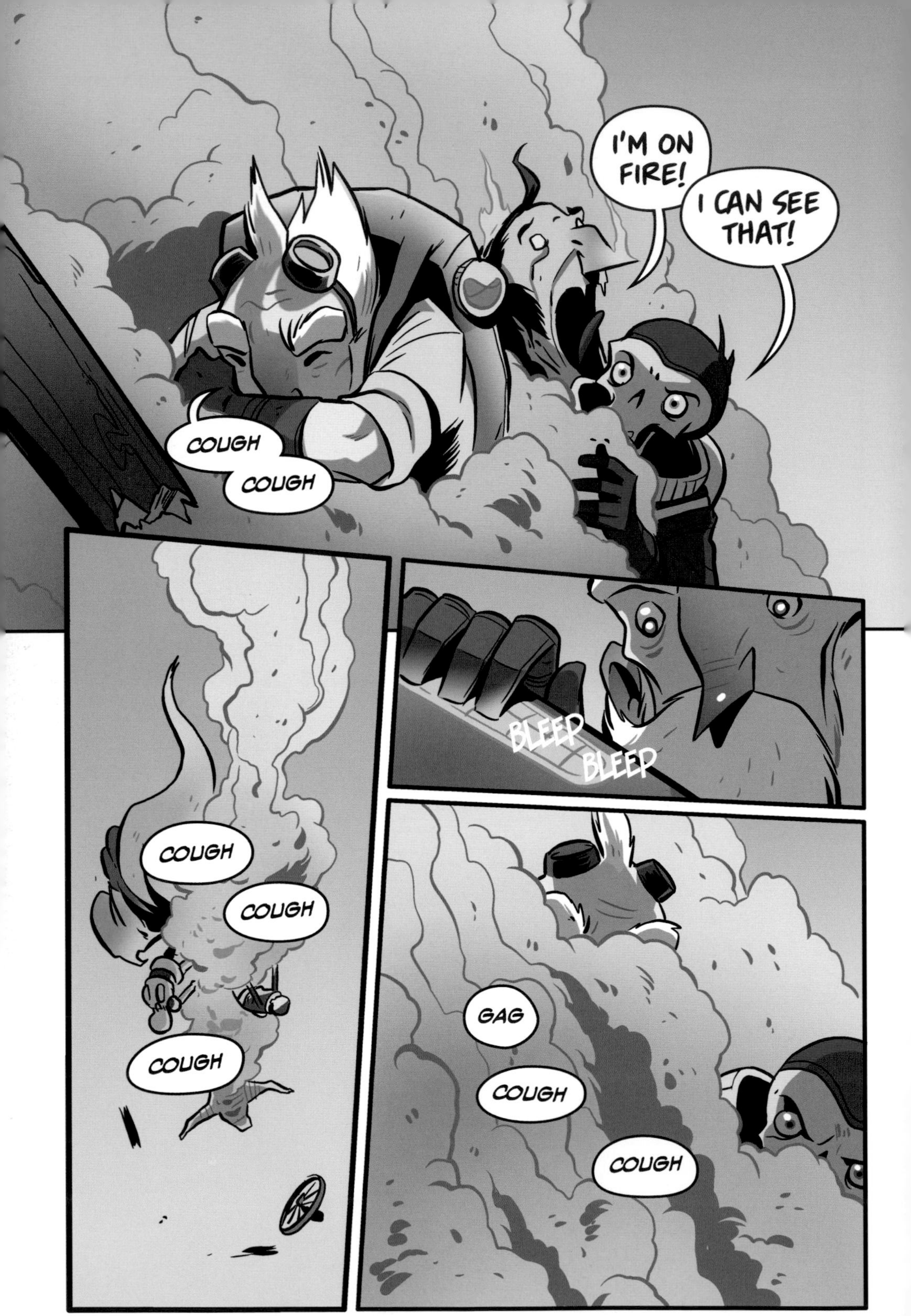
I'M ON FIRE!
I CAN SEE THAT!
COUGH
COUGH
COUGH
COUGH
COUGH
BLEEP
BLEEP
GAG
COUGH
COUGH

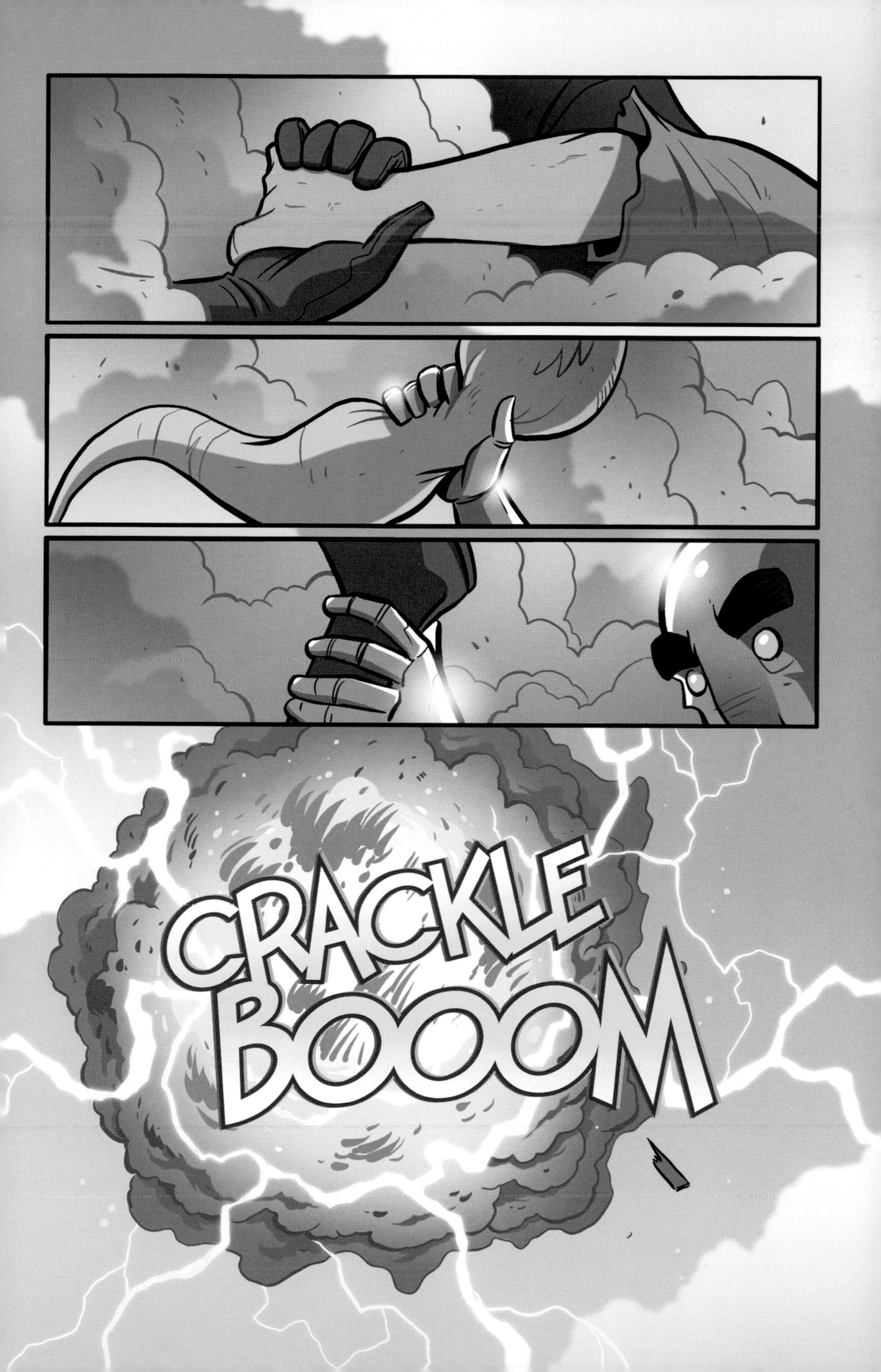
CRACKLE
BOOOOM

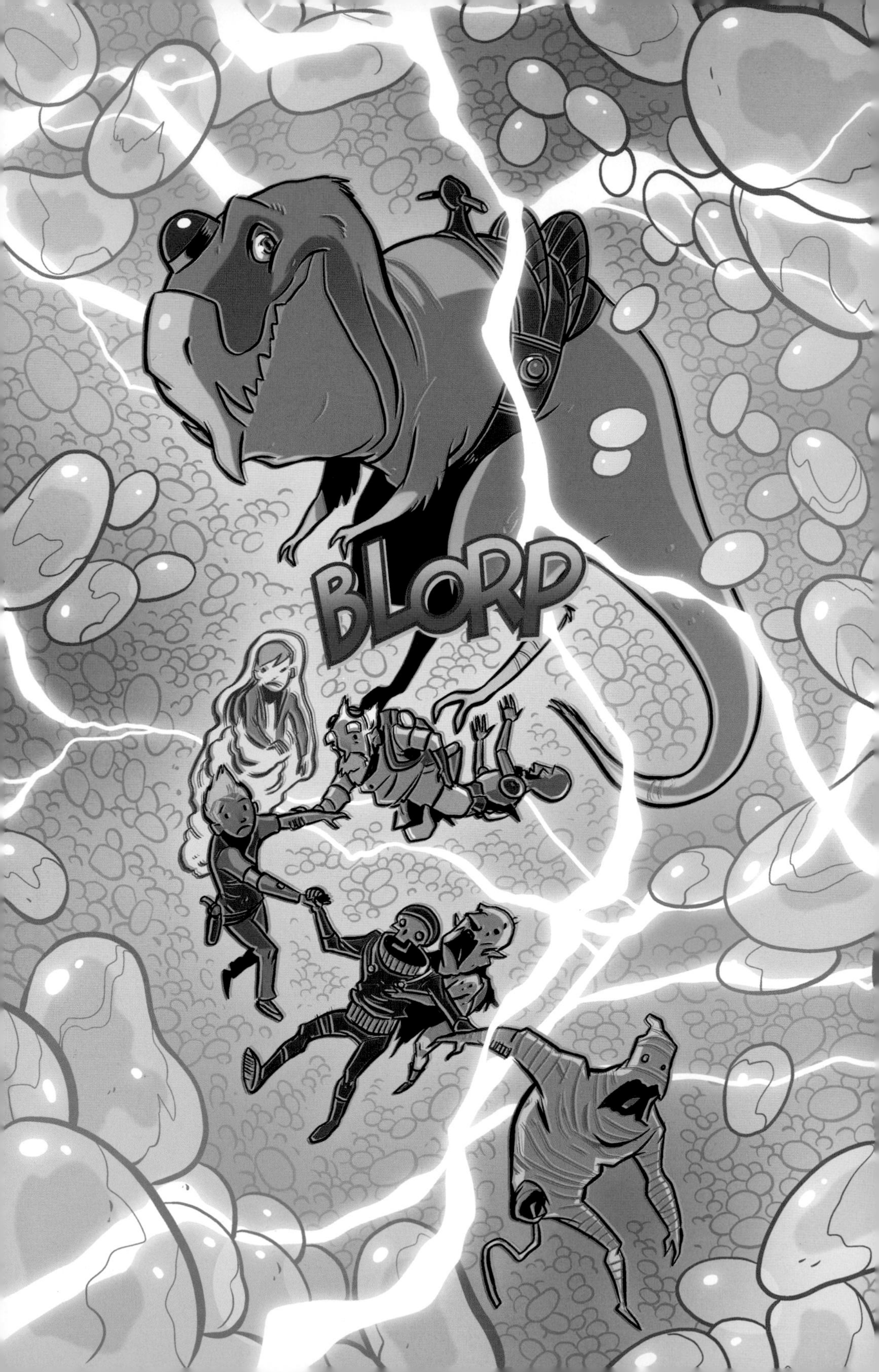
BLORP

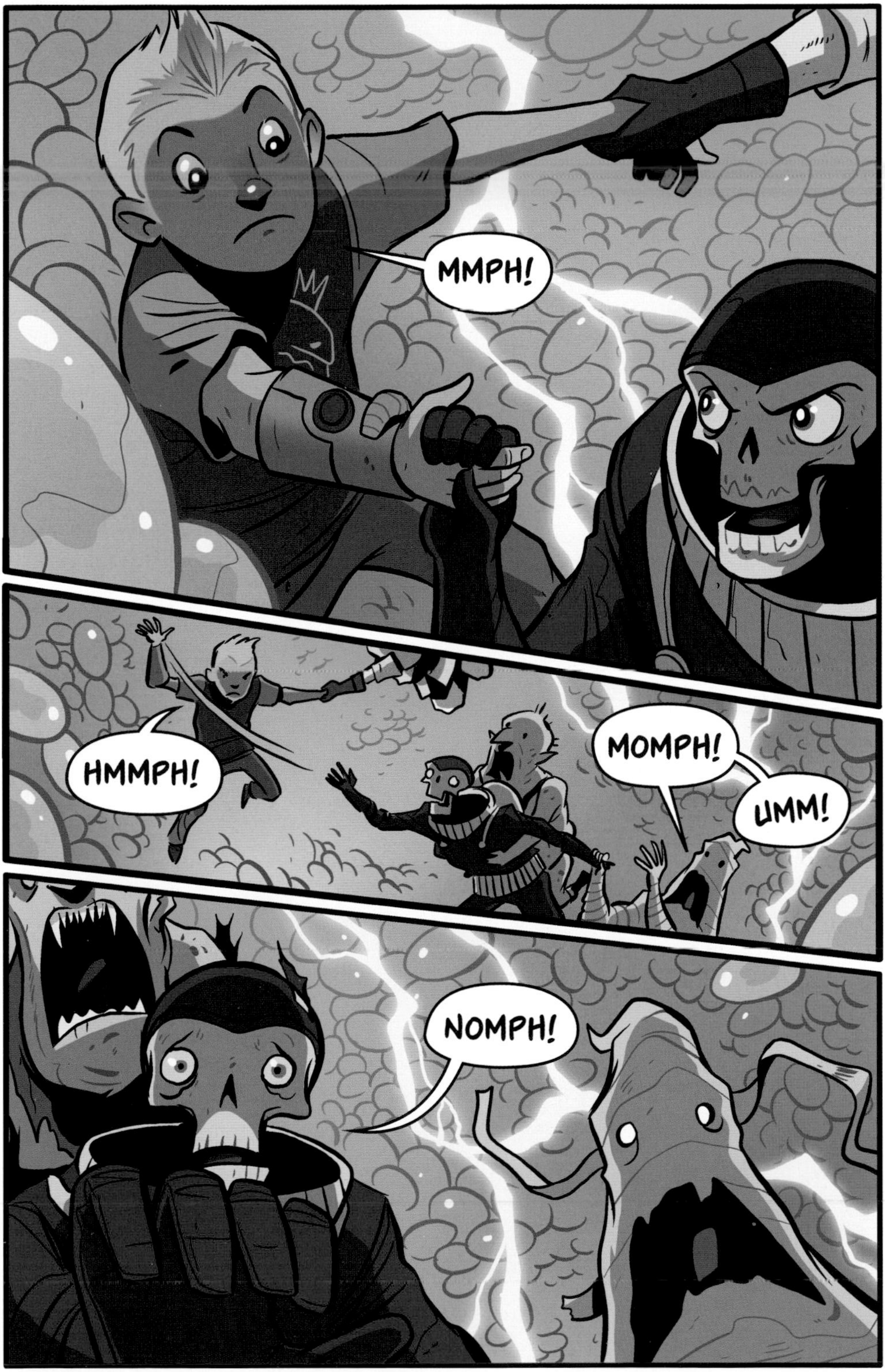
MMPH!
HMMPH!
MOMPH!
UMM!
NOMPH!

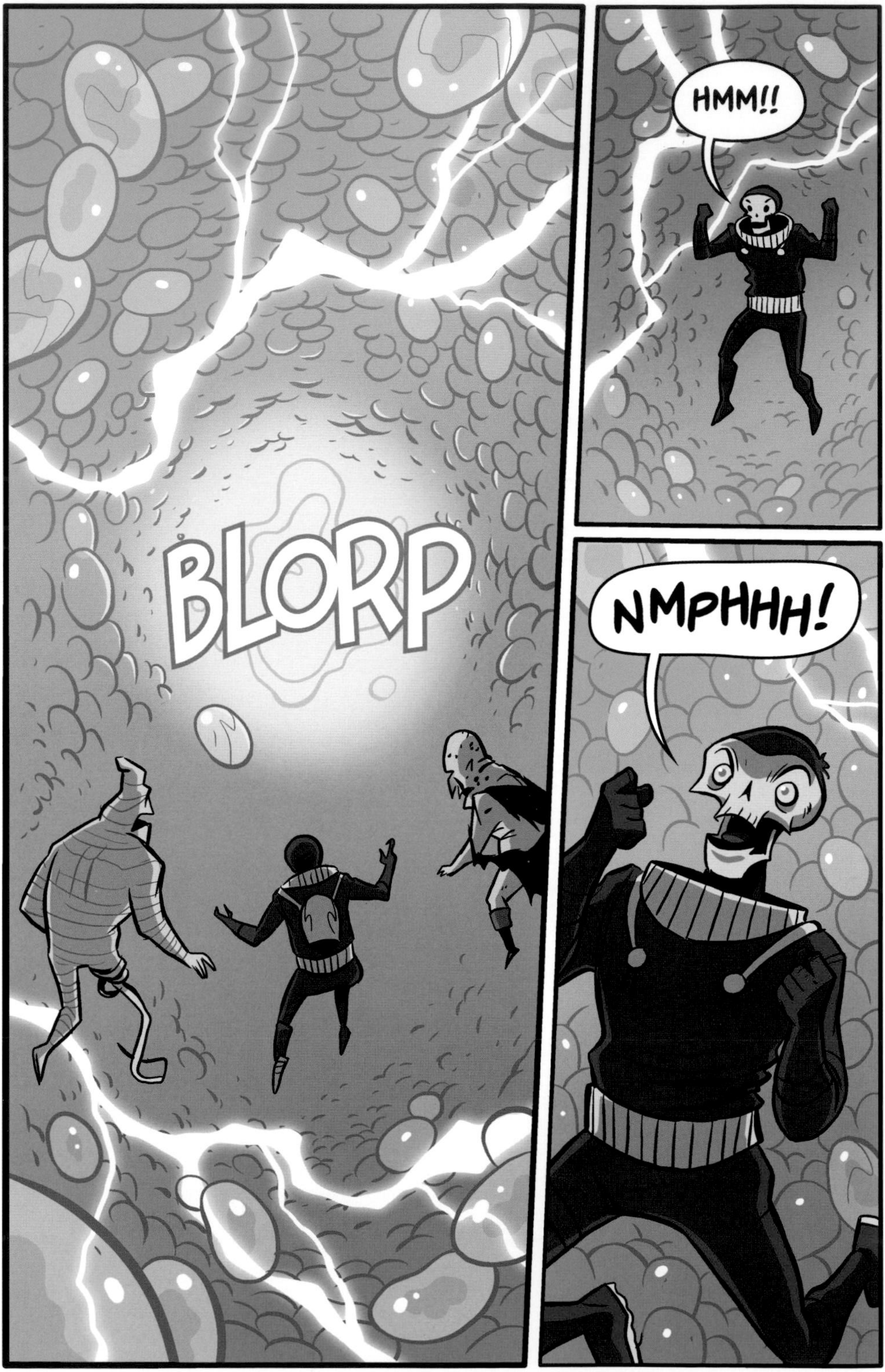
BLORP
HMM!!
NMPHHH!

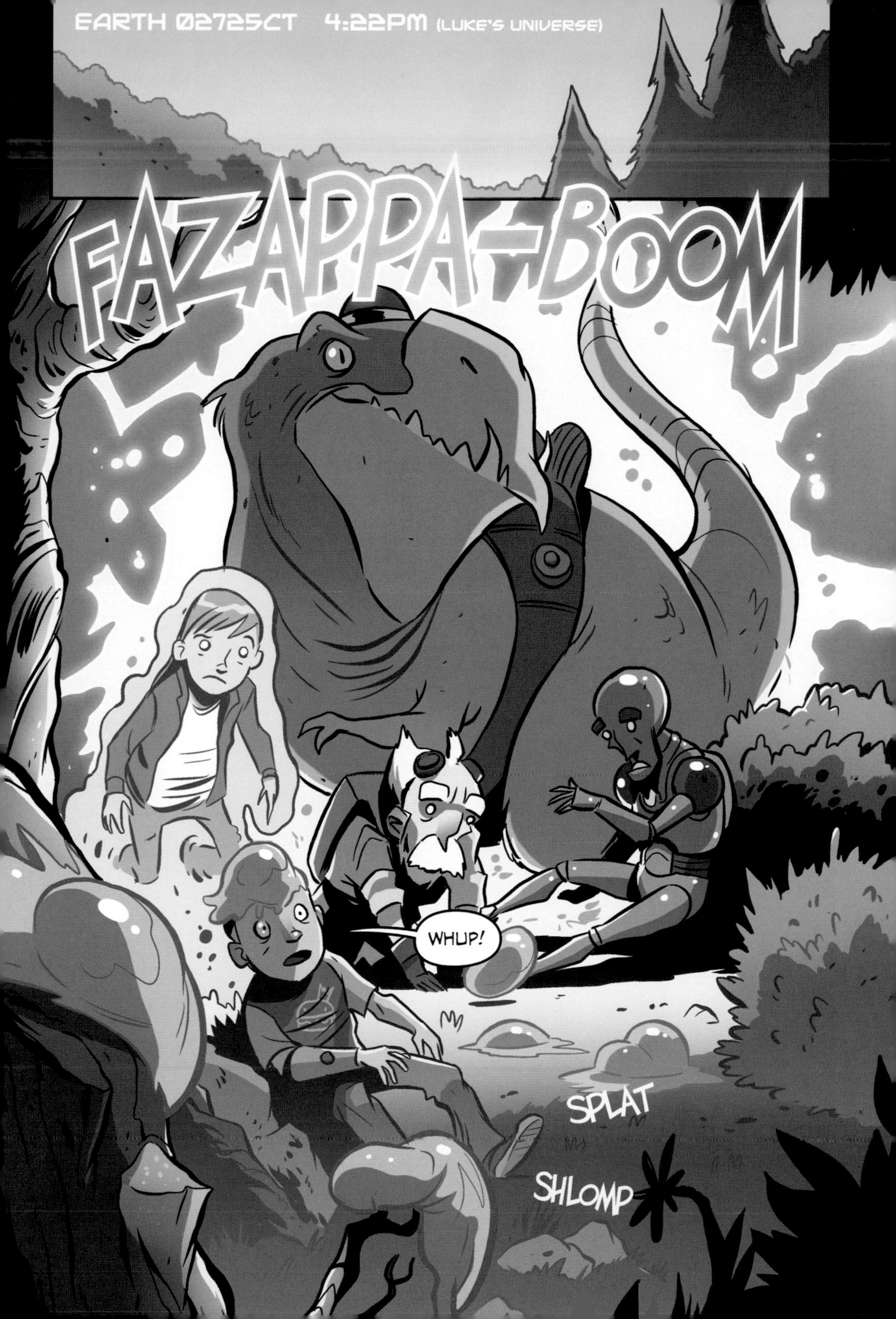
EARTH 02725CT 4:22PM (LUKE'S UNIVERSE)
FAZAPPA-BOOM
WHUP!
SPLAT
SHLOMP

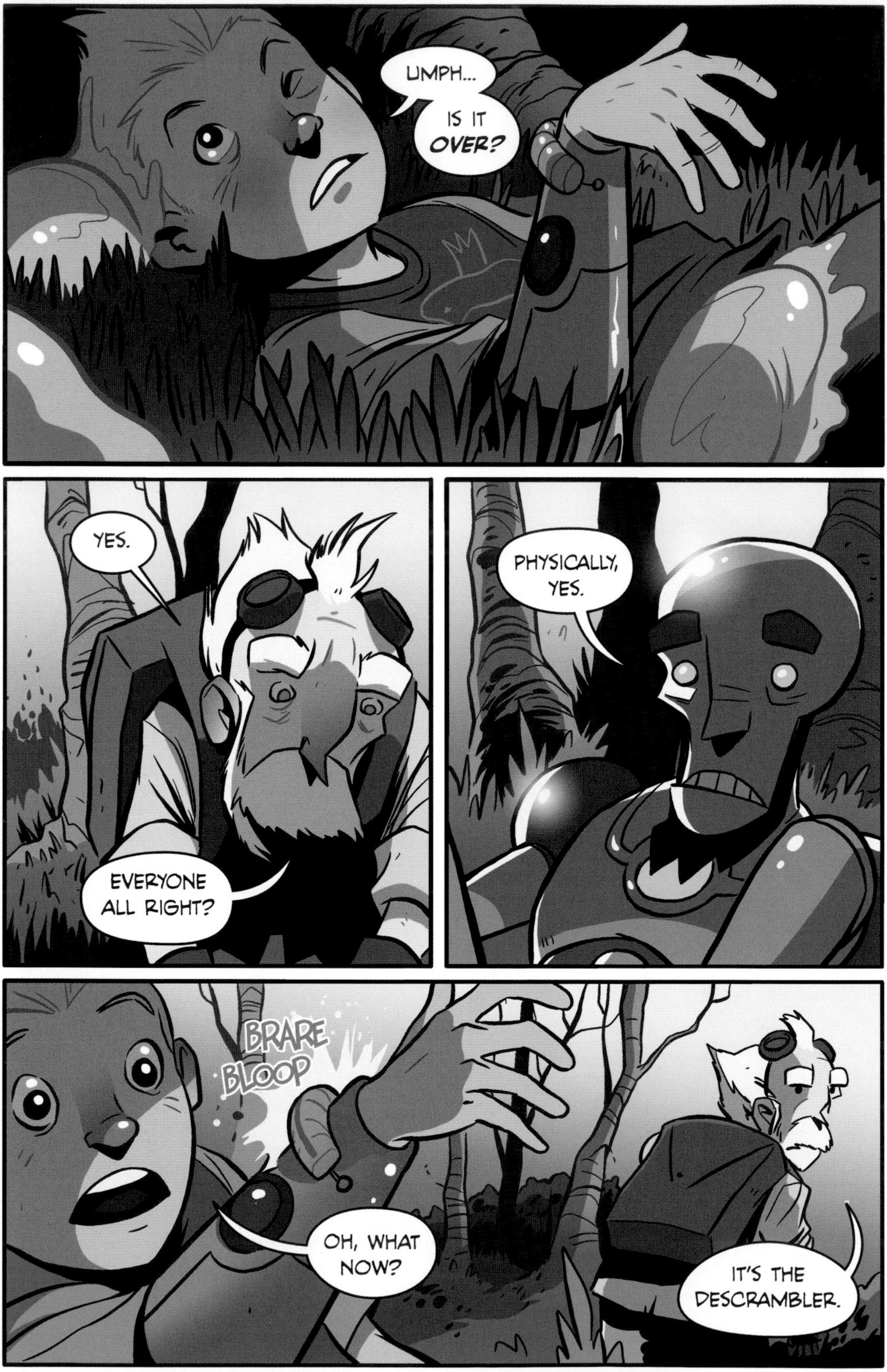
UMPH...
IS IT *OVER?*
YES.
EVERYONE ALL RIGHT?
PHYSICALLY, YES.
BRARE BLOOP
OH, WHAT NOW?
IT'S THE DESCRAMBLER.

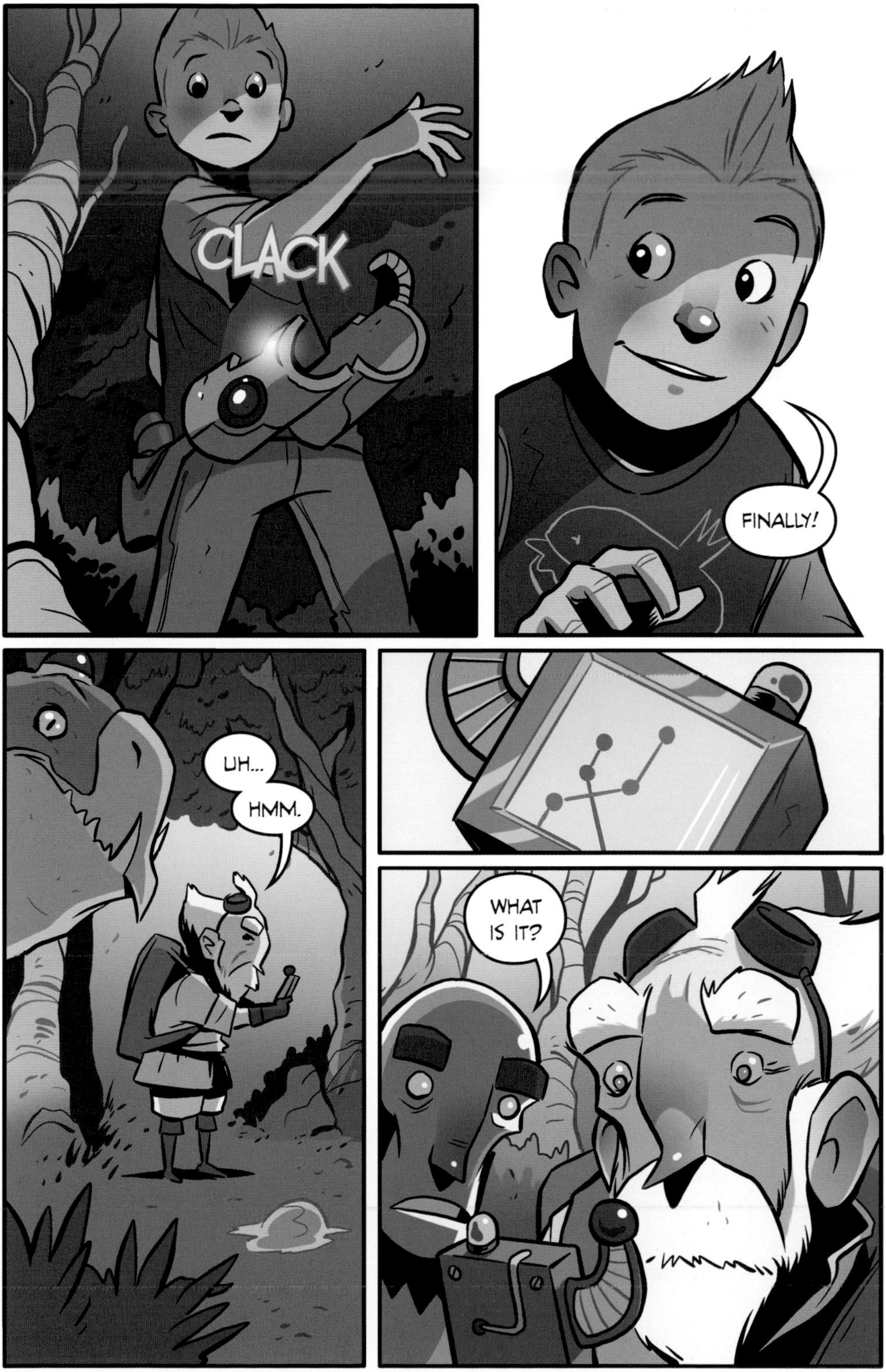
CLACK
FINALLY!
UH...
HMM.
WHAT IS IT?

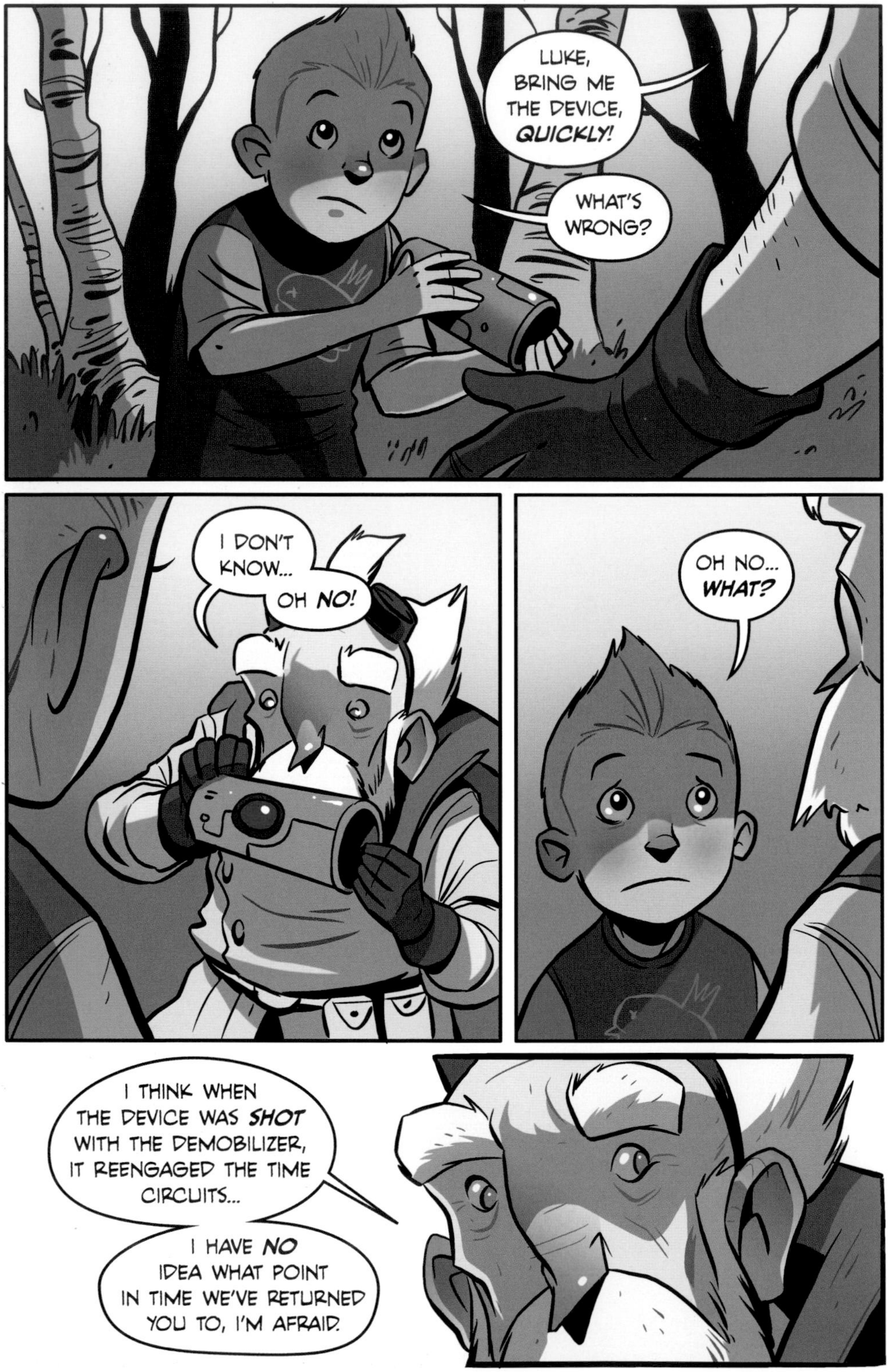
LUKE, BRING ME THE DEVICE, *QUICKLY!*
WHAT'S WRONG?
I DON'T KNOW...
OH *NO!*
OH NO... *WHAT?*
I THINK WHEN THE DEVICE WAS *SHOT* WITH THE DEMOBILIZER, IT REENGAGED THE TIME CIRCUITS...
I HAVE *NO* IDEA WHAT POINT IN TIME WE'VE RETURNED YOU TO, I'M AFRAID.

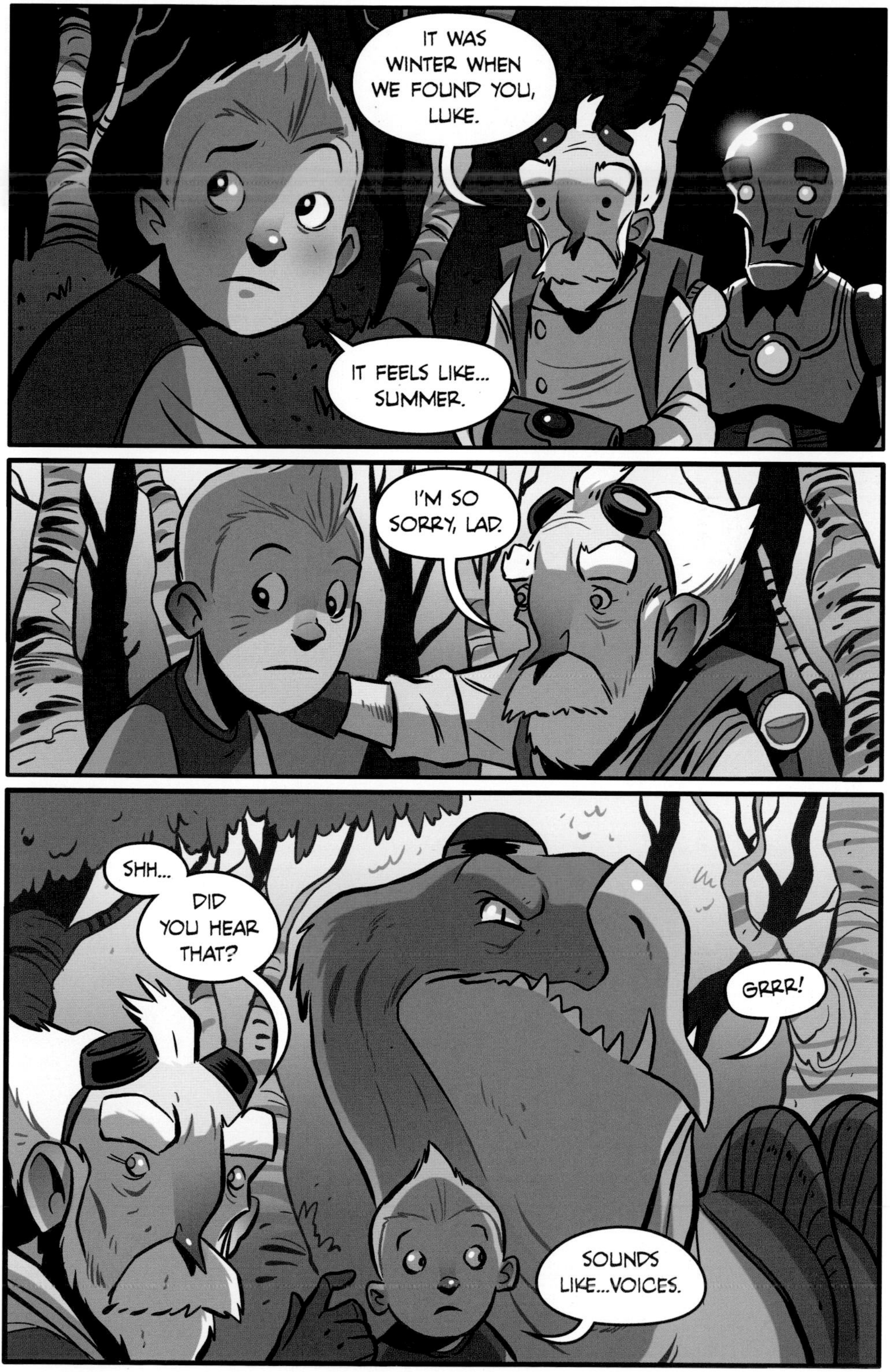
IT WAS WINTER WHEN WE FOUND YOU, LUKE.
IT FEELS LIKE... SUMMER.
I'M SO SORRY, LAD.
SHH...
DID YOU HEAR THAT?
GRRR!
SOUNDS LIKE...VOICES.

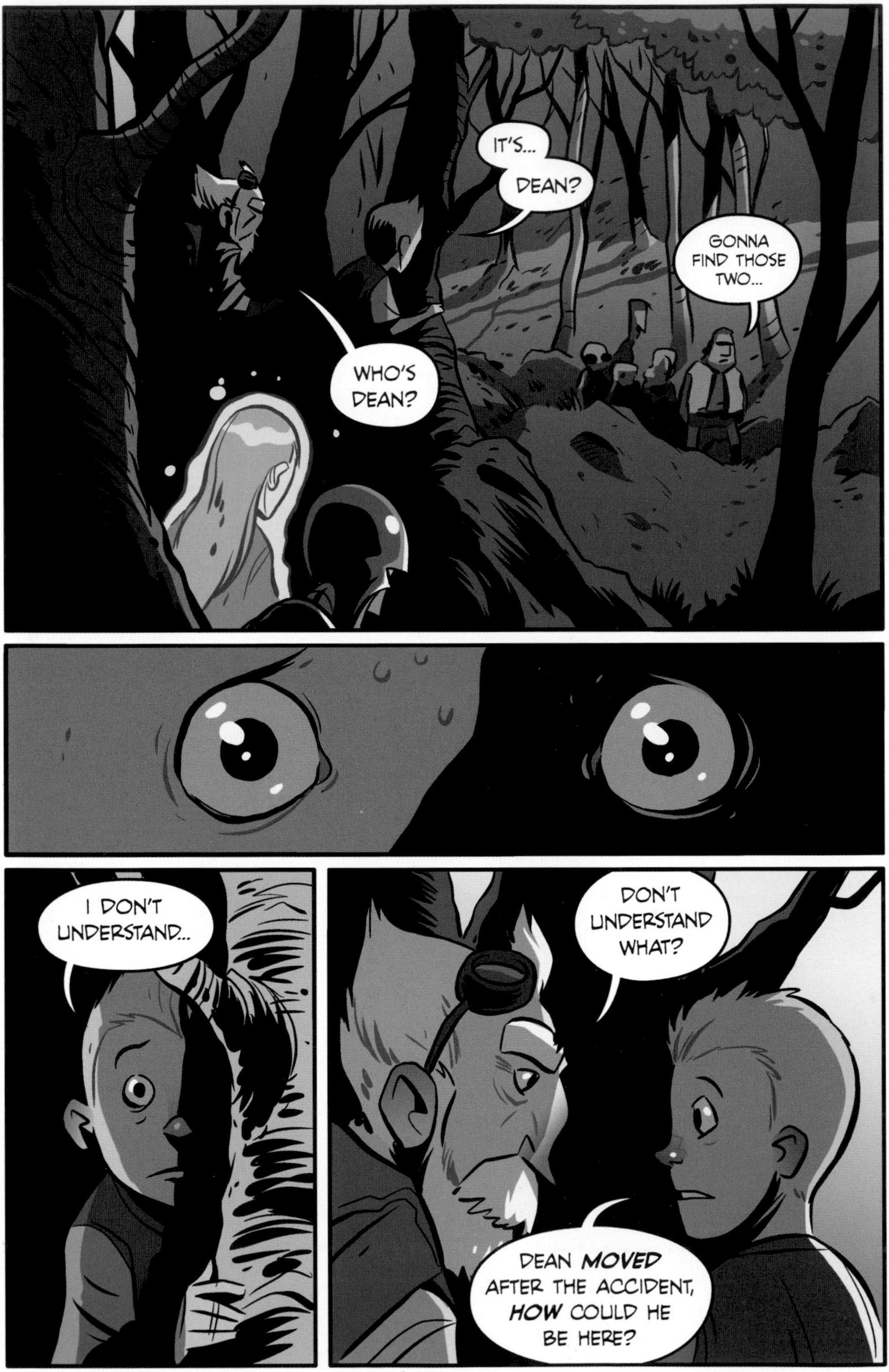
IT'S...
DEAN?
GONNA FIND THOSE TWO...
WHO'S DEAN?
I DON'T UNDERSTAND...
DON'T UNDERSTAND WHAT?
DEAN *MOVED* AFTER THE ACCIDENT, *HOW* COULD HE BE HERE?

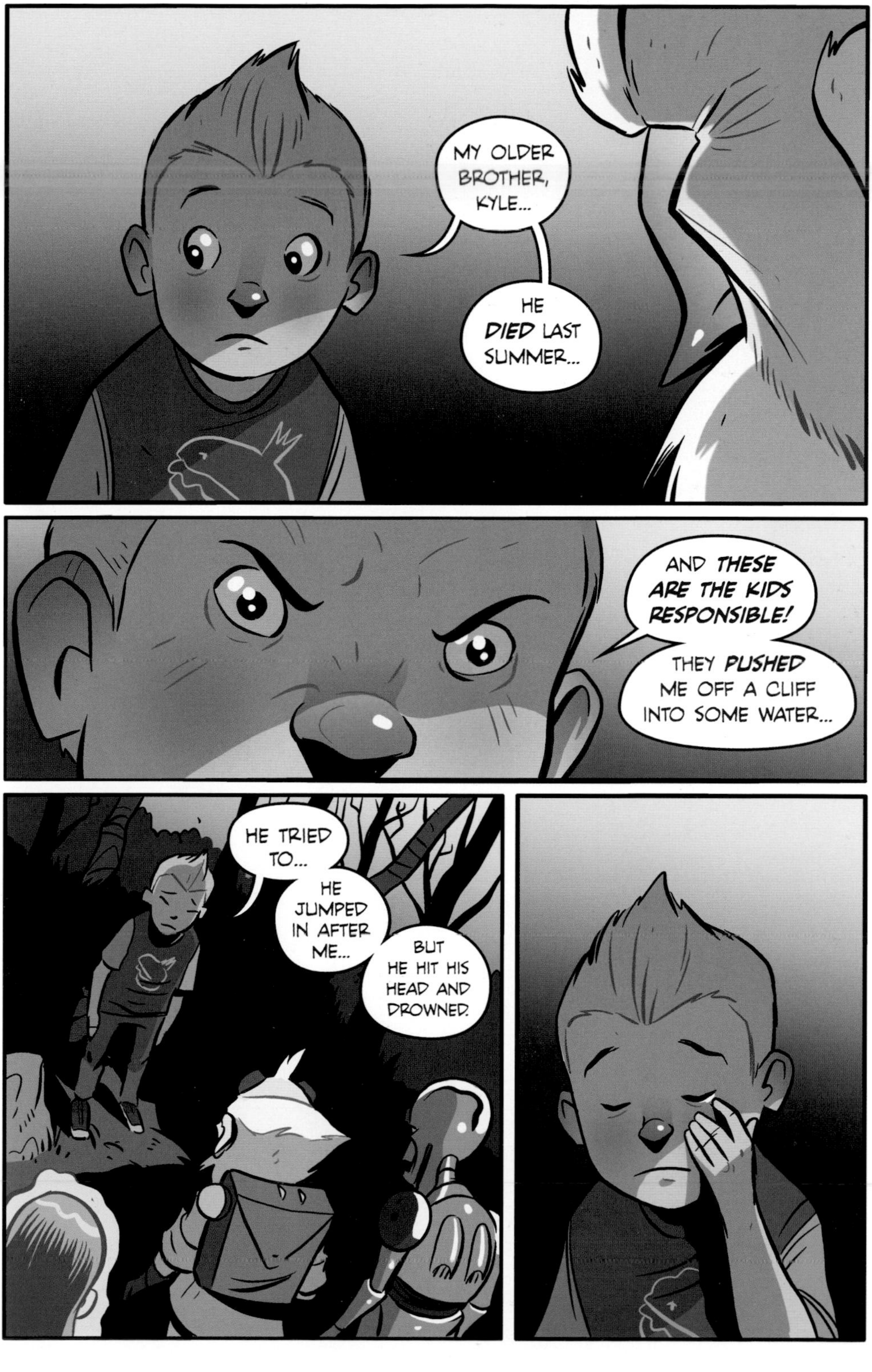

MY OLDER BROTHER, KYLE...
HE *DIED* LAST SUMMER...
AND *THESE ARE THE KIDS RESPONSIBLE!*
THEY *PUSHED* ME OFF A CLIFF INTO SOME WATER...
HE TRIED TO...
HE JUMPED IN AFTER ME...
BUT HE HIT HIS HEAD AND DROWNED.

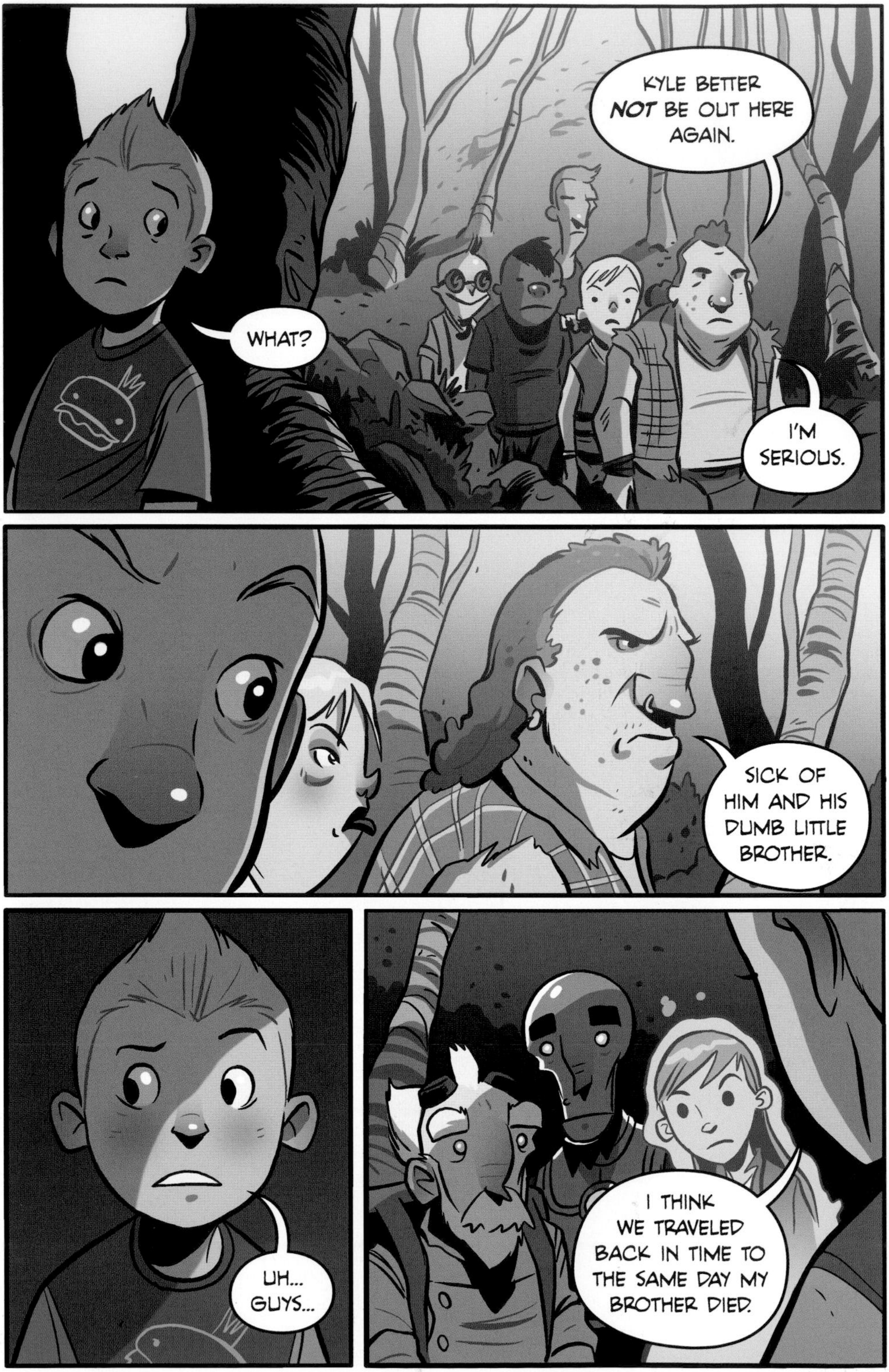
KYLE BETTER NOT BE OUT HERE AGAIN.
WHAT?
I'M SERIOUS.
SICK OF HIM AND HIS DUMB LITTLE BROTHER.
UH... GUYS...
I THINK WE TRAVELED BACK IN TIME TO THE SAME DAY MY BROTHER DIED.

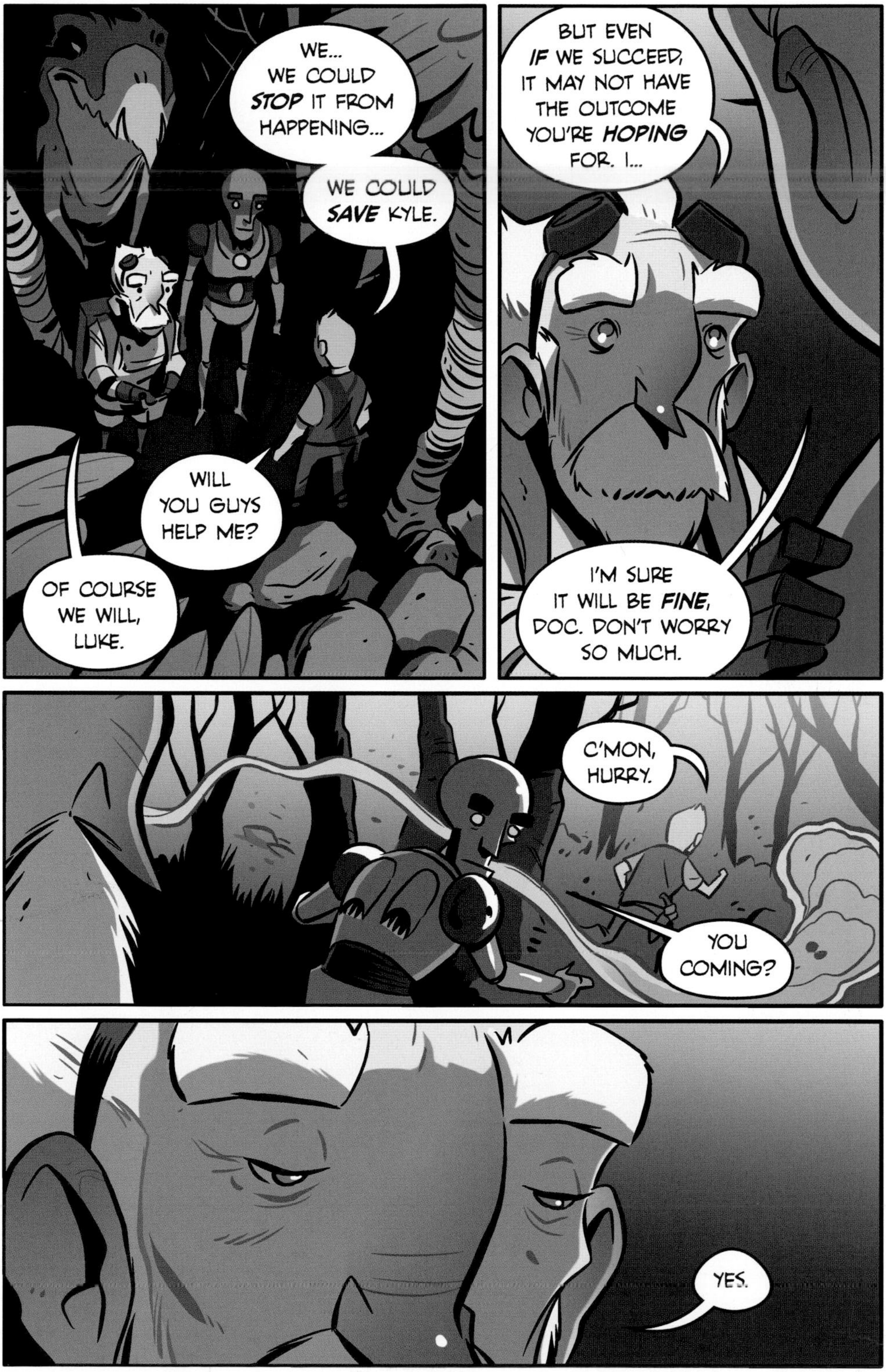
WE... WE COULD STOP IT FROM HAPPENING...
WE COULD SAVE KYLE.
WILL YOU GUYS HELP ME?
OF COURSE WE WILL, LUKE.
BUT EVEN IF WE SUCCEED, IT MAY NOT HAVE THE OUTCOME YOU'RE HOPING FOR. I...
I'M SURE IT WILL BE FINE, DOC. DON'T WORRY SO MUCH.
C'MON, HURRY.
YOU COMING?
YES.

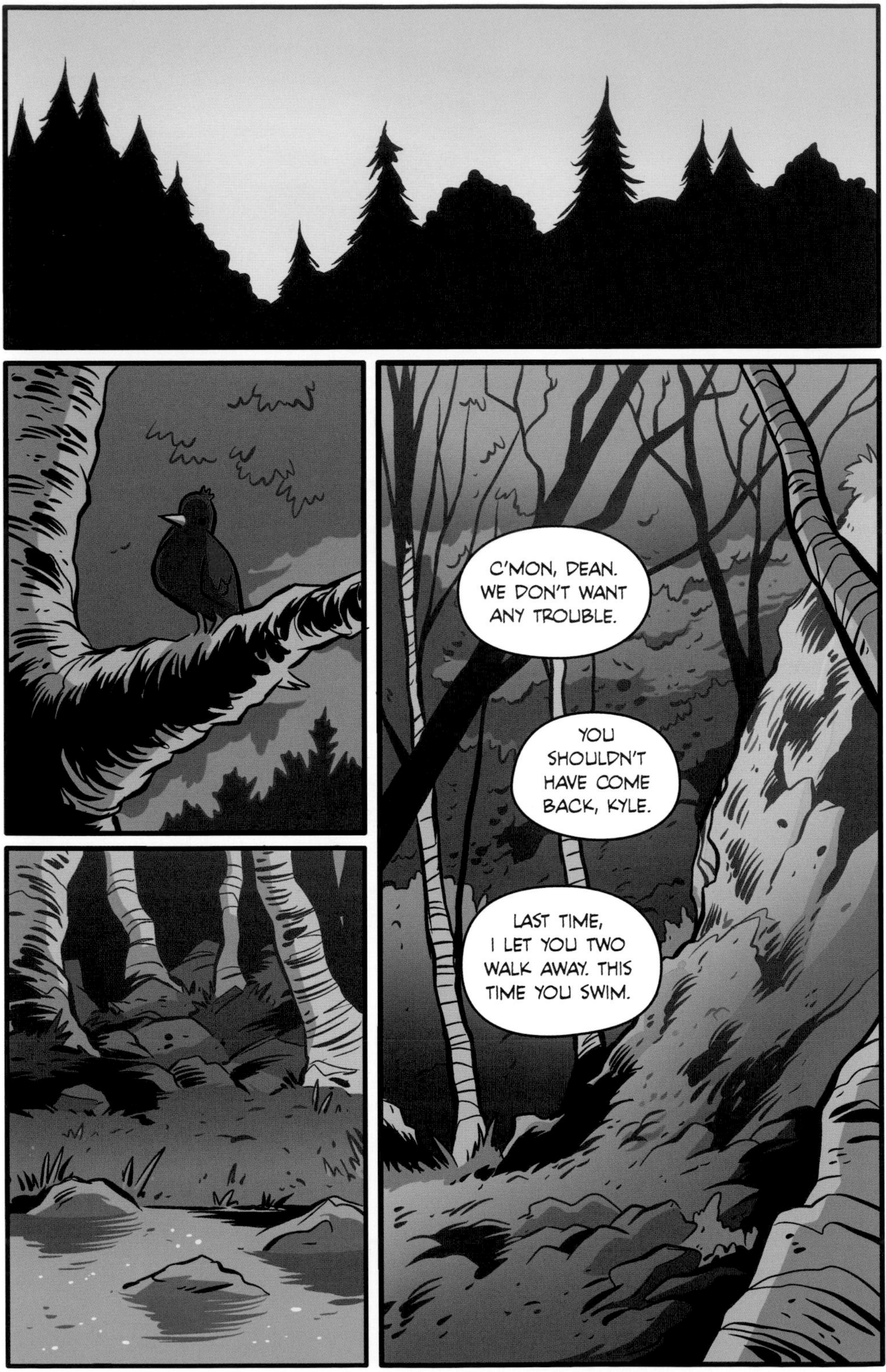
C'MON, DEAN. WE DON'T WANT ANY TROUBLE.
YOU SHOULDN'T HAVE COME BACK, KYLE.
LAST TIME, I LET YOU TWO WALK AWAY. THIS TIME YOU SWIM.

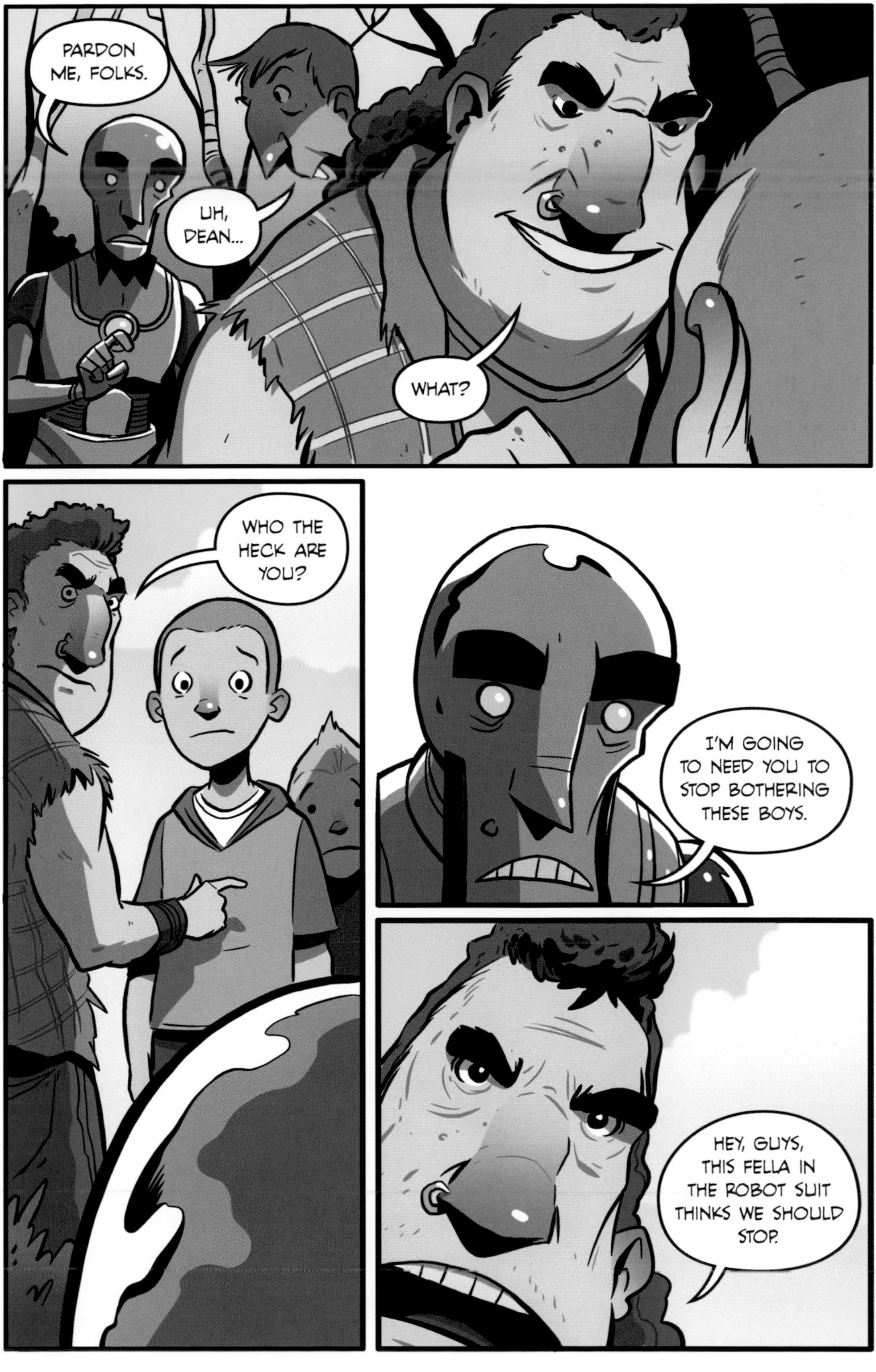
PARDON ME, FOLKS.
UH, DEAN...
WHAT?
WHO THE HECK ARE YOU?
I'M GOING TO NEED YOU TO STOP BOTHERING THESE BOYS.
HEY, GUYS, THIS FELLA IN THE ROBOT SUIT THINKS WE SHOULD STOP.

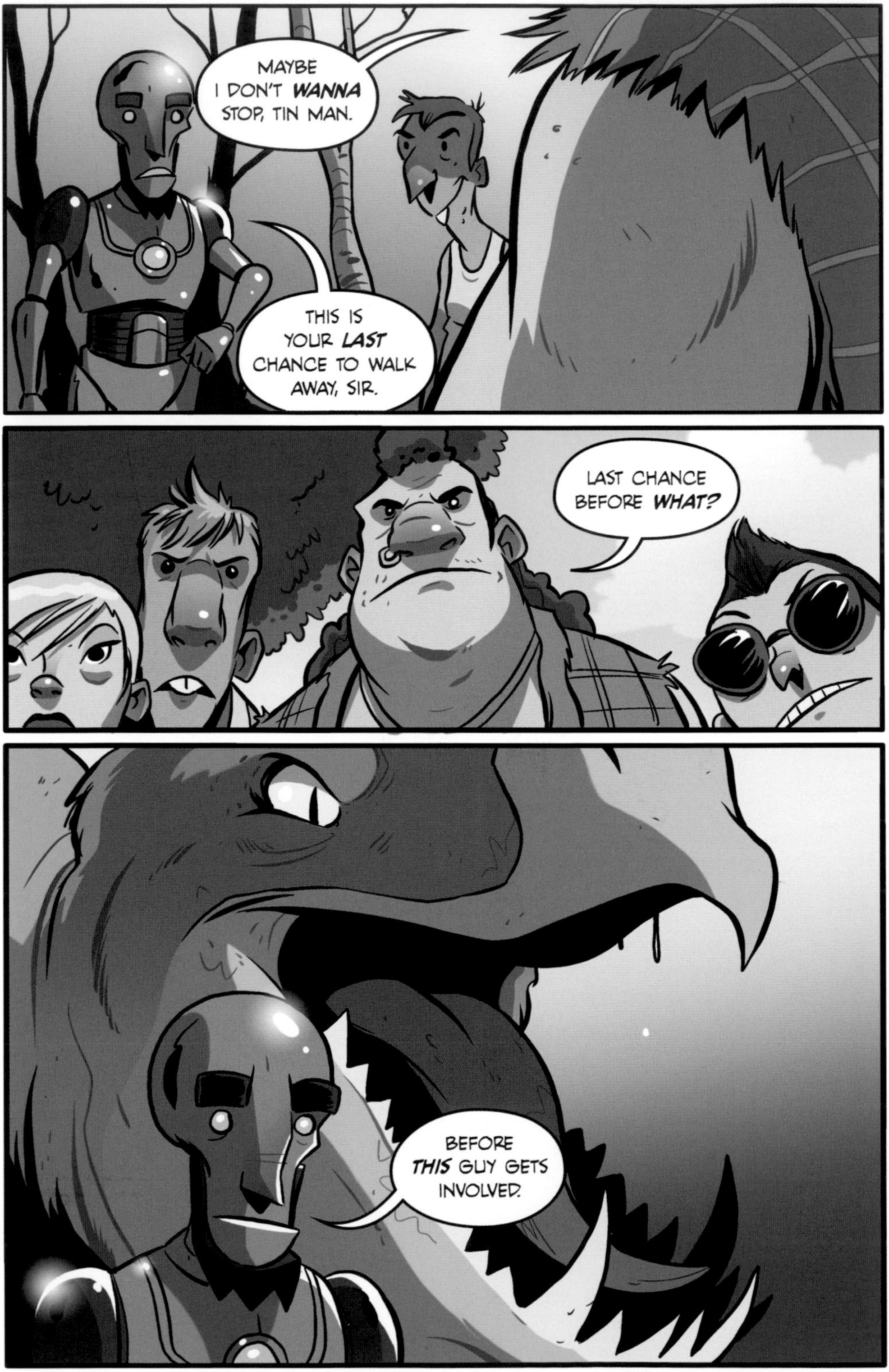
MAYBE I DON'T WANNA STOP, TIN MAN.
THIS IS YOUR LAST CHANCE TO WALK AWAY, SIR.
LAST CHANCE BEFORE WHAT?
BEFORE THIS GUY GETS INVOLVED.

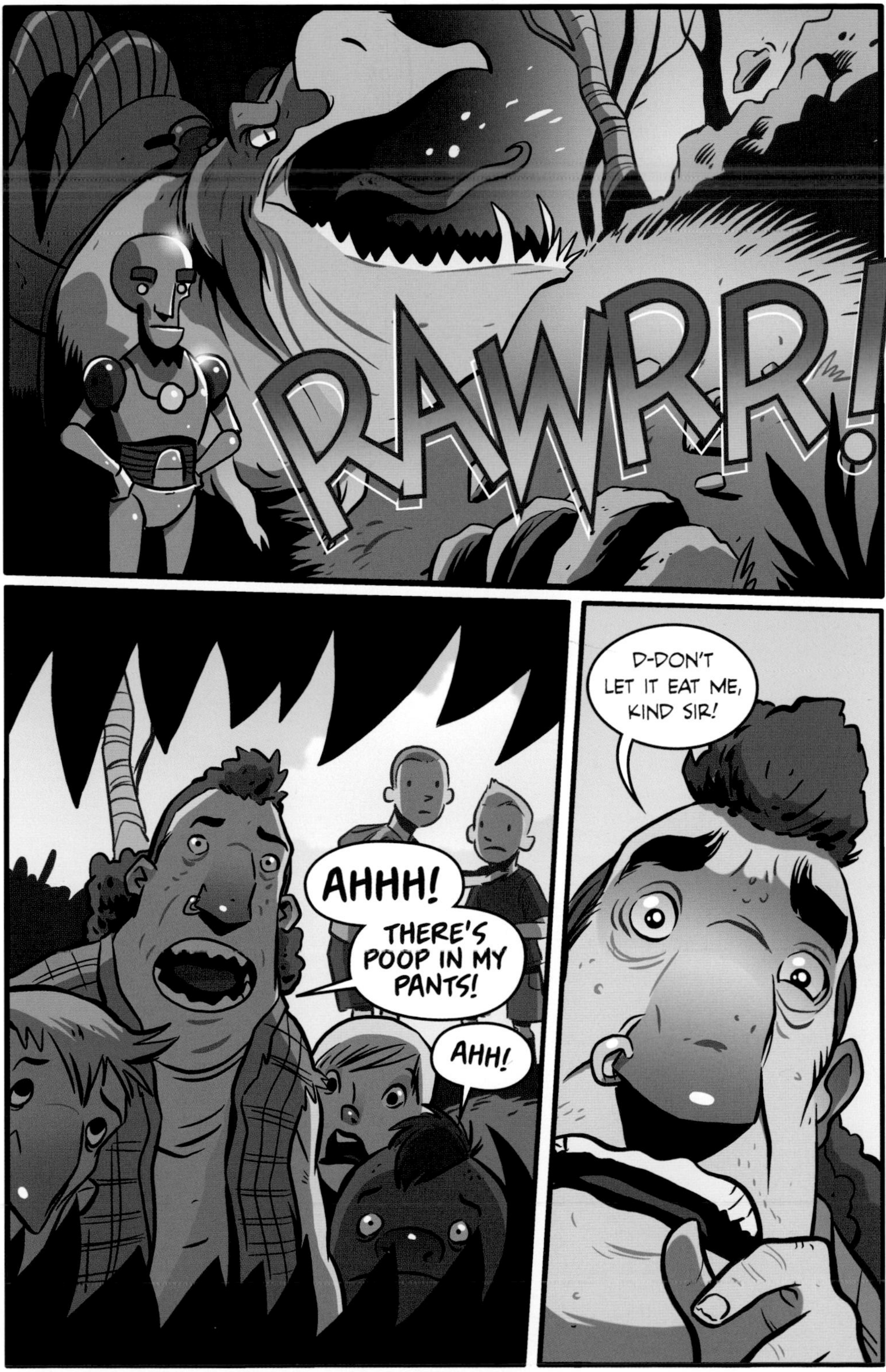
RAWRR!
AHHH!
THERE'S POOP IN MY PANTS!
AHH!
D-DON'T LET IT EAT ME, KIND SIR!

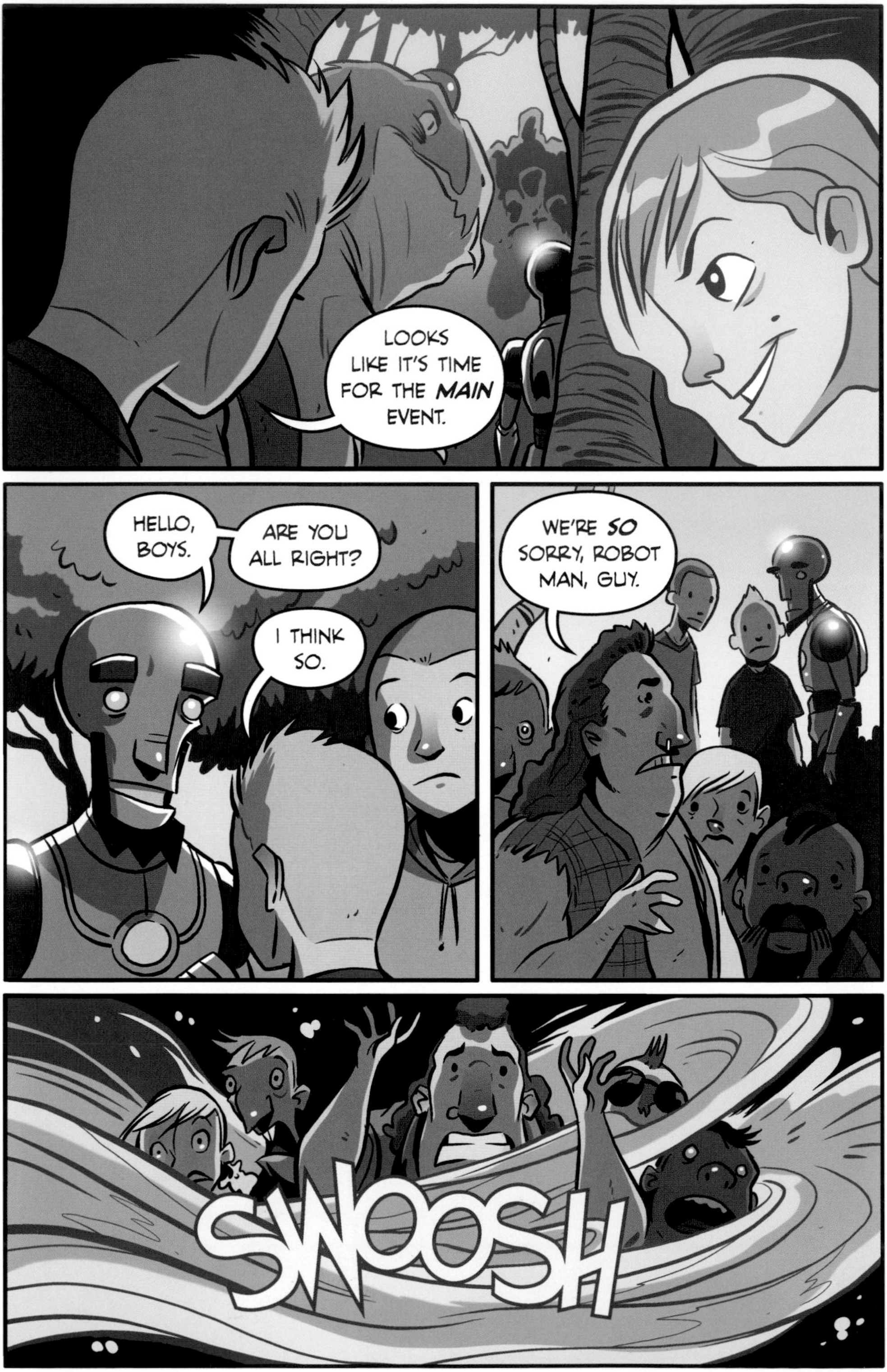
LOOKS LIKE IT'S TIME FOR THE *MAIN* EVENT.
HELLO, BOYS.
ARE YOU ALL RIGHT?
I THINK SO.
WE'RE *SO* SORRY, ROBOT MAN, GUY.
SWOOSH

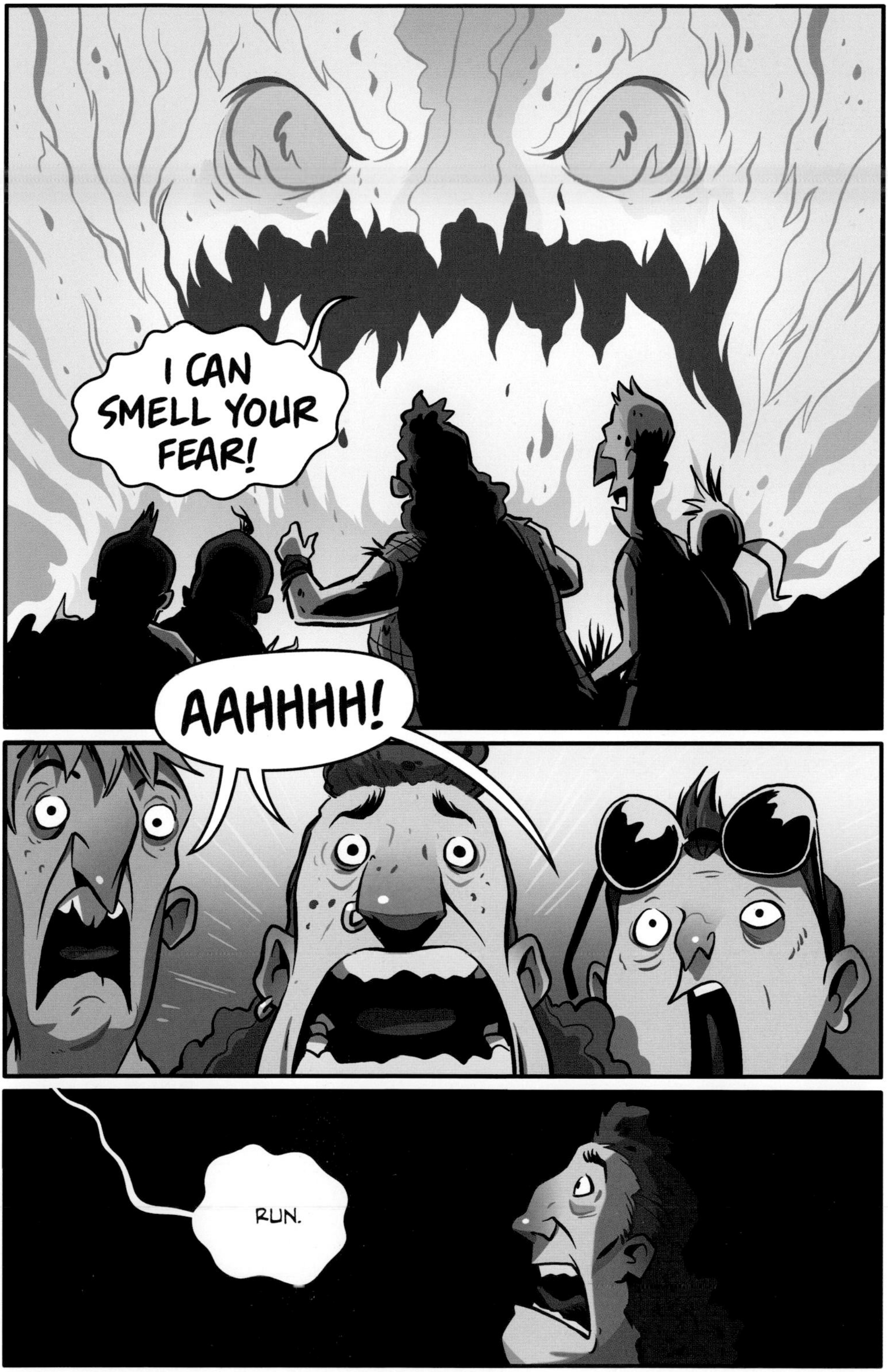
I CAN SMELL YOUR FEAR!
AAHHHH!
RUN.

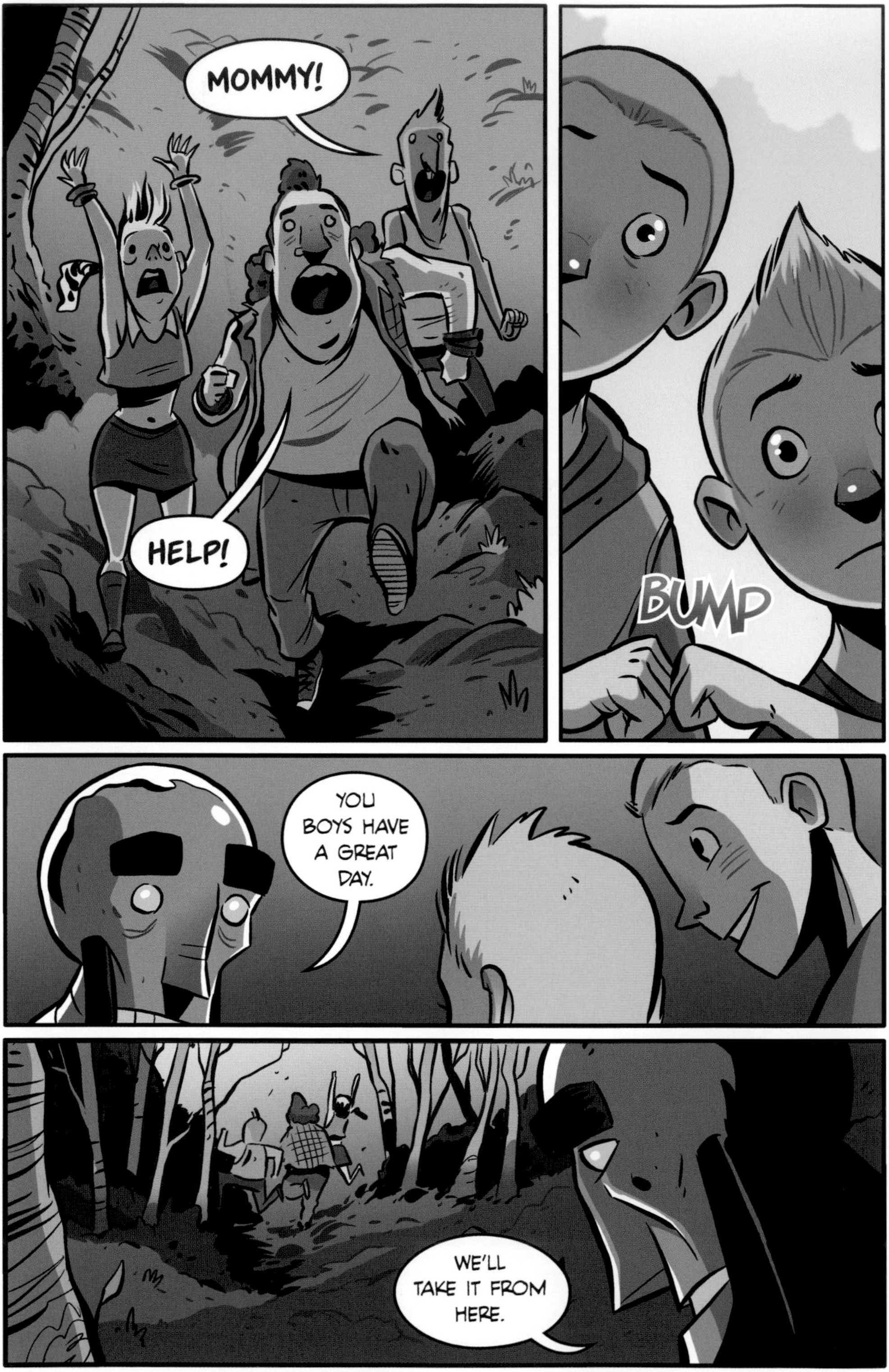
MOMMY!
HELP!
BUMP
YOU BOYS HAVE A GREAT DAY.
WE'LL TAKE IT FROM HERE.

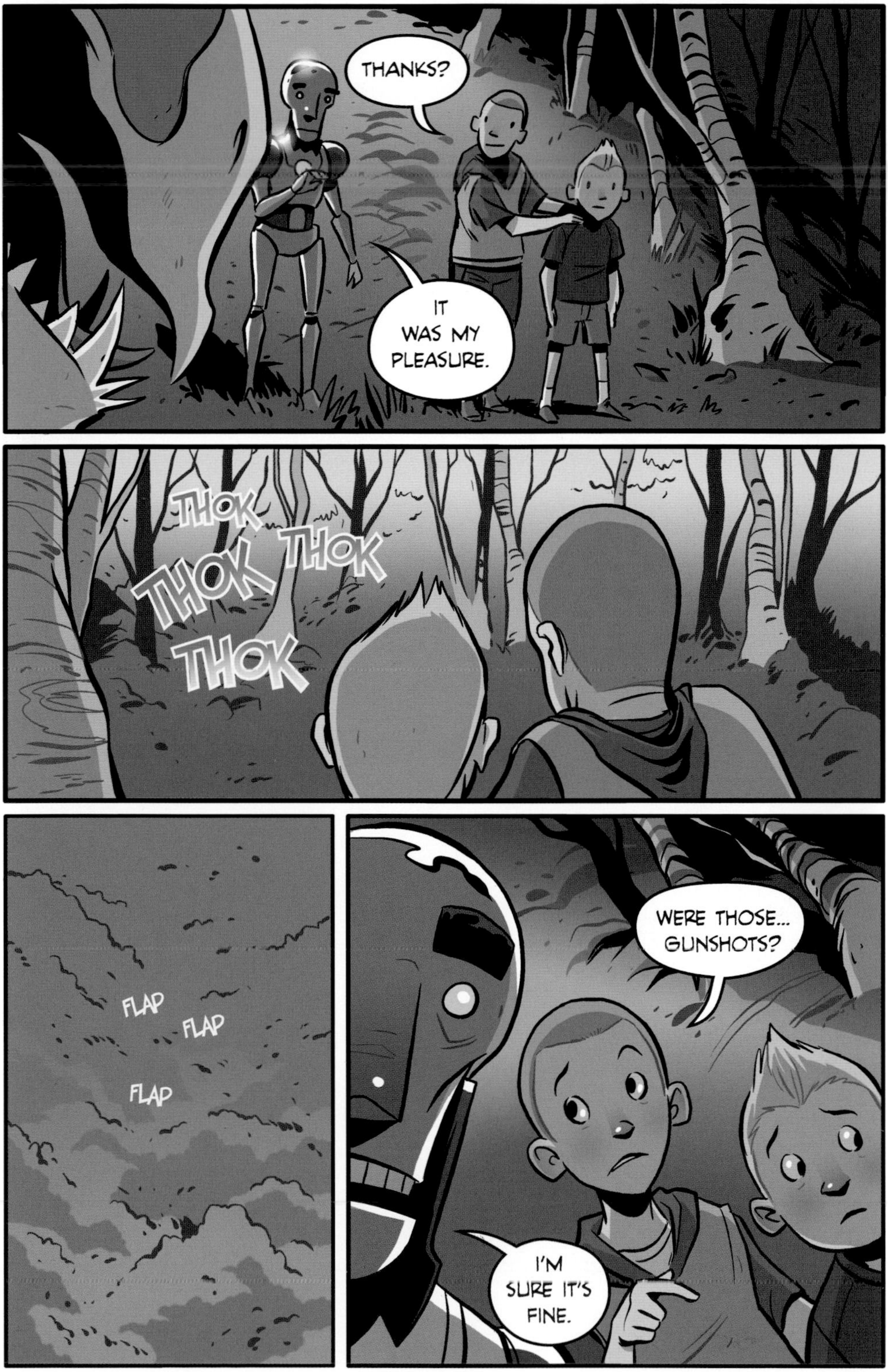
THANKS?
IT WAS MY PLEASURE.
THOK
THOK
THOK
THOK
FLAP
FLAP
FLAP
WERE THOSE... GUNSHOTS?
I'M SURE IT'S FINE.

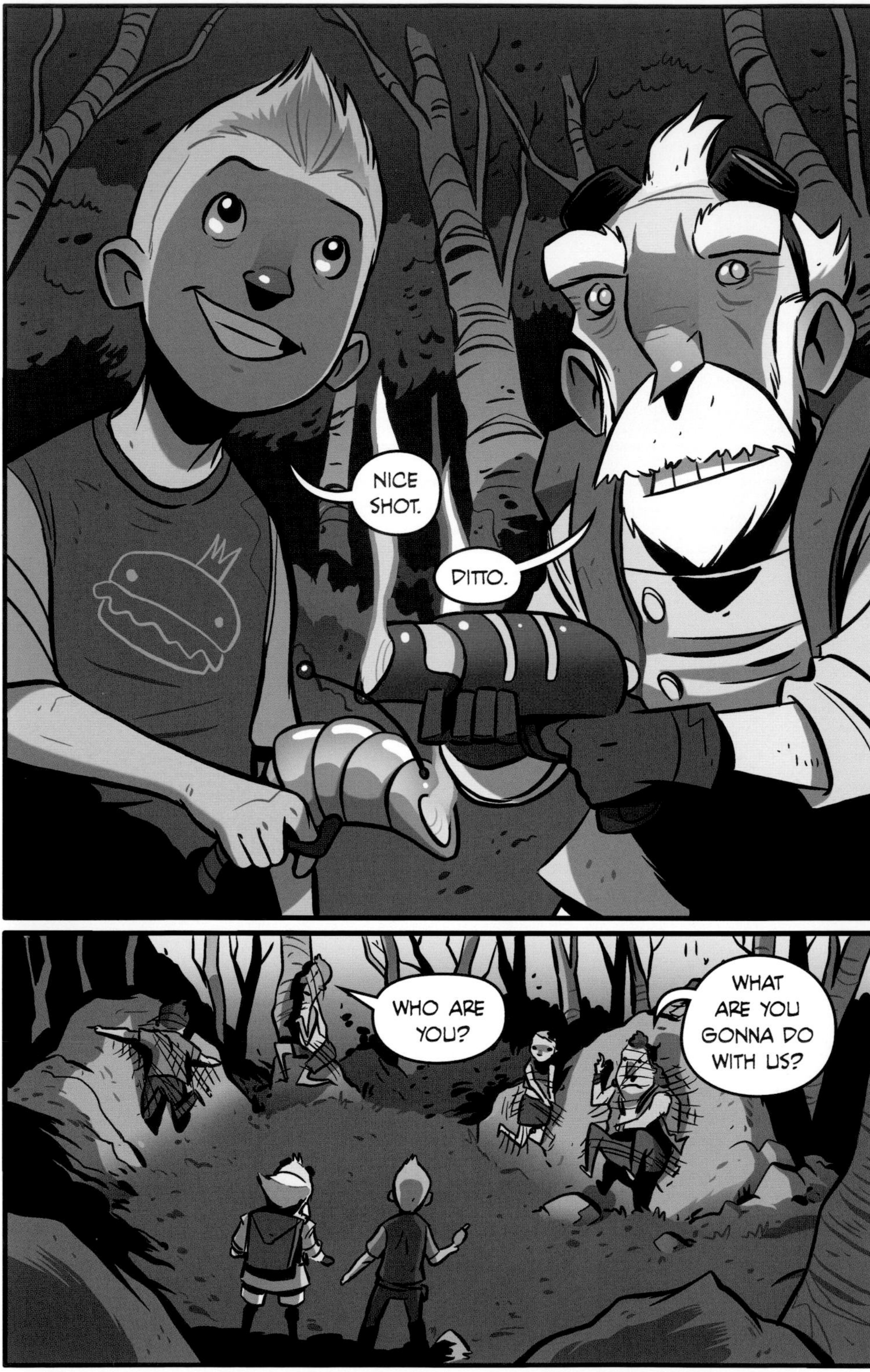
NICE SHOT.
DITTO.
WHO ARE YOU?
WHAT ARE YOU GONNA DO WITH US?

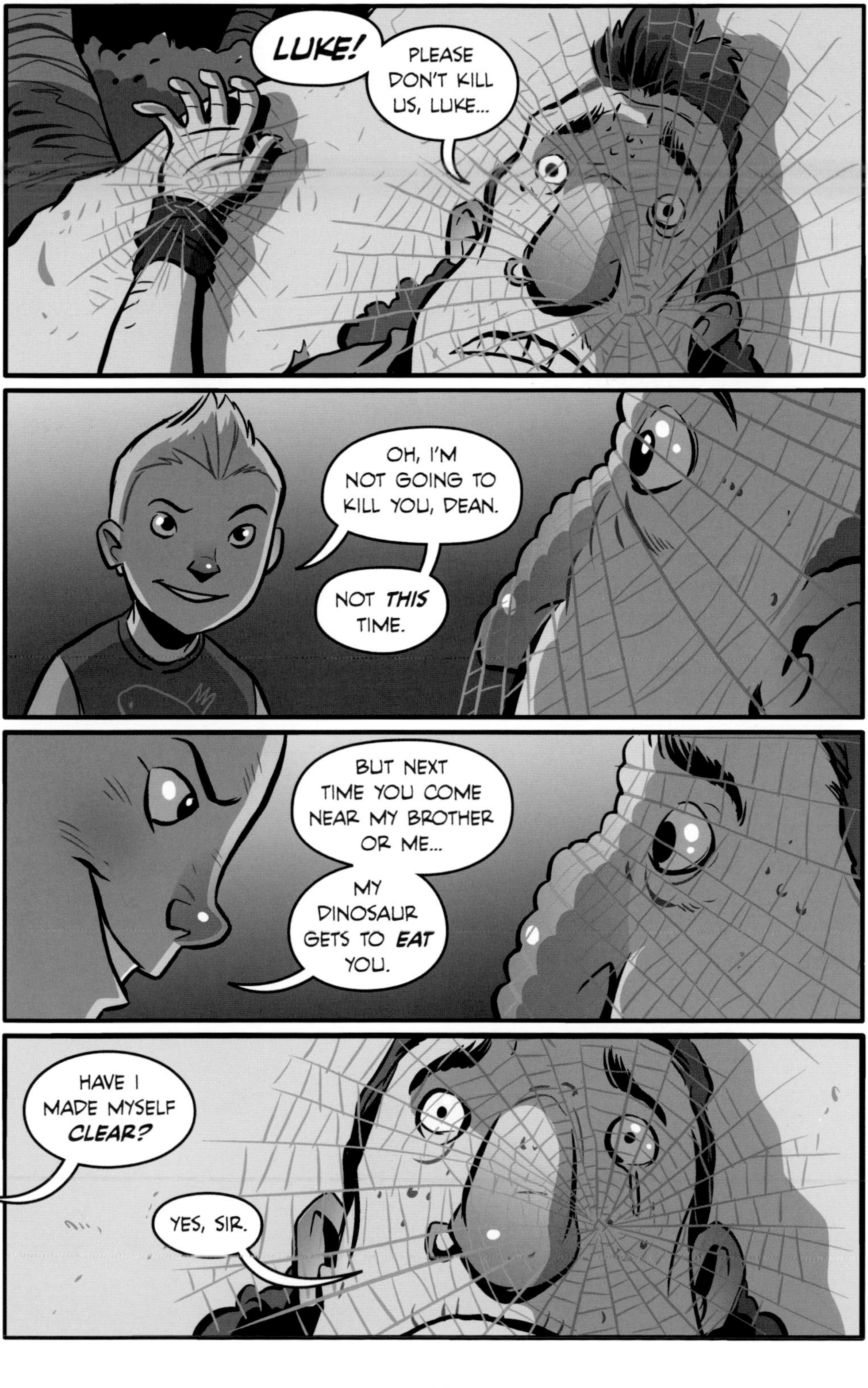

LUKE!
PLEASE DON'T KILL US, LUKE...
OH, I'M NOT GOING TO KILL YOU, DEAN.
NOT THIS TIME.
BUT NEXT TIME YOU COME NEAR MY BROTHER OR ME...
MY DINOSAUR GETS TO EAT YOU.
HAVE I MADE MYSELF CLEAR?
YES, SIR.

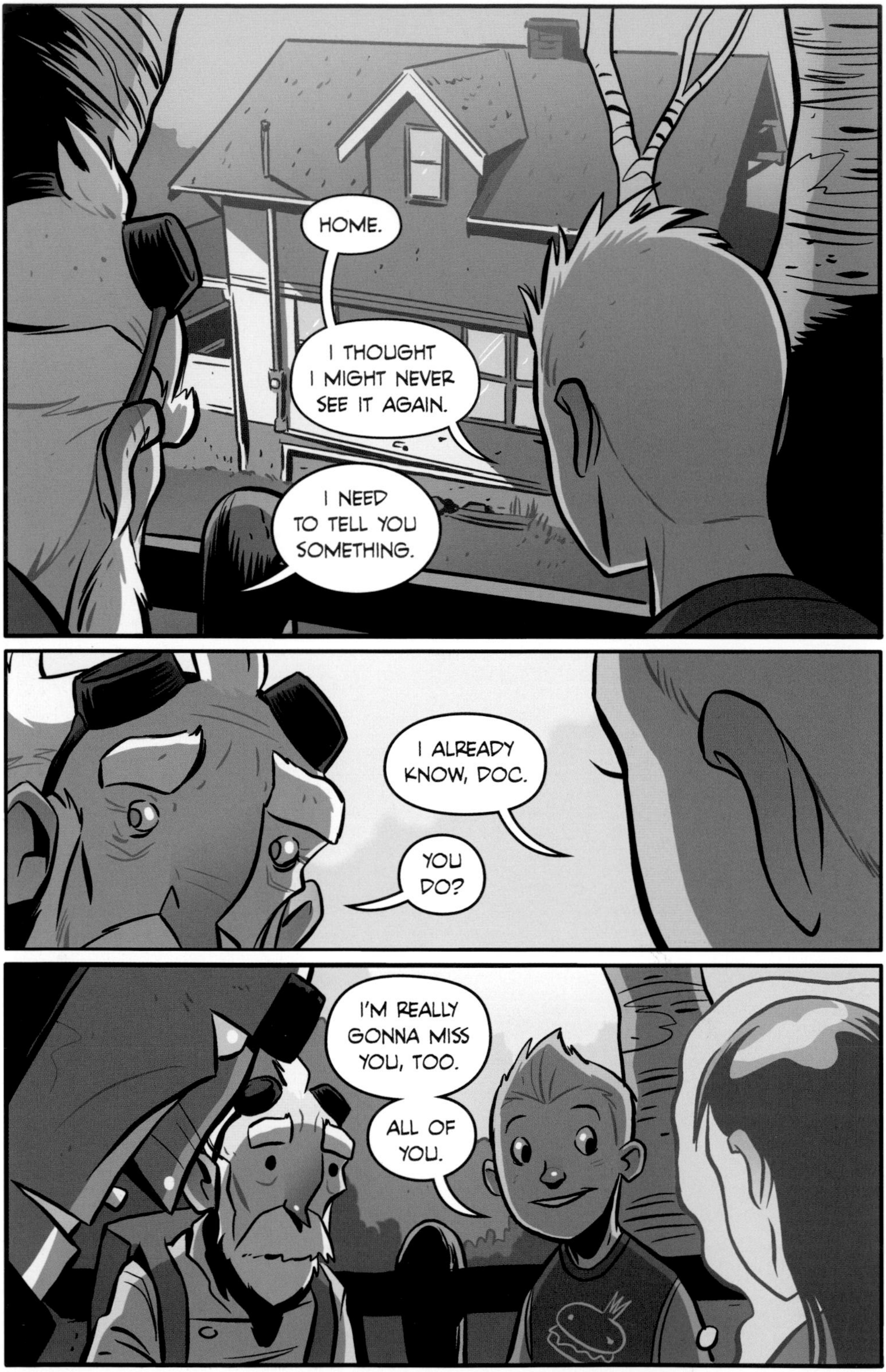
HOME.
I THOUGHT I MIGHT NEVER SEE IT AGAIN.
I NEED TO TELL YOU SOMETHING.
I ALREADY KNOW, DOC.
YOU DO?
I'M REALLY GONNA MISS YOU, TOO.
ALL OF YOU.

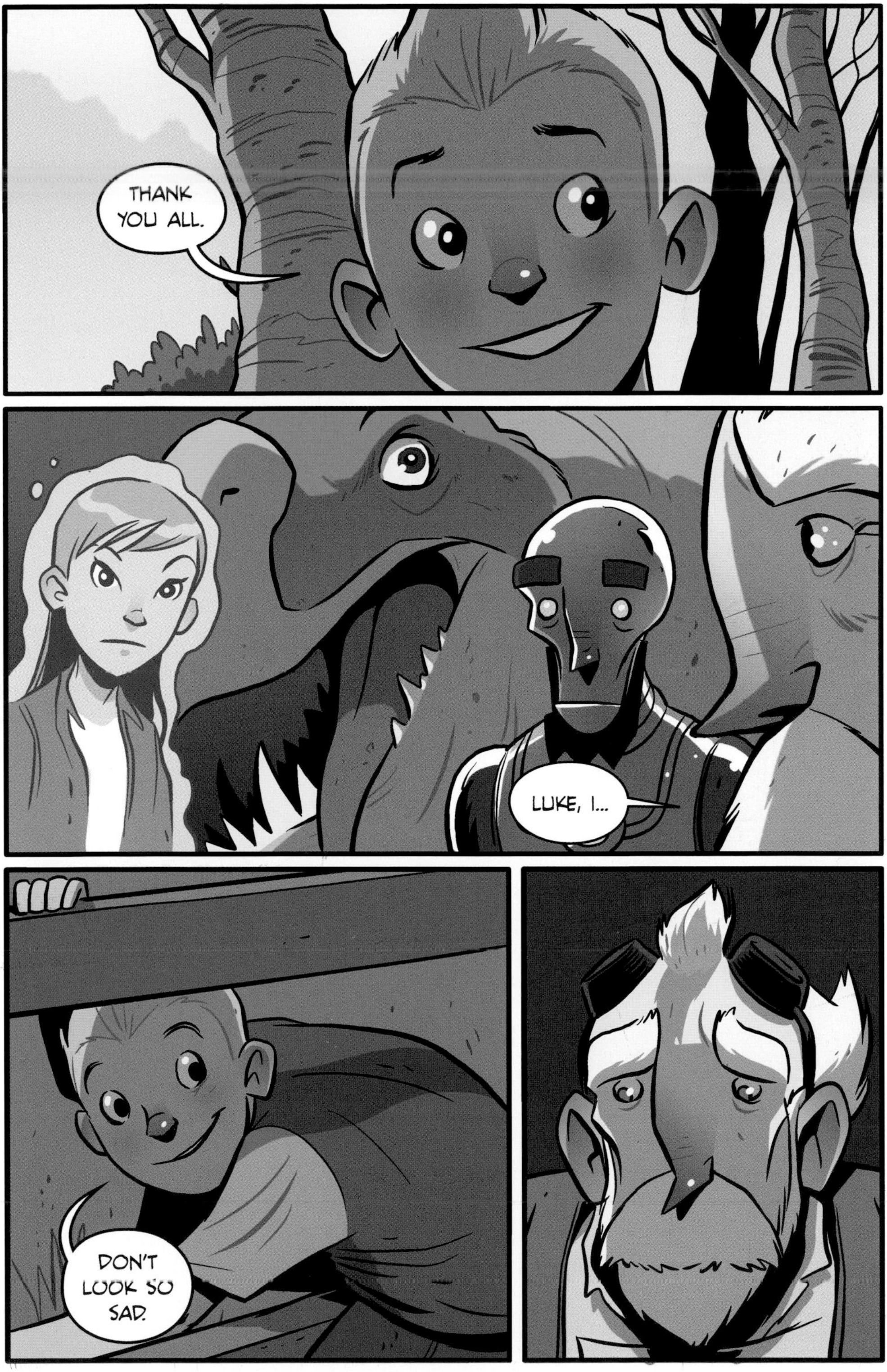
THANK YOU ALL.
LUKE, I...
DON'T LOOK SO SAD.

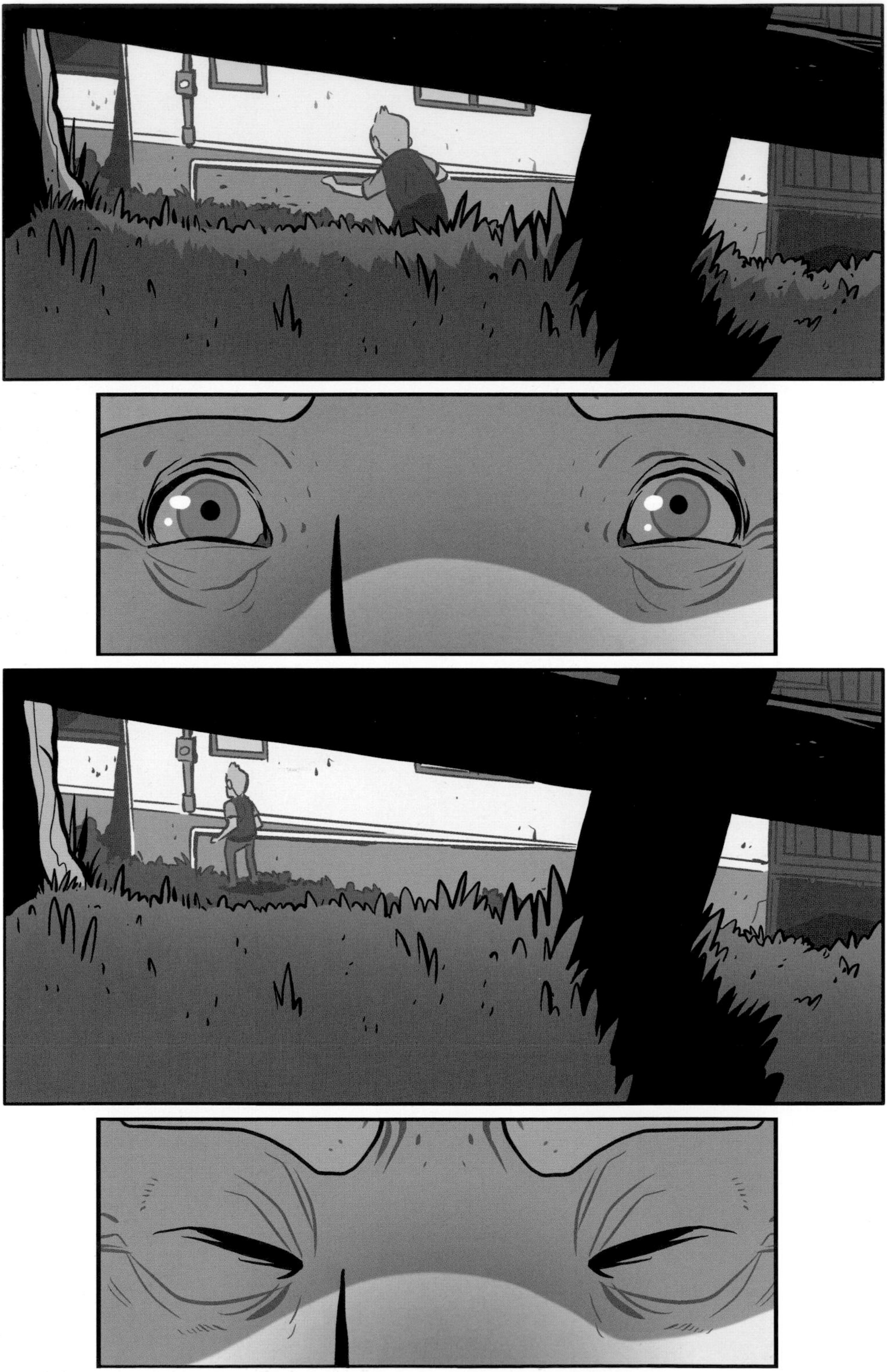

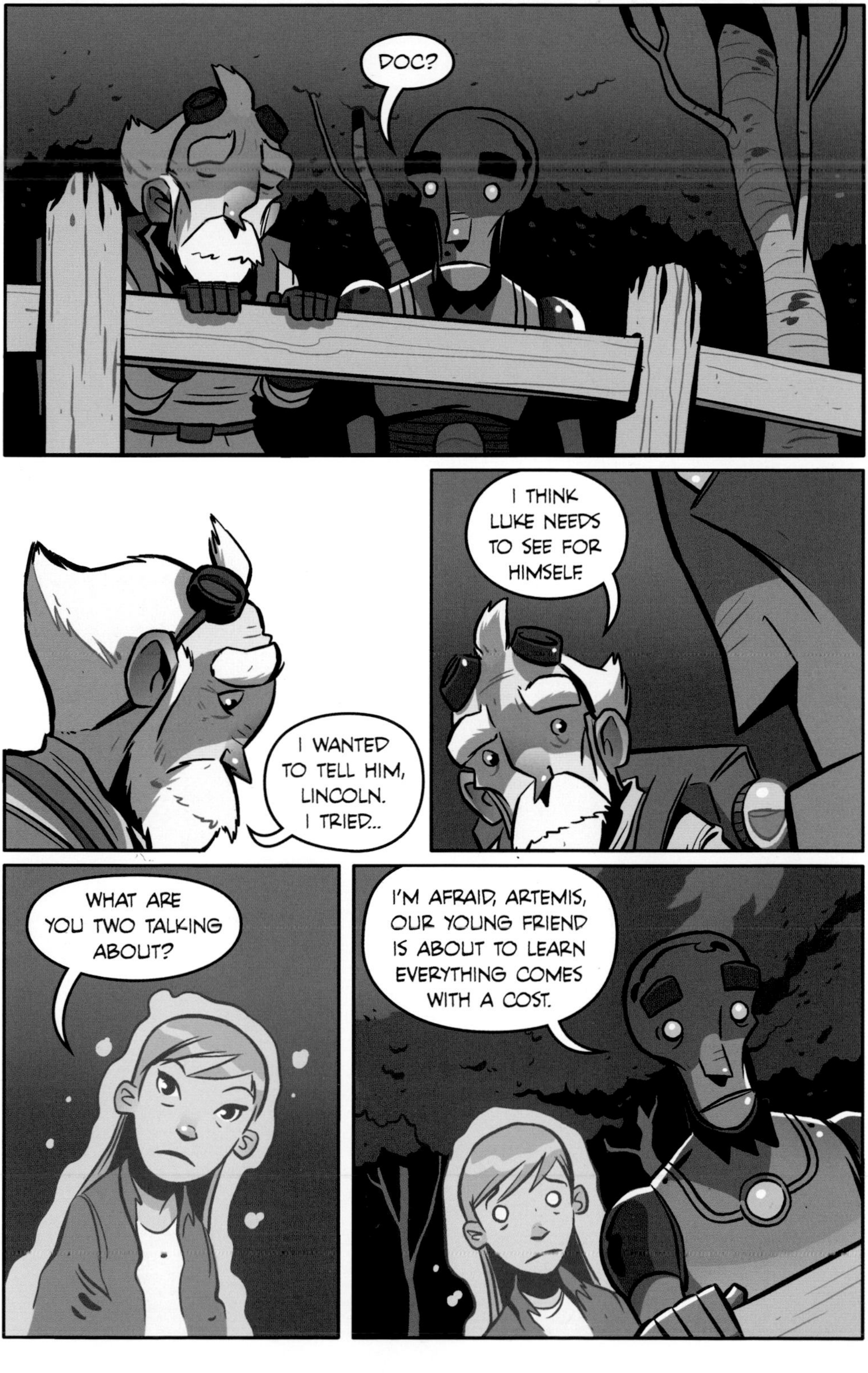
DOC?
I THINK LUKE NEEDS TO SEE FOR HIMSELF.
I WANTED TO TELL HIM, LINCOLN. I TRIED...
WHAT ARE YOU TWO TALKING ABOUT?
I'M AFRAID, ARTEMIS, OUR YOUNG FRIEND IS ABOUT TO LEARN EVERYTHING COMES WITH A COST.

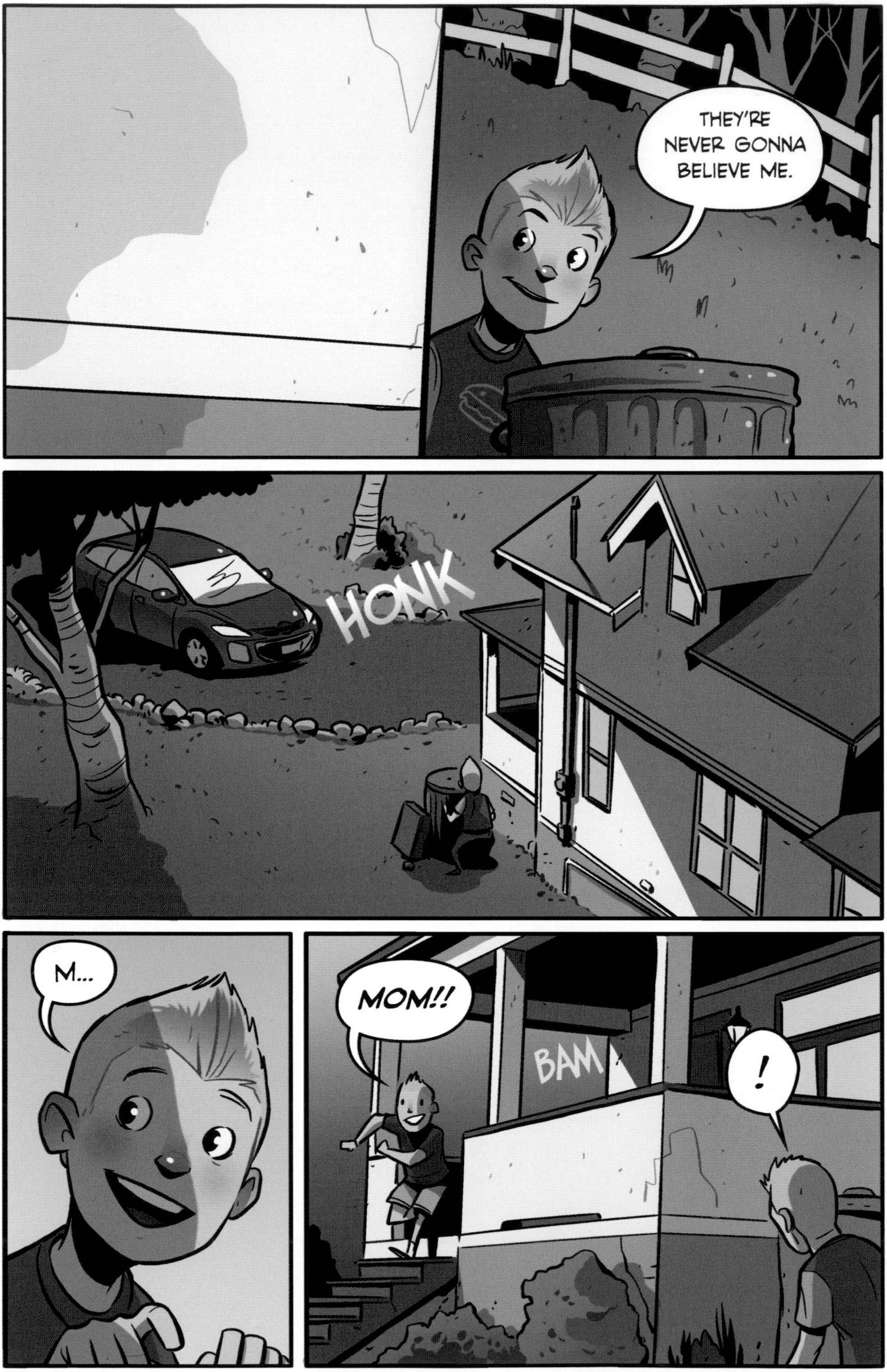
THEY'RE NEVER GONNA BELIEVE ME.
HONK
M...
MOM!!
BAM
!

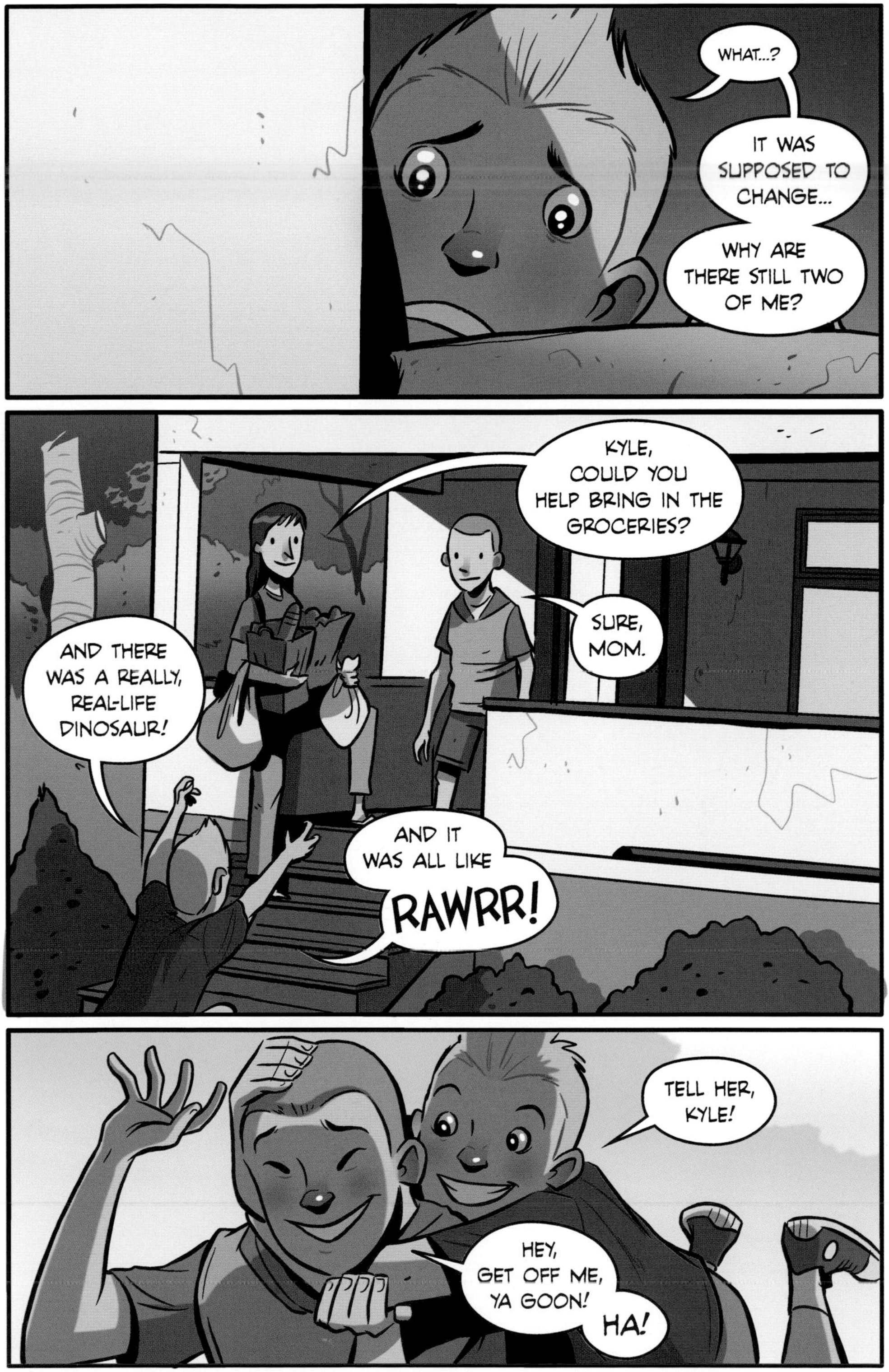
WHAT...?
IT WAS SUPPOSED TO CHANGE...
WHY ARE THERE STILL TWO OF ME?
KYLE, COULD YOU HELP BRING IN THE GROCERIES?
SURE, MOM.
AND THERE WAS A REALLY, REAL-LIFE DINOSAUR!
AND IT WAS ALL LIKE
RAWRR!
TELL HER, KYLE!
HEY, GET OFF ME, YA GOON!
HA!

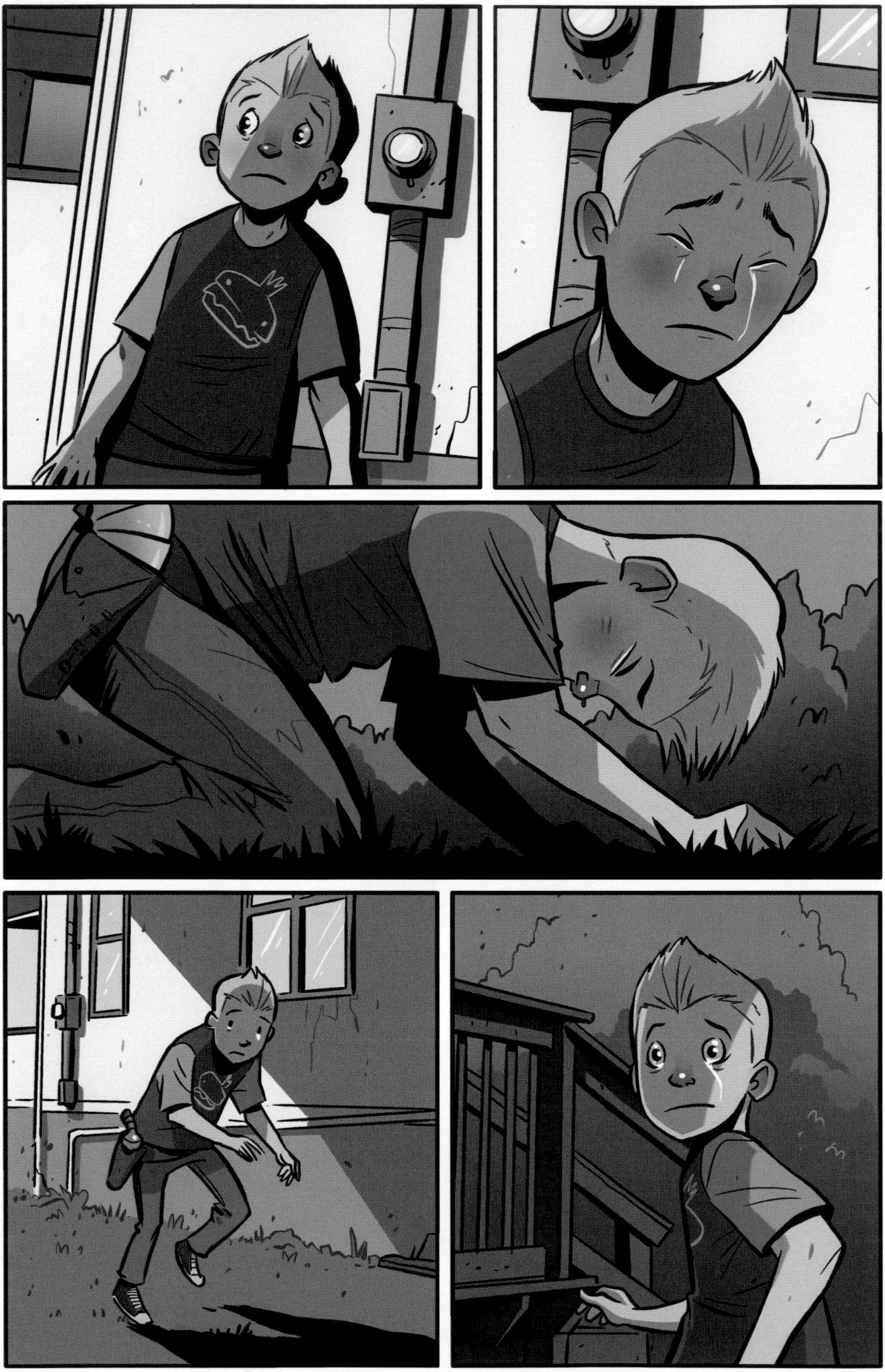

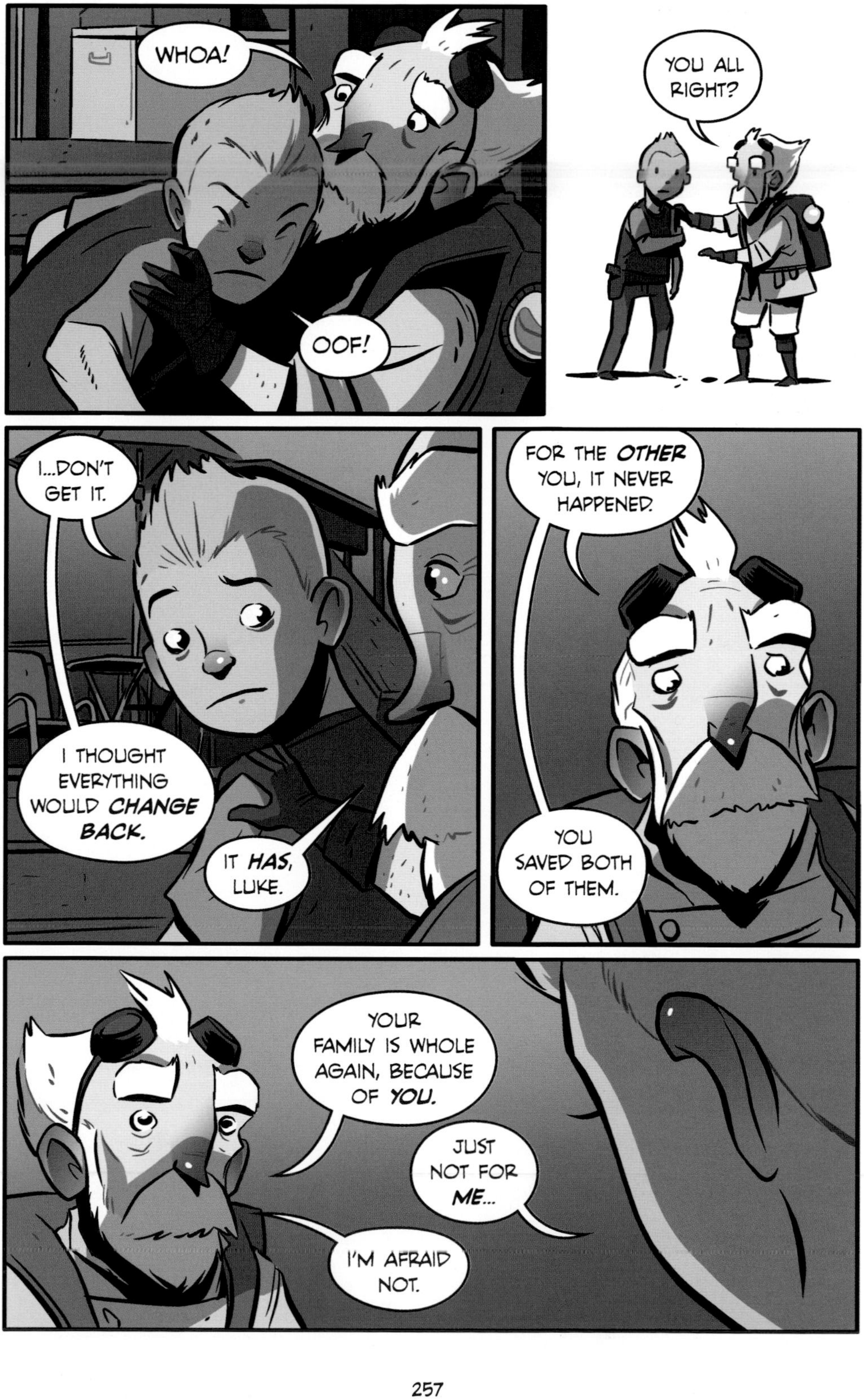
WHOA!
OOF!
YOU ALL RIGHT?
I...DON'T GET IT.
I THOUGHT EVERYTHING WOULD CHANGE BACK.
IT HAS, LUKE.
FOR THE OTHER YOU, IT NEVER HAPPENED.
YOU SAVED BOTH OF THEM.
YOUR FAMILY IS WHOLE AGAIN, BECAUSE OF YOU.
JUST NOT FOR ME...
I'M AFRAID NOT.

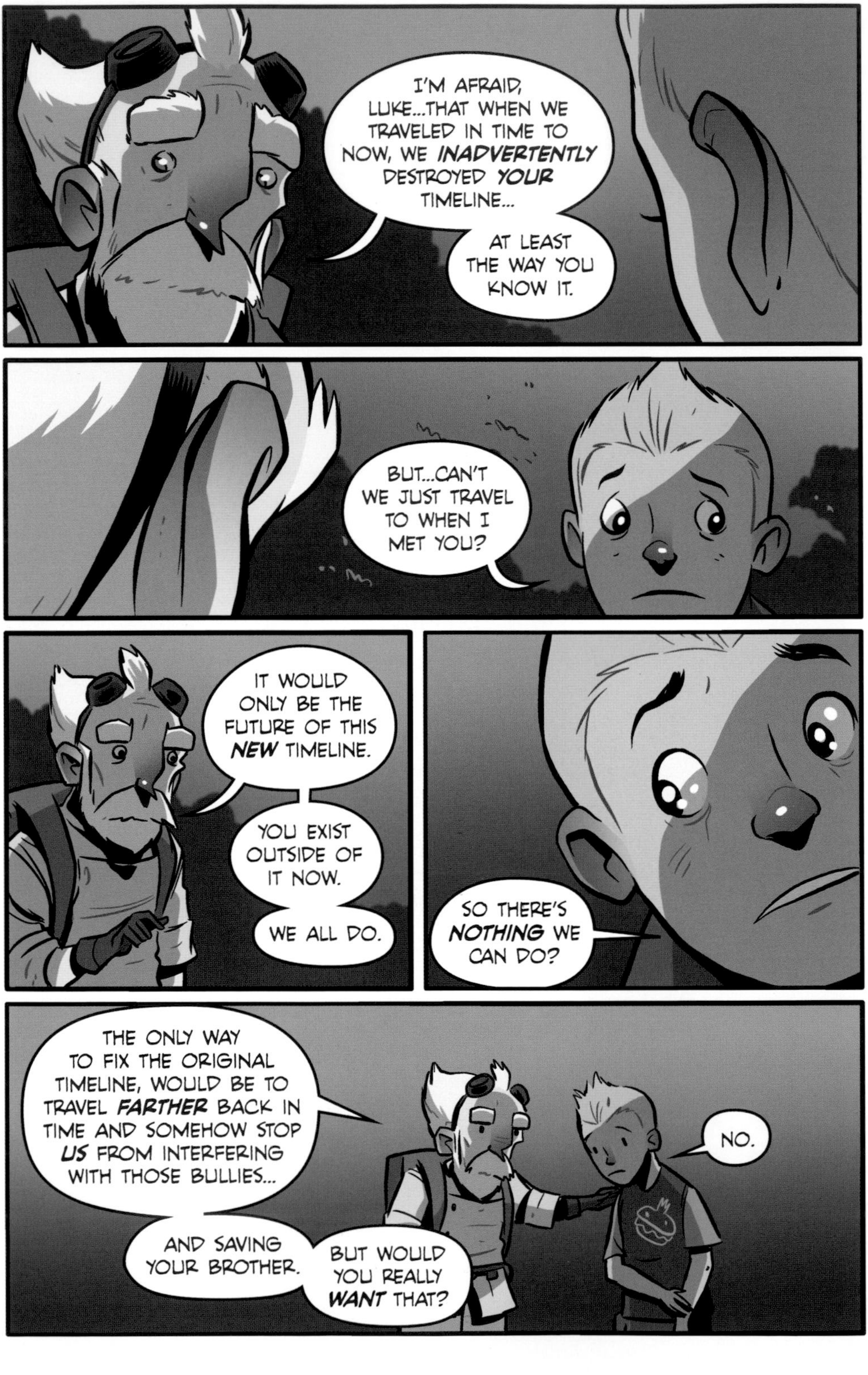
I'M AFRAID, LUKE...THAT WHEN WE TRAVELED IN TIME TO NOW, WE *INADVERTENTLY* DESTROYED *YOUR* TIMELINE...
AT LEAST THE WAY YOU KNOW IT.
BUT...CAN'T WE JUST TRAVEL TO WHEN I MET YOU?
IT WOULD ONLY BE THE FUTURE OF THIS *NEW* TIMELINE.
YOU EXIST OUTSIDE OF IT NOW.
WE ALL DO.
SO THERE'S *NOTHING* WE CAN DO?
THE ONLY WAY TO FIX THE ORIGINAL TIMELINE, WOULD BE TO TRAVEL *FARTHER* BACK IN TIME AND SOMEHOW STOP *US* FROM INTERFERING WITH THOSE BULLIES...
AND SAVING YOUR BROTHER.
BUT WOULD YOU REALLY *WANT* THAT?
NO.

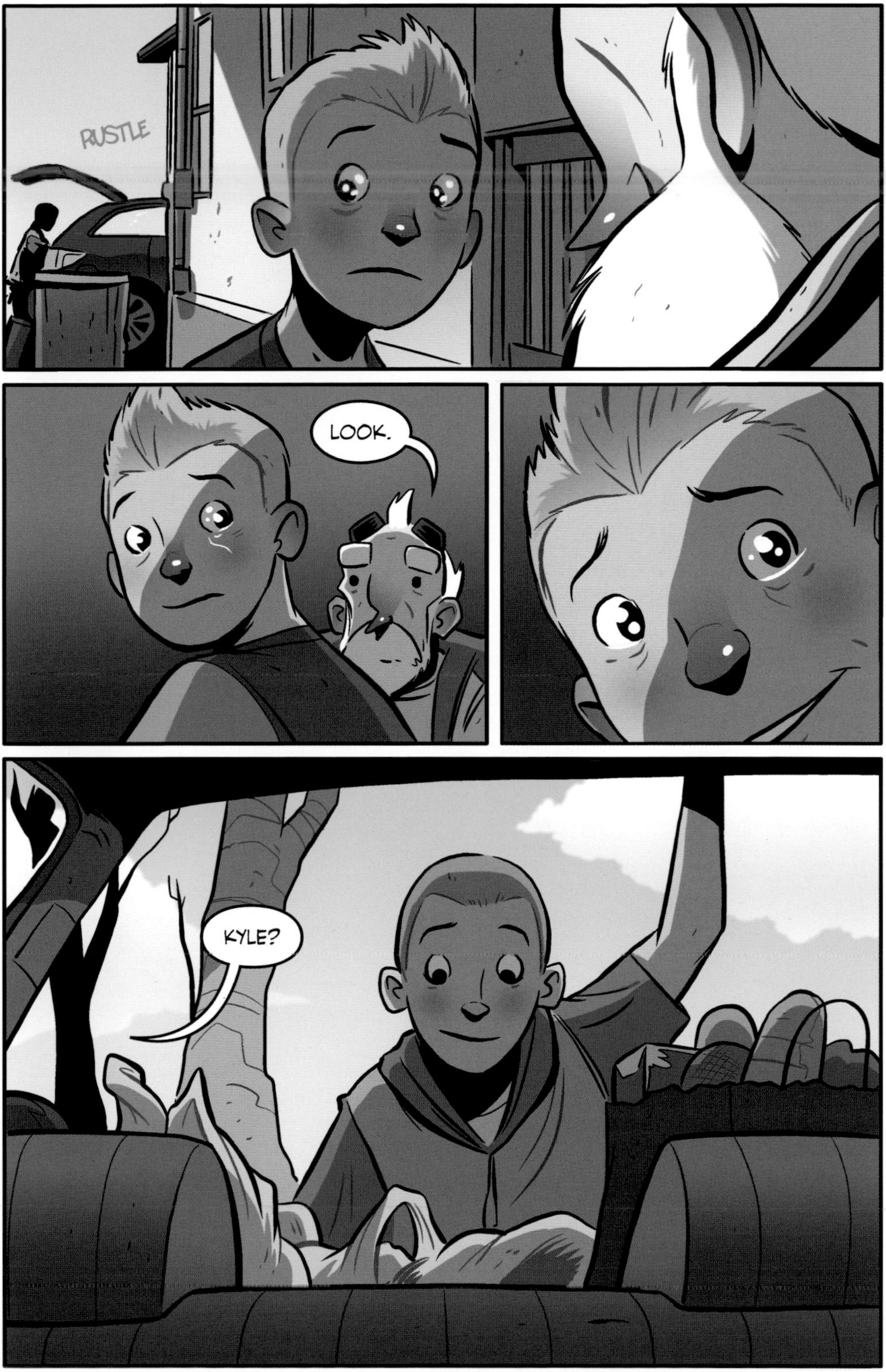
RUSTLE
LOOK.
KYLE?

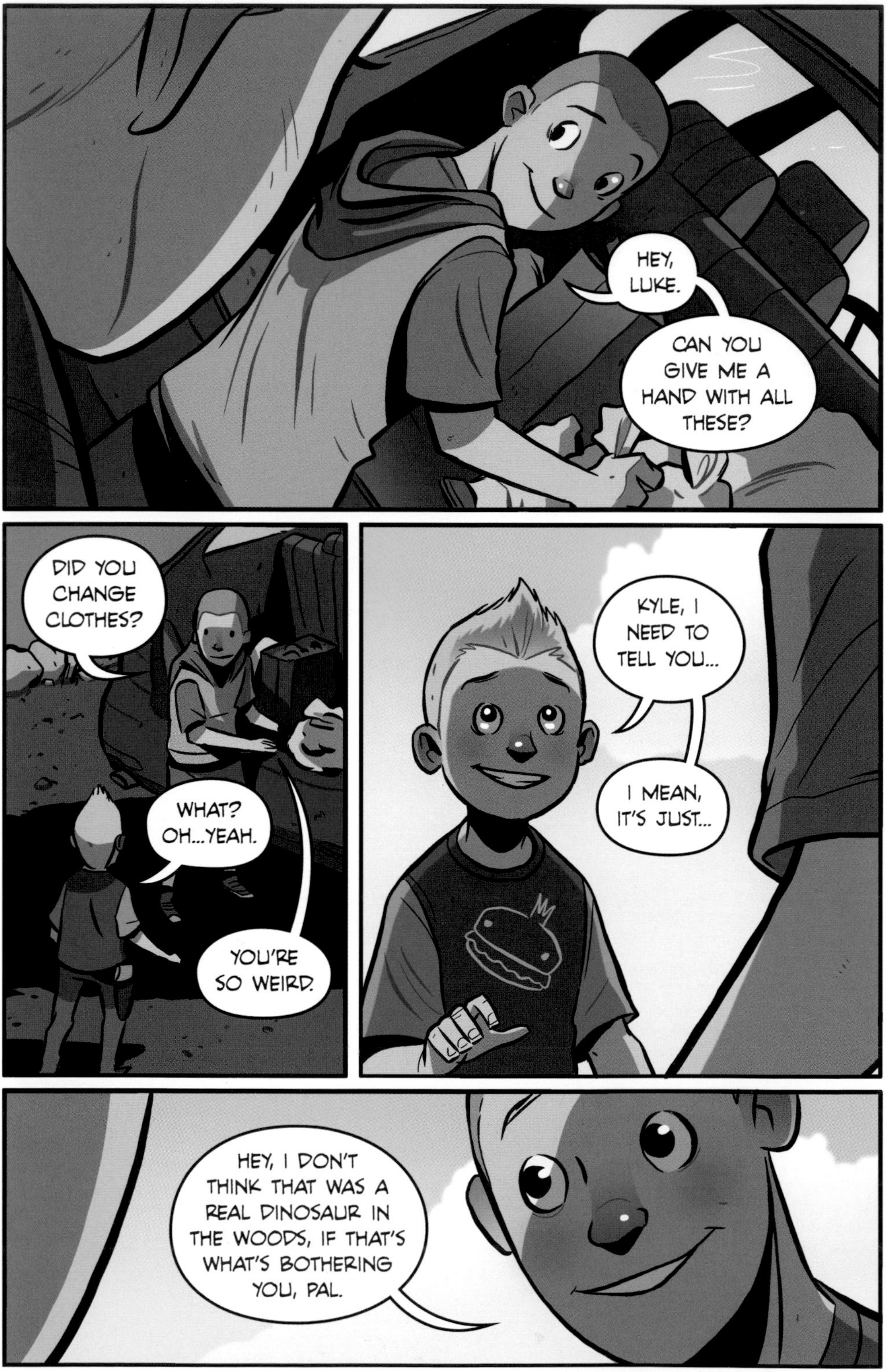
HEY, LUKE.
CAN YOU GIVE ME A HAND WITH ALL THESE?
DID YOU CHANGE CLOTHES?
WHAT? OH...YEAH.
YOU'RE SO WEIRD.
KYLE, I NEED TO TELL YOU...
I MEAN, IT'S JUST...
HEY, I DON'T THINK THAT WAS A REAL DINOSAUR IN THE WOODS, IF THAT'S WHAT'S BOTHERING YOU, PAL.

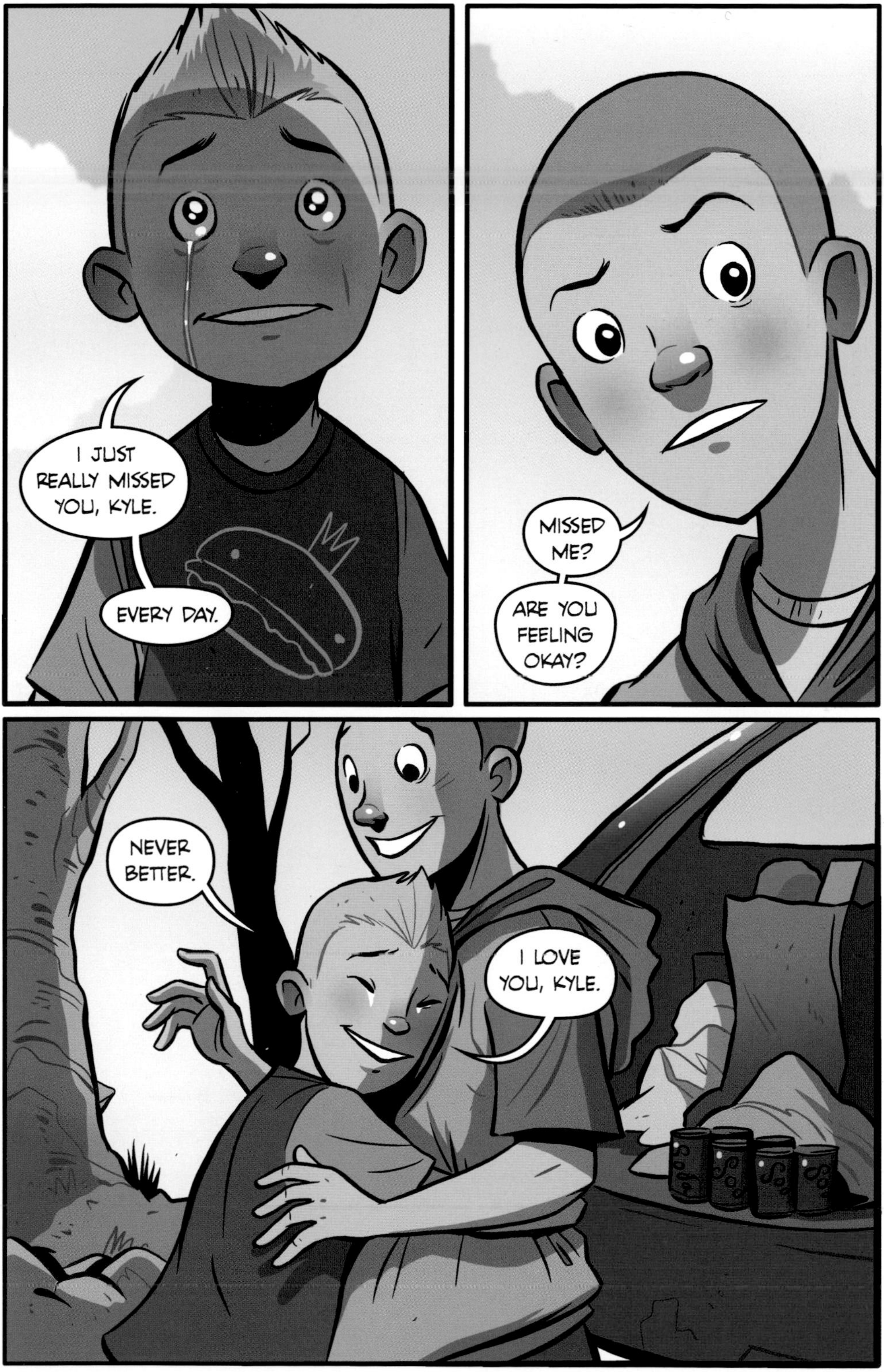
I JUST REALLY MISSED YOU, KYLE.
EVERY DAY.
MISSED ME?
ARE YOU FEELING OKAY?
NEVER BETTER.
I LOVE YOU, KYLE.

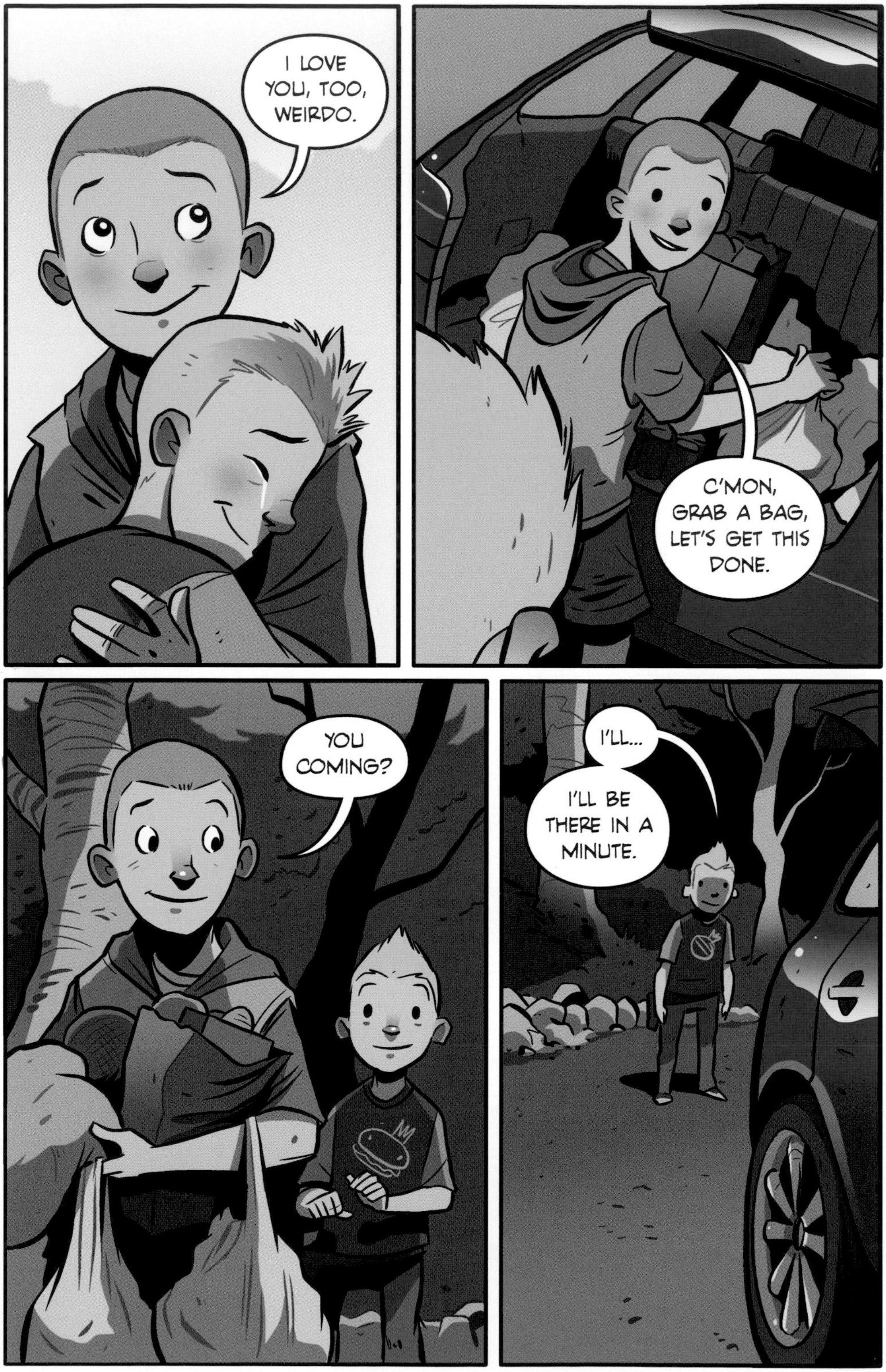
I LOVE YOU, TOO, WEIRDO.
C'MON, GRAB A BAG, LET'S GET THIS DONE.
YOU COMING?
I'LL...
I'LL BE THERE IN A MINUTE.

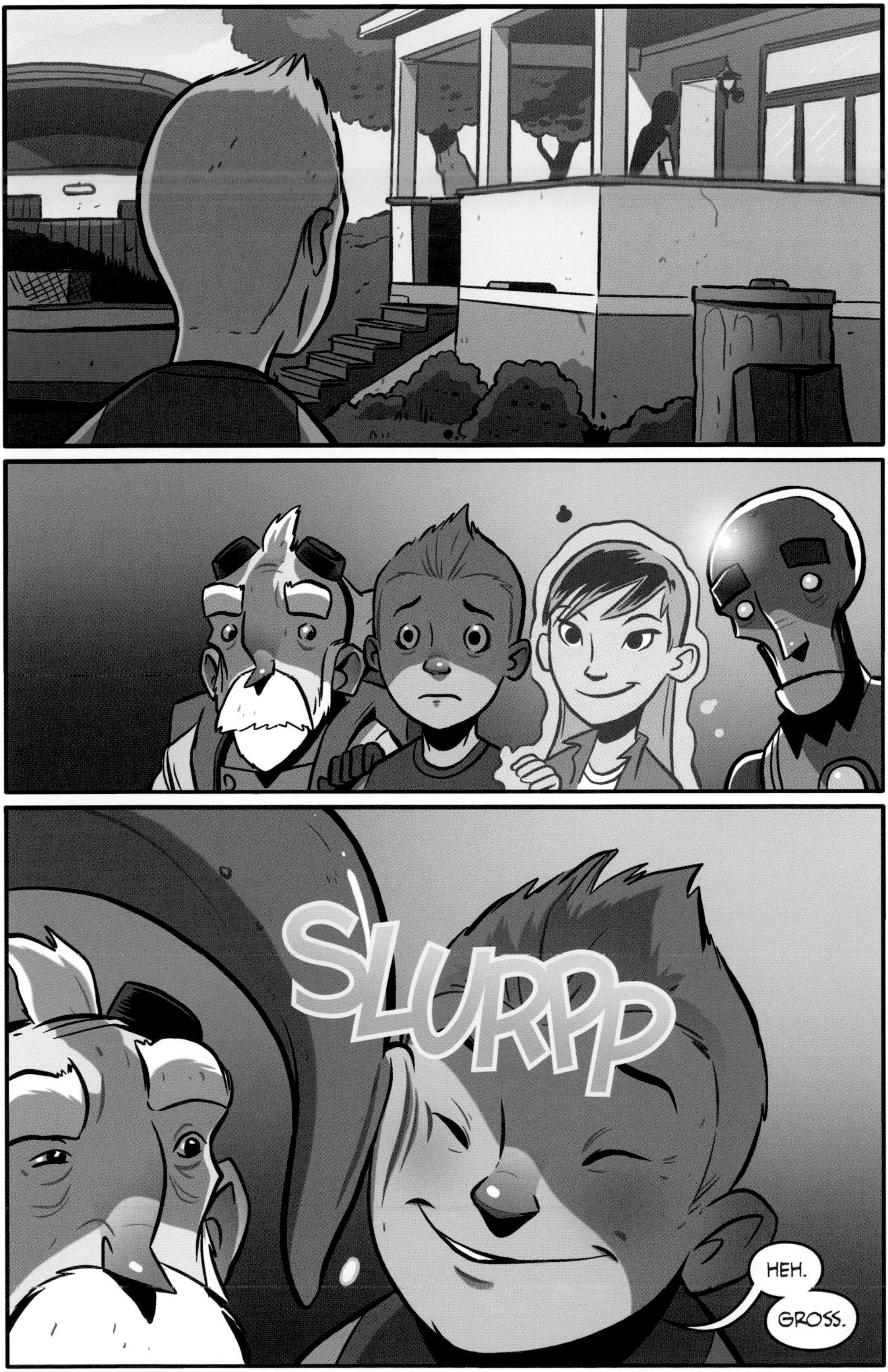
SLURPP
HEH.
GROSS.

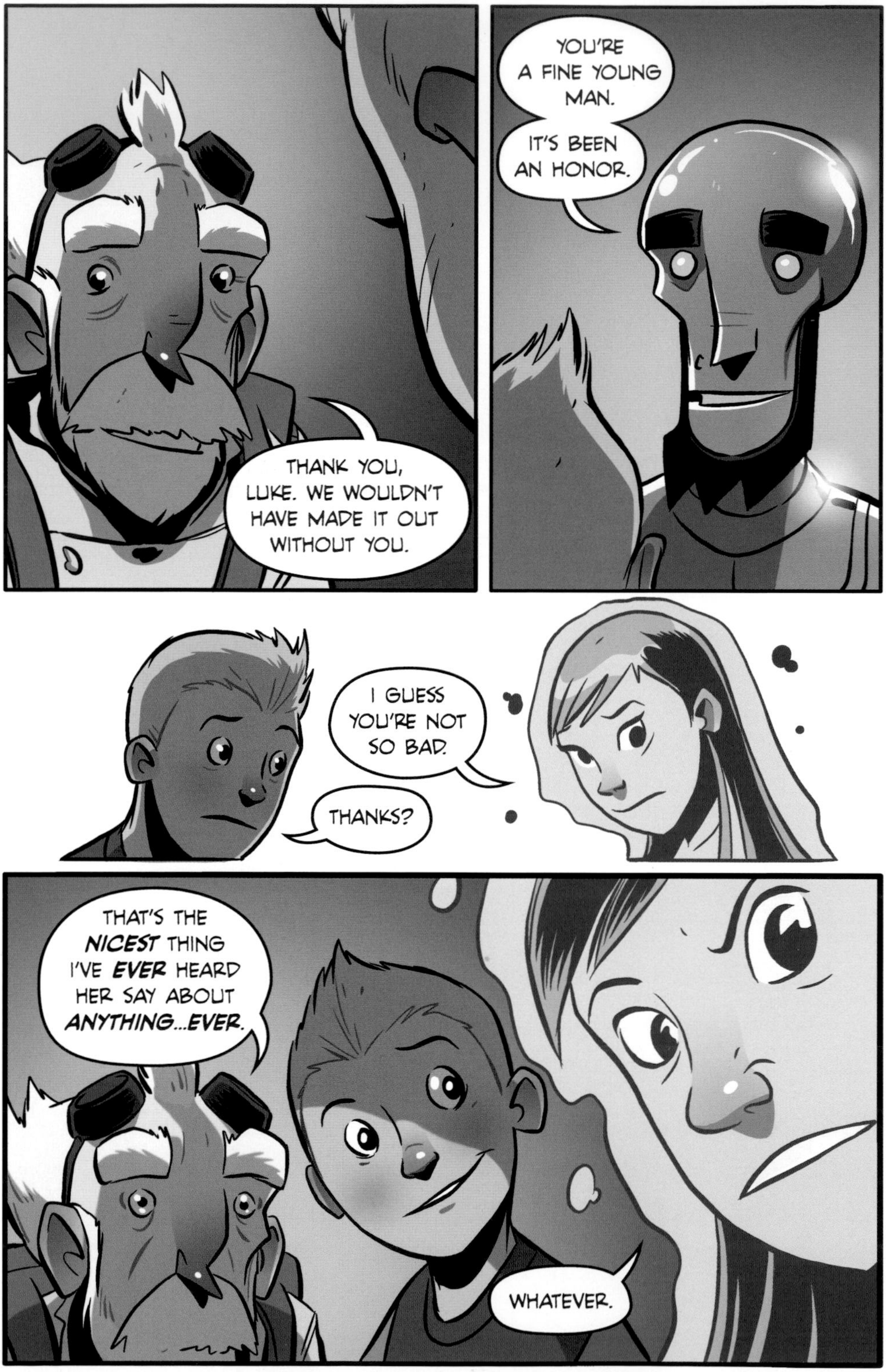
THANK YOU, LUKE. WE WOULDN'T HAVE MADE IT OUT WITHOUT YOU.
YOU'RE A FINE YOUNG MAN.
IT'S BEEN AN HONOR.
I GUESS YOU'RE NOT SO BAD.
THANKS?
THAT'S THE **NICEST** THING I'VE **EVER** HEARD HER SAY ABOUT **ANYTHING...EVER.**
WHATEVER.

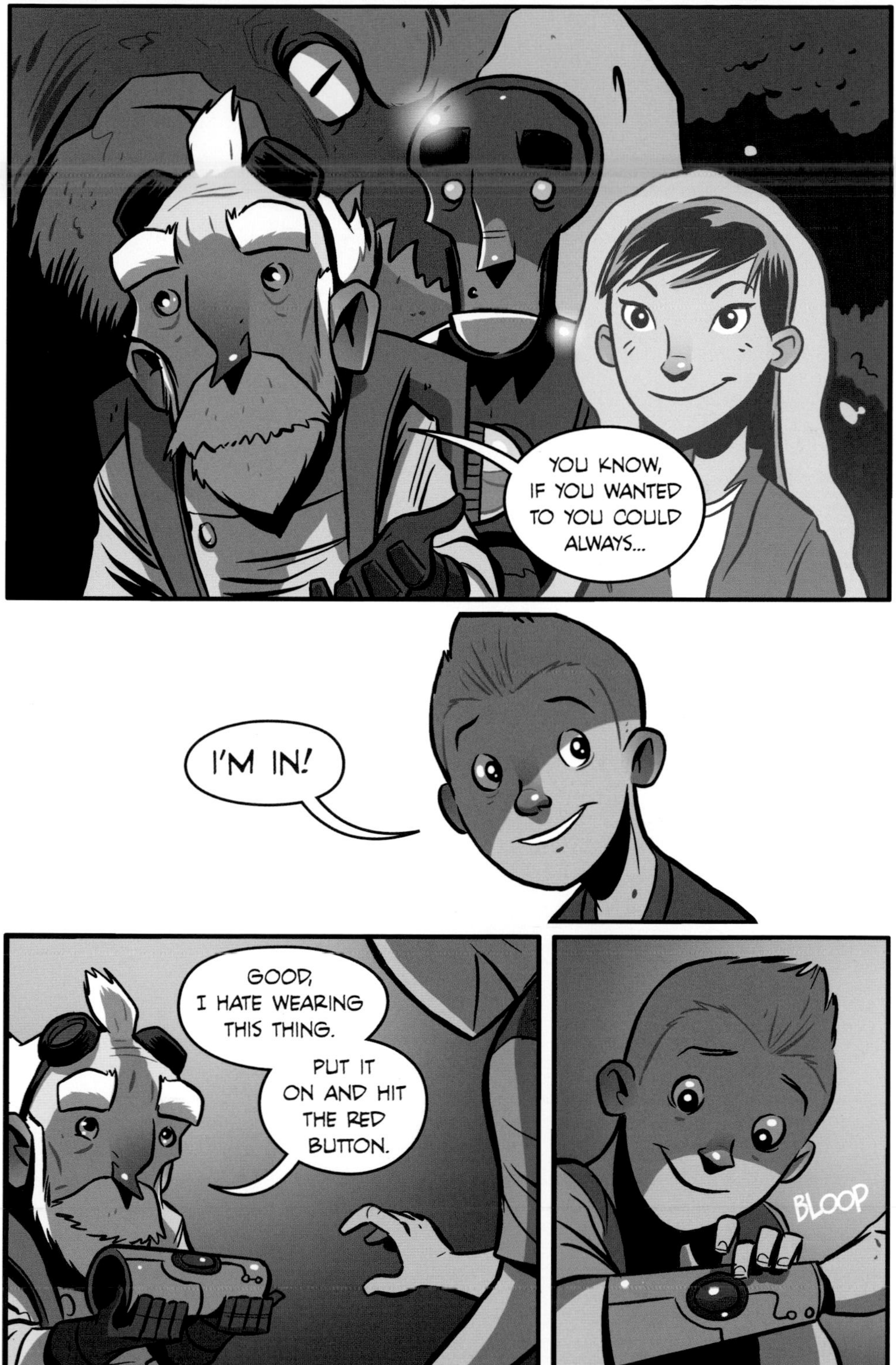
YOU KNOW, IF YOU WANTED TO YOU COULD ALWAYS...
I'M IN!
GOOD, I HATE WEARING THIS THING.
PUT IT ON AND HIT THE RED BUTTON.
BLOOP

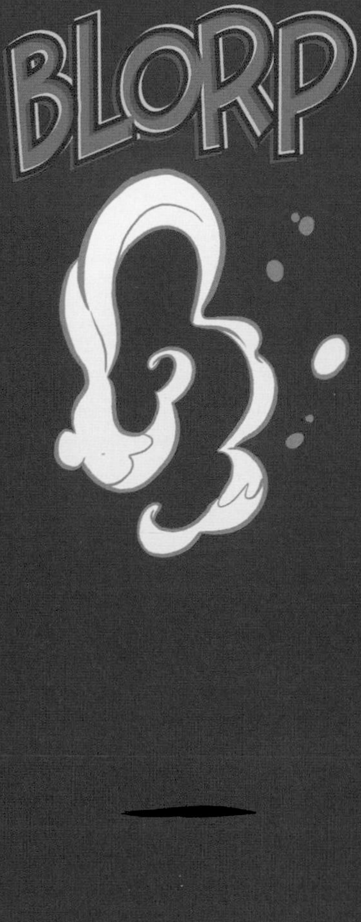
BLORP

CHRIS GRINE has been making up stories since he was a kid, not all of which were just to get out of trouble with his parents. Nowadays, Chris spends most of his time writing and illustrating books, drinking lots of coffee, and sleeping as little as possible. He spends free time with his wife, playing with his kids, watching movies, and collecting action figures (but only the bad guys).

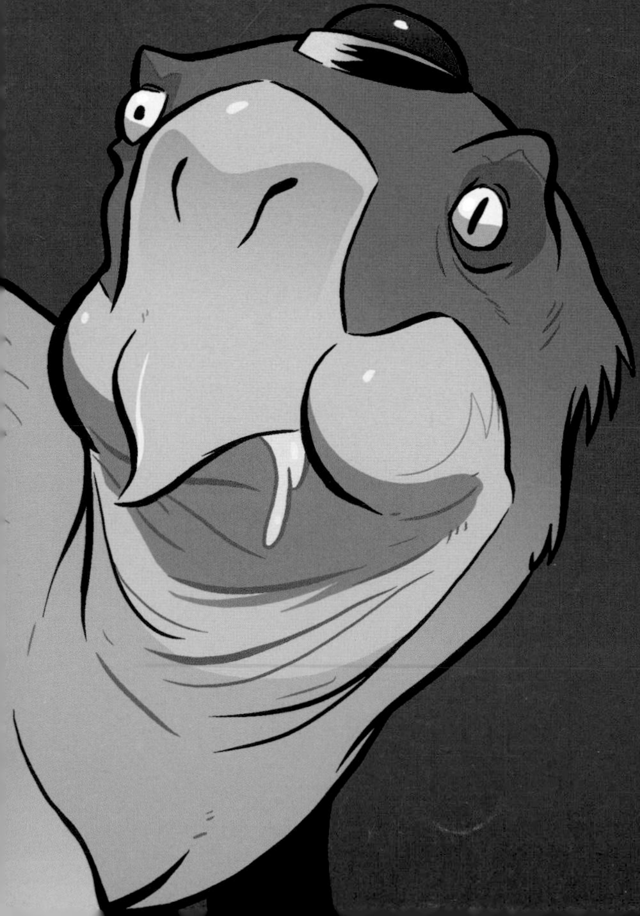